GENTLE MOON

月
負

The Story of Molly Lee

Deanna Windon

Gentle Moon

Deanna Windon

© 2016 Search for Truth Publications

Published by:
Search for Truth Publications
Midland, Michigan

Cover design & layout: Linda Lanning
Cover photo of Shwedagon Pagoda by Owen Lee
Map of Burma by Michael Malone
Portrait of Molly Lee *(on back cover)* by Lifetouch, 2010, used by permission

ISBN-978-1-939456-26-7

Library of Congress Control Number: 2016959220

Printed by The Print Steward.

Dedicated to the glory of God and Lord Jesus, His Son.

Contents

Introduction

As you read this story, understand that it is a true story, based on the memories of Molly Lee. We have tried to recapture the truth of the story with integrity, but we realize that in the process of recording it, the sequence of events may be out of order and some details may have been lost or reshaped by the fading of memory. I am aware of a few errors, which I could not rectify. For all of this we ask for grace. I hope you will find that the story is very much worth knowing, as I the author found it to be.

Also keep in mind that Molly often would tell me something and then say, "But don't write that in the book." She did not want to mention certain things, which reflected poorly on others, might cause offense, or might open old wounds. She wanted to cause no hard feelings and emphasized that some who hurt her before are so good to her now.

"I want peace!" she told me many times.

Some of these stories I could easily omit. For others, I asked Molly to let me write her story as she told it, and I promised to try to express it in such a way as not to blame or scold, but to show the culture and environment to help us understand choices made, and to fairly show both the qualities and failures of the characters, including Molly. I hope I have done this. Stories and life are full of conflict, and resolving conflict makes a well-told story and a well-lived life.

I have contacted many primary characters involved, showed them excerpts, and appreciate that they have allowed me to freely tell Molly's story as she remembers it and to show God's grace as He has given it. I would have liked to contact everyone involved, but this was not feasible. The story is, after all, from Molly's perspective.

The reader will notice that I have recorded stories from Molly that are hearsay. I decided to include many of these because the rumors are part of her experience, and many are impossible to verify, as is often the case during chaotic times.

In an effort to protect privacy, many names have been changed. Particularly, many of those with ongoing valued connections with Burma wished not to be named, not knowing how the book might be received there. No person, whether named or not named, should be assumed to be in agreement with opinions or versions of events given in this book.

The story is full of many dynamic people, and keeping track of them all can be difficult, particularly when a single individual could have more than one name. I was surprised to learn that Chinese people very comfortably took on a new name in a new stage of life, such as when marrying or attending school, but also, accommodating the English rulers in Burma, they often took English and Burmese names besides their Chinese names. I have listed the characters, both alphabetically and by relationship, in the back of the book for a reference. Also, I often repeat a character's connection to Molly, first known as Ngood. I hope this facilitates pleasant reading.

I have written in story fashion, because I find stories more engaging than straight biographies. Molly facilitated this approach by often telling her stories with animated dialogue.

Enjoy knowing the remarkable story and people of Molly's life!

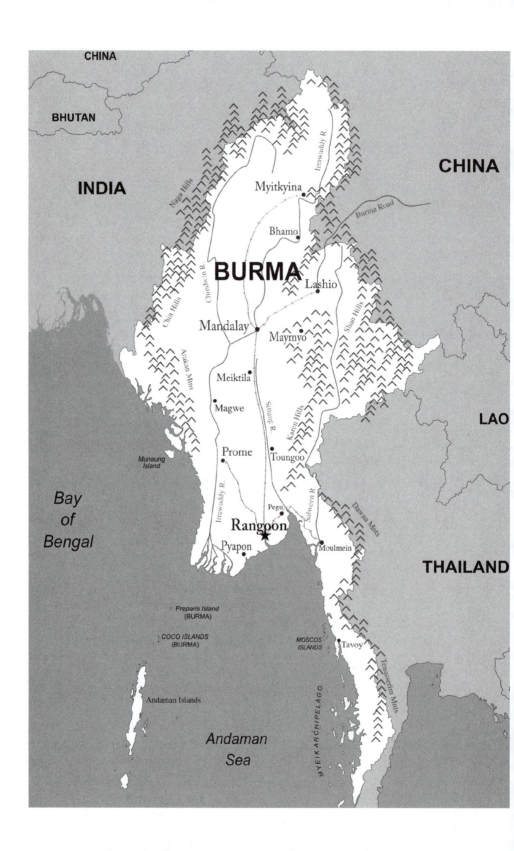

Chapter One

A Prosperous Beginning

Brightly colored kites swayed gracefully in the sky over Chinatown in Rangoon, and with long, undulating tails, they evoked images of Chinese ribbon dancers. Other kites in the same sky were engaged in fierce battle, strings chopping like quick arms of Kung Fu warriors. Sometimes a forlorn kite suddenly tumbled from the sky, a casualty of combat. The innocent kite-flying play of children unknowingly parodied fomenting violent forces that would threaten the seeming tranquility of Burma. For now, children attended their kites, engaged in the spontaneous art and exuberance of being children, and city residents looked up and smiled.

A dozen Chin children, siblings and cousins, were at play above, in, and around the four-story house. As usual, the grand teakwood doors were open to let in every movement of Burmese air, though children often flowed more freely than air. Young neighbors not invited inside the home would play at the cool, marble entrance between the front door and the decorative iron gate. The durwan, or doorkeeper, the Indian man hired to guard the house at night, would not come to close the gate until dark, so until then, this was a favorite gathering spot for neighborhood children. Rich and poor lived side-by-side, and the young children played all sorts of games together without exclusion.

Inside the house, Ngood's gentle Mama would never raise her voice or say, "No!" Only the maids would thwart Ngood and her sisters and little brothers, chasing them away from their kitchen realm on the third floor, where Ngood's family lived. Sometimes, from the second floor, rose the booming voice of Ngood's Number One Uncle, yelling to be heard by his nearly deaf Number One Wife. The children secretly called him *Lui Gong Sing,* literally, "Thunder Old Man Voice" – or, in the backwards way of words in the west, "Old Man Thunder Voice." But the loud rumblings of the uncle were known to be harmless, so there was little to slow the pace of the household. Even Grandfather Chin, who lived in the back of the first floor with his Number Two Wife and their young son, only smiled benevolently at the children.

On this day, the breezes off the Andaman Sea, twenty-five miles to the south of Rangoon, blew a steady breath north over the gaping mouth of the Rangoon River, whose current ran south. Many of the boys and the most daring girls, including Ngood and her cousin Len, took advantage of the wind and the four-story house, and from the roof-top they flew their prized, diamond-shaped, paper kites with bamboo struts and twine tails.

Like nimble mountain goats of their ancestor's homeland, the children scampered up the slanted metal roof that angled up from the concrete veranda above the fourth floor. They were daring little goats, but they weren't foolish. They played only on the part of the roof that sloped down to the open roof-top veranda on the back of the house, where slipping to the concrete floor might give a bump or scrape. No one dared go beyond the peak to the other side of the roof where the roof slanted toward the street, and the drop would be four stories down!

The children shared great excitement, being so high above the city and feeling the pull of kites reaching to the clouds. Ngood delighted in the experience, loving the freedom and thrill of it.

Ngood and Len were happy to keep their kites aloft and watch them dance. But the boys, Ngood's uncle's sons and their guests, were not satisfied with passive play, and they pitted their kites against others sent from lower, neighboring roof-tops or the street. The privileged ones had purchased special strings coated with rice glue and a fine, crushed-glass abrasive that glittered in the sun. When the strings of two kites touched, the boys would either pull the kite in or let it out quickly to saw against the opponent's kite string. Maybe the target's string was likewise coated, or maybe not. The ultimate coup was to cut an opponent's kite loose and send it helplessly tumbling down into the streets below while the victor's kite soared aloft. Oh, if a boy pulled this off, his celebration was heard throughout the block! Meanwhile the lost kite was considered fair game, so if the owner was not quick about it, the patiently waiting, ambitious, neighborhood child who retrieved it became the new possessor. On these kite flying days, the rickshaw and pony cart drivers had to be careful not to trample children who darted in front of them, children oblivious to dangers as they single-mindedly pursued their quarry.

The roof of the four-story house was in all ways the pinnacle of places to fly kites. No building in Chinatown was so high or so perfectly made for kite flying, except the identical four-story house next door; but the children in that home were too young for such adventures, and a certain unpleasant resident there made an invitation unlikely and access unwanted.

For the children on the roof, the view was expansive. From their high summit, they looked down at the red-painted corrugated metal rooftops which cut into the sky like a rugged mountain range below them. Ngood's sister Ah Ming, four years older and eminently more dignified, watched the kites from the roof's veranda, and Ngood called out to her, describing the sights she could see.

"Ming Dee! Big Sister Ming! I see the western hospital! And the hairdresser shop!" she called in her Taishan Cantonese dialect. Of course, Ngood could easily identify the large complex of Rangoon General Hospital across Canal Street to the north, to her right as she climbed toward the peak of the roof. Immediately next to the four-story house was the hairdresser's shop on the corner of Canal and Maung Khine Streets.

She continued to call to Ah Ming as she looked in each direction. Behind Ngood, to the back of the house, was the roof of the boys' Chinese school, which defined the eastern border of Chinatown. Beyond that was Twenty-Third Street, where beggars of several races, but mostly Indian, slept under cloth tents at night, and where the Chin children were not allowed to go alone. Prohibition aside, a disconcerting, long, wailing call came several times a day from the tower of an Indian mosque on that street, and Ngood had no desire to approach the place of the eerie sound that caused a few men in the street to mysteriously pull out a small rug or scarf, drop to their knees, and pray. Beyond Twenty-Third Street, on Pagoda Road, was the big Burmese market "Theingyee Bazaar," where the maids did the daily shopping at the fresh food stalls and which drew beggars looking for discards. Rangoon proper was further in that direction.

To the south was the identical four-story house where Ngood's mother's Number Three Sister happened to live with the family of her own well-to-do father-in-law. This house blocked much of the view south, and, as far as Ngood was concerned, there was nothing else for her to consider in that direction. A few blocks away were the busy docks along the Rangoon River.

If Ngood tentatively approached the peak of the roof, she could see across it to the two-story residences and clan houses across Maung Khine Street. Right across the street was the dong, the clan house, where middle-aged adult singles, recently emigrated from China, stayed until they found work. Nearly every day there was an Indian man sitting on the street with his blind son, who held out a cup for charity. Beyond the clan house were the rooftops of more Chinatown, and at the other edge of Chinatown, she knew, was her own school, Yuck Tuck.

Ngood recognized one more building particularly across the street, just south of the first dong. It was another clan house, but this one was licensed to sell opium. It was a curious place Ngood had often observed from her third floor balcony. From there she could see into the second floor open window, where long, raised wooden platforms with woven mats served as beds for rows of prostrate Chinese men smoking opium in long, curved pipes hour after hour, day after day. Sometimes it was hard to know whether the men were asleep or dead. The smell of opium was common in the street, but young Ngood was oblivious to the addictive, life-leeching peril it signified to its victims. To her, the clan house was merely a point of interest.

Ngood possessed by sight, if not by name, the more distant landmarks of Rangoon. Her life revolved around Chinatown, and this was the world to her. The rest of the city was painted on four walls as backdrops around her little story. But she did not feel the limit of her experience. Instead, she felt as if the whole world, as observed from her journey into the sky, belonged to her.

Wanting to share with Mama the jubilant kite-flying adventure, Ngood jumped from the roof to the veranda. "Tuck Sook," she bossed her Grandfather's young son, Hone Tuck. "Tuck Sook, 'Uncle Tuck,' Wind up my kite string and bring my kite to me when you're finished. Do not tangle the string. And be careful not to tear my kite." Then Ngood was momentarily distracted, peering over the veranda wall into the alley. A few beggars always lingered there, hoping to benefit from leftover scraps of food from the well-to-do residents of the four-story house. She also saw the hired city workers, Indian men, making their weekly rounds to shovel up the kitchen waste the maids had taken out to the alley. Some households would throw waste, kitchen or otherwise, from second story windows, and workers or pedestrians would have to be alert and agile to avoid being pelted with garbage. The Chin household was more careful; nevertheless, the alley was best observed from above and the children never ventured to play there.

Curiosity satisfied, Ngood continued to race down the steps to the third floor. She expected to find Mama expertly sewing clothes for her brood at the Singer treadle sewing machine. Ngood wouldn't get too close to her mother's work, though, and with that thought she was distracted again, her mind wandering a different path from her feet. As she traversed the steps, Ngood was remembering the time she was in her Mama's lap and, always curious, got her hand too close to Mama's work, and the sewing machine needle went right through her finger! Mama pulled the needle out right away. Ngood remembered the terrible pain, and the small dot of blood in the middle of her fingernail. She remembered how Mama crooned sympathetically and blew on the wound. Then Mama mixed Chinese herbs, applied them to the finger, and bound the finger in a cloth.

Ngood reached the landing to the third floor and stopped abruptly, suddenly wary, sensing danger! Next to the open doorway were the deliberately placed teak cane and brown shoes. These she recognized as sure signs of nearby peril waiting to spring upon the unwary.

The cane was simple, but sturdy and well-made. It was not a crutch for a limping man, but an emblem of prestige. The hand grip of the cane extended straight out from the shaft, polished smooth by the years of her father's stern grasp. The shaft was ornamented by a couple of rings carved around the circumference, and there was a copper tip at the bottom. The freshly polished shoes were also simple, but of unmistakable quality and comfort. These simple things, right shoe, left shoe, and walking stick, were symbols of much more: A tiger had entered the house and was treading in slippers somewhere nearby! Already the wordless news was spreading, and like wary prey sensing a predator, children were quietly slinking to their own homes.

How different the meals were when Papa was home from his travels! The usual lively chatter was not just muffled, it was silenced. Only Papa spoke, and his words were minimal and dignified. Rarely, as the oldest child, Ah Ming had the courage to speak to him. When the Chin children noticed the maids setting the dishes on the round dinner table, they quietly seated themselves without being summoned. Automatically they sat in order of age, Ah Ming next to Papa, then Ngood, then He'ung and the little boys, and Ah Ma. Actually, when they were small, the little boys did not often sit at the table. Instead, Pwa Pwa or Byu Goo would follow their active bodies, trying to slip a bite of food into their mouths.

The table was impressive, with a surface of white marble swirled with grey, and supported by four heavy wooden legs. The marble, like that of the front entry of the house, was imported from Yunnan China -- famously exquisite! The table was in the traditional circle shape of Chinese hospitality, where another chair for a guest could be added easily with the friendly invitation, "One more person, one more set of chopsticks."

The maids were instructed to make plenty of food in case an unexpected visitor arrived, perhaps coincidentally, at dinner time. The guest would be seated to the right of Papa, the place of honor. If there were too many guests to fit the table, the children would sit on cushions in the back bedroom, where the maids slept, and eat their suppers there. The maids ate together later in the kitchen, but Ngood did not feel sorry for them. They were savvy, Pwa Pwa and Byu Goo, and they helped themselves to as good a meal as any of them, gossiping happily together as they ate. Ngood would have gladly joined them, especially when Papa was home.

Papa was particular about meals served at his table. Always there was the excellent quality Burmese rice, served not in a pot, but in a fine porcelain rice holder. If the rice was not perfectly cooked, Papa would be mad. Then gentle Mama would have to confront the maids, making a show for Papa. She might say, "What did you do? Why does the rice taste smokey? Did you scorch the rice? You must pay attention to your duties! You must be more careful!"

Also with every meal there was soup and two meat dishes, usually chicken, fish, or pork, and a vegetable dish, all seasoned with curries. If a guest was expected, a roasted duck might be added to the menu. Beef was avoided, not so much because of a strict religious belief, like the Hindus, but because of a high regard for valuable, hard-working cattle that pulled plows and bullock carts on farms across Burma. "The cow sweats for us," went the old saying.

Parents and children always drank excellent tea from tea plantations in the Shan plateau in northern Burma. No one was fussy if the tea was neither hot nor cold.

Two of these large meals were served every day, and even in hot weather the food was served warm, for Chinese believed cold meals were difficult to digest. Even before the children left for school each morning, a full meal was served and the family ate together formally as in the evening.

The children usually had a small meal at school and a snack when they got home before three.

Ngood watched Byu Goo cater to her father's pleasure. How quickly she had learned to pacify him! She submissively offered him a personal plate of fried chicken gizzards and livers, and the barely cooked chicken fat he loved to eat. Byu Goo even had cut the meat in little pieces so Papa could eat them easily with his chopsticks.

As the platter of chicken was served to her, He'ung, Ngood's little sister, reached a little too far across the pile of chicken pieces to take a drumstick. This aroused the tiger, though the response was a quiet growl of warning. Hone Foo was a gentleman and did not raise his voice, but his words and frown clearly conveyed his frightful displeasure.

"He'ung. Do not reach for the chicken. Take the piece that is in front of you. You do not like it? You take it. Rude child! You disgrace me!"

Ngood felt the scolding with her little sister and sat still in mortification. Only when the tiger began to eat again did everyone else return to eating her meal in cautious silence.

Ngood was especially careful then to take small bites and to eat slowly, daintily, to avoid Papa's wrath. Only laborers ate quickly, the children were taught, so they could get back to work. The well-to-do would never rush a meal, especially not a girl. Genteel Chinese meals involved "enjoying life at leisure."

But the focus on leisure did not imply relaxing, as the children knew. Ngood would not dare rest her head on her arm or stir her food with her chopsticks. Children without manners were said not to have home teaching and reflected badly on their parents. Politeness required always that a little food must be left on the plate, although after spooning soup, the last of the broth could be quietly sipped from the raised bowl. Then each child neatly returned the place setting to its original position. Chopsticks were set parallel to each other on the right, and the soup spoon was placed horizontally behind the bowl.

After the evening meal, there was little time to get ready for the opera, a project of Ngood's father. He, the second son of Grandfather Chin, clearly had a good head for business, as his father before him.

Grandfather Chin had done quite well for himself. He had come from China to Burma as an impoverished teenager and worked hard until he could open his own little dry goods store in Chinatown. Profits from the store were diligently reinvested into more businesses and the little store sprouted another, and a hotel, and then the impressive three floor restaurant, Foo Nam Low, "Wealthy South Building."

The first floor of the restaurant was open in the morning to serve breakfast to people in a hurry, like carpenters, or anyone wanting to stop for tea. Here patrons could get oolong or jasmine tea, made with prime tea leaves. Also they could order pao, the Chinese dumpling, made with pork or chicken. Or they could order dim sum, which translates literally, "According to your heart." This was a varied menu, served in small portions of meat, seafood, vegetables, fruit, and dessert, and might include noodles, stuffed rolls, or meat on a stick.

The second floor was open after 4:00 in the afternoon. This was for organizations, conferences, or lavish wedding receptions, by reservation. The host might order twelve or even twenty courses, depending on what he could afford. The guests were served by waitresses who would begin by bringing perfumed towels for hand washing. Then the courses were presented one by one. Visitors from far lands to the west, from strange places like England or America, often didn't know to eat only a small amount of the first courses, perhaps cold meat or shrimp. By the time the last, and best, courses came, these greedy eaters were too full to eat any more. They ate too much, too fast, like common laborers. The businessmen of Chinatown enjoyed bringing their foreign associates here, and they joked quietly to themselves about the foolish fellows.

The most expensive item in the restaurant was swallow's nest. These were actual nests swiflets made from their saliva and attached to walls in limestone caves. Sources were limited to Thailand and Malaysia, and Chinese chefs used them to make soup or to flavor rice or other dishes. The nests were said to have many health benefits, including aiding digestion and keeping the body warm.

Yes, Grandfather Chin had done very well with his restaurant. And Ngood's father seemed to inherit the gift to create successful enterprises. Besides starting a men's recreation club and other businesses in Rangoon and Mandalay, he ran the Chinese opera on the third floor of Grandfather's restaurant, employing troupes from Singapore and Hong Kong.

Nearly every night Ngood would attend the show with her family. Performances were given nightly in all seasons, beginning at eight o'clock and lasting as late as midnight. Even when Papa was home, he would not sit with his family because he would be busy managing things. But the two front rows were always saved for Grandfather Chin, his wife and Tuck Sook, for Ah Ma, Pwa Pwa, and Byu Goo, and for Ngood and her sisters, brothers, uncles, aunts, and cousins.

Even though seating was always reserved for the Chin family, the children were sent early to hold the seats just to be sure. Enthusiastic patrons always wanted to sit close. While she waited with her sisters and cousins, Ngood wondered with anticipation what the show would be. She hoped for a historical opera. These were so popular in Chinatown.

Ngood chatted with her sister Ah Ming about the show of the previous week. Night after night the opera house had been full, with people standing in the back. The same show was performed four nights in a row, but Ngood didn't tire of seeing it. She didn't know what was legend and what was true, and that detail didn't matter at all to her. What mattered was that it was so exciting and so dramatic.

At last all the seats were filled, including the seats saved for Ngood's family, and the opera opened with a magnificent Chinese wedding. The actress portraying the bride was so beautiful, like a fairy from a divine place, and Ngood was immediately enthralled. The bride was brought onto the stage in the old-fashioned way, in a sedan chair carried by four athletic men. The chair was elaborately decorated in red satin and fresh flowers. The bride wore a breath-taking, long, embroidered silk Chinese dress, red for happiness and good luck. Her crown depicted the phoenix, a fantastic bird of Chinese lore, symbolic of everything beautiful and good, peaceful and prosperous. A red silk veil with long, jeweled tassels extended from the bride's crown and covered her face. Many attendants accompanied her, including a specially chosen woman, a human talisman of proven childbearing skill. Also came those who were carrying lanterns or waving banners, plus musicians, who played Chinese strings, pipes, and percussion. A spectacular lion, a pair of athletes filling the costume, danced exuberantly, thrusting his huge head in rhythm to drum, gong, and cymbal sounds. This welcome, scary beast was expected to frighten away evil spirits.

The bride dismounted gracefully and moved, like all skillful Chinese actresses, with tiny steps and so little up and down movement that she seemed to glide across the stage. Her elegant hands spoke with every gesture, whether held open with fingers up in the graceful lotus flower position, or pressed together, prayer-like, as she waited obediently for her groom.

The groom's arrival was announced with firecrackers, drums, and gongs. He too entered on a festively painted, teak sedan chair. A little boy rode with him as a charm for many sons. The bridegroom wore a long gown with a red silk sash and red shoes. On his head was a cap decorated with cypress leaves, symbolic of longevity, health, and fruitfulness.

The Chinese instruments continued to play until the bride and groom moved to face a platform on which were seated the parents of the bride on the left, parents of the groom on the right, and the clan elder in the center. The couple bowed three times to the elder, then to the groom's parents, then to the bride's parents, and then they bowed three times to the audience. They listened to the eloquent speeches and blessings of the fathers and the distinguished guest. The fates were entreated for prosperity and for many children for the couple.

The audience understood that the matchmaker had arranged this marriage, negotiating terms between families, assuring a lucky date for the ceremony, and delivering documentation of three healthy generations of long-lived ancestors. This celebrated community servant now stood to one side, watching the profitable union of the families, as the betrothed strangers married each other.

The wedding guests then exited to one side of the stage, and the bride and groom walked across to the other side. With a simple motion as if opening a door, the groom made known to the audience the threshold of his parents' home. The bride, hoping not to catch her long, silk dress on fire, jumped across an imagined flame lighting the threshold. All understood the real flame of a real wedding was supposed to prevent any evil spirits from entering the household with the bride.

Inside, the bride and groom kowtowed to the ancestor altar. First they stood facing the altar, then they kneeled and bowed so their heads touched the floor three times. Then they got up and repeated the ritual twice more. This was intended to reverently introduce the bride to the deceased ancestors so they would recognize and bless her as one of the family. Among Chinese, the kowtow, which literally means to knock the head, was considered the highest form of reverence. Such politeness and respect was of grave importance at a wedding and met the expectations of the audience.

Then the couple went before the groom's parents, for as any good Chinese person knew, the chief players of any wedding are these parents. Again the couple performed the kowtow, this time to the groom's parents, and then the bride served them tea, symbolic of her obedience and service to them. They gave jewelry to her, showing their ability to provide for her as she cut ties with her family.

This ritual completed, groom and bride were considered husband and wife. In real life, only when the bride was taken to the room she would share with her husband at the home of her in-laws, her veil would be removed and husband and wife would see each other face-to-face for the first time. Then the marriage was consummated. For the opera, however, the bride's veil was removed as the ritual ceremony ended, so that her dramatic face could be observed by the audience as traumatic events unfolded.

Suddenly, before any intimate touch between the husband and wife, trumpets sounded and soldiers thundered across the stage. They were immediately identifiable as soldiers by their military gowns, which were split at the sides but extended to the ankles, and by heavy boots up to the knees. The commander was known by the pheasant plumes in his helmet and by the way he walked across the stage, his steps making great arcs and his gait commanding much area. He announced he was conscripting young men for the emperor's work to build a great wall to defend China.

Ngood had learned in Chinese school about this Emperor Qin, of the third century B.C. He was famous for his cruelty, even commanding that scholars be buried alive for fear that the educated men would rebel against him. When this ruler died, Ngood knew, all of his soldiers were buried with him, as he had commanded. So, when young men were taken for the brutal Emperor's work, everyone rightly dreaded that the men would never come back; they would be worked to death. The soldiers on the stage forcibly dragged the newly-wed husband away as his bride cried piteously.

Quickly the bride was left alone on stage, and she swiftly and gracefully removed her now inappropriate red bridal gown to reveal the white one all knew represented mourning. By long, dramatic dialogue, the bride told of bitter months of loneliness and waiting for her husband's return. At last, she decided she must go and look for him, though she feared he was dead.

Some may have noticed by now that this actress was not young, but her representation of a young girl was flawless. She moved with such delicate, feminine grace and spoke so sweetly, with the high-pitched tones admired of Chinese women, she seemed but a helpless girl. The stage had few props and no backdrop, but the skilled actress used arm movements, exaggerated by long, scarf-like "water sleeves," to portray an arduous journey. She circled around and around the stage showing the great distance traveled, as she continued in soliloquy to explain her journey and purpose. The audience understood by her flagging posture the toll it took on her, and though everyone was shocked that she was traveling alone, everyone even more admired her courage and her loyalty to her husband.

At last she arrived at the Great Wall, represented by a cloth supported by bamboo poles. She plaintively approached one poor, ill-used worker after another, until she found someone who had known her husband. With extensive dialogue, this worker praised the husband to the woman, but confirmed her fears that he was dead. Still, no one could tell her where his body was, and she wanted to find her husband's bones. She cried and sang passionately as she offered fruit and wine to the gods. Then, kneeling at the wall, she begged the gods to reveal the bones of her husband.

The actress's voice was so beautiful, and she cried so much that mucous poured in long strands from her nose. Everyone in the audience was touched by her performance, and Ngood could hear the women near her softly crying too. People in the streets outside the theater, hearing the song through the open windows, were also moved, and asked each other, "Who is singing so beautifully? Oh it sounds so nice!" And they would want to come to the show the next night.

The fortunate ones attending the premier heard crashing sounds of thunder and saw flashing lights like lightening and knew that a sudden furious storm had overtaken the stage. Then the wall burst open to reveal the bones of the husband! The gods had shown mercy to the faithful woman!

The forlorn wife then did what the Chinese audience would greatly admire. She stepped away from the wall and then ran headlong into it to take her own life. Those left behind would bury her bones with those of her husband.

Well! It was a very satisfying performance, and the Chin family agreed that Man Geung Nwe Hook Pung Cheung Sing, "Dear Ginger, of the Man clan, Cries and Cracks the Great Wall," was one of their all-time favorites. The heroine was much admired for her silvery voice and her faithfulness to her husband, and Ngood saw tears welling in the eyes of every man and woman as they left the opera house. In fact, this opera won the hearts of Chinatown, and it would have many repeat performances, though the actress was so taxed she could not perform more than a couple of nights in a row. Alternate nights would offer lighter entertainment.

It was nearly midnight, and the children were hurried home and sent to their beds. They did not wear pajamas in those days, happily unaware of the need, and simply went to bed in their day clothes. Ngood climbed onto the woven mat of her four poster bed, and He'ung came up beside her. Pwa Pwa secured the mosquito netting around them.

Before Ngood went to sleep, she called to Pwa Pwa, "Please wake me at six o'clock tomorrow morning, so I can memorize my homework lesson before school."

Pwa Pwa replied, "You are a sweet, obedient girl. Foon cow cow, sleep well, little one." Pwa Pwa repeated the word for "little one," showing affection. Words to the young were often doubled this way.

Ngood pulled the light blanket over her head, not for warmth, but to protect her from ghosts. Byu Goo was especially good at pointing out these apparitions which seemed to linger in corners and behind doors. Secure beneath the blanket, Ngood slept soundly, and the night passed quickly.

Chapter Two

The Four-Story House

Ngood was still dreaming of a spectacular Chinese wedding when Pwa Pwa called her name softly, "Ngood.... Wake up, *Ah Nwe*, Dear Girl. It's six o'clock. "

Pwa Pwa and Byu Goo had been busy preparing the morning feast... two meat dishes, a vegetable dish, soup, rice, and tea. Ngood enjoyed the aromas drifting from the kitchen as she sat at the marble table with her studies.

Soon, she got up to go to the bathroom, which was through the kitchen. She knocked on the bolted kitchen door, appealing for entrance to the guarded domain of Pwa Pwa and Byu Goo. She knew that, as she crossed through the kitchen, she was being watched to make sure she did not linger.

But Ngood was observant enough after frequent passages to absorb every detail of the room. All the features were low, convenient for sitting to do kitchen duties. The kitchen stove was brick, decorated with pretty red tiles on top. It was heated with charcoal, which would be pushed in from one side, and had two burners.

On the wall above the stove, high enough to avoid the heat, was a frame in which was written the name of the kitchen god. Ngood knew three incense sticks were lit every morning and every evening to appease this tattle-tale god. In the eleventh month, tasseled sugar canes that stretched to the ceiling were placed to assist him on his climb to Heaven to report to the Jade Emperor, the ruler of the other gods. Sugar was hoped to motivate the kitchen god to give a sweet report about the family. Byu Goo would place the canes, which she had carefully selected with the best tassels and long length, next to the kitchen idol. She dared not offer a single cane, nor any odd number, and certainly not four sugar canes, because the Cantonese word for "four," *hlee*, sounds very much like the word for "death." Six or more canes in an even number would be fine. The family gave him a generous annual feast, as well.

The faucet was also low enough that one would sit to do dishes, which were placed in a tub for washing, then set on a table to dry. A drain in the floor conveyed the water out to the back alley.

Another furnishing was a shelved cupboard on four legs. Each leg rested in a little clay bowl of water to keep the black ants out of the stores. Ngood knew she dared not leave anything sweet out on a table, or it would soon be full of the ants. The cupboard doors were screened to keep out bugs while allowing air to circulate. In the morning, any leftover food was reheated before use. Refrigeration was unavailable, so foods were not kept for very long, and daily trips to the market were necessary.

Ngood opened the door to the modern bathroom. She crossed the narrow shower area, glad it was not occupied, or she would have to wait to use the toilet, or, if she was desperate, she would have to run to grandfather's bathroom two floors down. She took the two steps up to the little porcelain opening in the tiled floor. She untied the band of her Chinese pants and crouched over the opening. Then she pulled the chain on the water tank to flush away the unseen waste. She made sure her school uniform was in order, the black, straight-legged pants and white, mandarin-collar blouse with ornamental, fabric buttons. Quickly, she went through the kitchen and back to her studies.

****

Ngood loved Chinese school. When she was younger, living on Nineteenth Street, she followed Ming out the back door of their house into the alley and took the short walk to the Yuck Tuck "Producing Virtue" Girls' Chinese School on Twentieth Street. Fortunately, this alley was not as challenging to cross as some since there were not too many upper story windows expelling waste, but the girls still had to hold their noses. Soon, confident and enthused, Ngood couldn't wait for Ah Ming, and ran ahead to the school.

Her school was so much more to her than a three story white-washed concrete building with many open windows. It was even more than the institution that carried the names of her grandfather, uncle, and father as board members, though that was a very good reason not to be lazy about studies. But a love of learning came naturally to Ngood. Storehouses of information were open to her of which her mother never dreamed, and Ngood was hungry for it.

Ngood could hardly choose a favorite subject. She loved doing the mental math problems that were written in Arabic numbers on the teacher's big, slate board. Students sat with arms crossed so they couldn't count with their fingers, only taking the pencil out to quickly write their answers. Numbers written in Chinese calligraphy were too cumbersome to do mathematics, and so Ngood was also becoming fluent with Arabic numbers for longer calculations on paper. And she was proficient with an abacus, the calculator of the ancients, figuring complicated arithmetic problems quickly and accurately. In her mind, she chanted the sing song of her calculations as her fingers flew, whisking up and down the beads, two representing five each on top and five beads representing ones on the bottom.

She took pleasure in the drawing lessons, usually copying sketches or photographs of fruits and flowers from a book, and she was careful about her sewing lessons. Each semester brought a new project, and Ngood appreciated the challenge of each one, whether hand-sewing a vest, or tediously counting cross stitch, or crocheting, or knitting, or stitching artful embroidery. The girls were graded on the quality of their work, and when compared to her classmates, Ngood took pride in hers. Still, she would always aspire to the superior work of her big sister Ah Ming, and of course Ah Ma. A Chinese girl's greatest need was to learn to sew well, so she could sew for her own children one day.

All of the children seemed to enjoy the marching drills, when they were taught to march in disciplined patterns. They liked to take the stretching breaks too, when periods of seat work were divided by refreshing toe touches, reaches and lunges, and marching in place. The children also had exercise classes twice a week, marching around the large meeting hall, jumping, clapping, stepping, and crouching.

Ngood relished the Chinese history lessons, especially the recent history about Sun Yat Sen, the Chinese doctor who led a revolution against the imperialist Qing Dynasty in 1911, just eleven years before Ngood was born. His picture hung on the wall of the Chinese school. He developed the

"Three Principles" of governance, "Government of the People, Government by the People, and Government for the People." Ngood didn't recognize then the influence of the former American President Abraham Lincoln and these words from his Gettysburg address, but she learned from the adults influencing her to be glad of the reforms the patriot Sun Yat Sen brought to her homeland. Every morning Ngood and all of the other students of the school faced the Chinese flag and portrait of Sun Yet Sen and sang the Chinese National Anthem with conviction:

> "Three Principles of the People, The fundamentals of our party.
> Using this, we establish the Republic; Using this we advance into a state of total peace.
> Oh, you, warriors, for the people, be the vanguard. Without resting day or night, follow the Principles.
> Swear to be diligent; swear to be courageous.
> Obliged to be trustworthy; obliged to be loyal.
> With one heart and one virtue, we carry through until the very end."

Ngood respected the Chinese teachers. They were strict and demanding, which was to be expected for so important a task as educating children. Miss Lee Ting Hone was her Cantonese teacher from Hong Kong. She taught the Chinese calligraphy lessons, the Cantonese dialect, and the math, both with an abacus and with Arabic numerals. She also taught the English lessons for the whole school.

For Ngood's class, beginning English lessons came in a sing-song fashion. The children had learned the English alphabet, and that mastered, repeated after Miss Lee "A is for apple. B is for boy...." Next they learned to spell simple words, parroting after Miss Lee, "C-a-t, cat, d-o-g, dog...." As they recited, the letters were spoken in a lower pitch, and the word was said in a higher pitch. Later they would learn to recite easier tenses in the same sing-song way: is... was... will be. Ngood was barely aware of the world beyond Chinatown, but she did know that the British ruled the country of Burma, and that they spoke this foreign English language.

Some of the children didn't like Miss Lee. They thought she was too strict. She could be very particular about the students speaking the English noun-verb agreement correctly. "They were, not they was!" she scolded. But Ngood appreciated her high expectations of both behavior and learning. Ngood usually earned among the highest of numerical grades, reflecting the percentage of her correct answers. Behavior grades were given in Chinese characters representing "Excellent," "Good," "Fair," or "Poor," and Ngood's were always "Good." She didn't know anyone to receive an "Excellent" score.

****

After her large breakfast at home, Ngood gathered her school books and a few annas to buy her lunch. She hurried to school, a longer walk from Maung Khine Street, but she still did not need to wait for Ah Ming. Ngood had memorized the assigned passage, and she reviewed it in her mind as she walked. She knew she must be prepared, because the teacher, first thing, would make sure the children had done their homework.

Sure enough, after the children had sung the anthem, Miss Lee said, "Students, put your textbooks on my desk. Then return to your seats and prepare to write the passage from last night's homework."

Ngood obediently began to make the ink. Into her ink well she ground a little powder from the ink slab. Then she poured some water into the shallow well and mixed it carefully. Even before Ngood started learning to make the beautiful Chinese letters, she had learned to make this ink. She had practiced to get an ink that was not too thick and not too thin. Ink that was too thin would run, requiring a quick daub with blotter paper to stop it from spreading, but even so, a spoiled character would result. A thick ink would not flow well on to the paper, the character might be unreadable, and one had to frequently refill the brush.

When Ngood had mixed ink of the right consistency, she held her brush perpendicular to the paper by resting it firmly against her hand. Then she began to write the text from memory. Ngood tried to be very careful to keep her hand slightly above the work so she would not smear it and ruin the beautiful brush strokes.

When making a single Chinese character, Ngood was disciplined, as she had been taught, even as to the order of the strokes. First she drew a rectangle, wider than high, like a mouth: left stroke down, top stroke-- left to right, right stroke down, bottom stroke-- left to right. But she was careful to leave a little space between the left stroke and the top stroke, and careful to close all others. Then she drew a vertical line through the center of the mouth figure, the top of the line beginning slightly above the rectangle, and extending further below it. This completed the character for "central."

Below this she started the next character. First, three sides of a square box: a down stroke for the left side, a left to right stroke for the top, and a down stroke with a little hook inward at the bottom for the right side. Then, inside this box, she drew one short horizontal line, then another slightly longer one below it. Then she made a vertical line from the center of the first line, through the second line and about the same distance below the second line. The she put another horizontal line, slightly longer than the other two, at the bottom of the vertical line. Without the box, Ngood knew, this symbol meant "king." Now a simple dot to the right of the first line transformed the meaning of the symbol to "jade." Now, she closed the box at the bottom, stroking left to right, and Ngood completed the jade symbol inside a box, meaning "country."

China

The meaning of the two characters together, "central" and "country," means "China," called Joang Kok in Ngood's Cantonese dialect. So began Ngood's memorized lesson about the homeland of her people.

Ngood learned the symbol for other countries. For instance, she made the symbol for "beautiful." This was a combination of the often used "grass top" symbol of two strokes slanting together at the bottom, like a letter "v," though slightly open at the bottom. Beneath the "grass top," Ngood formed the symbol for "king," and then, closely below that, the symbol known as the "mustache," two strokes slanting down and away from each other. This character with the "country" symbol following it, meant "America," spoken in Cantonese Me Kok.

As she wrote the symbols in a series, Ngood arranged them top to bottom, right to left, building sentences in traditional Chinese order. Her left hand was always ready with the blotter, just in case. High scores and teacher approval were the goal, and blots and smears would deny that goal even if every stroke and dot was correct.

America

Truly, Ngood was overwhelmed in kindergarten and first grade. The teachers were demanding and the course work was daunting. But, as she progressed through the grades, she was able to conform to the high standards, and she took pride in her work. Seldom, any more, was she the focus of a teacher's strict reprimand for drawing the strokes in an improper order or manner. Still, whenever the teacher walked by, Ngood felt an inward shiver of fear of being singled out for stern correction.

During the lunch break, Ngood and her cousin Len took their annas to the hall where locals were permitted to set up stands to sell food. The girls really weren't very hungry after their big morning meals. While they were eating their little lunches, they hoped to catch a glimpse of Ming's teacher from Shanghai. Oh, she was so lovely! And so modern! She wore beautifully trimmed Chinese dresses and high heels. Her long hair was permed into gorgeous, shining waves. The little girls could hardly keep from staring at her.

****

After school, Ngood ran to the third floor of the four-story house to put her books away. After her snack, she looked for her cousin Len on the second floor. The girls were the same age and loved to play together. "Do you want to jump rope?" Len asked. Ngood and Len agreed to meet at the marble entry, and Ngood hurried down the steps to look for her Grandfather's young son.

"Tuck Sook, go and get the long jump rope. Len and I want to jump rope," she demanded.

Soon Tuck Sook was obediently dragging a long rope through the house and out to the street. Sometimes the girls used shorter lengths and jumped individually, but they knew if they appeared in the street with a long length of rope, they would soon be surrounded by dozens of neighborhood children ready to turn the rope or stand in line to jump, competing for highest number of jumps completed. Ngood ordered Tuck Sook to turn one end of the rope.

Unfortunately, teasing and bossing their grandfather's young son was another pastime of Ngood and Len. The boy was two years younger than the girls, and they used their size to chase him and frighten him. Other times, they simply took advantage of his usefulness to them. He took it all with a pleasant nature.

****

The four-story house of Ngood's childhood would always loom large in her recollections, like a revered mountain of her ancestors in southern China. The place of her birth, the little house on Nineteenth Street, with its high fan-shaped windows and pigeon emblems for luck, was quickly becoming a distant memory. She had a vague memory of her father's pleasure when swallows built their nests in the corners of the open windows in the old house as the four-story house was being constructed, a sure omen for good fortune.

The four-story house Grandfather built on Maung Khine Street was a local marvel of the times and was a testimony of Grandfather Chin's success in Burma. The home, and the twin peak beside it, had taken several years to build, with real concrete walls, iron beams, and expensive Burmese teak wood.

At street level, the first floor was set back so the upper stories formed a sheltering roof above the entrance. Supported on a track was a collapsing gate with closely spaced, vertical, iron bars. It was more than head high and stretched across the entire width of the building. Above the gate was a stationary ornamental grate that also extended across the building's width, so the entire entrance could be closed off with this imposing armor.

During the day, the gate was always left opened for neighborhood children. There were no grassy yards in Chinatown; the stifling streets were the playground, and the shaded entryway to One Fifty-Six Maung Khaing Street was an

Late photo of exterior of four-story house, taken after the arrival of cars and electricity

oasis, the marble floor staying cool even in the hot season, when the city often roasted in triple digits of the Fahrenheit scale.

Colorful tiles decorated the wall of the entrance, the top row of tiles displaying peacocks with showy tail feathers open like a Chinese fan. Like peacocks, the tile colors were fantastic, bright teal and green. The peacock was an emblem of dignity and beauty, and since the Ming dynasty it was used to represent a Chinese official. Indeed, two brothers who lived here were leaders of Chinatown.

The beautiful, heavy, teak double doors on the first floor were painted red for luck. Next to the doors was a tablet with the name of the god of the sky, to guard the doorway, and a shelf to offer incense and tea as appeasements to him. Above the first floor entry, upper floors also had double doors that opened onto balconies extending the width of the building. The balcony at each level had waist-high iron railings. Also, on both sides of the doors, tall windows, divided into panes, usually stood open, and vertical bars protected the interior. Transoms above the windows were also open, catching every breeze that stirred off the Rangoon River. The wood trim around the doors and windows was painted white. The building itself was concrete, tinted a soft, rusty brick color.

The doors opened into a living room, and to enter the room, one had to step over the threshold which was meant to keep out the ghosts. Here it was only about four inches high, but Chinese were known to make the threshold much higher, even a foot high, as a barrier to unwanted spirits. Inside, the large room had a high ceiling, which had a cooling effect. The perimeter walls were whitewashed concrete, but the wall across the room, where the ancestor altar was central, was wood-paneled and had arched entrances on either side to access the rest of the first floor of the house.

Above the two archways were huge enlarged photos of Ngood's paternal grandparents. On the right was the likeness of Grandfather Chin,  a bit younger than he looked to Ngood, but showing the wrinkles of age so admired by the Chinese. His portrait showed the distinctive round face and hairless head so familiar to Ngood, but the face in the photo was stern and dignified, not wearing the friendly smile that Ngood knew so well. The woman to his right was unfamiliar to Ngood. She was not the wife with whom Grandfather lived in the back of the first floor, the woman whom the children were told to call, Hlai Pwa, "Lesser Grandmother." The woman in the portrait wore the usual bun of an adult, married Chinese woman, but Ngood noticed her hair was pulled over her ears. These larger than life countenances presided over the room.

The ancestor altar was a critical fixture in every Chinese home, but the one on the first floor of the four-story house was of the best quality. Central on the solemn ebony table with inlaid mother-of-pearl designs was the ancestor tablet indicating the names and the dates of births and deaths of the deceased ancestors. Always there was an offering of fresh fruit here, usually arranged in a pyramid.

Those venerating ancestors are often not conscious that they have split the ancestor's spirit into three parts, and they cannot explain the rationale of this, but the origins of this custom might be influenced by the Yin and Yang concept of separate but equal parts. Two components of the deceased soul are said to reside one in the ancestor tablet and one with the bones in the grave. These parts are not considered to be immortal, and so descendants are required to provide nourishment for them. The third part of the soul is said to be immortal; it goes to judgment and roams the spiritual realm until it is reincarnated, entering a higher or lower level of mortal life, based on previous performance. The painful cycle into life repeats again and again until one perhaps reaches a state of careless oblivion in Nirvana.

Beside the ancestor tablet on the altar, was the representation of the goddess Guan Yin, Lady of Mercy, thought to be an ethereal influence of compassion. Some homes had a ceramic statue representing her, but in the Chin home, a framed picture depicted Guan Yin with flowing robes and holding a child, a sea god full of mischief, whom she only could control. She was portrayed standing on a lotus, the most sacred of Chinese flowers, which is said to grow in the mud while remaining undefiled as Buddha was said to be born of the world while remaining above it. In some pictures Guan Yin was shown with multiple heads or arms so as to better hear and help those in distress. Sometimes she was represented with eyes in the palms of her many hands, to suggest that she could see and relieve much suffering, or with very long fingernails, but these variants were preferred more in the Indian culture than the Chinese culture.

Below the altar, near the floor, was the red plaque representing the very important god of the ground, Who Ee, "property ground." This god must be appeased for successful harvest and prosperity of the household.

Above the ancestor altar was a tall painting depicting three gods of Chinese lore, said to be the three stars which are known as Orion's belt in parts of the world influenced by the Greeks. They were Fu-xing, Lu-xing, and Shou-xing: the happiness god, the prosperity god, and the long life god, representing qualities most desired by Chinese. In the portrait Fu-xing was dressed in the traditional blue robe of the civil servant, and Lu-xing was dressed in the robes of a Taoist priest. Shou-xing was always portrayed as an old man with a high forehead and carrying a peach, symbolic of long life.

Grandfather's housekeeper maintained the duties of appeasing all of the gods on the first floor, daily burning incense to each, offering tea, and keeping fresh fruit arranged. Ngood's mother was responsible for the same set of gods represented in the household on the third floor.

Against the wall on each side of the living room were matching carved ebony chairs with inlaid mother-of-pearl in intricate floral patterns. These stiff-backed, high-armed furnishings were not for comfort but were meant to show the style of those who could afford it. Two chairs in the middle were flanked by tables and two more chairs, so each person had access to a table. An enamel spittoon at each end completed the row, not that Chinese men used chewing tobacco, but because they often enjoyed the simple pleasure of spitting. The table tops were slightly higher than the chair seats and were always ready to hold the tea service. The beautiful red cushions that went with the chairs were stored away and brought out only for New Year celebrations. On each of the two walls above the arrangement of chairs was hung five long, red paper panels, perhaps a foot wide and three feet long. Ancient Chinese poems were written in black calligraphy on the panels. Such poems were beloved by the Chinese people, and one might take a new name for himself or his business from these poems. Other Chinese homes displayed four panels depicting Chinese seasons.

The second, third, and fourth floors were similarly designed. Entering from the staircase in the back of the house, one found a smaller living room than the first floor. Along one wall was the familiar sequence: a spittoon, an ebony chair, a table, two chairs, a table, a chair, and a spittoon. There was also a dressing table with drawers and a mirror. The servants' bedroom in the back was also sometimes used for hanging laundry to dry in inclement weather, as well as for overflow seating for a meal. Mama's often used Singer sewing machine was in this room too. The dining room, kitchen and bathroom completed the back of the house.

Toward the street, two long bedrooms with a hallway between stretched to the front of the house, and doors at the end of the hall opened to the balcony. Entering the hallway from the back, the girls slept on the left, and the master bedroom was on the right. When Papa was home, the master bedroom was divided by a curtain to separate the parents' area from where the little boys slept. The master bed was handsome, with a big bronze headboard of a modern, western style. Mosquito netting draped charmingly like a curtain around the bed, and stylish cords with tassels drew the netting to metal hooks in the wall when it was not in use. Pwa Pwa and Byu Goo would use big, grass, broom fans to chase away mosquitos from the bed area before the netting was pulled shut. Beside the bed was Papa's bamboo easy chair with a woven mat to fit the frame, which was much cooler and more comfortable than the ebony chairs. A wardrobe, a couch that made a spare bed, and a writing table and chair also furnished the room. On one wall was a very high shelf, big enough to hold the ancestor tablet with the ancestors' names written on a big red paper, a plaque of Guan Yin, and the plaque of the three star-gods, plus the incense holders and a pyramid of fruit. Who Ee, the god of the ground, was on the floor below.

Ngood sometimes witnessed her mother performing morning rituals. The rituals could be done any time during the day, but Ah Ma always did these early in the morning, a sign of her reverence. Climbing up on the chair of the writing desk, Mama would set a little tray on the shelf before the ancestor tablet. On this tray she placed the emptied and carefully cleaned small teacups without handles and the incense holder. Mama would light three incense sticks which were supported by sand in the incense holder. Then Mama would half-fill the three teacups with tea she had freshly brewed, because offering a brim-full cup to anyone was considered rude. Nearly always Mama kept fresh fruit stacked in a pyramid on the shelf, and as it began to dry up she replaced it with more fresh fruit. When Mama stepped down from the chair, she would kowtow and chant aloud her petitions to the ancestors for the well-being of her family. She must also pray to Who Ee for protection.

Certain holidays, like New Year's Day and Ancestor Day, required much more elaborate offerings. Also, on birth and death days of the ancestors, additional food offerings were made, particularly offerings that would not especially attract flies, most often more fresh fruit. On the first and fifteenth day of the lunar month, at the new moon and the full moon, as well as other special occasions, a decorative red candle would be set with a bamboo holder in the sand of the incense holder and lit along with the incense. On these days Mama abstained from meat as a sacrificial fast. Similarly, a white candle was used on birth and death anniversaries of ancestors.

Most often Mama's morning routine was done before the household stirred. But Ngood was sometimes awake and would help her mother by climbing up to light the incense sticks. On special occasions or when something good happened, the ancestors and gods must be especially thanked, and paper representing money and other gifts must be burned to the ancestors and gods.

The girls' bedroom had plenty of room for two double beds and a wardrobe, with shelves and a rod for hanging things, plus a couch that pulled out into a double bed and a small tea table with shelves underneath. The walls of the hallway between the bedrooms were highly polished wood partitions. There were glass panes at the top to let in light, and above that was open to the ceiling to let the air circulate. The rooms were private enough; only with a ladder could one have seen into the rooms.

There were no mattresses on the wooden four post beds. That would be much too hot! Instead, there were high quality, woven bamboo mats. The beds were low to the floor for coolness. Each evening the maids would put up the mosquito netting for the children by draping it over the four posts. During the day, each person's pillow would be placed on the bed with the folded light blanket.

****

The Moon Festival was held on the fifteenth day of the eighth lunar month. A special ritual was done by the women of the house every year at that time, and the little boys would join them when they were older. In advance of the full moon, each one, Mama, Pwa Pwa, Byu Goo, and the three girls, was given a plate to place around the dining table. A candle was placed in the center of each plate, water was poured at the base of the candle, and a mung bean was set in the water. Each of the women and girls was to keep her little bean seed watered. Before bedtime every night for a week or more, Mama beckoned for each one to observe her own bean sprout.

"Do not forget, if you want to be intelligent and clever you must watch your bean sprout grow bigger," Mama reminded. Ngood checked her bean sprout as she had done for many nights, and sure enough, the sprout from the bean seed had visibly lengthened. Ngood could feel her cleverness growing too.

Then Mama led the group to the balcony. The moon was full and beautiful. "Look carefully at the moon," Mama said with a little awe in her voice. She pointed, "There is the old man, cutting down the cassia tree. Can you see him?"

At first, Ngood could not see the scene at all. But after a bit, with Ah Ming saying, "Oh! Yes! I see him, Mama!" Ngood began nodding too. Well, maybe she could see the shapes of the man and the tree. Yes, yes, she thought she could.

"There is also a good and beautiful fairy that lives in the moon," Byu Goo explained. "She does kind things for people on earth. She can give you wisdom."

****

As a special event, the Chinese school was offering a field trip, and Ngood's class and Ming's class were participating. Lorries, trucks with long flat beds, and in this case affixed with benches, were hired to transport the children to the Shwedagon Pagoda. This was one of the most famous of the seven hundred pagodas in Burma, and though it was prominent in her birth city of Rangoon, Ngood had not yet entered it. The excited children rode several blocks down Canal Street, turned north onto Pagoda Road, and soon the stunning gold roof of the main stupa, a structure containing Buddhist relics, arrested their attention. They had not gone even two miles, and already they had arrived from Chinatown to this fascinating other world!

Needless to say, the children were awe struck by the size and extravagance of the magnificent Buddhist monument, which extended across fourteen acres. Built on a hill and elevated on a platform, the main pagoda towered over the other buildings of northern Rangoon and shone with a stunning golden brilliance in the sunlight. The pagoda was richly ornamented; the huge, tiered, umbrella-like roof was gilded with real gold and the tip studded with thousands of real diamonds and rubies.

The hill supporting the pagoda was said to be the burial site of relics of the four Buddha said to have walked the earth, including eight hairs from the head of Gautama Buddha. Surrounding the central feature were dozens of smaller structures, also radiant with gilding and repeating in miniature the umbrella roof shape. Tiny bells, moved by the wind, chimed a delicate, other-worldly sound. Even before climbing the stairs into the structure, the children were moved to reverence.

At the entrances to the Shwedagon Pagoda were many stalls containing items for purchase, both souvenirs and offerings to Buddha, including Buddha images, charms, candles, incense, streamers, and especially gold-leaf. Hawkers called out promises that purchasing gold leaf for Buddha would earn the buyer merit in Heaven. The children's teachers explained that deft pagoda keepers would climb the roof periodically to apply the donated gold-leaf.

In veneration, each girl and teacher removed her slippers before ascending the many uneven marble steps of the wide staircase to the top of the hill. Ngood added her sandals to the pile, but she also noticed racks where one could pay to have their shoes kept. The shoes looked odd to her. Few locals in Burma wore shoes; it was too hot! But foreigners could check their shoes and socks. Ngood did not know at the time, but the Shwedagon Pagoda was a site of repeated grave offense to the Burmese people, as prideful British occupiers often callously refused to remove their shoes as they walked around the revered site. This, besides other offenses and the desire for self-rule, fueled deep resentment and nationalist longings among Burmans.

Entering the elaborate gateway, which was guarded by a pair of huge, fantastic, winged lions, the children were instructed that they should walk together in a clockwise direction to visit the site. The marble floors extended throughout the open-air complex of ornate shrines, and the children found the marble was quite cool in the shade, though hot in the sunlight. They observed adherents placing flowers and prayer flags at the various stations and ringing small bells, whose sound was said to buoy prayers to the spirit world. Worshipers could pour water over a Buddha image as a sign of veneration. Numerous other Buddha statues were gigantic or miniature, portraying Buddhas seated on chairs, or with legs crossed and soles of the feet turned up, or standing, or reclining, some with crowns, some offering benediction, and many gilded in gold or clothed in gold gilded robes. There were also many other shrines of significance representing planets, animals, days of the week, guardian angels, and on and on.

Ngood was also impressed by two gigantic cast bronze bells, which towered over her teachers. She heard that one, weighing twenty three tons, was once plundered by the British invaders, who accidentally dropped it into the sea. Eventually it was retrieved and replaced at the Shwedagon. The second bell Ngood saw was one that weighed forty tons and was plated with gold. Ngood was told that a third bell was looted by Portugese invaders and also dropped into the sea, and it had never been recovered.

That evening, Ngood and Ming moaned about their sore feet from climbing all the steps and standing on the hot marble around the Shwedagon Pagoda complex. Byu Goo found a basin for each girl, careful to choose the dirty-use basins which were used to wash underwear and to soak feet. Byu Goo filled the basins with warm water and dissolved salt and herbs into the bath, and the girls were comforted as their feet soaked.

As they soaked, Ming commented, "The Burmese Buddha is the very best. The Chinese Buddha looks more Chinese and wears a Chinese hat. But the Burmese Buddha is prettier, and has the longest ears." Ming seemed to Ngood very wise. Long ear lobes, unattached to the face, were admired indications of long life, and the Burmese Buddha had wonderful, long ear lobes.

****

The Chinese had their own temple in Chinatown. Like all Chinese children, Ngood was taken to the temple before starting school. Her mother took Ngood to the altar of Confucius where Ah Ma kowtowed and worshiped and asked the long dead, very wise scholar to make her daughter wise.

Also called Master Kong, Confucius and his followers had prescribed a strict framework of proper relationships for stable society which required a subject to obey governmental superiors extending up the chain of command to the king. Similarly, in families, children were required to obey elder siblings, parents, and grandparents, and wives were to obey their husbands and his parents. This is where ethics began for a good Chinese citizen, though rulers and elders also had responsibilities, and it was thought that as one dutifully fulfilled his role, conforming to "the Way of Heaven," one would find harmony in life. One did not ask the elders "Why?" One simply obeyed.

Rituals to venerate dead ancestors and petition them to intervene favorably in the afterlife were an extension of this hierarchy of power. Elders, even after they were dead, were respected, and furthermore were thought to have the power to bring prosperity, health, and luck to the lives of the living. For these favors, the living were required to provide offerings of food, tea, and other items thought to be useful in the afterlife. Some items, including money, houses, and personal items were represented on paper and then burned with the intent of sending these things to the spirit world. Special ceremonies were expected on birth and death anniversaries of the deceased, and the first and fifteenth day of the lunar month were also treated specially. Misfortune of the living was thought to result from inadequately fulfilling the rituals required to serve the dead.

Confucianism was just one of several influences in the Chinese temple. For many Chinese, Confucianism, ancestor veneration, and social laws are mixed deeply with Taoism, which focuses on harmony with what are considered natural laws and on worshiping or appeasing spirits of nature. These spirits include humanized planets and stars, immortalized heroes, animal spirits, and spirits of human activities. This elaborate system of ritual is also called the "Way of Heaven," and by living properly with the spirits, one is thought able to achieve eternal life. Woven into both modern Confucianism and Taoism are the thoughts of Yin and Yang, meaning positive and negative, good and evil, light and dark, male and female, considered opposite things of equal value that must be balanced. So then, rather than work to eliminate evil, one should expect and accept evil, and passivity was thought the best way to cope.

To this, many Chinese add the influences of Buddhism, including beliefs that all suffering comes from earthly desire and that through reincarnation the cycle of suffering continues into the spiritual world and back again. These two more threads of fatalism were knit in to traditional Chinese life and death issues: suffering doesn't hurt if you don't care, and you can't help your unhappy circumstances anyway, because you must pay your debt for sins in previous lives. The best prescription, then, is to tolerate life as well as possible and not care too much about it, as long as requirements of the spirit world are faithfully satisfied. A better future life could be earned by good deeds, particularly by generosity to the temple system.

Of course, these are simplistic explanations of complicated systems of belief with many variants.

One could say the beliefs of Ngood's family had come from thousands of years of tradition and absorption of many influences, swirled together and hardened like marble.

Ngood often followed her mother to the Chinese temple. She never wondered why her sisters did not go along as she did. Maybe they were quickly bored with the rituals and did not care to see them repeated every full moon, at every ancestor birthday and death day, every anniversary of a deceased child's birth or death, or any time of special concern. Mostly the temple was filled with other Chinese wives, and Ngood seldom saw any men, except for the old monk who sold things needed for temple use.

Whenever they first arrived, Ngood would see Mama pay something, select a sea clam shell from a pile of many, then kowtow and worship at an altar. Then Mama dropped the clam shell on the floor. From the shell, a number written on a paper would fall out.

The old monk was available to help a novice, but Mama, like every good Chinese wife in Rangoon's Chinatown, knew what to do next. She went to a wall where were hung many sheets of paper several inches wide and quite long. She found the paper with the number that matched her number from the clam shell and read the fortune listed on it, including warnings and recommendations on everything from travel and business to lucky dates for marriage, burial, opening a business, or for naming and presenting a child to the world.

Mama also bought incense and a little brown boat made of folded paper with a square of gold leaf at the bottom which symbolized money. She put the money-boat before one of the gods represented in the temple. Mama lit the incense stick with a match supplied from a box at the altar, placed the end of it in a container of sand, and kowtowed before the idol of choice. Ngood did not pay attention to which altars her mother selected, but there were plenty from which to choose, including those representing sun, moon, planets and stars; weather; Chinese heroes; animals; prosperity, happiness and luck. Also vying for attention were patrons of business people, soldiers, performers, virgins, the elderly, and on and on. When Mama finished kow-towing, her last duty was to go outside with the little boat, and to burn the boat in a small furnace, sending the offering to appease and please the gods.

Occasionally Ngood saw other monks or nuns in the temple, conspicu-ous by their shaved heads and distinctive dress. The monks wore grey robes that exposed their bare arms, and the nuns wore beige short-sleeved blouses and longyis. Ngood observed to herself that these pallid robes were not as impressive as the lovely, deep-yellow robes worn by Burmese counterparts, monks who were often seen in the streets before noon, walking in lines through the city as they received charity. The Chinese monks and nuns wore necklaces of amber prayer beads, which sometimes attracted Ngood's attention as the devotee fingered the beads and quietly chanted something. Both monks and nuns lived at the attached monastery, but the nuns were careful not to interfere with the work of the monks.

The complicated mix of Buddhism, Taoism, Confucianism, and ances-tor devotion made an exhausting and frightful conglomeration of belief for a little Chinese girl in the early twentieth century. Yet, it was the only life Ngood knew, and she adapted to it.

****

Ngood turned eight in the western calendar year 1930, unless you reckon the Chinese way. Chinese traditionally add one year at birth and one year at death. "One for earth and one for Heaven," the expression goes. Long life was considered a blessing, and marrying into a family possessing the "long life gene" was beneficial. Hence, an exaggeration of a couple years was considered acceptable towards presenting your best, and starting at one was a comfort, however slight, to a mother during her child's precarious first year of life.

As this year began, Ngood, besides having the sister Ming, four years older, and the sister He'ung, three years younger, had two older broth-ers that died at birth. After He'ung, two younger brothers had survived, a baby sister had died, and Ngood's mother was expecting another child.

****

Grandfather Chin had built the four-story house for his four grown sons, born of his first wife, and their families. He planned that each son would have a floor of the house in which to raise his family.

Sadly, the number four brother of Ngood's father died young and left a poor wife and four little children. Ngood never knew how this uncle died; she did not remember seeing him sick and she never recalled seeing a body respectfully displayed for a period of mourning.

But Ngood vividly remembered the mourning of her aunt, weeping piteously, her long hair let down and sweeping the floor as she walked, hunched and swaying. Ngood even remembered hearing her cries from above on the fourth floor. The aunt did not stay at the four-story house after that. She went to a much smaller, older house on Maung Khine Street.

This aunt did very hard work on the street as a doobie, washing and ironing linens for patrons, including the Chin hotel and restaurant. To do the laundry, she had to make a coal fire, using three or four bricks as a makeshift stove and using a tall, empty kerosene can as a kettle to boil water. Then she would add soap powder to wash and bleach the linens. These linens must also be starched and pressed, and the iron must be heated with coal. The results of all her work were perfect and beautiful; her clients demanded nothing less. Ngood's carefree childhood was always troubled when she happened to see this unhappy aunt working so hard in the street.

Also, Papa's Number Three Brother never lived at the four-story house. Maybe his Hong Kong wife did not want to associate with the less refined, less fashionable, less educated Chinese women of Burma. This uncle rented a separate place, certainly at Grandfather's expense.

Still the four-story house became full, with Number One Uncle, Chin Hone On, "Abundant Peace," and his two wives, so far, and his maybe ten children, so far, plus Ngood's family, with five, so far, that survived birth, and her Grandfather Chin who lived in the back of the first floor with his Number Two wife and young son. Assorted servants and extended family members lived here as well. This was the sign of a successful Chinese man: a big house full of leisurely-living family members and hard-working servants, all supported by his own enterprises.

Ngood's father was the exception. Though tradition had led Chinese to believe avoiding employment was the sign of wealth and happiness, Chin Hone Foo did not accept a life of leisure. No doubt Hone Foo knew this warning of Confucious:

> *"The superior man, when resting in safety, does not forget that danger may come. When in a state of security he does not forget the possibility of ruin. When all is orderly, he does not forget that disorder may come. Thus his person is not endangered, and his clan is preserved."*

And this maxim:

> *"What the superior man seeks is in himself; what the small man seeks is in others."*

Certainly he knew also that his standing as the second son made his future precarious, as superstition prevented Chinese men from contemplating their own deaths, so they rarely left wills. Usually clansmen would support the claims of the eldest son in matters of inheritance. So this forward thinking Number Two Son could not afford to rest. Hone Foo, "Abundant Wealth," was often away from his family for one or two months at a time supporting the opera and other enterprises.

Pwa Pwa had been with the family for as long as Ngood could remember. She lived with them on Nineteenth Street and moved with them to the four-story house. She wasn't really Ngood's grandmother, but she was of the same clan as Ngood's father. Out of affection and respect the children called her Ah Pwa, "Elder Grandmother," or affectionately, Pwa Pwa. No one would think of calling her gung ngen, "work person," or "servant." Mama never ordered her around. Pwa Pwa was quite old and couldn't do heavy work.

After the move to the four-story house "Aunt," Byu Goo, joined the household. The children were never so rude as to call her anything but "Aunt." She was more distantly related than an aunt, but by this Cantonese designation for aunt, "goo," Ngood thought she was a relative on her father's side. She was younger than Pwa Pwa, maybe in her thirties, and she was very bright, but she was superstitious and quite old fashioned. She arrived from China in that big straw hat of Asian field workers that made Ming and Ngood giggle and secretly call her "jungley," a mocking name also used for the jungle people of Burma that sometimes awkwardly made their way into the big city. Also, Byu Goo wore the ridiculous fringe haircut in front, and she had tough, darkened skin from many hours, day after day, year after year, in the sun.

Other things made the children giggle about Byu Goo, like her absurd fear of the water faucet. In China, Byu Goo had carried pails of water on a pole across her shoulders, hauling it from a well, so she had never experienced modern plumbing. Ngood would always remember how water coming into the house with the turn of a handle seemed to Byu Goo frightening magic. In the first several months after her arrival, Byu Goo, forced by her duties to get water, always approached the faucet fearfully and jumped and yelled when the water came out. Ming and Ngood would squelch their laughter until they could run away to laugh in secret. As their elder, Byu Goo must be respected. Though the girls were amused by her, they soon learned to love her.

Byu Goo took good care of her Chin family. Besides daily duties of cooking and cleaning, she worked on hands and knees using cocoanut hulls and sand to scrub the cement floors of the apartment every week. She told Ah Ma this was no trouble and seemed to her light work after the time she spent hoeing and digging in the steep, rocky fields of China. Every few weeks she washed the mosquito netting that hung around every bed in the home, besides all of the other bedding and clothing. She was strong, and she was happy to take over the heavier house work for her family.

Chapter Three

A New Year

Ngood arrived home from school to see Byu Goo carrying an armload of books up the three flights of stairs. Ngood followed her to the girls' bed-room, where Byu Goo set the books and then stacked them neatly on shelves beneath the tea table. Ngood's eyes ran along the spines of the books, reading the titles in Chinese figures, like "A Dream of Red Mansions" and "The Romance of the Three Kingdoms." This aroused in her great curiosity and pleasure.

She heard Ah Ma calling and went to her room. "Ngood," her mother said, "This is my Number Four Sister, your aunt, Han Yee. She comes from Singapore. She will be staying with us and teaching in the Fokinese-Chinese school here in town."

Ngood was delighted to meet the im-pressive young woman. She was slim and attractive, much more modern than Ngood's

Han Yee, Ngood, and Ah Ming at Royal Lake in Rangoon.

mother, with permed hair and a fashionable long dress with a slit exposing her leg, instead of the typical shorter dress and pants her mother wore. Han Yee was also different from her sister in that she carried herself with unusual confidence and eagerness for a Chinese woman. Ngood bowed her head politely. She wanted to ask immediately about the books that apparently came with the aunt, but she maintained the formal composure of a child with home teaching.

Scarcely a week went by before Ngood came home to find her mother getting ready to go out. Mama going out? Oh my! This was a special occasion! Other than the opera, periodic trips to the Chinese temple, and a wedding now and then, Ngood's mother did not go out.

Han Yee said to Ngood, "We have been invited to visit Ah Goo at the shop *Kwong Hep Seng*, 'Spread out Very Strong Prosperity.' Would you care to come along?"

Ngood was always ready for an adventure, and she willingly joined her aunt and mother on the rickshaw ride. She was unsure whom might be the auntie mentioned, because most elders were called aunties or uncles or grandmas or grandpas, but she was happy to go along. The rickshaw driver was quite accustomed to pulling the weight of two adults and a small child in one trip, and soon they had traveled a few blocks down Dalhousie Street to the west end of Chinatown.

Above a shop, they entered a small apartment with linoleum flooring that Ngood admired. Ngood's mother presented their hostess with fruit. Everyone was seated, tea was poured for all, and cookies were offered to the guests.

Lee Htwe Khim gave Ngood a little packet wrapped in red paper. The Chinese frequently bestowed these gifts called *"Lai see."* Knowing to expect some money, Ngood opened the red packet eagerly and found six coins. For superstitious Chinese, six was a good number because the Cantonese word for "six" sounds like the word that means "expensive clothing," and "luxury," so besides the monetary gift was an implied wish for wealth. Ngood thanked Ah Goo, and gave the coins to her mother.

For a while Ngood listened quietly to the adult chatter, but she became bored. She noticed a ball on the floor, and she went to pick it up. She had hardly observed the boy before, except that he was about her age, sullen, and fingering a small whip. But as she reached for the ball, he purposely flicked it away with the handle of the whip! She scowled at the rude boy, and he stood defiantly scowling back at her. She went to get the ball again, and he flicked it again! With their eyes, they fought each other! Determined, she grabbed the ball, and he struck her on the hand and on the head with his stick!

Ngood was furious. "What?" she demanded. Hearing the outburst, both mothers intervened.

"Oh, Puck Ying!" Mrs. Lee said soothingly to her Number One Son, "You must be nice to the little girl. She is our guest, and besides, her mother is your godsister! Now go sit over there, and be a good boy!"

Ngood's mother tried to pacify her daughter, "Ah Ngood, you are alright! Oh, everything is fine! Where is your smile?"

Ngood wanted to please her mother, but her disappointing adventure had gone quickly from exciting to boring and then to upsetting. She sat politely, but her mind was filled with offense and dislike of the boy. Finally, the women finished their visit. Ngood was glad to start home again and hoped never again to see the rude boy with the big name.

"A Hundred Times Heroic," she thought, "is A Hundred Times A Brat!" After that, Ngood's mother and Han Yee would make other trips to visit Mrs. Lee, but Ngood did not care to join them.

Ngood thought smugly that even this boy wouldn't dare misbehave in a few weeks, because the New Year was coming. The approach of the New Year could not be ignored by any Chinese child, and surely even this naughty boy had heard the warnings Ngood often heard. A child's good behavior was terribly important at the turning of the New Year.

"Be respectful! Be good! The kitchen god will be reporting to the Jade Emperor soon! You must behave, or the kitchen god will give a bad report on this household. Then we will suffer!"

Ngood would try hard to be good. That brat would try too, or he would be sorry.

In the Chinese eleventh month, winter soup was made. Ngood wanted to help, and surprisingly, Byu Goo gave her access. "Go wash your hands!" the auntie commanded. Then Ngood helped her shape the balls of dough, rolling them with her clean hands. Byu Goo added these dumplings to broth with meat and bok choy. With this soup, everyone knew the year was coming to an end.

When the weeks had passed, Ngood was excited to see the final preparations for the New Year celebration. Her mother had been expertly sewing clothing for her family ever since the hot season ended. Now at last, the beautiful red cushions were placed on the ebony chairs in the living rooms, making their annual ten day appearance. Ngood did not sit on them, but she sat before them, admiring their beauty. They were made of red satin fabric and had skirts that draped over the dark wood. The embroidery on them was fantastic, with gold and silver threads forming splendid, regal peacocks. The tea tables also had matching cloths.

Ngood had been reminded for weeks to guard her words. If she happened to say something bad, she must go and rinse her mouth with sugar water and then come back and say something sweet. The sugar water was not at all considered a reward, but was a reminder of possible dread of consequences from the spiritual world for offenses at this critical time. No one wanted to risk upsetting any of the gods, and calamity always could be traced back to some infraction. The beginning of the year was thought to set the tone for the rest of the year, and so everything must be sweet. Not only bad words, but unlucky words, like the word "four," were forbidden.

In fact, a dizzying number of rules must be remembered. No knives or scissors could be used, for fear of cutting off good fortune. One couldn't wash her hair for fear of washing away good fortune. No one dared sweep, for fear of sweeping away good fortune. And those rules were just the beginning!

On New Year's Eve, a special large table, with its own lavishly embroidered skirting, was set near the ancestor altar, and it was loaded with food. Wine instead of tea was poured into the offering cups for this occasion. After the food was presented to the gods and ancestors and the family bowed at the ancestor altar, the family feasted. There was no meat at this meal, a personal sacrifice meant to atone for sin in the previous year. For the duration of the New Year celebration there would be much fruit filling the table, stacked in lucky pyramids before the gods and ancestors.

Ngood was thrilled when she woke up and realized it was New Year's Day at last. After the large family breakfast, Ngood's mother gave each of her children several new outfits, some for around the house, and some for special occasions. Ngood immediately put on her favorite, a white blouse matched with a sleeveless long dress that was pink with green stripes and decorated with green piping on the neck and sleeves. Her mother had purchased the handmade green floral buttons.

Then her mother brought out the special jewelry for the girls, which they were allowed to wear only on this one day. Ngood didn't realize at the time that one of the necklaces she wore was a United States one dollar gold coin hung from a heavy gold rope chain, in the bright yellow 22 or 24 carat gold preferred by discerning Chinese. The coin was embellished with gold filigree by local Chinese artisans. Dressed in her finery, Ngood tried to wait patiently for the New Year's Day parade, the pinnacle of the day.

Meanwhile, neighbors and relatives were stopping by, and they would bow with their hands folded in front of their faces, saying, "*Gong hee fat toy,*" meaning, "Wishing you great wealth." They presented red packets to the children. Ngood would open her packet with delight, find the coins or bills inside—in even numbers but never four--and give the contents to her mother. Some of the gifts were quite generous, and children wouldn't know how to spend money wisely, so they were expected to give them to their mothers. The visitations of friends and relatives would go on for ten days, and no one came empty handed. Fruit was the gift of preference to the parents, and red fruit, especially imported tangerines or red grapefruit, carried the additional implied wish for good luck. Candy was also given as a charm for a sweet year to come.

At last the time for the New Year's Day parade was near, and Ngood's family gathered on their balcony. Ngood could hardly keep still in anticipation, but she absolutely must behave. Papa expected perfect behavior from his children, particularly in public.

While she waited, Ngood noted her mother with admiration. Her mother's hair had been done by a special hairdresser. She wore it up, in the usual bun, but it was adorned by a beautiful gold hairpin with a jade stone and was held by a circle of smaller gold pins with rubies. Her sisters and the little brothers never looked finer, and Papa stood as the austere ruler over all. Ngood heard the chatter of relatives on the balconies above and below and sensed the excitement building in the street.

She could hear the parade approaching. First she heard the thrumming drums, coming closer and closer. Then she heard the horns. At last the band appeared at the head of Maung Khine Street and announced their arrival with a crash of cymbals!

Papa commanded, "Follow me!" The family hurried down to the street to watch the parade with the crowd. The girls knew to tuck their gold chains under their clothes so any bad men in the crowd could not rip the jewelry from their necks.

The children stood formally, as children with home training, but this was not easy because they were thrilled with excitement. Acrobats came with the first group of instrumentalists. They leaped and tumbled and flipped high into the air, all in rhythm to the music. Then the martial arts experts came, one group showing off impressive, unified Kung Fu moves and another making a frightening demonstration of flashing knives and spears.

Then Ngood could see the fabulous dragon, thrusting his head aggressively and shaking his horns and beard, his big eyes protruding and fierce teeth exposed in a scary, but benevolent, smile. His fantastically colorful, scaly body undulated down the road like a roiling river, flowing precisely to the beat of drums. She worried about the unsupervised children running barefooted around the dragon, oblivious to the danger of being trampled by the beast. As the dragon reached the four-story house, Ngood instinctively moved nearer her mother, claiming a piece of Mama's dress along with her little siblings. Ming stood bravely watching the dragon's approach, and Ngood took courage from her, though she did not release her grasp.

The dragon paused and then looked up at the third floor balcony with interest. Ngood didn't notice before, but there, fastened to the same balcony where she had just stood with her family, was a long string that dangled nearly to the street. On this string were tied many clumps of lettuce alternating with hundred dollar notes! As Ngood watched, the dragon began munching happily on the lettuce and also the money. Then, to her astonishment, the dragon began to climb up the side of the building, consuming lettuce and money all the way to the third floor balcony! The crowd cheered with pleasure! Then Ngood watched as the dragon returned to the street, and with flourish, flowed gracefully out of sight.

The dragon would find lettuce and money at other clan leaders' homes, but the spectacle could not have been what it was at the four-story house! The Chins enjoyed a "big face" in the community.

Only later did Ngood remember that the dragon was made of many men in costume. She marveled at the feat of the half-dozen athletes climbing on to each other's shoulders as they worked as a unit under the costume, making the serpent seem to magically climb the building. How did they do this while gathering the lettuce and money into the dragon's tummy?

Later, inside her house, Ngood noticed that Papa's shoes and cane had disappeared. "Woo-woo!" she sang in noisy delight. Papa had been home for a few weeks, and with the added challenge to behave well at the New Year, it was nearly more than the children, and likely the adults, could manage. Ngood knew he had gone for a walk and would return home soon. But the whole household joined Ngood in reacting to Papa's brief absence with some happy racket.

****

Ngood did not resist her aunt's books for long. She knew she should ask Han Yee for permission to read them. Instead she sneaked a look, and the stories caught her like a kite in the wind, lifting her up and away to the far off land and times of her ancestors. The gifted authors mixed fact and fantasy like herbs of a Chinese doctor's remedy, with a delightful result.

Ngood loved to sit with a book in her father's easy chair when he wasn't home, or she often strained in the dim light to read in her bed. Her mother was in her time of confinement, the last month of her pregnancy. She was to stay at home and rest, not lifting anything. Byu Goo had become a dear companion to her. The only time Ngood saw her mother laugh was when Byu Goo was telling her stories of her village in China. Byu Goo clearly enjoyed making Mama laugh, and developed quite a comic repertoire. Ngood realized by contrast that her mother seemed usually a bit sad.

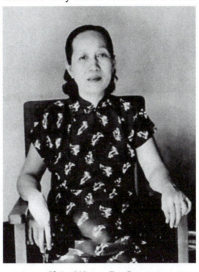

Chin Wong Po Sun

Ngood and her little sister He'ung were playing housekeeper in Mama's room. They were dressed in Mama's clothes, and they tenderly cradled their babies, bolster pillows wrapped in cloths. They took turns visiting each other at their pretend homes, a sheet or a measure of fabric providing a roof and a couple of chairs forming walls. They were pretending it was raining, so they had to use umbrellas to scurry between homes. Then, as each entered her sister's "house," she politely removed the sandals from her feet and made a bow. Byu Goo had given them each an orange to present to the other hostess, because no one would go visiting empty-handed. On a couple of plates from the kitchen they enjoyed their make-believe meals. Once in a while Mama's laughter caught Ngood's attention, and she stopped her own play to watch in pleasure.

Then Ah Ming came into the room and asked Ah Ma if she might play one of Papa's records. Once Papa returned home from a long trip with a record player and records. He had purchased these especially for his opera business, and he listened to the recordings to decide whether or not to book a particular opera. With Mama's approval, Ah Ming carefully put one of the records on the Victrola player and turned the crank so that the room was filled with sounds of the appealing melodies and dramatic words of Cantonese opera.

Hearing one mournful song, Ngood was reminded to ask her mother a question that had been troubling her for some time, "Mama, why does a bride cry so much at weddings?"

Her mother answered, "In China, when a daughter is getting married, the mother and daughter cry a lot because often the daughter must go to another village. Traveling can be quite difficult, and perhaps the mother and daughter will never see each other again.

"Besides, when a woman marries, she is expected to do for the other side, to become part of her husband's family. If they are well-to-do, it may be alright. But if they are poor, she will have to work in the fields. So, parting, the mother and daughter cry because they fear future hardship and that they might not meet again. Even if the parting is not forever, the daughter is not allowed to return to her parents for at least one month, as she adapts to her husband's family. In my case, I had to leave my family and my home to marry your father in this country."

"But Grandmother Wong lives here in Burma," Ngood observed.

Mama smiled, "Yes, only my Number Two Brother traveled here with me from my village in China. The matchmaker had arranged everything between my family and your father's family. I never saw your father before the wedding ceremony. A few years later, your papa brought my father and mother to Burma. They lived with my Number Two Brother. Your Grandfather Wong now teaches in the boys' Chinese school behind our house. You know my sisters are here in Burma also. Number Two Sister Po Swe lives with her husband in Moulmein. Number Three Sister Po Har lives in the four-story house next door. And Number Four Sister Po Han came from Singapore and is living with us now."

****

Ngood came home from school and found her mother's mother was there. Grandmother Wong was helping to supervise the care of Ngood's mother, instructing Pwa Pwa and Byu Goo in Mama's dietary needs during the last days of her pregnancy and making sure all the foods were assembled to feed Mama for the first month after she delivered. Ah Ma must build up strength after the delivery and produce plenty of milk. Byu Goo and Pwa Pwa had been preparing or purchasing the dried fish and dried duck, the sausages, and the best red wine. Pigs' feet would be cooked with ginger, sugar, and vinegar; the sweet and sour combination was said to aid with milk production.

When Grandmother Wong was satisfied that all was in order, she sat down with Ngood. Grandmother didn't visit often, and she often called Ngood by one of her sister's names first, but she always came to the right name at last. She said, "Ngood, I remember when you were born."

Ngood looked at her with interest. The thought that Grandmother was present for her birth was intriguing. She asked, "Did you come to help Ah Ma when I was born, Ah Pwa?"

Grandmother Wong answered, "Oh, Yes! And I will never forget. You were premature, born at only seven months." Grandmother held out her cupped hand, "I could put you in my hand. You were like a little mouse! I fed you arrowroot. I boiled and crushed the root and made a paste, and I put a little bit on my finger and put it in your mouth. Your mother didn't have enough milk, and you were so small, we dared not feed you anything else."

Ngood looked with wonder at the woman who told her things about herself she could not remember. She had often heard that two precious baby brothers had died, one before Ming and one after, but somehow she had lived. Ngood looked rather critically at the rough, old finger that had been in her mouth, but she suddenly felt very close to her grandmother. This loving and kind woman she hardly knew had helped her to live.

Before she went back to her home, Grandmother said fondly, "I will always think of you as *low-see doy*, my little mouse!"

A few days later when Ngood came home from school, the housekeeper Pwa Pwa shooed her, "Go out and play."

Ngood happily left her school books and went down to the second floor to look for Len. "Let's play locks!" she suggested.

Len agreed, "I'll get my lock and meet you downstairs."

The girls had invented a new game, taking advantage of the large marble squares in diamond orientation in the entryway. Each girl had found a little lock from a trunk somewhere in the house. Taking turns, a girl would put a lock on her forehead and lunge forward without moving her feet, hurtling the lock forward onto the tiles, with childish disregard to the value of the marble. Then she would jump in hopscotch fashion to where the lock landed, pick it up, and return to a happy line of noisy neighborhood girls eager to join the play. They kept a running score of the distance the lock was thrown based on the number of squares jumped. Ngood was always the smallest of playmates her age, but what she lacked in size, she gained in competitiveness.

While they were playing, they heard a commotion and curiously ran into the street to see a ferocious old woman several houses away storming toward them. Ngood recognized this unhappy thunder cloud as her mother's sister's mother-in-law who lived in the other four-story house. She was scolding unfortunate children, and they were scurrying from her. Ngood and Len and their friends were frozen in place, dreading the full force of the coming storm, but unable to turn their eyes from the wonder of its power. Just as danger seemed imminent, the woman turned in at her own home, opened the iron gate, and banged it shut.

When she recovered from her fear, Ngood was glad her own iron gate stood open for the children, and that they need not be afraid to enter it. She wondered what it was like to live in that other house, and she felt sorry for her aunt. Soon the girls resumed their game.

After a couple of hours of play, Ngood ran cheerfully up to the third floor. But cheer faded from her face as she found her home in chaos. Byu Goo was running from her mother's room calling to Pwa Pwa, "She's still bleeding! I can't get it stopped! I don't know what to do!"

Troubled, Ngood went to the girls' bedroom, where Ah Ming and He'ung were. She saw anxiety on their faces.

Ming explained, "Mama gave birth to a little boy, but something is wrong with Mama."

The girls tried to busy themselves with their sewing projects; even little He'ung could use a needle. They knew they must stay out of the way, but they could hear the fuss and worry. Ngood tried to be brave for He'ung as Ming tried to be brave for Ngood. The best ways they could help were to be quiet, to stay busy, and to be good.

Still, the concern was very real. Ngood remembered not long ago hearing a baby's ceaseless crying from an open window at a neighbor's home. This was not the familiar sound Ngood remembered of her own little brothers' crying when they were infants a few years ago. It was a tragic, incessant sound that could not be pacified day or night. Ngood had asked Mama what was wrong, and her mother explained that the baby's mama had died in childbirth. Old Man Thunder Voice's Number One Wife, the nearly deaf woman, had even heard the cries. The deaf aunt had taken pity on the baby and his poor father. She regularly sent one of her maids to take the father evaporated milk, cow's milk with much of the water removed and canned for long shelf life. With the precious, donated milk, the infant boy didn't cry so much and eventually began to thrive.

But, with this knowledge, Ngood was terrified by the very real possibility of losing her own dear mama. So it was that Ngood's industrious hands were busy crocheting the delicate little white flowers that would be worked together for a table cloth, the semester's sewing project for school. In and out, twist and around, each time her metal crochet hook caught the right strand of cotton thread and pulled it into the right loop. But the motions were reflexive. Her mind was busied with worry for her mother.

The Rangoon General Hospital complex just across Canal Street was unanimously ignored by the sick one and her caregivers. They would be as likely to think of going there as to a morgue.

The Chinese were very wary of "western" medicine. Their fears were reinforced every time the family of some terribly ill person, having tried all other remedies and desperate, would take the patient to the hospital when it was too late for anything to be done. The loved one would die, and his family would repeat throughout Chinatown, "Do not send an ill person to the hospital. You send them there, they die. Western doctors send you to your death."

The girls were comforted when they heard their aunt's voice. Han Yee had just gotten home from teaching. Ngood peeked out of the bedroom doorway, and He'ung and Ming joined her below and above, making a little tower of frowning faces. They saw their aunt, and heard her instruct the maids anxiously, "Why don't you go grill some ginger? Then pound it until all the juice comes out. I will get a big, white handkerchief and we will make a poultice. Quickly now!"

The girls saw Byu Goo and Pwa Pwa run to the kitchen, the panic on their faces masked with new determination. There was more scurrying between the kitchen and Mama's bedroom across the hall. Then all was quiet. Once they heard the weak cries of the newborn baby. Then more quiet. Time passed slowly.

At last Pwa Pwa came out of Mama's room, relief on her worn face. "Your mama is alright now, girls. She is sleeping. I will go and prepare your dinner."

Ngood felt such a wave of relief, she was a little dizzy. More than anything she wanted to see her mother. But she would continue to be a good girl and stay out of the way until called.

Late that evening, the call came for Ngood to meet her new little brother. He was tiny and wrinkled, his reddish skin contrasting with his black hair. Han Yee was holding him as she sat on the floor. Ngood knew that all babies were prized, but boys were considered extra special, and her father would be pleased. Her mother had now given him three little boys. The eldest boy, Chin Sen King, "New Scenery" was still a toddler, and so was Chin Sen Kee, "New Opportunity." When Father came home he would name the baby boy. The child would share one name with his father's clan, one name with his brothers, and the other name would be his own. The clan name always came first.

Ngood looked over at her mother, who was very pale. Ah Ma smiled at her weakly, hoping to reassure Ngood that she would be fine. Ngood knew Byu Goo would be burning paper money to thank the gods and ancestors that night.

The next morning, before school, Byu Goo reminded Ngood, "Do not tell anyone about your brother's birth. You don't want anyone to do black magic on him. If they know his birthday they can do magic to make a devil out of him, or even make him die. Especially, you must not tell the time of his birth. Remember, if someone has his time of birth, that person can steal an item of clothing, and with these things he can hire a black magic magician. The magician will make a doll to look like him and shoot a needle through the doll. Then your little brother will be in pain and slowly die."

Of course, no one would want to harm the baby. But someday, when he grew up, someone might have a grudge against him, and so his secret must be protected always. The responsibility of carrying this secret was heavy on Ngood, and she did not speak to a soul all day long, lest something slip out of her mouth that might one day endanger her brother.

Grandmother Wong had been brought and was taking care of the household when Ngood got home. Ngood wanted to find a way to help too. The housekeeper Pwa Pwa looked tired after helping with the delivery of her baby brother and caring for Mama. One of the woman's duties was to clean and change the water in the spittoons. Without being asked, Ngood took each spittoon to the drain in the kitchen and emptied the old water. Then she rinsed the spittoon and put into it a little fresh water from the low faucet. Often after that she would help Pwa Pwa with this chore. When working at this duty, she was not chased out of the kitchen.

According to common sensibilities, Mama did not leave the house for a month. Neither she nor the baby should be exposed to the outside air.

About a month after the baby was born, when the time of greatest risk to a newborn had passed, his birth hair was shaved off, he was named, and his birth was announced to the world. The announcement was made with food: a dish of yams cut in finger sized pieces and cooked with ginger, vinegar, and sugar. On top of the dish was placed two red stained boiled eggs. Eggs dyed red always signified the birth of a baby. This dish was given out to every nearby relative, and relatives reciprocated with little presents or red envelopes with money. Grandmother Wong had made for the baby a beautiful little hat with an embroidered band, and she attached a little sprig of blue pine and added a little laughing Buddha pin. Evergreen was a charm for long life, good luck, and wealth.

After that, Grandmother Wong went back to her home with Number Two Uncle in Kamayut, a village just north of Rangoon. Ngood didn't see her again for a long time, but she knew her grandmother was thinking of her "little mouse."

When Papa came home, he named the baby boy, "Chin Sen Phat," meaning, of the Chin clan, "New Abundant Riches." He was indeed pleased to have another boy. He held him briefly, but very clumsily, as if afraid of tender things. He was not at all involved in the baby's care, and soon was traveling again. When Sen Phat was old enough to respond with a smile, Ngood sometimes saw her papa lean over the baby and speak the nonsense words "Ahng-goo, Ahng-goo," in a tender voice Ngood had forgotten.

He had left something special for her mother. He said it was called "coffee." He told Byu Goo how to prepare it by putting a coffe bean in hot water in a metal container with a lid, letting it steep ten minutes, and then adding sugar and evaporated milk to the liquid. Soon, Ah Ma and Byu Goo wanted to drink coffee every day.

****

Ngood and Len were jumping ropes in the street in front of the four-story house. Grandfather Chin passed the girls in his rickshaw, looking very formal and dignified. Grandfather's permanently hired rickshaw man, an Indian man familiar to the girls, was pulling the two-wheel cart up the gently ascending road, likely to one of Grandfather's shops. Ngood felt sorry for the rickshaw man when it was hot, or when the trip was long or uphill, and she could see that the man often sweated uncomfortably beneath his turban. But, this late afternoon was not too hot, and the rickshaw man seemed to pull his plump patron with ease if not pleasure.

Rangoon depended on Indian men to do much of the hard work around the city. Escaping poverty in their homeland, these men were anxious to earn a wage to support their families. Sometimes, though, Indian Hindus and Muslims would clash, and more than once Ngood had seen one Indian man chase another, yelling threats, sometimes armed with red paint that was apparently an insult when thrown on the clothes of another, or worse, wielding a long knife. The British police were always having to watch them.

Ninety-eight, ninety-nine... "Puck." The girls counted their jumps to one hundred in unison.

Ngood was certain she could jump a hundred more, but a disturbance at the entrance of the four-story house distracted both girls, and they abruptly stopped jumping. Their durwan, the Indian man hired to guard their home at night, had arrived and spread his woven rope bed in a corner of the entry-way. But several neighborhood children were throwing something through the gate at him, and he yelled at them.

The children were also yelling at him, using a Burmese word for for-eigner, particularly an Indian foreigner. Ngood had not heard the word used with such intonation, as if a great insult. Ngood and Len ran to the entry, and the other children scattered. Inside the gate on the humble man's woven mat and on the lovely marble floor lay the greasy pork fat the children had thrown. The durwan, from Chitagong, India, was Hindu and did not eat pork. Nor did he want to touch it. Somehow the neighborhood children had discovered this and found cruel pleasure in upsetting the man. Ngood knew the children's parents were not aware of what they were doing and would not approve.

Ngood did not know what to say to the grown-up man. She was very sorry that the children would treat anyone so rudely and especially her durwan. She silently watched him at his unpleasant task of carefully cleaning the entry. Then he spread a light cloth over his rough rope bed. Ngood didn't think it looked as comfortable as the nice woven bamboo mat on her bed. She watched him remove his turban and saw his hair pulled into a short ponytail high on his head. When all the family had come home for the night, he would pull the gate shut and shoot the latch over on the teak door. Then he would spend the night in the entryway, protecting her family.

Sometimes on evenings after this, when Ngood was upstairs in her apartment, she would hear the raucous in the street below and know the children were harassing the man again. She wished they would stop.

Chapter Four

The Call of the Homeland

At school, Ngood's teacher Miss Lee Ting Hone wanted to speak to her privately. Ngood felt nervous to be singled out, even though she was the top student in her class.

"Ngood," Miss Lee spoke to her in a serious tone almost like she was speaking with a grown-up, "I have something important for you to do. Our homeland China is in trouble, and we must raise money to help. The school board has directed me to prepare you to give a speech at the big dong shared by several clans in Chinatown. I have a speech written for you, and I want you to memorize it. The theme is Que Kok, "Rescue China." You will speak not in the Hong Kong Cantonese dialect I teach at the school, but in your own Cantonese dialect, Taishan. When you have the speech memorized, I will tell you what to do. We will work together after school. Our homeland needs our help, Ngood. This is a very important duty, and I know you will do well."

Ngood answered simply, Hlen *sun, high lo*. "Teacher, yes." She took the pages of carefully written calligraphy from her teacher's hand. Ngood was proud to be chosen for the honor, and after school she began immediately to memorize the words. She told Ah Ming about it, and Ming was also pleased that her little sister was given the honor of this duty. She offered her assistance.

Before long, the speech was memorized, and as promised, Miss Lee coached Ngood. She said, "You will be speaking mostly to women, Chinese housewives, and remember, you want them to donate money for our home-land. Many of them are not well-educated, really, and you should address them casually, Ah sim and Ah mou." These were terms Ngood recognized as polite terms for younger and older "aunts," not necessarily of blood relations.

She continued, "When you give your speech, don't look only in one place. As you are talking, look all around. You are talking to many people, not just one person." She coached Ngood on which words to emphasize, when to raise her voice, and when to use a gesture.

Each night when Ngood came home from school, Ming practiced with her also. She had Ngood stand before her and recite the speech over and over.

Ming advised, "Ah Ngood, when you give the speech, don't think of the people in the audience as real people. Just think they are wooden dolls. This way, you will not be nervous." Ngood giggled at the thought of a room full of wooden dolls listening to her speech.

Ming also reminded her, "Speak louder, Ngood. Make sure the wooden dolls in the back row can hear you."

Soon the day came, and Ngood was ready. She wasn't afraid, because Miss Lee and Ah Ming had given her confidence. She went with her teacher to the large clan house. Ngood was small, and no one could see her behind the podium, so someone brought a stool. Ngood climbed up on the stool confidently and spoke distinctly and loudly so the women in the back of the hall could hear.

With the passionate words the teacher had taught her, she explained that Japan had attacked China and that overseas Chinese must help their homeland. "Do not buy Japanese goods," she called out. "Boycott Japanese products!" She raised her voice at the appropriate times, appealing to the housewives to "Save China!" At last, she concluded, "Donate money, Aunties, do not forget. Give generously to save your country!"

There was so much chatter among the women after the speech, Ngood could scarcely hear what was said. But once in a while she heard, "Isn't that Po Sun's daughter? Ha! Isn't that the daughter of Chin Hone Foo?"

"She's like a little chicken!" someone said.

She heard someone ask Miss Lee, "How did you teach her to speak so well?"

A woman said to Ngood, "Little brat, you did very well!"

It didn't seem odd to Ngood that her mother did not at-tend her speech, because her mother rarely left the house. But Ngood could hardly wait to go home to tell her. Mama loved to hear of her children's adventures in the world outside the four-story house.

After this, children from Ngood's school were sent out to collect money door to door. As she helped collect money, Ngood was surprised how often people in Chinatown recognized her and were friendly toward her.

****

Ngood arrived home from school to turmoil. She quickly understood that her baby brother was very sick. Her mother was frantic, Pwa Pwa could not console her, and Byu Goo had gone to get the medium. Ngood felt a chill run up her spine in anticipation of the medium's arrival.

The mysterious woman came in with great spectacle and ugency. She quickly assessed the problem.

She moaned, "Oh, there are so many unhappy spirits here! …Especially near the child! Aye ya! That is why he is sick!"

Ngood could not see the spirits around her little brother, but she was very much afraid.

"We have to appease the spirits," the medium continued gravely to Ngood's mother. "You must give me a piece of the child's clothing. And give me a bowl of rice. Uncooked rice."

Byu Goo was quick to cooperate with every command, glad to be doing something helpful.

"Now, give me the clothing," said the medium. "You are certain this has been worn by the child? It must belong to him."

Mama assured her that it was Sen Phat's jacket. The medium took the full bowl of rice and gently smoothed the surface. She put little Sen Phat's coat over it and twisted the end tight. Then she asked for string and tied it. She seemed very confident and professional in all she was doing. She smoothed her hand over the coat, again making sure the rice was level beneath the coat. Then the medium began to rub the bowl of rice gently, but firmly, on the baby's head, chanting something Ngood could not understand. This went on for some time.

Then the medium carefully unwrapped the bowl of rice. Her face was full of concern.

"See!" she said, "See how deep it is?" Sure enough, they all could see the deep well in the once level rice.

"The child is very much frightened. The deeper the dip in the rice, the more frightened is the child." The medium spoke very seriously, and with such evidence, she took for granted that everyone would follow her reasoning.

"You must appease these spirits! These spirits are making him sick!" Then she explained that many spirit papers must be burned and certain foods must be offered to satisfy the spirits. She would be back the next day, and meanwhile, the family could acquire the needed remedy.

The medium left, and Byu Goo went quickly with the list of items to purchase. The investment would not be small, but compliance was absolutely necessary. Sen Phat's life was at stake!

What a fitful sleep for all the household that night, knowing that displeased spirits were roaming freely! Ngood was convinced that they were upsetting her poor little brother, but she also imagined them hovering in her room, and they filled her dreams in spite of the little blanket pulled tightly over her head.

The next morning, Ming confided anxiously to Ngood, "I felt the weight of a ghost sleeping on top of me. I was lying on my back and was nearly gasping for breath. Really, the ghost was so heavy on me I could hardly breathe. I turned on my side, and the ghost could not rest so comfortably, and it finally got off of me. Then I could get a little sleep."

This new thought terrified Ngood more than ever, and she determined never again to sleep on her back. She would try to be an uncomfortable resting place for the ghosts.

Ngood could hardly wait to leave the house and go to school that day, but she worried for her baby brother. She did not like leaving him behind in that frightening place.

That afternoon when she was home from school, the dreaded appointment with the medium came. After much drama and anxious consideration, the medium chose the landing several steps down from the third floor apartment. There she set out all the items to offer the spirits... the silver colored papers that represented money, the elaborate paper house that would give the spirits an alternate place to live, plus the fruit offerings and full meal to sate the spirits' appetites. She seemed to have thought of everything.

The bowl of rice, wrapped again in Sen Phat's coat, was hanging from a stick. The medium set a big clay bowl and a candle next to herself. Then she chanted in an eerie voice and seemed to become half asleep, wedging herself somewhere between the reality in the stairway and the alarming, unseen spirit world. She slowly burned all the paper items in the clay bowl, still chanting. Her eyes rolled back in her head, and the effect was terrifying.

At last she said weakly, "See, the spirits have left." Ngood didn't see at all, but she felt some comfort that the medium saw that they were gone.

The medium seemed to waken, and then she took the coat off of the bowl of rice. She sighed with relief and said, "You see, now it is smooth."

Sure enough, there was no longer an indent in the bowl of rice; it was nice and smooth on top. And, indeed, the spirits must have gone, because Ngood could sense a difference in the room. She could see cautious relief slowly easing the tension in each face, that of her mother, Pwa Pwa, Byu Goo, Ah Ming, and even little Ah He'ung and the boys.

Still, Ngood did not like the medium. It was all very frightening.

The medium left the house, taking the fruit and food offerings with her. Seeming to find lingering ghosts on her way out, she coaxed them to follow her. Ngood ran to the balcony window to watch the medium until she was out of sight to be sure she was gone.

****

Ngood came home from school and found Mama resting, sitting on a mat on the floor, nursing little Sen Phat. He seemed to be better, imprinting in every mind the value of the medium. Ngood listened to Mama and Byu Goo chatting, Byu Goo trying to distract Mama from thoughts of the near disaster. Ah Ming sat with her drawing paper, making one of her beautiful ink drawings.

There was a break in the conversation, and Ngood said, "Mama, do you know the story of the woman that became a prime minister?"

Mama said, "Tell me the story."

Ngood began, "Well, there was a girl. Her father was a government official, and was well known. The girl had bound feet."

"Oh, yes," Mama interrupted. "Like your Grandmother Wong."

"Grandmother has bound feet?" Ngood asked.

"Her feet were bound for a while," Mama said, "There were reforms when she was nearly grown, and Grandmother's feet were unbound. But she has very small feet. Have you noticed?

"Yes, Ah Ma," Ngood replied. Curious, she asked, "How were her feet bound?"

Ngood did not mean to sadden Mama, but she noticed the grief in her voice when Ah Ma answered, "Like all the girls in her village, when she was seven years old her feet were broken by professional feet binders. Your grandmother's mother could not stand to watch her daughter suffer, and she had left her alone with them. Of course, Ah Pwa was just a little girl, and she cried and cried in terrible pain. The professionals waited, leaving the little girl to wail and moan alone, and then when she finally calmed down, they came back to tightly wrap her feet in cloth."

Ngood had not thought before of what was involved in binding feet, and she was shocked. She asked, "Mama, why would they do this?"

"The Chinese did this for a thousand years." Ah Ma hoped this would be explanation enough.

But Ngood persisted, "Why, Mama?"

Mama thought a while and said, "I think it was first done by order of an emperor, and the people had to obey him. If you disobey, maybe the whole family would be punished. For the worst crimes the emperor would chop the heads of family members nine times removed from the offender. But even after that emperor's time, the tradition continued. Men thought women with small feet were more beautiful, and they thought the shape of the foot looked like the revered lotus flower. Also, did you notice how Grandmother's hips sway as she walks? This is called the Lotus Gait."

Byu Goo added, "It was thought to make women more alluring to men."

Ah Ma agreed sadly, "Yes. But it was a cruel practice. Because of the foot binding, Ah Pwa must endure much pain when she walks. It was even worse for those who were older when the reforms came; they could not permanently remove the bindings without much damage to their feet."

Ngood was deeply troubled to think of her dear grandmother being tortured as a little girl. She couldn't understand why this horrible thing was done to young girls for the sake of supposed beauty.

She was lost in thought until Mama urged, "You were going to tell us a story. There was a girl with bound feet...?"

"Oh! Yes. Her feet were only three inches long. Her name was Meng Lijun, and she was the daughter of a government official. She loved a man named Huang Pu, but the son of an official of the Liu clan wanted to marry her too. This influential man was offended when Meng Lijun turned him away. In his shame and anger he framed Meng Lijun's father of a crime. Lijun wanted to restore face to her father, so she came up with a plan and disguised herself as a man."

Byu Goo interjected, "Disguised herself as a man! What? How could she do that? That would be quite difficult for a woman with bound feet!"

Ngood agreed, "Yes, you are right. She had to stuff wads of cloth into the ends of a man's boots, and she had to practice walking in them without the Lotus Gait. She had to practice a new way to talk as well."

Mama said, "It is surprising that, even with practice, the boots didn't slide off her feet and that she could walk with a man's gait."

"Yes!" Ngood continued, "Well, she disguised herself as a man so she could take the scholar's exam. When the results came back, her scores were better than all the men who took the test."

"Oh!" Byu Goo interjected, "She was a very smart woman! She was smarter than all those men!"

Ngood smiled, warming to the enthusiasm of her audience, "Yes, and so the Emperor made her his prime minister. But, of course, he thought she was a man. In fact, he wanted Lijun to marry his daughter, the princess!"

"Oh, no! She couldn't do that!" Byu Goo asserted, stumped by this predicament.

"Right," Ngood replied. "So, Lijun determined a solution. She had a friend who was the daughter of an honorable judge. Lijun had once rescued this noble woman from drowning when her boat capsized, so the woman was indebted to Lijun. This woman agreed to pose as Lijun's wife so that Lijun wouldn't offend the princess by not marrying her."

"Oh, that was a good idea!" Mama said.

"Then, the Emperor's mother, the Empress Dowager, became ill, and the Prime Minister was able to tell what to do to make her well," Ngood said, "and that made the Emperor like her even more."

"The friendship between the Prime Minister and the Emperor continued to grow. The Emperor loved to speak in poems, and the Prime Minister would answer back to him with poetry. This is where I am now in the book. I haven't finished reading it yet," Ngood said.

The women sighed, disappointed that Ngood's story ended there. "I wonder if Meng Lijun was able to restore her father's honor," Byu Goo said.

"Do you have very much homework?" Ah Ma asked. "Maybe after you finish your homework, you can read some more and then tell us about it. Of course, you must finish your school work first."

"Yes, Ah Ma," Ngood replied, and really she was eager to cooperate.

But, there were just a few days of school left before the hot season break, and Ngood's teachers expected a lot from their students in the last days. So it would be a little while before Ngood could finish her story.

****

At last, it was the end of the school year. Most children were glad to be done with lessons for a while. The hot season was so unbearable in

Rangoon that people usually stayed in the shelter of their houses much of the day to escape the heat. But Ngood had signed up for advanced Chinese classes during the season. Miss Wong, the school principal, was teaching the old style of Chinese writing, which was very complicated. In fact, what might be read in a couple lines of modern Chinese took a long paragraph

Simple and traditional characters for Ngood's other name "Yin"

to express. But Ngood was fascinated by it and looked forward to learning something new. Besides, Ngood was quite fond of Miss Wong and had great esteem for her. This educator was quite old, and Ngood trusted the teaching of Chinese ancients, that older members of society are a valuable resource, able to impart great knowledge, and always due deference and respect.

But before Ngood took on this new challenge, a few days after the last day of school, she joined her classmates in a bittersweet day. That beautiful teacher from Shanghai, the one who taught Mandarin to the older girls, the modern woman that charmed the little girls, had completed her contract and was returning to Shanghai. The children were only slightly cheered to

Some of the students with the lovely teacher from Shanghai. Ngood is in the print dress in front.

be invited to accompany her sightseeing and to the dockside as she boarded the boat to begin her long journey around Malaysia and then north into the South China Sea. Someone took a picture of the children with the teacher at the docks, and because Ngood was short, she was in the front row. Then,

育德女學校歡送梁琰先生回國

江干握別

The students at dockside see off the lovely teacher

too soon, the beautiful teacher boarded the boat and waved to the children as she disappeared down the Rangoon River.

****

Soon after that, Ngood confidently hailed a rickshaw. Ming had told her exactly what to do. Ngood told the driver, "Go to Twentieth Street." In case the Indian man did not understand her dialect, Ngood had learned the Hindi words, and called to him as he ran, *baayah*! "Turn left," or *tynah*! "Turn right," or *seedha*! "Go straight," or *hoe*! "Stop."

Some people cheated rickshaw drivers of their fare when they reached the appointed address, and then everyone around would hear the abused man's loud objections. But Ngood was taught to give the drivers a fair price, so they never complained. She paid the man and thanked him politely when he delivered her to the modern hair salon. Then she went inside for her first permanent wave treatment.

The stylist had a reputation in Chinatown for doing a very good job. Ngood was surprised that the man seemed to know her. He said, "I saw you when you went to the dock to send off your teacher."

Ngood said, "Really? The whole school was there because we like her, and we will miss her. She is so pretty and so modern." The man's friendly nature made her immediately comfortable, and she chatted with him easily.

He said, "Yes, I remember seeing you there. But I want to give you something." He brought out a little pin that had a picture of Ngood's face on it. Ngood recognized the picture.

She said, "Oh! You got it from that picture with Teacher."

"Yes," he smiled, "and I enlarged it. I wanted to give it to you because I heard your talk about rescuing China."

Ngood used good manners and thanked him for his kindness. She was impressed. She thought to herself, "Wow! Did I so influence him that he gave me something?"

The man did a nice job giving Ngood's hair the permanent wave, and she was pleased. When she got home, she could hardly stop looking in the dressing table mirror, fascinated by the bouncy curls that replaced her straight hair. After sufficient admiration of her image, she pretended she was a teacher from Shanghai taking a long journey on a boat. She convinced Ah He'ung to wave at her as if from the dock. Ngood walked on tip-toes, as if wearing high heels.

However, Ngood knew she would never really see Shanghai, even to visit. She had heard her father say many times, "I would never send one of my children to study in Shanghai. I cannot trust the people there. They are tricky. The place is not safe."

****

The hot season came over Rangoon like a smoldering blanket. The only relief came from the slight stirring of air up the Rangoon River. Every home had every window and door propped open like mouths gasping for air. Streets were empty, and even children were not seen playing in the streets at midday. Each afternoon, bamboo mats were spread on the floor for naps in homes around the city. Ngood went early in the morning for her archaic Chinese lessons with Miss Wong, and she returned home before late morning when rickshaw drivers retired for the hottest hours.

Ah Ma and Byu Goo kept asking, "Did you finish reading that book yet?"

At last Ngood finished reading about Lijun. Mama, Byu Goo, and Ngood sat in a circle on the rug in the bedroom, and Mama kept watch on the little boys while she heard the story.

She said, "Now, Ngood, you were saying that Lijun was speaking in poetry to answer the Emperor's poems...."

"Oh, yes," Ngood replied, "And Lijun was able to influence the Emperor of her father's qualities, without revealing to the Emperor that she was the daughter of the imprisoned man. The Emperor commuted the sentence of her father and restored him to his former position."

"But what about Huang Pu, the man that Lijun loved?" Mama asked.

"Well," said Ngood, "first I need to tell you that the Emperor had a eunuch as his personal attendant."

Ngood was uneducated about some adult subjects, even from her prodigious reading. She only understood that emperors liked to have eunuchs working for them in the palace. She didn't understand that these men were preferred servants because they would not be distracted by or competing for the beautiful women in the emperor's court.

Ngood continued, "This eunuch was suspicious of Lijun, even guessing her secret. He told the Emperor that the Prime Minister was deceiving him, but the Emperor would not believe it. To prove the deception, the eunuch thought of a plan and then carried it out. He made the Prime Minister drunk and let her sleep on a sofa in the library. While Lijun was asleep, the eunuch slipped off her boot and revealed the bound foot, proof that she was a woman."

"*Aye ya*! No! She could lose her head for deceiving the Emperor!" Mama interjected, knowingly.

"Did he cut off Lijun's head?" Byu Goo worried.

"Well, when Lijun was accused, of course, she feared for her life! But the Emperor had grown to love her. So, he forgave her. He even let her marry Huang Pu," Ngood finished abruptly with the happy ending.

Byu Goo sighed with satisfaction. Oh, she loved a good story!

Then Byu Goo had a story of her own. She told of the traumatic experience of an acquaintance.

"This woman's husband died some time ago, but he has an unhappy ghost. Just the other night he came to her in a dream, crying, 'Oh! I am so unhappy here!' He said, 'Oh! Please burn more money for me. Burn another house for me. The last one is not so good!' Then my friend-- of course, she doesn't want to be bothered by her husband's ghost– my friend burned SO many joss papers, and a BIG paper house!"

It was a hot evening, but when Ngood went to her bed, she turned on her side and pulled the cover tightly over her head. She tucked the cover securely around her so that no ghosts, happy or unhappy, could seep into her space and bother her. Still, ghosts found their way into her dreams.

****

The hot season went quickly. Ngood's mind was challenged with Chinese studies and engaged with reading stories to share with Mama and Byu Goo.

After the hot season came the rainy season with the monsoons. Most of the year's rainfall comes to Burma in this single season, and day after day drenching rain poured from the skies, and relentless wind thrust the rain into every corner. At last, window shutters were put to use and pulled closed against the barrage.

In Rangoon, life did not tread more slowly for rain as it had for heat, and activities went on apace. Umbrellas came out for lighter rains but were useless in monsoon winds that immediately turned such paltry shelter inside out, leaving one looking wet and foolish. Natives preferred to look wet only and knew when umbrellas should be put away, but foreigners often provided entertainment for the wise. Sandals were the only practical footwear, as they could be dried out quickly, and wooden sandals with a platform of an inch or two were especially useful for shopping in trampled, muddy, market areas.

For formal excursions, one might plan ahead and take along extra clothes. For transporting a change of clothes, a shan bag was indispensable. Shan bags were woven with heavy yarns by various Burmese tribes, and each tribe had a signature pattern. Ngood also carried her school books in a shan bag and the books arrived intact. She had finished summer school and was back in regular school, hiring good-natured rickshaw drivers to deliver her through the soaked macadam streets.

One good thing for Rangoon was that the British had built good roads so they were slightly raised in the middle sending water to the sides where open drains and curbs directed it away. This kept the streets from flooding, though pedestrians faced some risk with fast-flowing water as it drained.

As Ngood rode to school, seeing the flooded streets, she remembered the time when she was about six and Len had come to play with her at the Nineteenth Street apartment. The girls were playing happily outside near the stairway, running and splashing in the rain. Somehow, both girls got too close to the open drain and fell into it, caught and dragged by rushing water. They were able to scramble out of the drain and back into the yard, but each girl had hit her chin on the concrete. The people who lived in the downstairs apartment saw the accident and rushed up to the second floor to get Mama and Pwa Pwa, who hurried down to help the crying and bleeding girls. Each woman protectively whisked up a girl, holding her close as she fled back upstairs. Mama held a girl on each knee and spoke soothingly as Pwa Pwa poured into a little dish a Chinese herb that was reddish in color, in pieces about the size of sesame seeds. Even in her distress, Ngood was fascinated when Pwa Pwa added a little water to the herb, and the pieces became sticky and adhered to each other. Pwa Pwa put a rounded blob on

Len's chin and on Ngood's chin and then took long strips of cloth and wrapped each girl's jaw, tying the ends of the fabric in a knot on the top of each head.

"See," Mama said gently, consoling her daughter and her niece, "the bleeding has stopped. You will be fine. Why don't you rest for a little bit?" The bandages held the Chinese medicine in place and so were kept on the wounds for a few days. When the bandages were removed, the wounds were healing nicely already.

****

Ngood continued to study with teacher Miss Lee Ting Hone, but she had a new teacher for Chinese instruction this year. This woman, Mrs. Lee Go Wan, spoke incomprehensibly on the first day of school. Ngood stared at her, confused. She looked furtively at a few classmates and was somewhat relieved to see dumbfounded looks returning hers.

She looked at the teacher again. It sounded to Ngood that she was saying, "Shoo shoo shoo shoo shoo...." Ngood understood by the teacher's example to open her Chinese book. The characters were quite familiar to Ngood, but the words the teacher read were not at all familiar. Soon Ngood realized that the teacher was reading the universal Chinese characters in another dialect, and this was her introduction to Mandarin lessons. The teacher, from the Foking Province in China, spoke no Cantonese at all. As the days went on, the children began to recognize a few new words and attach them to the meanings of the familiar characters.

Mrs. Lee often repeated the phrase, *Dohn bu dohn*. Eventually, the children discovered this to mean, "Do you understand, or not understand?" But it was a strange sound to their ears, and in private moments, away from adult ears, they would repeat the phrase as the teacher said it and cover their giggles with cupped hands over their mouths. The children also learned the same phrase could mean, "Move or don't move," and they would stiffen in their seats, just in case.

During the next two years, Lee Go Wan's students learned to speak Mandarin quite well by following the familiar Chinese characters as the teacher read. This teacher also regularly gave the students a passage to memorize. Then she would say in the Mandarin dialect they were beginning to understand, "Put all of your books on my desk, and then write the lesson."

Once again Ngood would mix her ink just so and write the calligraphy from memory. The memorization and classwork were quite demanding.

In Ngood's class this year were a couple of Chinese girls from the port city of Pyapon, a swampy area of the Irrawaddy River delta southwest of Rangoon. The girls were in their late teens. Likely they were not able to find intermediate Chinese education in Pyapon. It did not matter that they were older. Students were ranked by level of education, not age, so classes were often of mixed ages.

He'ung was attending the Fokinese-Chinese school where Han Yee taught. She was also doing well in her studies. Ming continued higher level classes at *Yuck Tuck Girl's School* with Ngood.

When Ngood arrived home, Byu Goo was busy ironing. She had become proficient doing this chore while smoking cheroot, a Burmese cigar. Cotton was the most comfortable fabric to wear in Burma's heat, but cotton wrinkled and must be pressed for a neat appearance, so Byu Goo was often performing this sweltering duty, adeptly keeping cheroot ashes from spoiling her work.

Also, the preference was for starched clothing. By putting starch on the cloth fibers, clothing had more body and a nice sheen, and starch also kept dirt from penetrating the fabric so it came clean more easily. Many times Ngood had seen Byu Goo make the starch paste by cooking and mashing taro root. Then she would pour some boiling water over the extracted starch and stir it quickly to make a transparent paste that was then dissolved into the rinse water. She dipped the washed clothing into the water, and then, with strong hands, she would wring out much of the water from the clothes and hang them to dry.

When she was ready to iron, she would dampen the clothing, sprinkling water by hand, so the wrinkles would press out more easily. Ngood noticed Byu Goo had a new, helpful device, a little tin which was filled with water. Byu Goo would blow into one end of the tin, and a fine mist would come out the other side and onto the clothing. Not only was the method quicker than hand-sprinkling water onto the clothing, the device created such an even, light mist, that wrinkles could be wilted with less water and less pressing. Then Byu Goo pressed the clothes with the coal-heated iron.

Byu Goo looked up from her work. She asked Ngood, "Do you have much homework?"

When her mother saw Ngood, she asked about her day, then asked, "Do you have much homework? Why don't you finish it as quickly as you can? Then you can read more of 'The Three Kingdoms' and tell us about it." Ngood was glad to cooperate.

"The Romance of the Three Kingdoms" was written about the time period during and after the fall of the Han Dynasty in the third century. It was a chaotic era of civil war, disunity, and competing warlords. Oral stories had taken on mythological proportions by the fourteenth century, inspiring this novel. According to the Confucian thinking of the time, the bad men were those disloyal to the established Han Dynasty, and the heroes were those who remained loyal. The story is complex and introduces many competing characters who use various battle strategies. Ngood loved it!

Ngood recapped for her audience, "Now, you remember, the Wu, Wei, and Shu kingdoms were battling for supremacy, as were other weaker groups. Remember, Liu Bei was one of three brothers that swore allegiance, in the 'Oath of the Peach Garden', to the Han Dynasty. This Dynasty was represented by the Shu kingdom, and Liu Bei was titled 'Emperor's Uncle' for his battle successes and loyalty. His master war strategist was the brilliant Zhuge Liang.

"Well," Ngood continued, "In the 'Ruse of the Empty City,' Zhuge Liang needed to send an army to defend a strategic city that the Wei troops were going to attack. He asked his generals which of them would go fight for the city. Ma Su volunteered gallantly, and Zhuge Liang agreed to send him, but because he didn't trust him, he also sent Wang Ping, telling them both to camp near the city's water source. Zhuge Liang was left behind in the West City with just a few old soldiers.

"Ma Su disobeyed orders, thinking instead he would camp the troops at the top of a hill to launch his defense. Unable to change his mind, Wang Ping divided the troops, and took his men to the water source at the bottom of the hill as he had been instructed. Thus divided, the forces were doomed, and Wang Ping sent word to Zhuge Liang. Ma Su was able to escape with his life, but the troops of both Wang Ping and Ma Su were decimated.

Mama interjected, "Oh my! Oh dear! Ma Su should not have disobeyed the orders."

Byu Goo shook her head and clicked her tongue at the thought of the disobedient general causing the downfall of the troops.

"Zhuge Liang was also without protection in the West City," Ngood continued. "He was at the mercy of the oncoming Wei forces, because reinforcements were far away. But he came up with a desperate plan. He ordered his few old soldiers to dress as civilians, to open the gates wide, and to calmly sweep the road outside the gates. Zhuge Liang himself sat in plain view in an open window, playing a zither, with a couple of children beside him.

The opposing commander and his troops arrived. But seeing the calm setting, he was convinced of a trap and promptly left to consider his options.

"Ha!" Byu Goo cheered, "Brilliant! That was a good trick! It was very risky, but what else could Zhuge Liang do?"

Ngood added, "Yes, but there is more. The Wei commander sent out his scouts and found out the city really was empty, but by the time the Wei soldiers returned to the empty city, reinforcements had indeed arrived to set a trap, and the Shu army was able to defeat the Wei forces!

"Once things had settled, Zhuge Liang commanded that Ma Su be executed for disobeying orders. At Ma Su's execution, Zhuge Liang wept. One of his generals thought Zhuge Liang regretted the general's execution. But Zhuge Liang said, no, he regretted not listening to advice that he had been given that Ma Su could not be relied upon because his words often exceeded his ability."

"What was that story called again?" Byu Goo asked Ngood.

Ngood answered, "The Ruse of the Empty City."

"Ah, yes, that really was a good trick!" Byu Goo repeated. "I like that story."

Ngood was asked to repeat it often. She relished telling stories.

****

Ngood heard from her teacher, Miss Lee Ting Hone, "You have been asked to give another speech. This time, Ngood, you will speak to more people, men and women, and the speech will be more formal. And you will need to memorize the speech in Mandarin."

Many of the Chinese who would attend this speech were not from Chinatown, and they were generally more educated. Miss Lee's expertise was not Mandarin, but her previous success with Ngood made her the obvious mentor for the new speech. Ngood was able to memorize the speech fairly quickly. Instead of opening with "Aunties" in her address, she would begin formally, "Ladies and Gentlemen...."

Once again, Lee Ting Hone and Ah Ming were fine coaches. Miss Lee prepared Ngood, saying, "The speech will be given at Jubilee Hall. This auditorium has a main floor and an upstairs balcony, so make sure you look all around and up and down, speaking to all the people. There is no microphone, but Jubilee Hall has excellent acoustics. Still, you will need to learn to throw your voice out, without yelling, so everyone can hear you."

Every day Miss Lee worked with Ngood in the small auditorium in the Chinese school. At home, Ngood recited the speech over and over to Ah Ming, who continued offering helpful suggestions. Then Miss Lee took Ngood to Jubilee Hall a few times to practice. The hall was so big! Miss Lee sat in one of the seats far back in the auditorium, and encouraged Ngood to speak so she could hear every word. Ngood heard her voice echo like many voices answering her in the empty building. She spoke slowly, so her new words would not scramble with the old words.

When the day arrived, Ngood and Miss Lee entered the grand hall together and waited for Ngood to be introduced. Then Ngood walked on to the stage alone. She felt like a tiny little dot with so many eyes on her. She hadn't realized that thousands of Chinese lived in the Rangoon area. But she had been trained like a soldier to do her duty, and she did as she had been trained. Again, she was given a stool so she could be seen above the podium. Again she spoke clearly and movingly to the many wooden dolls, her urgent voice echoing through the auditorium, "Rescue China!" When she finished, the people clapped enthusiastically and gave generously.

****

Ngood received a diploma for graduating from the lower section of the *Yuck Tuck* Chinese Girls' school. Her age was marked by a cross, indicating she was ten years old. She also received a grade card showing her scores in Chinese and Arabic numbers. For studies of the Three Principles of SunYat Sen, she received a 98 percent. She also had very high marks for Mandarin, English, and drawing. In abacus and cross-stitching, her marks were sixty and sixty-six, respectively. But she had no cause for shame in those low numbers. In all subjects she was at the top of her class. The low scores reflected the demanding nature of the course work. As always, in conduct she received the grade of "good."

Chapter Five

Perseverance

Ngood was curious to arrive home and see her mother entertaining a visitor. "Ngood," Mama said, "Do you remember I told you that my Number Two Sister lives in Moulmein?"

Ngood answered, "Yes, Mama," wondering what that had to do with this visitor.

"She is married to a man whose family came here from the Canton Province before he was born. His two youngest brothers, Number Seven and Number Eight, attended the University of Nanjing in China and graduated from there. This is Number Eight Brother."

Ngood was impressed. This man went to university in China! She noted her mother's admiration also.

Mama added, "You may call him Number Eight Uncle, *Ah Baht Sook.*" Ngood greeted him politely and sat to listen as the young man spoke to her mother about his experiences in China.

Ngood thought he seemed very modern. He was dressed nicely in western style clothes, and his hair was smooth and combed back neatly. He wore glasses, and he spoke politely to everyone, even to little girls. He had a mustache like the two brush strokes often used in forming various Chinese characters. Ngood noticed he often quoted ancient Chinese sayings in conversation.

"Ignorance is the night of the mind, but a night without moon and star."

She wanted to remember the beautiful, wise words.

"To be able under all circumstances to practice five things constitutes perfect virtue; these five things are gravity, generosity of soul, sincerity, earnestness, and kindness."

Ngood left the room, and surely Ah Baht Sook assumed she was already bored with adult conversation. But she quickly returned with a notebook, a brush, an ink well and an ink stick so she could write down the quotes as he spoke.

One more chair and one more set of chopsticks were added to the table. At the evening meal, Ngood enjoyed hearing of Nanjing, meaning "Southern Capital," both an ancient city and a large and thriving present capital city of China on the Yangtze River delta. She remembered hearing in Chinese school about the city of Nanjing, which fell into and out of preference with various dynasties as the capital of China. Beijing, the "Northern Capital," was the alternate, as Ngood recalled. Just a few years ago, in 1927, Generalissimo Chiang Kai-shek again established Nanjing as the capital of the Republic of China. The great city was known as a cultural center, and Ngood was enthralled to hear someone speak who had been there.

Ah Baht Sook spoke of the Nanjing city wall, not to be confused with the Great Wall of China, but one of the longest city walls in China. It was built with beautiful, arching gates during the Ming dynasty in the 14th century. Ah Baht Sook had seen other stone walls in the city which experts had dated to more than two millennia earlier. He told of the historic campus of Nanjing University, which was founded by the Kingdom of Wu during the period of The Three Kingdoms in the third century. By the Number Eight Uncle's telling, Ngood shared his respect for centuries of human history and achievement in that place.

He also spoke of natural beauty that filled Ngood with awe. He told of the beautiful Purple Mountain, east of the city, whose peaks were often shrouded with clouds that glowed purple and gold at dawn and dusk.

When Ah Baht Sook rose to leave, Ngood heard him tell her mother that he would like to visit again. He planned to stay in Rangoon for a while. She was glad to hear her mother's sincere welcome.

****

For a couple more years, Ngood continued attending the Chinese school for advanced studies. After that, she could continue to go to the Chinese high school like Ah Ming. Ming was very smart and doing well in her studies, and Ngood could also learn much from the respected Chinese teachers. But she was curious about something else.

Ngood sometimes heard girls in the street speaking English. By now she had learned from Miss Lee a little grammar of this language. Ngood could recite the tenses, "is, was, will be" and "have, had, will have," and comparatives and superlatives, "warm, warmer and warmest." But Ngood could not at all follow the conversation of the girls in the street, and she was curious to know what they were saying. They also had uniforms Ngood admired, blue jumpers over white blouses. Ngood was eager to learn this new language and to wear the pretty uniform.

Finally, Ngood got up the courage to make a simple request of her father when he was home. "May I go to English school next season?"

Her father quickly consented, glad for his daughter's ambition and easily able to afford the fees. Then he was off on his travels again.

As the Chinese school year ended, Ngood's Number One Uncle announced exciting news. He had hired an English tutor for the hot season and was going to set up a small classroom on the fourth floor for all the children of the four-story house. He purchased desks and a chalk board, and Ngood was full of excitement as she saw the delivery men carry the furnishings up the four flights of stairs.

Ngood wondered why Ah Ming did not attend the English lessons during the hot season. She was certainly smart enough and willing to take on a challenge. A few years later Ming mentioned that she had sensed subtle signals which Ngood had missed. Ah Ming felt the Number Two Wife of Number One Uncle resented that the tutoring was provided for any but her own children. Of course, all of the money for tutoring came from Grandfather Chin, and it was his prerogative to include or exclude. Nevertheless, Ming was too proud to go where she felt unwelcome.

When the day arrived to begin summer school in the four-story house, Ngood eagerly climbed the stairs to the classroom. The new teacher was an older lady, very light colored and with English features. Seven of the Number One Uncle's children plus Ngood and her sister He'ung took their places at the desks. The teacher spoke in English, and she gave all the children English names. Ngood she named "Molly." Then she began to teach the children a word or two at a time.

But soon, instead of paying attention, the other children began playing, and Ngood felt sorry for the teacher. Morning after morning, throughout the hot season, Ngood listened to the lessons while her classmates played.

It was hard to pay attention when it was so miserably hot, but Ngood was motivated to learn; this was a stepping stone to the pretty uniform.

At the end of the hot season, Number One Uncle asked the teacher, "Who would you recommend for the English school?"

The teacher replied, "Only Ngood." Ngood was surprised; she didn't realize the teacher had noticed her interest. And so it was that Old Man Thunder Voice enrolled her in the third grade at the Methodist English Girls High School in Rangoon and delivered her to school on the first day of classes. She was twelve years old.

Ah Baht Sook had become a regular visitor at the Chin home. When he heard of Ngood's plans to study at the English school, he bought her a Chinese-English dictionary to encourage her effort.

****

The Methodist English Girls High School was founded on Lewis Street in 1882 as the Methodist Episcopal Girls School by those two Christian denominations and relocated to Lancaster Road in 1894. During Ngood's tenure there, the school offered classes from kindergarten to tenth standard for girls and only through grade four for boys. The first two years of education were called upper and lower kindergarten, and so the "tenth standard" corresponded to the twelfth grade in other countries. In Burma, a school that went through the upper grades was called a high school, even if lower grades were taught in the same building.

Learning came easily to Ngood. She had almost always come out first in her class in Chinese school, and sometimes she was bored with lessons that were too easy for her. But the first year of English school would challenge the girl like never before. All of the classes were taught in English, and no common written figures assisted her learning as with Chinese dialects. In fact, the writing was completely different, as was the language.

At least on the first day of school, Ngood could give her English name, in the English backwards order, "Molly Chin." But for the most part, she had entered an alien world. The exception was math, which was no problem; Ngood was familiar with the Arabic numbers and was adept at the universal process of arithmetic. In fact, most of the mathematic concepts were a review of the course work at the Chinese school.

However, until she learned English, Ngood would be lost in lessons of history, geography, literature, and composition. She was grateful that she had been exposed to some English over the summer. Nevertheless, she spent hours every night with the Chinese-English dictionary that Ah Baht Sook had given her, looking up nearly every word in her lessons, beginning with "the." She would study the definitions as well as pronunciation hints written in Chinese figures at the side. She struggled to carefully write out the lesson in the exotic English letters to give to the class teacher, Miss Gwendoline Durham

One evening she used the dictionary to look up her own Chinese name. Ngood? She looked at the Chinese clues to the pronunciation of the English word and said the word tentatively, "Moon." Then she found her

Characters above are Chin, Ngood-"Moon," and Yin-"Gentle," from top to bottom.

own second name: Yin. She found the Chinese calligraphy representing the word, and looked at the English word "Gen-tle." Studying the pronunciation key again, she slowly said out loud the foreign words of her own name, "Gentle Moon."

The English school also required learning the Burmese language. In twelve years, Ngood had hardly left Chinatown and could not speak the native tongue of the nation in which she lived. The Burmese-Anglo woman who taught all the Burmese classes at the school observed Ngood's struggles and took pity on her. Miss Reid met with Molly for an extra half hour of private tutoring after school each day to help her catch up with the Burmese alphabet and phonics. The phonetic sounds were then mixed into words, and slowly, Molly caught on to these first lessons. One thing she did notice quickly was that the name of the country called "Burma" by British occupiers, was pronounced Myanmar according to native spelling and phonetic cues. The literal translation of the country name is something like "Quick Health."

In class, Miss Reid spoke only Burmese, and little by little Molly began to pick up some meanings. Soon she was speaking simple phrases, like, *La! La!* the friendly Burmese invitation to hospitality, "Come! Come!" or, the more polite saying, which adds "please" and verbal punctuation, "La bahr dare." And she learned the inquiry to health, *Nay gaung tha la*, meaning, "(Do you) stay well?"

The Burmese language seemed complicated. There were so many subtleties of culture besides the language

"La bahr." The top figure is "la" and the bottom figure is the polite closure, "bahr." The parallel lines are the period.

itself. At least in English, Molly had only to learn the word "Mister" for politely addressing a man. But there were several variations in Burmese, and a slip could be construed as rude. Molly learned Maung is the term of address for a male youth, but it is also a humble term an adult man would call himself. A young adult man is addressed, *Ko*, "Brother" or *Ko Gee*, "Big Brother," although a young man of position is called by the respectful address for an older, established adult, *U*, meaning "Uncle," or *U Le*, "Younger Uncle," or *U Gee*, "Big Uncle." *PoPo* is the respectful term for a grandfather or polite address for old man. For addressing

Burmese script for "Myan-mar." Top figure means "quick" and bottom figure means "health."

women there is *Ni Ma*, meaning "Little Sister," for a little girl. *Ma* is proper for a young girl or woman, or one may use the more casual *Ma Ma*, meaning "Big Sister." Then for an adult lady the address is *Daw*, "Auntie," and for the older woman, the term of endearment *Pwa Pwa* is like the Chinese term for "Grandmother." The Chinese language has similar traditions, even more complicated by having to use different terms for an aunt on the father's side or the mother's side, but these were familiar and seemed more natural to Molly. Burmese seemed quite cumbersome, but she persevered.

Molly considered some of the things about Burmese and Chinese languages and cultures that were similar. The common Cantonese question of greeting, *heerch gore faun may ah*, translated, "eat, rice, finish?" is similar to the Burmese *hta min sar bebee tha la*, "rice, eat, finish?" Correct translation to English required the awkward phrase, "Have you eaten your rice?" In both Asian cultures, implicit in determining a person's well-being is whether or not he has had something to eat. Both Asian languages distinguish a question from a statement with a word at the end of the sentence, *ah* in Cantonese or *tha la* in Burmese, (the "th" sound is pronounced with the tongue further back in the mouth, not against the teeth). To indicate that an action has already taken place, *may* in Cantonese means done or not done. Similarly, *bebee* in Burmese means "finished."

Writing Burmese was all new to Molly. The Chinese calligraphy was made up of mostly straight or gently curved lines. Molly found that Burmese characters are all quite rounded, and include special cues to pronunciation. Two dots, one above the other, direct one to extend the duration of the sound. Parallel lines indicate the end of a sentence, though in conversation the words *bahr dare* might also be spoken at the end of a statement. Especially a short sentence, like *"Ho bahr dare!"* meaning "Yes!" utilized these extra words for good measure.

If all of this seems confusing, imagine a little girl learning two new languages at once!

English had its own set of challenges for Molly. *Aye-ya!* She thought she'd never understand how to conjugate verbs for different tenses! The Chinese language has no such encumbrances, but shows the past, present, or future of an action by other parts of the sentence. There was also the odd and formidable English perversion called "spelling." This use of an alphabet, in which letters represent different sounds, might give a novice a little help with pronunciation, unlike Chinese, whose written characters are universally recognized but are pronounced so differently that people of various dialects cannot understand the spoken language of another. But the pronunciation cues of English were not to be trusted, with arbitrary ways of writing same sounds or with "silent" letters absurdly thrown in apparently just to confuse students.

At least the Asian minds of Chinese and Burmese organized sentences in similar fashion. But to Molly, the English order of sentences seemed ridiculously backward and complicated.

Then there were the customs of English culture which complicated the language further. Molly discovered that one from a western country did not politely ask whether one had eaten as a form of greeting. Instead one might ask absurdly, "How do you do?" begging the response, "How do I do what?"

Thankfully, it wasn't complicated to show a question in English by ending a sentence with the odd question mark in writing or the higher voice in speaking. At least English do not change the meaning of a word by whether it is spoken in a high or low or ascending or descending tone, like Chinese. But by far the worst things about English were the complications of English tenses and subject-verb agreements.

Mama's Number Three Sister Po Har, living next door, was married to a man who spoke and wrote English quite well. So, when Number Three Aunt found out that Ngood was struggling in English, she made arrangements for Byu Goo to hand across Ngood from the third story balcony to her husband on their own third story balcony. The houses, with balconies clear across the front, were close enough and Ngood was small enough that this was easily done. The Number Three Uncle would then tutor Ngood in English. She was relieved she didn't have to come into the first floor entrance of the house next door and risk meeting the frightening mother-in-law. Being handed over from three stories up was much less traumatic.

One of Molly's classmates was a Burmese girl of the Kayin tribe whose English name was Gracie. As Molly became able to communicate with Gracie, she came to depend on her. During the brief lunch and recess periods, Gracie kindly helped her with both English and Burmese lessons.

The Burmese text book lessons revolved around someone called "Way Thun Theyaer." Gracie explained the story so the exercises would make more sense to Molly.

"The story began in India," she explained. There was a prince, the only child of a certain queen and king. They didn't want the son to see anything sad, so they sheltered him. When he grew up, he was married and had a son.

"Way Thun Theyaer wanted to go out and see the world. He had never been outside the palace. So, he disguised himself as ordinary folk and went out to satisfy his curiosity. For the first time, he witnessed beggars, sick people, and all kinds of suffering. He asked, 'What is this?'

"When he understood that the world is full of suffering, he was upset. He went back and told his wife he was going away to live in a woods as a hermit. He journeyed for six years, trying to find enlightenment. Finally, he sat under a banyan tree and said he wouldn't get up until he was enlightened. Eventually, he felt he was enlightened. He decided the way to end suffering is to end desiring."

Then Gracie mentioned, "This was the Buddha."

"Really?" Molly was surprised. Though her family members all considered themselves Buddhist, this story was unfamiliar to her. Gracie explained that most people in Burma were Buddhist, but that her family, like many Kayin, was Christian.

Molly had learned to understand the numbers spoken in English when Miss Durham read class standings. Of twenty five students in the class, Molly cringed when she heard, "Molly Chin, twenty-three." She was not accustomed to what she felt was a humiliating ranking. But each time the standings were read, Molly Chin moved up a little bit in the rankings.

By mid-year, her teacher was bragging on her, "See this girl? When she came, she didn't know much, and now she's doing so well!" With a lot of help and a lot of work, she was indeed beginning to do well. But it would be a while longer before the school principal called her to the stage for the monthly honor roll during a morning assembly.

At the first grading period, Ngood gave Ah Pa her report card to sign, and she saw the way he did it. At the next grading period, she was supposed to get a parent's signature again on her report card. But her father wasn't home, and her mother didn't understand what to do. So Ngood skillfully penned her father's signature, and from then on Ngood signed her father's name on all the school papers. She felt no shame. She wasn't trying to hide anything from her parents. In fact her grade cards were consistently good. She did not stop to think that she was deceiving her teachers. Under the circumstances, it was convenient to take care of it herself.

Paying the five *kyat* for tuition throughout the year was difficult, and sometimes Molly was very late in paying the fees. The problem was not in affording the fees, but her father would be traveling and her mother didn't know about these things, so Molly didn't have the money.

Soon she noticed her Japanese classmate, Judy Sato, was also not paying her fees on time. Molly asked her, "Your father is a doctor. You can get the five *kyat*. Why are you paying your fees late?"

Judy told her, "Because you couldn't bring yours, so I didn't bring mine." In this surprising act of friendship, Judy intended to keep Molly from facing the embarrassment alone.

Molly didn't appreciate the kindness as she should have. She was a little embarrassed by Judy's attention. It was a bit awkward for a Chinese girl to have a Japanese friend.

Rickshaw coins, at least, were always available from home, and Molly never cheated the drivers. She was a fixture on the road to and from school in all weather. The driver would put the rickshaw hood up to protect the little girl from monsoon rains or beating sun, or lower it for her to enjoy fine days. She always politely thanked the dependable drivers.

Unlike the summer tutor, Miss Durham was a strict teacher. As students were reciting multiplication tables, they must keep their arms crossed over their chests with fingers hidden. Some of the girls liked to talk in class, and Molly was shocked the first time she heard Miss Durham say, "Ida, if you can't be quiet, then stand on your chair, and stand there the rest of the period."

Ida was tall, and she looked so silly standing on the chair! Sometimes, if Ida still couldn't be quiet, she'd have to stand alone in the hall. Molly would have been mortified to be punished by the teacher. Moreover, she wouldn't think of disrespecting the teacher by talking in class in the first place. But a few of the girls didn't seem to mind the scolding or the humiliation, and they would talk anyway.

Molly was fascinated with what she learned in the hygiene class. She learned to identify female anopheles mosquitos, the ones that transmit the malaria parasite. The often fatal malaria disease plagued Burma, causing extreme flu-like symptoms of high fever and chills. Molly learned the three stages of malaria are "cold, fever, and sweating."

The mosquitos that transmit the parasite can lay fifty to two hundred eggs during their adult life spans of one or two weeks. Eggs hatch in as few as two days. Larvae live on the water's surface, then they form pupae before becoming adults, at which time they crave blood and spread disease as they suck blood. The entire life cycle can take as few as five days, but usually takes ten to fourteen days. Molly learned that still, standing water in tropical Burma was ideal for breeding these mosquitos. Mosquitos were more than a nuisance; they could be deadly. Now Molly understood the importance of sleeping under mosquito netting.

Molly also learned about something called "germs" that cause diseases like typhoid and dysentery, common in Burma. Miss Durham described typhoid, which she said was a disease usually caused by drinking water contaminated by human waste or spread by flies. The symptoms last four debilitating weeks, beginning with rising fever, slowed pulse, discomfort, headache, and cough. The second week brings high fever, sometimes with delirium, swollen abdomen, and green colored diarrhea. In the third week, high fever continues, perhaps with the patient muttering and picking at clothing, and with the possible complication of encephalitis, swelling of the brain. In the fourth week, fever subsides slowly in the survivor. After all of this, the patient is usually quite weak.

But as Miss Durham spoke of dysentery, Molly was haunted by the familiarity of the symptoms: diarrhea, bloody stool, abdominal pain, fever. Molly thought of stories she'd heard about the two brothers before her that had died, and about precious little Sen Phat who had nearly died as well. More recently, Molly's new baby sister had died, her fragile life ending with the same, horrible symptoms. Molly remembered the poor suffering infant drawing her legs up with pain. The medium's ministrations had been futile and the baby girl's weak cries were forever silenced, leaving only a sad memory of her brief and tragic life.

Now in the hygiene class, Molly was hearing about the importance of showering, washing hair, washing hands, and cleaning fingernails to keep from spreading germs. She learned that because microscopic creatures live in some water, boiling contaminated water was necessary to kill the creatures and keep them from infecting people who drink the water. This was all new to Molly, and she wondered how this information related to the capricious gods and ancestors that wreaked misery on her family. She didn't mention any of this at home; it was all rather confusing, and it was not her place to advise Mama. But she began to wonder.

The children at the school would seem to get "pinkeye" often. Molly thought, "Oh, you only look at someone with pinkeye and you have it too." When she came home with pinkeye, her mother instructed Byu Goo to take some of the thick jade leaves from the tree on the veranda on the roof, pound the leaves until the juice came out, put the mass in a white handkerchief, and put it on her eye. It really seemed to help. The teachers kept telling the girls not to rub their eyes or touch others, because they could spread the disease this way.

The principal of the school was also Miss Reid, called "Big Reid" to distinguish her from "Small Reid," the teacher that taught Burmese. She was American, maybe the only American teacher at the school, and she lived on the school premises. She spoke at the school assembly in a big hall every morning. First she would open with a brief, calm prayer, then give announcements, and then she spoke what Gracie called, "devotions," which contained moral lessons and challenging words that Molly admired.

Most everyone would also sing something called, "hymns," and each child wanting to participate could buy a little hymn book. Molly eagerly took hers home and studied it, looking up unfamiliar words and trying to remember the tunes. These songs were so different from any she had experienced, and some of the words were so touching:

> "Sweet hour of prayer, sweet hour of prayer,
> That calls me from a world of care,
> And bids me at my Father's throne
> Make all my wants and wishes known:
> In seasons of distress and grief
> My soul has often found relief,
> And oft escaped the tempter's snare
> By thy return, sweet hour of prayer."

As Molly looked up the words, some of them didn't make sense to her. But even in her short life, she could think of times she had known distress and grief. She imagined a powerful Father on a throne who could help one find relief. She wondered about this lovely sounding, "Sweet Hour of Prayer." She had never observed anyone to experience "sweetness" in prayer.

Another simple song touched her heart:

> *"Jesus loves me. This I know,*
> *For the Bible tells me so.*
> *Little ones to Him belong.*
> *They are weak but He is strong.*
> *Yes, Jesus loves me!*
> *Yes, Jesus loves me!*
> *Yes, Jesus loves me! The Bible tells me so."*

"Hmm?" Molly wondered at the little song full of mysteries. "The Bible? Jesus? Does he love me too?" She didn't understand, but she liked the sound of it.

There was also something called a Scripture class. The girls who were not from Christian families did not have to participate and could quietly work on homework while the rest of the class studied Scriptures. But Molly was curious, and she listened to every word.

"I see that you all have a book in front of you. What is that book?" Molly asked Gracie, practicing her English.

"This is a Bible," Gracie replied in a tone of reverence. "When we have Scripture class, we are studying the Bible. It contains messages from God. It is God's Word."

Oh! A Bible! Molly knew from the song that this was the thing that told of Jesus' love! But who was Jesus?

Molly was moved by something called "The Beatitudes," that was read from the Bible. She copied these words when Gracie showed them to her, and Molly often read them slowly, as if she were savoring every bite of a fine meal.

> *"Blessed are the poor in spirit: for theirs is the kingdom of Heaven.*
> *Blessed are they that mourn: for they shall be comforted.*
> *Blessed are the meek: for they shall inherit the earth.*
> *Blessed are they which do hunger and thirst after righteousness:*

for they shall be filled.
Blessed are the merciful: for they shall obtain mercy.
Blessed are the pure in heart: for they shall see God.
Blessed are the peacemakers: for they shall be called the children of God.
Blessed are they which are persecuted for righteousness' sake:
for theirs is the kingdom of Heaven.
Blessed are ye, when men shall revile you, and persecute you, and shall say all
manner of evil against you falsely for my sake.
Rejoice, and be exceedingly glad: for great is your reward
in Heaven: for so persecuted they the prophets which were before you."

"These are the words of Lord Jesus," Gracie informed Molly.

"Oh!" Molly felt the opportunity, and asked, "Who is Lord Jesus?"

Gracie answered, "He is the Son of God."

Now that was curious. Molly pondered, "Which god? What son?" Molly didn't understand about these things, but in the words of this Lord Jesus she sensed a tenderness for those who suffer and encouragement for those who suffer because they do the right thing.

How did all this fit with her understanding that suffering came because of bad behavior in another life? How did it fit with unpredictable gods and unhappy ancestors who caused suffering to punish people for not burning enough paper money?

Molly had no idea, but she liked listening to these new things. Lord Jesus, the kind Son of God, intrigued and appealed to Molly.

Molly could also ask Gracie many questions about the foreign culture which she found outside of Chinatown. "What is the thing like a lamp post without a light? I see this in front of many houses in Rangoon."

Gracie thought a moment and then understood Molly's question. "Oh, yes, this is at the front of every Buddhist house. The people use it to give offerings to Buddha. They open it and put a plate of sticky rice inside."

Molly also learned new games at the English school. Oh, she loved to play musical chairs! When the music stopped and there was one fewer chairs than children, Molly, small and quick, could often slide into a chair as a bigger classmate was just beginning to sit down. Only Molly's Japanese friend Judy was smaller, so Molly often won this game.

****

Ngood's life was very full. Besides her studies, Ngood continued to enjoy the opera with her family every evening. Papa's recordings had been played over and over again on the record player, and Ngood and Ming had memorized every word. They usually sang along with the records, Ming always singing the girl's part and Ngood always singing the boy's part. And Mama and Byu Goo continued to encourage Ngood to finish her homework so she could read more of Han Yee's books and tell them the stories.

Now she was reading "Journey to the West." For her rapt audience, Ngood reviewed, "Remember, the monk is traveling on horseback from China to the west to get the Buddhist writings. You know, Guan Yin, goddess of mercy, had chosen him, Xuanzang, at Buddha's request. There were many dangers on the road, so Guan Yin gave the monk helpers to give him protection along the way.

Ngood continued, "Now, his helper the monkey was tricky and very naughty, and so, in this part of the story, Gaun Yin decided to teach him a lesson. One day, the monkey was rather desperate to empty his bladder. Seeing five mountains, some smaller and some bigger, he decided to go there for privacy to relieve himself. Then he tried to get back to Xuanzang, but he couldn't get back through the mountains. He jumped up and down, having a tantrum and saying bad things in his anger.

"Then he realized some super power was preventing him from getting out of the mountain range, so he demanded...." Ngood changed her voice to imitate what she thought a cocky, talking monkey might sound like, " 'Who is doing this to me?' "

She went on, "Then he heard a voice say..." and here Ngood changed her voice to sound very commanding, " 'You think you are powerful? If you can jump over my fingers, then you can go,'

"The monkey said, 'Fingers? Whose fingers?'

"Then he looked up and saw Guan Yin. He was amazed.

"Guan Yin said, 'You are naughty, so I put my five fingers out. They look like mountains to you. See, you dirtied my hand when you relieved yourself!' "

At this, Mama and Byu Goo gasped in surprise. How rude! How shameful!

"So Guan Yin made him apologize. At first he didn't want to, but Guan Yin gave Xuanzang a power over the monkey. Whenever the monk would say a particular prayer, the monkey would get a terrible headache.

The monkey would be in pain, but trying to resist, he would kick his feet on the ground. At last he had to bow down and do the respectful things.

Guan Yin told him, "Do not boast about yourself, but do your task. You must go and protect this monk all the way to India and back to China."

Mama concluded, "Aye-ya! What a naughty monkey he was!"

Byu Goo added, "It is a good thing Guan Yin was patient with him. Maybe tomorrow night you can tell us more."

Ngood returned her smile and nodded.

****

Usually Han Yee and Ah Ming would shop together. By now, Ming was entrusted with selecting the fabrics for all of the clothing for the family, both the casual wear and the fancy clothes. Ngood noticed the sister and the aunt sitting side by side in a rickshaw looking angry. Sometimes they argued. Other times Ming would say to Ngood, "I'm not speaking to her!"

Ngood wondered why these two did not get along. Well, maybe they each had strong opinions. So, if they didn't get along, why did they ride together to go shopping?

Sometimes Han Yee took Ngood shopping instead. Some days they would go to one of Grandfather's dry goods stores. Ngood was fascinated to see all of the things stacked any-which-way: candles, incense, and spirit money for the gods and ancestors, dried foods and aromatic spices, bolts of beautiful silks and brocades as well as the every-day cottons, and other fascinating imports from Hong Kong. Many items were in jars or bags, with one item on the lid or on top of the bag to show what was inside. Big sacks of rice sat open to display the quality. Often, charges for a family were listed in books and would be billed later. In this way, maids could do shopping without carrying money.

Grandfather's shops were disorganized, but they were clean and dry. Not so with the outdoor Burmese markets.

Neither were the markets quiet. Besides the loud haggling and hawking, shop owners were known to have heated arguments. Occasionally a furious, old, market woman would loosen her longyi and expose herself, a gravely insulting gesture comparing her combatant with excrement. Ngood understood why people in her circles sometimes called a hot-tempered woman a market-woman.

But this was the exception. Most Burmese were quite self-controlled and were known for being exceptionally kind, hospitable people. One time when Ngood followed Han Yee to shop, they passed one of many Burmese houses with an awning in the front. A little table was set up in the shade of the awning. The mistress of the house beckoned to them:

"*La bahr! La bahr!*"

Han Yee explained, "She is inviting us to come and sit with her to have some tea and sweet cake."

Han Yee accepted graciously in Burmese, "*Jay-zue din bahr dare.*"

Han Yee explained in Cantonese to Ngood, "*Jay-zue din* means thank-you. *Bahr dare* has no meaning, but politely ends a sentence."

Ngood would not be so rude as to say to her aunt that she already knew some of this, and anyway the native tongue was still mostly foreign to Ngood. She watched with admiration as Han Yee expressed fluent blessings to the woman.

In this fashion, Ngood often experienced the hospitality of a Burmese Buddhist. As her aunt explained, Ngood was helping devotees to earn merit in Heaven by accepting the hospitality they showed to strangers.

****

Pwa Pwa did most of the grocery shopping for the family. She would go daily to the fresh food market and put the purchases on the Chin account. One day, Ngood heard her very gentle Mama scolding Pwa Pwa. "You have been buying groceries for your family on our account. And then you are taking the rickshaw man to your son's house to deliver food to him on your way home. You must not do this again! Mr. Chin is very displeased!"

Following the necessary chain of command, the grocer had mentioned his suspicions to Grandfather Chin, who through a servant confirmed the breach of trust and then spoke to his son, who spoke to his wife, who must then speak to Pwa Pwa. Ngood could hardly blame Pwa Pwa for wanting to help her son when there was a seemingly endless source at her disposal, and she felt sorry for Pwa Pwa. The correction was mortifying, and of course, Pwa Pwa never did this again.

Han Yee took Mama and Ngood to the British Scott Market. Built just a few years before, it was a huge brick building, three stories high, with room for more than one thousand six hundred different stalls, where people sold whatever goods they had to sell. Shoppers could browse comfortably without fear of rain or wind and could find everything under one roof. There was no particular order of shops, and one never knew what surprises would be in the next stall. Ready to eat ethnic foods were available, as well as hats, shan bags, baskets, produce, sandals, spices, jewelry, Persian rugs, pots and pans, and bolts of splendid fabrics. Ngood also noticed with admiration the high heeled shoes. Whereas most of the sellers in Burmese markets were Burmese women selling fresh foods, most of the Scott Market sellers were Indian men selling goods.

Han Yee was an expert at bartering at the market. She would ask the price of something and the shopkeeper might say, "Ten annas." She would say, "What! Ten annas! Oh, that's too much!" And she would turn to walk away.

The shopkeeper would say, "But for you, seven annas."

Han Yee would slowly turn and say, "Four annas!"

The shopkeeper would complain that the price was unfair, but before Han Yee could walk away he would say, "Five annas!"

Han Yee would say, "Now you are being reasonable. Yes, I will pay you five annas."

Han Yee also liked to go to the Lee family dry goods shop on Dahlhousie Street, Kwong Hep Seng, "Spread out Very Strong Prosperity." Sometimes Mama would join them in the short rickshaw ride around the corner to visit the Lees. The shop was much like Grandfather's shops, with a random mix of items for sale. But the Lee shop was famous for one special thing: the most excellent soy sauce, very black and rich with flavor. Ngood thought it was curious to always see Mrs. Lee, not Mr. Lee, keeping an eye on workers in the store.

Mrs. Lee was always delighted to see them, and she encouraged them to go upstairs to visit Choon Fong, her oldest daughter. Mrs. Lee clearly admired Han Yee and valued her influence on Choon Fong.

The family lived on the two floors above the shop, which were dusty and full of a complex mix of odors from below. On the top floor, Ngood was fascinated watching dust swirling in the rays of light coming from the skylight. She enjoyed seeing Choon Fong, who was a couple of years older than herself, and they always seemed to get along well. Sometimes Ngood would see the spoiled boy and would think smugly, "A Hundred Times a Brat." But she didn't speak to him.

That boy, because of Ngood's misfortune to have to share her grandmother as the boy's godmother, also sometimes came to visit her mother, his godsister. He loved to fly kites on their rooftop, chopping away at the other kites, and because of his official relationship to her mother, he could come to the four-story house freely. It was a minor irritation, and Ngood was usually too busy to pay attention to him.

100 | GENTLE MOON

Ngood once asked her mother why Grandmother Wong was that boy's godmother. She said simply, "Your grandmother is an admired friend of Mrs. Lee's, and a delicate child is thought to need a godmother, someone of great age, as a lucky charm for protection."

Ngood wondered to herself, "What delicate child?" But she didn't say anything.

****

The English school was not in session on Saturdays or Sundays, but the boys' Chinese school behind the four-story house met on Saturdays. On those days, Ngood enjoyed looking out the back window of her home, from where she could see through a window of the school into one of the boy's classrooms.

Han Yee, wearing the more comfortable dress and pants she wore only at home, came into the room and noticed Ngood studying the boys' school. She put her students' workbooks on the table, preparing to check them, but first she went to stand next to Ngood.

She said, "Your Grandfather Wong taught in that school. Now he has gone to Mandalay to open a school there. Did you know his name is Wong Ngood Lao, 'Pavilion to Enjoy the Moon?' You girls were named for him, and also because Ngood Ming was born in the month of the harvest moon. You know we Chinese like the moon very much. Every fall, when the lovely harvest moon is shining, Chinese poets drink wine, contemplate the moon, and write poetry."

"Yes, Han Yee," Ngood answered politely. She humbly accepted repetition of these cultural facts by her elder, acknowledging her wisdom.

Han Yee added, "And did you know, Grandfather Wong is an Excellent Scholar?"

"What is an Excellent Scholar, Han Yee?" Ngood wanted to know.

"In the days of the emperors of China, an examination was given to interested young men of every class to give them a chance to excel. It was a demanding, week long test, requiring answers to many difficult questions, some involving long essays. The scholars could not leave the premises until the examination was finished. The man with the top score was called *Jong Ngoon*, Number One, and he would be rewarded with wealth and position as a magistrate or governor, or some such thing. Maybe even he would be given a princess to marry. Number Two, *Hum Far*, would also be given a prestigious position and an estate. Number Three, *Bong Ngan*, would be rewarded similarly. The other scholars who placed well on the test were given the title, *Sue Toi*, Excellent Scholar. Your Grandfather Wong is an Excellent Scholar. It is a great honor."

Ngood was impressed. She remembered seeing a few things Grandfather Wong had written to her mother, and understood, now, why his calligraphy was so beautiful and why his wording was so compelling.

Ngood also realized, with fondness, that her Grandfather Chin was named, *Chin Mung Yee*, Great Scholar. She was amused that this grandfather really didn't look like a scholar and wasn't particularly known for his intellect, but she knew he was a hard-working and very successful businessman. She was proud to be the granddaughter of each man.

****

Ah Ming had discovered a new store called Rowe and Company, and she introduced her sister to it. Ngood had never seen anything like it; for the first time, she saw ready-made clothing that one could find in a specific size and purchase to wear right away, just like that. Lately, her mother had been hiring a seamstress to do some of the sewing for her growing family. But this was even more convenient.

Ah Ming suggested, "Let's buy Papa something for his birthday!"

Birthdays were not celebrated as a rule, because of superstition. But it was appropriate for parents to give a child a red packet with some money on his birthday and to honor him with the preferred leg and thigh of a chicken at mealtime. It was not unknown for children to buy a small gift for their parent's birthday. So Ngood was eager to join in the surprise.

After much looking, Ming settled on a nice pajama suit. Like everything at Rowe and Company, the pajamas were very expensive. The girls did not consider buying anything so extravagant for themselves, but they wanted to do something special for their father.

When the birth date arrived, the girls were anxious to see their father's pleasure as he unwrapped the gift. He began to open the gift with a pleased look on his face, but when he saw the pajamas he did not smile. He did not thank them or praise them for their gift. He was very solemn.

Confused, Ming and Ngood waited for an opportunity to ask their mother in private, "Mama, what did Papa say about the gift? Did he like the pajamas?"

Mama answered gently, "Well, he was not too happy.... Maybe he was a little angry. He is afraid the pajamas are a bad omen. Pajamas are for sleeping, and he thinks such a gift will make him go to sleep and never wake up." She added delicately, "He is afraid the pajamas will make him die."

They girls were ashamed that they had made such a mistake. After that, they did not buy him anything but food. He liked to eat, and food was always well received.

Chapter Six

Adventures

The next school year came quickly, and Molly was glad to be back with her friends and her studies. Number One Uncle was seeing the value of Molly's education, so her cousins Mary and Nellie were taking classes at the English school also. Miss Gwendoline Durham was again Molly's classroom teacher. Miss Durham's elder sister taught all the math in the upper grades, and she was even stricter than her sister. All the girls were very

much afraid of her, but Molly really enjoyed learning algebra.

The elder Miss Durham also taught all of the geography classes. Molly was finally to learn about the country in which she lived. Seeing the map of her homeland, Molly thought the shape of the country was like one of her kites with a long tail. She saw that Burma is bordered generally by India to the northwest of the diamond kite-shape, China to the north and northeast, and Laos and Thailand to a section of the southeast.

Molly's Cousins Mary and Nellie

The waters of The Andaman Sea bound the rest of the southeast line, and the Bay of Bengal laps the southwest shores, so that coastline provides a third of Burma's total perimeter. The very long strip of land of Burma's kite-tail extends southward from midway of Burma's southeast border and is shared with Thailand.

Molly learned that natural barriers, thickly forested mountains and deep gorges, separate Burma from its neighbors. Indeed, Molly knew her own relatives had come to Burma around the long way, by sea. In northern Burma, the Naga Mountains have the highest peaks at around twelve thousand feet. The Chin range to the west has peaks in the eight to ten thousand foot range, and south of this range are the lower Arakans. The Shan Hills fill much of the eastern part of the kite. They rise steeply from the central plain to form the high Shan Plateau and then rise steeply again. Molly learned that many of Burma's famed gemstones come from this area. South of the Shan Hills are the Karen Hills and the Dawna Range, and further south the Tenasserim range extends down the Burma tail, effectively dividing Burma and Thailand.

Molly could not have imagined then how the wild Shan Plateau region of Burma would provide a haven for her in a desperate time of her life. For now, she enjoyed a calm existence as a city girl whose greatest concern at the moment was to label the map of her home country so she could get a good grade on her test paper.

The elder Miss Durham explained that Burma is split by three great rivers that flow north to south. The greatest is the Irrawaddy in the central plain, and the less important Sittang is further east, south of the Shan plateau. Still further east, the Salween River, whose waters originate in mountains of Tibet and Thailand, cut steep, nearly impassable gorges through Shan mountain ranges before exiting at Moulmein, a port city high on Burma's tail.

The Irrawaddy's headwaters begin in the Himalayas, from which melted ice rushes through winding mountain gorges into the wide river valley. The waters bring fertile soil into the lowland, and with tropical temperatures and Irrawaddy irrigation, the area provides prime rice-growing land, hence Burma's nick-name "The Rice Bowl of Asia." In central Burma southwest of Mandalay, the Irrawaddy is joined from the west by its main tributary, the Chindwin River, which has also come roiling from northern rugged mountains and jungles. The combined waters of the two main branches form a river that spans several miles wide in some places. Molly learned that only one bridge, the Sagaing Bridge near Mandalay, recently completed by the British in 1934, was the only bridge crossing the Irrawaddy. Ferries were required for all other crossings.

From the ice melts in the mountains to the Andaman Sea, the Irrawaddy traverses more than a thousand miles, and more than six hundred miles of that distance is navigable. As the Irrawaddy drains to the south, still more than a hundred miles from the sea, it splits into a wide river delta, with nine major outlets and many lesser ones pouring into the Bay of Bengal and the Andaman Sea. Some of these branches come within a few miles of feeders to the short, but important, Rangoon River, on which was built the great city and current capital of Burma. The Irrawaddy, Sittang, and Salween Rivers are considered the great rivers of Burma, but the wide mouth of the Rangoon River and location of the port city made this another vital shipping lane.

Before Molly's geography education was finished she would learn to draw the Burma map from memory. She could draw and label all the important details including rivers, mountain ranges, cities, and railroads. She also marked the seven hundred mile Burma Road, which was being built by two hundred thousand Chinese and Burmese laborers to give the British a supply route into China during the Second Sino-Japanese War.

Molly was taught that the tribes of Burma varied widely. She learned that the Kachin were a warring tribe and that the women sewed coins onto their clothing for decoration. The Arakan, coastal people and dark-skinned, were generally more educated and often produced Burma's doctors and lawyers. The Mon people were light skinned. The Shan people live in the plateau area. The Nagar were wilder, and the women were said to live bare-chested in the thick, hot forests. The War were also forest people, known to use fatal poison arrows against outsiders who entered their territory. Then there was the Kayin tribe which was very much influenced by Christian missionaries. One segment of Kayin, the Padaung, were known for tribal women who wore many rings of heavy brass coils around their necks, compressing the collar bone and rib cage and making their necks appear very long. The Burman tribe had become the ruling tribe. For formal occasions, Burmans traditionally wore hats of silk over bamboo woven frameworks. These are brief, oversimplified descriptions which Molly learned of just a few of the many great tribes of Burma.

Burma's history is full of wars among tribes within and conflicts with neighboring countries. In spite of the intimidating natural barriers, which offered protection from neighbors, the country's rich lowland soil, navigable river system, and long coastline were coveted possessions which must be defended. Also the fierce tribes within Burma were in the habit of exercising force against each other for the prestige of military achievements and acquisitions.

Burma's history of conflict with Great Britain extends back into the late eighteenth century when tribal groups harassed and attacked British outposts in India. Aggression and hostilities between parties continued through the next century. Also driven by Anglo greed for Burmese teak, oil, and rubies, three Anglo-Burmese wars were fought from 1824-1826, in 1852, and in 1885, and each time greater territory was occupied by Great Britain until the whole country was annexed. Burma was first managed as a province of India. While Molly was attending English school in 1937, Burma would become a self-governing English colony apart from India.

British influences, for better or for worse, were all around Burma. Roads, bridges, railroads, and schools had been built by the Empire. Molly found out that Jubilee Hall, where she had given her speech for China, was built in 1897 to commemorate the Silver Jubilee, the twenty-fifth anniversary of Queen Victoria's coronation. Many of the roads were named for the subjugators, including officers like General Dalhousie and Major Phayre, who had a history of conquest and consequent governing appointments in Burma. The British knew how to seize and exploit the hidden wealth of Burma, mining the world's most magnificent jade, as well as rubies and silver, and harvesting the forests of resilient teak wood.

****

At last, Molly felt she was able to keep ahead of her studies, so she could consider an extra-curricular activity. She noticed that every time there was a school program, her classmate, Alice, an English girl, was asked to dance. She was very good! Molly admired her very much but was too intimidated by her to tell her so. Then she found that Jean, a Chinese girl a grade ahead of her, took dance lessons at the Diocesan Girls' School, which was close to the Methodist English Girls High School. Molly was eager to learn to dance, so Jean took her along to meet Miss Reed, the instructor, and Alice was a dance student there. Molly eagerly enrolled in the class. Miss Reed was an older woman, so she often asked Alice to demonstrate various dances. Alice and Jean were the only girls Molly knew at first.

Another Reed! Molly concluded that Reid and Reed must be the biggest clans in the western world as Chin, Wong and Lee clans were the largest of the Chinese.

Soon Molly was learning to do graceful ballet steps. She was excited to also learn some acrobatics, like backbends and cartwheels. Oh, the cartwheels! She would do one after another through the long hallway in the four-story house.

Molly and Jean became good friends. Jean was an accomplished young woman, very intelligent and talented. Molly often visited Jean at her home, and Jean's mother liked Molly. She encouraged the friendship, glad to have a companion with good home training for her only daughter.

Molly was also selected for the drill team. Some girls from her class and the older class met during one of the school periods to practice daily. The drill instructor, Miss Davies, taught the girls to march, lifting their knees high with every step, and to turn this way and that in very specific formations. Sometimes Molly was instructed to follow another girl, and sometimes she would veer off on her own assigned path. Each girl remembered her own unique moves and followed through with precision, creating impressive, orderly patterns. Molly enjoyed being a part of a team effort, where each one depended on others for a most beautiful result. The Diocesan school was the biggest rival with Molly's school in the competitions. But the accuracy and unity of the Methodist English Girls High School drill team was difficult to match, and soon

Drill team posing with award. Principal, "Big Reid," is in the center, and Miss Davies is to her right. Molly is standing behind and between them.

Molly was attaining the level of her peers.

＊＊＊＊

Ngood noticed something was different about Papa. She used to be glad to escape his notice. Now she thought that he seemed proud of her and wanted to exhibit her talents. She was cautiously pleased by his pride.

Every few years he would buy a new car. Papa's cars were used almost exclusively by himself, driven by a hired driver who would take him on his travels. Occasionally, when he was home, he would send the driver to take the children to school, but only if the weather was very bad.

One day when Papa was home and entertaining a very tall British car salesman, he introduced Ngood in limited English.

To Ngood, Papa said in their Taishan branch of Cantonese dialect, "Say something to him in English."

So Ngood greeted the man, "Hello. How are you?" Then she wished him, "Happy New Year."

The man was very impressed and told Papa his daughter was very accomplished. Similar scenes were often repeated after that. Of course, salesmen wanted her father's business, and they would say, "Oh! How smart she is!" Ngood enjoyed showing off for them.

Papa allowed the children to sit for a little while in his new, unmoving car. They sat very politely, enjoying the smell and feel of it.

****

Molly learned to match the three seasons of Burma with the months of the English calendar. The hot season went from March to the middle of May, and schools were closed for the two hottest months. The Burmese celebrated the New Year in April, and schools reopened in May with the beginning of the rainy season, which went from May to October. The heavy monsoons came during the months of July and August, but much rain and humid air were expected throughout the season. The most pleasant time, the dry season, extended from November to February, and cooler temperatures in the mid-sixties and seventies Fahrenheit were enjoyed.

After the rainy season had passed and the weather became delightful, Gracie proposed, "Molly, next Saturday, why don't you and Yim Sie come to my house?"

Molly knew that Gracie lived on a dairy farm in a rural area far from the school, near Insein, north of Rangoon. Molly considered this. She had been on a bus with her aunt, Han Yee, and in fact, with Han Yee's help, even Molly's mother had gotten up the courage a few times to take her brood on the bus to visit her mother in Kamayut. Anyway, Gracie managed to make the bus trip to and from school nearly every day. How difficult could it be?

Yim Sie was a new friend and classmate of Molly. She recently had been adopted from Singapore by the childless woman that lived across the street from the four-story house. The girl's mother often enlisted Molly as a companion, and she registered her daughter to attend the Methodist

English Girls High School with Molly. Both girls eagerly agreed to visit Gracie at her farm.

The next Saturday, Molly and Yim Sie boarded a motorized bus to Insein and sat on one of two long, hard benches that faced each other. Molly didn't mention the trip to Mama. Molly didn't think of this as naughty; she had become used to getting around by herself, and her mother knew less about the world outside Chinatown than she did. The girls were careful to follow Gracie's instructions and had no trouble finding the farm.

What a thrill for a couple of city girls! Everything was new and fascinating! There were so many trees! One could pick fresh marian fruit right off a tree! The girls were curious about the small animals. The dog barked at them wildly until he sensed Gracie's acceptance of these strangers, and then he was friendly. Rabbits hopped happily in the yard. Gracie's father owned many cows, and Molly had never been so near such a big animal. They were intimidating at first, but Gracie's familiarity with the animals calmed Molly's fears, and she decided the beasts were really quite gentle.

After a couple of hours and a very enjoyable visit, the girls thanked their hosts and boarded the bus back to Chinatown in Rangoon. When they paid the bus driver, he said, "I'm sorry, but this is only enough to take you as far as the Insein jail."

Molly said with childish bravery, "Okay."

She told Yim Sie, "I'm familiar with the area. We can walk the rest of the way."

So they got off the bus at the jail and started walking toward home. She thought they were fairly close to Chinatown; at least the distance between Chinatown and the Insein jail had seemed pretty close as they rode the bus.

Yim Sie and Molly kept walking. The road was a highway, made for vehicles, not at all like a city street that was easy for pedestrians to navigate. Buses and trucks flew by them, along with various pony, horse, or cattle carts, each vying for space and taking their own pace, so the girls had to walk on the side of the road. Their feet were hurting, but they could only keep walking.

Yim Sie began to cry. Molly tried to comfort her, saying, "I know the way. I am going to help you get back."

But Yim Sie was not convinced, and Molly had more trouble convincing herself. She was beginning to wonder if they could be home before dark. She did not see any familiar landmarks. Molly realized too late that they could have gone to see her grandmother and uncle in Kamayut if she had known how far they were from home. But they had passed that area some time ago, and it didn't make sense to go back.

Yim Sie continued to cry. Molly continued to urge her to keep walking.

At last, a Burmese man driving a pony cart came up beside them and asked, "May I give you girls a ride?" Molly had heard of men in Rangoon who would kidnap children and ransom them to their parents. She was afraid at first, but the man explained, "I can only take you as far as the Rangoon jail at the end of Insein Road. I work for the Catholic missionaries at the orphanage near there."

He seemed kind, and the girls were desperate. Molly thought they could jump off the cart and run away from him if necessary. So they took the risk and climbed onto the cart.

It was a two-wheel cart and rather flimsy. The sides and back were open, and Molly and Yim Sie sat at the back with their sore legs dangling, immensely relieved and thankful to be carried. Thus transported, they rested while covering the miles in good time. After a while, Molly noted the high curved walls of what she now realized must be the Rangoon jail, and the man stopped. The girls were most sincere in their thanks to him for his kindness. Molly wanted to pay him something, but of course, she had no money, and profuse thanks was all she could give.

Not knowing anything but the bus route, the girls walked the few blocks east to Pagoda Road, turned right and walked for a block to Canal Street, where the bus stop was. Then they walked the last half block back-tracking on Canal Street to lovely Maung Khine Street. They barely made it back in time to wash up before the evening meal, their families unaware of the girls' ordeal. Molly never told Mama, thinking it better not to worry her. But after that she always made sure she had enough money for bus fare.

****

Ah Baht Sook was visiting again. He seemed pleased that, when he came, Ngood always got her notebook to write down the quotes he spoke.

"Forget injuries, but never forget kindness."
"To see what is right and not do it is want of courage."

He would often say quotes especially for her benefit, to add to her growing collection.

"Respect yourself and others will respect you."
"Study the past if you would define the future."

Ah Baht Sook noticed that Ngood's face was close to the note paper as she penned the Chinese letters. He said to Ah Ma, "I wonder if Ngood needs glasses?"

Mama was immediately concerned. "Glasses? I do not know how to get these for her."

Ah Baht Sook said, "If you want me to help, I could take her to Rangoon to get her eyes tested by an 'optician.' If she needs glasses, I can order them for her."

Mama was pleased with his offer, and so it was that Ah Baht Sook helped Ngood to get her first pair of glasses. Ngood had not recognized her own need and was delighted to be able to read the chalk board at school.

Soon after that, Ah Baht Sook asked Mama if he could take Ngood to the circus. The circus! This was entirely new to Ngood. It was a western circus, meaning it was from the west, from England or America, but it incorporated acts from many parts of the world. Ngood saw huge elephants doing tricks, like standing on their hind legs! They walked in a long parade, biggest to smallest, each holding the tail of the elephant ahead! But what took Ngood's breath away was the trapeze act. One man was swinging high in the air, hanging upside down by his knees. A woman was also swinging, but she was holding the swing by her hands and hanging below it. She swung higher and higher, with huge arcs that swept her nearly to the top of the tent. Suddenly, the woman let go of the swing, flipped in mid-air and caught the waiting hands of the man on the other swing! Ngood could hardly believe what she had just seen! After her initial gasp and moment of disbelief, she laughed and applauded with the rest of the audience. Then costumed men called "clowns" did the silliest things, and Ngood laughed like never before in her life. She was thoroughly delighted with the circus!

A few weeks after that, Ah Baht Sook took her to a movie that was in English. He called it a "western," and the heroes were called "cowboys." Ngood enjoyed it very much! She had seen Chinese movies a few times, but the movies were long and the pace was slow. Indian movies also had scenes that dragged on, and the actors and actresses were forever singing. But these westerns were exciting! There was so much action, rarely a slow moment! Ngood saw several westerns with Ah Baht Sook at either the Globe Theater or the Palladium.

Then Ah Baht Sook wanted to see another movie called, "Tarzan." He invited Ngood to come along. When they went to buy the tickets, there was such a crowd of people! Men were even on the roof of the theater, trying to get the ticket seller's attention and waving money at him. Ngood didn't know how they kept from falling. She was going to stand in line with Ah Baht Sook, but he told her to wait for him some distance apart. There was some fighting in the crowd, and soon British police came to keep order. At last Ah Baht Sook got two tickets, and they went into the theatre to see the movie.

Before the lights went off and the movie was shown, music cued everyone to stand and sing the British Anthem, "God Save the King," in honor of King George VI. Ngood had come to find this routine repeated at every theater before the show:

"God save our gracious King,
Long live our noble King,
God save the King!
Send him victorious,
Happy and glorious,
Long to reign over us;
God save the King!"

The Tarzan movie was exciting, and Ngood was captivated. The Tarzan character was a young man who had been raised from a toddler by apes in the jungle. He was a friend to many of the animals and could speak their languages. He was very muscular and could quickly move from place by swinging on long vines. Tarzan met an American woman whose party had become marooned, and she became his wife. The movie was memorable for the dramatic battles between animals and the thrilling rescues by Tarzan. When Tarzan himself was in need of help, his resounding jungle call would bring a herd of elephants or a tribe of apes to his rescue. Also, the housekeeping arrangements of the jungle couple entertained audiences as Tarzan kept making rustic inventions to improve the tree-house home.

The movie was in English, so after the movie, Ngood asked Ah Baht Sook about a few things she didn't understand. She chattered excitedly as they rode home.

****

Byu Goo had an addiction besides cheroot cigars. She had become quite a fan of the opera stars, and because of her place in the Chin home, she had unique access to them. She had also become very attached to Sen Phat, and even when he would get down from her lap to play, she would pull him back on to her lap. He had grown now to seven years old, and still Byu Goo liked to carry him. Ngood joked secretly to Ah Ming, "Our brother is sticking to her!"

So, Byu Goo and Sen Phat would go together to visit the opera stars. She would say, "Sen Phat loves this actress and wants to see her, so I will take him for a visit." Sometimes they would be gone for hours, and Ngood guessed Byu Goo was cooking for them as an excuse to tarry. It seemed a harmless, amusing addiction, and Sen Phat cooperated with Byu Goo.

****

At the end of the school year, Ah Baht Sook spoke to Ngood's mother, "Ngood is a smart girl. It is too bad that she has never been outside of Rangoon. May I take her on a train ride to Mandalay? It will be a good experience for her, and you can be sure I will take care of her. I have contacted her father, and we can stay with him in Mandalay."

Her mother agreed, and Ngood was excited. Not only would she visit another city, but she would have her first ride on a train!

On the appointed day Ah Baht Sook picked her up very early in the morning, before dawn, and took her to the train station. He directed her to the proper platform and they boarded the passenger car, put their luggage in the racks above the large windows, and took their seats. Ah Baht Sook and Ngood sat on one of the long benches facing the windows so Ah Baht Sook could sometimes point out sites as they traveled. Windows were usually left open in the trains, as in the homes, to let the tropical air circulate.

Ngood heard the train whistle blow, then felt a little jerk as the car ahead pulled their car forward. The train moved slowly at first. She glanced at Ah Baht Sook and smiled with anticipation. As the track curved, Ngood could look out the window and see the steam engine. In the dim morning light, she could see the black cloud of smoke pouring from the smoke stack. The mighty engine began to accelerate, and Ngood, standing to peer through the window, saw the wooden ties heaving with the weight of the train on the rails.

As they moved through the city, Ngood was already in unfamiliar territory. They were moving quickly, much faster than any rickshaw man or pony cart, and faster even than a bus. Soon they were racing along, sometimes reaching speeds of nearly forty miles an hour, and the cool morning breeze rushed through the windows as the train rattled and jiggled along the track. The motion, the sounds, and the sights all added to the thrill of the journey.

City sights gave way to shadowy trees very near the train, passing quickly. Then dawn came and shone its light on a big, new world to Ngood. For the first time in her life, she saw wide expanses of land. She saw farmers in fields urging cows or water buffalo harnessed to plows. Other times she could see cattle or deer grazing on the grasslands or drinking from the Sittang River. Often she would see clusters of thatch houses, sometimes raised playfully on stilts as if the houses were wading on long legs through the shallow water. She saw the deep blue silhouettes of distant mountains, mysterious in the haze on the horizon. Pagodas would gleam from far sites and near.

As they sped past Pegu, fifty miles northeast of Rangoon, Ah Baht Sook told her about this ancient capital of the Mon tribe. He described a reclining Buddha image, stretching nearly 180 feet long, and another statue of four giant Buddhas seated back-to-back which towered nearly ninety feet high. Also quite famous were the ancient ordination hall for monks and several notable pagodas.

All day riding in a train tired even the most enthusiastic traveler, and Ngood napped a little in the evening hours. At last, the train arrived at the Mandalay station and Ah Baht Sook arranged for a rickshaw to take them to the second home of Chin Hone Foo, Ngood's father.

Papa seemed pleased with his visitors. In the morning, Papa's personal Indian cook fixed them a fabulous western style meal of fried eggs, over easy, and bacon and toast. Ngood had never tasted such a meal. She admired Papa's small but very modern house. Then Papa took them to the shop he owned in Mandalay. Whereas the family shops in Chinatown carried imports primarily from Hong Kong, this shop had goods from around the world. Most of the items were in tins, stacked on shelves to the ceiling. Papa gave them a sample from one small decorative tin containing eight precious shortbread cookies from Denmark. At lunch time, Papa took them to a Chinese restaurant.

Grandfather Wong was teaching his students during the day, but he joined them for a meal in the evening. He didn't seem too well and didn't speak much.

Ah Baht Sook took Ngood sight-seeing in Mandalay. They toured the Royal Palace, which was built during 1857 to 1859 when Burmese King Mindon Min moved the capital to Mandalay. The palace was surrounded by a moat and protected by high walls. When the British conquered upper Burma, many of the artifacts of the Royal Palace interior were plundered, but Ngood was impressed to see some remnants of royal trappings, including the king's imposing throne on a dais. Behind it were tapestries worked in gold and silver threads and ornamented with many tiny mirrors that reflected light magnificently.

Ah Baht Sook told Ngood some of the cruelties and tragedies of late Burmese royalty. Popular King Mindon had come to power by overthrowing his half-brother King Pagan. Then as Mindon was dying in 1878, one of his queens, Hsinbyumashin, arranged for nearly all of Mindon's possible heirs to be murdered so that her daughter, Supayalat, and her son-in-law Thibaw, a son of Mindon and a lesser queen, could succeed as queen and king. Then in 1885, the conquering British exiled Thibaw and the remaining royalty to India.

When she returned home, Ngood told Ah Ma all about her adventures. Mama was happy for her daughter.

****

Ah Baht Sook had another idea. He wanted to take Ngood to Moulmein where his brother and sister-in-law lived. Moulmein is a coastal city, not too far down on Burma's long tail. Mama had never been there to visit her sister, but she was delighted for Ngood to go.

Once again Ah Baht Sook and Ngood traveled by train. It was another scenic ride: long sweeps of grasslands ornamented by clusters of stately palm trees, miles and miles of rice paddies, fishermen wading with nets in the waters, and blue hued mountains filling the horizon. Ah Baht Sook began to describe the city of their destination to Ngood.

"Moulmein is famous for its tropical fruits and for excellent seafood," he said. "Do you remember having the durian fruit, that smells terrible but tastes quite good? Durian fruit grows very well there. Also, Moulmein has several sawmills for cutting the teak wood brought down the Salween River from the forests. Rice is also transported from the plains to the rice mills here. From the Moulmein seaports, Burmese teak and rice are transported around the world. Also, there are many rubber plantations around the city. Shipbuilding is a big enterprise at Moulmein. The city is an ideal port, not only because of its location at the mouth of the Salween, but because the Bilugyun Island shelters it from rough seawaters.

"Some people call Moulmein, 'Little England', because of the large Burmese-Anglo population. Many British have come here over the years to run the plantations and mills.

Ah Baht Sook also told Ngood about the city's history and landmarks. "Moulmein was the first British capital of Burma as lands were annexed. It is also a very ancient capital city, and I will show you some of the ancient structures while you are here. In the hills around the city, we will also see some of the many ancient pagodas. I want to take you south of the city to see the world's largest reclining Buddha."

At the train station Ah Baht Sook's older brother was there to meet them. He was a big man, definitely Chinese with Chinese features, but he dressed like a Burman, with the longyi skirt tied in front, and he spoke fluently with the natives. Unlike Ngood's family, this man had assimilated to the native culture.

Soon they were greeting Ngood's Number Two Aunt and were made welcome in her home. Unlike her husband, she was more traditionally Chinese in her dress and habits. She wore the Chinese pants like Ngood's Mama. She was very sweet and soft-spoken and obedient to her husband. The house was made of the strong and durable Burmese wood, pyinkado.

While there, Ngood noticed on the ancestor altar a statue of Buddha, about five inches high. Her aunt's husband saw her studying it.

"Ngood," he said, "Keep looking at this piya, god. If you look long enough, his eyes will move."

With irresistible curiosity, Ngood stared at the statue's eyes. She looked, and looked, and, suddenly, she saw the eyes move!

The uncle told her, "He is the living god!"

"Yes, Cheung, 'Auntie's Husband,'" Ngood answered meekly.

In spite of the fright it gave her, Ngood went back later to try it again. The uncle was not with her this time as she stared at the Buddha. It did not seem to her this piya could be alive. But after a while, she saw his eyes move again, and she thought, "It must be alive!"

Still, she doubted. She did not dare to touch the object, but she viewed it from every angle. Since her uncle was not present, he could not be moving the eyes, and she could see no wires or anything to make them move. Besides that, he seemed very sincere in his belief that the Buddha statue was alive.

The English school was causing her to question and to reason, but she had no answer for this and felt a chill of fear. She did not know then that after staring so long her eyes could play tricks on her.

They had been visiting for several days when Ah Baht Sook got a letter from Ngood's Grandfather Wong. As Ah Baht Sook read the letter, Ngood saw his cheerful face cast with concern. Ngood wondered what was wrong. She hoped he would explain to her, but he did not.

Soon after that Ah Baht Sook said to Ngood, "We must go back." Many of the sites he had promised to show her were left unseen. Ah Baht Sook was very quiet on the train ride back to Rangoon. He dropped Ngood off at her home and left quickly. She did not see him very often after that, and whenever he saw her again, he acted differently, very self-conscious. She would not understand the reason for this until later.

Chapter Seven

Cow Head and Horse Face

Yim Sie no longer attended the English school. Ngood heard from her mother that Yim Sie was sent back to Singapore by her adoptive parents. Frankly, life had been so busy for Ngood that she had hardly missed this little friend and fellow traveler to Insein. But she did wonder what would make the parents send her back, and she felt concern for her friend. What she heard later from her mother was chilling news. Yim Sie's adoptive mother, once again childless in a culture where a woman finds her own value in her children, had killed herself.

Cousin Mary, a daughter of Number One Uncle's Number Two Wife, was not well. She was rather sickly and had a strange rash all over her body, and she had to leave her studies at the Methodist English Girls High School. The Chinese community gossiped that Mary had leprosy, and because the fourth floor of the four-story house was not used, Mary's mother hid her there. Surprisingly, Ngood was unconcerned about contracting a contagion, and no one told her not to go to visit. So, because she missed her cousin, she often went to the fourth floor to see her. Mary was a very bright girl who very much enjoyed Molly's visits. But, too soon, Number One Uncle moved Mary to a home he purchased in Golden Valley, to remove her further from Chinatown gossips. Molly heard later that her cousin and friend died there.

Another daughter of the Number Two Wife was Nellie. She contracted tuberculosis and became very ill. Her mother took Nellie to Madras, India hoping to find treatment and a sunny, dry climate better suited to healing. They were gone for some time, and then Number Two Wife returned to

Rangoon without her daughter. She was distraught and tearfully explained that Nellie had died on the long boat ride to return home. She told how the boat managers would not allow a dead body to remain on the boat. She woefully described the lifeless body of the precious girl as she last saw it lowered into the sea and sinking beneath the waves.

Ngood heard the cruel gossip of servants at the four-story house. They said Buddha was punishing Number Two Wife for having low morals. But Ngood thought the auntie seemed nice enough.

****

One day, Ngood was in the street playing with Len, Tuck Sook, and many other children. She had learned the English word "duck" or "ducky," and she thought it sounded like her Uncle Tuck's name, so she and Len were calling him, "Ducky." He didn't seem to mind.

The children were playing a favorite game they called simply, "Run!" Ngood often played this at school as well. Dividing into two teams, each one with a base, players would try to run past the other team's line of players to reach the base without being tagged. Then they would be aung thu, Burmese for "victorious person." Ngood's small size and speed worked well for her in this game.

Han Yee was coming home from teaching school, carrying the stack of children's workbooks. A frightening man came from around the corner of the house. Ngood had seen him before; he was a crazy man, half Chinese and half Indian, and quite unpredictable in his actions. Sometimes Ngood had heard and seen him howl and beat his own chest with a brick.

This man pointed at Han Yee and yelled in Chinese, "Long-necked goose! Long-necked goose!" Ngood saw Han Yee's face flush with shock and embarrassment.

Ngood was also stunned. She didn't think her aunt's neck looked too long at all. In fact, Han Yee was an attractive woman, slim and graceful, and very stylish. But the man's words clearly hurt Han Yee.

After that, there was no stopping him. Daily, lovely Han Yee had to endure his taunting. "Long-necked goose! Long-necked goose!" It became a constant aggravation and embarrassment to Han Yee. Ngood hated to see her dear aunt so shaken by this rude man. But what was to be done?

****

These days Ngood sometimes spoke with Puck Ying when he visited her mother. He was not the rude boy she remembered from their younger days. Ngood knew he was attending an English school, St. Paul's Catholic School, and she was too eager to practice her English to bear a grudge against him. He seemed to enjoy practicing his English also.

"What is your English name?" Ngood asked him one day.

He replied, "My name is Mariano. What is yours?"

"Molly," she answered. "Do you like your studies at St. Paul?"

"Very much," he answered. "Do you like your studies at the Methodist English Girls High School?"

"Yes! I love my school work!" Molly answered. "How is your sister, Choon Fong?"

Puck Ying answered, "She is very well, thank-you. She goes to St. John's Convent. She goes by the English name of 'Anita.' She is interested in the dancing school you attend. Maybe my other sisters would like to learn to dance too."

Molly said, "I will tell my teacher."

When she did so, Miss Reed said cheerfully, "Bring them along."

Soon Anita, Number Two Sister Fe Lan, now with the English name of "Lily,"and Number Three Sister Fe Yone were coming to the dance classes. Molly and the other girls learned a range of dances from around the world. They did a very fast Russian dance in a line, with arms crossed over their chests and kicking their legs in high kicks from side to side. They learned tap dancing as a group and were motivated to be very precise, for if someone made a mistake, the others could hear the errant "click" right away. They all loved the graceful ballet that Miss Reed taught, and periodically the students would perform various styles at dance recitals. Molly was more advanced than most of the girls now, but Alice was still the most experienced, and Miss Reed always asked her to demonstrate to the other girls.

****

Han Yee told Ngood, "I have been asked to join the Lee family for Ancestor Day. They will be worshiping at the cemetery, at the grave marker of the Lee grandfather. Will you go with me?"

"Of course," Ngood answered. She never missed an opportunity to tag along with Han Yee.

Most Chinese worshiped several times a year at the cemetery, especially on the anniversary of the death of the deceased, and sometimes on the birth day as well. Also very important was the third month of the Chinese year, when good Chinese citizens would certainly visit the grave sites of their ancestors. Ancestor Day, also called Grave Sweeping Day, *Ching Ming Jie*, was celebrated to honor the dead and to do maintenance on the cemetery grounds. Surviving relatives would remove leaves and clean the tiles or concrete at grave markers; surely the ancestors would be impressed with such loyalty and attentive care. Grave Sweeping Day was even more important to a good Chinese citizen than the Chinese New Year.

Ngood's own deceased ancestors were buried in China, and so the family worshiped primarily at the ancestor table. These were enjoyable occasions, for after the worshiping and time for the ancestors to have their fill of the lavish spread of food before the altar, the family could partake of what was left, and there was always plenty. On these occasions, Grandfather Chin's restaurant supplied all that was needed for the feast, and the family enjoyed quite a party.

So it was that Ngood curiously followed Han Yee to the cemetery and found herself gazing at the impressive grave marker for the Lee Grandfather. A wide, circular apron of concrete, the size of a well-to-do living room, spread before the grave. Many young children, the offspring of Lee Wat Hong and Lee Sit Hong, were playing happily on this patio, their presence giving a big face to the ancestor. On the far side of patio was a concrete monument, which was a foot-thick, an arm span-wide, chest-high, and rounded on top. This marked the site of the Lee Grandfather's buried bones. The front of the monument was covered with beautiful blue and green decorative tiles, framing an inset in the center. On this engraved plaque, in gold calligraphy on a red background, were written the grandfather's name and the impressive number of years he lived. No grave site in the Chinese cemetery was as imposing as this one. Most of the other grave markers were much smaller, with only a short upright concrete or teak headstone and the identifying red placard with gold letters.

The amount of food being set before the Lee Grandfather's tombstone was daunting, and the offering was not only big, but decoratively displayed. Flowers also brightened the area.

Ngood considered that the concrete apron would make this grave easy to sweep. The green lawn was well cared for, and the few weeds and dead leaves would be pulled and removed easily by so great a crew.

Han Yee and Ngood were the only guests, but family members and maids filled the space, and Ngood enjoyed seeing all of the activity, but Mrs. Lee was the main attraction. Ngood had never seen her like this. The admired woman maintained her dignified composure, but her face was taught with tension as she barked orders to the maids.

Ngood feared for those directly encountering Mrs. Lee's quiet power, seeing that no one could stand up to her, no one could please her, and no one could placate her. Even her precious children, usually coddled, were wary. Should a hapless child forget and approach her, she snapped, "Go away! I cannot talk to you now!"

As Ngood watched from a safe distance, she realized the stress upon this woman to assemble a lavish feast for the great Lee Ah Poi. Ngood understood for the first time that her own mother did not experience the stress of most families, especially well-to-do families, whose ancestors would have very high expectations. Ah Ma was fortunate to have a husband well-connected with restaurants, and so she and her maids were not responsible to do any of the excessive cooking required of the day. Ngood and her family experienced all the festivity and none of the severe duties of Grave Sweeping Day.

Ngood pictured the frequent lavish events at the four-story house, when Chinese men walked from the restaurant, bringing many round tables, carrying them on their shoulders, and many chairs, as well as table cloths and napkins, dishes, bowls, platters, and chopsticks. Then came more men, usually Indian laborers, pair by pair, one in front and one in back, bearing poles on their shoulders which conveyed covered wooden trays laden with course after course of fragrant food. All was accomplished according to Grandfather's orders and by his gold. The parade of workers from the restaurant was the festive initiation of every event, which the Chin family had only to enjoy.

But Mrs. Lee, as Ngood saw, did not have this advantage. Instead, she and her young maids must have had to buy, kill, dress, and cook a flock of chickens, an ordeal in itself. But this was just one aspect of the food preparation duties, because the Chinese were never satisfied with one main course. So, the pork must be roasted and the seafood prepared, along with bushels of vegetables and fruits. The women, likely occupied for days in preparation, began their final, frenzied push long before dawn. Mrs Lee's expectation was very high, as required by her position as daughter-in-law of the rich Ah Poi. She must provide an extravagant show, in cooperation and competition with the widow of Wat Hong. Of course, Wat Hong's widow was distracted somewhat by her duties to her own dead husband.

Not only must the Chinese community be impressed by Mrs. Lee's ministrations, but, more importantly, Ah Poi himself must be pleased with her efforts so that he would be swayed to improve her state from his position in the world beyond. The strain upon the woman was considerable.

A low table was set before grave and spread with the lavish feast. Incense sticks were burned, along with paper money and three-dimensional paper constructs of items the ancestor might need or want. Then everything was packed up and taken to the Lee home above the shop, to be set up again before the ancestor altar. Mrs. Lee also set up a feast before her own father's altar.

After the appropriate amount of time for the ancestors to partake, Mrs. Lee opened the tables of food to all, generous in her hospitality. Duties to the ancestors finally completed, Mrs. Lee could look to her guests and family, saying, "Come! Eat! Have you eaten enough? Have some more!"

****

Grandfather Chin was very old, and he was not getting around too well. When he walked, an odd bulge sometimes showed underneath his clothing in the private area between his legs. Ngood thought she should not look at this, but she could not help what she saw. This thing seemed to be causing great discomfort to Grandfather. He rarely came out from his rooms in the back of the first floor of the four-story house, and when he did appear, he did not smile. Ngood missed him.

****

Molly's cousin, the oldest daughter of the Number One Wife of Old Man Thunder Voice, had lived with an aunt and studied in Hong Kong from the time she was very young. She came back to Rangoon like a beautiful phoenix, and no one could keep his eyes off her. She was modern, lively, gorgeous, and even shocking. She had permed hair, and wore a fancy, sleek, long dress of fine material, with a slit provocatively higher up the side than the women of Chinatown wore. She had taken the English name of Dolly.

Cousin Dolly said she was going to drive a car! Women in Burma did not drive cars! And when she did drive a car, she drove herself to the university swimming pool to swim! Women in Burma definitely did not swim! Molly wouldn't think of wearing a bathing suit! If her father saw her in a bathing suit, he would furiously send her to her room and never let her out! She shivered to consider his anger. Molly suspected Old Man Thunder Voice did not know what his daughter was doing.

A young man, Sammy Ng, met Cousin Dolly at the pool, and he fell quickly in love. Then his older brother Stanley Ng became a life guard at the pool, and he fell in love with Cousin Dolly too. The older son went to the Number One Uncle to make his appeal, and he got himself engaged to Uncle's daughter. When the younger brother heard the news, he was broken-hearted.

Another Ng son, the eldest, had died in an airplane crash, and his wife and son still lived in the Ng house. The young widow's mother was closely connected to the Lee family. In fact, the woman was Anita's godmother, and so she was expected to be helpful about such matters as a prospective good match for Anita.

She spoke to Mrs. Lee knowingly, "You know the Ng family. Number Three Son, Sammy Ng, is quite eligible, and he's studying to be a doctor. He's in his final year of medical school. He would make a good husband for Anita."

The ladies began to scheme about joining the two. Instead of going through the matchmaker for the headstrong girl and the pining boy, the women planned to host a nice dinner at the Lee home and invite several guests, including the promising boy. Anita didn't know about this until the plans were already made.

Sammy certainly did not want to go to the dinner! He knew his sister-in-law's mother was trying to fix him up with a girl. He knew she thought Anita could help him forget about his lost love. But he did not want to forget her; he wanted to mourn his loss. He was sure no one could compare to Dolly.

On the other hand, Stanley thought it was a wonderful idea for his brother to have dinner with the Lees. He told his brother what he had heard of Anita... so smart, so beautiful, of a good family. With all parties so insistent, Sammy could not find a way to refuse politely, so the invitation was begrudgingly accepted at last.

Han Yee was also invited to dinner at the Lee house, as the recognized companion and mentor to Anita. As she often did, Han Yee took Molly along.

When they arrived ahead of the dinner, Molly heard Mrs. Lee tell Anita enthusiastically, "Choon Fong, go wash your face, dear, and put on some make-up. Put on one of your best dresses."

Molly followed Anita to her room. Anita was quite irritated with her mother's scheming. Influenced by the English school she attended, with wild ideas about the dignity of women, she did not intend to be traded off like property.

To Molly, she said stubbornly, "I am not going to put on make-up! I am not going to wear my nice brocade! I'm going to wear my oldest dress!"

Indeed, this is what she put on, and this is what she wore to the table. Molly wondered if Sammy Ng would be offended.

Dr. Ng was late in coming, and when he arrived, he was not so nicely dressed either. In fact, he had some blood stains on his white pants from delivering a baby! It was an awkward evening, as Anita was cool, refusing to speak, and Sammy was brooding. Like the days of her childhood, Molly did not mind when Han Yee was ready to leave the Lee home above the dry goods shop.

The next week, Molly noticed a young man watching the dance lesson from the doorway. Then she realized it was the young Dr. Ng watching them! What a surprise to see him there!

When Anita noticed him, she became very shy and embarrassed. Anita left and Dr. Ng followed her. They walked around outside talking about something. The Lee car had been sent to pick up Anita and her sisters, and Molly was to ride along, but they all had to wait for Anita to come back. She didn't seem as cool toward Sammy when she returned.

****

Mama received a letter from Grandfather Wong. She was very quiet after reading it. Ngood

saw that Grandfather's letters could have a big effect on people.

Later, Ngood found the letter in her mother's wardrobe. It was a beautiful letter, both in style and content. All the calligraphy was done artistically and the words were creatively chosen and sensitive, the words of a poet. In the letter, he gently told his daughter that he was in poor health and was moving to Singapore for his last days. He told her not to cry for him, not to grieve. He said that he was old and it was time for him to go. He said that his soul was at peace, and that she should also find peace. Ngood understood why Ah Ma was moved by the letter, but she wondered why Grandfather was going to Singapore to die.

****

Ngood's mama had found courage, and she was taking her brood by bus to the home of the Grandfather Wong's Number Two Son in Kamayut. Mama knew her brother would not be there, for he spent much time in

Mandalay with his father. Mama wanted to visit her mother. Ngood knew that for Mama to take the bus without Han Yee was a brave undertaking.

As they were traveling Ngood remembered that Mama had said this Number Two Brother had escorted her to Burma when she came to marry Papa, and then he cared for his parents in Burma. Ngood reasoned, "Something must have happened to the Number One Son, because it was his responsibility first to take care of his parents in their old age."

The bus delivered them to a bus stop near the home, and they walked down a hill and crossed a wooden bridge over water. What fun it was to tramp across the bridge and to peer over the edge into the swampy water! They arrived at a little wooden house that was raised up on stilts to keep it above flood waters. Water cress grew abundantly in the shallow pool all around the home. Ngood knew this home was part of a community of hard working Chinese, and they grew the cress and other vegetables to sell in the markets.

Ngood also knew she would be treated to fresh cress. Ah Pwa would pick it, wash it, and steam it quickly. Then she would serve it with a little sauce seasoned with fresh garlic, Chinese chili, and onions, and some steamed squid. Ngood loved to eat this, but she smiled to remember that afterward she should not go talking to people because her breath would smell bad from the garlic.

Ah Pwa was delighted to see them. She was especially anxious to see how baby Ngood Haing was growing, and she had a few words of advice. Though Mama had experience caring for babies by now, she listened respectfully to Ah Pwa's words. When Ah Haing was born several months ago, Ah Pwa had come again to help Mama bring this little sister of Ngood's into the world. Ah Haing had thrived, and Ngood enjoyed seeing her mother and grandmother fussing over her. The little boys had grown too, Sen King, Sen Kee, and Sen Phat, and Ah Pwa greeted each one affectionately.

Then she sat to continue her work while she enjoyed the play of the little ones. Ngood sat with her and helped her to pull the tough strings off of green beans.

"Hello, low-see doy, my little mouse," Ah Pwa smiled at her. Mama and Ah Pwa chatted. After the string beans were done, Ah Pwa began to rinse bean sprouts.

Ngood noticed the family wasn't well off. Though Ah Pwa never complained, Ngood thought she didn't seem very happy. Her daughter-in-law seemed to speak with annoyance at Ah Pwa, and this made Ngood feel very sorry. Daughters-in-law should be kind and respectful, she knew.

Ngood wondered how often Grandfather Wong came to see his wife. She wondered if Ah Pwa would go to Singapore with him, and if she would be happier there.

****

Soon after that Han Yee told Ngood, "You know, my father, your Grandfather Wong, is moving to Singapore."

Finding her opportunity, Ngood asked, "Yes, but why is he going to Singapore?"

She answered, "He has a lot of stomach pain and is not well. He is going to live with his other wife in Singapore."

"His other wife?" Ngood was surprised. Stunned. She didn't know about this.

"Yes, his other wife and their son and daughter-in-law and grandson all live in Singapore." Han Yee answered.

"Is Grandmother Wong going too?" Ngood asked innocently.

"No, she will stay with Number Two Son in Kamayut." Han Yee said.

This made Ngood think of another question. "Do you know where is my Grandmother Chin, the grandmother whose picture hangs above the ancestor altar in the front room downstairs?"

A tone of sadness colored Han Yee's attempt to answer matter-of-factly, as she knew Ngood was beginning to understand the grief endured by Chinese women whose husbands thought it glamorous to take multiple wives.

"When your Grandfather Chin took his second wife, Hlai Pwa, your grandmother Chin moved to Hong Kong," she said.

Ngood could tell there was more to the story, but Han Yee changed the subject to something that clearly had been on her mind. "Remember when you were in Moulmein with Ah Baht Sook?"

Ngood replied, "Of course." That trip continued to trouble Ngood as she wondered what had happened to her friend. Why did the cheerful man now seem unhappy? Did Han Yee know something that would help Ngood understand why Ah Baht Sook did not come to visit anymore?

"Did you know that Grandfather Wong wrote him a letter?" Han Yee asked.

This gave Ngood encouragement to hope for answers. She replied, "Yes. But I don't know what the letter said. After he read it, Ah Baht Sook was sad."

Han Yee said, "Before your trip to Moulmein, you went to Mandalay. Remember?"

Ngood nodded.

"And you saw Grandfather Wong there."

Ngood nodded again.

Han Yee explained, "Grandfather Wong was angry with Ah Baht Sook for traveling with you. Ngood, you are becoming a woman. Your Grandfather wrote to him, 'Why do you want to take Ngood Yin along with you? Have you not noticed she has started to become a grown-up girl now? This is not good for you to be traveling with the niece of your brother's wife. I expect you to stop this inappropriate behavior immediately!'

"Your grandfather reminded him of the Chinese saying, as you remember, Ngood, 'An unmarried man and woman must not have a close relationship. This is unacceptable.' After that scolding, Ah Baht Sook quickly brought you back."

Ngood thought quietly for a little while. She could picture the well-known series of Chinese characters in her mind: the characters for "unmarried man" and "unmarried woman," then the characters for "consider the acceptability" and "acceptable" and "not," and the character for "close relationship." She understood Ah Baht Sook's reserved behavior now, but knowing did not comfort her. She felt awkward and embarrassed.

"But Ah Baht Sook did not do anything bad," Ngood protested quietly. "He treated me like a little girl. He always treated me very nicely."

Han Yee replied, "I know, Ngood. Ah Baht Sook is a good man, and you are a good girl. Your innocent mother trusted Ah Baht Sook and was pleased that he was teaching you so much and showing you new things, many things that she will never see. He gave vision to your eyes by helping you to get glasses, and he gave vision to your mind by showing you more of the world and teaching you wisdom. But my father is concerned that we behave properly."

Ngood understood that proper behavior is very important. But she was sorry to lose her friend. She would miss Ah Baht Sook very much. Whenever she saw him again at family gatherings, they spoke only briefly and formally, never referring to the old days.

Ngood had only begun to lose precious people from her life. She would have to adapt to many more losses.

****

Grandfather Chin also became deathly ill. He was dressed in his best clothes, and he was put on a bed in the front room of the four-story house. According to Chinese custom, his feet were facing the ancestor idol so that after he died, it was said, his spirit would be ready to join the ancestors. Thus prepared, Grandfather Chin died in the four-story house. Then his bed was turned the other direction, facing the door, to ease his spirit's exit through the door into the other world.

Ngood's father came home and joined his brothers to mourn for their father. They dressed in sackcloth, loose wraps of rough fabric, as a show of discomfort in sorrow.

At the foot of Grandfather's bed, his obedient grandchildren sat for hours at a time for a full week. The presence of these descendants, especially boys, was important, as they represented Grandfather's prosperous life, must help Grandfather in his next life, and must carry on the name and household of Chin.

Mourners, hidden beneath beige, coarse, sackcloth hoods, cried and chanted in trembling voices. "Oh Grandfather! You left us and went to Heaven!" Then they petitioned, "Bless your grandchildren to have prosperity."

Ngood cried too. Oh, she cried! She felt she was supposed to cry. She did sense the loss of the familiar, cheerful face she would never see again. She also felt anxious about this new, potentially oppressive spirit whose name would be added to the ancestor tablet on the altar as an object of his family's praise and appeals for favor. The mourners carried on for some time, wailing as though their hearts would break. They must have dearly loved Grandfather!

At last the hoods of the mourners went up, and their faces were calm and tearless! Mystified, Ngood watched them closely. Soon they were chatting and laughing together. Ngood felt a bit cheated by what appeared to be phony expressions of sorrow. She did not know they were professional mourners, hired to help make a good show of grieving.

The family members kept their long vigil, leaving Grandfather's body only to take their meals, to relieve themselves, and to sleep. For meals, they would go through the arched doorways on either side of the ancestor altar and assemble in the interior room at tables full of food.

After a couple of days, the decorated wooden coffin was delivered, and Grandfather's body was lifted into it. Ngood did not like the looks of the box, with red paint at the head and the foot of the casket and black paint on the sides. Sometimes coffins were set in the street for a week so mourners could pass by at their convenience, but Grandfather's open coffin remained in the front room of the first floor, with his head near the ancestor altar and his feet facing the front door. Relatives and friends streamed into the house to mourn. At last the black lid was put on the box, and it was nailed shut, leaving a lingering impression of Grandfather sealed away in the dark box.

Extravagant efforts were made to send things with Grandfather that he might need in the next world. His favorite foods were placed on a table near the altar, with fruit and wine. Spirit money, or joss papers, made of bamboo or rice paper with little triangles of actual gold leaf, were burned in a big clay bowl, along with paper mache images representing Grandfather's personal belongings, like his rickshaw and driver, his servants, and his house. The facsimile of the four-story house was as tall as a man! All of these items were purchased at great expense at a Fokinese shop which specialized in this personalized service.

Spirits of the deceased were thought to be arrested by monstrous creatures, human-like but for their heads, as described by their names. Always spoken in low tones were the titles, *Ngow-How* "Cow Head" and *Mar-Meng* "Horse Face." These frightening beasts, armed with pitchforks, drug the deceased to the King of Hell, who judged the degree of the soul's wickedness. Very bad people were said to go into the lower ground to be tortured. The worst offenders were fried in boiling oil in a big wok. Other evil men were forced to roam a mountaintop with peaks covered with upward-facing, finely-sharpened knives, causing a second painful death. These terribly bad people had no opportunity for reincarnation. A mean person who regretted his sins might go on to the next cycle of life as an animal, such as a dog. It was said that a wheel-shaped illustration was consulted by the King of Hell to identify the offense and the level of penalty in reincarnation. Those to be reincarnated were taken to the Yellow River to drink from it, causing them to forget their previous lives. Ngood had seen all of these things portrayed in a comic book from Hong Kong.

Everyone hoped that Grandfather Chin qualified as a good person and would go to the next life as a human of even greater rank than he enjoyed in this life. Maybe even he would be a monk. Hearing this was of some comfort to Ngood. Nevertheless, she was quite frightened by the thought of death, and she sensed the fear of the adults around her as well.

After several days, Ngood noticed that the odor around the casket became very unpleasant, but she knew better than to say anything. At last the day considered propitious for burial arrived, and Grandfather's coffin was placed on the flat bed of a clan-supplied truck and hidden behind lovely embroidered silk tapestries supported by a framework. The noisey mourners followed the truck in a slow parade through Chinatown and past Grandfather's establishments, and people lined the streets to watch. The sons, especially the oldest, showed a good display of emotion to prove their love for their father. Still wearing sackcloth, they cried and wailed until mucous poured from their noses. The oldest son was privileged to carry the incense burner, and he held it so close to his face that Ngood thought the smoke must nearly choke him. But she also wondered if the incense helped to cover some of the nauseating smell of the casket as the men followed closely behind it. Hlai Pwa, Lesser Grandma, and her son Tuck Sook followed in a car.

Chinese monks used sticks to beat on temple blocks as they marched and chanted blessings over the deceased soul. These percussion instruments were called moke ngwe, "wooden fish," because the hollowed-out wooden blocks were carved to look like fish. Fish were erroneously thought never to sleep, so pounding on this image was thought to keep one alert to spiritual things.

The boy grandchildren were waiting at the end of the parade route, and they and the parading mourners got into cars to go to the cemetery where speeches were made and monks again beat on the *moke ngwe*. At last, Grandfather's casket was lowered into the ground.

The offerings at the ancestor altar for Grandfather would continue for forty-nine days. This was said to be the period of judgment between death and rebirth. The wife of the deceased must wear mourning clothes, only in the colors of black or white, for one hundred days.

In three years, when most of the flesh had decomposed, Grandfather's body would be dug up again. Indian men, eager to earn a living from the Chinese traditions, were hired to wash the bones of the deceased. Then the bones were arranged in a sitting position in a decorative jar, porcelain for the rich and pottery for the poor. This jar was then buried in another part of the cemetery, always with consideration to the right environment, the *fung shwe*, as advised by a hired fortune teller. The expert carefully selected

GENTLE MOON | 135

the proper place, the proper direction for the bones to face, and the proper time for the second burial. The family must attend the second burial with another great feast of many courses.

Every detail about the burial ceremonies must be right, for an unhappy ancestor could imperil generations. Each household could produce stories of happy or unhappy ancestors blessing or cursing their heirs, proving the urgency of cooperation even to the most rebellious children, particularly the eldest sons.

Chapter Eight

Reversals

Like the proverbial rippling effect of a stone thrown into water, Grandfather Chin's death continued to disturb the peaceful waters of Ngood's life. Almost right away, Grandfather's widow and her son Tuck Sook were sent to live in an older home not too far away. Ngood rarely saw her playmate after that.

It was also necessary for Ngood's family to move from the four-story house. The reason for this was not discussed with Ngood, but it seemed reasonable to her that the Number One Uncle needed more room for his ever growing family. He brought two more wives to the four-story house, so now he had a floor for each wife. Number Three was a Burmese wife, and Number Four was the older sister of the silvery voiced actress who starred in "Ginger Cries and Cracks the Great Wall." To have four wives in the four-story house gave Number One Uncle a very big face.

Grandfather Chin, keeping with Chinese superstition, never wrote a last will and testament, fearing that this would make him die prematurely. As expected, then, most of the inheritance went to the oldest son, and younger brothers were left at the mercy of the eldest. Daughters had no expectation to share any inheritance. Married daughters had been given a dowries at their weddings and then were considered the responsibility of their husband's family. "The daughter's face is turned outside," the saying went, meaning a daughter would eventually be focused on her husband and his family, so there would be no advantage in giving her an inheritance. A younger brother could bring a suit in the British court system, but that would reflect poorly on the family face, and Ngood's father would not consider this option. Ngood was vaguely aware of some tension between her father and his oldest brother during this time, but it was not her concern.

What was of great concern to her was Han Yee's disturbing announcement. "Ngood, I have decided to move to Singapore. My father and his Number Two Wife have invited me to live with them, and I have decided to go. I do not like the rude people in Chinatown insulting me, and there will be excellent opportunities for me to teach in Singapore. But, I will miss you."

Ngood could hardly express her sadness in losing this woman who had so influenced her life.

Adding to the loss of Han Yee herself was the loss of the precious collection of books Han Yee would take with her. Ngood watched Byu Goo packing up the treasure, and each book disappearing into a shan bag was like another friend slipping away.

****

The second floor apartment on Canal Street had one bedroom for Ngood's parents. The rest of the family slept at night in the one long living room. The girls had beds that dropped down from the wall, and two could sleep in a bed. The boys and Byu Goo slept on good quality woven mats on the floor. Windows were protected with iron bars for security so they were left open. The ebony tables and chairs and the dining table with the marble top had moved with them to their new quarters, and these, at least, were comforting in familiarity. The kitchen and single bathroom were equipped with modern faucets and drains such as the family had enjoyed at the four-story house.

As much as Ngood had enjoyed living at the four-story house and would miss it, the adjustment to the apartment was not as great for her as for the others, because her life was so full of distractions. Still, she would miss Pwa Pwa very much. Pwa Pwa had become old and stooped over. She would live her final years with her children.

****

The Chin girls found a new pastime at the Canal Street apartment. Papa had several sets of Mahjong tiles, including good quality bone sets and best quality ivory ones. Often, even in Papa's absence, the tiles were left on the table. Taking advantage of the access and finding willing teachers, ever-resourceful Ming had learned to play quite well. Four players were best, but three were satisfactory, so she taught her sisters Ngood and He'ung to play and engaged them often. They did not gamble as the adults did, but they spent many enjoyable hours at the game, caught up in the challenge of strategy and the unpredictability of chance. Soon Ngood was so familiar with the tiles she could recognize them without looking, feeling the Chinese calligraphy representing numbers, four wind directions, red, green, and white dragons, four flowers, and four Chinese seasons imprinted on the one hundred forty-four tile surfaces.

****

Ngood's mother birthed another beautiful, healthy boy. Soon, the same ominous symptoms weakened the helpless infant and filled the family with dread. Disappointed with the powers of the medium, Ah Ma called a Chinese doctor this time. The woman doctor felt the boy's forehead with her hand to see if he felt hot. She held the baby's wrist for a while and frowned, perhaps as she had seen western doctors do. Then she wrote down a list of traditional herbs, and Byu Goo was sent to the Chinese pharmacy to get the remedy. But it was not long before the pathetic cries of the wee one fell silent, and he breathed his last breath.

Why? Oh, why were the gods so unhappy and the ancestors so displeased with Ngood's mama? Did she not burn enough incense and spirit money? Did she not serve enough tea at the altar, or was the fruit unsatisfactory? Did she not cry enough petitions or give enough money to the temple? Was she so wicked in a previous life to deserve this sorrow? Ngood suffered to see her dear mama suffer.

What would become of the poor, tiny, unnamed brother in that terrible place of the spirit world? Would Ngow-How and Mar-Meng be rough with him? Why must this little one be taken away by them?

****

Old Man Thunder Voice was now managing the opera and Ngood's family did not attend very often. But Ngood and Ming still loved singing the opera songs with Papa's records. Ming continued to sing the woman's part and Ngood sang the man's part. Papa never let on that he heard them singing. But his homeland was in need of his assistance again. The Japanese had attacked and taken Nanking, with excessive brutality toward women, children, and the old, and the cries of the native land were heard once again by the overseas Chinese.

Papa continued to profit from the recreation club he founded, where men could go to play billiards, Mahjong, and other games. As head of this club, he was asked by other leaders of Chinatown whether his daughters could sing something for the fund-raising concert to "Rescue China." He said with reserve, "Maybe they could sing one or two items." But the organizers asked them to sing several songs.

One very patriotic song on Papa's records was called, "March of the Volunteers." The lyrics were performed as part of a Shanghai play in 1934, and the next year the words were put to music and made the theme of the Chinese film "Sons and Daughters in a Time of Storm" about an intellectual who was moved to fight against the Japanese. It had become a very popular song among Chinese as a call to resistance:

> *Rise up! All who refuse to be slaves!*
> *Let our flesh and blood become our new Great Wall!*
> *As the Chinese nation faces its greatest peril,*
> *All forces expend their last cries.*
> *Rise up! Rise up! Rise up!*
> *Our million hearts beat as one,*
> *Brave the enemy's fire!*
> *March on!*
> *Brave the enemy's fire!*
> *March on! March on! March on! On!*

On the day of the concert, the theatre house was full. Ngood was given the costume of a little boy and Ah Ming was given a girl's dress. The girls never had any coaching from adults and had not rehearsed at the venue, but these were songs they knew very well and could sing with enthusiasm. Ming also had a wonderful sense of performance and led Ngood in the rousing song "Rise up!" Chi Lai! They also sang several other songs from the operas, all with a patriotic theme. Mama was not in attendance, but Ngood saw Mrs. Lee and her family in the audience.

Ah Ming had matured into a beautiful young woman. She was alsdgifted in making the most of her beauty and dressed to accentuate her figure and complexion. Her hair was always shiny and coiffed, and she carried herself with style and grace. She gave special attention to her long slender fingers, manicuring her nails and applying fashionable polish to accentuate them. Soft, manicured hands were a sign of the wealthy class.

Matchmaker made regular visits to the Chin home, and the calls were never rushed. As she "drank down the teapot," she was full of gossip from the neighborhood. She also pried for the latest gossip from the Chins.

Ngood knew that Byu Goo was waiting for Matchmaker to leave so she could ask Mama, "Why does she have to have the chicken from the head to the tail?" expressing her displeasure at the busybody. But before Byu Goo could speak so freely, she must wait for Matchmaker to take a nap, resting her tired legs and tongue. And when she awoke, no one doubted how she would respond to the inevitable invitation to make use of, "one more set of chopsticks."

Matchmaker apparently was not offended that everyone called her "Number Three Sow," a reference to her birth order and to her hefty weight, which was a condition of her line of business. And no one minded too much about her nosiness or her opportunism, because these too were necessary for her line of work, and she provided a service to the community. Sometimes her duties required great sacrifice; a boat trip to China would take her a month or more.

Naturally, Matchmaker had taken a special interest in Ming. It is no surprise that the lovely girl had many admirers, especially after she and her little sister Ngood sang so adorably at the theater and enjoyed some fame in Chinatown. Many love-struck, mooning men could not wait for Matchmaker and approached Papa directly. But Papa would quietly turn suitors down, either because of the breach of propriety or because none lived up to the expectations he had for his eldest daughter.

Also Ming did not return their affections, which was a significant factor because she, for one, had much persuasive power over her father. Ah Ming was in no hurry to limit herself to the attentions of one man and take on the comparative drudgery of becoming a wife. She did not want to give up her freedom nor her power. As Ngood observed, she liked to have men chasing her, but she did not want to be caught.

Her suitors persevered. One persistent fellow was a well-educated man with a good job as a reporter, but he was from the Hakka class of Chinese, and this alone classified him as unworthy in Papa's eyes, prejudiced as he was to certain other clans. The unfortunate man had gone past the house and seen the girl, and already he was in love. He wrote many love letters, testifying of his devotion and his ability to provide for Ming, pleading for her affections. But Ah Ming did not care for him, and his lovesickness was in vain. Even after he was refused, the hapless man continued to long for her, and he became quite ill.

It was customary that if a man was lovesick for a girl, someone would ask the girl for an item of her inner wear, like a camisole. The representative would boil the under garment in water and give the water to the suffering man. He would drink the water and perhaps be cured. So, Matchmaker came to the four-story house and asked Ming for a camisole, but Ming refused. The poor man continued to languish, and eventually he died.

People in Chinatown said, "She has a cruel heart!" and blamed Ah Ming for his death.

Ming was sorry he died. But she defended herself, "I didn't do anything to him!"

****

Molly's school was having a concert. Students who had special talents were asked to perform, and Miss Reed's dancers were eager to participate. As usual, Alice played an important dancing role, but Molly was also given a good part. She was invited to play the solo part of a dancing fairy, and with her wand she would touch all of the dolls and toys in the toy shop, and they would appear to come alive. Molly wore a special fairy costume and carried a shiny, silver wand. She did some ballet steps, but not with toe shoes; she walked on tip toes.

On the night of the show, Molly paid the rickshaw driver to take her to the auditorium at the school. She performed very well, and many people congratulated her after the show, including her friend Jean and her family. Jean was not performing in the concert because she was preparing to leave Burma and study in England, but she had come to enjoy the show and support her friends. So Jean and her family enthusiastically praised Molly.

Jean's parents, who knew Molly's father, said, "Molly! You did so well! But where is your family? Why didn't they come to see you? Why did nobody come?"

Until this question was posed to her, Molly never thought that it was unusual that her family didn't come to watch her. Papa was not home, and Mama did not go out. These were usual conditions. After chatting with Jean's family, Molly went out in the cool evening air and confidently hired a rickshaw driver from the long line queued up after the program. She went home and told Mama all about the evening, and Mama's eyes shone with pride.

****

Mrs. Lee's son visited Ngood's mother at the apartment. Since they had moved from the four-story house, they were no longer so convenient to Chinatown, but Puck Ying seemed to find the trip worth the effort to see his god-sister. Ngood could understand that; she enjoyed spending time with her dear Mama as well. Still, she felt a little annoyed with him. He would come nearly every day and just sit.

Even Papa sometimes said with irritation, "Why is that boy here? Why is he always sitting in my house?"

The boy had a new apple green Morris open coupe, very practical with no roof for the Burma heat, but also very stylish. He parked his car in front of the Chin apartment, and it was a beacon for gossiping neighbors.

One particular day, even Molly had to agree it was a very good thing that Puck Ying came to visit at the apartment. Ah Ming had trouble with acne, and someone told her the remedy for acne was chrysanthemum tea. Byu Goo brewed some for her, boiling the leaves in water for hours and then cooling and straining the liquid. But instead of drinking a little of the concentrated potion as instructed, Ming drank the whole pot to make sure she would see results. Soon after, she began to hemorrhage heavily and continuously. She suffered for several hours, becoming weak and faint. Already neighbors, hearing of her symptoms, were gossiping that she was having an abortion. Chinese remedies to stop the bleeding had not helped, and the situation was becoming grim. When Puck Ying came to visit, he found the household full of concern for Ming, and indeed she appeared to be losing her life.

Puck Ying hurried home to tell his mother, who then rushed to see Ah Ming. By then it was night, but Mrs. Lee urgently sent Puck Ying to fetch her "western" doctor, Dr. Sato, a kind Japanese man who had received a western medical education. This was the father of Molly's compassionate classmate Judy.

After examining Ah Ming, Dr. Sato determined that he needed to give her an injection. Ming had never seen a needle and syringe, and she was frightened. But she trusted Mrs. Lee, who gave her the confidence to trust the doctor of suspicious race and foreign ways. Soon after the injection, the hemorrhaging stopped and a crisis was averted, though Ah Ming was pale and weak for many months after this.

Molly and Moonlight, shortly after Moonlight's illness. A seamstress made the dresses, yellow with red trim and floral buttons. Photo taken in a studio.

It is no wonder that Ah Ming trusted Mrs. Lee. She was known in Chinatown as nwe' jaing foo, "as good as a man," and a hero among women. She spoke in refined language in monotonous tones considered dignified, like a lawyer, and she was famous for being smart and wise. Her speech was seasoned pleasantly with compliments, with rhymes, and with ancient Chinese poetry and philosophy.

She was also known in Chinatown for her generosity; as the saying goes, "she does not count every pice," or penny. Sometimes a person would approach Mrs. Lee, delicately acting on behalf of a poor family unable to afford to bury a relative. Mrs. Lee was quick to offer the cash for a casket. No woman in Chinatown was so well regarded, and Ah Ming and her family were now among those greatly indebted to her.

****

He'ung had developed her own medical problem, and though it was not life-threatening, it caused physical discomfort and emotional and social pain. Periodically, a terrible rash would spread over her body. She was quite fashionable, but, in shame, she resorted to wearing long sleeves most of the time. Cruel gossips had already taken note and whispered "leprosy," so that, Ngood noticed, even Ming avoided He'ung when the rash prevailed.

****

Molly was entering the high school at the Methodist English Girls High School. The elementary school, through grade four, and the middle school, through grade seven, were on the first floor of the building. Now Molly was on the second floor, which held grades eight through ten, or more correctly, the eighth through tenth standard, which was the terminology in some British colonies corresponding to grades ten through twelve in other countries. Two early grades were called kindergarten.

Eighth grade at the Methodist English Girls High School brought Molly a new teacher. Miss Bartel told the students, "Say Bar-TEL, not BAR-tle."

She was young, and pretty, and very English. As much as Molly loved all of her teachers, this one would be her favorite.

The girls studied Shakespeare's "As You Like It." The play was written in English, but the wording was unlike any English Molly had seen before, and her grasp of the language would be pushed to new limits. Molly and her classmates found that what first seemed overwhelming could be understood with Miss Bartel's enthusiastic coaching. Just as Molly had admired the poetic writing in Chinese literature and Grandfather Wong's letters, she became intrigued by Shakespeare's creative use of words.

Miss Bartel would ask, "Judy, what do you think Shakespeare meant when he said, through the character of Jaques, 'All the world's a stage, and all the men and women merely players?' "

Then she would ask, "Molly, how does this seem true to you, and how is it not true?"

And then, "Gracie, can you give an example of what is 'Too much of a good thing?' "

Miss Bartel also enjoyed making the girls laugh, even as she broached sensitive subjects. In "As You Like It," mischievous fairies meddled with men and women and made them fall in love. Miss Bartel joked, while giving a gentle caution, "Be careful when choosing a boyfriend. You might have little cherubs flying around you." Molly admired the joy in her.

History was a subject that Molly knew could be rather boring, but Miss Bartel made it exciting. She told the story of the Battle of Hastings in 1066 AD when Edward the Confessor died leaving no clear successor, and a battle ensued between Harold II of England and Duke William of Normandy. She told of factors preceding the battle and nuances of the war strategies. She explained that, by one account, it first seemed the English would prevail by protecting themselves with a wall of shields, and they rained rocks and javelins down the hill on the Normans. But as front-line Normans started to retreat, the English broke ranks to pursue them, allowing Normans to then turn and penetrate the line. The English, on foot with simple shields and hand weapons, could not defend against the Norman's might, including troops and mercenaries from as far as southern Italy, and varied weaponry, including the first use of the crossbow and a well-trained cavalry. Miss Bartel helped the girls to understand the long-term influences of this Norman victory, including the English language which is full of words deposited from the French-speaking Normans.

Miss Bartel transported her students to the sixteenth century and the drama of the cruel, tyrannical, ostentatious, and egotistical Henry the Eighth, who, two days after his coronation, ordered the beheading of two of his father's ministers. Molly learned of spunky Anne Boleyn, second of six wives to Henry, whose lack of submission to her husband the king and her failure to produce an heir were fatal strikes against her. Henry imprisoned her in the infamous Tower of London and had her executed by beheading along with five men accused by Henry of adultery with his wife. Miss Bartel told the stories with passion and made the girls feel the tragedy of this brutal time in history. Molly's own thought was that Chinese emperors, Burman rulers, or English kings alike could be very cruel and place little value on human life.

Again the Scripture classes were optional, but Molly was attracted to the talk about Lord Jesus. She listened from across the room, soaking up every word, and often wondering, "What is this love they are talking about? It sounds like romantic love, but it is not. I think it must be holy love." When passages of Scripture were assigned for memorization, she eagerly memorized them.

The hymns sung by the Christian girls and teachers continued to call to her heart, almost as if wooing her, touching a deep need. Miss Bartel

Miss Bartel's eighth grade class. Molly is the first girl on the left, in the second row from the front.

sang the hymns beautifully and passionately as she accompanied herself on the piano. Molly learned the songs and often sang them at home. She sometimes noticed the sweet melodies and touching words were soothing her in the background of her mind.

Molly had become fond of many of her classmates by now. Many of them had continued with her since the third grade. Gracie remained Molly's closest friend. Besides providing friendship, she continued to be very knowledgeable and helpful to Molly. She could explain much about two foreign worlds to Molly, about Burmese customs and about the Christian faith. Judy Sato was always kind friend, though Molly, having participated in raising funds to fight the Japanese, was resistant to accept close friendship with someone of that race. Anna was a Jewish girl, and several times she had invited Molly to her house for a meal. Molly thought the food rather greasy, but she liked Anna, and she was interested to hear Anna explain about kosher foods, and why she couldn't eat certain things. One Chinese girl was called simply, "Tan." Miss Bartel couldn't pronounce her Chinese name correctly, as it contained sounds not used in English. Instead of taking an English name, the girl went by her clan name.

Carol was a new girl that had joined the others in high school. She was Anglo-Indian and was very bright. Molly could consistently surpass her test scores only in math. Carol was so much fun to be with. Her family owned a radio and they tuned it not to the local Burmese songs, but to a station that aired new American songs, and she taught the songs to the other girls. She would come to school and announce, "This is the latest song! Listen to this!" Most of the girls were eager to learn songs like Benny Goodman's "Sing, Sing, Sing," Leadbelly's "Goodnight Irene," The Sons of the Pioneers "Tumbling Tumbleweeds," and Bing Crosby's "Pennies from Heaven." Only the native Burmese girls were not too enthused, Molly noticed, preferring local tunes.

Miss Bartel was teaching the girls other things as well. She taught Molly to think for herself and to think big thoughts. A simple question like, "What do you want to do with your life?" implied that Molly might have some choice about her future. This was a radical thought in a culture where women were taught three stages of obedience in life. Molly had heard these many times. Stage one: when you are young, obey your father. Stage two: when you marry, obey your husband. Stage three: when you are old, obey your son.

A gradual change was coming over the girls as they became educated. No one told them to judge the ways of their culture, but as they learned to understand and reason, they also began to question.

Ngood wondered silently, "Why build a high threshold to keep out ghosts? If ghosts exist, why can't they go over the threshold? If a threshold keeps them out, how do they get in to a home?

"...And pressing a child's head into a bowl of rice naturally makes a dent in the rice, right? It doesn't show he is haunted by ghosts, right?"

She noted with secret, heretical dissatisfaction, "It is profitable to be a medium or a fortune teller in Chinatown."

She continued to question, "How can knowing someone's birthday and sticking a pin in a doll make someone sick? Are not illnesses caused by viruses and bacteria?"

Molly was even quietly critical of her own Chinese name. "Gentle Moon?" she thought to herself. "How can a moon be gentle? The moon is just a big rock satellite going around the earth. It is not gentle."

She reasoned further, "Now, Ah Ming's name makes sense, 'Moonlight.' The moon does reflect light from the sun, so that is a good name. But 'Gentle Moon?' No."

The girls were influenced in other ways. Miss Bartel had taught them about a man by the name of William Wilberforce, who, because of his devotion to the Lord Jesus, worked tirelessly to abolish the slave trade in Great Britain. Molly thought of families she knew who owned slaves, or who mistreated servants, and she was finding she did not quite approve. The maids in her own household were certainly not slaves, but once, recently, Molly had seen Ming motion angrily as if to swat Byu Goo on the head for lacing her shoes too tightly as the auntie put the shoes on the toy gee lo gah-nwe, the "money's owner's daughter," or "rich man's daughter." Molly did not think this was right. She didn't understand why a capable person could not put shoes on herself, and besides, Molly felt that everyone, servant or not, elder or not, should be treated with respect. The sisters were learning different world views as their paths diverged.

****

Molly had to admit she admired Puck Ying for standing up to Byu Goo's ridiculous fascination with ghosts. Byu Goo would point into a corner with fright, crying, "Look out! Don't go over there! I see a ghost in the corner! Stay away from that corner!"

Because of the woman's hysteria, the household would be in a panic, but Puck Ying would march bravely into the corner and stomp around, demanding, "Where is the ghost? I don't see a ghost!"

Terrified, Byu Goo would cry, "No! Do not go there! You will anger the ghosts! Something terrible will happen to you!"

But Puck Ying would repeat with bold defiance, "I don't see a ghost!" As he continued to fill the very corner, he would ask, "Now! Where is the ghost? Do you see any more ghosts?"

Molly had to admit that Puck Ying was also handsome and manly, but he was a bit of a dandy for Molly's sensible tastes. He admired the suave American actor Tyrone Power and slicked his hair back like him, using the men's hair pomade "Brylcream." His clothes were expensive; he always wore American-made Arrow shirts and stylish western suits ordered from

Hong Kong. And he looked quite the modern man driving around, without a hired driver, in his apple green Morris open coupe.

These attractions caught the sly, admiring looks of many eligible young ladies, and even ineligible women took notice. But these were only casual observances of one who noticed everything, for Molly's interest was in her studies.

Like boys and men around the world, Puck Ying also admired Charles Atlas, the American body builder who transformed himself from the skinny, sickly, and bullied Angelo Siciliano into the ultimate, muscular, virile hero. Puck Ying more than admired Mr. Atlas, he imitated him. He went regularly to a weight lifting club for body building and conditioning for boxing. He told Molly that he had been taking martial arts lessons since he was eleven years old. The dong house diagonally down the street from the four-story house offered a youth club with such instruction.

Molly noticed one other thing about Puck Ying, though she was too polite to say anything. He seemed to always be sniffling. In fact all of his brothers and sisters seemed to sniffle too. She remembered visiting his family apartments above the dry goods shop and seeing the thick dust in the beams of light coming through the skylight. The rooms were also filled with the various odors of the shop below. Molly had learned in school about germs and irritants and she wondered if there was a connection between the dust and the sniffling of the children. Were they having allergic reactions?

Molly continued to enjoy practicing her English with Puck Ying when he came to visit her mother. He seemed to enjoy speaking in English with her as well.

Puck Ying confided, "I want to be an architect someday, like my father's sister's husband. He has been advising me. I plan to take some architecture classes through a correspondence course from England."

"Oh, that will be so nice! I want to be a doctor someday," Molly announced. She added, "...a western doctor, not a Chinese doctor."

Puck Ying replied, "I see."

Indeed, Molly and three of her classmates had determined to be doctors. Sharing the passion were Gracie, Sally--a plump Persian girl from a rich family, and Louise-- whose Burman father was a judge. They studied together and were the only girls to take all of the science classes the school offered, which consisted of botany and biology. These determined girls weren't even squeamish about dissecting a cockroach or a frog in biology class, accepting every challenge from their science teacher, Mrs. Linsdale.

The world of medicine fascinated and motivated Molly. She wondered what was in the scientific injection Dr. Sato had given Ah Ming. Molly pondered about the chrysanthemum tea and its effect on Ming. Did the tea have some anticoagulant properties? She wondered what scientific explanation might be given for He'ung's rash and what carefully researched cure might remedy it. Was she having an allergic reaction of some kind? And, importantly, was there a western cure to keep babies from dying?

****

Puck Ying's sister Anita was seen walking down the streets of Chinatown with her hand tucked into the crook of Sammy Ng's arm! Ngood had heard of their engagement, but this rumor of such an open display of affection, even for an engaged couple, was shocking! Before long, Ngood saw it for herself. "Oh, my!" she thought. "Nobody does this!"

****

Like so many other days, Ngood took the rickshaw home from school and paid the driver two annas. Carrying her school books in a shan bag, she entered the apartment and climbed the stairs with a sprightly step to the second floor. In spite of the heat of the day, she had an appetite for both a little snack and to be at her lessons.

When she entered the apartment, she was startled by the sight. Mooncakes! Hundreds of mooncakes! These dense Chinese pastries, about four inches in diameter, were stuffed with lotus seed paste or sweet bean paste and held an egg yolk "moon." Molly stood and stared at the piles of them on many trays. These were not small trays, but big ones that could be attached to poles and carried on the shoulders of delivery men. Stamped into the top of each crust was the Chinese character for "Double Happiness."

Ngood felt the ominous significance, but she wasn't too worried, yet. She asked her mother, "Ah Ming?"

The way her mother smiled at her, Ngood knew even before Mama shook her head.

Ngood knew. "Me?" She asked.

Mama nodded, tears of joy welling in her eyes.

"Anyone I know?" Ngood asked, trying to keep dismay from her voice.

"Puck Ying!" Her mother rejoiced.

And that was the first Ngood knew of her engagement to Puck Ying.

She saw Mama's exultant look. Ah Ma was certain that she and Papa had done well for their daughter. Ngood tried to return Mama's smile.

How could Ngood complain? This engagement was so much better than her precious mama's distressing experience. Ngood could not forget that Mama had traveled hundreds of miles from her village in China, left all that she had known and loved, to go to a foreign country and marry a man she had never met. Only Number Two Brother had escorted her. At that time she didn't know if she would ever again see her family. There was no period of courtship. She did not even meet the groom before she married him. At her wedding ceremony Ah Ma had worn a heavy veil. Afterward, she went alone to a bedroom to wait for her husband to come in and lift her veil, and only then did the eyes of husband and wife first meet without concealment. And just like that, she was his.

Such difficult things had not happened to Ngood. She already knew this boy Puck Ying, and since he had grown, she actually liked the young man. He lived in this same city, so Ngood wouldn't have to move to some far off place never to be seen again. In these modern days, there could be some time for courting. Mama was certain Ngood would find these happy circumstances. She expected Ngood's gratitude and joy. This dear, uncomplaining woman could not be disappointed. And, of course, Papa could not be opposed. All of the important people were in agreement.

With resignation Molly thought, "My fate is sealed."

Unable to completely hide her resentment, Molly told Mama softly, "You got me engaged. Okay. But I want to finish college." She sat at the marble dining table and tried to focus on her studies.

Mama noticed Ngood was not overjoyed. Trying to appease Ngood, she said, "Mrs. Lee told me you will never have to do labor. She says she can afford plenty of maids."

Maids? That was not Molly's concern right now. Nevertheless Molly was able to give her mother a slight, but genuine smile, if not for the circumstance in which she found herself, at least for the love and concern of her dear Mama. Molly determined to guard her countenance for Mama's sake.

Molly found it difficult to concentrate on her books. She was irritated by the Byu Goo's silly felicity and wished the woman would just get on with the inevitable work of delivering the mooncakes to family, friends and neighbors, announcing her engagement. Periodically Molly chided herself for not seeing the warning signs. Now she understood why the boy was always hanging around her house. And, yes, Matchmaker had joined the Chin family for dinner recently, but Molly was caught off guard thinking Ah Ming would be first. Then Molly remembered Byu Goo making foolish faces at her and giggling like a young girl. She should have recognized that these signals, taken together, warned of danger.

That evening her parents and his parents continued to make fast the bond. Matchmaker happily mediated between the homes, delivering the three-generation documents testifying to the health of Ngood's and Puck Ying's ancestors and exchanging rings.

Molly never saw the documents, but hearing of them, she thought critically that if an ancestor had leprosy no one would admit to it anyway. She also knew that women were not mentioned in these documents except by clan name, because--and she felt the sting of it deeply now--women were of little importance in these matters.

Her mother would keep for her the diamond engagement ring Match-maker brought from the Lees. It was too valuable to be worn in public. Her father had ordered another ring in 24 carat gold, instructing the jeweler to engrave it with Molly's Chinese initials in English letters, "CNY." Papa gave the ring to Matchmaker, and she tucked it into her pocket to deliver to the Lees.

Next day at school Molly did not mention her engagement to her classmates. It was not something she wanted to discuss.

But that evening Puck Ying arrived at her door wearing his best clothes, an expensive off-white, western style suit from Hong Kong. "My mother says we should have our picture taken. She made arrangements with the photographer. Will you please get dressed and come with me?" He was polite, and all necessary parties had agreed, so Molly obeyed.

She went to her bedroom and put on a fancy velvet brocade dress with a high collar and stylish slits at the sides. Ming had chosen the fabric for Ngood, and Mama's seamstress had sewn it. The fabric had a beautiful pale orange background with white raised velvet decoration. Molly wore high heeled shoes with lacing up the ankles.

Puck Ying led her to his apple green Morris open coupe and opened the door for her. As he helped her delighted brother Sen King into the back seat to act as a chaperone, Molly glanced at the second floor apartment window to see the faces of Mama, Byu Goo, and two sisters grinning at her.

Well, Ah Ming wasn't smiling too much. And why should she? Every-one knew Ming was supposed to go first, even if she wasn't eager to get engaged. Ming never said anything to Ngood and was lov-ing and gracious as always, but she must've felt the slight to her dignity that she was not the first engaged. Of course, Molly was in no hurry to get engaged either and would have been most happy to wait for Ming. Anyway, she would put off marrying Puck Ying as long as she could.

But she was afraid Puck Ying had other ideas. Molly could see now what she had been blind to before. He was really, intensely in love with her. She remembered the Chinese expression chi' ting, meaning "crazy with love" and understood now what those words described. Puck Ying's thoughts seemed to be so focused on her that he couldn't function normally.

Soon Puck Ying was coming to the Chin apartment nearly every night wanting Molly to go out with him. It was hard for Molly to keep up with her studies, but she was determined. She was nearly eighteen and in the ninth standard at the English school. She still had another year of high school after the present one, and then she would begin college.

She did enjoy riding in the apple green Morris open coupe with Puck Ying and Sen King to the movie theater. Puck Ying grinned shyly at her.

He was anxious to explain, "I heard my mother talking to Matchmaker. She was asking the matchmaker if she knew anyone suitable for me that is my age or a little younger, or whether she thought of finding someone in China. When Matchmaker left, I followed her. I told her, 'Don't you dare match me with any other girl!'

"She asked me, 'Oh, do you have someone in mind? Tell me, and I will see if I can work it out with your mother.'

"And I said, 'I want Chin Ngood Yin.'

"Matchmaker was pleased, 'Oh! That is easy! Your parents and her parents know each other already. And your parents and her parents are in the same business class.' So she told my mother, and my mother agreed."

Ngood didn't know what to say. She was flattered, really, by Puck Ying's attention. She tried to smile and answer pleasantly, "Oh."

Chapter Nine

Dancing and Milk Shakes

Puck Ying loved the American movies, and over the next year or so, he and Molly saw many movies together. They saw "The Wizard of Oz" and "Gone with the Wind," and movies starring Jeanette Macdonald and Nelson Eddie, or Fred Astaire and Ginger Rogers. They saw Dorothy Lamour in "The Jungle Princess," a film similar to the Tarzan movies Molly had seen with Ah Baht Sook, but with a woman in the lead role.

Like Ah Baht Sook, Puck Ying liked the Tarzan movies. Molly was amused to hear Puck Ying imitate the savage Tarzan yell the jungle man used to call the wild animals, and he could do it very well. But sometimes he was so very loud that she would have to try to shush him.

And they saw "Show Boat." Puck Ying loved the song "Ol' Man River," which was sung in the film by Paul Robeson, a man of African descent with a rich bass voice. Mr. Robeson played the character of a stevedore on a riverboat which entertained patrons with a theatre production. In the song, he complains that the Mississippi River just keeps rolling along, careless of the tragedies and toiling of human experience. Puck Ying imitated the singer, crooning in his lowest range and perfectly mimicking the language. His effort always got a giggle from Molly.

Puck Ying did not yet understand the pathos of the song. He just liked it.

He told Molly, "I don't like the Burmese movies or Chinese movies. One scene takes so long."

Molly laughed. She remembered Ah Baht Sook saying the same thing. Of course, the couple always took a little brother or sister to ride along in the car. It was not nice to see a couple going out alone. Most often Molly's sister He'ung was the one to happily tag along.

Puck Ying had a small camera, and he loved to take Molly's picture. At first she enjoyed posing for him, obeying his instructions to stand here or move her arm thus.

Molly poses with the Lee character on the grill of the Morris

Molly with Terence's Number Three Sister Fe Yone on the back of a bus hired by Mrs. Lee for an excursion

Soon Molly tired of this amusement. She never knew when Puck Ying might snap another picture of her. He was particular-ly annoying to her when she was trying to study, and her counte-nance reflected her displeasure. When Puck Ying took the film to be

Terence's father, Lee Sit Hong, in the front seat of the apple green Morris open coupe. Terence's Number Two Sister Lily, Molly, and Ginger are in the

developed and received the printed photographs a week or so later, he surely noticed that he was accumulating a number of Molly's displeased looks across her books. But he seemed not to be discouraged, and he continued to record for posterity the glares of his beloved Molly.

****

Ngood enjoyed teaching English to He'ung and to Sen Kee. Sen King was not interested, and Sen Phat and Ah Haing were still young, but in the two siblings Ngood found eager pupils. Ngood enjoyed the role of teacher, imitating the women she much admired.

Molly decided it was time for her siblings to have English names, and all eagerly agreed. In fact, the Chinese were comfortable having multiple names. For instance, Molly's aunt Han Yee gave herself a new name when she began to teach professionally. A new name, often selected from Chinese poetry, might be taken at marriage or after a special event or milestone in life. So it was not at all unusual to take on a new name, and Molly knew the advantage of having an English name in culture ruled by the English. Besides that, everyone knew how pitiful the English were at pronouncing some Chinese sounds, so accommodating the English by providing an alternate name they could say was sensible. Molly's siblings were pleased to have Molly's help and proud to have a name that influential people would be comfortable to use. Ming had already taken the name of "Moonlight," because it was an easy translation of her given name.

This was an enjoyable exercise for Molly and for her brothers and sisters, and American movies provided the inspiration for the names she selected. He'ung she named "Ginger" for the dancer Ginger Rogers. Sen King was very good looking, and already he was turning the heads of the girls, so Molly named him "Clark" for the handsome actor Clark Gable. Next was Sen Kee, and Molly named him "Johnny," for the actor Johnny Weismuller, who played the Tarzan role. Next was Sen Phat, and Molly chose the name of "Wayne" for him, after the actor John Wayne. For her youngest sister Ah Haing, Molly chose the name "Dorothy" for the actress who played the Jungle Princess.

Mama was expecting again, and this little brother or sister would need an English name. Molly was happily considering her options.

Molly also mentioned to Puck Ying that she did not particularly like the name Mariano that he had chosen for himself. After all, it was not really an English name, was it? She thought it sounded Italian. So, what name would she choose for him, Puck Ying wondered. She liked "Terence." He liked it too.

****

Molly was concerned for her brothers. Clark had become the proverbial rich man's eldest son, spoiled by wealth, spoiled by position, and spoiled by his own beauty. He was quite vain about his looks. He, like Terence, combed his hair with Brylcream, styling a pouf in front and slicking back his hair.

Most unfortunate, in Molly's view, Clark did not see the benefit of an education. One time he and his brothers were absent from school for several days, and it was discovered that they had used their lunch money to take a rickshaw to the zoo. Molly knew Johnny and Wayne had been influenced by the older brother, and she still had high hopes for them. But she was very concerned for Clark's future.

****

Terence and Molly often went together to dances hosted in private homes. Usually they went to the home of a Chinese medical doctor. Terence was acquainted with a Fokinese gentleman who was a friend of the doctor and in this way they were invited.

"You don't know the dances?" the man told Terence, "Come along anyway and we'll teach you." He told Terence, "Bring your friends. We want the young people to come and dance." So Terence invited his siblings, his cousins, the Chin girls, and several others.

Not many in Chinatown knew how to dance. So those who could already dance were especially welcomed to these parties.

Molly loved to dance, and after so many years of lessons, she was quite good at it. She had a nice figure complemented by a stylish dress with a slit up the side and high heeled shoes. She learned the latest dance steps very quickly and was eager to show off her ability. The Fokinese man was heavy in stature but light on his feet, and he taught the young people the newer dances like the tango, a provocative dance from Argentina, with long elegant steps, minimal up and down motion, and dramatic head movements. Even Ginger, who never had dance lessons, learned to dance the tango with the man whose wife seemed content to watch her husband dance with the young women.

Soon Molly was an expert at these new dances, and she enjoyed herself immensely. She might have traded English names with her sister He'ung because she felt like Ginger Rogers on the dance floor. She would dance with Terence for a while, and then someone would tap him on the shoulder and say, "May I cut in?"

Terence would grudgingly release Molly to dance with another man, but he watched sullenly, angry to see Molly enjoying herself with someone else. He had no desire to dance with anyone but her.

Soon Terence would say grumpily to Molly, "Let's go home." Often, the party wasn't even half over! Molly sometimes argued with him but stopped when she realized that they were making a scene.

Someone would say, "At least let Moonlight and Ginger stay! We'll bring them home later!" But Terence and Molly needed a chaperone, so most often Ginger had to go with them. Molly and Terence would ride in the Morris open coupe arguing all the way back to Molly's house.

Terence would say resentfully, "I don't like people tapping me."

"These are older men!" Molly would answer, thinking Terence's jealousy was foolish. "They are my father's age! And the young men are your own cousins! I'm not in love with them! I don't flirt with anyone! I'm only dancing! You are being ridiculous. You are not being a good guest to our hosts. You are so grouchy everyone is glad to see us leave. Your foolish jealousy is already well-known in Chinatown!"

It is true that Molly did not flirt with other men. But she was insensitive to Terence's love, and that he wanted her to return his affections. He longed for her attention, her closeness, and her touch, and it pained him that she was giving these precious things to other men.

Their outings were often embarrassing, and the ride home in an open car was hardly a private place for an argument. Recalling this at a much later time, Molly's face warmed with embarrassment as she guessed that neighbors looked up as they passed and thought, "There goes that handsome young couple in the splendid car... arguing again." And poor Ginger, the unfortunate chaperone, got an earful, expanding her English in a novel way.

One night, the three sisters were together when they arrived home from a dance, and Byu Goo met them at the iron gate. She looked fearful.

"Hush!" She cautioned in a loud whisper. "Be very quiet! Your father is at home. Someone told him you were dancing! He was so angry! He was pounding his walking stick so we thought it would go through the floor! He was threatening to beat you all! Your mother... you know she never says anything to him... but she tried to sooth him.

"Eventually Ah Ma was able to calm him down and talk him in to going to bed. She said, 'Oh, I'm sure it is not too bad! Oh, I am sure they will not go again! Oh, you look so tired after all your travels....'

"Finally he went to sleep. So you must take your shoes off and sneak up the steps. Be very quiet when you go in so you don't wake him!"

Suspecting the rumors were at least partly true, Byu Goo also had to scold, "Why do you want to hug those men? Dancing? Have you no shame?"

The frightened girls did as they were told. The next day they were especially respectful to their father, fearing his wrath to shoot out like hot coals at any moment. But he did not mention the dancing.

It was more peaceful for everyone when Terence and Molly went to the movies, or went into the city with Sammy and Anita. They especially liked to go to Fraser Street where there were rows of stalls that opened at five o'clock in the evening. Mostly Indian people ran the enterprises in this part of town. Strolling down the street, Molly would notice Sammy folding Anita's hand into the crook of his arm. Terence tried to do this with Molly, but she was too embarrassed to show affection so openly in public, and she made it clear to him she did not approve.

But Molly did approve of the milkshakes Terence bought for her. The Indian man would mix fresh mangos, bananas, and milk, and he would pour this over ice he had shaved from a big block. Or, Terence could always pacify Molly with falooda, a beverage of rose syrup, vermicelli, tapioca seeds and milk. He discovered another weakness of hers was the Indian paratha, a layered fried bread that was topped with seasoned ground beef. Though Terence didn't eat meat, except seafood, he was happy to accommodate Molly. Well, sometimes he had paratha too.

Often they would start their dining experience in Chinatown, ordering fried noodles. Terence loved to order squid, which was chopped and boiled quickly, then mixed with water cress that was also quickly boiled, something like Grandma Wong had often made for Molly. It was served with an excellent sauce that was both sweet and sour, with garlic and hot chili. Molly agreed it was so good, "You feel like you want more!" But no matter how the meal began, the strollers often seemed to end up on Fraser Street for a milkshake.

They explored other shops around Rangoon, exotic and exciting to Molly, though she had grown up in this very city. Mogul Street was famous for selling gold and the workmanship of the well-to-do Indian goldsmiths was admirable.

Sometimes as they walked along in the streets, they would hear loud music coming from a radio blaring from an apartment window. In those days in Rangoon, anyone fortunate enough to own a radio would turn it on loud for the world to know it, giving the owner a big face. Mostly they heard Burmese songs, not the American ones that Molly's classmate Carol sang.

Molly became a bit more aware of the Burmese culture surrounding her. She remembered how she had taken shopping trips with Han Yee and enjoyed the hospitality of Buddhist women with charitable instincts to earn merit in Heaven. Again Molly and Terence accepted hospitality in the cool shelter of the awnings, and if the hostess was present, they practiced their Burmese.

Often as they walked, they would see the ever familiar beggars in the streets, usually impoverished Indians. The Burmese believed in being charitable to them, and Terence also shared his coins.

But Terence confided a troubling rumor to Molly. "I have heard that parents will intentionally blind their children or beat and cripple them so they can earn more money for the family as pitiable beggars."

"No!" Molly said.

But Terence feared the rumor was at least somewhat true. She wondered about the father and his blind son that used to beg near the four-story-house. Did that father harm his child? This was a very troubling thought. But as Terence and Molly discussed the possibility, they agreed that even if the rumor was true they must show mercy to the disadvantaged children.

Some of the Burmese holidays, usually associated with full moons, were now more apparent to Molly. As she strolled with Terence in October, the Burmese month of *Thadingyut*, she observed colorful strings of lights, on homes with the benefit of electricity, to celebrate the *Tazaungdaing*, the lighting festival. Pagodas and public buildings were also illuminated, and people often carried candles, creating quite a sparkling spectacle in Rangoon. The festival was meant to celebrate the legend of Buddha returning to earth after preaching about his law to celestial beings in Heaven. It was also a celebration of the end of the rainy season and a special time to honor monks and elders. Especially during this time the charitable tables were extended in front of homes for passersby.

Molly enjoyed seeing various street entertainments up close. She and her sisters had observed these from their Canal Street apartment windows when the roadway was full of celebration. Sometimes events were casual, as informal as a small crowd around a single story teller, who could be rewarded for telling a good tale by tossing coins into his cup. Other shows, called *pwes*, were quite elaborate affairs with stages that blocked a street. These might be associated with holidays, but were often charitable events given by the wealthy attempting to earn passage to Nirvana. The shows might involve dancing, singing, skits, puppet shows, white-faced clowns, or dramas. Sometimes carnival rides were featured, such as a carousel or a ferris wheel, and sometimes there were games of chance. Performances could run very long, and entertainment might run past midnight. There was much jocularity, and Molly watched with interest as the audience often laughed and laughed. Molly recognized the Burmese words, but she often did not understand the jokes. There seemed to be a lot of insider references.

In April, or Tagu, the Burmese New Year, the *Thingyan* festival was a raucous time of celebration, notable for the tradition of throwing water on friends and strangers in the street. It was during the hot season, and the drenching with cool water was not unpleasant. No one got upset, and in fact, no one went out unless prepared for a shower. Some Buddhists associated the dousing with washing away sins, but the holiday appeared less serious than joyous. Pagodas and monasteries were also washed. The elderly were honored by washing their hair.

When not going out for entertainment, Molly and Terence could sit together in the living room of her home. But there was definitely no hugging. And no kissing. *Aye-ah*, no!

One day when they were sitting together, Molly said to Terence, "When we were children you hit me on the head. Do you remember?"

"Oh, yes," Terence laughed, "I remember."

Molly teased him, "Now I will get my revenge on you!"

****

Molly really liked Terence's sister Anita. Sometimes the young women would stick up for each other. Anita was always having to beg Terence for the use of the car. She could not drive herself and would have to hire a driver, but this was much more convenient than other modes of transportation open to Anita. Molly overheard her complaining to her mother, "I have an appointment tomorrow to see a dentist, and Puck Ying won't let me use the car."

Molly was able to use her influence for Anita, not that Anita needed help persuading her mother. As the oldest daughter, she was clearly favored. But Molly had great influence over Terence. If Molly asked for something, Terence was too smitten to resist.

Anita and her sisters were now attending the Diocesan school where the dance lessons were given. Anita explained to Molly, "We changed schools because the nuns from St. John's were often coming to Mama's shop and taking things without paying. They expected Mama's charity. Ah Ma got tired of that."

****

Molly scolded Terence, "I don't like the way you boss your maids around! You should respect them. They are people too."

Terence grinned at her, "When I was a boy, even eight years old, I would come home from school and just sit down and stick out my two feet. Two maids had to take off my shoes and socks. One maid for each foot."

Molly was agitated. "It sounds like you were a puppet! Or a doll! Someone had to dress you and undress you?" She clucked, "What a spoiled boy!"

Terence knew it was true and could only answer her with a sheepish grin.

****

Terence bought Molly a swim suit! What? A two piece! What? This was absolutely inappropriate, and she let Terence know this. She would never wear such a thing! She could not imagine her Papa's response if he saw this thing! But she kept it.

****

Before school, Molly held her new baby brother and walked around the apartment living room, bouncing him very gently. He was such a handsome, sweet baby, and Molly had already grown accustomed to carrying him and singing him to sleep. She leaned close to him, caressing his soft face with her nose. She was careful not to touch the boy's head, because Chinese tradition holds that a male's godliness resides in his head, and a woman must not pollute him. The head of a man is "only for Buddha," the saying went.

The baby was crying a little, and he had a little diarrhea before, but *piya*! Thank god! He seemed to be much better this morning. Once again, Mama didn't have enough milk, so Byu Goo had fixed goat's milk for him.

"Go to sleep little one," Molly cooed. Then she sang softly to him a song she learned when she saw "The Wizard of Oz" with Terence, "Somewhere Over the Rainbow."

****

The girls at the Methodist English Girls High School were very much surprised. The elder Miss Durham had married! Now she was Mrs. Morgan. They wondered, "How did this happen?" She seemed to them rather old and cross, and they were quietly confounded that anyone would want to marry her.

Molly was working diligently towards her diploma. After she finished the classroom work, she would have to sit for the test, the "matriculation examination," which was the same for the whole country. To graduate from high school, everyone had to pass sections in English, Burmese, and three areas of mathematics: arithmetic, geometry, and algebra. Molly was determined to do more than pass these and other subjects. She intended to excel so that she could go on to college and medical school.

For the classroom work Molly now had Mrs. Wells. Her teaching style was very different from that of Miss Bartel. Mrs. Wells was old, maybe in her seventies, and she was quite bent over. She taught Shakespeare's Macbeth, but she didn't really do much teaching.

When someone asked a question, she would respond, "You are big girls! Look it up yourself!" But their resources were very limited; they did not have a library. Often in confusion the girls could only look at each other blankly.

Somehow they muddled through on their own. Each day they would read the assignments and work together to try to figure out the answers. Mrs. Wells was very stingy about grades. One had to write a perfect composition, with correct grammar and punctuation. Mrs. Wells wouldn't, absolutely would not, accept contractions.

After a challenging day at school, Molly came home to the apartment on Canal Street. As she carried her books up the stairs, she thought the rooms seemed unusually quiet. Byu Goo met her as she came in and told her mournfully, "He is gone!"

"Who is gone?" Molly asked urgently.

"The baby," Byu Goo answered, her voice cracking. She looked sorrowfully at Molly and then across the room at Mama. Molly thought her mother never looked so weak and broken.

Molly had held the treasured little boy and sung to him that very morning! He seemed fine then, but now he was gone! Why? What had caused the animation to leave his little body? Why would he never have the chance to grow and to learn and to be?

She thought about what she had learned at the English school about the spread of germs. Was the goats' milk contaminated? Or the water? Had someone not washed her hands and spread the dysentery? Or were the gods or ancestors angry? Had this little one been guilty of some past offense in a previous life? Was her mother being punished? None of these lines of reasoning could provide any real comfort to Molly now, and she could not shake her sorrow of the tragic loss of her little brother. Nothing could be done to bring back the precious boy. Nothing could comfort her mother.

Someone from the Chin clan house had come and gotten the body and buried it quietly. There was no funeral procession, no public acknowledgment of their loss. The sorrow was too great. The shame was too great.

Somehow the family must go on without the precious baby. Somehow, Molly thought, she must become a doctor and learn how to stop the suffering of the little ones and their mamas.

****

Molly was finishing her last year at the Methodist English Girls High School, the tenth standard. It was nearing the end of the English year of 1941, and Molly was 19 years old. All of the class material had been covered, and the students were reviewing all of their lessons in preparation for the country-wide exam to be given at the end of the school year in February. Molly and her friends Gracie, Sally, and Louise continued to immerse themselves in their studies, determined to go on to college and become doctors, and the committed teachers at the English school were doing all in their power to help the girls achieve their goals.

Molly knew the British were at war with the Germans and Italians and that China continued to fight Japan. On December 7, Japanese airplanes bombed the naval base at Pearl Harbor, Hawaii, of the United States and invaded Hong Kong and Malaysia the same day, December 8 local time. But those were distant concerns for a girl so focused on her studies and her future.

Chapter Ten

Houses Falling Down

The English school was closed for Christmas break at the end of December. Molly had learned about the Christmas story, about Lord Jesus' birth—in a stable? What a hard and humble place! This was unexpected to an Asian mind. Buddha was born in a palace and was shielded from the outside world. Instead, Jesus' mother wrapped him in clean strips of cloth and tucked him into an animal's feeding trough. Really?

Angels announced the birth of God's Son to shepherds and a bright star announced his birth to wise men. Molly pondered these things in her heart, much like the baby's mother Mary first pondered. Molly heard that Jesus, Son of God, was sent to the world by God because God so loved the world. Hmm. This was respite from her studies, to let her mind wander to these curious thoughts.

But, she really must study. Even Terence was busy studying now and had little time to enjoy with Molly; they both had many notes to review before the final tests in February. Their future depended on these tests, they thought.

It was December 23, and the day seemed quite ordinary: another pleasant, cool-season day in Burma. Molly was concentrating on her notes, which she had spread out before her at the marble table. Hours had gone by as she reviewed formulas, definitions, lists, and dates.

Molly came slowly from her studious trance, disturbed by a commotion. She looked up and saw Ah Hem, the Sino-Indian boy who worked for Papa at his recreation business on Lanmadaw Street. Molly knew Papa put a lot of confidence in this young man and trusted Ah Hem to manage things in his long absences and to act as his personal assistant when he was in town. Ah Hem didn't come to the apartment very often, but Molly knew him immediately. He was neatly dressed as usual in western clothing, a shirt and long pants.

Unfamiliar, however, was Ah Hem's countenance. Something had clearly upset him. He was fluent in Cantonese, and the ladies of the house gathered around him.

Moonlight asked him, "What is it, Ah Hem? Why do you look so concerned?"

He said, addressing them all respectfully, "I have come from the club to warn you. Something has happened on Pansodan Street."

Molly was familiar with Pansodan Street, or Phayre Street, as the English called it, the primary business district of Rangoon. The son of one of her father's friends had opened the Green Hotel on that street. Molly wondered, "What could have happened on Pansodan Street that would cause Ah Hem to run all the way over here to tell us?"

Moonlight urged him to go on.

Ah Hem explained vaguely, "People are saying houses on Pansodan Street are falling down and that pieces of the buildings are scattered everywhere. Everyone is talking about this." As he spoke, he frowned in puzzlement, as if he could not make sense of his own words. "They say that people are dying in the street. Many more people are running here and there like they are crazy. That is all I know. No one knows what happened."

Molly could see that Ah Hem was both alarmed and puzzled. She received his words with the same confusion; the words were recognizable, but they expressed a situation too unfamiliar to be understood.

Mama, always hospitable, asked Byu Goo to get Ah Hem something to eat. Molly glanced out the window and noticed groups of people in Canal Street talking excitedly. She went down to see what she could find out.

She heard bits of conversations spoken in Burmese. "What has happened in Pansodan Street?" "What could make houses fall down and make people die?" "Who knows what this means?"

Molly thought with frustration that everyone here could ask questions, but the only answer anyone gave was, "I don't know."

At last, a few brave young men decided to run toward central Rangoon to see for themselves.

Molly went back into the apartment, unable to add anything to Ah Hem's information. She wished Papa was home. The boys had been out playing somewhere, but they came home when they heard the same inadequate bits of incomprehensible news. The family waited together nervously, hoping for a reassuring explanation, but other pieces of news they heard later in the day did not comfort them.

"People saw an airplane! It looks like a bomb must have been dropped in Pansodan Street!"

To this news, the response was invariably the same, "A bomb? Why would anyone want to bomb Phayre Street in Rangoon?" It was too strange to be believed. And yet it was too terrifying to be ignored. No one spoke of anything else.

A few people in the neighborhood owned precious radios, but at first it did them no good. Though they listened intently and blared the sound into the street, no information was broadcast about the mystifying events.

Molly had never been so glad to see Papa when he arrived home the next day. He tried to calm the fears of his family, telling them not to worry, assuring them they were safe. They wanted to believe him, and his composed presence and soothing words were reassuring.

But the following day, the English holiday of Christmas, it became impossible to believe there was nothing to worry about. More airplanes came to Rangoon with more bombs, causing more falling houses and more people dying in the streets.

As time passed, the horror of the situation cut more deeply into each one's dazed mind. "What friends and acquaintances have died terribly?" each wondered but could not know. "Where will the next bombs drop, and when?" "Why is this happening?" The whole city was in a panic.

In a few days, there was no question as to why the bombings had happened. The British rulers explained over the radios that the Japanese had invaded Burma. Not only were they continuing to fight China, but now they wanted to take over all of East Asia, including Burma. In fact, Burma was key to Japanese designs on China. This, the British explained, was war.

So, there was the explanation, but the reality was a difficult concept to understand. War? What does this mean? Even those with some concept of war knew nothing of this kind of warfare. What defense could there be against airplanes dropping bombs?

Messages from the British continued to come over the radio. Those who owned radios informed their neighbors, and word spread quickly. If they were able, people were to find shovels and dig trenches. When they heard the airplanes, the people were to run to the trenches and lie face down for protection. If they had no trench to go to, they should run to the lowest part of a building and stay away from windows. Like many residents of the city, the Chins had no place to dig a trench, so when they heard the airplanes, they ran to the first floor, huddling helplessly in the stairwell.

The people were told to follow a curfew, but no one knew at first what a curfew was. British officials explained: no one could be in the streets after dark, and no one should use candles or lights of any kind. One dim little light might be allowed in a home, but the people were warned that a light could mean a target if the Japanese planes came at night. The atrocities and horrors of the bombings were recited throughout the city, so no one would risk being a target.

Soon the British had established a city-wide system of air raid sirens, which blew when airplanes were sighted. Local Air Raid Wardens would watch the sky for in-coming planes and sound hand-cranked sirens from rooftops. These wardens could vary the pitch of the sirens, cranking faster to produce higher pitches, and so two different signals were devised to communicate to the neighborhoods.

Citizens were trained to run for cover when they heard these sirens sounding a long, mournful wail, slowly rising and descending in pitch:

"ooooOOOOooooo ooooOOOOOoooo!"

Each time, the sound penetrated Molly's nerves and instantaneously catapulted her to her feet. She would grab the hand of little Dorothy and run for the stairs. They were to stay still in their hiding places as they heard the throbbing engines of the Japanese airplanes overhead, "RHmmm! RHmmm! RHmmm!" Sometimes they heard whining sounds and explosions. Who knew what was happening outside?

When the planes were out of sight, the wardens would make a different sound, to signify "All clear," to the citizens. This siren rose quickly in pitch and held the note constant:

"oooooOOOOOOOOOOOOOOO!"

As it sounded, those who had escaped harm warily lifted themselves out of the trenches and corners. The terror was over for a little while, but the fear was never over.

So began a different sort of existence for Molly. Between moments of panic, a sort of numbness settled in; nothing was very funny or pretty, nothing tasted good, and no distraction was engaging. Even her schoolwork couldn't take her mind off of the danger, the constant, wearing, worry. Every noise was a concern, every thought was weighed down by another exceedingly oppressive one, and every sleep was haunted by ghastly Japanese soldiers.

Molly tried to be brave for the younger ones and tried to be a help to her mother. Still, she could see that each beloved face in her home was drawn with tension. Molly worried not only for herself and her family but for her classmates and teachers. Were they safe? Were they alive?

Even when curfew was not in effect during the day, few people ventured out into the street. People were afraid to go out to buy and sell, and the formerly robust city took on a hushed and solemn tone.

Terence was often at the Chin home now. Papa was also home and resented the boy who was always hanging around. The apartment seemed smaller as tensions grew.

After a few weeks, the report came from British officials that the residents of Rangoon should evacuate to rural areas. The administrators explained that the Japanese were targeting cities with their bombs so they could do more damage and kill more people. For this reason, people would be much safer if they dispersed to the country. What the people didn't know was that Japanese forces had already come over the mountains from Thailand. They had taken Moulmein and were marching to Rangoon to cut off strategic supply lines to China.

Papa said to his wife, seven children, and Byu Goo, "Hurry up! Pack a few things! We have to go north!" He continued, "We will be gone for just a short time, a few weeks, a few months at the most, until things calm down in the city. So pack only what you need. Take just a few clothes. No need to bother with trunks or suitcases. Just put a few things into your shan bags and roll your clothing into a bundle."

He added, "I am taking you to a small village, where we will be safe. The Japanese will not want to waste a bomb on a town with only one street."

With unusual excitement, Papa urged them, "Quickly! Quickly! The sooner we can leave this place, the better. We must be on our way by morning!" The usually calm and quiet tiger made an impression on his family with his animation and often repeated words.

Molly looked through her belongings. She gathered a few clothes, an extra pair of sandals with two straps, and her school text books. Papa would understand that she must continue to study for the exam in February. Certainly this business with the Japanese would be over by then.

She looked at some things she would have to leave behind. Among these was the precious calligraphy book, one of her most treasured possessions. For a moment she held these pages on which she had carefully written many wise and ancient Chinese sayings as Ah Baht Sook recited them for her, and then she gently tucked them into the wardrobe. The book would be safer left here until the family returned in a few weeks; it might get damaged on the long trip to the wild places of Burma. She did slide a few special photographs into the pages of her school books.

Whereas Molly packed text books, Moonlight and Ginger packed their make-up and high heeled shoes. They also took a supply of tong-like metal hair curlers; the girls were experts in heating these in charcoal till they were hot enough to curl but not singe their hair.

Terence intervened in Papa's plans. He begged him, "Let Ngood stay with my family for a few days. I promise I will bring her myself to join you before the end of the week. Please let her stay with me. I want to make sure nothing happens to her. I can't bear for her to be so far away from me."

Papa didn't like it, but he relented. He could not have doubted the sincerity of the young man or his will to protect his daughter at all costs. Besides, the car hired to take them from Mandalay into the hill country would be crowded with all ten of them. This was never mentioned, but one fewer in the car would make the journey a little more tolerable, particularly if that one left behind carried a stack of school books.

So, very early the next morning, Papa locked the apartment and hustled his family toward the train station on Phayre Street. Ah Hem was left behind to watch Papa's recreation business. He could surely fend for himself for a few weeks with plenty of food and a modern bathroom. Papa was never stingy and would reward him well for his effort.

Molly was dropped off at the Lee dry goods store and apartment. Reluctance showed on the faces of the one left and the ones leaving. Molly would room with the Lee girls until Terence arranged for their journey north. Meanwhile, the Lee household was in its own turbulence, waiting for Mrs. Lee to decide if, when, and how to leave the city. Mrs. Lee was very hesitant to leave their holdings unattended in Rangoon.

While Molly was not physically with her family, her mind was on them constantly. Her emotional attachment at this frightening time was especially to them, and she did not like to be separated from her loved ones. But she did not complain.

Papa had said they would travel by train to Mandalay, spend the night in his house there, and then hire a car to take them into the hills. They were to take refuge in a remote village called "Namhsan" in the Shan Plateau.

As she waited, Molly recalled her lessons from English school. Though she had not heard of the little village of Namhsan before Papa named it, she had learned about the Shan States. Molly thought again of Burma's diamond kite shape and tail, and of labeling the whole right-hand corner section as the Shan Plateau. She remembered the data: averaging three thousand feet above sea level, peaks over seven thousand feet high, independently governed by Shan, Pa-O, Intha, Taungyo, Danu, Palaung and Kachin tribes. The region is more temperate than tropical Rangoon, she recited to herself, and it is known for its agriculture: for teak, tea, millet, fruits and vegetables, and at higher altitudes, for opium and heroin. It is most famous for its gems, sapphires and rubies, and for mining lead, silver, and zinc. Molly recalled that while people often think of a plateau as being fairly flat, the Shan Plateau, or highlands, is certainly not flat, but undulating with steep hills and mountains and cut by deep gorges.

Well, those were a few facts, but Molly realized she really didn't know about the area. She wondered what her brothers and sisters were finding in Namhsan. Were the jungle people of the Shan States primitive and savage? Would the family be living in crude huts or tree houses? Her sisters were so delicate; how would they fare?

****

True to his word, by the end of the week Terence had arranged for their passage north. Like Molly's family, they would take the train to Mandalay, and from there they would hire passage to Namhsan. Driving his own car was not an option, as the unmarried couple could not consider traveling together unchaperoned, and the car was not designed to navigate the rough terrain of the hill country.

Terence's family was continuing to resist leaving the area, concerned to protect their business interests in the city. Molly heard mention that they may move to the soy sauce factory they owned eight miles north of Rangoon. While the Lees vacillated, Terence dared not delay in keeping his promise to the formidable Mr. Chin. Neither did he dare ignore his mother's demand that he return to Rangoon immediately to care for his family. She was not happy that he was leaving them even for a few days.

So Terence took Molly to the train station, and they boarded the train to Mandalay, sitting on one of the long benches running down the length of the passenger car. Molly sat next to Terence, with a wide space between them. They would not sit too close to each other, for that would be shameful.

Again remembering her English school lessons, she carried the map of Burma in her mind as they headed north toward Mandalay. The road, railroad, and Sittang River travelled north together. The scenery was unchanged from the trip Molly had taken with Ah Baht Sook, but the world had changed, and what a different trip this was! This was no happy childhood adventure.

The train passed through Pegu, the home of the reclining Buddha and the four sitting Buddhas. Molly thought it was strange to think of them reclining and sitting there quietly, when so many people were fleeing. As the train charged north, Molly noticed the hills that slept mysteriously in the distance. In her travels with Ah Baht Sook, the hills were only a back-drop to her adventures; she had never entered them.

Molly saw the familiar houses on stilts in the Sittang river flood plain. Sometimes she saw women bathing, longyis knotted across their chests, splashing water on their shoulders and faces. Sometimes women were standing in the water to wash laundry, lifting the brightly colored fabrics in and out of the water. Cattle continued to pull plows at farmers' commands, fishermen still stood in the waters with their nets, and other farmers continued to work in their paddy fields as if nothing had changed. Did the people here know what had happened in Rangoon? Did they know the Japanese were coming? Well, Molly thought, maybe the Japanese would never get this far, with British forces defending Rangoon.

But this would not be the case. The train left behind town after town to wait for the Japanese: Toungoo, Pyinmana, Pyabwe, Thazi, and Meiktila.... The train stopped in several of the towns, and again, Molly observed people calmly behaving in usual ways. Neither Molly nor the villagers could imagine the vicious fighting that would come, in some cases within a few weeks, to these strategic cities. The winner of the battles would control the vital supply line and route into Burma's interior and then have access to China via the singular Burma Road, the narrow and rugged seven-hundred-mile road connecting Lashio in northern Burma to Kunming, China. This road had only been completed by British direction a few years ago, to supply China in its war with Japan.

Molly had been too busy to pay close attention to world events, but the Japanese had cut off supply routes on China's coast, making the challenging route through Burma critical to China. Finally realizing their desperation to hold Burma, the British had recently accepted Chinese help, and even now the Chinese were, with difficulty, making a push south to make a brave stand at Toungoo against Japanese foes fighting their way north.

At Pyabwe, feeder-rivers began to drain north into the great Irrawaddy River instead of South into the Sittang. These waters too would eventually double back and drift south, swept by the wide Irrawaddy into the Andaman Sea. The waters of these great rivers of Burma continued their unperturbed, customary journey south as Terence and Molly were pushing north into the unfamiliar and unknown. The ol' man rivers just kept rolling along, as the song said.

Arriving at the great city of Mandalay in the early morning hours, Terence and Molly found an unoccupied bench at the train station, where they sat until daylight. They couldn't sit too close to one another, so unsupported and uncomfortable, Molly endured hours of a traveler's intermittent sleep. As her weary body relaxed and called her to slumber, her head would fall a little, and the unfamiliar movement would jerk her awake. When she woke, she didn't dare get up from her seat and walk around, or someone would take her place.

At last, dawn brought locals selling the steaming hot Burmese dish *bey byu*, "beans boiled," similar to chick peas. Terence bought some for Molly and himself, reasoning that hot food would be safer to eat than fresh foods from people of unknown hygienic habits. The *bey byu* had been cooked with onion, tasted good, and was quite filling. This was important, for it could last them a long time.

Then Terence found a passenger lorry that included Namhsan in its route. This bus had a big engine powerful enough to grind through the hills. Luggage was thrown onto the roof of the vehicle and was held in place by a railing and ropes. As was typical, long benches ran the length of the bus, and glass windows could be slid down to open or up to shut. At first, the windows were open. Soon the bus was rolling, and, after a while, the travelers were leaving the flat land of the Irrawaddy tableland and were climbing into the Shan Plateau.

For the most part, the Burmese bus driver said nothing except to call out the stops. A couple of times on the trip, he stopped the lorry, called *"Twag la bah!* Come out!" and pointed to the forest. The passengers were to find a place to relieve themselves and re-board quickly. Molly was young, able, and determined to hold her bladder as long as possible. Her Chinese jacket and pants were not conducive to modest crouching as with native longyis, so for any privacy she would need to venture into the forest. She was not yet that desperate, even though she knew she was facing a continuing long and bumpy journey.

The road headed gradually northeast by various combinations of north, south, east, and west as it wound through the increasingly rolling topography. Also, as it ascended into the elevated plateau of the Shan States, the road led generally upwards, but the trip to the heights required repeated dives into the depths, and so the climb must be repeated again and again. The roadbed continued to decline in quality as it inclined in grade. Rarely was the path straight, and sometimes it zigzagged in steep switchbacks, adding miles to keep the incline somewhat manageable.

As they went higher and higher, Molly felt an unexpected pain in her ears. Terence was experiencing the same. No one told them about ears "popping" as changes in air pressure at higher altitudes creates unequal pressure on either side of the ear drum. No one told them yawning or swallowing could allow the pressure to equalize, relieving the pain. Adding to that discomfort, jostling and stress produced uneasy stomachs in the passengers.

Once again, road and railroad toward Lashio were often close traveling companions as they ascended into the hills, but sometimes the two trails separated for a while and found their own meandering way around a jungle-covered hill before reuniting. Sometimes the railroad may have been quite near, but hidden by thick vegetation, no one could know.

Paved roads were left behind, traded for packed earth. The speeding lorry left a long tail of dust behind them. They were going quite fast, in fact, even when roads were poor, steep, and winding. The driver was clearly familiar with the route and knew at what rate he could likely take the turns without peril. And, if the bus should go over a cliff... or not... well, that was all a matter of fate or luck. Molly knew that when the Burmese invoked the expression, "It is your goo tho gan, your fate!" no argument could prevail against it.

A vehicle coming from the other way had to pull off the road for the lorry to pass on the single lane highway, and then the lorry plowed through the haze of dust left by the oncoming vehicle and returned the favor. Soon, everyone and everything in the truck wore a layer of dust, and, though windows had been shut and Molly kept her mouth closed, she felt the invasive grit even between her teeth. Now that they were in higher altitudes, and in this season, at least the windows could be closed without causing the bus to become too stuffy.

One concession for safety was made by the lorry driver at the sharp turns. At these times, his view completely blocked by thick vegetation, he blared his horn repeatedly to announce his presence to anyone coming from the other direction.

Molly had studied her text books a little bit on the train ride from Rangoon, though it was hard to concentrate. But there was no way she could focus on a bouncing page of words on this stretch of the trip. She and Terence could not talk easily with the rumble and grit of the bus, so they watched the scenery and kept to their own thoughts.

Molly could not disconnect from the stress of the journey, and she could not help but worry about the Japanese, about the truck driver, or about her family. But, as a flat-lander and always curious, she was a little in awe of this craggy region. As she and Terence continued to ride, the jungle growth sometimes reached so near it would brush against the truck. Other areas would open up and flatten out, and Molly could see areas sectioned into small, irregularly-shaped, adjoining rice paddy fields, each one framed by earth piled up to hold water in shallow pools.

Molly knew Mandalay was in a dry zone of the country, and she knew that rice required a lot of rain and rich soil. She guessed that the plains and valleys tucked into these hills must receive more rain than Mandalay, enough rain for rice.

They came to an elevated flat area and a pretty colonial city with tidy British houses and gardens. This vision of gentility seemed out of place in the rugged terrain that surrounded on every side. Molly saw a sign saying, "Maymyo," and watched until this curious oasis was out of sight.

Miles later, the travelers came to the most steeply declining of switchbacks with the sharpest and most numerous turns, and the speed of the lorry was compensated only slightly. The driver used just the pressure on the gas pedal and just the spin on the steering wheel to make the turn, with what he considered tolerable sliding and acceptable tipping. He was heedless of the comfort of his passengers. If the driver misjudged, no barriers or railings gave a hint of safety. The imminent threat for Molly was not the Japanese, but the precipice, and one could not help but think that if the bus disappeared over the edge into the canyon below, no one would ever discover how these souls met their tragic end.

A timely distraction helped Molly place the present danger to one side in her mind. They were descending into a wide, lush valley, and as they did so, she caught glimpses of a magnificent span of silver lacework, shimmering in the sunlight, extending across the width and depth of the great valley. The scale of the structure was spectacular, and it seemed to hang like a giant, woven fishing net pulled across the valley from rocky cliffs on either side. Molly and Terence had seen bridges before, but this was an amazing structure, and they were in awe each time the bus switched back so they could observe it. Molly's special interest was the structure's size and beauty, but Terence was intrigued by its design. Their comments to each other reflected each one's focus, and with the perspective of the other, the experience of each was enriched.

It was impossible for two curious people not to be captivated. Neither knew such a structure existed, nor expected to see such an engineering marvel in the wilderness of Burma.

Once in the valley, they continued to stare, peeking from between forest trees to see the looming structure in the distance. But here the jungle was often so thick that the truck seemed to be passing through a tunnel of green, trees branches arching from either side, with clear, blue sky peeking between the lush leaves overhead. They crossed a small bridge across the insignificant river that had somehow carved this vast, rich valley.

Soon they were traveling hundreds of feet up the other side of the gorge by more tedious and treacherous switchbacks. They watched intently for a few last looks at the marvelous bridge, and then they were speeding away from the fascinating valley left behind.

****

The hours of driving dragged on and Molly thought again of her family waiting for her in Namhsan. She continued to wonder about the secluded place Papa arranged for their refuge.

As usual, Papa had said very little about it. He did mention that their host would be a Chinese associate, a Mr. Wong.

He added, "The ruler of the area is called the *sawbwa*, and he gave us permission to enter his domain. No one can live there without his permission. We are fortunate."

Molly thought of those words, "We are fortunate." At this moment, on the dusty road in the Shan Plateau, it was difficult to feel so. She worried about what was happening back home in Rangoon. She worried about taking the final exam. She worried about what was happening in the little village of Namhsan.

Molly remembered that Moonlight had the courage to ask, "What is the house like, Papa?"

Ah Pa answered simply, "I don't know."

****

They had been on the road for many hours since leaving Mandalay when the lorry driver turned off the main road. The route they left continued northeast with the railroad to Lashio. If they had continued on that main road, they would have seen that the northeast branch of the railroad ended at Lashio, and there the southern end of the Burma Road into China began.

Instead, they were taking a dusty path that headed generally more due north, and they soon entered the town of Kyaukme, "Chalk-may," where Molly could see a thriving market. Molly remembered her Burmese lessons and knew incidentally the name of the town meant "Stone black."

Quickly through the village, they escorted a stream fed from hills and mountains on either side, and the trail was more winding than ever. Obviously, the path was constructed in the easiest possible way, not with concern for quick or easy navigation, and every natural obstacle was respected. That is not to say road construction had been simple, for the stream had not carved a wide floodplain, and walls on either side of it were often quite steep, sometimes requiring a cut into the rocky bank the width of a single lane. The bus driver was honking his horn frequently at blind turns.

Once again, the vegetation around the stream often concealed it from view, though the trees were not towering over the bus as they did in the thick jungle valleys at lower elevations. The worn path exposed reddish brown or yellowish brown earth. The high peaks sometimes glimpsed now were not lush with forest vegetation, but were sparsely dotted with determined shrubs.

The road was rough, full of ruts and wash-outs that indicated rainy seasons could make this route impassable. Fortunately, Molly was unaware that sometimes during a rainy season a truck would become stuck in the mud. The road could be blocked for days, as the truck plugged the small space between rock wall on one side and a few spindly trees growing from a cliff edge that dropped to the stream on the other side. The effective stopper in the route would leave a short line of hapless, stranded drivers who didn't know any better than to travel to Namhsan by motor vehicle in the rainy season.

Several streams of various sizes were crossed. Some had the dubious benefit of a so-called bridge that did not warrant confidence. Other streambeds were shallow and needed only a couple of thick planks to traverse them. Still other streams were crossed brusquely by the rambunctious lorry bouncing over the rocks and splashing up mud.

Molly felt the jarring of the lorry on the rough path and considered that it had been some miles since she had seen any sign of human life. She imagined the village of Namhsan must be at the very end of the world. Only because her family was there, she was anxious to arrive at the said end of the world. She rather wished she was a little girl and not expected to greet her loved ones with dignity.

It had been nearly a week since she had seen her family. She pictured the precious face of each one huddling together in a little village hut. Papa would be quietly ruling his brood, keeping each one on his best behavior. Mama, far from the comforts of a home she rarely left, would be faithfully focused on her family, attentive and nurturing. Moonlight must be quite unhappy in the rustic setting, but staying strong and setting a good example for her siblings. She was twenty-three years old and was quite a responsible lady. Ginger, sixteen years old, would be quietly doing what was expected of her. Clark, the fifteen-year-old, would be looking around for girls to impress. Fourteen-year-old Johnny would be making the best of this new, wild adventure and had probably explored a wide area around the village. He would be leading ten-year-old Wayne, who had finally grown too big for Byu Goo to carry and was doing quite well getting around on his own two feet. Dorothy, just nine years old, would be attached to Mama and protectively watched by Papa.

After a while, the lorry climbed, grinding and quaking, away from the stream and made its way to a mountain ridge, 6000 feet above sea level. From this perch, Molly could see many rough mountain ridges, one layered behind the other, each one paler and less distinct in the distance. A few airy clouds draped like shawls around the shoulders of some of the mountain peaks, resting motionless in the calm atmosphere. Here the vegetation was scrubby, not lush, so no great trees or dense shrubbery interrupted the impressive view. The valleys between the ridges were rich shades of deep green, but the peaks were predominately brown, with only small patches of pale greenery.

The disinterested bus driver once called out "Namhsan," and pointed off to the right. Molly strained to focus in the indicated direction, across a wide, craggy valley. An irregular line of buildings appeared as a tiny, rusty red and brown caterpillar, its motionless body bent to the contour of the distant ridge.

As if avoiding Namhsan to the east, the bus continued snaking north, following the ridge. Long after Namhsan was out of sight of the anxious novice passengers, the bus finally wound slowly east, and then, at last, south. Molly craned her neck for a look at the village which would be her home, as Papa said, for the next few weeks or months.

Eventually, from their high approach, Molly saw a single, dusty street lined on each side by jumbled rows of corrugated metal roof tops. Most were painted red or maroon.

The bus drove into Namhsan and stopped, allowing the trail of dust to billow in a fog around it. Molly observed houses of various size and design, but she noted with surprise and relief that the houses were nicely made of wood and not at all shabby.

She was eager to be looking for her kin, but she got up slowly, letting her legs adjust. Terence took her heavy shan bag, and she clutched her roll of clothing, as they climbed down from the lorry. The air was chilly, but Molly found it refreshing and, in her sleeved blouse, she did not feel too cold. They were able to learn which house to approach in the small village, and a knock on the door brought friendly, but unfamiliar, Chinese faces.

After a quick call, a beautiful flow of loved ones poured in from the open door in the back of the building. At last, Molly was smiling at the dear faces she had so missed for nearly a week! Tears brimmed in the eyes of the women. Cultural formalities made hugging adults taboo, but embraces were not necessary for Molly to feel warmly welcomed by her mama and sisters.

Papa greeted Terence in the expected dignified manner. Then he added proudly, "You see, this is a safe place. No one will waste a bomb on this little village. You should tell your family to come here. I can obtain the permission and make the arrangements."

Papa's satisfaction with Namhsan was evident. "When you go back to Rangoon, I want you to convince my brother to bring his family here also. Tell him to come as soon as possible."

Terence and Molly were introduced to their hosts, the Wong family. Molly noticed immediately that, though they were Chinese, they were quite "Burmanized." Mrs. Wong wore the Burmese longyi, a brightly dyed fabric woven into a tube and simply knotted at the waist. Unlike Burmese men, who tied the knot in the middle, women tied the knot on the left side. With this skirt, Mrs. Wong wore a long-sleeved white blouse. Even more surprising than her Burmese clothes, Mrs. Wong spoke stammering Chinese and fluent tribal Palaung. Molly understood at once that her poor cloistered Chinese mother, who spoke not a word of Burmese, would have difficulty communicating with this woman who was Chinese by race, but Burmese by culture. Indeed the two women smiled genuinely and nodded in a friendly way but could not engage in a satisfying conversation. This did not prevent Mrs. Wong from being quite hospitable to her guests.

Mr. Wong greeted them in the dignified manner of a gentleman, speaking only to Terence and scarcely acknowledging Molly with a slight nod as she bowed to him. This exchange was not at all rude, but proper, distant formality between men and women. He was very thin and tall, quiet, and reserved.

Molly met the five Wong children and Mrs. Wong's mother, who, it was quickly apparent, supervised the maids and the children. Molly's amazement continued as she heard Mrs. Wong's mother also speaking Palaung! A Chinese woman even a generation older than her mother had adapted to local culture! This old woman smoked a long, thin cheroot cigar that Molly would discover was very popular with the local women, and so Byu Goo would have no trouble continuing to feed her craving. Mrs. Wong's sister also lived with the family. Completing the household were local maids to serve the family, a cultural necessity for the well-to-do and employment for the poor.

Moonlight offered to show Molly to the bathroom facilities, which was of immediate interest. She led her to the back part of the house, which was the guest quarters for the Chins. In the back of this section of the building was a small room with a planked wooden floor in which some holes were cut. Moonlight explained, "Squat over the hole to relieve yourself, but this is for urinating only. We also bathe in this room, and after bathing, we pour the basin of water on the floor and into the hole to clean away the odor."

She pointed to the outhouse behind the building which was to be used for sterner business.

Moonlight cautioned, "Toilet paper is very difficult to obtain here. What we do get, we must cut and fold ahead of time. Papa says when you need to use it, take only two or three pieces."

Moonlight pointed to a basin and a pail of water. "Scoop a little water into the basin to wash yourself. We must be very careful not to use too much water. All of the water must be carried from the stream by Byu Goo."

After Molly freshened up, Moonlight showed her the rest of the Chin's quarters with a few gestures: besides the bathroom, there was a single main room and a small bedroom for their parents. The walls and floors were made of the weather resistant pynkado wood, cheaper to obtain than teak, but quite long-wearing. Simple, shutterless glass windows let in beams of light, and could be slid open for air. Nice, thick, woven mats and pillows were pulled out for sleeping, then rolled up and tucked in a corner during the day. The boys would line up to sleep on one side of the room and the girls and Byu Goo on the other. They were given the familiar mosquito netting to drape over themselves, and between themselves and the netting ... quilts! Now this was quite unfamiliar! No one ever needed such a heavy cover in Rangoon.

The next day, Terence was on his way back to his family. Who knew what was happening in Rangoon now? Molly was concerned for him, and oh, he was so sorry to leave her! At least he was comforted to have seen for himself the remoteness of Namhsan and so could leave Molly in her father's care. But there was no doubt that he was anxious to bring his family here and so keep his duty to them and be near his Molly. He left on a mission to convince his mother to come to Namhsan. He would not forget his duty to approach his future father-in-law's brother as well.

Chapter Eleven

Refuge in the Hill Country

It was one thing to say the place at the end of the earth was not as bad as most of them feared; it was quite a different thing to claim anyone was comfortable. No one was happy with the circumstances, and it was not long before complaints were verbalized. The toilet paper was rough, the outhouse was inconvenient and smelled bad, the air was cold, the quarters were crowded, and so on, and so on.

Papa said firmly, "Do not grumble. You are lucky to have this." It was a reminder he would have to repeat often to his children, who were used to finer things.

He also quoted one of his favorite Chinese sayings: yew ngen yew moth, literally, "have people, have things." All understood his meaning, "If you have your life, you can replace things." The implied unspoken corollary was also understood: if you lose your life, material things will do you no good. This was a saying the Chin children heard often during their stay in the hill country.

The family was barely aware of Papa's work the next few days, securing necessary permissions and adequate quarters for others. He was expecting quite an influx of Chinese relatives and friends to Namhsan.

Indeed, back in Rangoon, Old Man Thunder Voice was frantic. He hesitated leaving his varied properties, but he also had a very large family to protect. Like many Chinese, he was trying to make arrangements to move his family out of Burma and in to China, but, even for a man of means, the journey between the countries, through thick jungles and rugged mountain terrain, was extremely harsh and dangerous. With so many women and children to move, this would be a difficult, risky endeavor. The first wife of Number One Uncle had died, but he still had three wives and sixteen or so children. Molly had lost track of exactly how many cousins she had, but she thought there were four children from Number One Wife, eight or nine from Number Two Wife, and four or five from the Number Three Wife. Number Four Wife had no children.

The local people were delighted to make some money renting out places to the well-to-do Chinese from Rangoon. The villagers and farmers also had plenty of fresh produce and chickens and pigs to sell. Millet was grown locally and rice was not difficult to obtain, so moneyed refugees were able to get enough food. The Palaung people were used to trading for goods, and also they accepted Burmese-British notes. Sometimes high-priced goods were brought in by truck from other areas as well. Every five days, a well-supplied market was set up in the street, attracting quite a crowd from the surrounding area. Actually, the Chins ate quite well, and Byu Goo still cooked chicken fat for Papa.

Molly was fascinated by the Palaung people, though she had little opportunity for personal contact; the people spoke the Palaung language, and Byu Goo did all of the shopping and necessary interaction. But Molly was especially impressed to observe the women skillfully balancing on their heads large baskets of family laundry or garden produce to sell. They didn't need to use their hands to steady the baskets, even when walking on uneven terrain! In fact, Molly watched them closely, and she never saw anyone drop anything from her basket.

Molly observed the local fashion. Women wore vibrant, colorful clothing and woven leggings with embroidered designs, and they were well-adorned with silver jewelry, with many bracelets, necklaces, and belts, and big hoop rings in pierced ears and noses. The men wore the familiar longyis, though the longyis were often tied differently for the working tribal men versus the city dwellers, with the hanging skirt pulled forward between the legs and tucked in at the waist to shorten the length to above the knee. Molly was amazed to see the people wore no shoes, no slippers, and no sandals, even on the coldest mornings, with the exception of an occasional, homemade, simple sole tied to the foot. On frigid days, natives often wore knitted hats pulled completely over their heads, little openings revealing only their eyes. Molly sensed even these masked ones were returning her shy smiles by the friendly shape of their eyes and the slight bob of their heads as they passed her.

The uncovered faces of women and children were usually smudged by tha na kah, a paste made of ground tree bark and mixed with water. Sometimes Molly had observed this yellowish, tan stuff marking the cheeks of children in Rangoon, and she understood the paste was thought to protect skin from sunburn and to moisturize and cool the skin. It was a very popular treatment in this village.

The sun shone brightly at this high altitude, but temperatures could be quite chilly, sometimes dipping into the forties at night. On the coolest days Molly would pull a shawl around herself, but she also found the cooler air invigorating.

Moonlight filled in a few details about their host, Mr. Wong. "Many years ago Mr. Wong obtained permission from the sawbwa to organize a carnival in Namhsan, providing many items for sale, feasting, and games. The people love this, and they save their money to participate. Mr. Wong hosts a small casino at the carnival, and the Shan people respond enthusiastically. This is a popular draw to the carnival, and this is how Mr. Wong made his fortune."

"What is a 'casino'?" Molly asked.

Moonlight, having the advantage of nearly a week's education in Namhsan, explained, "In the favored game of chance, words are printed on cards, words for different animals like monkey and dog... but not rat." Already Moonlight was an expert. She confided knowingly, "The Shan people hate rats! If Mr. Wong printed "rat" on a card, they would probably throw things at him or destroy his casino."

Moonlight continued, "The game works this way: people risk money on their favorite animal. Somebody might say 'Five kyats on monkey,' and pay five kyats. When it is time to show the card, which was chosen in advance of bidding and remains hidden under a bowl, a big crowd of people gathers to see who has won. Then the card is revealed, and if the monkey card comes up, everyone that bid on monkey, plus the casino, gets a share of the money. The sawbwa permits Mr. Wong to hold this carnival and casino several times a year, and Mr. Wong pays the sawbwa for the privilege."

"Mr. Wong is on very good terms with the sawbwa, and, as the Burmese say, has become na-te, super rich. He is also very generous, to the local people and to us, and we are privileged that he is allowing us to stay in his house."

Parroting Papa, Moonlight instructed, "We should be very grateful."

****

On January 15, the Japanese captured Tavoy and its airfield, giving the Japanese three airfields on the long tail of Burma's kite shape and facilitating the movement of bombers and fighters into Burma. On February 23, the British-Indian brigades were defeated at the Battle of Sittang Bridge, leaving Rangoon vulnerable to the Japanese advance. To slow the Japanese, the bridge was blown up, but the explosion came too early, before all of the Indian division of British forces had crossed the bridge. The stranded soldiers tried to cross the Sittang River by any means, but they had to leave much equipment behind. Those who survived regrouped at Pegu.

The Japanese were slowed at the Sittang River because of the ruined bridge, but eventually soldiers and artillery were ferried across the river. After heavy fighting, the Japanese were able to push through Pegu on March 6 and 7. The British, who had been moving or destroying tons of army supplies, hastily evacuated all remaining personnel in Rangoon, and when the Japanese forces arrived in Rangoon on March 8, the invading soldiers were surprised to find the city was deserted. There was no Ruse of the Empty City nor cunning trap to resist their incursion, only capitulation.

****

Old Man Thunder Voice arrived in Namhsan with his family. Then after a few more weeks had passed, the Lees arrived. Mrs. Lee had hired a fleet of trucks to bring her family, associated families, maids, and their most needed possessions to Namhsan.

Terence was visibly moved to see Molly; he had been deeply worried about her. She was also quite relieved to see that he had not come to harm.

Terence told Molly his family had moved from Chinatown to the soy sauce factory his grandfather Lee Ah Poi had built eight miles north of Rangoon. His mother had instructed that a bomb shelter be built on the premises, but even so, the situation had become frightful. The property was very near the Mingaladon airport which had been constructed for the

Relatives peeking from an upper story window at the rented Namhsan home of Old Man Thunder Voice.

fledgling Burman air force to serve Rangoon in 1940. Now it had been taken over by the Japanese air force, and even though the soy sauce factory was not being bombed, the frequent traffic overhead of Japanese fighters and bombers was disconcerting.

Adding to the danger, the airport itself had become a target. The British Royal Air Force (RAF) and the Flying Tigers, an unofficial American and Chinese cooperative, had been forced to retreat to the Magwe airfield on the Irrawaddy River between Rangoon and Mandalay. From that position, on March 21, the RAF conducted a raid on the Mingaladon airfield and destroyed many Japanese aircraft on the ground.

Terence told Molly, "My mother wanted to escape to China. We drove many days to get to Lashio and then found the Burma Road was blocked. The sawbwa of Lashio refused to let us stay there. I convinced my family to come here. The roads were so bad it took us another day to get the trucks here from Lashio."

In the Lee entourage were Mrs. Lee's mother and the mother's daughter-in-law and two grandchildren. The grandmother's son had died in China, and she doted on his wife and two sons. The old woman was a suffering victim of foot binding, and Molly winced in sympathy as she watched the effort with which the old woman walked on her heels. Molly felt she needed to be ready to catch her even as she swayed on level surfaces, and on the uneven ground around the village, the poor woman wobbled frightfully. Molly knew the cold air must be especially hard on her, though she did not complain. She was kind to Molly.

Also, the Ng family had come with the Lee troupe. Anita married Dr. Ng in Rangoon before coming to Namhsan, and her mother had given her one of her maids. Engagements and marriage had tied these families together, the Chins to the Lees and the Lees to the Ngs.

Some of the poorer class of Chinese also followed the Lee family to Namhsan, hoping to continue to find a way to make a living. They survived by cooking and selling food to the Lees and other Chinese in the village. One of Molly's favorite foods was a fried meatball seasoned with chili, salt, and vinegar. The cooks would go house-to-house with the ingredients, plus a pot of fire, a stove, and charcoal, and would fix the hot meal on site.

Terence and Molly would take evening strolls through the village, joining Anita and Sammy, and Cousin Dolly and Stanley. Anita would place her hand in the crook of Sammy's arm and Cousin Dolly and Stanley walked with the same attachment. Terence would coax Molly quietly, "I want you to do that too." Molly put him off for a while, but at last she conceded and tucked her hand under his arm. Even in this remote village, Terence was quite proud to be seen this way.

As they walked, they often came across groups of Palaung huddled around woks full of lighted charcoal for warmth, sipping tea and chatting. Other Palaung walked past them carrying little tins with handles, similar in size and shape to lanterns, but full of hot coals and held for heat, not light. Their bodies were bundled in warm clothing, but, again Molly noted, the bare feet of the natives showed below the footless socks, exposing flesh to the cold ground. No wonder they were chilled!

Terence had gleaned some information for Molly, knowing he would be appreciated for satisfying her curiosity. "Molly, do you remember that gigantic bridge we saw stretched across the valley on our way to Namhsan?"

"Of course," Molly replied. "We stared at it all the way through the valley!"

"I found out some details about it," Terence began, expecting her interruption.

"Tell me! What did you find out?" Molly asked, forgetting to be dignified.

"It is called the Gokteik Viaduct. Gokteik is a nearby village, and a viaduct is a structure that carries a road or railroad across a valley. It was built by an American company, The Pennsylvania Steel Company, as part of the British railway system to upper Burma, which goes as far as Lashio. When the Gokteik Viaduct was completed in 1900 it was the largest railway trestle in the world, and it's the highest in Burma. It rises three hundred thirty five feet above the jungle floor."

Molly was quite impressed. "It is a wonderful structure! It must be very strong to carry a train all the way across the valley! And it's so high! I don't know how they could do it! It must have taken a long time to build."

Terence continued to offer tidbits of information, "The viaduct is 2,260 feet long, and the trestlework is made of steel. The bridge is supported by fourteen single towers and one double tower, as we saw."

"I am so glad you told me!" Molly replied. "In a few weeks, when we drive back through the valley on our way to Rangoon, I will look at it again."

"I found out something else," Terence said.

"What else?" Molly asked eagerly.

"Do you remember the colonial village we passed through? The sign said, 'Maymyo.' "

"Oh, yes!" Molly remembered seeing the English homes and gardens.

Terence said, "The British built it as a resort, a hill station, they call it. The British aren't used to the heat of the summers in the cities of Burma, so many of them retreat to Maymyo for the hot season. At the elevation of over thirty-five hundred feet above sea level, the weather stays cool and pleasant all year round."

Molly was pleased to be informed, and Terence was delighted with her pleasure. He wasn't finished yet. "There are silver mines near here. The local women love the silver, as you have seen, but the people are afraid of nats, ghosts they say are all around and inhabit the trees, the earth, the animals.... They say ghosts live in the mines and guard the treasure. These must be appeased before the treasure can be removed, or better yet, they are happy to let the Chinese work the mines. The Chinese get rich because the locals are afraid to go in the mines."

Terence added, "The Chinese are very superstitious too, but they like to get rich, and that overcomes their fear."

Molly quoted the saying, "If there is wealth to be had, the Chinese will not be far from it." She had heard another saying too, but she didn't repeat it. She knew that some people said Burma was like a dog in a manger; the dog doesn't eat the hay, but he doesn't want anyone else to eat it either. They were absurdly implying that locals did not care to profit from the great wealth of their country. The British and others used such arrogant comments to rationalize their exploitation and oppression of local owners.

Returning to her conversation with Terence, Molly observed, "It is a pleasant evening."

Molly enjoyed talking to Terence in English, and she appreciated the stimulating conversation. She had to admit that she had missed him, and she was feeling affectionate towards him.

But Molly's evening was spoiled when she returned to the Chin wing of the Wong house and Mama had some uncharacteristically stern words for her. "Papa saw you walking in the street and holding Puck Ying's arm! Papa says this is disgraceful behavior! You must not do this again!"

Molly was embarrassed and ashamed. Later, she scolded Terence for getting her into trouble with her father and forcing her mother to speak sternly to her. So quickly Terence lost the ground he had recently gained with Molly in his diligent information gathering.

Soon after that, Papa's words were even more serious. Mr. Wong heard about deteriorating circumstances in Burma. The British were unable to stop the march of the Japanese, and invaders were quickly working their way north. Already Mandalay was being assaulted. Mr. Wong cautioned Papa about his daughters, "The Japanese are taking unmarried women. They especially like to harm Chinese girls, and your daughters are pretty...."

Papa understood his meaning, and without unnecessary details, told his daughters, "You must stay inside the house at all times. If you need to go to the outhouse, someone must guard the street and make sure there are no Japanese soldiers around."

Byu Goo insisted, "I will continue to bring all of the water to the house, and I will do all of the shopping in the street. No one will want an old woman like me."

Byu Goo was likely only in her early forties, but she appeared much older. Well experienced with hard work in China, she hauled water adeptly and without complaint, using a pole across her shoulders so she could carry two heavy buckets of water at a time. Molly felt a twinge of remorse for making fun of Byu Goo's country ways when she first came to the four-story house. What would they do without her now?

Because of the seriousness of the situation, Papa superseded his usual delegation of command and repeated his rules sternly to all of his children, "We are ten people, and I do not want Byu Goo to carry any more water than necessary. When you bathe, use only one pail of water. When you finish, use your pail of water to rinse the bathroom floor. It is cooler here, and you do not need to bathe so often. Every few days will be fine."

Molly was moved by Byu Goo's faithfulness to her family. As Molly watched her efforts, she wondered why her strong, healthy, teenage brothers couldn't help Byu Goo's with the chores. But it was not Molly's place to make such a radical suggestion.

"Anyway," she told herself, "It will be for just a short while, and then we'll go back to Rangoon. Then Byu Goo will have water from a faucet again."

Already Molly had lost track of the time. She had no calendar, so days and weeks and months had piled up in a jumble at the bottom of a deep gorge. Even the weather was different from Rangoon, so Molly couldn't be certain of the season. She was sure that enough days had trickled past the February examination day. She hoped that, under the circumstances, a make-up exam would be scheduled very soon. But how would she know about the test date while stuck in Namhsan? What if things were settled in Rangoon before she knew it? She continued to review her text books, but concentrating was difficult.

Over the next tedious months, the Chin girls were confined to the house, imprisoned for their own protection. The boys were able to go out and play, but the girls must find something to occupy their time inside. A young Chinese widow, the daughter of a rich man from Kyaukme, came with her young children to visit the girls. She had a place in Namhsan, perhaps because she was a refugee as well, fleeing the Japanese from the more accessible Kyaukme. She was very friendly and spoke Cantonese fluently. The Chin girls looked forward to her coming, both enjoying her company and eager to learn more advanced knitting techniques from her. She always supplied them with yarn and knitting needles and taught them to do four-needle knitting, which could be used to construct socks without a seam. Sweaters and blankets, unnecessary in Rangoon, were also very practical items to have in Namhsan, and though they had no plans for a long stay, such things would be immediately useful. In fact, none of them even owned a sweater prior to coming to Namhsan. In the dreariness of the day to day confinement, this weekly visit was much anticipated. The girls also spent many hours cutting and folding toilet paper from the rough sheets. Despite these distractions, time passed wearily.

The door between the Chin wing and the Wong residence was often left open. When Mr. Wong was home, Molly noticed he was usually smoking a long pipe. This brought pleasant remembrances of her Grandfather Wong, who also had this habit, looking very wise and scholarly as smoke rose in thin wisps around him. But there were also upsetting views beyond the door when the grandmother took to beating a maid with a broom, screaming insults, before remembering to shut the door to block the view, leaving muffled sounds to the imagination. Molly tried to calm herself by thinking the maid must have stolen something to receive such severe treatment, yet this violence was quite unsettling and foreign to Molly.

In the days of her sequestering in Namhsan, Molly had plenty of time for thinking. She reminisced of many things: the golden years in the four-story house, playing with Len and the small uncle Tuck Sook. She

Molly and Cousin Len at Royal Lake. Terence photographed this picture of his fiancé and their chaperone a few years earlier, in 1939.

remembered her grandmother's affection, and wished she could hear her again calling softly, *low-see doy*, "my little mouse." She thought of her mentors, Han Yee and Ah Baht Sook. Ah Baht Sook had come to Namhsan with the extended Chin clan, but his friendship was lost. Thoughts of home were so distant from her present circumstance they seemed almost to belong to someone else. Still, memories were comforting to recall and diverting like a good book.

Molly thought a lot about her English School and missed her friends and teachers. She reviewed in her mind many experiences at the school, and among these, she remembered the devotions she had heard in the big assembly hall. Molly found her thoughts lingering on the intriguing Lord Jesus. She observed her mother was doing her best to maintain her duties toward the ancestors and gods, but Molly had the uncomfortable feeling that these efforts were futile. Instead, Molly found herself often praying to Lord Jesus. She did not consider herself a Christian, but she was pleasantly drawn to the Christ. She prayed to Lord Jesus as one speaks to a friend, the way she had heard the teachers at the English School pray, although her own prayers were never spoken out loud. Didn't her teachers say that prayers to Jesus could be silent, and that He could still hear every word?

So, Molly prayed to this fascinating Son of God, who came to the world because he loved. This pledge of love gave Molly courage to pray to Him passionately, "Oh, please Lord Jesus, spare us! Do not let my family and all our relatives be bombed! Do not let the Japanese soldiers take my sisters and me away!" As she prayed, she sensed the comfort of a compassionate Lord.

News from outside was sporadic, but Mr. Wong sometimes had more information about the war for Papa. The Chinese men refugees regularly gathered to play games of chance and to talk of the war. So it was that news of the bombing of Chinatown in Rangoon was passed around with deep concern. Everyone worried more than ever about the conditions of their homes and neighborhood.

Often Molly did not hear of these things from Papa. He strove to protect his family with ignorance. Usually her news of the war came from Terence.

One day Papa did have a story to tell his family. Mr. Wong had introduced him to the sawbwa and his wife, who came into Namhsan with a host of maids. Papa said the Queen was a British woman, though she wore native dress. The people referred to her with the borrowed Indian phrase, *mahadevi*, "Great Goddess." The sawbwa, "Lord of the Heavens," had studied in London and brought her back as his wife, Papa told them. The local people greatly esteemed their rulers and always bowed deeply in their presence. Even the poorest people gave a portion of their best resources to the sawbwa and his mahadevi, even if they could afford to give only a few eggs. No doubt, Papa had also given an appropriate gift as gratitude for being allowed to come to Namhsan for safety.

****

Mrs. Lee gave birth to a baby boy, Number Six Son, and in the month to follow she put much thought into naming him. She worried that the shared name of his brothers, *Puck*, meaning "A hundred times," had been too big for them, and they were seemingly crushed under the weight of the name. After vigorous Number One Daughter Choon Fong came the delicate infant, Number One Son Puck Ying, "A Hundred Times Heroic." The next child was a boy, Puck Hee, "A Hundred Times Great," who also struggled, though he turned out to be very smart. The next daughters, Number Two and Three Fe Lan and Fe Yone, were strong babies. However, the Number Three Son Puck Hong, "A Hundred Times Healthy," had died before living out his first year, and Number Four Son Puck Koon, "A Hundred Times a Gentleman," was also sickly at birth. A healthy girl, Number Four Daughter

The surviving first six children of Mrs. Lee. Two sons did not survive childhood. Photo taken before the births of two more daughters before the war and two sons during and after the war.

came next and was named Fe Heng, "Wise Fill-In," to try to fill the void of the lost baby. The next boy to be born, Puck Hem, "A Hundred Times Add-On," died at age five. The loss of each child was clearly felt deeply by Mrs. Lee, and she grieved. A thriving Number Five Daughter came next and was named Fe Yin, "Wise Swallow."

With this evidence, healthy girls and ailing boys, Mrs. Lee was burdened with the belief that she may have caused the illnesses and deaths of her sons by giving them too great a name. Not only was she suffering the loss of two sons, she bore the guilt of her failed duty. Now feeling grave responsibility in naming the boys, Mrs. Lee would not risk crushing them with heavy names. Especially in the harrowing circumstance of war, Mrs.

Lee would choose something for good luck, for this was desperately needed in Namhsan.

Much later, Molly, having lost all track of time, would learn that this newest sibling of her fiancee had been born in May. Molly also didn't know then that by May the Japanese were occupying Mandalay.

One day, after talking to Mr. Wong, Papa commanded the girls, "You must cut your hair short, like your brothers. And from now on you must wear your brothers' clothing." Papa insisted, "Do not dare to go near the windows! At all times you must stay away from the windows! Do not speak loudly so as to be heard outside the house. Do not speak in high tones. Keep your voices low."

The girls did not think of objecting, and they solemnly sat one by one before Mama's scissors. As Mama combed out each strand of hair and snipped, the other girls watched their sister's feminine locks fall to the floor. Obediently the girls put on the masculine shirts and long pants. Molly took these changes stoically, but she was aware that it was harder for Moonlight and Ginger. Her sisters were very fashion conscious, and Molly observed them as they silently mourned this humility. She saw their downcast looks as they tucked away their make-up, manicuring tools, and fingernail polish. She saw them look with dissatisfaction at their reflections in the mirror as they combed what was left of their hair: chopped above the ear, razor-shaved up the back of the neck, no bangs, and the hair above the forehead combed to the back.

Papa could not bring himself to tell the girls, but Mama told them later, so they would be very cautious, "The Japanese are going into the houses looking for girls. If you are unattached, they take you. They do not care what your father or mother cry. They are wild. They are without law."

Indeed, it is reported that the Japanese army forced tens of thousands of kidnaped women to follow their military camps. These brutalized prisoners were called by the evil euphemism, "comfort women." There were not enough patriotic Japanese women willing to supply the demand of Japanese soldiers for prostitutes, the supposed need fueled by the perverse myth that a man would perform better in war after debasing a woman. Women from occupied areas were kidnaped and forced to work at "comfort stations" where they endured horrific conditions, repeated beatings, and dozens of rapes a day by Japanese soldiers. It is thought less than one fourth of these women survived the war, and many were outright murdered when they became ill and at the end of the war. Japan's history with China made women of the Chinese race an especially desirable target of cruelty.

Quickly the Chin girls came to appreciate tedium, for it was far better than utter terror when the Japanese soldiers came strutting and parading through the village. As remote as Namhsan had seemed, the same road that transported the Chins to this refuge also sometimes brought the occupying soldiers, who were flooding the main route from Burma into China and washing up into these intersecting roads.

On those days of terror, a verbal alarm, triggered by watchmen, spread quickly through the village. Hearing the warning, the terrified Chin girls would move as far as possible from view of the windows, turn their backs, and remain noiseless, lest feminine sounds be overheard. Molly could not bear to look at her sister's faces, their features contorted and complexions pale with fear. At these times, the minutes and hours ticked by with agonizing slowness.

Once again, Molly did not know it was November when Anita had a baby. Anita's father-in-law named him Ng *Get Lee*, "Everything Fortunate." This *Lee* is unlike the clan name and is spoken in a lower tone, and the emphasis is on "*Get*." Surely Mr. Ng too was feeling the need for good fortune.

No one would say these babies were born into good times or circumstances, but something about having babies in the village gave everyone a small feeling of normalcy and tiny reasons to hope for a better future. Terence took a picture of his mother with her carefully named infant son *Foke San*, "Lucky Mountain," and her grandson Get Lee. Perhaps these babies and their lucky names would bring a turn of fortunes to Namhsan.

The girls had a new occupation, which was knitting little socks, sweaters, and blankets for the babies. Their Chinese knitting friend from Kyaukme was able to show them how. Molly began with adorable little pairs of socks for her fiancee's brother Foke San and his nephew Get Lee.

Anita didn't have enough milk for Get Lee, and the infant looked red and thin and wrinkly. But Dr. Ng quickly negotiated with some tribal people to purchase a few goats to provide milk for his son. Sometimes Anita was able to come to visit with the Chins, and Molly would hold Get Lee and feed him his goats' milk from a bottle. Fondly, she called him, *mah-lau doy*, "Little Monkey."

Ah Baht Sook, Molly heard, had gotten married. He met a Yunnanese girl in Namhsan, and he was helping her with a shop selling rice and tea. This surprised Molly. She had heard the shameful expression, "Yunnanese worm," meant to insult the intelligence of those from Yunnan province in China. Molly knew it was a cruel and untrue stereotype; even so, she found herself wondering, could the rural girl really be a good match for wise Ah Baht Sook?

On the other hand, Ah Baht Sook's archaic Chinese studies were of little use in Burma, especially now, and Molly heard that his wife was prosperous and had a good mind for business. She supposed it was foolish to hope they could be happy in a time and place such as this, but she hoped anyway.

Despite Papa's preference to conceal bad news from his family, his children heard the devastating news: The British had abandoned the country, and the Japanese were occupying all of Burma. There had been much destruction and looting in Rangoon and elsewhere. The only comfort was that at least the bombing had stopped.

How long had they been in Namhsan? A year... or nearly two? It seemed intolerably long.

At last it was too much for Mrs. Lee, for the Ngs, and for Old Man Thunder Voice, and they all made arrangements to take their families back to Rangoon. They felt that, since the bombing had stopped, they must risk going back to check on their possessions in the city.

Papa had no intention of joining them. He was not willing to risk lives to protect his interests, nor would he waste time grieving over what was lost. Molly heard him remark, "Actually, the situation is not good. Nothing is settled yet. There will be plenty of time to rebuild after the war." He repeated his favorite saying, "*Yew ngen yew moth.* Have people, have things." When the time came, he would start again to build wealth.

Molly with Terence and his mother in Namhsan

The Lees were not persuaded by his wisdom and continued to pack. Perhaps it was a disadvantage that they had more property left to secure in Rangoon than Papa.

The opposing pulls of passion and duty tore apart poor young Terence. He longed to marry Molly right away and take her with him, but she was not to be swayed nor was her Papa. As the eldest son and as the brother of young siblings, Terence was desperately needed by his family. At last, duty ruled, and he painfully left Molly behind in Namhsan and accompanied his family to Rangoon.

****

Molly was secretly relieved Terence had left Namhsan. For a time, she had a break from his pestering to get married.

But her reprieve was short-lived. Terence was back!

He was accompanied by a traveling companion, Lo Lui, for protection. Terence renewed his quest to marry Molly right away. Things he had seen and heard made him even more fearful for her. But Papa was satisfied to wait, and Molly wished Terence had stayed with his family for a while longer.

Now they had nowhere else to stay, and Terence and Lo Lui, the cook of Terence's father, shared quarters with the Chins. No one but Molly seemed to mind having Terence so near. Byu Goo had no problem accommodating Terence and his finicky eating habits. When she found any seafood for sale in the village, she quickly snatched it up for him despite the expense. But for Molly, Terence's proximity made it even more difficult to avoid his relentless pressure.

Terence confided to Molly about the devastation he had found in Chinatown. Among the ruins, the building that was both his home and the dry goods shop that had provided the family's primary means of support had been bombed and looted. There was nothing left to salvage. Terence then helped the family go to the soy sauce factory. But when they arrived, they found the Japanese were occupying the compound! So they went back to Chinatown and found that Grandfather Lee Ah Poi's Burmese wife's sister's family owned a couple of houses on Maung Khine Street, near where Molly had lived in the four-story-house. A rental agreement was made, and Terence helped his family settle in to one of these homes, hoping the soy sauce factory would be returned to them soon. In any case, Terence assured Molly he would take good care of her, and they could be very happy together there until he was able to start working as an architect.

Molly knew Terence was a good man. Truly, she considered him one of the best. He was smart, ambitious, hardworking, loyal, and honest, and she knew he would try to make her happy. But she was not ready to let go of her dream of going to college, and she felt quite safe in her papa's care.

Papa also remained stubborn. His daughter was valuable, and he was too proud to acquiesce to a small, rushed wedding for her. Terence dared not pressure Mr. Chin too much, but he continued to beg Molly.

Letters were not easily delivered in those difficult days, but Terence received several from his mother. Mr. Lee signed the letters, but Molly recognized the words of Mrs. Lee. Each time she was more adamant that Terence was needed. She wrote impatiently, "Hurry and come! Marry her quickly and come back! Have a simple wedding, and then you will have the right to travel with her. We need your help! You are being selfish, thinking only of yourself! Your brothers and sisters are so small! Come quickly! We need your help! You must not abandon your family! This is not right!"

Molly and Terence in Namhsan

They tried other arguments as well. Knowing that Terence did not need convincing, they surely intended for him to use the appeals to sway Molly. "You have been engaged over three years already. You don't want to be separated. So much is uncertain in these times. What if you don't find each other again when this is over? Get married quickly and join us, so you can be together."

Molly used her own arguments to try to persuade Terence differently, "You had better go back. They need you. I will be fine here. Wait for things to calm down. We will get married after I go to college."

Terence insisted, "No, Molly, I can't go without you! I don't want you to be taken by the Japanese! I can't bear to leave you here! I worry about you every moment you are out of my sight." And so it went for several more months.

****

The women were knitting, as usual, and Papa came in and sat with them. He was silent for a long time. Then, to Ngood, he said matter-of-factly, "We have been here two years already, and no one can tell the future. It is not good for you and Terence to be separated." He hesitated, as if convincing himself, and then repeated firmly, "It is not good for you to be separated." Ngood knew what was coming.

Papa finished decisively, "We cannot have a big wedding or a banquet feast. We cannot invite a lot of relatives, of course. Anyway, who knows where they are? We will have a simple ceremony here in the house."

Ngood knew it wasn't her decision to make. She answered obediently, "Yes, Papa."

Here in this lost little village of Namhsan, dreams were slipping away from her, tumbling down the mountainside and into the river and washed out to sea. Going to college, becoming a doctor, even the expectation of a big wedding with lots of friends and relatives, feasting, and gifts... she sensed all of these things were falling from her reach. Instead, she was going to have the shame of a small rushed wedding, like a girl in trouble, with no prospects for a bright future in these traumatic times.

****

What to do? There was no Chinese lady to do the ear-piercing, so Mama sent Ngood to the English hospital in Namhsan to see if the doctor could bore holes into Ngood's ear lobes. Such preparation was necessary for a Chinese bride, so she could wear pierced earrings at her wedding. Moonlight and Ginger had their ears bored long ago, but the studious Number Two Sister could not be bothered with such things.

Molly, Ah Ma, and Wayne in Namhsan, the village hospital in the background

When she went for the procedure, Ngood was mildly surprised to see the small western hospital implanted in the obscure, rustic village. Even here in Namhsan were the clear marks, and Ngood would say, benefits, of British occupation. The doctor was Anglo-Indian, trained in England, and Ngood wondered if he also had to hide from the Japanese.

Ear-boring was not his specialty, and as a result the hole was a little higher on one lobe than the hole on the other, askew like everything else in Ngood's world. Then, even with sterile precautions, the holes became septic, and Ngood had to go back for antibiotics.

In a few more days, when a propitious day for the match had arrived, Ngood was kneeling at the ancestor altar with Terence. Only Ngood's immediate family, including Byu Goo, and Mrs. Wong attended the ceremony.

Ngood was wearing a simple Chinese top and matching pants with tiny maroon squares, clothes ready to travel, nothing to attract attention. She was also wearing the typical Burmese slippers, which looked odd with the Chinese formal attire but were much better suited than heels for running to trenches. And who knew when she might have to run?

She served the tea and obediently kowtowed to the ancestors and then to her parents. Terence also kowtowed to Ngood's parents. Before the ceremony, influenced by western thinking, he had told Ngood he didn't think it was necessary for him to make the bows. But Ngood argued with him sternly, "You had better do it, or they will think you are very rude."

If Moonlight had been married, tradition dictated that Ngood would have bowed to her as well. But Moonlight was not married. Reflexively, Ngood gave her an apologetic glance.

Ngood's Mama gave the blessing for wealth and prosperity, and of course: "May Ngood have many children, and especially many, many sons." The marriage certificate was signed by Papa and stamped in red ink with Papa's official ivory seal. Terence's father would add his seal when they saw him. That was that.

Ngood knew the date had been chosen carefully and that the Chinese date was printed on the certificate. But she would never see the certificate and would never know for sure the date of her marriage.

Mama gave Ngood a beautiful dark emerald ring in an elegant gold setting. The metalwork shone in the rich, yellow hue of fine 24 carat gold as the Chinese preferred. No goldsmith was to be found in Namhsan, so Mama also gave Ngood some small loose pearls and rubies, and a jeweler could be hired to make something later. Moonlight gave Ngood a dainty, light-weight sweater she had knitted. Ngood tucked the sweater into her small shan bag, and she carefully wrapped the jewels and put them into her hand bag.

Mama did not cry as in the weddings of Chinese opera. Surely Mama thought Ngood would be in good hands until they were reunited. Papa kept reassuring everyone the fighting would be over soon, and they would all be together again in Rangoon.

False money was burned to the gods. This was thought necessary so that the daughter would not take her parents' money with her from their house.

As Ngood left her Namhsan home, she leaped across a flame lit over the threshold. She must not be allowed to leave with any evil spirits to invade the home of her husband's family. The leap was rather frightening for her, but at least the traveling clothes were less likely to ignite than a longer Chinese wedding dress as she jumped over the fire.

Chapter Twelve

Honeymoon

Terence had made arrangements with a friend of his, a former classmate at St. Paul's, who drove a truck for his father's tea business. The tea plantation was near Namhsan, and, even in war time, the boxes of tea leaves must be delivered to a warehouse in Mandalay. Terence and Molly would ride with him that far and then take the train back to Rangoon to rejoin his family on Maung Khine Street or at the soy sauce factory. After the wedding ceremony, the native man was waiting for them outside the home.

Terence introduced the young man to Molly, speaking the wonderful words for the first time, "This is my wife, Molly." Molly nodded her head and then took Terence's hand as he helped her up to a bench on the back of the tea truck. Terence would ride inside the truck cab with his friend. Molly was relieved that Terence was not beside her as she tried to control her emotions.

Molly could hardly bear the sadness of leaving her family. She didn't know if she would ever see any of them again. But now she belonged to his people, and she must follow him.

She tried not to make a scene, because she knew it was hard enough for her family to see her go. Especially for her mother, she tried to wear her most natural smile and speak in light tones without a break in her voice. She spoke the Cantonese farewell that implied she expected to see her family again, "*Doy woi.*"

Again, the rugged beauty of the scenery in the Shan Plateau might have inspired Molly in other circumstances, but everything seemed harsh and unfriendly. Molly recalled coming up this very road to Namhsan. Now it was even more difficult to think happily of the future. As frightening as it was coming to Namhsan, at least then Molly thought she would be gone from the familiar things only a short while; then all would be back to normal. Now she knew that nothing would ever resemble the "normal" of her life before the war.

She thought of her Papa's words, "Pack only a few things. We'll be away only a few months."

"Well," she thought, as the truck ride rattled her body, "What happened to 'only a few months?'" She didn't want to be bitter, but she couldn't help it. She did not want to blame Papa for the duration of the war, nor for letting her go with Terence. But, at the moment, without realizing it, she, a good Chinese girl, silently resented her father.

If she thought the bus ride to Namhsan had been rough, the return trip to Mandalay, riding in the back of a truck, was pounding. Molly felt her inner parts were scrambled. The physical shaking matched her emotional upheaval, and she could not find a solid thing to give her security for either. When the earth fell hundreds of feet just beyond the sharp turn of the road, Molly fought her fear, and she did her best to cling to the bench to keep from sliding off it. Then, when the darkness of night cloaked the dangers, cliffs were more fearsome than ever, left to the imagination, like the future. The huge and beautiful viaduct was also passed unseen.

They drove much of the night, but it was still dark when the truck stopped. The driver and Terence left the cab and came to talk to Molly.

"We are approaching Mandalay, and there is a Japanese checkpoint we must pass," the driver said. "This is the only way to get to Mandalay, so it is a very strategic area, and the Japanese soldiers heavily guard this road. Soldiers stop every vehicle and inspect it. They will stop my truck too. They will use their bayonets to poke some boxes to make sure I carry only tea."

Concerned, Molly asked, "How do we know the soldiers will not harm us?"

Molly's heart quickened as the man continued, "We will have to take our chances. But we will have to be careful, because the Japanese are very suspicious, and if they find you two riding on this truck, they might think you are spies, and they might kill us all."

Molly's heart leapt in fear. The man did not make eye contact with Molly as he added, "This area is secluded except for Japanese soldiers. They might do something when no one is watching."

He added gruffly, eyes still diverted, "So, you and Terence must ride in the center of the tea boxes until we pass through the check point, and you must stay still and quiet."

Molly could hardly believe what she was hearing! She looked at Terence, hoping for comfort, but even in the darkness she could see fear on his face, and she knew they were about to face great danger. She sensed he had not known about this checkpoint when they left Namhsan.

He choked quietly, "Come on Molly. We need to do it."

Her body tensed with terror. She wanted to run away! But where could she go? She must not think such thoughts! Now that they were here, it seemed they had no choice but to trust this friend of Terence. With all the years of her good training, piled on top of generations of well-trained Chinese women, she obeyed her husband, nodding bravely.

She watched the driver move the boxes on the tea truck to hollow out a tiny cave in the center. Then Terence climbed on to the truck bed and crouched into the small cavity, leaving a tiny space for her. Molly slid into the opening beside Terence and squeezed next to him, bowing her head to her knees. The man replaced the tea boxes against them, so that they were completely concealed.

The man cautioned them again, "Just be very quiet. And do not move. They will poke the boxes with their bayonets, but don't worry, their bayonets will not reach you. Don't let them know you are here. Whatever happens, you must be quiet."

"Don't worry?" Molly's mind hung upon the ridiculous admonition. And did he say, "Whatever happens…"? What if the Japanese soldiers had gotten longer bayonets? What if they decided they must check the load more thoroughly and move boxes? What if she couldn't keep quiet?

She felt the truck moving again, and impulsively, she cried inwardly, "Lord Jesus, help us!"

If they were discovered, she was certain Terence would protect her with his life, but what could he do against many soldiers with guns? If the soldiers killed Terence, they might do worse to her! Aye-ah! *"Bu yao pahr,"* she told herself firmly, "Do not be afraid!" She must not think about what could happen. She must calm herself.

Terence cautioned her, "Just make sure you stay quiet!" Of course, she had heard this instruction already and would do everything in her power to obey it. Still, Terence needed to repeat the warning because he was helpless to do anything more to protect his wife.

After riding a few miles, Molly felt the truck slow and stop. She heard an unfamiliar and frightening language, commanding loudly and roughly, "*Row! Row, row, row, row!*" The sounds seemed cruel and unnatural.

She could not hear Terence's friend, but she imagined he must be mortified too. She wondered how he could stay calm, as if nothing was unusual about his cargo. What if his fear aroused suspicion?

She prayed, "Lord Jesus, please give him courage!"

They were no longer in the cool hills and mountains of the Shan Plateau, and this tiny space she shared with Terence was stifling. She longed for fresh air and freedom from the confining space, but she tried to stay small and motionless. She was afraid her breathing might move the boxes or be heard, but she quickly discovered that not taking enough air was more dangerous, for this caused her to need to gasp. So she concentrated on breathing quiet, unruffled breaths.

Then Molly heard alarming boot steps, "Clop! Clop! Clop! Clop!" as the soldier walked around the truck. "Chaunk!" Molly fought tremors of terror as she felt the boxes move with the stab of the bayonet! "Chaunk!" How could she sit still? What if she did not sit still? "Chaunk!" The bayonet was not long enough to reach her heart, but with each thrust her heart felt pierced, and it pounded as if it would explode from her chest! She felt the ridiculous impulse to leap from her hiding place!

She prayed again to Jesus, "Oh, Lord! Help me!"

More clopping of the boots! More terrifying, unintelligible words! What were the soldiers saying? Agonizing minutes felt endless....

At last the truck began to move slowly. Molly wished the driver would go faster. She told herself that at least they were moving away from this treacherous place, and apparently without pursuit. But were they safe? Or, terror! Had the Japanese commandeered the truck?

The truck was driven a few more miles. Then it stopped. The driver's door opened and closed. Footsteps approached.

Molly heard the calm voice of Terence's friend. "We are safe! We are at the warehouse in Mandalay!"

In the dark cave, Terence and Molly breathed gratefully, "*Piya! Piya!* Thank God!"

The friend removed some boxes, and fresh air filled the hole. Terence and Molly uncoiled and climbed down from the truck bed. Molly found her legs did not work too well, but she didn't want the men to notice, so she leaned against the truck for a few minutes. Then she tried to walk normally.

The friend took the couple into the warehouse where they could sleep a few hours before taking a train to Rangoon after sunrise. In the dim lantern light in the warehouse, Molly was surprised to see many people resting on a sea of mats and a few bed islands among high stacks of boxes in storage.

The men went to see the tea agent, the *pwe sah*, or broker, and Molly noticed they were talking rather excitedly and kept looking in her direction. Maybe they were telling him about the terrifying experience at the checkpoint.

Terence came back to where she was waiting. She couldn't quite read the expression on his face.

He said, "The *pwe sah* is very generous. He wants you to be comfortable, so he will provide us with a bed." This seemed like good news, but Molly could sense something was wrong. Terence was not forthcoming with an explanation.

They took a small lantern to find the little twin bed given them, and they stretched together on the narrow space and closed the light. Terence wordlessly made his intentions known to Molly.

"What?" she whispered, "No, Terence! Not here! Not in this open place!"

Terence whispered, "It doesn't matter. It's very dark in here. No one will see. You are my wife now. We had an official ceremony at your parents' home. We have your father's signature. All that is missing is the signature of my father. Everything is official."

Terence added emotionally, painfully, "Molly, if we don't start acting like a husband and wife, the Japanese will take you. I won't let those Japanese have you. Why should I let them have you? You are mine!"

Molly couldn't say, "No!" to him. Indeed, she was his. But she worried that people would hear them. This honeymoon was nothing like wonderful thing American couples experienced, as Molly knew from watching the American movies. There were never graphic bedroom scenes in those movies, but it was always implied that the wedding night was superlative, and very private, joy.

****

Having arrived exhausted at the warehouse just before the opening curtain of dawn, and now in the darkness of the warehouse, they were oblivious when the full light of morning shone on Mandalay. So they slept late. When she woke, Molly worried that they had surely missed all of the daily trains to Rangoon. At last, Terence confessed to Molly what he couldn't tell her when they arrived at the warehouse.

"The Japanese have taken over all of the trains to move troops. No one but soldiers can ride. We will have to wait here in Mandalay a little while, until the train lines are open for business again."

Now Molly understood why so many people, maybe two hundred or more, were in the warehouse. "These people expected to use the trains also," she observed with concern, as the implications for herself penetrated her mind. "They are stranded... like us."

She looked around the huge warehouse with the very high ceiling. All of the people here looked fretful and unhappy, clutching their small bags, looking ready to run. They sat awkwardly hunched in family groups, most sitting on the floor.

Terence agreed with her observations. Then he added, "But we are lucky...."

Molly did not feel lucky, and Terence could see the worry on her face. But he hurried on, "As I said, the pwe sah is very generous. He is a good Buddhist and will earn his way to Nirvana with his generosity. You know, the Burmese people love to do this. They often take in travelers and show hospitality. We don't need to worry."

Terence was talking a little too fast, like a hawker in the street market trying to sell Molly a cure for her doubts. "The *pwe sah* is allowing people to sleep here, and he provides meals-- rice, vegetables and tea-- for everyone. He knows Chinese women like to sleep on beds, so for you he provided a bed instead of a mat. He is not charging us, or any of these people, for his care."

This was impressive generosity, but Terence sensed Molly was not impressed, so he tried another approach, "But we don't have to stay here during the day. Let's go look around. Anyway, I don't care for the *nga-pyi*, the fermented fish. The Burmese love this, but I don't like the smell of the fish or the lingering smell on the breath. Let's see if we can find some *mohinga*."

Terence could not cope with waiting in the warehouse all day, and he wouldn't think of leaving Molly, so each day they walked around the dusty, strafed city. Though Mandalay was in the so-called dry zone, accumulating little rain during the year, Molly would hardly call the humid air dry. Sweat was inevitable, and dust stuck staunchly to damp skin. Clothes also stuck, and chaffing made her skin itch. Oh, how Molly longed for a refreshing bath!

The beautiful city of Mandalay was unrecognizable. Disconcerting signs of war were everywhere: grotesquely wounded buildings exposing jagged skeletons, pocked and littered streets, patrols of terrible Japanese soldiers, cowed civilians. Molly was not embarrassed now to hold Terence's arm, anxious as she was to make clear that she was attached to him. She kept her head down to avoid unwanted attention as she stepped over rubble. She wouldn't think of wearing high heels or make-up, and she was not sorry that she still had the chopped haircut. Often the sirens sounded dreaded wails, and the couple ran for cover as planes thundered above the city, dropping terrifying bombs.

Even in her fear, Molly noticed immediately something was different about these planes. These were not the small planes that she heard in Rangoon. These airplanes were bigger, and the engines sounded much more consistent and powerful.

Terence explained, having conversed with the *pwe sah*, "These planes are coming from the Allies: The British, Americans, Canadians, Chinese...." Molly felt a moment of relief when she heard the names of these countries she thought of as friendly. She thought of the gallant heroes of the American movies and pictured the likes of Gene Autry, John Wayne, and Errol Flynn in the pilot seats of the planes. Quickly the dream was reframed by the reality that she and Terence were still in grave danger, no matter who was dropping the bombs.

When the bombing stopped, the "all clear" siren would sound, and people would slowly appear in the street again. Hearing the sirens, Molly sometimes thought of the brave local men who, even after the British retreated, manned the sirens to warn their neighbors of danger. She wondered, "When they see the airplanes, don't they want to run and hide too?"

As people came out of hiding, vendors were quickly ready to sell them *mohinga*, a catfish (*nga*) soup with rice noodles (*mok*), seasoned with garlic, onion, chili, and ginger root, and served with battered and deep fried squash and lemon wedges. This, or a fried rice with vegetables, made a filling meal for breakfast or lunch. Vendors would call out their specialty, *mohinga*, or *bey-byu*, the familiar chickpea dish, or *oh-no cow-sway*. The latter was a curried fried chicken with coconut milk (*oh-noke*) gravy thickened with chickpea flour. This was served with yellow egg noodles (*cow-sway*) and several optional garnishes such as hard-boiled egg, lemon wedges, and chopped cilantro.

Terence always seemed to have enough money to buy food from local vendors. Molly was completely dependent on him. She didn't have even an anna in her handbag, though she always carried the precious little collection of wedding jewels from her mother.

The local people were quite happy to take Terence's British-Burmese notes on the sly, though they risked their lives to do so. The Japanese had been printing their own money, but it was cheaply printed on cheap paper and no one thought the bills had any worth. The Japanese were forcing people to exchange the old trusted bills for the newly printed ones, but the people were resisting. If the Japanese were watching exchanges or if Japanese soldiers wanted to buy something with their contrived money, the vendors were compelled to take it.

Sometimes Molly would try to talk Terence out of roaming the streets. "What are you going to find in the streets? Bombs are dropping left and right! People are running everywhere!" She felt a little bit safer in the warehouse, although she was aware that the huge warehouse might become a target if bombers thought that it housed military supplies and soldiers instead of tea and refugees. She tried not to think about it, but if a bomb did hit the building, she knew many innocent people would die.

Molly's argument for staying in the warehouse did not reflect pleasant conditions there. It was crowded with people whose faces were frozen masks of stress from extended trauma. No one in the warehouse chatted with others. No one felt normal curiosity or friendliness toward their forced companions, nor had enough concern left to give others when each one's attention was consumed by his own difficult state. Between moments of utter terror, the people sank into a sort of semi-aware numbness, barely able to murmur minimal courtesies, only able to focus on mundane tasks needed to survive.

So Terence and Molly had two unsatisfactory choices: to walk the bombed and blasted streets of Mandalay, always prepared to run for cover, or to huddle in a warehouse full of traumatized refugees, blindly hoping to avoid bombing. Terence preferred to be out where he felt he had some awareness and control over his circumstance, however slight.

Terence occasionally heard a little more information about the war from the *pwe sah*. In this way he knew that the Sagaing Bridge, the only bridge to cross the wide Irrawaddy River, had been bombed by the British on their retreat from Burma. By this strategy, the Japanese were prevented from using the railway system's northern route from Mandalay to Myitkyina. Also, he heard that a section of the Gokteik Viaduct, which had so impressed him and Molly on the trip to Namhsan, had been bombed and was impassable.

Terence had said they would have to wait a few days in Mandalay, but days piled up into weeks, and weeks piled up into several months. Molly did not want to resent her husband. She knew it was not his fault that the trains had stopped taking passengers. But it was hard not to blame him for her unhappiness. She wondered how her family was fairing in Namhsan, and, honestly, she wished that she had not been rushed into this marriage. Her imprisonment in Namhsan had been more tolerable than this. She reminded herself that Terence was doing his best to protect her, and there was no question that he loved her deeply.

Someday, she consoled herself, though she may not become a doctor, Terence would be a respected architect and builder in a peaceful Rangoon and would provide her with a lovely home in which to raise their children. Chinese stories often ended in tragedy, but she was counting on a happy ending like one of the American movies she and Terence loved. Still, it was getting harder and harder to believe even the revised dream.

****

Three months and more passed dismally and dangerously in Mandalay, when at last Terence heard good news for the refugees. The trains could begin taking some civilian passengers. Terence purchased tickets, and he and Molly boarded a train for Rangoon.

The duration of the trip seemed longer than ever, but at last the weary travelers were relieved to be in Rangoon. The latest message from his parents, over three months ago, informed Terence to meet his family in Chinatown in Rangoon, where they were renting the home on Maung Khine Street.

At the train station in Rangoon, the couple boarded a bus. Though familiar with the shattered war zone the city of Mandalay had become, Molly was unprepared to see the devastation of her home town. Many familiar buildings of her memory were crumbled heaps of wood or concrete. With trepidation, Molly rode with Terence toward the familiar street of her childhood, seeing ruins and rubble along the way.

Soon the bus was turning the corner, and she caught her breath as she saw the four-story house still intact! Relief swept through her like a cooling wind. She saw the third floor balcony where she had observed the approach of the New Year's Day parade, and she was moved with a wave of memories from those happy years. She noticed the beautiful tile entrance was not clean, lacking Grandfather Chin's maid's vigorous scrubbing with coconut shells. She thought again of her childhood play with her cousin Len and small uncle Tuck Sook, as they enjoyed the cool oasis with many neighborhood children. Her throat tightened with sadness as she mourned the loss of those days, but at least the building was there. At least this one thing remained much as it had been. Such emotions!

At last they came to the designated house on Maung Khine Street. They went to the door and knocked, but there was no response. Something must be wrong. The home seemed too quiet for a houseful of children, even in war time. Maybe the family had been able to return to the soy sauce factory.

Terence continued to knock, and at last a married maid of Terence's mother came to the door. The family was not there, she explained. She said they were worried about renewed bombing and had fled, south this time, to Pyapon. Terence and Molly were to find them there.

Terence's disappointment was less than his fear of Molly's disappointment. He tried to tell her everything would be fine. All they needed to do now was to book steamship passage to Pyapon. No problem.

Molly was exhausted, and it was more and more difficult to hide her anger. Nothing went according to plan and nothing resembled normalcy during these long, fatiguing years of war. Things had only gotten worse since marrying Terence. He was not to blame, but Molly blamed him anyway. Her anger and frustration with her situation could not be directed at the culpable villains, and so she found her anger focused on the convenient target.

How she wished she were still with her family in the relative safety of Namhsan! Why did Terence have to drag her along? Why didn't he just go help his family and leave her be?

Then, as angry thoughts tend to do, a fury of angry thoughts raged and tumbled one upon another in her mind. Why did he rush her to marry him? Why did he risk her life in a tea truck? Why did he make their first intimate night together in a warehouse full of refugees? Why did he make her stay in the warehouse and in the streets of Mandalay, with bombs dropping all around, for more than three long months? And now this! The in-laws who were so anxious for them to come weren't even here! And now he was going to drag her off to Pyapon, and who knew what was next?

True to years of training to be a good Chinese wife, Molly didn't say a word. But Terence quickly understood her silent language and knew better than to try any more to cheer her.

****

Terence was quick to book passage to Pyapon, but a quick booking did not bring a quick passage. It should have come as no surprise to the couple that the war had also complicated steamboat transportation in Burma. They would have to wait several weeks to acquire two spots on the crowded boats.

The Scottish-owned Irrawaddy Flotilla Company, established in 1865, predating British occupation of Burma and originally cooperating with Burmese royalty, had built the largest fleet of river boats in the world. The service ran from the Irrawaddy delta nearly a thousand miles north to Bhamo, just 130 miles from the Chinese border, incorporating many navigable feeder streams as well. The company had an active patrol keeping channels marked and waterways clear of shifting sands and debris. Just before the war, the flotilla carried over eight million passengers and over a million tons of cargo annually. But that was before the war.

When the Japanese invaded Burma in 1942, nearly the entire fleet of six hundred vessels was scuttled by the company's personnel, a drastic move ordered by the owner to prevent confiscation and use by the Japanese. Now, the few remaining riverboats were crowded, and passage was limited, tedious, and expensive. Private cabins had been removed from these vessels to give more space to pack in passengers. This was no luxury cruise.

Also, waterways were not maintained after the Japanese invasion, so many of the systems were no longer navigable. Significantly for Terence and Molly, the Twante Canal, which provided a shortcut due west of Rangoon to one of the fingers of the great Irrawaddy River, had filled with silt and was impassable by steamboat.

Eventually, Terence and Molly left the docks of Rangoon and journeyed by a paddle wheel steamboat south toward the mouth of the Rangoon River. About halfway to the Andaman Sea, the steamboat turned into a tidal stream connecting the Rangoon River to the eastern outlet of the China-Bakir Creek, then upstream to Dedaye, and across the connecting Podok River, then into the Pyapon River at Kyaiklat, and downstream to Pyapon. Thirteen miles here and twenty-seven miles there folded and bended the fifty mile straight southwest distance from Rangoon into many miles more, passed monotonously at ten or so miles an hour.

Sometimes the vessel was moving easily with tidal waters and sometimes it fought against. What difference did it make? Either way Molly was always moving against her will toward more uncertainty, more difficulty, more distance from the security of her former family.

Molly was little aware of this journey. She was in no mood for sight-seeing and was so fatigued, tense, and ill that she slept much of the way even in the press of fellow passengers. When she was awake, she saw more and more mangrove trees lining the steamy banks of the waterways, passing by hypnotically mile after nautical mile. The mangrove limbs slouched with dampness in the ghostly fog, and in such environs, it was not difficult to imagine and fear the Burmese nats haunting the rivers. So, the steamship ride to Pyapon was shrouded with a misty veil in Molly's memory, like a vague dream when one awakens to an oppressive feeling without clear consciousness of the dream itself.

Chapter Thirteen

Refuge in the Irrawaddy Delta

In peacetime, Pyapon was a busy port village on the Pyapon River, an Irrawaddy River tributary, about ten miles inland from the Andaman Sea. Even now, the number of docks and boats showed that this remained an important shipping town. The area was very marshy, mangrove trees grew thickly in the soil seasoned with salty sea water, and rice paddies surrounded the village. Most of the residents were of the Kayin tribe, though many tribal Burmans lived here as well.

At last, the worn travelers found Terence's family living on Eighth Street in a spacious two-story house built of white brick. Ngood obediently leapt across a flame into her in-law's home to keep the evil spirits from following her.

Mrs. Lee attempted to greet them cordially, but then she scolded Terence for taking so long and told him how his absence, his abandonment, had put his family at risk. She didn't directly blame Molly, but her meaning was clear. Already she was quite displeased with her daughter-in-law.

Mrs. Lee informed them that she would host a quickly assembled wedding ceremony for them so the Lee relatives could participate. She showed Molly the wedding dress she had ordered from Hong Kong before the war and which Anita had worn to her wedding in Rangoon. She told Molly she could borrow this dress for her wedding.

Privately to Terence, Mrs. Lee said, "I see Ngood is pregnant. Is the baby yours?"

Terence replied angrily, "Of course the baby is mine! Who else? I have been with Ngood all the time! She has not been out of my sight!" Terence knew better than to mention this insult to Molly until many years later.

But until his mother's observation, neither Terence nor Molly had realized she was pregnant. She had been vomiting a little in the mornings, but life had been so stressful, she assumed that this explained her sickness. Times were precarious and days difficult to account, so she hadn't kept track of her menses. Molly was small and thin and by now had been married almost four months. Mrs. Lee's practiced eye could immediately spot a pregnancy of that duration.

Terence and Molly would live with Terence's parents and six youngest siblings on the second floor of the white brick house, where rooms were separated by cloths. Molly would have a private room, something quite new to her and quite an accommodation. The bed was the familiar style, nicely draped with mosquito netting that could be pulled back and fastened to hooks on the wall during the day. Terence, always sniffling, had difficulty breathing and slept in another area near an open window for fresh air. Several maids also lived on the floor, including one very young girl, Haung Se'ung. All of the cooking was done outdoors.

Mrs. Lee's mother lived on the cooler first floor with her daughter-in-law and grandsons. Molly doubted Terence's grandmother could climb the steps to the upper story on her wobbly feet, deformed as they were. For some reason, there were many student desks on the first floor.

Water was piped to the house from a large community pond protected by high fences and netting, so water for the family was no problem. An outhouse behind the house met other needs.

The family of Mr. Lee's deceased brother, Wat Hong, was also established at Pyapon. Apparently, the Lee Wat Hong family had evacuated here directly when Rangoon was bombed. Molly had never seen Wat Hong in person, as he had died long ago, but she had seen a picture of him. He appeared to weigh over three-hundred pounds, and Terence thought his death was linked to obesity. Lee Wat Hong's widow was very sweet to Molly. She had many children in her household.

Word among Chinese had spread about this haven in Pyapon. Many Chinese families had found safety here.

****

Out of respect, Molly bowed her head whenever she approached her mother-in-law. She noticed the maids always bowed deeply to their mistress.

Mrs. Lee did not let the war stop her from setting up a nice ancestor altar, with all the necessary representative pictures, ancestor tablet, incense, and teacups. Her favorite icon was Guan Yin, goddess of mercy, and she had carefully carried the porcelain image from Rangoon, to Namhsan, back to Rangoon, and then to Pyapon. Molly understood from Mrs. Lee's dignified hinting that it was now her duty, as daughter-in-law, to wake up early every morning, make a fresh pot of tea, and serve the ancestors tea and incense.

Molly woke early the next morning, obediently rising to perform the ritual. She emptied the old tea and washed the cups. Then she boiled the water, but as she poured the water to fill the teapot, she filled it too full and hot water spilled from the spout and burned her hand. It was all she could do to keep from crying out in pain.

Why hadn't someone showed her what to do? She had never had to do this before! Byu Goo had always boiled the water for her mother to make tea for the ancestors.

Terence continued to sleep, unaware of her misery. Tears filling her eyes, Molly wrapped her burned hand in a cloth, because neither her mother nor Byu Goo was there to do it for her. If she were here, Mama would coo soothingly and prepare some Chinese herbs to ease the pain.

Molly put tea leaves into the pot and let them steep until the water changed color, then filled the three little handleless cups on the altar for the ancestors, then one for Guan Yin, one for the ground, one for the door.... She lit the incense for each one. Then she returned to her room and silently cried herself to sleep.

Later that day Terence stretched out in his chair and commanded Molly, "Bring me a glass of water!"

Molly answered, "Get it yourself!" She would put a stop to such foolishness right now! His mother had spoiled Terence, and he could be very bossy, lording over others. Well, she had no intention of spoiling him, or of being his maid, and the sooner he found out, the better.

"Don't ask people to do things you can do yourself! You are not a puppet! You are not a doll! Nobody is your servant... least of all me!" she lectured angrily.

Molly suspected her mother-in-law would not approve of this resistance to Terence, even though Mrs. Lee was the boss in her home. It was not the traditional Chinese way, and Molly remembered the old saying, "Obey your father; obey your husband; obey your son."

Maybe Molly's western teaching was coming out. The words of gently liberating teachers like Miss Bartel had made an unmistakable influence, and she told Terence, "Everybody is equal."

Terence was surprised by Molly's speech. But he did not argue.

To be sure he understood, she repeated, "I am not your maid. Remember that."

****

Mrs. Lee owned her own personal get sing "book of stars," the astrology book of good omens. Molly always thought of the book with dread; it seemed that some days were forecasted to be so bad, one had better not do anything. But Mrs. Lee carefully consulted it to determine the luckiest time for the couple to marry. All was done in the Lee house in Pyapon; there was no point in renting a hall for the few relatives in the city able to witness the ceremony. There was no celebrity or dignitary able to attend the event.

Molly was dressed in Anita's traditional bridal outfit. It was very expensive; only the well-to-do could afford such a thing. The top dress was black with lavish embroidery in silver and gold thread. Slits in the sides of the dress showed the under skirt, which was red and also beautifully embroidered with peacocks worked in silver and gold. The Lee parents did not have a stage on which to be seated, but they were arranged prominently at the front of the room. Wat Hong's family attended also.

After hearing the speeches and petitions for wealth and children, Molly kowtowed to the Lee ancestor altar so that the Lee ancestors would now recognize her as part of the family. She knelt on the cushion before the altar and touched her forehead to the floor three times. She stood up and then knelt again to repeat the thrice bowing. She stood again, and then again she knelt and repeated the bows, so that her head touched the floor a total of nine times. Then she and Terence knelt on the cushion before his parents and repeated the kowtow to them, submitting to their authority.

Molly's mother-in-law presented her with a beautiful gold bracelet. Later, her mother-in-law gave her other jewelry including diamond earrings, and her father-in-law gave her a diamond bracelet, but it was thought rude to show off too much at the ceremony. Molly received jewelry from other relatives too. Considering the circumstances, the gifts were quite generous, for everyone worried about finances, not knowing how much longer the war would drag on and deplete stores.

Molly knew she should be grateful, but this second attempt at a wedding ceremony was still nothing like the magnificent event expected in the days before the war. The celebration was further dampened by a curfew order, now imposed by the Japanese, and there was no getting away from the underlying fear of bombs that pervaded all activity.

Terence asked others to use his camera to take a few pictures of the event. There was no place to have the pictures developed now, but someday he and his bride would have these treasured reminders of the day. The size of the wedding didn't matter to him; he was just glad Molly was his wife.

As evening came, a few dim candles were lit; even for a wedding celebration no one dared to use bright lights that could endanger everyone. The men were prepared to extinguish even those few lights if planes were heard. But Mrs. Lee had prepared a very nice wedding feast.

Mr. Lee added his signature and red seal on the marriage certificate along with Papa's name.

Mrs. Lee offered the progressive, familiar approach with Molly and said, "You may call us Mama and Papa."

Not long after the wedding, Terence overheard the rumors as Molly's pregnancy began to show, but again, he didn't tell Molly about the confusion until many years later. Some did not know of the marriage ceremony in Namhsan, and so they thought less of Molly, thinking she had relations with Terence before she was married to him. Consistent with the double standard of the age, Terence was not judged badly under those mistaken terms.

Molly understood by indirect comments that her mother-in-law had expectations of her besides duties at the ancestor altar. Molly was anxious to please her mother-in-law, particularly this nwe' jaing foo, hero among women. So Molly obediently took over some of the care of her mother-in-law's young children, bathing and dressing her sister-in-law Fe Yin and brother-in-law Foke San. Molly did not mind this, and she was quite fond of the children. The greater challenge was that sometimes Molly was also expected to help the maids with kitchen duties. For someone who had always been chased away from the kitchen, this was a difficult obligation. Though Molly balked, she could not refuse.

Once again, getting enough food to eat was not a problem in Pyapon. Before the war, the area had been famous for its seafood, and even now shrimp and fish were plentiful. Rice was available, and fresh vegetables were usually not hard to find.

****

Molly mentioned to Terence she wasn't feeling well. She had recently recovered from a case of German measles, several days of rash, swollen glands, and joint pain. Now, in the wee hours of the morning, she was having stomach pains, and felt she needed to go to the bathroom.

Terence told his mother, and she said to Molly, "Come and lie down on your bed."

Molly did not realize she was in labor. No one told her what to expect. Her mother-in-law tied two pieces of shawl-like fabric together and draped them over the mosquito netting rods that linked the posts of the bed. Her mother-in-law told her, "When you think your baby is coming out, pull on these straps to strain."

This was the only instruction Molly was given. In the old Chinese way, it was considered shameful to talk of things like childbirth, even to a woman about to experience it for the first time.

In spite of the late hour and curfew, Mrs. Lee sent Terence to bring the Kayin midwife. Terence was a typically nervous new father and ran all the way to the midwife's house. Water was put to boil, and in a couple of hours a baby girl was born in the partial light. She was a big baby, over eight pounds, a credit to Mrs. Lee for feeding Molly well during the latter part of her pregnancy.

Molly was sore and tired, but she held the newborn and immediately loved this little one, her own little one. Molly whispered prayers to Lord Jesus for protection for this sweet, fragile life brought into a hard world at a frightening time. She was grateful that she could talk to Lord Jesus at any time from the privacy of her own heart, without ritual or benefit of an altar and offerings.

The next day the midwife filled a metal tub with water, then boiled hot water to add to the bath to warm it, and then she added some healing herbs. Molly was to sit in this pleasant, warm bath to heal the torn flesh of childbirth.

It was after this that Molly was told her baby had a fever, a rash, and even sores oozing pus on her back. The poor infant had contracted German measles from her mother. Molly was very concerned for her baby, but the situation could have been much worse, for risks of German measles to an unborn baby are grave, especially when the illness strikes early in the pregnancy. The baby could have been blind, deaf, retarded, miscarried, or stillborn, so rash and fever were trifling matters, and this child would be spared of worse.

Mrs. Lee asked a maid to prepare a small tub of lukewarm water, and then she sprinkled medicinal herbs into this bath, herbs which she had gathered from the yard. She held the baby face-down over the water and gently bathed her back. Despite her grandmother's very tender and compassionate treatment, the baby cried pitifully, and Molly could hardly wait to hold her, soothe her, and nurse her. When Mrs. Lee rested the warm cloth on the baby's back, the girl seemed comforted and stopped crying. Mrs. Lee bathed the baby daily, and, after a week or so, Mrs. Lee showed Molly how to give the bath.

The softer fabric used for diapers was difficult to find in those days, so Mrs. Lee gave her maids pieces of stiff canvas and told them to wash and boil the fabric many, many times. This made the fabric softer, but it was still poor diaper material, rough against the baby's tender skin and not very absorbent.

Mrs. Lee gave the fabric to Molly and said, "Use this on the baby," without instructions on how the diaper should be folded or fastened. Perhaps Mrs. Lee assumed Molly would know what to do, but Molly was embarrassed to ask for instructions and felt very clumsy about diapering her baby.

For the next month, Molly was treated to special care and special foods and drinks to insure she would have enough milk for the baby. By custom, if a woman gives birth to a boy, her care is especially attentive. Considering the war time and the baby girl, Mrs. Lee made remarkable concessions to Molly. Somehow she was able to find the Chinese delicacy of roasted duck, which had been split open and hung over a fire to slowly cook all day. Also, she found the traditional pork sausage. And to increase breast milk, Molly was fed pickled pig's feet which had been cooked with garlic, onion, peanut, vinegar, sugar and a little ginger, and served with gravy colored with thick, black soy sauce. Molly remembered Byu Goo shopping and Grandmother Wong feeding these same dishes to Ah Ma after she gave birth.

Molly appreciated that Terence was the proudest of fathers. His child could not have been more precious to him or more loved, boy or girl, rash or no, hard times or easy. Together, he and Molly studied their daughter's precious little features with wonder. The mystery of a newborn child transfixed these parents, as new parents have been transfixed generation after generation.

Molly would never know for sure the anniversary of her wedding at Namhsan, but her daughter's birth would give her a clue. Figuring about nine months prior to Ah Hing's birth, she assumed she had been married in August. Knowing that the Chinese greatly regarded the bright full moon in August, she thought she and Terence might have been married on August fifteenth, 1943.

After the month of gravest concern for the infant had past, Mrs. Lee named the girl, *Ngwan Hing*, which translates, "Lasting Grace." This word *Hing* is not to be confused with Dorothy's name which is pronounced in a high pitch and means "fragrant." This baby's name was pronounced in a lower pitch, and is most accurately translated "moist" or "repeated," the latter which reflected Mrs. Lee's observation of the leap month of the leap year. The use of the word for "Moist" or "Grace" was also a good omen, signifying, "Let's hope you will bring a brother." So much meaning in such a little word! Clearly, Mrs. Lee chose the name carefully. She presented the baby with a good-luck bracelet made of a curved piece of dark brown cane and closed with a gold clasp. With Mrs. Lee's attentive bathing routine, the rash on the back of Ah Hing had scabbed over.

By now Ngood was taking care of her own baby, after she cared for her mother-in-law's children. Understanding what was expected, Ngood cared for Fe Yin and Foke San before she attended her own infant daughter Ah Hing. Ngood knew of this old-fashioned Chinese custom, and she did not argue.

But Wat Hong's widow was critical of Mrs. Lee. One day she said to Ngood, "Huh? She gave you this fabric for diapers? Huh? She didn't teach you how to diaper your baby?"

Ngood didn't want to appear disrespectful, and in deference she said, "Oh, *Hlum Nye Nye*, Number Three Respected Madam, well, it is war time. Maybe she couldn't find better fabric. Maybe I didn't learn too well."

Wat Hong's widow startled Ngood with her angry tone, "She couldn't find better? Hmpf!"

She muttered something else and added, "I had better keep quiet."

Then the woman patiently instructed Ngood in the care of her baby. She showed her how to fold the square diaper into a triangle, place the baby with her waist in the middle of the folded edge, and bring the three points together in front and pin the fabric. This worked so well!

Ngood noticed Wat Hong's widow's children called their mother in the old-fashioned formal way, instead of the familiar "Mama" or "Ah Ma." That gave her an idea, for Ngood was painfully aware of the tension between her mother-in-law and herself.

Ngood understood that Mrs. Lee was pleased for her own children to call her "Mama." But Ngood had started off poorly with Mrs. Lee, because Terence loved her too much and had abandoned his family in their time of greatest need to chase after her. Perhaps Mrs. Lee would always resent Terence's *chi' ting* lovesickness for Molly and would always blame Molly for distracting him.

But Ngood admired her mother-in-law tremendously. After all, she was rightly one of the most esteemed women of Chinatown. Ngood had so often heard wonderful things said about this great woman's capabilities, her wisdom, and her generosity. Ngood wanted very much to please this highly regarded woman.

Addressing her by a formal title was a small, but perhaps, significant thing, so she told her mother-in-law, "If it pleases you, I will call you, '*Nye Nye*,' and my father-in-law, '*Lo Yeahr*,' out of respect."

Nye Nye did seemed pleased. Ngood was happy to address them with the deferential terms, "Respected Madam" and "Old Dad."

****

Bombing in Pyapon was increasing. The targets were usually buildings and attacks usually came during daylight hours. So, by Nye Nye's wisdom, the Lees took on a daily routine, traveling to a nearby cemetery to spend each day. Lo Yeahr had been able to buy a pony cart, with which he hauled groceries from market to the home and then to the cemetery. Much food was needed to feed the large group for the day. Early in the morning, the food was cooked and packed in tiffin boxes, large stacking containers designed to carry several courses.

Terence had to have his own special meals prepared. Nye Nye confided proudly to Molly, "We think he was an Indian monk in a previous life." She shared her reasoning, "Monks don't eat meat, and he has never wanted to eat meat. Just shrimp. I cook his meals separately to keep from mixing any meat with his food."

When the food was ready, the cart was packed with supplies for the day, and the women and children climbed aboard. Besides the driver, the cart could hold six adults at a time on facing benches, so two or more trips were made to transport everyone to the cemetery, where the party took shelter in a pavilion. Most of the men would walk the few miles each way, though someone would usually stay behind to protect the house from looters. Wat Hong's family came too, and the Ng's. They had to return to their homes before the evening curfew.

Nye Nye had made a baby carrier for Molly to hold Ah Hing on her back while she went about her few chores. The carrier was made in the traditional way, with scraps of brightly colored fabric, prints in blues and reds, sewn together like a quilt, and with four long strips of red-checked fabric sewn at the corners. These strips were pulled under Molly's arms and at her waist and tied in the front. It was a very practical tool and gave Ah Hing the comfort of her mother while freeing Molly's hands to work. Yet, Molly would often consider that the bright colors seemed both a beacon and a target to those fearful, noisy, war birds overhead.

According to Nye Nye's philosophy, the cemetery was a refuge because no one would waste bombs blowing up dead people. It seemed to Molly wise reasoning. She noted again that Nye Nye led the Lee family wisely and capably.

One day Molly was watching Nye Nye in action, taking command of the husband, the children, the maids, and other relations with military authority. Molly was quite impressed, and she herself was comforted to be in Nye Nye's confident care.

Terence noticed that Molly was watching his mother, and he whispered to her in English, "Imagine if your father had married my mother!"

Molly had to smother a laugh. She whispered back, "They would be very successful, but, oh! There would be fireworks!"

Terence laughed, causing a quick, stern look from his mother. But she was too busy to ask questions.

When she looked away, Terence risked another whisper to Molly, "And if my father married your mother?"

Molly smiled and whispered back, "Poor things! Who would take care of them?"

"Terence!" Nye Nye called, irritated by their secret and suspecting they were being impudent. "Go check the kitchen and make sure all of the food has been loaded!" Terence smiled at Molly and then obeyed his mother.

This would be an often repeated, very secret joke between them. Maybe they were being a bit disrespectful to the parents, but the picture was amusing. A smile is welcome anytime, but in war time each grin was a valuable commodity.

The pavilion at the cemetery was open on the sides, but it had a roof to protect from the searing sun and the torrential rain. There were a few tables and benches.

In this place, each day dawdled as if it had nowhere to go, no purpose but to pass slowly after others just like it, rudely dragging people along at this slow, repetitive pace. Everyone ached for something new.

Each one went habitually to the same bench and sat staring at the same nicks and stains in the pavilion floor and posts. Molly often found her eyes drawn to the pitiful, deformed feet of Nye Nye's mother. Though covered by the binding cloth and ornamental shoes, the misshapen feet were apparent to Molly's imagination. She knew that women whose feet had been bound so long must keep them wrapped; the feet had become accustomed to confinement so that to free them exposed them to great risk of injury. The fancy, toy-like shoes in other circumstances would have seemed very pretty, but Molly could see only the horror and cruelty the shoes represented.

Sometimes this grandmother would get up and step precariously after a young grandson, waving an item of clothing. She would call, "Wait! Here! Put on this shirt so you won't be chilled."

In her attempt to walk quickly she would wobble dangerously on her heels, often with a step back to catch her balance. Molly was sure the woman would fall and automatically jumped up to stand beside ready to catch her.

Nye Nye scolded her mother, "Sit down! You'll hurt yourself! The boys are big enough to take care of themselves!"

While no one seemed to have the energy otherwise for anything but basic conversation, little squabbles like these came up often. There was also the ongoing tension between the sisters-in-law Nye Nye and Wat Hong's widow. One day Wat Hong's widow confided to Molly, "Your mother-in-law says poetic things that hit from the side. I know what she's saying. I just ignore her." But Molly observed that she could not always keep quiet.

Molly could stay out of the quarrels with her elders, but her temper was short with Terence. She did not like this about herself, but she couldn't seem to help it.

Day after day, bickering words were spoken, children were tended, meals were prepared, and the cycle to and from the pavilion was repeated. The monotony was exhausting to the soul.

Nye Nye did often mention her concern for Puck Hee, the child born next after Terence. At age 13, this bright son had filled out the English application on his own and was accepted into a college in Bengal, India. He had sailed there with a guardian, with plans to earn a four-year medical doctor's degree. Nye Nye hoped the war had not gone to India, but she had not heard from this son, and she worried.

Molly also observed Nye Nye's particular attention to one poor maid. She scolded all of the girls, with stern, dignified commands, but especially she scolded Haung Se'ung, the young girl charged with watching Foke San. Molly thought Haung Se'ung herself needed care; instead the poor eight-year-old looked overwhelmed as she walked with the toddler balanced on her hip. Nye Nye was especially concerned that the girl keep Ah San's bamboo mat with her at all times.

"Haung Se'ung, do not leave Ah San's mat behind!" she would say. "Haung Se'ung! He may need to lie on it! Keep it rolled up neatly when he is not using it, and carry it with you. Haung Se'ung, do not forget Ah San's mat!"

Another maid, as Molly knew, was Nye Nye's own sister-in-law. Molly called her, as instructed, "Number Three Aunt," but despite the familial address the woman was treated as a servant, not as a family member. Molly remembered her own father's widowed sister-in-law who washed laundry in the streets to survive. There was little doubt that in Chinese culture the options for a young woman whose husband dies, even in a wealthy family, were limited. Number Three Aunt seemed grateful to be provided for along with her sons. She was very good natured and obedient. Molly couldn't imagine doing menial work for relatives all of her life.

Tedium was replaced with sudden fear when the family heard the hum of Allied plane engines and the whine and explosions of falling bombs. Morbid note was made of the location of the boiling cloud of smoke rising above the village. While one could be relieved at not being killed, one could never forget that people likely were killed, possibly innocents among them. Nor could one forget that the next bomb could maim, mutilate, or disintegrate his own flesh, sending his spirit into the next world to meet *Ngow-How* and *Mar-Meng*. When the catastrophic event seemed near the white brick house, all were in a panic for the relatives guarding it and concern that this home and possessions were lost.

Afterward, with apprehension, the refugees would return to their home on Eighth Street. One time, they returned to find Ninth Street had been bombed, and another time, they found Seventh Street had been bombed. The proximity to disaster was harrowing.

In these unlikely circumstances, Terence's Number Two Sister Fe Lan, or Lily, fell in love. Myo Khin was a half-Burmese half-Fokinese friend of Terence who lived in Pyapon. The former classmates happened to meet in the village, and Terence invited him to come for a visit. It was one of those rare evenings that the family came back to the house a little early, willing to risk danger for some socialization. That evening led to others, and Myo Khin took little time to decide he wanted Lily for his wife. Myo Khin was a very bright young man, and though part Burmese, Nye Nye said, he was cultured in Chinese and could write in Chinese, and his father was a shop owner of rice and dals, so she was pleased. The matchmaker was contacted, Myo Khin's father consented to the attachment, and Nye Nye planned the wedding. It all happened very quickly, and the young bride and groom seemed very happy. Conforming to tradition, the newlyweds lived with Myo Khin's father's household.

****

One day, when there had been no explosions for a while, Lo Yeahr bought a pig to butcher and everyone stayed home from the cemetery that day. In the courtyard of the house on Eighth Street, several people were just beginning to do the work of cutting the meat, planning to preserve it with salt. Molly was busy in the house with Ah Hing, but she occasionally glanced at the proceedings through a window. Suddenly the "in coming" sirens sounded, and Molly saw the men running for the cover of the lower level. For a moment Molly did not react, so odd was the vision of the men fleeing from the carcass of the pig. Soon, only the pig was left in the open courtyard, and still Molly stared, entranced, strangely curious to see whether or not the pig would explode. Bombs sounded nearby, and at last she remembered the danger to her and to her daughter, and she clutched Ah Hing and ran to the lower level.

The family heard a bomb explode very near their house. Maybe the Allies thought Japanese soldiers were butchering and wanted to destroy their provisions. Nye Nye scolded her husband, "You put us all at risk!"

But when the planes left and the "all clear" siren sounded, the pig was found to be intact, while buildings in the next street were aflame. The men went back to the work of preserving the pork.

Molly noted that her father-in-law was quite skillful in preserving food, and she wondered where he had learned these skills. Often, Lo Yeahr purchased a large number of high quality fish from local fishermen. He removed the head and gutted each fish, then salted it, stacked it, and let it ferment in a salt brine for a couple of weeks. When salt penetrated through the fish so that the flesh was translucent, he removed the fish from the brine and rinsed it. Then he pressed the fish to remove excess moisture and to flatten the flesh so it would dry better. Then he spread the fish out on a big, round, bamboo tray and left it to dry in the sunshine for about a week. These fish had very little bone and much tasty meat. In fact, the enterprise was so successful, he bought more fish by the box, and produced enough extra salt fish to ship to Rangoon to sell. Perhaps Lo Yeahr was not as wise and ambitious as Molly's father or his own driven wife, but this man was determined and able to help his family survive.

Still, there was never any question who was in charge of the Lee household. One night, Molly saw her in-laws in the backyard of the house. Lo Yeahr was digging and Nye Nye was bossing him. One of Nye Nye's nephews was helping them. Molly was too tired to worry about what they were doing, but she thought absently about the spongy, water-logged soil of the delta area, knowing that if Lo Yeahr dug very deep, the hole would fill with water.

****

Terence was sent on a trip to Rangoon for some family business. He didn't tell Molly about the purpose of the trip until he came back to Pyapon, not wanting to worry her more than necessary. When he returned after a few days, he was quite ill.

He waited for an opportunity to speak to Molly alone and explained, "My mother wanted me to go to Rangoon to exchange a gold bar for cash."

Terence complained, "You know no one wants to use the Japanese bills! You just look at them, and you can see they are worthless! We keep only a few to use when the Japanese are watching."

Terence went on, "Most shopkeepers still prefer to take the British bills, so we did not turn in most of our currency for the fake Japanese bills. But we must use the British bills very secretly."

Molly remembered walking around Mandalay with Terence. She had noticed then his secretive use of British currency.

She agreed. "We dare not risk angering the Japanese. They will kill people for any reason or no reason."

"Yes. So we were running out of Japanese bills, and my mother wanted me to go to Rangoon to get more," Terence continued. "She made me a special belt so I could keep the gold bar concealed under my shirt. She warned me never to remove the belt."

"Oh," Molly said, "Nye Nye is smart, very savvy. But were you in danger? What happened? Why are you so ill?"

Terence explained, "For the trip to Rangoon, I stood on the open deck of the steamboat. The monsoon winds blew, the water was rough, and heavy rain soaked all of the passengers, including me. I was afraid someone would see that I had something hidden under my wet shirt. I was wearing my longyi, and I hoped the knot in front would conceal the belt."

Molly commented, "...good idea that you wore Burmese clothing, Terence, not Chinese or western. That was better to hide the belt."

"Also, I didn't want to stand out as being different and attract attention," Terence continued. Concern marked his face as he recounted the difficult journey, "Even with the longyi, I was afraid to move and risk exposing the bulge of the belt and gold bar. When the rain stopped, I didn't dare remove my wet shirt because the belt would have been exposed. These are desperate times, and robbers are everywhere ready to steal. They don't think twice about killing to steal.

"I didn't dare move," He repeated solemnly. "No matter how wet I got, I had to stand there. I got chilled and could hardly stop shaking. Later, after I got to Rangoon, I got very sick."

"Oh my...." Molly was full of concern for him. She was glad Terence had returned safely from the journey. What if something had happened to him? Now she found that she could bring her husband a glass of water.

Terence recovered very slowly, but never to his previous health. After that, he often told Molly he could feel his heart beat irregularly.

Poor Terence. He had not wanted this life for Molly or for his daughter. The war was wearing him down. And now with the lingering effects of illness, he was finding difficulty in keeping his spirits up.

But Terence did find a comfort for his frustrations in singing. He discovered a Kayin neighbor who was a very talented piano player. So Terence and a friend, another Chinese refugee from Rangoon whom Terence happened to meet in Pyapon, would go to the neighbor's home to sing as she played piano. Terence had a good, strong, tenor voice, and he sang with boisterous, operatic style. At that time, his favorite song, made famous by Enrico Caruso, was "Santa Lucia," sung with Italian lyrics. Terence seemed to be cheered when belting out this song about a beautiful city and an evening boat ride, moonlight reflecting in the water, sailboats sailing softly in the gentle breeze.

Those in the streets and neighboring houses of Pyapon could hear him, and, though the words were foreign, they were cheered by Terence's exuberance. Molly, occupied with duties at the Lee home, could hear through the window the longing for freedom in his voice. She shared his longing.

****

But freedom was a dream and oppression was the reality. One day as the family was making the evening return from the cemetery to the house on Eighth Street, Molly was to experience one of the most terrifying moments of her life.

Not only would she fear for herself. For all the inconvenience and irritation he caused her, Terence had become dear to her, and already she couldn't imagine living without him. Now also Ah Hing was knit to her heart, and young brothers-in-law and sisters-in-law were owning her affections.

After another long day in the cemetery, Terence hitched the pony to the cart and loaded the supplies. Then he helped Molly into the cart and gave her Ah Hing to hold in her lap. Terence helped his mother and the other children into the cart, then climbed to the driver's bench with his father. The trip to the cemetery had become too difficult for Nye Nye's mother, her bound feet continuing to cripple her, so she and her devoted daughter-in-law and grandsons risked staying in the lower level of the Eighth Street house for the day.

Terence called in American cowboy vernacular to his Burmese pony, "Giddy-up!" and the bilingual pony began his slow journey pulling the full load the few miles back to village.

Suddenly, Molly heard the whine of approaching aircraft, flying low, and she tensed with fear. She knew that when the Allied planes came flying low this way, they fired machine guns at their targets instead of dropping bombs. Sirens started wailing! The little party was completely exposed! Molly's stomach seemed to jump to her throat and her bowels to her feet!

Terence stopped the pony and yelled to the adults and children, "*Fie ya! Fie ya!* Hurry! Hurry! Get out of the cart! Get in the ditch! *Fie htwe ya!* Really hurry!"

"Ya" was the Cantonese verbal exclamation point, and at Terence's command, each one obeyed. Molly leapt from the cart with Ah Hing and fell face down into the muddy ditch, instinctively covering Ah Hing with her body to protect her. Her mother-in-law scrambled into the trench near her, clutching Foke San, and Lo Yeahr pressed his large frame into the ditch. The man and the two women used arms and legs to pull the other children under the shelter of their bodies.

Molly heard Terence racing away with the pony cart, urging the pony to gallop faster. "Giddy-up! Giddy-up! Ha!"

What was he doing? Why didn't he take cover in the trench with them?

As one plane passed very low overhead, Molly looked up to see that it was chasing her husband down the street! The plane swooped lower, like an eagle after doomed prey.

Her mind cried out, "No!" but no sound came from her gaping mouth. She waited in horror for deadly machine gun to erupt. The cart was careening from side to side as the pony, now spooked by the terrifying, howling predator chasing him, ran for his life.

Molly realized that her husband was drawing the plane away from her, away from his daughter, away from his parents and siblings. It was all happening so fast, and yet, for Molly, it seemed to materialize in torturous slowness as she lay helplessly in the ditch, clinging tightly to her daughter and watching her husband's impossible attempt to flee from the killing machine.

As terror stretched the moment intolerably, the pursuing plane finally swept over Terence and the pony, angled its nose upward and, to Molly's wonder, climbed into the sky. Not a shot had been fired at Terence!

Would the plane circle back to attack? No. *Piya!* The airplane gained altitude and joined in formation with the others, and the sound of their engines slowly faded in the distance.

Molly felt faint with relief. She was overwhelmed with gratitude to whatever Power had protected her husband. She was also thankful to the gunner who restrained his trigger finger as he carefully discerned that her husband was not his enemy. A less heedful eye, a less cautious gunner, a less steady finger and.... Molly was ill to think of the horror that so nearly occurred.

Terence slowed the gasping pony and turned him around as the sirens sang "all clear." More than ever the swelling sound seemed to call to those who survived, "Come, you are still alive!"

Terence returned to where he had left his passengers in the trench and found them moving slowly, as they dimly comprehended that the ordeal was over. He helped Molly to stand. They brushed mud off of Ah Hing, and Molly tried to reassure her daughter and stop her from crying. But Molly's voice was quavering uncontrollably, and she had to give up cooing to Ah Hing. With trembling hand, she tenderly brushed debris from the clothes of the other children. Nothing was said as the shaken group reassembled in the pony cart to return to the white brick house on Eighth Street.

****

Word came from the village chief that the Allies had retaken northern Burma and were chasing the Japanese army south. The Japanese were leaving as much damage as they could in the wake of their retreat. Soldiers with a reputation for brutality were more violent and destructive than ever as they withdrew angrily, with lost face, from Burma.

Among the expected instructions for heightened caution and security, the village chief gave this unusual order, "Anyone with a camera or film must throw it into the pond. The Japanese are accusing anyone with a camera of being a spy for the British, and he is shot instantly and also those who are with him. They are searching houses. You must throw your camera into the pond or you are jeopardizing yourself and this community! No exceptions! Throw all cameras and all film into the pond!"

Was the rumor true? There was no choice but to obey. With regret, Terence took his little camera, which still held the film that recorded his and Molly's second wedding ceremony, to the railing that surrounded the village pond. He hesitated only a moment. Even if he wanted to risk hiding it, other people already knew about the camera and might report him. Few in Pyapon had cameras and no one would tolerate his endangering others to keep his. So, he sadly tossed the camera into the pond.

The message about the Japanese retreat and the Allied pursuit had come quickly. The process to reach the end of hostilities took much longer. Now, when freedom from the Japanese occupation seemed near, each day continued to pass with aching slowness. With bombing from planes halted and ground troops expected, the trips to the cemetery were stopped. Instead, citizens of Pyapon, the Lees included, confined themselves in their homes, and waited. Each day was filled with fear that at any moment the stillness would be shattered by a terrible pounding at the door and a terrifying search by cruel Japanese soldiers. No one could stop them from taking whatever they wanted or from doing whatever they would do. Molly knew that Terence, having both abundant love and abundant bravery, would defend her to the death. She passionately prayed to Lord Jesus that it would not come to that.

****

One early evening, it happened suddenly: a dreadful pounding at the door thundered through the house! Everyone, young and old, stood still, immobilized in cold fear! Everyone watched the door, each one picturing the very thing he hoped against: the door thrust open violently and furious Japanese soldiers plunging through it!

Molly pulled Ah Hing close to her chest, and Terence moved himself protectively between Molly and the door. The sound came more firmly, "Boom! Boom! Boom!"

Molly felt her knees weakening. Moments stretched to interminable lengths, enveloping past and future. Memories, seeming in the distance to belong to someone else, peeked through the fog at Molly and drifted near, almost touching, but not quite, as if the displaced faces and events were too painful to fully own and let go in their passing... loving Mama and frowning Papa... Moonlight in her dancing dress and heels... the sweet young sisters and brothers... never to be seen again. Then in the same fog came the ir-revocable, impending future: Japanese soldiers, faces contorted in hatred, a horrible explosion of warriors, bursting through the thin wooden barrier and killing all of these loved ones!

Lo Yeahr could no longer ignore the knocking. He collected his cour-age and went bravely to answer the door and be the first to die.

Unable to see what he saw, everyone in the house watched as Lo Yeahr opened the door and flinched. Then he stood at the door, staring, his face pale. The moments continued to pass slowly, bloated as they were with fear.

At last Lo Yeahr's expression changed, and he graciously motioned for the soldiers to come into his home. He had lost his mind!

The soldiers came flooding in, and Molly cried out! But, as even as the sound of her fear went forth, she was realizing that the reality didn't match her expectation.

Slowly, as dawn exposes the fiction of what seems real in darkness, the angry faces of Japanese soldiers turned into the kind and grinning western faces of soldiers wearing the uniforms of the long lost British! She stood, clinging to Ah Hing, as Terence turned and looked at her, his face a mystery of tension and relief. Love and jeopardy had nearly wrung his heart to its painful limit.

Nye Nye was not slow to react to the situation. Once again, Molly watched with comfort and admiration as her mother-in-law went to work. Calling Terence to translate into English, Nye Nye invited the soldiers to stay for dinner. She ordered the maids to their duties, preparing food and a place on the ground floor for a party. She instructed that all the desks in the room must be slid together along the wall to form a long table, and a feast was quickly assembled from Nye Nye's generous stores. Fish and shrimp, pork and chicken, rice, and, even now, fresh vegetables and fruits appeared by Nye Nye's magic.

When the preparations were completed, Nye Nye announced grandly, translated by Terence, "You fine soldiers have worked so hard. Now eat your meal leisurely."

And the festivities began! The odd comrades, Chinese civilians and British soldiers, took great pleasure each in the others' company to celebrate the monumental occasion. No one of them had experienced anything that paralleled this present joy. After so many consuming years of obligatory warring in the most intolerable conditions, the soldiers knew that they could soon leave their perilous service and go back to happier lives, simply being husbands and dads, laborers and businessmen. And the Lees could stop running, stop hiding, stop fearing, and begin to work, to rebuild, and to thrive again. In this atmosphere, Terence continued to translate occasion-ally, but the shared smiles, the mutual appreciation, and the unanimous joy needed no interpretation.

Molly was fascinated watching the soldiers. She had never before observed soldiers this closely, and these men were nothing like she expected. They were joking and laughing, full of friendliness toward each other and toward their hosts. Oh, they enjoyed eating! It occurred to Molly that perhaps it had been a while since these men had eaten well.

After the meal, the soldiers graced their hosts with entertainment they would never forget. A couple of soldiers started playing harmonicas, filling the room with a sweet and mournful sound that made Molly want to laugh and cry at once. Then other men sang another, cheerful song with the harmonicas, "You Are My Sunshine."

Then several of the men sang songs in the four-part a capella harmony of a barbershop quartet, the lead singer warbling melody, a tenor harmoniz-ing in a pitch above, and bass and baritone completing the chord in notes below. The audience laughed when the tenor sang falsetto high notes or when the bass rumbled as if from the bottom of a well. The talented men sang expertly, tingling ears as they slipped sweetly from major to minor to seventh chords. It was so enjoyable!

Then, oh, the dancing and carrying on! The men were waltzing with each other, in time to the happy harmonica tunes, and next they were linking arms and circling in a country square dance. They danced a funny Irish jig, arms straight down at the sides, feet turned out, stepping and hopping. Then the harmonicas played a tune with a Spanish flair, and Molly recognized the dance as several of the men paired up for exaggerated long steps and quick head snaps of the Argentine tango. Oh, they looked so comical! The more clownish they were, the more their hosts laughed and encouraged them to more antics. One man dipped his partner, holding him in a deep back bend, and the spectators roared. Molly was pleased to see how much Nye Nye and Lo Yeahr were enjoying themselves, as was every soul. Even little Ah Hing was laughing at all the merriment.

It was long past evening and going in to late night when the soldiers prepared to leave. They had work to finish in Burma in the coming days. But, they were sorry to leave their hosts, and the Lees were sorry to let them go.

"Cheerio!" called each of the Englishmen.

Nye Nye mimicked in the foreign tongue, "Cheerio!"

Little Foke San echoed his mother, "Cheerio!" Oh, it was good to laugh!

****

The family had endured much danger and hardship during the war, so they were cautious about returning to Rangoon. But that changed the day Terence came to the house, breathless and his face flushed with joy, announcing, "The war is over! The Japanese have unconditionally surrendered to the Allies!" Someone had heard the report on a radio, and news spread through the streets faster than if phone lines had connected the homes. The news was echoed and celebrated throughout Pyapon.

The Japanese accepted surrender to the Allies on August 14, 1945. The ceremony of official surrender took place in Tokyo Bay aboard the American battleship the *USS Missouri* on September 2, 1945. High ranking Allied military officials from China, the Soviet Union, The British Empire, France, Netherlands, Australia, New Zealand, The United States of America, and Canada were present to receive the surrender of the Japanese Empire from the foreign minister of Japan. Allied Commander, American General

Douglas MacArthur, read a speech that was broadcast around the world: "It is my earnest hope – indeed the hope of all mankind – that from this solemn occasion a better world shall emerge out of the blood and carnage of the past, a world founded upon faith and understanding, a world dedicated to the dignity of man and the fulfillment of his most cherished wish for freedom, tolerance, and justice."

This broadcast reached Pyapon, and Terence heard it with a group huddled around a neighbor's radio. He brought the news back to his family.

On September 13, 1945, the Japanese in Burma also surrendered.

Chapter Fourteen

The New Normal

Now there was an urgency to return to Rangoon. The Lees knew that their home and dry goods shop were lost, but the soy sauce factory must be possessed as quickly as possible. Who knew whether squatters might move in and whether laws would be enforced immediately? A few loose ends must be tied in Pyapon, including arranging to have someone sell the house.

So as soon as they could, the Lees packed up and headed back to the capital city. Before they left, Molly saw Nye Nye hovering over Lo Yeahr as he dug in the yard and pulled up an old kerosene can.

"Oh, I see!" Molly said to herself, admiring them with the realization, "This is must be where they hid their valuables... gold bars and jewelry."

The few ferries were busier than ever, bringing the waves of cautiously eager refugees back to the city. Maybe Molly was better prepared than some, for she had seen the devastation of Mandalay and was aware of the extensive damage to Chinatown in Rangoon. Still, the return to Rangoon was oppressive. Most of Molly's grandfather's businesses, including the dry goods store and the restaurant and opera house, as well as her father's club, were all destroyed. Somehow the Number One Uncle's four-story house remained, as did his restaurant and hotel. But it was hardly a jubilant homecoming for anyone.

The ravaging effects of four years of war were everywhere. She did not see for herself, but Molly heard from Terence that the Chin apartment had been bombed, so that only partial walls remained of the second story, and anything that survived the blast had been looted. Molly imagined that

Papa's Anglo-Indian boy, Ah Hem, may have had to sell furnishings to survive, and no one would blame him if he did. Harder to consider, the loyal young man may have been a casualty of war. In any case, he was never seen again.

Molly asked Terence specifically about the wardrobe in the second floor apartment, and he had to tell her it was gone. So there was no precious copy book containing Molly's careful calligraphy of the wonderful old Chinese sayings Ah Baht Sook had recited for her.

The suffering and loss of life from the war was almost too big to think about and too big to feel, but the loss of her copy book... this small thing represented the greater losses to Molly, and this she felt deeply. She had worked so hard to save those wise sayings and now they were lost to her forever. Those carefree, gentle, innocent days of her childhood were also lost.

Molly thought of other precious things. She missed her hymn book with the beautiful, touching words. She missed the book of encouraging Scripture verses from the Bible. And she knew that the lovely letter Grandfather Wong wrote to Mama before he died also had been tucked away in Mama's wardrobe. Molly longed to see and hold these things again, but all were gone.

People did not speak of these material losses. Everyone had lost so much, no one really wanted to talk about it or hear others talk about it. And of course, to complain of material things when so many innocent lives had been taken was callous. In Rangoon, as in many of the war zones of World War II, one needed to acknowledge the current reality, to accept that things could never again be as they were before the war, and to make the best of the present circumstance. By focusing on the present and working for the future, one could maybe gain emotional distance from the horrible events of the recent past

Molly's thoughts were never far from that distant village of Namhsan. She was sick with worry. She had no idea how her family had fared since she left. Now she belonged to Terence's family, but her heart was tied also to the family into which she was born. She frightened herself with the thought that she did not know even whether or not they had survived. She remembered her long ago prayer to Lord Jesus. Had he heard her prayer? Was he able to protect her family? Would he care enough to do this?

****

When they arrived at the soy sauce factory compound on Prome Road, the Lee caretaker showed them around the grounds, first pointing out a large crater where a bomb had been dropped and pieces of sharp metal had scattered great distances in the yard. The old, bent-over man described a terror that had not diminished with time. Fragments of the bomb had shot out in all directions when it exploded, and if he had been near it, he could have been maimed or killed. Fortunately, he had heard the plane coming and was hiding inside a giant wok on the premises. He showed them the wok, and sure enough, Molly thought, it looked big enough to cook a man, like the one described in the hell of Chinese tradition. The bitter thought flashed through her mind that boiling in oil would be fitting punishment for the aggressors who had caused the terrible war.

Terence showed Molly the bomb shelter his mother had ordered to be constructed, where the family stayed until conditions got so bad that they no longer felt safe even in this refuge. Molly noticed it was nicely paneled, and it would have been a relatively comfortable place to hide and protect the Lee children. Once again, she admired her mother-in-law's foresight and resourcefulness.

Terence asked the caretaker how he was able to get food to survive. The caretaker told them he was fortunate that soybeans continued to ferment in large pots on the grounds, providing him with something of value to swap for food. Every few days he would collect a couple bottles full of the renowned soy sauce to trade.

He also showed them the sign that the Lee's Japanese friend Dr. Sato, the doctor who had treated Moonlight and perhaps saved her life, posted to Japanese soldiers, asking them to respect the property. He had printed in Japanese characters, saying, "Soldiers, you are welcome to stay here. Please do not damage or confiscate this house. Signed, Dr. Sato." The soldiers had honored the doctor's request.

As the caretaker was speaking with them, they suddenly heard the close sound of airplane engines. It was not the distant sound of planes approaching from overhead. The noise was immediately upon them, and they instinctively looked for cover. The caretaker explained that the Mingalandon airport that served Burma's capital was very close, and Allied planes were still taking off from there. No wonder the Lees did not want to stay here during the war when sounds of one airforce or another came frequently.

****

The soy sauce factory became the permanent home of the Lee family. The family referred to it as "Eight Mile" because it was eight miles from the city of Rangoon. It was relatively unharmed, except for the one crater and bomb fragments. There were several buildings on the ten acre property, including a tiny guard shack, a pawn shop, a big house built for the family as a hot season retreat, an old house where soy sauce factory workers once stayed, and a few other old buildings. All of the buildings were one story, but they were raised many feet above ground level, a necessary precaution for monsoon season flooding. Paddy fields and water buffalo could be seen near the compound.

Molly realized she had a vague childhood memory of this place. She remembered the big house decorated with ribbons and recalled people throwing confetti. Then she realized that she and her aunt had attended the ceremony to dedicate this house when it was built, back when she was a young girl attending Chinese school. She remembered that rites were made to appease the gods and that a lavish banquet was served to guests. Tradition held that only after such a ceremony was it considered safe for a family to move in to a home. The Lee family could then enjoy these hot season quarters when they needed a retreat from the city's oppressive heat.

Now the Lee family stayed together at the big house. The elder Ngs lived in the old house on the property. For a short while, Anita and Dr. Ng and their two sons stayed on the grounds as well. Dr. Ng continued to keep a goat for milk for his children, but Nye Nye had a short temper about the goat. She would leave her clothes to air out in the sun, and the goat took pleasure in dashing them to the ground with his horns, stamping on them, and chewing them.

Molly heard her angry words, "Lock up your goat! He has damaged my clothes!"

Really, Nye Nye could not be blamed for her ire. Clothing was precious. But, so was the goat. Before long, Dr. Ng bought a house for his family in Golden Valley.

Nye Nye's mother also left the soy sauce factory. She decided to go back to China, taking with her Nye Nye's sister-in-law and nephews. Likely, wartime experiences in Burma made memories sweet of a poor little Chinese village. So Nye Nye was left to do the patriarch's grave-tending duties, and the others went back to their homeland. Molly didn't hear about them again.

****

Molly continued her duties to the ancestors early every morning, making fresh tea and filling cups: three cups for the ancestors to win their favor, one cup for Guan Yin to appeal for mercy, one cup for the god of the earth to secure prosperity and property, one for the door guardian to bargain for protection, and one for the kitchen god to solicit bounty. As Nye Nye preferred, Molly burned three incense sticks for each god. Then, each morning, Molly presented Nye Nye with a hot cup of tea. She continued to help care for her mother-in-law's young children. Sometimes she couldn't avoid helping in the kitchen, but Molly knew she never did enough to please Nye Nye.

Her mother-in-law never bossed or scolded Molly. In fact, she rarely directly asked Molly for help. She was too dignified for that and spoke in the low, even tones becoming her station. But Molly quickly understood Nye Nye's look of displeasure. And Nye Nye communicated volumes in the way she made mention of the Chinese ways since ancient times and of strict loyalties and duties. Both women knew, "Respect for one's parents is the highest duty of civil life," and Molly's duty was now to her husband's parents.

Also Nye Nye could make her expectations known by referring to other daughters-in-law who were of more help: "The wife of Puck Ken works so hard for all the family! She cooks! She cleans! She washes clothes! She irons! She is a wonderful daughter-in-law!"

Nye Nye did not expect her own children help with household chores, as this would reflect poorly on her status. But daughters-in-law were often considered servants in traditional Chinese culture. Molly knew the saying, "The patience of a daughter-in-law results from her desire to become a mother-in-law of the future."

But Molly resisted. Frankly, not only was Molly inept in the kitchen, (challenged even to boil water!), but she was too proud to split wood, tend fires, and cook meals. Molly accused Terence of being spoiled, but maybe she had been rather spoiled herself. Byu Goo and Pwa Pwa had chased her out of the kitchen saying, "You hinder us!"

She knew her mother-in-law was aware that she had never done labor, but she would not dare remind her. She knew Nye Nye had promised her mother she would never have to do labor, but she would not dare remind her. Surely, Nye Nye felt that the present situation had changed everything. She needed help, Chinese tradition was in her favor, and her own laudable adaptation to disintegrating circumstances were unspoken arguments that Ngood should serve her.

Molly's upbringing did include training that a woman should respect and obey her mother-in-law. So, besides the tension between Nye Nye and

Molly, there was always tension within Molly to both respect her elder and to maintain her dignity. She tried to compromise and do what she could do to please her mother-in-law.

Sometimes it seemed that Nye Nye was two different people. She could be angry and scolding, even slipping occasionally from her usual dignified demeanor. Other times she could be so very sweet and thoughtful. Molly heard Wat Hong's wife using the Chinese saying, "The mouth is two pieces of flesh," in referring to Nye Nye. Truly, the same mouth could say good and bad, and Molly never knew quite what to expect.

Terence sometimes intervened for Molly, but Molly would later scold him. "Don't argue with her! She is your mother! You must give her respect. Besides, it only makes things worse. After you argue with her, she thinks I am to blame."

Often, Molly continued to lecture him, "Maybe the elders of the house are wrong, but that's okay. Stay quiet. And if you must say something, Terence, please be diplomatic. You are too frank with your mother."

Now sometimes Terence reacted with anger to Molly's scolding. He would curse and answer, "Yeah! That's what you think!" Later, when he had time to cool off, he would apologize to Molly. But, truly, Molly felt the heaviness of duty to her demanding mother-in-law, and Terence felt the unhappiness of his wife.

****

Ngood noticed that after a meal, Nye Nye would begin talking while sipping Johnnie Walker scotch whiskey. Whiskey was thought to be beneficial to a nursing mother, and Nye Nye had done enough nursing over the years to have grown accustomed to drinking regularly. Molly noticed that Lo Yeahr and the children slipped away one by one as Nye Nye began to talk, leaving Ngood to listen.

Nye Nye could be talkative with *chiung hee* "too much air," as the Chinese expression went, or with *shah shay* "long tongue" as the Burmese would say. Molly herself could share these tendencies at times, but she could also listen. She really enjoyed hearing Nye Nye's stories, so she was pleased to show respect to her mother-in-law by listening and learning of family history.

"My father lived in *Me Kok*, 'Beautiful Country' for many years," Nye Nye would say. "He started a laundry business in *Khem Sun*, 'Golden Mountain.' Every six years he would come back to *Joang Kok* to visit my mother and give her another baby. While he was away, he regularly sent money home to the family."

Not realizing that the United States of America was quite big, the Chinese stories about Me Kok reflected the notion that "The Golden Mountain," or San Francisco, was typical of the wealth throughout nation. The San Francisco gold rush of 1849 continued to fuel exaggerated stories of the wealth to be found in the country.

"You know, we do not say *Khem Sun* for no reason," Nye Nye continued. People there sometimes find gold nuggets lying on the ground, and they only need to pick up the things and they are rich. My father did not find gold nuggets, but he did well in his laundry business. When my father became old, one of my brothers took over the business at *Khem Sun*. My father returned to *Joang Kok*, 'Central Country.' "

Though most people did not find gold nuggets in the street, many Chinese did find wealth in the United States through opportunity and hard work. Nye Nye's father was one such man.

Nye Nye continued, "Then a few years after I came here to Burma, my father brought my mother and their children here also. My father died long ago. You never met him. He was an excellent man."

Ngood remarked, "My father also brought my mother's family out from China."

"Yes," replied Nye Nye. "Life in the villages of China could be very difficult. Floods and famine are common there. For many Chinese, Burma offered better opportunities and even wealth." Nye Nye was quiet for a moment, reflecting.

Molly also learned more about the Lee ancestors to whom she had been introduced at her second wedding. Nye Nye showed her pictures as well.

"The father of Sit Hong was a very wealthy man. You cannot dream of such wealth," Nye Nye continued in dignified monotones and formal language. "My father-in-law Lee Ah Poi came here from China, looking for a better life. He had seen his own mother die of starvation in the village. I am told that she had only pretended to eat so that enough food would be left to feed the men and the children, while she herself starved. After his mother died, Ah Poi, fifteen years old, left China by junk to Singapore, a long and dangerous journey. He then made his way north to Penang, Malaysia where he learned carpentry skills. A British contractor offered him carpentry work in the Andaman Islands, and from there he came to Burma. He always worked very hard. Even in his spare time, he made boxes to earn extra money. When other carpenters took time off, he continued to work. Because of his work ethic and workmanship, he won the attention of British authorities and was hired to build barracks for British soldiers. Again he worked hard, and he invested his money until he could buy a teak timber mill, then a rice mill, and later many other businesses including this soy sauce factory. Also, he opened the pawn shop here at Eight Mile."

In the hesitation, Ngood asked politely, "Pawn shop?" This was unfamiliar to her.

"Yes. People could pawn clothing or jewels for cash, and if they could not redeem the items in the agreed amount of time, the possessions became the property of Ah Poi. In all these businesses he made his fortune. Ah Poi was so well-off, he brought many relatives from China to help him.

"Long before I came to Burma, Ah Poi married a Burmese woman, but she could not give him any sons, only daughters. Ah Poi adopted an Indian boy for good luck, so the son could show the way for new sons to follow, but still his wife produced no sons, only daughters, five in all. Everyone told him, 'Ah Poi, see, you have made a lot of money already and you have no one to inherit it. You must have a son so you can leave him your fortune. Find another wife so you can have a son. Get a wife from China.' That is what they told him."

This line of reasoning was not a shock to Ngood. Though she had been educated enough to feel the injustice that daughters were thought of as lesser offspring and that wives were blamed for not bearing sons and were replaced callously, Ngood was sadly familiar with these hard customs. She nodded, not in agreement, but in understanding.

"So, he was quite old, but he brought out a young woman from China and married her. This wife also bore him many daughters, but she did give Ah Poi three sons. So, Number One Son of Ah Poi was the Indian boy. Number Two Son died at age twelve. The remaining sons of Ah Poi were Number Three Son Wat Hong and

Chinese wife, Lee Ah Poi, and Burmese wife.

your father-in-law Number Four Son Sit Hong. Lee Ah Poi was more than

Chinese wife with children, including adoped son to far right, Sit Hong on far left, and Wat Hong seated right of his mother.

sixty years old when Sit Hong was born.

"Sometime after the Chinese wife gave Ah Poi his sons, she heard from gossips that the Burmese wife was jealous and doing voodoo magic against her, trying to make her die. The Chinese wife, your father-in-law's mother, was afraid and felt she had to leave Burma. She took her children and went back to her village in China. But she could not stay there."

"Why couldn't she stay there, Nye Nye?" Ngood asked curiously.

"She heard rumors that bad people had taken notice that she was wealthy and were planning to kidnap her sons for ransom. So she took the young sons and her daughters and walked a difficult journey at night to Doushan, a town of Taishan in southwestern Guangdong, China. A short time later the Chinese wife died there in the smallpox epidemic. When Ah Poi heard of this, he set sail to get the children and bring them back to Burma. Sit Hong was only 11 years old then."

Lee Wat Hong and Lee Sit Hong

Nye Nye continued, "When Sit Hong was old enough to marry, the matchmaker came to my village looking for a wife for him. Matchmaker came by boat, and the journey took her more than a month, she told us. She told my parents that the family of Sit Hong was very wealthy. So, of course, my parents arranged the match. I had never left my village except to visit my sister in another village, and it took me several hours to walk to see her, so I did not go often.

"When I first came from China and married Sit Hong, my ten fingers never touched the water. My hands were soft and beautiful. I had many maids to serve me, many beautiful clothes to wear, and many parties to attend.

"When Lee Ah Poi was eighty years old, his son Wat Hong gave him a birthday party," Nye Nye said. "It was an extravagant party! Many, many people were there. Each guest received a fine new suit of clothing from Ah Poi."

Lee Chin Htwe Khim

Nye Nye didn't describe the suits, but Ngood pictured the likely clothing, probably for the men guests only, Chinese pants and a jacket with a Mandarin collar. Perhaps the jacket was double breasted, but certainly it was adorned with traditional, fancy, filigree, hand-made button clasps. As the wealthy host, Ah Poi's own suit likely had buttons hand-carved from jade or perhaps even molded from gold. Likely the dong had been reserved and a lavish luncheon served.

As Ngood imagined these details, Nye Nye was quiet, contented, picturing that opulent occasion. Then she concluded the story and added her comentary.

"Live chickens in cages were given to Ah Poi as birthday gifts. Ah Poi was concerned that the chickens were not being given proper care, and he went to feed them, but he slipped and fell," she said, shaking her head slightly. "He never recovered from the fall and died three days later. You know what they say, 'Never celebrate your birthday, or soon after you will die.' "

Nye Nye added, a sudden bitterness in her voice, "Wat Hong got everything. We had to fight for what little we got."

****

At another after-dinner-chat with Nye Nye, Ngood learned things she did not know about her spouse. Nye Nye began with familiar lines one day, "I am sure that Puck Ying was an Indian monk in an earlier life. That is why his dietary needs are special."

Ngood answered patiently, "Yes, Nye Nye." She knew her mother-in-law had a very high opinion of her eldest son. Molly did not mention that Terence had confided to her that a maid who hand fed him when he was a young boy would scold him if he ate meat. In this way he learned to refuse to eat meat. When he was grown, he guessed that the maid herself had wanted to eat his meat. Nye Nye never knew of this.

"Yes," Nye Nye continued, "Even when he was a boy, he did not want to eat meat. I knew then he was exceptional. But, he was not an easy child to raise. He was *kai seung*, a 'naughty child.' He kept me very busy paying the mothers of Chinatown."

"What?" Ngood asked, curiosity aroused.

Nye Nye shook her head slightly as she envisioned the wild boy of her memory. "You remember visiting our dry goods store *Kwong Hep Seng* with your aunt, Han Yee? And we lived above the shop?"

Molly nodded. "Oh yes. We often went there to visit Choon Fong."

"Yes." Nye Nye sighed and said what Molly knew already, "*Kwong Hep Seng* was bombed in the war."

For a moment, Nye Nye's face showed that she mourned the lost business and home. Then she repeated the Chinese saying, "Earth people always calculate, but the gods calculate more," meaning, "whatever you plan, the gods are in ultimate control."

After a sympathetic nod from Ngood, Nye Nye went on, "One time the mother of one of Puck Ying's playmates came angrily into the store, dragging along her son. She said, 'See! Your son beat my son! Oh, yes! Your Puck Ying hit my boy! Just look at his bruises! My poor boy came home crying and told me what your son did, and I said, 'I know his mother! She should know what her son is doing!' Puck Ying is such a menace! You should deal with him harshly!' "

Recalling the confrontation, Nye Nye smiled slightly, "She was a rough one and ready for a fight."

Nye Nye continued, "What could I do? I said..." and Nye Nye's voice became high and patronizing, " 'Oh, I am so sorry. Oh, I hope your boy will be all right.' Then I reached into my pocket and brought out a few notes. I said, 'My son has no manners. He should not be fighting with other children. Will this help? Maybe you can buy some medicine.'

"Right away she shut her mouth. She took the money, perhaps to buy Chinese medicine, but likely not. Anyway, she was satisfied.

"Then we had to discipline Puck Ying. Imagine the disgrace of having someone come to the shop to complain about Puck Ying fighting! I told his father, and you know, Sit Hong did not beat his children. But when he found Puck Ying hiding upstairs, he did beat him because he was so angry that Puck Ying had disgraced us. Puck Ying did not resist the beating. His father was still so angry, he took Puck Ying to the roof and chained him there to punish him."

Ngood exclaimed, "Oh my! How old was Puck Ying then?"

Nye Nye replied, "Oh, I think around twelve years old.

"Later that same evening, another parent came to complain, 'Your son beat my son! Just look at his bruises!'

"But I said, 'No, it could not be Puck Ying, because his father chained him to the roof.'

"The woman argued, 'No! No! Listen to what I am telling you! Your son beat my son! Go look for yourself! He must have flown away from your roof, because he fought my son!'

"Sure enough, Sit Hong sent one of the maids to look, and she came back and said, 'Puck Ying is not there! He has slipped away!'

"What else could I do?" Nye Nye asked, and then she answered her own question. "I had to reach into my pocket again and apologize for my son. Somehow, while he was up on the roof, he had managed to get free of the chain. Then, because he did not dare come back into the house, I think he jumped from our roof to the roof of our neighbors."

Young Terence and friend

Nye Nye was shaking her head again. "After that, we could not stop Puck Ying from fighting. I always had to keep money in my pocket to pay the mothers of the beaten boys. They would come in very angry, but as soon as I reached into my pocket, they were quickly mollified. In fact, they left smiling, no longer worried about the injuries of their sons."

Later, Molly told Terence that his mother had recounted this story. "You were a bully!" she accused him.

But he said, "No, Molly. I was a bully's bully. I would fight boys that were picking on others. The ones who got hurt would come and tell me, and I would go to confront the bully and sometimes it would lead to a fight. Then, after the kids found out their families could get some money from my mother, some of the boys would pick fights with me. My father thought he could stop me by chaining me, but I worked out of the chains."

Molly believed Terence, that he was not picking fights, but she gently scolded, "You were a naughty boy!"

Terence answered, "Well, at that age you learn to do a lot of stuff. I wanted out of the chains, so I got myself out. Then I jumped to the next roof and found my way out of that building."

Molly replied, "I hope your son will not be like that, if you have a son!" Then she softened, "Did your father ever beat you and chain you again?"

Terence said, "No, he knew I could get free anyway. Soon my parents figured out that people were just trying to make some money at our expense. Their sons would come to challenge me, and after I gave them a few punches, they would run home crying. I never beat anyone too badly. But they made it a big affair, and my mother paid them, and then others would hear about it. Sometimes, I never even touched a kid, and his mother would come to my mother and say, 'Oh, Puck Ying hurt my boy!'

"But," Terence repeated, anxious for Molly to understand, "I never bullied anyone."

Molly frowned, "You bullied me! You hit me with a stick!"

Chastened, Terence smiled sheepishly, "Oh, yeah.... I'm sorry about that."

****

From Nye Nye, Molly also learned more about the history of the family of her birth.

"You don't remember your grandmother Chin," Nye Nye said one day.

"No," Ngood said. Again her curiosity was aroused. "I don't remember her. I only remember seeing her great picture in the four-story house on Maung Khine Street. Grandfather Chin's picture was on one side, and Grandmother Chin's picture hung on the other side. Did you know her?"

"Of course!" Nye Nye exclaimed. "She was a friend of mine."

Ngood had not considered that Nye Nye might be familiar with her absent grandmother.

"As I recall, you were quite young when she left for Hong Kong," Nye Nye explained. "It was about the time your grandfather Chin Mung Yee took a second wife. He was very prosperous, and to make a big face, he took another wife."

Nye Nye recounted the scene, "Your grandmother was furious! She went to the balcony of the second floor of *Foo Nam Low*. She beat on a gong to attract a crowd. As soon as a big crowd of people stood under the balcony, she cried out, 'My husband was not faithful! He has taken a second wife!'

"She would not be consoled. Chin Mung Yee was angry with her and sent her to Hong Kong with a daughter and a maid," Nye Nye said abruptly.

Ngood didn't say anything out loud. She felt the brokenness of the grandmother she never met. So, both of her grandfathers had taken second wives and had abandoned, as Grandfather Wong, or banished, as Grandfather Chin, their first wives. Molly wondered if her father, in all of his travels and months at a time away from home, had remained faithful to her mother. She did not like to think about it.

She never discussed this with Terence, but she was certain he would not take another wife. She was certain he would always be faithful to her. This was a great comfort.

****

Nye Nye told Ngood with unusual animation, "Number Two Son Puck Hee has been found!"

"Nye Nye, this is wonderful news," Ngood responded. "How is he?"

"Oh, he is well!" Nye Nye told her.

But Molly heard the rest of the story from Terence. "We've heard from Stanley Ng. He went to India with the British army. He happened to meet Wat Hong's oldest daughter there. You know, some of Wat Hong's family escaped to India during the war. My cousin and her husband went to India soon after the war broke out. She told Stanley that she ran across Puck Hee in Calcutta, though she hardly recognized her cousin. He was terribly thin, nearly a skeleton, and he had picked up mannerisms of the local Indian people, like cocking and shaking his head as he spoke."

"My goodness!" Molly exclaimed. "I wonder what happened to him."

"My brother Puck Hee was so young, and he has always been timid. Also, he's not too flexible, so he had a hard time being stranded in India when the war began. In fact, my cousin said that when she found Puck Hee, he told her that he had eaten grass to survive."

"He ate grass?" Molly was incredulous. "What? Really! Like a goat or a cow?"

"Yes," Terence replied. "In fact, Stanley said because of a widespread famine in India during the war, many people in Calcutta were eating grass to keep from starving, so that even the lawns of homes were grazed bare."

"Oh!" Molly could not comprehend such hunger.

"It was a good thing my cousin and her husband took Puck Hee home with them and cared for him. Stanley told me that Puck Hee was surprised by her kindness to him. He had always heard our mother and her mother arguing, so he thought she would not like him." Terence added, "My mother is sending money to support him now."

****

Another family member was found to have survived the war. Nye Nye discovered that Ngood's Grandmother Wong was still living safely with her son and daughter-in-law in Kamayut. Nye Nye had made contact with her, the respected godmother to Terence.

After that, Grandmother Wong sometimes would come to visit Ngood and Puck Ying at the big house at the soy sauce factory. She always brought one of her grandsons along to help her navigate the buses, as age continued to bend and cripple her body. Nye Nye always welcomed them warmly, and they would spend one or two nights. For a guest to stay longer was considered rude, unless pressed by the host to remain.

Even now, when Ngood was grown up, Grandmother said fondly, "Hello, *low-see doy*, my little mouse." Ngood was warmed by her affection, grateful to have this steadying relationship.

****

Nye Nye hired an Indian man, and he and his family moved into one of the buildings at the soy sauce factory. He was always referred to with a derogatory term for "Indian" and by his occupation, "Gardener," never by his name. Regrettably, this was the accepted cultural practice of the time.

The big house at Eight Mile had been plumbed for water, but pipes had never been connected to a water source, so Indian Gardener was always busy not only with using a curved knife to cut grass on the groomed portion of the ten-acre compound, but also with hauling the water for all the households at the soy sauce factory. He filled buckets at a well at the back of the compound and carried them on a pole across his shoulders as Molly had seen Byu Goo do in Namhsan.

Again, Nye Nye made do with what was available. From some of the hundreds of giant pots that had been used to ferment soybeans at the soy sauce factory, she instructed that a few be carried into the bathrooms of each of the buildings. These pots were about chest high and round, easily big enough inside to hide a man, though the openings would be too small for most grown men to squeeze through. Indian Gardener had to keep all of these designated pots filled with water. To use the water, one drew it with a very long-handled dipper for bathing, cleaning, and removing waste. Once again, water must be used sparingly so as not to abuse the hired man, but he had to periodically dump the water from the pots to keep it fresh, and then he must refill the pots.

He also hauled water for drinking and cooking, but this he brought from a restaurant across the street where the water quality was better. Still, the British now informed the citizens of Rangoon that drinking water always should be boiled before use, and boiling water was one of the many duties of the young maids.

Sometimes Molly would hear Nye Nye berating Indian Gardener. Molly thought, "This man works so hard all day and well into the evening. So many of us depend on him. Why must she scold him?"

Molly remembered the durwan, the nice Indian man who guarded the four-story house of her childhood. She knew Indians could be very hard-working, satisfied to eat the yellow dahl beans, boiled soft, without meat, and that they saved every pice, every quarter of an anna, to send to much poorer relatives in India. She admired their work ethic, family loyalty, and frugality.

But Molly kept her thoughts to herself. She would not dare to say anything to Nye Nye. Nor would she tell Terence, because he would speak to his mother about it, and that would make things worse.

Who could say, afterall, what anyone might do in Nye Nye's position, when so much responsibility for so many people lay on her shoulders? Nye Nye continued to be greatly loved and respected in the community, and rightfully so. Neighbors often came to Nye Nye for help and she would generously share her wisdom or her purse.

For instance, Molly once observed a distraught woman who came to Nye Nye. She was upset that she could not become pregnant

Nye Nye said, "I can help you. Do you trust me? Do as I say." Then she gathered wild herbs from the yard and said confidently, "Boil these in water. Then strain out the herbs. Drink this three times a day."

Molly was surprised later to hear that the woman was pregnant. Many such people came to Nye Nye for help.

****

Soon after they were settled at Eight Mile, Lo Yeahr brought an unusual guest to dinner. Molly was immediately struck by this impressive man. He was clearly Chinese, though very tall and of a stronger build than any Chinese man she knew. She had heard that men of Northern China were framed this way, but it was a little breath-taking to see this one in person. Lo Yeahr explained that the gentleman was a colonel of the famed Flying Tigers, Northern Chinese men who were trained as pilots to fly with Americans in American-made bombers even before America was officially involved in World War Two. Terence nearly worshiped these heroes, and to meet one in person was a great thrill for him!

During the dinner, Terence listened intently to every word the colonel spoke and conversed happily in response. Molly silently listened to the men, trying not to stare at the colonel but catching a discrete glimpse when she could. The pilot was grateful to Lo Yeahr for letting his contingent stay at the soy sauce factory during the last part of the war. He was looking forward to returning to his homeland.

****

While Terence was out, he picked up stories about the war and brought them back to Molly. It was in this way Molly first heard about a frightening new weapon.

Terence told her, "It was the Americans who forced the Japanese to surrender to the Allies."

"Yes," Molly replied as if Terence was telling her nothing new. "When the Americans entered the war, everything turned around." From her perspective, the Americans had saved the world from the tyranny of some of the most brutal despots in history.

Terence said, "No, I mean the Japanese had no choice but to surrender to the Americans. The Japanese Emperor was determined not to lose face. He told his people to fight until every samurai warrior, every kamikaze pilot, and every civilian was dead. In fact, he had told his people to commit suicide rather than surrender."

"Then, why did he surrender? I don't think every Japanese person is dead," Molly observed.

"Because of a new bomb. It's called, the 'atomic bomb.'" Terence answered.

"What is this, 'a-tom-ic bomb'?"

"The Americans made this weapon, and it is much more powerful than any other bomb." Terence explained. His voice conveyed the weightiness of this news. "They dropped one bomb on a Japanese city, Hiroshima, and everything was completely destroyed for a one mile radius. Damages extended for several more miles from the site. Sixty thousand buildings in

264 | GENTLE MOON

the city were completely destroyed or badly damaged. Tens of thousands of people died at once. Later, more people died of burns and sickness from the bomb. This was all from one single bomb, Molly."

Molly stared at him in disbelief.

Terence added, "Still the Japanese would not surrender..."

"What?" Molly interjected.

"... So three days later the Americans dropped an atomic bomb on another Japanese city, Nagasaki."

"Woe! Another one?" Molly spoke quietly.

"Only then would Emperor Hirohito surrender. If the Americans had not done this, who knows how long the Japanese would have drug out the war?"

"Wow," Molly didn't verbalize anything more, but she thought of many things. She continued to be grateful for the end of the war and for the American contribution in ending it. She was also astonished to consider a bomb of such force. She had never heard of anything that compared to the power of this weapon. She had observed for herself that even after many, many terrible bombs were dropped in the cities of Rangoon, Mandalay, and Pyapon, the devastation was nothing like Terence had described. A bomb of such power was frightening to consider in any hands, and she was glad the Americans had thought of it first. She also felt sorry as she imagined that so many innocent people, even children, likely were hurt or died from the horrible bomb. In fact, over one hundred thousand died instantly from the two bombs, and tens of thousands died later from radiation poisoning.

****

Another day Terence mentioned to Molly, "Some of the local Chinese are secretly calling the Burmese leaders two-headed snakes."

"What?" Molly asked. "Why are they so insulting?"

Terence explained, "We have heard that some Burmese leaders were involved in helping the Japanese army invade Burma."

Molly was shocked at this news! How could Burmans have brought such devastation on themselves?

Aloud, she exclaimed, "No! Why would they do that?"

"They resented the rule of the British over them," Terence said. "They thought the Japanese would liberate them from British occupation."

Molly answered angrily, "That is crazy! The Japanese were much worse than the British!"

"Yes." Terence agreed. "Much worse. Now everyone knows this. The Burmese thought Asians would treat Asians better. When the Burmese leaders realized what a terrible mistake they had made, they switched sides. They joined the Allies to defeat the Japanese."

As a person who had so recently experienced traumas of war as a consequence of such a strategic error, Molly could not immediately accept how this could happen. In fact, she had gotten along quite well under British colonialism, and it was difficult to relate to a Burmese citizen feeling the oppression of occupation and longing for liberty and self-rule.

Terence concluded, "That is why some people are saying the Burmese leaders are two-headed snakes. They say the men cannot be trusted, that Burmans go to this side, and they go to that side."

"I see," Molly said.

"At least," Terence pointed out, "they learned from their mistake and adjusted. And not all the Burmese sided with the Japanese. Some worked with the Allies from the start. In fact, some thought to be spies for the British were tortured by the Japanese."

"Tortured?" Molly asked. "How were they tortured?"

Terence hesitated, unsure of how much he should tell his wife. But unlike previous generations of Chinese men, he thought of Molly as his friend, and in some ways his equal. So he decided to tell her frankly, "Broken glass. The Japanese would break glass into small pieces. People thought to be spies were made to kneel on the glass. Then they were forced to crawl on their knees through it."

"No!" Molly couldn't believe her ears. "They did this?"

Terence said solemnly, "Yes. I believe it is true. And something else. They would pull out a person's fingernail to get him to confess to something or to force him to give information."

"Oh!" Molly shook her head as the words made an unwanted picture in her mind. She was shocked by the cruelty of it. The couple was silent for some time. If not for the sweet distraction of Ah Hing, they might have remained mired in disturbing thoughts.

A few days later Terence came with more shocking news of a more personal nature. "Molly, sit down. I have something to tell you."

She saw the concern on his face and immediately sat down, asking, "Now what?"

"It's about your Number One Uncle, Chin Hone On," Terence said.

"Yes? What is it? What about Old Man Thunder Voice?" Molly asked urgently.

"He was tortured by the Japanese." Terence told her quietly.

"No!" Molly whispered. "What happened to him? Glass? Fingernails? Oh, is he dead or alive?"

"The Japanese took two of the leaders of Chinatown, your uncle and a Fokinese man, Mr. Chun. They accused them of being spies and took them to prison for interrogation."

"Oh, my!" A chill ran through her. Molly thought not only for the safety of her uncle, which was of great concern in itself, but of all his wives and children. If anything happened to him, what would become of them? She was afraid to know what happened, but not knowing was worse.

"Go on," she said deliberately, but a catch in her voice gave away her fear.

Terence spoke the hard words as gently as he could, "They put a tube into his throat, pushed it down into his stomach, and pumped his stomach full of water."

Tears welled in her eyes as she thought of her poor, dear uncle, helpless in the hands of brutal captors. "What? Why did they do that?"

Terence said, "They made the water go and go non-stop into the stomach. Slowly the stomach became bloated. If the interrogators didn't get the answers they wanted, they did not stop the water. Then the stomach would burst, and the person would die."

"Oh!" After a pause, Molly's voice broke as she asked, "Tell me, Terence! Did my uncle die?"

"He survived," Terence answered, then he added solemnly, "Mr. Chun did not."

Molly was unable to respond.

Terence added, "Maybe your uncle was stronger. Or maybe he confessed to something he didn't do just so they would stop the torture. Anyway, somehow he survived."

Molly could not shake the image of her uncle's torture. She was stunned to consider such cruelty. She was pained to think her own uncle was treated so. She was silent.

Terence wondered if his wife had the same thought that occurred to him, "If your father had left Namhsan when your uncle and my family came back here to Rangoon.... As a leader of Chinatown, your father...." Terence didn't finish his sentences, knowing by his wife's expression it was not necessary to say the dreadful words.

Trying to lighten the oppressive thoughts, Terence mentioned, "Your uncle and his family are now living at the *On Lok* restaurant, one of your grandfather's restaurants on Dalhousie. Of course, it is not a restaurant any more with all the family staying there."

Terence added, "He has rented the four-story house to The Freedom Press."

Molly liked the name of "Freedom Press." She had felt a painful lack of freedom in recent years. But she didn't know anything about this organization.

Actually, it was satellite of an anarchist publishing house founded in London in the late nineteenth century. Anarchists were generally against any centralized government, and some were willing to violently overthrow rulers of any political persuasion. For these people, freedom was prized over all other considerations of safety, comfort, and morals. Founders of "The Freedom Press" were not so extreme and did not advocate violence, but insisted, maybe naively, that people could live happily together without rule. The founders felt people could be convinced to voluntarily cooperate with each other for mutual good.

Molly did not know how much her uncle knew about "The Freedom Press." But the very sound of the word "freedom" in any language must have been a comforting thought to Old Man Thunder Voice after being so wrongly and cruelly abused by those in rule. Surely, he would continue to long for the simple freedom to openly speak his opinions.

Chapter Fifteen

Reunion

News to Eight Mile usually arrived at the pace of an old pony with a heavy cart, but there was nothing slow about the news one day in July of 1947. When Terence brought the fresh news to Molly, he was clearly upset.

"What is it?" She asked.

"Do you remember I told you about some Burmese leaders that switched sides during the war, first helping the Japanese, then helping the Allies?"

"Yes, of course."

"Aung San was one of the main leaders of the Burmese Independence movement. He and twenty-nine others were called the "Thirty Comrades" that trained with Japanese and fought with them to take Burma. Then, when the Japanese broke promises, these men joined the Allies to defeat Japan."

"Yes...?"

"Well, you know the Burmese have not forgotten their desire for independence from Britain. Even before the war there were hunger strikes, protests, and armed rebellion. Since the war, Burmans are even less patient. Last year the Burmese police force went on strike, forcing the British to cooperate for independence. Since then, Aung San has been working with the British, and an agreement was reached in January to begin taking steps to transfer rule to natives. Then, Aung San and his socialist group won assembly elections in April, preparing for Burmese Independence."

Molly wasn't sure what this had to do with her husband's agitation. He was about to tell her.

"Aung San was meeting with six members of his cabinet today."

"Yes...?"

"They were all murdered."

"What?" Molly was shocked, "Who would murder them? People should think of Aung San as a hero if he was helping them to get independence from the English."

"Yes, well, many agree," Terence answered. "However, from what I understand, there are many factions wanting to take over Burma when the British leave. Socialists. Communists. Conservatives. And many minority tribes, the Arakans, the Kayins, and many others, don't want to be ruled by the ethnic Burmese tribe again. They want their own independence. Also there is competition among ethnic Burmese. In fact, I heard that a political rival, U Saw, the prime minister of Burma before the war, may have been responsible for the assassinations."

"Now what?" Molly wondered.

"Good question. For the answer, we must wait and see."

Molly was expecting a child in October. To what sort of world would he or she come?

****

Molly's life was stressful in many ways, but she was able to keep herself doing what she must do. One thing that seemed to most challenge her ability to hold back tears was Ah Hing refusing to eat. Molly would chase her, trying to slip a bite into her mouth now and then as she had seen Pwa Pwa and Byu Goo do with her little brothers when they were toddlers. But Ah Hing would not eat, and this was too much for the young mother. Molly would sometimes collapse on the floor in tears, worrying that she was not a good mama, worrying that Ah Hing would not thrive, and helpless to know what to do about it.

****

Nearly two years after the war ended, Molly gave birth to a son. She enjoyed her month of respite and special care. Most importantly, the baby was quite healthy. After the critical month passed, Nye Nye gave the boy his name, Eng Koon, meaning "Supreme Power."

"Eng Koon?" Molly thought, "That is a very big name."

Molly knew that according to Chinese tradition a child's name foretells his future, yet a child given a name too big for him will die under the weight of it. Molly remembered that Nye Nye had chosen a different name in common for her own boys for that concern.

But now, "Eng Koon?" Clearly Nye Nye had big expectations for her little grandson and was confident he would meet the challenge of fulfilling the destiny of his big name. After all, this was the first son of the first son, and the child's father was showing great promise to live out the big name of Puck Ying.

Terence, Molly, Ah Hing, and Eng Koon on an excursion to Rangoon, in front of the four- story house of Molly's childhood

Once again Terence was a proud papa, and as the stress of war faded somewhat, Molly could begin to enjoy her little family. Still, there was cause for concern. Competing factions continued warfare leading up to the independence of Burma, and Molly sometimes heard gunshots and explosions near the soy sauce factory.

****

Lo Yeahr brought his next door neighbor to talk with Terence. The neighbor was a well-to-do Indian man, and he informed Terence that he had gotten a contract to deliver goods to China. He was going to need a lot of truck drivers to keep up with the demand. He wanted to sub-contract Terence to hire and manage drivers, while he himself would supply trucks, receive orders, and obtain goods for delivery to China. Terence was eager to accept the arrangement.

Since the war, Terence's health had not been very good. After his frightening boat trip from Pyapon to Rangoon to exchange the gold bar, he often seemed short of breath. But this job managing the truckers seemed to suit him well, and he pursued it with energy, anxious to be making an income.

Soon, profits were coming in and Nye Nye was delighted. She said that the infant Eng Koon was good luck and was bringing them success. She was proud of her little grandson.

But after a while Nye Nye seemed displeased with them. Molly realized Lo Yeahr seemed uncharacteristically angry with Terence as well. Finally Nye Nye said something that hinted of her offense to Molly, mentioning a commission someone was rightly paying someone else.   Accepting the bait, Molly later asked Terence, "Do you pay your father something of the profits from your business?"

Terence answered, "I gave him a little bit."

Molly argued, "Terence, pay him something! Give him a percentage of your profits... five percent or ten percent. He got you the job. You were hired because of the reputation of your father. Besides, if you don't pay them enough, they blame me."

Terence gave Molly a quick smile of understanding. "Okay. I'll take care of it."

****

Terence handed Molly a letter from Maymyo. This was a puzzle, because letters rarely came from anywhere. How did it get to her? And Molly didn't know anyone who lived in Maymyo. She was uncertain as she opened the envelope. The hand writing did look familiar, but Molly was afraid to hope.

Ah! Piya! Thank God! It was a letter from Moonlight! Finally, some word from her family! Molly was overjoyed to have news from her sister and rushed to read every Chinese character in Moonlight's lovely handwriting.

Molly eagerly chattered details to Terence as she read, "My parents bought a home in the British hill station of Maymyo. Yes, I remember when we went to Namhsan we passed by Maymyo, the town the British built in high country. Remember, Terence?   Moonlight says it is beautiful there. Oh. Moonlight says Papa is working for Mr. Wong, and Papa will run the carnival for him in Namhsan."

Terence said, "Good for him! That will be a good way for him to rebuild himself."

"Yes, it is very kind of Mr. Wong to help my father this way," Molly agreed.

There was more news. Molly spoke with laughter in her voice, "Oh, Terence, remember when   you came back to Namhsan to get me, you came with a traveling companion?"

"Yes, of course. He was an older man, but he was tall and strong," Terence replied. "He was a cook for my father.

"You'll never guess!" Molly chuckled.

"What is it?"

"Apparently this gentleman spent a lot of time in the kitchen in Namhsan. He developed a romance with Byu Goo!"

"Really?"

"Yes. Well! And they had a son!" Picturing the happy family, Molly was delighted for her friend.

"The boy's name is Ah Hop, 'Agreeable.' " Reading on, Molly added, "Oh, the boy is about the same age as Ah Hing."

But as she read further, her face clouded and her voice fell. "The new husband is dead already."

"Oh, no." Terence responded. "What happened?"

"He was returning to Rangoon ahead of the others and disappeared. No one knows what happened. Papa thinks he met up with robbers. It was so chaotic right after the war."

Terence was sorry to see his wife's joy turn so quickly to sadness, and he changed the subject. "How is your family?" he asked hopefully.

After reading a little more, Molly smiled again. "Moonlight says everyone is fine. Ginger is well, and the boys and Dorothy are really growing, she says."

Tears welled in her eyes as she said the words again, softly, "Everyone is fine." The relief was indescribable.

****

Terence (seated by driver) with workers in one of the trucks for the delivery business at the entrance to Eight Mile.

Terence had no trouble finding men wanting to work as truckers. One snag in the business venture was that petroleum stations were not conveniently placed on the route to China, so it was necessary to obtain five-gallon cans, fill them with petroleum, and give them to the drivers so they could complete the trip without running out of petrol.

Terence rented a big, one-story building across the street from the soy sauce factory. It was a long building, but not very deep. He moved his family into one side, and he filled the other side with row after row of cans full of petrol, which had to be stored inside to protect the precious commodity from theft. More empty cans were stored outside. The building also had a yard that provided a place for the trucks to park. On payday, once a week, drivers came to receive their paychecks from Terence.

Molly didn't care for business traffic in the home or the smell of the petrol, but she was grateful for the income and happy to see her husband's success. This newer, bigger house also gave them room for their growing family.

An odd mix of odors filled the home across from the soy sauce factory. The unpleasant smell of petroleum fumes permeated the air, and cheroot smoke was constant incense, for it seemed the maids were always rolling or smoking cheroots. Terence knew enough to insist that the maids not smoke the cigars near the gasoline cans, but, in hindsight, the home was at risk of bursting into flames from the dangerous mix of petrol fumes and smoldering cigar. Many years later, Molly would reflect that the family's bedroom was a thin wall away from the rows and stacks of cans filled with petroleum. Besides petrol and cheroot scenting every inhaled breath, spicy fragrances from the cooking competed with mixed results.

Molly with Ah Hing, Eng Koon, Kayin maids, and petrol cans and drums in the yard of the home across from the soy sauce factory.

****

Molly was pleased with the maids she had hired. These two Kayin women worked so well together, like sisters, as they chatted together happily in the privacy of their Kayin tongue. These two were also Christians, as Kayins often are, and Molly loved to hear them singing the Christian hymns that she had learned in the English school. The words of the songs continued to touch her heart.

The maids divided the work and shared duties well. The older woman, Ma Seng, did most of the cooking and was very responsible about making sure all the household chores were done. Daisy was from the jungle area around Pyapon and was rather backwards and clumsy, but she was very attentive to Ah Koon, and she often sat cross-legged, cradling the baby in her skirt the whole time he slept.

Once Molly heard Ma Seng ask Daisy for help, and she argued, "You do it! How can I do it when I'm holding this baby? He is more important!" Molly felt it best not to interfere, and most of the time Ma Seng did not seem to resent Daisy's leisurely work and let her be. Only rarely did they argue.

Ma Seng, on the other hand, loved to do the shopping. Every day Molly would send her by bus to Insein to the fresh market. Ma Seng, always smoking cheroot, took the money for food, along with bus fare and a little extra to buy mohinga for her own meal. In those days, five kyat would cover it all. Ma Seng came back with fresh meat and vegetables, along with fresh gossip she had gathered from her daily meeting with friends.

But good maids were hard to keep. Unlike Nye Nye, who bought young Chinese girls that were required to complete a decade or more of service, Molly continued to hire local girls. Daisy was needed by her relatives in Pyapon and could no longer continue serving. Before leaving, Daisy asked Molly if she could take any old clothes or shoes to share with her poor family members. Molly was surprised that she wanted to take even the old broom, worn nearly to the binding. Startled to consider such poverty, Molly gave her the new broom instead, and as many clothes and shoes as she could spare.

****

The "Union of Burma" gained independence from Britain on January 4, 1948 at 4:20 am, a date and time carefully chosen by an astrologer. U Nu, an Aung San cabinet member that had not been present during the murderous rampage of the previous year, became the prime minister of the newly birthed nation. But government officials had a tenuous hold on the nation, as they attempted to unite disparate tribes which often controlled roadless wilderness, jungles, and mountains practically impossible to patrol. Bribery of tribal leaders by the government had brought some areas under the "Union of Burma" umbrella. Others groups were not to be bribed or cajoled or threatened, tired of subjugation and broken promises by the British, the Japanese, or the Burman. Rebel forces of various tribes and competing groups continued to fight each other or government forces. As communists took control of China through 1949, factions of Nationalist Chinese retreated into Burma, adding to unrest.

Molly understood that some things are worth fighting for, and she supposed that some of these groups had rightful causes. But, when she heard the gunshots, she was frightened for her children and was emotionally exhausted to endure so many years of proximity to armed conflict. She just wished for peace. She could not know at what cost the guns would be silenced.

****

When Eng Koon was several months old, Terence had a surprise for his wife. He felt Molly needed a change.

He said casually, "Molly, you know that since the war there are many military planes left over in Burma. Also, there are RAF pilots still here willing to fly them."

"Yes," Molly answered absently, hearing the information shallowly, as an impersonal matter of interest.

Amused by his wife's indifference and willing to open his gift slowly before her, he went on, "And during the war, new landing strips were built so soldiers and supplies could be moved quickly."

"Yes."

"So airplanes are now available to transport civilians on regular routes to various cities," Terence said.

Molly nodded and made an effort to be conversational, "Hmmm. That explains why every day we hear so many airplanes coming and going from Mingaladon Airport."

"Yes," Terence agreed, unable to prevent a grin from stretching across his face. "Planes have been flying to Mandalay... and Moulmein... and recently they've started a route to the hill station of... Maymyo." He waited for Molly to react and was pleased to see that at last he had her full attention.

"Maymyo? That's where Mama and Papa are living," she explained, as if Terence might have forgotten.

"Yes," he smiled, "I know. I've booked a flight for you, Ah Hing, and Eng Koon to go to Maymyo to visit your family."

"What? Oh! Terence!" Molly was rarely at a loss for words, but this news was too wonderful! Finally she could ask, "When...?"

"At the end of the week. That will give you time to pack what you'll need. You'll be gone for several months, maybe longer. I will get our trucking business established while you are gone, and I'll drive up for a visit when I can. When you are ready to come back to Rangoon, we will all come back together in my jeep."

Surplus military jeeps were very popular after the war, as was, incidentally, clothing made of parachute fabric. Molly thought the fabric too hot, but she often saw both Burmese men and women wearing short jackets sewn of the dark fabric.

Trying to maintain his composure, Terence added practically, "Remember to take warm clothes for you and the children. It will be much cooler at the hill station."

Molly could only nod in response. She would hurry and knit sweaters for the children.

"Your parents will be glad to see you and to meet their new grandchildren," Terence said, smiling. "I wrote to tell them you are coming. They will pick you up at the airport."

Molly was a strong woman, and she did not often complain. But Terence knew by the tears filling her eyes that he had given her a great gift. He never mentioned this to Molly, but with gunshots often sounding nearby and assassinations in Rangoon, surely he was also concerned for the safety of his family.

What Molly did understand was the sacrifice Terence was making. He didn't like for Molly to be out of his sight, and yet, didn't he say she could be away for several months? He would miss her and the children terribly! She didn't ask about the financial cost of the plane trip. Surely his mother would not be happy that she was going to Maymyo. Everyone knew a Chinese girl is supposed to leave her family and become a part of his family. Yet, regardless of all the arguments against it, Terence did this lovely thing for her.

****

At last the necessary purchases were made and the bags were packed. Terence took his precious little family to the airport and helped Molly carry luggage and children up the steps to the airplane, which still looked like the military transport it was. Long benches had been installed along the sides of the interior, and other passengers had already taken places. Molly sat, holding Eng Koon, luggage beside her. Terence set a tin of cookies on the floor between Molly's feet. Ah Hing sat on the canister at her father's instruction and obediently wrapped her arms around her mother's calves. Molly drew her legs against Ah Hing to secure her, and so Terence confidently left his little family to their journey.

Uninformed about aerodynamics, Molly warned Ah Hing, "Hold on to Ah Ma! Don't let go! If the plane stops suddenly in the sky, you may fall down from your seat." Molly assumed that, as with a car, the plane might stop suddenly in the air, causing the passengers to jerk forward.

"Yes, Ah Ma," Hing answered obediently, clutching her mother's legs tightly.

Molly did not expect the airplane to be so loud and was unprepared for the disconcerting jostling inside the belly of the metal, motorized bird. She was unnerved when the plane bounced over unseen objects in the air and her stomach lurched uneasily. Air turbulence provided good reason for Ah Hing to heed her mother's warning to keep her grip. Passengers could not converse over the noise, and there were no windows to see outside. It was not a pleasant journey.

But, my goodness! In less than two hours, they were landing at the airstrip near Maymyo. Why, just the trip to Mandalay by train could take fifteen hours, and Maymyo was several more hours by taxi. She could not have taken such a journey alone with two very young children.

Molly's brother Clark and sister Moonlight met her at the airport in Maymyo. Clark was looking quite the modern man in his father's new, sporty car. With his stylish hair and expensive clothes, and as handsome as ever, he made an impressive figure. Molly immediately noticed with concern that people treated him as if he were a movie star, and he enjoyed the attention. Moonlight greeted her with joy, and the sisters chatted happily as Clark drove them to the Chin home.

Clark, Johnny, and Wayne with their father's car in Maymyo

Molly had a great surprise when she arrived at the house and saw her parents. Papa smiled! Ah Pa actually smiled at her! Molly had never seen him do this before. She was both shocked and honored.

Mama was overjoyed to see her Number Two Daughter, and she was moved to meet her first grandchildren. She spoke to Ah Hing, admiring how pretty she looked. Then she took Eng Koon from Molly and sat on a mat on the floor, gently swaying with her infant grandson. From this place, she quietly took in the mirth of her reunited family, a portrait of happiness.

Byu Goo served them tea, and her adorable son, Ah Hop, trotted around the room cheerfully, especially curious about Ah Hing. Everyone was bursting with questions about Molly's ride in the airplane, and Molly obliged with a dramatic description of the noisy, shaking flight. When she described Ah Hing sitting on a tin of Danish cookies, and Molly squeezing Hing with her legs while holding on to Eng Koon, everyone laughed at the imagined picture. Molly was always a good story-teller.

As all continued to sip tea and chatter in multiple conversations at once, even in Papa's presence, Molly noticed details about her family. Moonlight was stronger than ever in her position as the eldest, and supervised the household like a feudal lord. Papa seemed more mellow, tolerating the noise, and he was content to let Moonlight rule, though, of course, she did not boss him. Mama was as ever the gentle mother and quiet, obedient wife. It saddened Molly to observe the boys: well-dressed, but lazy, lounging, spoiled, rich man's sons. Whereas their experiences in Namhsan might have strengthened their characters, instead they had been pampered even throughout the war. Now that they could finish their educations or do some productive work, they had no interest.

Especially, she worried about Clark. He was quite a handsome fellow, and he had a magical way over people. He would only mention something and people would run to please him. Molly worried that this apparent gift was also spoiling him.

Molly was amused to observe Dorothy. She, more than any other, was influenced by Burmese culture, specifically the Shan culture of Maymyo. Papa's Chinese cook lived in separate servants' quarters with his Shan wife and their young daughter, and Dorothy loved to visit with the wife and had even learned to speak some Shan dialect. Most obviously, Dorothy wore the Tha na kah paste smeared on her cheeks. Molly watched Dorothy deftly use a rock to grind the tree bark with a little water to form the paste the local women used to cool their skin and improve their complexions.

Molly learned that Dorothy also had a rather wild habit of showering in the cool air in an enclosed outdoor shower stall. She could have showered in the modern indoor bathroom where it was warmer, but Dorothy, wrapped in a Burmese longyi, liked the cool, refreshing, outside air and water. Dorothy was blossoming into a beautiful young woman, and Molly thought her less refined habits were appealing. She thought of Dorothy as a jungle princess, wild and independent, strong and lovely.

Perhaps Ginger was the one most changed since Molly had seen her last. She was always rather shy, but now she seemed quite timid and somewhat helpless. Molly noted that she herself had less courage and independence than before the war, but it hurt her to see Ginger seeming so insecure.

Byu Goo was, as ever, a constant, devoted companion to Mama. And Mama clearly delighted in Ah Hop. As expected, Byu Goo and her son lived in the main house with her family

The next day, Ah Ma and Byu Goo were busy loving the children. The brothers had dressed nicely, but sat in the house doing nothing. Moonlight asked Molly to join her for a walk in the gardens in the cool morning air.

The house was of the British style, with a big yard and gardens and the separate building for servants. As the sisters strolled alone together, they shared things face-to-face which had been too difficult to write in letters. Each was anxious for the other to tell about experiences during their separation.

"How did you fare after you left Namhsan in the tea truck?" Moonlight asked her.

Molly spoke with an agitated, high-pitched voice about her ordeal: the Japanese check point, the delayed trains, the bombing in Mandalay, the warehouse, the trip to Rangoon and finding the in-laws had gone, hiding in the cemetery in Pyapon, more bombing, and the war plane chasing Terence. Then she concluded by telling of the great party with the British soldiers.

Moonlight responded with big-sisterly compassion at each new fright Molly recited. After laughing about the British soldiers' antics, she said gently, "I did not like to see you go. You looked so fragile and forlorn as you bounced down the road with all those boxes. You tried to smile, but I knew you were unhappy. We all worried about you." She smiled, "I'm glad to see you looking so well!"

Molly asked her, "How were things after I left? Was it very quiet in Namhsan?" She imagined that if she had stayed with her family, she would have fared much better through to the end of the war.

"For awhile," Moonlight said. "But the situation was much worse toward the end. The sawbwa got word from his people that the Japanese were retreating and looting homes and..." she added solemnly, "...raping women. He told us to hide in his tea plantation during the day. So every morning, we got up very early and walked to the tea plantation to hide among the tea bushes. Byu Goo stayed behind with Ah Hop to look after the house in the village. She said she was so old no one would take her.

"Ngood, it was terrible," Moonlight's voice trembled as she recalled the memory. "As we walked to the tea plantation, we often saw the dead, decaying bodies of the poor Palaung people, lying beside the path. We didn't know before that these people were starving. Merchants had stopped taking Japanese or British bills, considering one as worthless as the other. Instead they would only trade for goods, or for gold, silver, or jewelry. As you remember, these tribal people often wore silver jewelry from the local silver mines. But when that was gone, if they had nothing left to trade, they starved to death."

Molly shook her head at the thought. She recalled the friendly village women she had seen when she first arrived in Namhsan. She also thought of how well she had eaten throughout the war. In Pyapon, she had access to plentiful fish and rice that were scarce in the mountains and jungles around Namhsan. Molly saw the sorrow on Moonlight's face, and she realized that, though she had many terrors during the war, she was not exposed to starvation. In spite of all the nearby bombings, she had not seen dead bodies. She understood that her terrible experience was not as bad as some.

"Then after the long walk, carrying our supplies, we came to the tea plantation, isolated and surrounded by forest trees. We spent day after day, hiding in the rows of tea bushes on the hillsides. No one could approach us without being seen, and the plantation workers continued to work around us, making the scene appear quite normal. The sawbwa still had much power in the hill country, and the Japanese did not interfere with his business."

"You were day after day hiding in a tea plantation, and I was day after day hiding in a cemetery," Molly observed. She was well acquainted with the fear and tedium that Moonlight described of her experience.

"We prepared all the food very early and carried enough with us for the day," Moonlight said, and Molly could relate to this as well.

"Did the Japanese ever come?" Molly wondered.

"We did not see any Japanese soldiers at the tea plantation. But in the village... Byu Goo...." Moonlight's face was ashen.

"What?" Molly asked, "What happened? Was Byu Goo alright?"

"The retreating Japanese came to Namhsan, and they were angry! You know, when you were there, the Japanese sometimes came marching in the street. After you left, they were more and more daring. Sometimes they asked women in the street, 'Are you married with children?' By the time they were retreating, they would violently break through a door and storm through a house, taking whatever they wanted, including girls." Molly remembered the rumors and warnings they had heard while in Pyapon and realized these terrible things had actually taken place in Namhsan.

Moonlight continued, "Byu Goo was sitting outside with her baby when the Japanese came and raided the Wong house. She was terrified! One of the soldiers found my high heeled shoes, and he came to her, holding one of the shoes on his bayonet!"

Molly felt a chill of fear. Later she reflected on how little they understood of refugee life when they had packed their bags for Namhsan. High heels? What were they thinking?

Moonlight's voice tightened as she described Byu Goo's ordeal with the angry soldier, "He said... somehow he knew the words in our dialect... Gun yong! 'Young Miss!'"

Molly understood his meaning. He was demanding, "Where is this young virgin?"

Moonlight exclaimed, "Ngood, they were hunting for girls like us, like a predator after its prey!" Even now Moonlight's eyes reflected the terror of being the object of pursuit by soldiers with cruel intentions.

Molly impatiently urged Moonlight to continue, "What did Byu Goo do?"

Moonlight said with a mixture of fright describing the terrible scene and of obvious admiration for Byu Goo, "She pretended to be old and dumb. You know, with her dark, wrinkled skin, she looks older than she is. She shrugged her shoulders, shook her head, and said with slow words and hand gestures, '...Not my house. I just came here. I have nowhere to stay.' "

"Did he believe her?" Molly asked.

"He dropped the shoe angrily and put his bayonet to Byu Goo's throat!" Moonlight continued to narrate the ordeal, and Molly felt faint as she thought of the threat to her friend.

"For some time he held the blade against her neck. But, Byu Goo would not tell him anything. She told us that she was shaking with fear, but she did not speak. One stroke and she would be dead! She expected to die at any moment, with Ah Hop in her arms! Suddenly the soldier released her and left to see what damage he could do elsewhere."

"Oh! She risked her life to protect you!" Molly exclaimed breathlessly. "Of course, you and Ginger and Dorothy are like daughters to her."

"Yes," Moonlight acknowledged.

Molly said with admiration, "She is a brave woman and very loyal."

"She is," Moonlight agreed simply.

Molly pondered the relationship between Moonlight and Byu Goo. Moonlight clearly loved and admired her, and yet she continued to boss her.

Mama had not given Moonlight that example and clearly did not think of Byu Goo as a servant, but somehow Moonlight had taken the role of an overlord, second in command after their father. For her part, Byu Goo seemed happy to cooperate in this arrangement. It occurred to Molly that without influences at the Methodist English Girls High School, this interaction might seem normal to her as well.

Moonlight, Dorothy, and Ah Hing in Maymyo

When they returned to the house, Byu Goo was in the big yard watching the three-year-olds play together. Byu Goo was amused, "Look, Ngood! Look at Ah Hing and Ah Hop!"

Molly watched the children playing happily. She didn't notice anything unusual.

"Look at Ah Hing ordering him around!" Byu Goo pointed out. "They are only three years old, and already they know their class! They know their destiny."

Molly tried to argue, but she watched as Byu Goo had instructed. Sure enough, little Ah Hing was bossing poor Ah Hop, and he obeyed contentedly.

Byu Goo said, "Already my son is eager to please your daughter. Watch him. He is always ready to do what she commands. And Ah Hing knows how to command him."

Molly had to admit that the children seemed to have taken these roles. Molly wasn't happy about it. She thought defensively, "Hmm, Ah Hing has picked up this habit from her father."

Later she recalled how she had bossed Tuck Sook, her Little Uncle. Children were not so much fulfilling their roles, she thought, as following their human natures, one exerting power over another just because one could.

****

Molly greatly enjoyed her time in Maymyo, and the days went quickly. How lovely it was to have grandparents, aunts, and Byu Goo doting on Ah Hing and Eng Koon!

Terence patiently allowed Molly to be away for many months, and he made regular visits to see his family. But at last he drove his jeep to Maymyo for a final week-long visit before taking his family home. He was so glad to be with Molly!

Another visitor joined them at Papa's house as well. This was Papa's sister's son. Molly was delighted to meet one of this branch of relatives from Hong Kong, where her mysterious Grandmother Chin had retreated with her daughter when Grandfather Chin took a second wife.

Molly learned that her cousin had been an interpreter for the Allied army and followed his unit to Burma. Somehow he had discovered his uncle in Maymyo. Molly observed that her cousin was tall and very bright, and she admired that he was hoping to attend medical school.

The adults were enjoying the lovely Maymyo climate, visiting together in the yard as Ah Hing pattered around the flower beds. Ignoring the big, lush blossoms, the little girl carefully picked small flowers and brought them to show her mother. Molly admired each of her daughter's selections and then watched fondly as Ah Hing trotted away to pick another.

After observing this exchange, Molly's cousin asked, "Have you given her an English name?"

Molly thought, "Oh, he is from Hong Kong. He is so up-to-date. Naturally he would think a three-year-old should have an English name."

She replied, "No, not yet. I haven't thought of one yet. Do you have a suggestion?"

He was ready to advise her. "How about Charlene? This is a French name meaning 'small beauty.' Your daughter is going around the yard picking only the small flowers to bring back to you, and Ah Hing is herself a small beauty. Why don't you call her Charlene? It seems a fitting name for her."

Molly said, "Oh that is a very pretty name. I like the sound of it." She was pleased with her sophisticated cousin's observation.

Terence agreed, "I like it too. Okay. Charlene it is."

****

Clark was delighted with Terence's jeep and obtained permission from his brother-in-law to drive it during his brief stay. He also got permission to borrow some of Terence's clothes and combed his hair with Brylcream shaping the fashionable puff in front. He created quite a stir motoring around town, and Molly frowned with disapproval.

Before Molly left Maymyo, she felt there was something she must do. She knew she must gather her courage and face the tiger. She waited

for the opportunity, and at last she found her father alone in the garden.

"Papa," she said, bowing her head respectfully. Then she spoke before she lost courage, "I am concerned about your sons." Wary, she waited briefly to see if her father would be angry with this first broaching of the subject. He did not look at her directly, but he was listening to her.

She continued, "Times have changed, Papa. Your sons need a way to make a living. It is not good for them to be so carefree.

Molly in Maymyo. The sweater was made by Moonlight.

"You and Ah Ma are getting older, and how will they eat when you are gone?" Oh my! Did she really say that to her father, touching upon the taboo subject of his death?

"How long can you sit on the carnival money, Ah Pa?" Molly asked the daring words as respectfully as she could, never forgetting that the tiger could turn on her at any moment.

Then Molly spoke the words she never thought she could say to her father, "You should..." She was nearly stopped by her own audacious words.

But Molly finished her thought, "Papa, you should help them find something they can do."

Molly sensed few words were better than many, and she waited a moment to gauge her father's reaction. He said nothing, but he did not appear angry with her and looked as if he were watching something far away. She was cautiously relieved that her advice had been heard. She would have to be patient and see if her advice would be taken. Wordlessly and cautiously, she walked back to the house, still amazed that she had spoken so to Papa. And he had not so much as growled at her.

****

Terence was not aware that he was matchmaking during his visits to Maymyo. He had discovered that a school chum a couple years older than himself was living at the hill station. Several times he had invited Frank to visit at the Chin home while he was there, and this last trip was no exception. Frank continued to visit the Chins after Terence went back to Rangoon.

Chapter Sixteen

Abundant Life

So much had happened while Molly was in Maymyo! Nye Nye had another son, and she named him Foke Loke, "Lucky Good Material Things." Molly had not been present to care for her mother-in-law after the baby was born, another dereliction of duty. Terence's Number Three sister Fe Yone had married an older man, William, who had been her tutor. Also, old Mr. Ng had died.

Nye Nye was still willing to chat with Ngood, and she was happy to listen. Nye Nye explained that Mr. Ng had asked permission to die in the old house at the soy sauce factory. Nye Nye was practical about it. She said it was good fortune, not bad fortune, to have an old man die in your house. To have a young man die in the home would be very bad luck, and Nye Nye would have forbidden it.

Then Nye Nye offered to tell Ngood more about her new brother-in-law's family. "Do you remember when you came to meet us at the house we rented on Maung Khine Street during the war? Of course, you remember, at that time we were not there. As you recall, Puck Ying had abandoned us to go marry you in Namhsan, and he should have returned quickly, but he was delayed. So, he did not meet us before we left Rangoon and went to Pyapon. Remember? We had to make that terrible journey without Puck Ying to help us care for the little children." Nye Nye's look was full of meaning.

Oh! Suddenly the casual conversation had swung to barb her with reproach! Molly answered quickly, before further mention was deemed necessary. "Yes, Nye Nye. I remember." She bowed her head, accepting the blame.

After a moment of uncomfortable silence, Nye Nye continued, "The house was owned by the family of the sister of my father-in-law Lee Ah Poi's Burmese wife. Fe Yone's husband is the grandson of this sister. He was living with his family in the house next to the one we rented. That is how he first met Fe Yone. He gave her academic tutoring, which was so difficult to find in wartime."

"I see," Ngood answered. Molly had not met William's grandmother, the owner of the house, but she knew William's mother was a commanding Chinese woman, even more so than Nye Nye. She also remembered that his mother had bound feet and had much difficulty in walking.

"During the war, William's family tried to escape from Burma, planning to reach China by the Chindwin River. Two of William's sisters died there."

Died there? Suddenly recovered from the recent sting, Ngood was touched by the sorrow of such loss. She pictured the tragic scene of the family in the rugged jungles of Burma, desperately trying to escape the Japanese soldiers. The trek must have been terribly difficult, and surely at least part of the trip had to be taken on foot through very rough terrain. Ngood wondered how a wobbly old woman with bound feet could have walked it. No wonder some of the children did not survive.

Terence told Molly more about the ordeal. "As my mother said, they went up the Chindwin River, hoping to get to China through India. Following the river up from the plains area, travelers must go through treacherous areas of steep mountains and dense jungles. Wild tigers and elephants live in some places. It is hot and damp and full of disease, like malaria and dysentery. William's family got black fever, caused by a parasite transmitted by a blood-sucking fly. It is called black fever because it sometimes causes the patient's skin to turn black. Often it is fatal, and when someone is already in a weakened state, he is sure to die of this illness."

Terence knew Molly liked to hear scientific explanations of diseases. She did appreciate the details, but her response reflected the compassion she felt for those who had suffered.

"Oh, Terence! Those poor girls! What a terrible thing!" she cried. "If my father did not take us to Namhsan, we might have gone the same way to escape the war. I could have died or lost some of my family to black fever."

Later Molly would learn of the area's terrible consequences to American soldiers during the war. American General Stillwell ordered a secret unit of three battalions of American volunteers into northern Burma in 1944. Led by Frank Merrill, this unit of men were called "Merrill's Marauders." After a grueling 65 mile trek through jungle, they fought the Japanese valiantly at Myitkyina, but they were decimated by fevers and dysentery. General Stillwell did not permit evacuation of troops for recovery, as was urgently recommended by medical staff. After the battle of Myitkyina, the 5307th Marauder force, originally numbering nearly three-thousand, was reduced to one hundred thirty men able to continue combat.

****

While his family was in Maymyo, Terence had indeed been working to develop the trucking company, and he was quite successful. In addition, he was making use of the architecture classes he had taken while in high school. Though Terence's plans to become an architect were disrupted by the war, his brief education in this area was useful. Much of Rangoon was in need of repairs and rebuilding, and projects were going on all around the city, so Terence was able to find work as a building contractor, and he could find skilled carpenters ready to work. As the building work increased, Terence sold his trucking business.

One of his first big contracts was to help rebuild a church in Moulmein. Terence was gone from home for long periods, but he enjoyed his work and was glad to be supporting his family. He told Molly he was working for a Mr. Howard Chrisman, an engineer who had left his job in America to come to Burma as a missionary with the American Baptists to help in the rebuilding of mission buildings damaged or destroyed in the war. Mr. Chrisman and Terence got along very well. In fact, Terence soon came to think of Mr. Chrisman as a friend as well as a business associate. But in the formal, respectful way of the culture, he always addressed him as "Mr. Chrisman."

****

Molly enjoyed visits from her sister-in-law, Anita. One time Anita's mother observed the two young women happily chatting in English. Nye Nye commented matter-of-factly, "Neither of you has ear lobes. See, the bottoms of your ears are fastened straight across to your heads. You know this means you will have short lives. Both of you will die young."

Anita told Molly after her mother left, "I don't believe in those superstitions anymore, Molly. I am a Christian now."

That was interesting to Molly. But she answered simply, "Oh." She was still thinking of the words of her wise mother-in-law and expecting, with some concern, that she would die young.

Anita and Molly

Anita had given her boy Get Lee an English name. Molly sometimes fondly teased the little boy. "Gabriel, when you were born, you were red and skinny. You looked like a little monkey, so I called you, *mah-lau doy*. I sometimes fed you goat's milk from a bottle."

Gabriel seemed to enjoy his aunt's good natured teasing. He and his siblings played happily with their cousins.

Anita commented to Molly, "You know the Chinese guy that opened the opium shop? I happened to see him the other day, and I got into a big argument with him. I told him the Chinese are the bravest fighters, but the Chinese government doesn't provide for its soldiers. There are so many people, officials don't care if they lose many men. The soldiers' own commanders don't care if they die. They don't consider the men are worth the expense to protect them. Well, all I said is true, but the businessman did not like my comments."

Molly agreed with Anita, "I see what you mean! The uniforms and provisions for the poor Chinese soldiers is of low quality. You see the American soldiers, and they have beautiful leather boots. The English, the Canadians, the French... they always have nice uniforms. They look so pretty!"

Anita chimed in, "Exactly! Just what I'm saying. Also the weapons are far better. But you are right. I too noticed the shoes especially. The poor Chinese guys don't even have shoes. Just little slippers made of grass! Poor things! But they are tough."

Molly observed, "I agree. The Chinese men are dutiful soldiers, but the commanders do not put a great value on their lives like the Americans and the English value their soldiers. The western people put so much value on one life, they will risk others' lives to save one man. Asians think that is foolish."

"I know! That is what I said in my arguments. Unlike the Chinese, the Americans care about each person," Anita said with approval.

Molly had to admire Anita for speaking up. She couldn't imagine getting into such a debate with a gentleman acquaintance, even though she felt Anita was correct.

Molly did not join Anita's conversation on one subject: mothers-in-law. Anita often complained about her demanding mother-in-law, but Molly thought it best not to mention her own difficulties.

****

Terence mentioned to Molly, "I hear there is a Christian church in Rangoon that has services in English. Why don't we take a look? Next Sunday morning we can take my jeep into town and see what they do. We can practice our English."

Molly would enjoy that. She and Terence often spoke to each other in English, but it would be nice to converse in English to others as well.

As the day approached, Molly realized that she was looking forward to other things as well. Maybe she would hear again some of those touching hymns she learned in the English school. She would love to hear wise and encouraging Scripture verses and learn more about God's Son, Jesus. She did not realize before Terence's invitation how much she longed for those things. She had often thought of Jesus during the war, and when she was in danger, she had not thought to pray to the ancestors, or to any of the Chinese gods, or to Buddha; instead she had prayed to Jesus. How curious!

Immanuel Baptist Church was in downtown Rangoon, within sight of the Sule Pagoda. Compared to the ornamental and gilded pagodas of Burma, the church was quite plain, a brick structure with a peaked roof between the spires of twin bell towers. At the peak of the roof was a cross, which Molly recognized as a symbol of the Christian faith. Something about the simplicity of the church appealed to her. The inside of the church was also plain, with high-backed benches called "pews," another large wooden cross, a tub of water, and a speaker's podium.

During the service, Molly and Terence joined in singing some of the familiar hymns. The pastor stood at the podium and spoke an understandable message about God. Molly and Terence found the words so interesting!

Most of the people in the church were English, but there were also Indian, Kayin, and mixed-race church members. Everyone was very friendly to the Chinese newcomers. Molly was happily reminded of her days at the

Methodist English Girls High School, when people of all races and social classes interacted pleasantly.

****

Part of the initial appeal of the church to Molly and Terence was the American influence. They both had high opinions of Americans who, in their minds, had rescued the world from the belligerence of the Japanese, Germans, and Italians. Americans were associated with Christianity as Indians were associated with Hinduism and Persians with Islam, so Terence and Molly felt that the apparent heroism and goodness of Americans must result from universal belief in the Christian faith. In fact, Molly heard that the Americans were helping their enemies, the Japanese, rebuild their country devastated by war.

"Who does that?" Molly asked herself rhetorically.

She heard in church that the Christian God wanted people to show love and forgiveness, even toward their enemies. This explained the American policy, she thought. At the pastor's challenge, she wondered if she could love and forgive her enemies also. She didn't think so, but Molly could see the benefits, and she wanted to try. She would like to know and to please this loving Christian God who considers each human life of value, who wants each person to know Him personally, and who wants people to live holy lives in harmony with others. She liked this God very much.

Molly was again taken by the simple, conversational prayers Pastor Eastman prayed. He didn't chant repetitious phrases, nor did he beg for prosperity. He talked to God as one might speak to an affectionate father or a deeply admired friend. Molly was reminded of her desperate, sincere prayers to Lord Jesus during the war, and now she understood that He really had protected her even though she had not then thought of herself as a Christian.

On the way home from the church service, Molly thought again of the simplicity of the church building. The many pagodas of Burma were far more beautiful, lavish, and expensive. But, she observed to Terence, "I think this church is not about a show. It's about the heart."

Terence and Molly felt drawn back to the church several times, though it was an inconveniently long drive on a Sunday morning. As the Pastor spoke, Molly's eyes were often drawn to the cross behind him. She began to wonder about the terrible, mysterious day represented by this symbol, the day in which the Lord Jesus, sinless Son of God, was actually nailed to a cross to die-- how horrible!-- as he willingly gave His own life to redeem people from the mortal debt of their sin and rebellion against Holy God. Molly scarcely understood this, but somehow God had planned from the beginning to let His Son's substitutionary death satisfy both His need for perfect justice and his passion for love and mercy.

The terrible war was still very fresh in Molly's mind. As she heard the words, "All have sinned and fall short of the glory of God," she knew it was true. So much hatred and cruelty in the world!

Molly thought that compared with many people, she herself wasn't too bad. But when she thought of God's holiness, she felt that all her passions, motives, judgments, and choices were corrupt. Often her own thoughts shamed her, and she was sorry that God could hear every one.

Contrite, she whispered simply, "Yes, Lord God! I am sorry for my sins. Please forgive me!"

****

An acquaintance of the Lee family was the sawbwa of an area of Burma called the opium triangle, where poppies grew profusely. He was a Yunnanese Chinese, from the province directly northeast of Burma, bordered to the south also by Vietnam and Laos. Puck Hee was now working as a doctor for this sawbwa. Molly's father also knew the sawbwa, and she remembered seeing him and his family in Maymyo.

In Rangoon, Terence had contact with this sawbwa's brother. Then he came to Molly with a proposition.

"Jimmy Chow and his wife have a second home here in Rangoon. They have asked if we will move into the home and take care of it while they are gone. Jimmy says it is a big house with room for all of us, so we can keep living there when they come back. Let's go have a look at it."

So Terence took Molly to a very nice section of Rangoon. He turned onto Ady Road, then to Duberin. There Molly saw an impressive, modern home with a wide, groomed lawn. Inside, she found all of the modern conveniences of a western style home, including a water supply and a flushing toilet. Indeed, there would be plenty of room for everyone.

"Really?" she asked Terence, her eyes shining with delight.

Losing no time, they moved in to the home. Mr. and Mrs. Chow would stay in Rangoon for a month or two, and Terence and Molly would host them as honored guests. Then the Chows would go back to their home in northern Burma. The arrangement was mutually satisfying, and they all got along very well.

The only problem was that when the Chows were gone, their Indian gardener obviously did not like having Terence and his family around. His expressions of displeasure and his outright rudeness were impossible to miss.

Molly thought, "Before we came, the gardener was king of this place whenever the Chows were away." He was undeniably master over the other servants caring for the house.

Other than this tension, the home suited the family perfectly. An added benefit was that it was much closer to the Immanuel Baptist Church, so Terence and Molly could attend regularly.

****

It was 1949, and often when Terence and Molly returned to visit Eight Mile, they continued to hear distressing sounds of gunshots and explosions. Alarming sound waves erupted primarily from northwest of the Lee compound, toward Insein. Indeed, these were sounds of the Kayin rebellion which would go on for decades in Burma, the Kayin responding to broken constitutional promises of Burmans. These failed guarantees would have given tribal states some level of autonomy from the central government. The Kayin had lost patience and were more determined than ever to achieve independence from Burman rule. This particular siege, called "The Battle of Insein," lasted several months.

****

Terence's work on the Moulmein church was finished, and Mr. Chrisman was completing his many projects in the Rangoon area. The Chrismans would be returning to the United States.

Terence would greatly miss this American friend. He bought a pair of lamps with shades as a gift to Mr. Chrisman. But Terence wasn't feeling well, so he asked Molly to run the errand for him. Molly took a *dong ping*, a motorized, three-wheel taxi, to the Chrisman home to deliver the gift. She found the Chrismans busily packing for their return to the United States.

Molly liked Mrs. Chrisman immediately. The gentle, American woman graciously accepted the gift, and the two shared pleasant conversation. Mrs. Chrisman told Molly that she would be sorry to leave Burma.

Mrs. Chrisman seemed around Molly's own age, but she confided, "I have arthritis, and the hot air here is a comfort to me."

Terence had instructed Molly to ask Mr. and Mrs. Chrisman for their address in the States so he could stay in touch with his friend. The Chrismans were glad to share a mailing address.

****

After attending the Immanuel Baptist church for many weeks, Terence and Molly agreed that they wanted to be baptized. Actually, Molly wasn't too sure what baptism was, but she wanted to know God better, and He said in Scripture that believers should do this, so she was eager to participate.

Terence and Molly knew there was much they didn't understand about the Christian faith, but they were drawn to it. The words of the Lord Jesus touched them: "Come unto me, all ye that labor and are heavy laden, and I will give you rest." The overwhelming message seemed so personal, so passionate: "God loves you." The sacrificial love of God was so great: "God so loved the world that He gave His only begotten Son, that whoever believes in Him will not perish but have everlasting life."

More than anything they wanted a close relationship with this loving God. What a privilege! What a thrill! Of course they believed in Jesus and gratefully accepted His gift of atonement! Of course they wanted Him to be their Lord! Who wouldn't?

"This is a faith for the living, not for the dead," Molly said.

When the couple told Pastor Eastman they wanted to be baptized, he was delighted. However, he suggested that Molly, seven months pregnant, could wait a few months and be baptized after her baby was born. Molly told the pastor she did not want to wait.

Mr. Eastman conceded, "Okay, Molly. Usually, when I baptize, I tip people back into the water, but I want you to go forward. It will be easier for you."

On the auspicious day, Pastor Eastman and Terence stood in the tank of water at the front of the church, facing the congregation of people. Pastor Eastman said, "I baptize you, Terence Lee, in the name of the Father, and of the Son, and of the Holy Spirit." Then he lowered Terence backward into the water, a simple act representing death and burial of the old life. The pastor helped him to stand again, the triumphant rising from the water symbolic of Terence's embracing newness of life in Jesus. Terence looked so joyful, and Molly's heart was full.

Then Molly stepped into the water, and the pastor baptized Molly, repeating, "I baptize you, Molly Lee, in the name of the Father, and of the

Son, and of the Holy Spirit." He helped Molly bend forward in the water, and she came back up without slipping.

Terence and Molly went to private rooms to change into dry clothes. When they were reunited, they could only smile broadly at each other. Words could not describe their joy! They felt new, cleansed, refreshed, and glad to be children of God!

Pastor Eastman counseled them that some people try to hold on to parts of their old religion, even when it is in conflict with Christian faith. By doing this they spoil truth with untruth, as pure water can be spoiled by a little impurity. Other religions have many grains of wisdom, implanted by a God of Truth wooing people of every race and tribe. But God Himself must be the final arbiter of what is wholly true, and Christians believe that is perfectly expressed the Bible, which contains more than wisdom; it is God's own living, transforming Word.

Pastor Eastman mentioned that God calls Himself a jealous God, and that His perfect love carries an element of perfect jealousy. God loves us too much to be neutral about attention and affection that should belong to Him only. He is not threatened by other gods, but unfaithfulness spoils relationships, and Our Creator wants us to have a pure relationship with Him. This is to our great benefit.

The pastor didn't need to warn them, really, for the old ways held no appeal. They gladly embraced the Christian faith. Interestingly, God's jealousy for her was not something Molly resisted.

As one immediate benefit of the new faith, Molly no longer feared ghosts. She no longer felt the urge to pull covers over her head for protection. She believed, "The Lord will protect me," and she slept without fear.

Terence and Molly were excited to tell others about their commitment to God, but they quickly found that most people didn't want to hear them. Perhaps Terence had an inkling that his mother would not be pleased, but he was not prepared for her fury.

She raged, her voice uncharacteristically raised, "You will anger the ancestors! You disrespectful son! You must change your mind! Recant your foolish words! Serve the ancestors, or something terrible will happen!"

She fumed, "This is the influence of that wife of yours!"

When Terence told Molly, she wondered, "Why didn't she get mad at Anita when she became a Christian?"

Terence answered with what Molly already knew, "Anita belongs to her in-laws now. They are responsible for her. In the same way, Ah Ma does not think you reflect poorly on your parents. She thinks you dishonor her. You know what they say to the parents about their son's wife, 'If the daughter is out of her father's house, the trouble is all yours.' "

Molly nodded sadly. She said defensively, "I didn't make her son a Christian. Anyway, she is the one who sent you to a Christian school." But Molly would never say such things to Nye Nye.

Terence responded angrily, "Of course, you did not make me a Christian! I made up my own mind. But she wants to blame you. She thinks I also have dishonored her, and she worries that I will not worship the ancestors, including herself, after she dies. As the oldest son, I am particularly expected to maintain the traditions.

"Well, Ah Ma is right! I won't do it! I won't worship the ancestors, because I worship the one true God now. I must be faithful to Him. And you must not make tea for the ancestors and gods. I won't let you do it!" Terence could be very stubborn, or very faithful to his beliefs, depending on the point of view.

Molly felt he was right. She didn't want to further incite Nye Nye's wrath, but it seemed wrong to pretend to serve the ancestors. She could never go back to the old ways that she no longer believed were valid and which were so unsatisfying to her soul.

When Nye Nye realized the two rebels were serious, she did not hesitate to express her displeasure to everyone. No wonder she was angry! Her eldest son, in whom she had such high expectations, persuaded, she thought, by his strong-willed wife, had turned his back on her most dearly held beliefs and the cultural traditions of centuries upon centuries of Chinese ancestors! Furthermore, her eldest daughter-in-law was no longer fulfilling her household duty to appease and appeal to the gods and ancestors. Nye Nye was deeply offended, and she was certain of grievous consequences from the spiritual realm.

✳✳✳✳

Antia's husband Dr. Ng had studied in England, learning a specialty in tuberculosis. Besides managing a hospital for tuberculosis patients, Dr. Ng opened a clinic with a Burmese woman doctor. Molly was pleased with the sanitation of the clinic and the modern approach to medicine. So Molly went to this woman doctor for the birth of her third child. It was the first time Molly had a doctor's care for the birth of a child.

Between contractions Molly told the doctor that she liked the medically advanced clinic. The doctor said, "Yes. We hope to educate local people about safe practices. Did you know that Burmese people often burn charcoal in the room when a woman is in childbirth? They think she needs to be warmed, even in these tropical conditions. They think the smoke is healthy to breathe, but, in truth, the burning charcoal can give off a gas called, 'carbon monoxide.' It is dangerous to inhale this gas."

"Oh!" Molly remembered that when she was a little girl with chicken pox, her mother burned charcoal in the room, thinking she was helping her daughter.

Molly appreciated this doctor talking to her about medical science. Molly felt the doctor not only had expertise, but that she respected her mind. There was so much to learn and to know, and with this child, Molly was getting both expert medical attention and an education she craved.

Soon the baby was delivered, and the doctor told Molly, "She's a girl! And, oh! She's such a cute little baby! Just wait until she grows up. She will have many admirers."

This was, indeed, a cute and thriving baby. Molly had taken vitamins and minerals during the pregnancy, and she and the baby continued to take these after the baby was born, because the doctor had explained the importance of minerals like calcium to growing children. Ah Hing and Eng Koon had not benefitted as this infant did. After the superstitious month had passed Nye Nye named her, *Ngwan Har*, "Lasting Glory."

A pastor at Immanuel Baptist Church, Mr. Zimmerman, dedicated the baby at a church service. He gave her the Biblical name of Lois. The pastor explained that the Lois mentioned in the Bible was a woman devoted to the Lord.

****

Molly enjoyed living in the modern home of the Chows. It was so convenient to things of the city of Rangoon. She enjoyed managing the home and entertaining the Chows when they returned. Other than the rude treatment of the gardener, everything seemed to be working out just fine.

Molly had been busy making lovely clothes for her daughters and son, and after the children wore the outfits, she would wash them carefully. To dry the clothes, Molly placed a couple of chairs near the bay window and put a sturdy bamboo pole across the backs of the chairs. Then she draped the clothing on the pole. The breezes through the window dried the clothes effectively. But, one day after leaving the clothes to dry, Molly returned to find all of the clothes were gone! Stolen!

She had no proof, but she would always wonder if the rude gardener had taken the clothing. Maybe he was trying to make them leave.

Soon after that Mrs. Chow came alone for a visit. She was a pleasant British woman, always dressed in fashionable Chinese clothes. As always, Terence and Molly enjoyed acting as host and hostess. They gave Mrs. Chow the use of their jeep and driver.

Molly noticed that Mrs. Chow had their chauffeur carry her heavy handbag for her. She was also not careful about hiding the wealth in her bag when she purchased goods. One morning, Mrs. Chow was distraught, and she confided to Terence and Molly that a gold bar was missing from her handbag! The couple felt sorry and even felt in some way responsible for not protecting Mrs. Chow and her property. The police were called, and they found bare footprints in the grass leading to a locked window, as well as grass inside the window. This made them conclude that someone inside had helped someone outside with the theft by opening the window. The house servants, gardener, and chauffeur were all under suspicion, but the police were never able to charge a thief or thieves.

Feeling the shame of letting down their benefactor, Molly said to Terence, "We should not stay here any longer." With apologies to the Chows, they regretfully moved back to the soy sauce factory at Eight Mile.

Chapter Seventeen

The Old House

The gunshots persisted north of Eight Mile. The tensions with Nye Nye persisted. One thing that did change was the living arrangement.

While Terence and Molly were away, Nye Nye decided she and Lo Yeahr and the children would move into the pawn shop. She had the sign removed and the building remodeled, adding a large extension on the back with a dining room and two other rooms on one side. An outside stair-case, trimmed nicely in teak wood, was built up to the entrance of the raised building. The kitchen had a nice built-in cement stove with two burners, one for a wok and one for a pot. Charcoal was pushed in from the side of the stove.

Nye Nye, always resourceful, had the big house remodeled and rented out as a restaurant to help support the family. It was called *Mahn Neng Ting,* "Ten-Thousand Year Green," or more comfortably in English, "The Evergreen Restaurant."

Moonlight, Molly, and Charlene

Terence, Molly, Ah Hing, Eng Koon, and Ngwan Har moved into the oldest building on the grounds, where the elder Ng's had lived for a time. This inferior accommodation for the first son was likely intended to create an uncomfortable situation for him and his rebellious wife. Until Terence was feeling better and found work, options were limited.

It was a roughly made building, meant for workers at the soy sauce factory, not for a family. In the hot season, the living area inside the building became nearly unbearable as the sun heated the uninsulated tin roof, turning the place into an oven.

The family found refuge beneath the house, which was raised on stilts nearly ten feet off the ground. One solid wall supported the back of the house and several upright beams secured the other corners and sides of the house. This perimeter was covered with an open lattice, allowing breezes to move freely through the enclosure, creating a pleasant haven. A large opening in the front formed a doorway. A staircase on one side of the shelter went up to the house, and the large beams supporting the house were visible from below.

The Evergreen Restaurant. Molly is in the back row between Number Four Sister Fe Heng and Number Five Sister Fe Yin; in the front row are Ah Hing, Eng Koon, Number Seven Brother Foke Loke and Number Six Brother Foke San.

Inside the old house were two main rooms and a bathroom. As usual in Burma, the ceilings were high to keep the rooms cooler, though the tin roof cancelled the effect. One room acted as the living room, dining room and bedroom for Molly and the children. The other room was reserved for the maids. Terence felt suffocated inside and slept on the broad balcony that extended across the front of the building.

For bathing in the bathroom of the old house, an oval aluminum tub with handles on each side was filled with water from a soy sauce pot, which had been filled by Indian Gardener. The tub was not big enough to sit in, but it was set on a stool so one would not need to bend too far. Water was then dipped from the tub with a little pot with a handle and poured over one's body, and the water rained down into a drain in the wooden floor. Usually, because of the tropical climate of Burma, Molly was content to use the water at room temperature, and it felt refreshing to her. But Nye Nye said she was always cold because her body was stressed from having so many babies. So at her house she had one of her maids boil water to add to her bath. Occasionally in the cool season, Molly asked her maids to do this for her as well. Other personal duties were done in an outhouse. Molly missed the conveniences of the automatic faucets, showers, and flushing crouch toilets to which she had grown accustomed in her childhood home and at the Chow house.

Molly looked at the house with a critical eye. It was not very satisfactory. Really, the house was not well built to begin with and had become dilapidated. But she was in no position to complain, and so she gave it her womanly attention, bought some basic furnishings, and tried to make the home as clean and comfortable as possible. She could not afford anything resembling the grand, round marble table of her childhood home. Instead, she bought a low, rectangular, wood table with four chairs. She bought the necessary beds for herself and Terence and two maids, mats for the children, and basic stoves and utensils for the cooking area under the house. Molly also found a table and cane chairs for the balcony, where Terence loved to sit with her and watch the children play in the cool evenings.

****

In the Chin home of Molly's childhood, the children wouldn't think of calling Byu Goo and Pwa Pwa "servants;" they were always addressed respectfully. By contrast, Mrs Lee sent away to China to purchase young girls, seven or eight years old, orphans or children of impoverished parents. In this culturally acceptable practice, desperately poor families rationalized that a daughter placed with a rich family would not starve, and the income helped the rest of the family to survive. The girls were fed, clothed, and sheltered, and in return they were expected to work for their masters until they were of marriageable age. Sometimes, even at eleven o'clock at night, Nye Nye and Lo Yeahr would get a taste for *hlew yeah*, a "night treat." Sometimes they themselves would cook, both seeming to enjoy this task, but other times the girls would have to make whatever the masters wanted. Sometimes they had to make a hurried up version of a favorite dish, boiled cabbage soup. At least Nye Nye always found a husband for each maid when she came of age and often provided a generous dowry for her, including a set of twenty-two karat gold jewelry and several outfits of clothing. She gave even more gifts to favored ones.

Molly realized that Nye Nye was helping these girls and their families to survive. But the girls were often so young Molly thought they themselves should be cared for, not responsible for serving others.

Molly would find local maids, counting on Terence to ask around for referrals. They would usually want to work only a year or two before returning to their villages, and then Molly would have to find replacements. She quickly found out that two maids from the same tribe worked best; otherwise they would be much more argumentative. For instance, a tribal Burmese maid felt superior and a Kayin maid resented the Burmese woman. The discord between maids naturally spilled over to create an unharmonious home.

Molly especially liked to have two Kayin maids. Though girls from the same tribe could also have disagreements, most of the time they got along well and even sang together in their native tongue as they worked or as they relaxed in the evenings. Molly enjoyed the happy songs and often Christian hymns. She paid the girls 30 kyat per month plus room and board. They did the shopping, cooking, cleaning, and laundry, and helped with children.

Molly's maids were wary of Nye Nye and quickly found something energetic to do when she approached. "The old lady is coming!" they would cry in warning. Then they might start sweeping a swept floor or re-washing clothes they had just cleaned, just to look busy. Sometimes, Nye Nye would scold them anyway.

All of the maids bowed very low when Nye Nye passed, or if they had to walk in front of her. Molly did not dissuade them, recognizing the prudence of this submissive act. But Molly did not want her maids to bow to herself or Terence. "We do not have this custom," she told them.

Molly found the maids to be good cooks, and she enjoyed the Burmese cuisine, although she quickly made two adjustments: not too much chili and no fermented fish. Molly and Terence agreed that even the smell of the latter was unpleasant. Sometimes Molly asked the girls to make a Chinese dish, but usually she did not interfere as long as they did their jobs well.

Inevitably, new maids would hear that Mr. Ng had died in the old house. In spite of Nye Nye's belief that it was a good omen to have an old man die there, Molly's maids did not share this conviction. The country girls had backgrounds steeped in that belief, and even the Christian girls sometimes clung to superstition and spiritism. They often disrupted family happenings with frightful sightings of Mr. Ng's ghost. Once again, Terence was angered by their irrational fears and tried to show them their foolishness, but they were undeterred.

The hot season in the old house forced the occupants to seek cooler shelter below, but the monsoon season had its own challenges. The worst storms were usually in the afternoon, when rain would pound on the tin roof like a hundred drums and the wind would press itself against the old house as if shoving with a strong shoulder to knock it down. The sudden boom of thunder and flash of lightening would always cause a fright, sometimes with unhappy remembrances of wartime explosions. But the feel and smell of wetness was so customary in Burma, this condition was hardly noticed. One learned to do what needed to be done in soggy conditions.

During monsoon storms, the stoves and fuel under the old house were covered until meal time, and then the maids did the best they could against the deluge in the partial shelter. Meals were eaten tolerably at the table in the old house, with tin roof cacophony and wind induced tremors.

In all seasons, the open-air refuge under the house was the place for cooking, and wood and charcoal were stacked to make the fires in two small, hand-carried stoves. Each stove had an opening near the bottom for small pieces of firewood. Or, charcoal could be placed in a basin above. Either way, heat would rise to the top of the stove and ash would fall below to be emptied. Charcoal was more expensive, but the maids preferred it, because it was ready to use, and wood must be chopped and split into small pieces. Three clay supports held a grate above the coals, and the cooking pot was set on the grate. Even in those days it was an old-fashioned way to cook.

Terence had his particular tastes, and even in her anger Nye Nye continued to dote on him. She often sent Foke San over with something special for Terence to eat.

****

One hot afternoon when they were all sitting under the house trying to escape the heat, Terence asked Molly, "Remember the days we spent hiding in the cemetery in Pyapon?"

"Of course." Molly was surprised Terence brought up this subject. No one liked to talk about the war days.

"Do you remember Haung Se'ung carrying Ah San and his mat?"

"Yes," she replied. "Every day Nye Nye would scold, 'Haung Se-ung! Do not leave Foke San's mat behind! Haung Se'ung! He may need to lie on it!' "

Terence smiled and asked, "Did you know that my mother had sewn two bamboo mats together?"

"...to make Ah San's mat?" Molly asked. "No, I didn't know. It looked like an ordinary mat to me."

"That is what she intended. Ah Ma had sewn British notes between the two mats," Terence confided, a sly grin on his face as he admired his mother's cunning.

"Really!" Molly answered, her mouth gaping with surprise. As close as she was to the situation, she had never suspected the ruse. "I see! That is why she watched Haung Se'ung so closely! She wouldn't let the poor girl out of her sight!"

Terence nodded.

Who would think a little servant girl was carrying around a small fortune in the mat of her charge? Surely the girl herself did not know. Once again Molly marveled at her mother-in-law's ingenuity and realized the weighty responsibility this woman had to keep many family members alive and well during the war.

****

Molly was surprised to see a nephew of Nye Nye walk into her tiny house, bringing all of his possessions. He was clearly intending to take up permanent residence.

As soon as Molly could talk with Terence alone, she accused, "Why did you invite him to come here?"

Terence said, "I did not invite him, Molly. I never knew he was coming."

"What about the children?" Molly said. "You know he has tuberculosis! You know this disease is caused by a bacterium and can be spread with a cough! He may not know this, but what if he passes it to your children? They could die, Terence!"

Indeed, the frail man coughed a lot, and Molly could imagine the fearful, unseen germs floating through the air and into the noses of her precious little ones. While Molly felt sorry that the man was clearly ailing, she could not put her daughters and son at risk.

Terence also could not bear the thought of his children contracting tuberculosis. The disease, which first attacks the lungs, was commonly called "consumption," because it seemed to slowly eat away at a person. Reminded by his wife of the danger and nudged to do the difficult thing, he gently confronted the man.

He said kindly, but firmly, "My children are young. Your cough may spread the tuberculosis to them. I think it is better for you to live in the guard shack."

The young man quickly agreed and moved to the tiny building on the grounds. To Molly's great surprise, a little while later the man took a wife and she bore a daughter. Not long after that, the young family moved back to his village in China.

****

Terence's mysterious illness was getting worse. He always seemed to carry a low grade fever, at least 100 degrees or as much as 102 degrees. He was weak, his joints ached, and he tired easily. Terence took some time off of work to rest, hoping to rebuild his strength.

Molly began a long and frustrating journey with Terence, accompanying him to many doctors and specialists, including cardiologists and lung specialists. No one could find the cause of his illness. One doctor thought he had intestinal trouble. Another thought he must have tuberculosis, like his cousin. But after Terence had an x-ray, another doctor said his lungs were clear.

Every doctor had his own diagnosis and prescribed a new remedy. The doctor that diagnosed Terence with tuberculosis, unconvinced by the chest x-ray, prescribed injections of a new wonder drug, streptomycin. Oh, the results of that were terrible! Terence became dangerously ill. He couldn't get his breath, was nauseous, and couldn't sleep. Now these are known to be common side effects of the drug, but for a terribly sick man, this was too much!

Finally Terence said, "I'm not going to those doctors anymore! I can't stand their treatment!" He refused to finish the course of injections, and Molly was glad he quit them.

Terence would not consider going to the Chinese folk doctors, though they had learned to mimic western physicians by convincingly wielding a stethoscope. After acting the part, they prescribed their usual, traditional mixtures of herbs.

Molly agreed with his decision. She told Terence, "You take their medicine, and then you live or you die. Who knows whether or not the medicine will have any effect, or even make you worse?" Chinese medicine, she knew, did not require the rigorous scientific testing of the west and was often anecdotal.

But as far as Terence was concerned, the British trained Burmese doctors weren't doing any better. None of their treatments seemed to help, and some made him worse.

Nye Nye had her own diagnosis. "Because you became Christians," she ranted, "that is why you are sick! You do not worship the ancestors! They are punishing you! I told you something bad would happen!"

Day after day Nye Nye would walk into the home scolding and walk out scolding. Often she accused Molly directly, "You have done this to your husband! You should have followed me to worship the ancestors!"

Molly knew she was not the cause of Terence's illness. But she dared not defend herself, and she would not talk back to her elder. Day after day Molly took the verbal pounding, languishing beneath the relentless anger of this great woman.

Really, from Nye Nye's view, she had nothing but trouble with her daughter-in-law. First Ngood Yin addled her son's mind with *chi' ting* romance so that he could not focus on his duties to his family in their time of greatest need and danger. That was a great strike against Ngood, but Nye Nye had tried to be patient with the girl. Then the rich man's daughter was fussy about kitchen work, unlike some daughters-in-law. In fact, hadn't Nye Nye herself been forced to adapt when her husband's fortunes were diminished? Then this Ngood shamed the family by becoming a Christian and was failing to perform the religious duties expected of all daughters-in-law for many, many centuries.

Now this! Nye Nye's precious eldest son Puck Ying was quite ill, and Ngood must be to blame. Nye Nye knew she had raised Puck Ying well. Ngood surely influenced him to become a Christian, causing grave offense to gods and ancestors who retaliated with this illness. Even with all this evidence, Ngood remained stubbornly Christian.

Puck Ying, her very promising eldest son, was ruined. His inexcusable Christian belief and the sickness proving the displeasure of the gods made him a liability and an embarrassment to his family. In fact, he was seriously damaging the family's excellent reputation. Ngood was responsible, and Nye Nye had lost patience with her.

Nye Nye did not raise her voice, but she had one mission: to bring the rebellious couple to their senses. It was for their own good, for the good of the family, for the good of the race, for the ancestors, and for the traditions. Perhaps if the rebels would renounce their Christian beliefs and appease the gods, there might be some hope for them. Therefore, Nye Nye had no intention of making life comfortable for the family of her eldest son. It was actually a kindness, she thought, to make their lives difficult, so that they must reconsider. She was required to express her displeasure, and, by her lawyerly arguments and parental scolding, she must correct them in their error. This was her duty.

If Nye Nye was the only one to relate differently to them, as difficult as that was, the couple might have been better able to cope. But now, friends and relatives stopped coming to visit, and acquaintances avoided Puck Ying and Ngood. No one wanted to maintain a connection with the pariah couple who seemed so clearly to have upset the gods and ancestors. Each one feared he would incur wrath by associating with the cursed ones. Whether or not Terence was carrying a deadly contagion, he and his family must be avoided as if he were.

Eight miles on a crowded, bouncing bus was a long trip for a sick man, and the parents would not want to loan the jeep for trips to church, so the couple was rarely able to attend. In those days it was also a great distance for church friends to come to visit, friends who might have supported them. Terence and Molly were thankful that Pastor Eastman came sometimes to pray with them and encourage them, and more than ever Molly looked forward to visits from Anita, who was now her sister in Christ. But, for the most part, the couple was very much alone to suffer.

In desperate need and separated from other comforts, Molly cried out to Lord Jesus, speaking to Him as a loving friend. She spoke, not with flowery words, but from a broken heart.

"Oh, Lord," she prayed. "You heard what my mother-in-law said. She said it is because we believe in You that Terence has become so ill! Please help us. I don't know what to do. My husband is sick. My mother-in-law is angry at me. Our friends have left us. If something happens to my husband, I don't know how I can take care of my children."

The thought came to Molly, "Even Lord Jesus suffered. He can help me face my suffering." This brought her great comfort. But she knew that God could fix her circumstance, and she desperately wanted Him to do so.

She had no Bible of her own, but she did have a small booklet of Scripture verses, which had come in the mail from the church. Molly would read the words and think, "Oh my! God Himself is talking to me! I am moved by His attention to me. I can feel His love! It's so wonderful!"

These personal encouragements from God comforted her and kept her from going crazy with worry and sadness. She kept the booklet with her at all times, so that any time she could read and find refreshment, encouragement, and tender words of love.

She found one Scripture especially comforting, and every day she would reread the two promises of God in Hebrew 13:5 "I will never fail thee nor forsake thee." She knew God could be trusted to keep His promises. God, Almighty and Wonderful God, was with her! He knew every detail of her life, and He loved her. No matter what, He would not abandon her. What could matter as much?

Molly found she must read Scriptures every day. The words were like spiritual food to her soul, helping her to survive. If she didn't eat them, she worried about her husband's illness, feared losing him, felt lonely from social ostracizing, and felt demoralized by Nye Nye's harping. Looking at her troubles, she could quickly become hopeless and defeated.

Yet, when she became aware of God's glory and the downpour of God's abundant love over her, she felt her soul was refreshed. She could feel the joy of being near Him and a mysterious peace in His care. She could feel a strengthening power and understood a higher perspective. Oh, maybe this was the work of the Holy Spirit inside of her!

Molly also found she must repeat the verses about forgiveness. Good Chinese girl that she was, she was surprised to recognize her own resentment toward Nye Nye for the way she was treating her. She would remind herself:

> *"Put on then, as God's chosen ones, holy and beloved, compassion, kindness, lowliness, meekness and patience, forbearing one another, and if one has a complaint against another, forgiving each other; as the Lord has forgiven you, so you must also forgive. And above all these put on love, which binds everything together in perfect harmony." Colossians 3:12-14*

She discovered that she had to choose to forgive, and then she had to have help to actually do it. She often prayed, "Lord, please forgive me for not forgiving. Help me to forgive and to love others."

As she did this, she often felt the heavy burden of bitterness lifted from her like a kite floating to the clouds. But the next day, as if she had pulled the bitter kite back by its string and clutched it sourly to her chest, Molly would have to pray again and forgive again, releasing her hurts to God.

She realized that she did not feel close to Lord Jesus when she was bitter, and she very much wanted intimacy with Him. Slowly, she found she could release anger with more ease, anticipating the beautiful results of sensing the fullness of Christ's presence and sharing His pleasure. In this way, day by day, she sensed the power of God's word and His Holy Spirit working in her, changing her, gradually shaping her to His likeness as she depended on Him.

Molly realized that Terence was angry. Not only was he suffering day after day with his debilitating, mysterious illness, he was feeling the frustration of a weakened man unable to support his family and needing to be dependent on his parents. Plus he was forced to endure the anger of his mother, hear her scold his wife, and feel the deep loneliness of abandonment by his friends.

When Pastor Eastman came to visit, he sensed Terence's anger. The pastor did not scold him or preach at him, but he sat with him and listened quietly, allowing Terence to vent his frustrations. Then Molly could hear the pastor reading from the Bible with Terence and praying quietly with him. Terence seemed at peace after the kind pastor's visits.

But Pastor Eastman had been in Burma for twelve years and was making plans to return to the States. Terence felt well enough one day to load his family into the jeep and drive to see Pastor and Mrs. Eastman at their home before they set sail on the nearly two month journey to America. The Lees found the Eastmans in a small house with sparse American furnishings. Before they left, by Terence's request, Pastor Eastman used Terence's camera and took a picture of Terence and his family standing in front of

Molly and Mrs. Eastman, left, and Molly, Terence, Ah Hing, and Eng Koon, right

the Eastman's house and car. Terence also took a picture of Mrs. Eastman with Molly.

Then all said, "Good-bye." Another friend was gone.

****

The months of Terence's illness had turned into a year and more. His health continued to worsen, his mother continued to accuse, relatives continued to spurn the couple, and Molly was in a constant state of concern for his life.

One day, Nye Nye suggested to Ngood, "Why don't you bring all of your wedding jewelry to me? I will lock it away for you, for safe keeping."

Oh! Molly did not want to surrender the jewelry to Nye Nye. She guessed that Nye Nye was foreseeing an on-going drain on resources to provide for her son's family, particularly in the event of his death, and who could blame her for securing collateral? At the time, Molly did not know the extent to which Nye Nye had previously boldly saved her family from financial disaster, besides carefully protecting dwindling fortunes during the war. From Nye Nye's view, Molly's rebellion could thwart all of her efforts and bring down the family wealth along with its social standing.

It was a difficult thing to do. If Terence died, the jewelry would be Molly's only, meager economic security. But Molly obediently gathered the gold bracelet, the diamond bracelet, the diamond necklace, and other jewelry her in-laws had given her after the wedding ceremony in Pyapon. She also collected the jewelry she had been given by the Lee relatives and handed it all over to Nye Nye. But she kept the emerald ring and the loose pearls and rubies from her mother.

****

Molly heard about the new hospital in Rangoon opened by American Seventh Day Adventists. Though Terence had tired of fruitless trips to the doctors, Molly convinced him to take advantage of this new opportunity. Americans had helped win the war against the Japanese; perhaps they could help win the war against the illness that was ravaging Terence. So, Terence was admitted into the hospital for a week of tests. He and Molly were buoyed with high expectations of finding out what was wrong and of Terence becoming well.

At the end of the week a doctor spoke to Terence. "We were able to diagnose your illness."

What a relief! Terence looked at the doctor hopefully. But Molly noticed right away that the doctor's countenance did not reflect hope.

"You have rheumatic fever and a rheumatic heart. Your heart is very much enlarged, and the mitral valve has been so damaged by persistent fever, that it will not close and open properly. The heart is not able to circulate blood as it should. If we had seen you sooner, we might have been able to do something...."

At the last sentence Molly knew in her breaking heart *mow hee mong... mow* meaning "no," *mong* meaning "wishes," *hee mong* meaning "look forward to good things." She thought dismally, "No reason to look forward to good things." And so she despaired in two languages, "*Mow hee mong*. No hope of recovery."

"I'm sorry," the doctor said sincerely.

The doctor spoke aside to Molly, "Take him home and try to make him as comfortable as possible...." As he spoke, the doctor's words were kindly spoken, but his dire meaning was clear. Terence would hang on as long as his heart would allow him, but death was imminent. Doctors could not save him, nor could they offer him relief or buy him time.

Terence and Molly were devastated. They feared the terrible pain of separation Terence's death would cause them. Neither discussed other fears, but they both knew that life would be extremely difficult for Molly and the children with Terence gone. Molly foresaw with dizzying anxiety that she would become a servant, a disliked one, doing kitchen work for her mother-in-law. She would be alone to face the anger of Nye Nye about her Christian faith. She would feel like a beggar toward her in-laws for every tube of toothpaste for her children unless she found some means of support. Molly also feared the alternative, the looming prospect of working on the street doing laundry like her poor aunt when Number Four Uncle died.

As a Christian, Terence was not afraid to die, but he was devoted to his family, and he knew they still needed him. He insisted to Molly that he was not ready to die.

Chapter Eighteen

Death Watch

It was November, the most beautiful time of year in Burma. It was not yet too hot, and the monsoon rains were finished drowning the country for now.

Ready or not, Terence was clearly near death. His every breath was a battle of will and his hands and lips were puffy and blue. His face was so round, it was unrecognizable. His whole body was swollen, and his stomach was so bloated, he looked like a pregnant woman. Molly had endured the heart-rending agony of seeing him worsen day by day. As the illness took its toll on Terence, Molly was consumed by caring for him and the three young children. Her face was hardened with stress and fatigue, and her figure was starkly thin with neglect.

Dr. Ng came to visit Terence. He looked serious and said little. Afterward, using the traditional Chinese chain of communication, he told Anita, who told her mother, that Terence was not likely to live through the night.

Immediately Nye Nye took command: "Indian Gardener! Indian Gardener! Come here right away! Carry Puck Ying's bed to my house and place it before the ancestor altar. Then carry Puck Ying to my house and put him on the bed, with his feet facing the altar.

"Ngood! Now! Bring Puck Ying's suit... his best suit of clothes. Bring the children."

Nye Nye ordered someone to go to buy Terence a pair of new shoes. Molly understood this concern of her mother-in-law. She knew the Chinese traditionally believed the dying individual should be wearing new clothes for the formal entrance into the next world, but especially the shoes should be new for all the endless walking required in the next life.

Nye Nye continued giving orders, "Indian Gardener! Put mats around Puck Ying's bed.

"Ngood! You and your children will sleep around your husband's bed tonight."

Terence heard the commotion and was angry. He said weakly to Molly, "She thinks I'm going to die. But I'm not going to die. Don't worry."

Molly was too distraught to argue. She said simply, "Okay."

But in her mind she thought, "Did he say, 'Don't worry?' Of course, I am very worried! All I can do is worry! Look at my husband! He looks as if he cannot hold on to his life much longer. I cannot help it! I am very worried!"

Molly did not want Terence to be taken to his mother's house or to face the ancestor idol. Nor did Molly like seeing Terence disturbed with his mother's unnecessary and taxing ministrations. Why couldn't she leave the dying man in peace? How could she subject his poor swollen body to dressing in a suit that no longer fit him? Terence was angry, but he was too weak to argue with his mother, and Molly was too afraid of Nye Nye to object.

Of course, Nye Nye thought she was doing the right thing for her son. She had never stopped loving him, even in his disobedience. She was fulfilling her duty as she understood it.

Terence told his wife gently, "It's okay, Molly. Do as she says. Anyway, I'm not going to die."

Molly's attention, even in the stress of the situation, was caught when the new shoes arrived. The shoes were not like the black dress shoes that Terence usually wore with his suit. They were white canvas tennis shoes.

"Tennis shoes?" Molly thought. "How odd. That doesn't look nice. Who bought these? Why tennis shoes?" Later, Molly would conclude that these were chosen either for economy or for comfort as Terence began his supposed long walk into the spirit world. But at the time, she was so exhausted with concern for Terence that her mind seemed to stick there, unmoving, thinking, "Tennis shoes?"

Before the day's end, a string of relatives came to see Terence. In her grief, Molly thought resentfully that at last they had overcome their fear of associating with him to satisfy morbid curiosity in the bloated, failing man struck by the gods. Some relatives were likely truly concerned for Terence and wanted to offer kind words. But Molly felt others had a sideshow interest, and she suffered to see her husband put through this.

Molly overheard the whispers, "Look at him! Can a man live long like this? Surely he will 'go through' tonight. He should not have angered the ancestors."

She was distraught. Again Terence assured her, "They think I'm going to die. But I'm not going to die."

****

Night time had spread deep darkness across the Asian world, but Molly could not sleep. She was on the mat by her husband's bed. He was squeezed into his suit, with tennis shoes on his feet, facing the ancestor idol.

Before going to her bed, Nye Nye had spent much time at the well-stocked altar, asking the deceased relatives to prepare for Terence and to be easy on him. She also asked that Terence's misbehavior not be taken out on herself or her other children. In the oppressive atmosphere, Molly could only cry quietly to her own God.

Now alone with her dying husband and her doomed children, Molly lay quietly, tears flowing in rivulets onto the woven bamboo mat. She was feeling the impending loss wrenching her heart as if Terence were dead already. Unlike the wailing Chinese actress whose long strands of mucous streamed from her nose, Molly wiped the stuff with many handkerchiefs, noiselessly so as not to disturb her husband and children. She could hear Terence's labored, raspy breaths, and this pitiful sound was the small comfort of her circumstance. If the room fell silent, how could she bear it?

Through the night and into the early morning hours she cried desperately, noiselessly to God, "Lord Jesus, please don't take him away now! The children are so small.... They're not even in school.... The children need their father! Please, let the children grow up first.... Perhaps when they finish school... or finish college.... Perhaps then they will be able to stand on their own feet.... Perhaps then they can get along without their father. Lord Jesus, please have mercy on us and let Terence live!"

In moments of slight courage, she wanted to be faithful to God in any case. Afterall, He had not answered her prayers for Terence to be healed so far. What if He did not let Terence live? She cried, "Lord Jesus, I'm asking for help from you. You said, 'Seek and you shall find. Ask and it shall be given. Knock and it will open.' I remember these three things.... I can't remember from what part of the Bible this is," she apologized, "but I remember the words, and I'm seeking You, and I'm asking for help, and I'm knocking on Your door. Show me the way. Show me how to do and what to do."

But her little bit of courage in asking for help in the pending unmentionable circumstance always dissolved into the desperate cry, "Oh, Lord Jesus, please let Terence live... for his children. Perhaps after they finish college...."

She also argued respectfully, "Lord Jesus, Nye Nye thinks the gods and ancestors are causing Terence to be sick, because they are angry with us for worshiping You only. Lord Jesus, if Terence dies, everyone will say it is because we are Christians. But You are the True God. You have all the power. Please save Terence so they will know Your power. If he dies, they will think the gods and ancestors are powerful and that You have no power."

Molly cycled through her arguments and petitions hour by hour. Intent on own her desperate prayers, she hadn't been paying attention to Terence's breathing. Suddenly, about three o'clock in the morning, he called to her softly, "Molly! Molly! Come here! Hurry!"

Fearing he was calling out as he breathed his last breaths, Molly frantically responded. Leaning close to his face, she asked urgently, "What is it? What do you want?"

"Molly, you must remember this for me," Terence's voice sounded stronger than she expected, and he was full of excitement.

"What? Remember what?" Molly asked.

"Just now.... I wasn't sleeping. I wasn't dreaming, Molly. I was half awake... and this... Being... came and stood by my bed. He was wearing a white, gauzy robe, you know, like Arabian people wear, but it was very bright and flowing. And He looked at me with the most compassionate eyes. Blue eyes. The kindliest, blue eyes, Molly. He didn't say anything to me, but this Being held His hand above me and... He didn't touch me, but He did this: He stroked his hand over me, up and down above my body, three times. Stroke. Stroke. Stroke." Terence demonstrated to Molly, holding his hand above his torso and slowly motioning three times from his shoulders to his hips.

Then Terence added with awe, "He looked at me again, his blue eyes full of compassion.... Suddenly He disappeared! This was not a dream, Molly. It happened to me just now."

Molly was speechless with awe, and Terence was quiet with wonder.

Then he repeated, "Molly, you must remember this. I don't want to forget it. I must never forget."

Terence spoke earnestly, "Will you help me remember?"

"Of course, Terence! I won't forget," Molly assured him.

Terence relaxed and said, "Oh…. I am so tired."

Soon he fell asleep. He slept very deeply, very quietly, much more comfortably than she had seen him rest for some time. She was consoled and grateful to see him resting so.

But Molly could not rest. She lay on her mat again, her mind carrying her on a wild ride from thought to thought. She was certain Terence was not making this up. How he disliked the apparitions and ranting of Byu Goo! How he scolded the Burmese maids for their fantastic stories! He was too honest and too scientific to be imagining or making up a story like this.

But, Molly wondered, who was this Being? Blue eyes? Nobody in Burma has blue eyes! She was almost afraid to hope. Could it be that Lord Jesus had made an appearance in Nye Nye's home, right here in the room full of idols? Did Jesus have blue eyes? Could Jesus have blue eyes? And if The Being was Lord Jesus or His Messenger, what did this mean? Why did He come?

As wonderful questions and thrilling thoughts tumbled through her mind, Molly's heart raced with excitement. No way could she sleep! She kept considering each of Terence's stunning words. She wanted to keep her promise and remember every detail, and besides that, she wanted to savor the event and wonder of its meaning.

"Kindliest blue eyes…" she reflected. "Full of compassion…" she considered.

After about an hour, Terence woke and called to her again, "Molly, bring me the night pot!"

His urine ran like a faucet and nearly filled the pot to the brim! Molly precariously emptied the pot, and when she returned, she found he was asleep again, his fragile body resting with the contentment of a satisfied baby.

Molly watched his peaceful sleep. In the dim light, she looked closely at his fingers. She thought the swelling appeared to have gone down. She looked at his stomach and thought, "Oh, my goodness! The bloating has subsided! Right in front of my eyes!" His face looked better too.

She watched Terence's serene countenance and observed his easy, quiet breathing. She whispered, "Lord, did you do a miracle for us? Did you answer my prayer? Did you spare my husband's life?" Still she could not sleep, her mind filled with awe.

The next morning Terence was much better, and Nye Nye consented to let him go back to his house. He continued to gain strength, little by little, day after day. Molly spoke passionate, grateful words to her Heavenly Father. She was moved that He had heard her cries and intervened with tender mercy.

But Terence and Molly didn't tell anyone about the visitation. At the time, the experience seemed to them too sacred of which to speak. Like Mary, the mother of Jesus, who treasured the words of angels and shepherds at Jesus' birth, Molly "kept all these things, pondering them in her heart."

****

Days, weeks, and months passed, and Terence continued to gain strength. Every day when Molly woke and found him alive, she poured out thanks to God. Still, Terence was not well enough to work, and Molly knew their situation was tenuous.

Molly confided to God, "Lord, when I was growing up, I depended on my father to take care of me. Now we are depending on Terence's parents, but they are getting older. How long can we depend on them? It isn't fair to expect them to do everything for us. I can't watch the older folks doing the work, and me not doing anything. I'm no help in the kitchen... and, Lord..." Molly added cautiously, "I want some freedom from my mother-in-law. I cannot bear her anger with me. I want to please her, but she is so unhappy with me. I feel so burdened by her displeasure."

Knowing she must be honest with One who already knew her heart, she added, "And besides this, Lord Jesus, I know I am spoiled, but, please, I don't want to be her cook."

Molly continued to confide to her best friend and gracious, all-powerful benefactor, "I don't know if Terence will ever work again; he can take a few steps now, but then he starts having heart palpitations. I think I must find something to do to support my family."

Now that, Molly knew, was a problem, as she continued to discuss with God. "I don't know what I can do. I finished all the school work, but I never got to take the final test and get my diploma from high school."

Molly knew God was already very familiar with every detail about her. She was not informing   God, but conversing with Him. She felt very close to Him as she shared both mundane thoughts and deepest concerns.

Molly knew He listened lovingly to every word. She asked her attentive Heavenly Father, "Please help me again. Help me find some work I can do."

Molly found comfort for her plight in the verses of the hymn, "Count Your Blessings":

When upon life's billows you are tempest tossed; When you are discouraged, thinking all is lost,
Count your many blessings, name them one by one, and it will surprise you what the Lord hath done.
Are you ever burdened with a load of care? Does the cross seem heavy you are called to bear?
Count your many blessings, every doubt will fly, And you will keep singing as the days go by.
When you look at others with their lands and gold, Think that Christ has promised you His wealth untold;
Count your many blessings. Wealth can never buy - Your reward in Heaven, nor your home on high.
So, amid the conflict whether great or small, Do not be disheartened, God is over all;
Count your many blessing, angels will attend, Help and comfort give you to your journey's end.

Each verse was followed by the encouraging refrain:
Count your blessings, name them one by one, Count your blessings, see what God hath done!
Count your blessings, name them one by one, and it will surprise you what the Lord hath done.

The words of the hymn were so moving and so personal. She did feel tempest tossed, discouraged, and burdened with a load of care. She did feel her poverty. She often felt all was lost. But, as the song said, she had many blessings to count. She had a husband who loved her very much, and God had miraculously and graciously spared his life. So she was not alone to care for their three precious children, each one a great blessing. They had a roof over their heads and food to eat.

And she was especially blessed to know the true God. She was grateful to know that He is always loving, always good, and always faithful. She was blessed that He was amazingly attentive to her needs. She was so thankful to know He would help and comfort her until her earthly journey came to an end. She also knew that the trials she faced were temporary, and that one day she would face her wonderful Lord Jesus and live with Him eternally. She would not trade the wealth of knowing Him for any material reward. Yes, she thought, the song said it all so well.

****

Terence said something to Anita, and Anita took the risk of confronting her mother as tactfully as possible, "Do you think you should return Molly's jewelry now? The family is in a difficult circumstance, and they may need it."

Only Anita could have spoken so to Nye Nye. Some of the jewelry was returned: the cat's eye ring and the large red stone ring, which was not ruby but called "French stone," and others. But Molly would not see the diamond jewelry again. From Nye Nye's perspective, it was small compensation for the trouble she had with Ngood, a catalyst of loss of face and fortune.

****

Molly's family in Maymyo moved back to Rangoon. They found an apartment on Forty-Fourth Street, a predominantly Anglo-Indian neighborhood, very near the Rangoon River. Molly was glad to have her parents and siblings living nearer, though she was now of the Lee family and had first duties to them. She could not be away from Terence for very long, but she sometimes took the children by bus to visit them.

Molly was pleased to see her brothers Johnny and Wayne were improving themselves and making a living. Johnny was doing accounting work for a family friend who owned a restaurant and ballroom, and Wayne was selling insurance, mostly to Anglo-Burmese or Anglo-Indian buyers. Chinese and Burmese people were generally uninterested in insurance. They knew no one of their race who had purchased insurance in the past, and Wayne could not convince them of the need for it. Of course, Molly was an exception and purchased insurance to encourage her brother's efforts. Clark, sadly, was still so coddled by everyone, he had no motivation to earn his way in life.

Ginger had married Terence's classmate Frank, the frequent visitor to the Chin's home in Maymyo. This couple returned to Rangoon as well, and lived near Molly's parents. Molly was impressed to see that Frank was attentive and helpful to Ginger and very protective of her. Ginger was quite insecure and rarely let her husband out of her sight.

****

One day when Molly visited her family, Papa gave her a package and asked her to deliver it to the British ambassador. So, another day she made another trip to the city. She made sure Terence was comfortable before leaving him and gave the maids orders for his care. She dressed in Chinese formal wear, appropriate for meeting a dignitary. Then Molly took the bus into Rangoon, bringing Charlene along.

Charlene took every opportunity to tag along with someone. She often followed her mother on errands, and she loved to go with the maids when they did their shopping. She was a bright youngster, absorbing all that went on around her.

Molly had no trouble finding the impressive home of the British ambassador near the Methodist English Girls High School. She was met by a guard, who curiously evaluated her and the quiet, lady-like little girl in tow. Molly asked to see the ambassador's wife, and the guard showed them to the formal living room, where they waited patiently.

Molly had a few moments to wonder about the envelope. Her father could not write English, so Molly guessed his Jewish friend must have written it for him. A real estate broker, this friend had helped her father with many things over the years, including helping him find the home in Maymyo after the war. Distractedly, Molly remembered years ago, when her father proudly stood Molly before his friend to show off her English. He had been very complimentary of her few English phrases.

Molly noticed that Charlene was entranced. Hands folded politely in her lap, she observed every detail of the well-decorated room.

After several minutes, the ambassador's wife joined them, warmly apologizing for the wait. Molly explained the purpose of her visit, and the woman accepted the envelope for her husband. The meeting was cordial and brief. Molly would never know what was in the envelope.

Since her mission was completed so quickly, Molly decided she would take this opportunity to visit the Methodist English Girls High School. She had heard that Miss Bartel was now principal of the school.

Renamed the Methodist English High School, the school was empty when Molly arrived on this Saturday. She and Charlene wandered through the building, their footsteps echoing through the hallways. They went up the steps to the second floor, and there Molly came face-to-face with her dear teacher, Miss Bartel, herself!

Miss Bartel was thrilled. "Molly! Molly Chin! Oh, I'm so happy to see you!"

"I am happy to see you too!" Molly grinned warmly at her teacher and corrected politely, "I am Molly Lee, now, Miss Bartel."

"Oh yes, of course. I too have married, and I am now Mrs. Logie." She repeated more slowly, "Low-jee." Immediately drawn to Charlene, and stooping to admire her, Mrs. Logie asked, "And who is this young lady?"

"This is my daughter, Charlene," Molly answered.

"Hello, Charlene," Mrs. Logie smiled. "What a lovely name! You are such a pretty girl!"

She turned to Molly again, "Oh, Molly! I can't tell you how glad I am to see you have survived the war! What has happened to you since I saw you last?"

Molly told her a little about her war time ordeal and years following as Mrs. Logie listened sympathetically. Mrs. Logie asked softly, "Did you know that Miss Gwendoline Durham was killed during the war?"

Molly shook her head sadly. She thought of her strict but devoted third and fourth grade teacher at the English school, who had opened to Molly so many new worlds of learning.

Mrs. Logie added, "Likely others of our teachers and students are also lost. I am always relieved and overjoyed to see one of my co-workers or one of my dear children...." Mrs. Logie's voice cracked with emotion.

Molly thought of her three fellow classmates who planned to be doctors. She had not seen Gracie or Sally since the war. Louise, alone, was pursuing her dream of becoming a doctor, but what had become of the others?

"You were such a good student and hard-worker, Molly." Mrs. Logie repeated, with a tender voice, "I am so glad to see you."

Mrs. Logie told Molly, "Did you know the school was badly damaged in the war?"

"No!" Molly shouldn't have been surprised to hear it, for she knew much of Rangoon had been bombed. But everything looked fine. She said this to Mrs. Logie.

"Yes," Mrs. Logie replied. "American Baptists as well as Methodists sent money to rebuild the school. Come and have a look."

"Will you be opening soon?" Molly asked.

"Oh, Molly, we have been operating for some time!" Mrs. Logie responded enthusiastically.

The ladies toured the building. Inquisitive Charlene was content to walk between them.

"The auditorium was completely destroyed," Mrs. Logie explained as they looked at the large hall. "A young man by the name of Mr. Chrisman, from the United States, came and hired local workers to do the repairs. He has returned the building to the way it was before the war. No one can tell it was terribly damaged. He also made a living quarters on the second floor for my husband and me."

"Oh, was it Mr. Howard Chrisman?" Molly asked, having resisted interrupting with this urgent question.

"Yes, Molly, do you know him?"

"My husband worked for him!" Molly exclaimed. "My husband Terence subcontracted work for Mr. Chrisman. Terence had a big job in Moulmein, hiring and supervising all the carpenters."

Mrs. Logie laughed at the coincidence. "Well, Mr. Chrisman and his workers did a fine job here."

They walked through the familiar building, full of good memories for them both. Then Mrs. Logie asked Molly about her children.

Then she asked, "Where are they attending school, Molly?"

Molly had to confess, "They are not attending school."

"What?" Mrs. Logie was startled, "How old is Charlene?"

Molly admitted, "She is seven years old. Eng Koon is four, and Lois is two."

Mrs. Logie insisted, "Oh, Molly! What are you doing? You must get Charlene into school! You know education is so important! Why don't you send your children to school here? We are coed through high school now, which is why we are now called the Methodist English High School."

Molly felt the admonishment of her teacher. Mrs. Logie was quite right, and Molly suddenly felt she had neglected her daughter. Frankly, with trying to adapt after the war and coping with Terence's illness, Molly was embarrassed to realize she really hadn't given it thought. With Charlene being seven years old already, it was certainly time to think about her schooling.

Indeed, Molly wanted very much to have the best education for her children. But, she could never ask her in-laws to send her children to the Methodist English High School.

"You are right, Mrs. Logie. Education is so important. But, I'm sorry to say, my husband is ill, and he is not able to work right now. We cannot afford to send the children here," Molly confided sadly, but firmly.

"Let me see what I can do," Mrs. Logie urged. "Maybe I can find some scholarship money for them. Bring Charlene in to register as soon as possible, and I'll see if I can get her enrolled. And when Eng Koon and Lois are old enough, you must bring them to see me."

****

Now that Terence's condition had improved somewhat, his Number Three Sister Fe Yone and her husband William risked a visit with Terence. This visit was quite an event for Terence, and though he maintained a proud countenance, Molly knew he was grateful to see them.

While Terence was chatting with his relatives, Molly thought, "William is educated. He is a Rangoon University graduate. He knows of the world outside of the soy sauce factory and outside of Chinatown. Maybe he can help me."

As the couple prepared to leave, Molly said abruptly, "William, I need to find work. Do you know of anywhere I can find a job?"

William was startled, "Work? You? What work?"

Molly sighed. "I don't know. I have to find something." This wasn't going to be easy, but she was determined. "Puck Ying is not too well yet, and I need to find some work. I can't depend on his parents to help us forever. But I don't know what I can do."

Recovering from his initial surprise, William quickly understood, and replied, "Oh, sure. Maybe I do know of something. Why don't you go to the USIS Library? It just opened. My sister Rita got a job there."

Molly had never heard of this. "The USIS Library? What is that?"

"Do you know where the Chartered Bank is downtown?" William asked.

Molly was familiar with the building.

"Just go to the Chartered Bank. The Americans opened a library there. Look for Rita. She can tell you what to do. She told me they are hiring more people, so maybe you'll find something," William encouraged.

After William left, Molly saw the anguish on Terence's face. He cried aloud to his Heavenly Father, "Oh, Lord! Why did I get sick? I don't want my wife and children to go out and work! I want to take care of my family!"

Molly tried to console him, "Terence, I know you would work if you could. You are not a lazy man! But I don't want you to try to work now. I am so afraid that if you go to work you will die. You know you can't even go a few steps without heart palpitations. Terence, I don't want you to die!

I need you, and your children need their father. You must stay at home and rest and take care of yourself. When you are well, then you will go to work.

"Look, it will be okay, Terence. I will work. I don't mind. It is better than taking charity from your parents. I don't like to beg for every pice. And I won't go running back to my parents asking for money. I can't do that." Molly thought of the shame of asking her parents for money. She couldn't bear to see their looking-down faces.

She added firmly, "I have my pride."

Terence winced, as if Molly had struck him with her words.

Molly quickly added, "I know you are proud too, but..." She said his name with two drawn-out, earnest sylables, "Te-rence... you don't need to be ashamed that your wife is working. You can't help it! It isn't your fault that you got sick. It isn't your fault! You are doing the best that you can for your family. I must do the best that I can too.

"I cannot be your mother's servant. I can't do the chopping of firewood. I can't do the cooking. I won't get on the floor on my hands and knees to scrub with cocoanut. Do you want me to do that? Do you want me to work like that for your mother?"

He shook his head sadly.

To be sure he understood, Molly added defiantly, "I'm not going to do that! Besides, your parents are getting older. It is not fair for us to take advantage of them. We should be able to take care of ourselves."

This was not the traditional way of Chinese. But Terence had no reply.

Molly was concerned to leave Terence alone even for a few hours, but she felt she must respond quickly while there might be a job for her at the mysterious place where Rita worked. The next day, she wore a neat Chinese dress and high heeled shoes, and she carried her most fashionable handbag. As Molly rode the bus into Rangoon, she wondered what was done at a library, and she wondered about the letters "USIS." Mostly, she worried about what she was qualified to do. She hadn't even finished high school, and she knew William's sister Rita had finished college. The prospect of doing laundry in the street still loomed in a corner of her mind like one of Byu Goo's dreadful ghosts.

Molly found the Chartered Bank without any trouble and saw a sign saying "USIS Library." Apprehensive, she climbed the steps to the front door. Just inside was a long desk, and Rita herself was seated at the desk.

"Rita!" Molly called, relieved to see the familiar face. "Oh, I'm so glad to see you sitting right here by the door! Your brother told me to come and see you!"

Rita looked uneasy and put her finger to her lips. She said quietly, "Molly, speak softly please. This is a library. People are studying."

Molly realized many eyes were on her, and she was quite embarrassed. She said in a lower voice, "Oh, I am sorry. I didn't know. Your brother William said I should come," she repeated. "I want to find some work. He thought maybe I could get a job at the U-S-I-S Library."

Rita smiled. She said, just above a whisper, "Oh, good. They are needing more people. You should go to the US Embassy to get an application."

Molly felt weak. This was a complication she had not foreseen, and she was losing her courage. But she tried to hide her discomfort and asked, "Application...? Embassy...?"

"Yes," Rita said still speaking very softly, "The embassy is not hard to find." She gave Molly directions, "Just go back outside and go around the corner and...." Molly lost all remaining courage when she heard about a United States Marine guarding the building, and she scarcely heard the something about "...personnel office..." and "...ask for Miss Westbrook." Her mind seemed to retreat into a dark jungle.

When Rita finished speaking, Molly said, "Thank-you, Rita." Then, taking the small steps befitting a lady, but taking them quickly befitting her anxiety, she went back outside and got on a bus and went straight home!

She was no longer the fearless little girl who hired rickshaw drivers to transport her to new places throughout Rangoon. It had taken all her courage to go to the familiar landmark of the Chartered Bank. She was not prepared to go looking for an embassy, whatever an embassy was, guarded by a United States Marine.

As she was jostled on the bus, she alternately scolded herself and made excuses for herself. The excuses took over, "It's getting late. I don't want to leave Terence alone any longer. Already I have been away nearly two hours. He will be worried. I will have to come back another day." Postponing the trip to the embassy would give her time to pray for more courage.

Clearly, the reality had not settled with her yet, that if she got a job, she would be away from Terence much longer than two hours at a time. She hadn't figured out how to manage the children either. First she must get a job, and then she must find a way for the rest.

Molly told God of all her concerns. She acknowledged her weakness and her need for His help again. Gradually she was able to give her concerns to Him so that she could focus less on her need and more on God Himself, and then she felt the peace of His Presence wash over her. She did not know what her future held, but she knew she could trust God to take care of her.

****

Less than a week went by, and Terence had another visitor. At once Molly recognized the man as the new American missionary pastor of Immanuel Baptist Church. What with Terence's illness, she had only been to church a couple of times since Mr. Brown had come to Rangoon, but she immediately liked the new pastor. He was friendly and took time to listen and understand others, and Molly sensed in him a sincere concern for people. This was his first visit to their home, and he wanted to pray with Terence.

She took the pastor to him, and Mr. Brown greeted Terence graciously. She knew his words of encouragement would be good medicine for Terence, and she was grateful to hear him pray for Terence's health. But she also anticipated approaching the pastor before he left. Because he seemed a kind man, Molly felt she could ask him for help.

When her opportunity came, she spoke nervously in one rapid, long sentence. "Pastor, I wonder, sir, if you can help me because I need to get a job to help support my family because my husband cannot work, and the USIS Library is in the Chartered Bank in downtown Rangoon and my husband's sister's husband's sister got a job there, and she's says maybe I can work there, but I have to go to the embassy to get an application, but I don't know where the embassy is or what an application is, and I don't want to leave my husband alone to go and look for it."

Guessing at last what Molly wanted, Mr. Brown's look of attentive concern changed to a big smile. "No problem! I know exactly where the US Embassy is, and I can pick up an application for you!"

Relief spread across Molly's face, and then she remembered a few important details. She was all seriousness as she determined to recite the details accurately, "My brother-in-law's sister said to see Miss Westbrook." She spelled out the name. "Rita said to go to the personnel office to see Miss Westbrook to get an ap-pli-ca-tion." She said the last word slowly.

Mr. Brown smiled again, "Yes, I know about the personnel office. And I know about applications. I can get a job application for you, Mrs. Lee. No problem."

"Oh, and..." Molly added, "...the embassy is guarded by a United States Marine." She looked to see if Mr. Brown would be dissuaded.

"It's okay. He will let me pass to get an application for you," Mr. Brown assured her. He added, "You have no need to fear the marine, Molly."

Molly reflected later, "I asked the Lord to help me, and already He has sent me help!" Her heart was full of thanksgiving to Him.

****

True to his word, Mr. Brown returned a week later, driving eight miles from town. He handed the job application to Molly.

He told her, "Fill out this paperwork, and then you can send it to the embassy. You won't have to make a trip to town to drop it off. I have the address for you right here."

Molly thanked him profusely. She glanced at the precious form he gave her.

"After they have read your application, they will send you a letter telling you when to come in for an interview," Mr. Brown added.

Molly wished she still had her English dictionary. It would be helpful to look up some of these new words she was encountering. She had heard of this latest word, but she didn't know what to expect. She decided she must expose her ignorance to Mr. Brown.

"Interview? What is an interview?"

He did not look as if he thought less of Molly for her question. He replied kindly, " 'Interview' means they will have you come to the embassy and ask you some questions about what you can do. They want to meet you and talk with you before they decide if they want to hire you."

Molly was grateful for his help. Later, as she carefully filled out the application, she felt again the inadequacy of her qualifications. She thought defensively, "Who can sit for the exam during the war? Bombs going off! Running here and there!" Nevertheless, praying to God as she filled each line, Molly determined to be truthful; she would not exaggerate her abilities.

No longer superstitious, she wrote her birth date without fear. This bit of information seemed important to those of the west.

She also wrote a personal note explaining, "I really need this job. My husband is sick...." She sent the letter and the application to Miss Westbrook at the embassy and waited for a reply.

There was no daily mail delivery; the mailman came only when he had something to deliver. Several days had passed when the mail carrier pulled up to 116 Prome Road and saw a maid hanging laundry on a clothesline in the latticed enclosure under the old house. Terence was also there leaning back in his cloth lounge chair. Seeing the mail car arrive, Terence went to accept the envelope, and he noted the official return address of the United States Embassy.

Terence called to Molly, and she hurried down the stairs to see what was wrong. Terence held out the envelope to her.

Molly read the enclosed letter aloud. Miss Westbrook thanked Molly for sending the application and requested that she come to the embassy for a personal interview, setting a date and time for Molly to meet with her. Thanks to Mr. Brown, Molly had an idea of what to expect at the interview.

Terence was anxious. Again, Molly tried to comfort her husband, "God spared your life. You must stay home and protect yourself until you are stronger. I will work. I don't mind, Terence. Your job for now is to take care of yourself."

****

On the appointed day, Molly made the trip to downtown Rangoon. Outside the embassy, she shyly showed the official letter to the intimidating marine guard, who smiled and let her pass.

Carefully following the instructions in the letter, she found the personnel office and asked for Miss Westbrook. The secretary replied, "Yes, Mrs. Lee, she told me to look for you. I'll tell her you are here." So far, so good.

Miss Westbrook was friendly. She offered Molly a seat across the desk from herself, and she began going over the application with her.

Molly felt the need to apologize almost immediately. "I could not finish high school. It looks like I dropped out, but I did not drop out. I completed all the course work, but I did not get a high school diploma because I never got a chance to sit for the final exam because the war came, and we had to retreat to the Shan States, and then I had children to care for and my husband got sick..."

"Yes, I see Molly," Miss Westbrook said. Looking at the application, she inquired, "You say here that you can speak several languages?"

"Yes," Molly replied, unaware of the significance. "My family is Cantonese, and I spoke the Tai-sun dialect at home. I learned the Hong Kong dialect, which is similar, and the Mandarin dialect at the Chinese school. Then I went to the Methodist English Girls High School and learned English and Burmese."

"Hmm," Miss Westbrook said in a non-committal tone. They spoke a little longer, and Miss Westbrook explained, "Mrs. Zelma Graham is the director of the USIS Library, but she is on vacation for a few weeks in the States. So I would like for you to speak with her temporary replacement, Miss Rosenfeld. Molly, I'm sending you over to the USIS Library. Do you know how to get there? Yes? When you finish, come back and speak with me before you go home."

Molly left the building, explaining to the marine that she was instructed to return to speak with Miss Westbrook. The marine responded politely that he would be expecting her.

Just around the corner, Molly found the USIS Library, and with a little help from Rita she found Miss Rosenfeld, who reviewed her qualifications. Miss Rosenfeld said, "I'm going to ask you to go to the junior library to see Martha Khin."

Recognizing the Burmese surname, Molly followed directions to the junior library expecting to find a Burmese woman. Instead, she found an American woman dressed in Burmese attire, although her hair was cut short like Molly's. Her curiosity was aroused, but Molly was too polite to ask questions. Instead, she responded to the questions of Mrs. Khin. Like Miss Westbrook, Mrs. Khin seemed very interested in the languages Molly spoke.

At last Mrs. Khin explained, "We are very much in need of someone who can speak English, Burmese, and especially Chinese."

Molly said with cautious eagerness, "Yes, I can speak these." She repeated the languages and dialects she knew and how she had learned them.

"That's fine," Mrs. Khin replied. "Can you type?"

Again Molly felt inadequate. "When I was a child I learned to type on my father's old type writer. I just use my two fingers." She held up her pointer fingers apologetically.

Mrs. Khin gave Molly a few small paper cards she called "catalogue cards" and some books. "Can you find this information in the books and type the information on the cards? Each item-- author, title, book description, and so on-- needs to be placed just so on the card." Mrs. Khin showed Molly a sample card and where to find the information on the books. "Follow this formula, please."

Molly put the cards one by one into the typewriter and pecked out letters and numbers in the proper places on the cards. She was very slow, but she thought she was accurate.

Then Mrs. Khin wanted to know whether Molly could file the cards alphabetically. Molly knew the English alphabet well, and she was pleased to be able to perform this task quickly.

After taking some time with her, Mrs. Khin told Molly. "Fine. That's all I need from you today. Now you can go back to see Miss Westbrook at the embassy."

The marine waved Molly through the checkpoint. He seemed a little less frightening now.

Miss Westbrook asked a few more questions. Then she told Molly, "Thank-you for coming today. You can go home now. I will speak with Miss Rosenfeld and Mrs. Khin, and you'll be hearing from me soon."

"Will you hire me?" Molly asked anxiously. "Mrs. Khin said you were looking for someone who could speak Chinese." Molly repeated her abilities in this area and reminded Miss Westbrook that she really needed to work because her husband was sick. She was desperate, but she tried to maintain respectful politeness.

"Your qualifications seem a good fit for us, Mrs. Lee, but I can't make any promises," Miss Westbrook answered kindly. "I need to speak with the library staff first. I will write to you either way, whether we offer you a job or not."

"Thank-you, Miss Westbrook," Molly bowed slightly. "Thank-you for in-ter-view-ing me."

Once again, Terence was anxiously waiting for the bus to bring Molly home. As soon as she walked in the door, he questioned her urgently, "What happened? What did they say? Did you get the job?"

Molly explained every detail of her interview. Neither Terence nor Molly was prepared to wait again, but this was unavoidable. At least Molly could tell him that her language abilities might be useful. But what if they decided against hiring her? She didn't know what else she could do.

Meanwhile, Molly said nothing to her mother-in-law. She was too afraid to mention the subject to her. Terence could tell his mother if he wanted, or if Molly got the job, Nye Nye would figure it out soon enough. Likely, she would not be pleased. Having a daughter-in-law working away from home was not going to help the Lee face.

Chapter Nineteen

Providence

Again, the mail carrier arrived at 116 Prome Road with an official envelope from the United States Embassy. Once again Terence called Molly to open the letter.

Molly read aloud the few words that would greatly alter her future, "We are pleased to offer you a position with the junior library of the USIS Library.... You may report for work a week from next Monday. You are assigned to work between the hours of 8:15 to 5:15. You will report to Martha Khin...."

The words penetrated Molly with significance. Her eyes filled with tears of grateful relief.

"Thank-you God," she spoke in her heart. "You have made a way for me to help my family."

Molly became aware that Terence was frowning tragically; he could not meet her look. Understanding that she must ask Terence to make the final decision, Molly asked him, "What do you think?"

He said, broken, "I suppose you have to take it."

****

The timing of Molly's job and Charlene's school worked out well. Lo Yeahr kindly suggested to Molly that he could drive her to work and Charlene to school.

338 | GENTLE MOON

This was a big help, as they wouldn't have to worry about taking the bus, and Molly could be with Charlene on the way to school. Molly would send a maid by bus to pick up Charlene in the afternoon. Molly was much relieved.

Lo Yeahr eagerly rode in his surplus military jeep with his hired chauffeur, having his own reasons for wanting to leave Eight Mile for the day. Officially, he had shopping to do and directions to give the chauffeur. But Molly also knew weather could be stormy for him at home, and ten acres was not enough space to escape it.

Each morning Lo Yeahr had a car full. First he instructed the driver to follow Kabaya Pagoda Road south toward town to drop off his younger children at their grade school. Then they crossed over University Avenue to take Number Four Sister Fe Heng to Rangoon University. Then he took Charlene to the Methodist English High School on the corner of Lancaster and Signal Pagoda Roads. Then he dropped off Molly at the Sule Pagoda from which she walked to the embassy. Then he was off to the market.

Lo Yeahr took his time shopping at the fresh market, selecting meats and vegetables daily. At the market he would hire an Indian boy, maybe ten years old or so, to help him. The boy would accumulate Lo Yeahr's purchases in a huge basket and follow him, balancing the basket on the turban on his head. Lo Yeahr would give the boy a kyat for his services, and the boy was happy.

Usually, then, Lo Yeahr spent the morning with his Number Two Daughter Fe Lan, Lily, at the import-export shop she and her husband Myo Khin owned in town. When it was time, he would pick up his children at the school and take the groceries home to the maids.

Each morning before she left, Molly would remind her maids of their duties, particularly in the care of each of the children. She was comforted that Terence was at home to make sure the maids fulfilled their responsibilities. The maids were not mean spirited, but were sometimes forgetful or distracted, and Molly was a protective mama. She was not at all happy to be leaving her children in the care of others. Moreso, she did not want her children to grow up in poverty or dependence.

Just when Nye Nye thought her face could get no smaller, her daughter-in-law took employment outside the home. And Terence was left much of the day to face his mother's displeasure alone.

****

Molly's first day of work was May 21, 1951. Dates were important in this new culture, not for superstitious reasons relating to the moon and the Chinese horoscope and calendar, but for things like seniority, raises, vacation eligibility, and retirement plans, none of which were understood or mattered to Molly at first. She was relieved to be employed and glad to give all necessary attention to dates.

Molly began her first day with no small amount of fear, and she was praying constantly to God for strength and guidance. She didn't know what to expect and had much to learn.

Molly walked up the steps to the entrance of the imposing cut stone building of the USIS Library. The building was indeed impressive and intimidating, but the doors stood open wide in welcome. Molly passed a Burman seated on her right, and then noted the long adult circulation desk extending down the wall on her left. She waved quietly to Rita who was sitting in the first chair. Rita returned her wave and smile. A couple other ladies sat with Rita at the desk and they looked up curiously. Molly gave a little nod to each, but continued toward the junior library. As she walked, Molly looked in awe at the shelves and shelves packed full of books in the large, brightly lit room. She supposed she had seen the vast treasure when she came here to be interviewed, but she was so nervous and distracted then, she hardly had time to consider it. Now, she had to pause a moment and be amazed. Right here in Rangoon, right here in this building, were more books than Molly had ever imagined could exist in the whole world!

Molly remembered back, so many years ago, when she watched Byu Goo stack Han Yee's collection of books on a shelf at the four-story house. Those few books had brought her hours of great pleasure. The excitement was fresh as Molly imagined the vast wonders expressed in these many books.

Molly continued across the great room of the adult library to the entrance to the children's library. Mrs. Khin, the Junior Library Director, greeted her and said warmly, "I'm so glad to have you here, Molly. We have often seen Chinese children come to the library and look around with curiosity. We had no way to make them understand about the library and to help them to use the books. That is how you can help us."

So that was why Molly was needed! She said sincerely, "I am glad to be here. I will try very hard to do a good job."

Mrs. Khin said in a friendly tone, "Come with me, Molly. I'll give you a tour of the library and introduce you to the staff."

"Yes, Mrs. Khin," Molly answered respectfully.

"Oh, Molly, call me Martha."

"Yes, ma'am," Molly replied obediently, but she felt the resistance of her Asian upbringing to be so familiar with an authority figure.

"Let's go back to the Library Director's Office. Do you remember meeting Miss Rosenfeld when you came for the interview? You may recall that she is filling in as director while Mrs. Graham is gone. Mrs. Graham is the one who opened the library a few years ago. She had to go back to the 'States' for a few weeks."

Martha led Molly back through the adult library. At the library entrance sat the Burman she had observed earlier. Martha told Molly, "That is one of our page boys. He takes attendance for us and keeps statistics."

Molly was puzzled about the words "page boy." The man was not old, but she certainly would not call him a boy. And, she wondered, why was he called a "page" like a sheet of paper bound in a book?

"He and other page boys shelve books, repair them, put labels on the back of the books, and do other things for us in the library."

As they passed the adult circulation desk, Martha introduced Molly to the ladies sitting there. The head of circulation was a fair-skinned Burmese woman whose long hair was curled into a bun and adorned with a fresh jasmine blossom. She greeted Molly formally.

Martha then took Molly past the extraordinary book-lined aisles and past long study tables with rows of empty chairs. Martha commented, "Soon these chairs will be full of students, young and old, bending over books in concentration. You will see, this library is a very busy place."

"The adult non-fiction section--books about true things such as texts and biographies--is over here, and the fiction--you know, books about imagined things like novels, poetry and plays--is over there." Martha took in whole swathes of the room with sweeps of her arm.

Molly was truly in awe. All that fiction? By the time she had finished high school, Molly felt she was quite familiar with Chinese literature, Burmese literature, and English literature. What could be left? And non-fiction! Just imagine! Those many hundreds of books contained information about things people discovered about the world! Molly felt an excitement just walking past all the intriguing books.

Still walking, Martha pointed, "There to your left is the loan collection department. The women there pack boxes of whole sets of books which are loaned to schools throughout the area."

"And over there are the periodicals. Current magazines are available for patrons to read here in the library. Older copies, filed below, can be checked out."

Molly heard the odd words, "Periodocals," "Magazines," and "...can be checked out," and didn't quite understand. But she didn't say anything.

Martha then pointed up to the second floor in the back of the building, which overlooked the adult library. "Up there is the mezzanine. That is where we keep the reference section. All of the encyclopedias, dictionaries, technical papers, and so on are kept up there. Those books must not leave the library. There are more long tables up there for studying. Our library is actually better equipped than Rangoon University library, I'm told, and we have law students, business students, medical students, and many others who come here to learn. I'll take you up there later and introduce you to the head of reference. The cataloging department is also there, but it is reached by a separate staircase and is closed to the public. They prepare all the new books for the library. Among other things they make file cards for the card catalogue so that people can find a book by title, author, or subject."

At last they came to the back of the adult library and entered a spacious office. Miss Rosenfeld smiled warmly at Molly, "I'm so glad you could join our team, Molly. You will be such a help to us. Your qualifications are a perfect fit. I'm sure Martha will help you get settled in, but if you need to see me, my office is always open."

Molly was impressed by Miss Rosenfeld's casual, friendly style. She did not treat subordinates in the stiff, reserved fashion for which the British were known. Instead, almost immediately, Molly felt as if this American, Miss Rosenfeld, treated her almost as a friend.

Martha introduced Molly to Miss Rosenfeld's office staff, two Kayin women, a secretary and a typist. Molly wondered why one of the Kayin women had a Chinese name.

Then Martha took Molly back through the adult library to the junior library. "This is where you'll be working Molly. We want you to work here at the junior library circulation desk. There is the card catalog, which you'll learn to use so you can help the children to find the books they want. That area over there has picture books for the very young children. The books for older children are separated into fiction and non-fiction. If a child wants to look at a book here in the library, and he doesn't remember the proper place to put it back, he may leave the book on the table and a page boy will replace it."

This part of the library was clearly meant to be inviting to children. There were four low tables with low benches for dozens of little children. Colorful pictures and displays decorated the walls.

Martha explained, "Hazel Johnson comes over from the embassy and arranges all the displays and decorates the big bulletin board. She does a nice job, doesn't she?"

Molly was impressed, "Oh, it's beautiful!"

Martha commented, "Our theme changes every month."

Molly knew Charlene would love to come here! Eng Koon too! And even little Lois! Molly wondered whether she could bring her children here some time, and whether it would be expensive to do so.

Martha said, "Let me show you the music room. Come this way."

She led Molly to the back of the junior library. There, Molly saw a raised stage with a piano, an American Flag, and a podium. Portable chairs were arranged facing the stage area. Molly thought more than a hundred people could be seated here.

Martha explained, "This is where we have programs for the children. Staff members plan the singing and story-telling. Ei May Tun leads the singing, but we all sing along, and we teach the songs to the children. Oh, they love it! Another staff member, Polly, plays the piano. We do a lot of story-telling; Ei May Tun tells stories in Burmese and English so the children learn to understand some English. A screen can be pulled down along the wall behind the stage, so we can show films. Also, we have staff meetings here.

After pointing out the bathrooms, Martha led Molly back to the junior library circulation desk. As they walked, Molly admired the shelves and shelves of children's books.

Martha introduced Molly to the head of the junior library circulation, Ei May Tun. As she exchanged greetings with the pleasant, dark-skinned women, Molly recalled this woman was mentioned as the story teller and song leader.

She recalled that Burmese did not have clan names like the Chinese, nor family surnames like the English, and that women often did not change their names when they married. Family members, then, often had no names in common.

"And these are your co-workers, Polly and Clara." Martha added, "Remember, Molly, I mentioned to you about our piano player, Polly. And Doris will be here later. She is working the afternoon and evening shift.

The morning and afternoon shifts overlap several hours of the day, so Doris comes later and stays later. Many of our patrons come in the evening."

Martha said, "We all pitch in with what needs to be done. You may need to do some typing. Remember the cards I had you type when you came for your interview? The cataloging department does most of the typing, preparing the pockets to paste in the books and the cards for the catalog. But when a pocket is torn or dirty we must type a new one, indicating fiction or non-fiction in the corner, and listing the title, author and subject, and giving a summary, just so. Also, we need to type the cards that go into the pockets, which become full of the childrens' names who have borrowed the books. The page boys paste the pockets into the books."

Martha hardly stopped for a breath, "Now, Molly, I want to explain the labels on the back of each book. See, right away there is an indication for fiction or non-fiction. Fictional books are identified with the first three letters of the author's last name, and the books are filed on the shelves alphabetically by the last name of the author. Non-fiction books have this Dewey Decimal Number printed. Are you familiar with the Dewey Decimal System? Well, see, the numbers help us to organize the books systematically. If someone wants to find a book about philosophy, he can go to the 100's. See, Molly, those books are over there. And science books are in the 500's, history in the 900's. See? Within each of those categories, numbers indicate divisions within the category. See, the 700's indicate the arts, and architecture is specified by the 720's. 727 identifies books about buildings for education and research. The decimal points after the number divide each of the categories further. See? This system is used in libraries around the world. You will need to familiarize yourself with this so you can help children find the books they want."

Molly had just a moment to consider the section of books Martha happened to pointed out. Architecture! Terence would love to read about architecture! Maybe the adult library had architecture books for adults. Maybe Terence could come to the library too.

"Now, if a child comes in and knows the title of the book he wants, or if he knows the author, or if he only knows the subject he wants to read about in a book, he can go to the card catalogue and look up where to find the book. That's over here. See? Three cards are typed for each book, one for the subject, one for the author, and one for the title. See?"

Molly nodded hesitantly. She was fascinated by the organized method of sorting books, and she understood the concept, but it was all rather overwhelming.

Martha smiled, "It's alright Molly. We'll give you time to study the card catalogue so you'll feel comfortable helping the children. And don't hesitate to ask me or the other ladies for help. I'm sure you'll do fine."

Molly was eager to begin researching the card catalog right away. But Martha continued, "You'll also need to help in circulation. Ei May Tun will explain this to you."

Ei May Tun told Molly enthusiastically, "Oh, we can use your help! Sometimes so many children come in all at once, especially after school, and we are all so busy!

"Every child may borrow books from the library if he or she has a library card. If someone doesn't have a card we can give a card to him. See, each child must give us this information: his name, his parents' names, his address, and so on."

Molly was trying to give Ei May Tun her full attention, but part of her mind circled the statement, "Every child may borrow books...." She wondered silently, "Does this mean children can actually take the books out of the library? They can take the books home? What a great thing! Could my children take books home too?"

Ei May Tun continued, "All of this information needs to be typed and the cards filed alphabetically. Then, see, the child receives one of these cards. Then he can borrow books for one week. If a child is late in returning the books, we send out these reminders. The cards are already printed. We fill in the date, address the card, and give it to the mail room."

Again, Molly pondered the thought, "Children can take the books home for one week?" She waited for Ei May Tun to explain the cost of this privilege. Molly probably could not afford it.

"Of course, we need to keep a record of who has the books, so we need to take the card from the back of the book, and the child puts his name on the card, and we file it. Then, we put another card in the pocket and stamp it with a date, to remind the child he must return the book by that time. A child may renew the book if he brings it back and checks it out again. If the book is late, then we must charge a small fine.

"Now, Molly, this is important: reference books cannot leave the library. They are marked so. Children must use the reference books here in the library. That way, if someone needs to look up something, he can be sure the book will always be here.

"When children return the books, they place them over there. Then we take the 'date due' card out and return the book card to the pocket." She pointed out the book cart and explained, "The pages push these carts around the room and return books to the proper places on the shelves."

"Do you have any questions, Molly?"

"Yes," Molly answered. She had a question more important than why the men were called 'page boys.'

"How much do you charge for this service? What does it cost to get a library card?" Molly asked, her interest surging beyond job training.

"Oh, it's free! There is no charge to borrow the books. Only, we charge a small fine if a book is returned late. Of course, there is a charge if the book is lost or damaged." Ei May Tun smiled at the startled expression on Molly's face. "Any more questions?"

Molly had to know, "May any child get a library card?"

Ei May Tun answered, "Any child whose parent fills out an application. Adults can get library cards for themselves at the adult circulation desk," she added, kindly.

"How many books are there in this library?" Molly asked.

"In the whole library, more than ten thousand," Ei May Tun answered. "And we're getting new books all the time."

Molly was quiet as she considered what this would mean to her family. She knew each one would benefit greatly.

Empathizing, Ei May Tun asked, "Would you like to have a library card, Molly? It will be good for you to understand the process for yourself; you'll be better able to help the children. I'm sure you will find books you can enjoy. Why don't you go to the adult library and have a look?"

Molly nodded, afraid to trust her voice. She was very excited, and though she doubted she would find much time to relax and enjoy a book, she could hardly wait to bless Terence and the children.

"Oh! Thank-you, Lord Jesus!" she prayed silently. "I asked you for a job, but I never imagined there was such a place as this! And you have allowed me to work here! Miss Rosenfeld said my qualifications were a perfect fit! You were preparing me to work here, and I didn't even know it! Thank-you."

****

Terence was watching for her to come home. At last he saw her, carrying an armful of something, and he was filled with relief.

Molly spoke to Terence excitedly, "Look! I brought you books about architecture. And...!" From the stack of books Molly proudly pulled a thickness of bound, slick paper with a gold colored border on the front cover. "... this is called a magazine. This particular magazine is 'National Geographic.' It's produced in America. Terence! Just look at the pictures inside! Pictures from all over the world! Some are in color! A new magazine, called an issue, comes to the library every month. Each one has completely different pictures and stories. The new magazines are kept at the library, but I can bring older ones home. There are other magazines too. We can borrow the books and magazines for one week. Then I will take them back, and I can bring different ones!"

Answering Terence's look of concern, Molly added, "It doesn't cost us anything at all! I have books for the children too. They must be very careful with them. If they do any damage, we will have to pay a fine." This would not be a problem, because Molly's children knew they must be careful with books.

Molly proudly showed Terence her library card. "You and the children can get cards too. There are special programs for children. I hope I can take our children. Oh, Terence, the library is so beautiful! And there are more than ten thousand books!"

Terence was pleased with the books Molly handed to him. But, as he observed Molly suspiciously, he was concerned. He had not seen his wife look so happy for quite some time.

Chapter Twenty

"I Can't Do It!"

During her first few weeks of work, Molly often heard about Mrs. Graham, the Library Director temporarily in the United States. The library employees were clearly fond of her and maybe a little bit in awe. Molly had heard the descriptions and comments, but she was eager to meet this dynamic woman for herself.

The library seemed to hum with a respectfully quiet air of expectancy. The citizens of Rangoon had already embraced this place as their own, and, like Molly, they were excited by the prospect of access to so many books. When she saw the number of people using the library, she wondered whether she and her relatives were the last people to know of it.

Molly was pleased to watch her co-workers lead the children's programs in the not-so-quiet music room. Ei May Tun, with the support of others, was teaching songs written by a nineteenth century American named Stephen Foster. The songs were so much fun to sing:

> *Camptown ladies sing this song, doo-da, doo-dah.*
> *Camptown racetrack's five miles long, oh, de doo-da day.*
> *Goin' to run all night. Goin' to run all day.*
> *I bet my money on a bob-tailed nag.*
> *Somebody bet on the gray.*

Another nonsensical song delighted the children as they learned the meaning of the English words:

> *I come from Alabama with my banjo on my knee.*
> *I'm going to Louisiana, my true love for to see.*
> *It rained all night the day I left. The weather it was dry.*
> *The sun so hot, I froze to death, Susanna, don't you cry.*
> *Oh, Susanna, Oh don't you cry for me*
> *For I come from Alabama with my banjo on my knee.*

Every night, Terence was anxiously waiting for Molly. He always seemed relieved to see her, yet he usually met her with a scowl. If she was a few minutes late, he was even more anxious and questioned her, "Why are you so late? I thought you were never coming home."

Molly dismissed his concerns, "Of course I have come home! Where else would I go?"

"Will you massage my neck?" Terence would ask. "My neck hurts very much today. You know just how to do it." Molly felt her own neck needed attention, but she would patiently rub her husband's neck and shoulders while instructing the maids and talking to the children.

Terence thoroughly enjoyed the architecture books; he studied them and was inspired to make his own plans and sketches, dreaming of his future as an architect. He greatly admired the work of American architect Frank Lloyd Wright. Terence's drawings were always beautiful and creative; Molly was much impressed by the designs he would show her.

He couldn't get enough of "National Geographic" magazine. He lingered over every glorious picture, letting the wonder of the photograph speak poetic volumes into his soul. Terence read every article, usually more than once, and he told Molly fascinating details as they ate their evening meal. His conversation would jump from a Chinese pilgrimage to the Kunming Temples in the Yunnan Province in China, to the Ohio River in the United States, to flying machines called helicopters used to fly above and photograph ancient sites in Panama, to Birds of Paradise in Papua, New Guinea, to the Island of Formosa-- the name given to Taiwan long ago by Portugese mariners. And that was from a single issue! Each time Molly came home with more books, Terence looked first for the magazine with the solid yellow border, white oak leaf trim, and table of contents on the cover.

The children were also delighted with books that Molly brought for them, and they were excited to see what she would bring home next. Before they went to bed, she often read to them, and even little Lois would sit quietly with the others, listening to her mother's voice. Molly read about the boy Christopher Robin and the adventures of his life-like stuffed animals Winnie-the-Pooh, Rabbit, Owl, and so on. Also, The Little Engine That Could, Make Way for Ducklings, and Curious George were soon favorites of her own children, as well as the children at the library.

Such literature especially written for children was new to Molly. She thought as she read the books, "The authors are so good. They inspire the imaginations of children. They know just what appeals to children."

****

One morning upon arriving at work, Molly sensed excitement from her co-workers even before anyone spoke a word. Then she overheard, "Mrs. Graham is back."

Molly busied herself at her work, filing the cards no one had time to file the day before. Then she heard the chorus of greetings from co-workers, "Good morning, Mrs. Graham," "Good to see you, Mrs. Graham," "Glad to have you back, Mrs. Graham."

A compelling voice responded, "It's so good to be back with you all!"

Molly looked up to see a tall, sturdy, western woman in her forties. She wore a bright red suit, and between her smiling teeth she gripped a pipe with a very long stem. The woman noticed Molly and walked over to her.

She removed the pipe and said, "You must be Molly Lee! Miss Rosenfeld told me about you. So glad to have you on board! I am Mrs. Graham, USIS Library Director."

"I am pleased to meet you, Mrs. Graham. I am glad to be working here in your library," Molly answered.

"Oh, it's not my library, Molly," Mrs. Graham replied. "The library is shared by many people. The Congress of the United States established this and other libraries around the world, 'To disseminate abroad information about the United States, its people, and policies...' and, 'To promote a better understanding of the United States in other countries, and to increase mutual understanding between the people of the United States and the people of other countries.' "

Mrs. Graham smiled, "That's the official language. So in a way it is a library of the people of the United States. But as you can see, Molly, the library really belongs to the local people."

Mrs. Graham surveyed the junior library with obvious pride. Already, a stream of youngsters was eddying around the bookshelves. Mrs. Graham repeated, to no one in particular, "It's good to be back."

Molly would find that Mrs. Graham often enjoyed standing in the children's library, a big smile on her face as she watched the crowd of eager faces. She may have claimed to Molly that it was not her library, but she had birthed it, and she nurtured it like no other.

To Molly, Mrs. Graham said, "I'm so glad to have someone here with your linguistic abilities."

Mrs. Graham held her pipe as she spoke, "So many times I've seen Chinese children come in here, and they look around with great interest, but they don't know what to do. We didn't know how to tell them. They can't speak Burmese or English, and none of us can speak or understand Chinese. Do you see our problem? Now, with you here to help us, our problem is solved! I want you to help the Chinese children to enjoy the library, Molly! Explain to them what to do! Tell them how to get a library card! Tell them how to use the card catalog and how they can borrow books! Tell them about the programs here at the library! And teach them some English too, Molly! It might be useful to them."

"I will, Mrs. Graham," Molly answered eagerly. With a slight bow of her head, she added, "Thank-you."

****

Molly quickly learned the routine at the library. Quite a lot of the children were Cantonese, and word spread quickly among friends so that more and more Chinese children came to enjoy the library. Molly was very busy helping them become adept in using it. Most of the books were in English, though quite a few were written in Burmese. Even when the children couldn't read those languages, they could always enjoy the

Molly seated at circulation desk in the junior library. Embassy photo, used by permission.

pictures. When she had time, Molly read to them and translated key words and phrases.

Molly also advised them in Cantonese, "Wear shoes or slippers when you come to the library. It is not impolite to wear shoes here, and people will think you look nice. Make sure you wash your face before you come, and dress neatly. Take pride in how you look when you come to the library. You do not want to bring disgrace to your race."

The children told their parents, "We must wear our shoes or slippers to the library."

Molly at the library. Embassy photo, used by permission.

So it was that the Burmese and Indian children continued to come with bare feet and sometimes without shirts, but the clean Chinese children wore shoes and nice clothes. Perhaps this private coaching was unfair to the other children, but, after all, Molly had been hired especially for the Chinese, and she wanted to do well for them.

Sometimes there were long lines of children, Burmese, Chinese, Indian, and a few English, waiting to check out books. The ladies, Clara, Doris, and Molly, would be working quickly to stamp dates and to file cards, though Doris sometimes found it necessary to go to the bathroom ahead of the rush and would return feigning surprise that she had missed it.

The library was open evenings and Saturdays. Molly was sometimes asked to work these hours, but she didn't mind because she was paid extra, something called "overtime," which compensated her at a higher rate than her usual pay. Her family could always use something extra.

****

On school and work days there was a flurry of activity around the Lee compound as all the children and Molly got ready to pile in to Lo Yeahr's jeep. The arrangement was working out well; everyone was getting to where they needed to be and Lo Yeahr was enjoying his duties orchestrating the daily routine.

There was one problem. Molly sensed, in these close quarters of Lo Yeahr's jeep, the resentment of Nye Nye's children. It was no surprise that they would imitate Nye Nye and reflect her displeasure with her face-depleting daughter-in-law. But it was hurtful.

As she rode in the silent car, Molly took this new concern to the Lord. "Oh Lord Jesus! My mother-in-law has many branches. She doesn't need the branch of her eldest son any more. She considers that our branch is broken off, because Terence is sick-- and because we have trusted You. She is angry with us, and she is turning her children against us."

Molly reminded herself as she spoke with God, "You have told us to forgive seventy-times seven. You have said, 'Do not return evil for evil.' You have said, 'Vengeance is mine.' I have no right to get mad. But I can't help it. Lord Jesus, help me to forgive, as You forgave. Help me to love those who hurt me. Help me to pray for those who want to be my enemies. This is too hard for me, and I need your help."

She was humbled as she recognized her own faults and her desperate need for Him. As she submitted to Jesus and His Spirit in her, she gained new perspective, new determination, new strength, and the fruits that come from Him: Love. Joy. Peace. Patience. Kindness. Goodness. Faithfulness. Gentleness. Self-control.

She realized that if she focused too long on the problem, she became more agitated. Molly remembered words of Scripture: "Cast all your anxieties on God, for He cares about you." She needed to freely and honestly tell God her concerns, but at some point, she needed to lay her burden down and trust Him. Then she could turn her full attention to Him. She could enjoy being with Him, praising His attributes, and loving and worshiping Him. Focusing on Lord Jesus, who could remember troubles?

In this way, by His power, she could forgive. She could give up the anger that churned in her stomach. She could let go of the offense and its power over her. The troubles did not quickly end, and hurt feelings kept coming back. But the remedy was always available to her when she humbled herself before God.

She could also walk the half mile from the soy sauce factory to the bus stop instead of riding in Lo Yeahr's jeep. The walk would be good for her.

****

Molly was a few minutes later than usual getting home. Terence was anxiously waiting for her.

With too much irritation he asked, "Why are you so late? Where have you been?"

"The bus was delayed. Anyway, I'm only a few minutes late," Molly said defensively. "What's the matter?"

"I don't like you working at that United States' Library!"

"What? Terence, we have talked about this! It can't be helped. I have to work," Molly felt impatience rising in her voice.

Terence sulked, "I don't like you being with all those American men!"

"Men? What men? I don't work with men! I work with children!" Molly exclaimed. "My co-workers are women. A few Indian men and a Burman work at the library, but I have little contact with them. There are no American men at the library."

"Well, I don't like it!" Terence repeated, tension in his voice.

Matching Terence's anger, Molly said, "Even if I did work with American men, you don't have to worry about me. I don't flirt around! I'm not that type of woman!"

"It doesn't matter. Everyone knows American men always flirt." The frown on Terence's face showed no sign of relenting. "I don't trust them with you."

Molly was too insulted to pity Terence's insecurity. She repeated curtly, "I'm not that type of woman! I'm not going to leave you! I wouldn't do it! You don't have to worry. Don't be so jealous!"

Many times they would fight this same battle! The very same words were repeated over and over, exposing the same weaknesses and trampling over the same hurts. Terence remained resentful and grumbling, exposing his jealousy. Molly was too irritated and offended to sympathize or to have patience with him.

One evening soon after that, Terence came to Molly's bed.

"Terence, no!" Molly whispered. "You are too sick! We should not do this!"

Terence persisted, "I'm not too sick to be your husband!"

"Terence, you don't have to prove anything to me. Don't worry." She insisted, "I don't need you to do this. I will remain faithful to you, no matter what."

Terence would not be dissuaded.

In a final, weak plaint, Molly cried, "I don't want you to die!"

Terence was adamant, "I'm not going to die!"

****

Predictably, monsoon winds and rain continued to sweep in from the southwest from May to October. Because Molly was walking to bus stops, she sometimes carried an umbrella with her during the five months of rainy season. When she was a child in Chinatown, she didn't mind getting wet in the rain and she thought those wrestling an umbrella in the wind looked ridiculous. Now, becoming soaked before work was not pleasant and the effort of carrying an umbrella, even for a little protection, seemed worthwhile. But when the wind blew, umbrellas still turned inside out, and Molly could not afford to replace hers. Instead, when reckless winds gusted, Molly faced them with her umbrella protectively folded under her arm.

In the worst storms, she did what she learned from the other women. They would bring from home a spare set of clothes and shoes, and then they would change into dry clothes in the bathroom at work. Her tightly woven shan bag kept the spare clothes surprisingly dry. Wet clothing was stuffed back in to the shan bag, and in the evening the stale clothes were given to the maids to wash.

September, Mrs. Graham told Molly, was "Sports Month" at the junior library. Molly tried to be cheerful as Mrs. Graham enthusiastically explained to her about the favorite American pastime of baseball, along with the newer sports of basketball and football. Hazel put up the sports-themed bulletin board, and the staff taught the children about the athletic games. Molly was helping the Chinese children especially, as duty called.

Also, there was another subject to teach the children. Already they were learning to sing Christmas carols in preparation for that most antici-pated of holiday celebrations at the library. The junior library staff members were teaching one or two songs at a time until the songs were very familiar to the children.

But Molly wasn't feeling well, and she had a disconcerting suspicion. By October, she was certain. She didn't say anything to Terence, but she confided to her maid.

"I don't know what I'm going to do!" Molly spoke in the Burmese tongue. She also communicated her great distress in the universal language of emotion.

"Three children already and now four! And my husband sick! The future will be so hard for us! How am I going to go to work when I have a newborn? But I must work, because we need the income! What if they fire me when I miss work to have the baby? How am I going to ride the bus when I get so big? But how else can I get to work? And I must work! Oh! I can't have this baby! What am I going to do?"

Molly blamed Terence. "My husband is a dreamer! He doesn't have a grasp of the reality of our situation! He thinks he has to prove he's a man by producing children. Now look where he's got us! Now I have to get big and bounce on a bus!"

Again she was overwhelmed by the impossibility of her situation. "I can't have this baby! What am I going to do?"

The maid, an older woman, had patiently listened to Molly. Then she said softly in Burmese, "Ma Ma, Big Sister, if you don't want this child, I can help you."

Molly was confused at first. She had not expected her maid to help her with the problem, only to listen sympathetically. She asked, "What do you mean?"

"I can make the child drop out. I have helped many others in my village."

"Oh!" At first Molly was shocked by what the maid was suggesting. It had not occurred to her to try to end the pregnancy. When she said, "I can't have this baby," she meant it, but she did not mean that she intended to do anything to stop it.

Still, as she thought about it, Molly felt she had no choice. She was desperate and confused, and the problems seemed insurmountable.

She asked, "How do you do it?"

"Oh, I will show you," the maid answered calmly. "Don't worry."

Molly continued to feel troubled over the next several days. But she found a measure of comfort when she thought that there might be a way out, an escape from peril that seemed to loom over her.

The following weekend, when Molly was home from work, her maid said, "I am ready. The children are napping. Terence is resting. Go lie down on the bed."

Molly felt there really was no reason to hesitate. The maid seemed to offer the only solution to the impossible situation, and waiting would only make it harder to do what had to be done. She had done hard things before. She would do this difficult thing for her family. So, with her face hardened into a determined frown, she went to her bed.

Molly braced herself against the physical pain as the woman began the procedure. But even the physical pain could not block out the agonizing turmoil in Molly's mind and the sorrow in her heart.

"I can't have this baby," she told herself. "I can't see any way to do it. This is my only choice. I really have no options."

Tears came in a heavy flow. The late storm battering the thin walls of the old house seemed to share in Molly's mourning. She wanted to wail out loud with the howl of the wind, but she didn't dare disturb her husband or children. How could she explain her cries to them?

Molly spoke silently, defensively, to Jesus, "I can't do it, Lord. You know, I can't have a baby now. How could I go to work and do the job You gave me to support my family?"

For an instant, she blamed Him for her predicament. Why would He put her in this difficult situation?

Then, for some reason, Molly thought of the Chinese opera. She remembered how, when a baby arrived into a family, it was brought on stage with great fanfare by the hands of fairies. For generations this had been the traditional operatic representation of birth. Molly's Chinese ancestors believed that children are a blessing from Heaven.

Chopped verses from the Bible whispered in Molly's mind, " 'Lo, children are a blessing from the Lord...' something, something.... 'Children are like arrows in a quiver.... Happy is the man that has his quiver full of them.' " Molly couldn't remember all of the words, but she remembered enough.

Suddenly Molly knew, "Oh, Lord! This is a life inside me! Why should I kill him or her? This child is a gift from You! Why should I not accept the gift?"

Out loud Molly shouted in Burmese, "Daw-bee! Daw-bee! Enough! Enough! Please, don't do it! I want to get up!"

She blurted out, "Gayin chia! Sinful sin! Big sin! My God may not like it!"

Quickly concerned that she might have offended her maid, Molly added meekly, "Thank-you. Thank-you very much, but I think I will be able to take it. I want to think it over. I think I want to have this baby." Oh, she hoped her family had not heard anything! And she hoped the baby was not harmed!

To God, she prayed, "Lord, please forgive me!"

Remembering another Bible verse, she prayed, "I know You will work all things together for good for those who love You! I'm sorry I didn't trust You. Help me to trust You."

****

Terence was delighted to know Molly was carrying a child! He proudly told everyone he knew.

Soon Terence also had some news for Molly. "I'll be starting work next week. I will be supervising construction in Rangoon." He spoke with nonchalance, but Molly could not miss the pride in his voice.

What could Molly say? She was terribly afraid for Terence to work. He was not yet very strong. And who would keep an eye on the maids caring for the children, especially the new baby?

But she understood her husband. He needed this job. He could not easily sit at home and depend on his wife. In fact, the very thing that frustrated her about Terence, that he would not stay home and take care of himself, was also one of the things she admired about him. He was not a lazy and dependent man. If he could provide for his family's welfare, he would do so.

Still, Molly would keep her job for now.

****

Molly overheard the Burmese women chatting at the library. "Everyone comes to take what they can from the Burmese people. We are too polite to defend our resources. The British take from us. The Chinese take from us. The Indians...."

Another put in, "Well, at least the Chinese give something back. They will build a nice pagoda or something. The Indians make money in Burma and then send it to India."

Molly wasn't trying to eavesdrop, but she couldn't stop her ears from hearing. She hoped the Indian page boys didn't hear. She did know that Chinese business people often sent money back to relatives in China, but they also built pagodas to please the natives, and she felt a moment of pride in the generosity, or at least the business wisdom, of her race. But who could blame the generosity and loyalty of Indian people sending money home to impoverished relatives?

****

Molly was shocked and embarrassed! She had been busily working at the children's library, confidently helping children find things in the card catalog, proudly leading children through the wonderful maze of books, happily checking out books for eager readers to take home. Suddenly she saw him, standing there in the entrance of the children's library, wearing his construction clothes and dirty, heavy construction boots! She was mortified!

Her eyes met his, but not with the delight of one whose sweetheart unexpectedly appears. Her mien of shock and embarrassment quickly became the face of anger, which met his look of determination. If Terence expected a fond welcome and tour of the library, he did not get it.

After a moment's hesitation, Terence strode firmly to one of the small chairs made for the children. He sat down heavily as if he intended to stay as long as he pleased, daring anyone to tell him otherwise!

How foolish he looked in the child's chair! Molly turned her back on him and pretended to ignore him. She tried to focus on her work.

At last Molly could not contain her anger any longer and went to Terence, demanding in a stern whisper, "Why are you here?"

They exchanged a few cross words. Then Molly, shamed to find herself arguing with him in front of her co-workers, insisted that she had to get back to work.

Hoping to dismiss him as she stomped away, she scolded, "If you want a book, you should go to the adult library!"

After observing the exchange, Martha came to Molly and nodded in the direction of Terence. "Do you know that man?" she asked with concern.

Humiliated, Molly replied, "Yes. That's my husband. He came to check on me."

"Oh." Martha seemed satisfied and didn't pursue the subject, to Molly's relief.

At last, Terence got up. He left the library feigning the same aristocratic air in which he entered it.

When Molly arrived home that evening, she was ready with a furious string of accusatory questions: "Why are you spying on me? Why must you humiliate me in front of my boss? Why do you come and sit in a child's chair? You are a grown man! Do you want to make everyone think you are a fool? Why do you come in your work clothes and your muddy construction boots? Why were you were so disrespectful?

"Where are the American men I am flirting with, Terence? Where are they? Did you see them all around me? Why don't you trust me? Now are you satisfied? You see, it's just as I told you! There are no American men in the children's library! Anyway, I am not that kind of girl! Why do you insult me?"

Terence had no chance to reply to any of the questions before his wife fled to be alone with her anger. He did not spy on Molly again.

It was not until her fury cooled that she remembered, as she pictured the scene when she first saw him, Terence had been clutching his heart as he stood there spying on her. She was moved with compassion, but she was too proud to show him. Terence! Why was he so stubborn to take this construction job?

Once again she was overwhelmed with fear of losing him. She prayed again that God would preserve the life of her husband.

****

The days flowed swiftly, and in a moment it was December. For months, Molly had been hearing excited chatter from other employees about Christmas at the USIS Library. Molly's anticipation was building as wonderful changes were transforming her workplace.

Hazel had done a delightful bulletin board with a snow scene and Santa Claus. This was foreign to Molly. What was snow? Who was Santa Claus?

Evergreen garlands were draped over all the doorways and windows and a huge, fresh-cut spruce tree was placed prominently in the music hall. Molly wondered from where such a tree had come. She had never seen one growing in Burma, though Nye Nye could manage to get little sprigs of spruce to pin to a baby's cap for luck. Delightful things were hung on the tree: sparkling silver tinsel, colorful glass balls, little decorative figures, and glorious sparkling lights of many colors. Oh! The children loved all of this!

In the weeks leading up to the holiday, the junior library staff members were busy planning the program, learning and teaching the Christmas songs, and wrapping little gifts packages for all of the children. Special, colorful paper was used for the wrapping, and each gift was adorned with a ribbon tied into a bow. As she was helping to wrap the hundreds of little gift packages,

Embassy photo, used by permission.

Molly noticed that, like the Chinese red gift packets, red was prominent on the Christmas wrapping paper and décor. Green was also a favored color for the holiday.

At last the holiday week came, and each day lines of children extended for several blocks from the library entrance. This was the highlight of the year, and eager, scampering children had spread news of the event throughout Rangoon. Just in case of trouble, the page boys were assigned to keep order in the crowd where excitement churned, but the children waited patiently for their turn, the reward clearly worth the wait. Besides, the risk of offending the Americans and missing this event was too great even for a rowdy child. Many of the children wore their nicest clothes, especially the Chinese children.

Mrs. Graham asked one of the Indian page boys to dress up like Santa Claus. The white cotton beard and mustache, with his white, smiling teeth, contrasted brightly against his dark skin, making a striking appearance. The featured book *'Twas The Night Before Christmas"* was read to each group. Then, the red-suited, pillow-plumped Santa gave the children the little wrapped presents, which they opened carefully to find pencils and little pads of paper printed with "United States Information Services" at the top. Oh, they were so pleased!

Molly said to Clara, "You would think they were getting gold, the way they stand in line so long to see Santa and get their little gift."

"Some children come back again to get another present," Clara noted. "The page boy is taking attendance as the children come in to the library, but Mrs. Graham doesn't say anything if they come back and get more than one gift."

"I see that no one wants to leave. The children want to stay all day." Molly commented.

Mrs. Graham also had children of staff members dress as the characters of the Nativity to portray the scene of Jesus' birth: Mary and Joseph, angels, shepherds and kings. They put on a little skit of the first Christmas, and as the wise men came from afar, the staff led the singing of "We Three Kings."

The programs were repeated many times to accommodate all the children. Molly was singing so much, she was losing her voice. In fact, all members of the staff were hoarse. But Molly loved to hear the Burmese children singing, "Jingle Bells," in the foreign English tongue. She wished her own children could also participate. Next year she must find a way for them to do it.

Mrs. Graham invited the library staff and their families to her home in Washington Park. Terence was unwell and could not go, but it would be rude for Molly to decline the invitation, and she took the children along. The home was quite large as a residence for one person, an indication, Molly thought, of Mrs. Graham's rank. It also helped Mrs. Graham's diplomacy efforts in Burma, as she could entertain large groups. Molly admired the modern bathroom, and she marveled to hear that the home had both heating and air conditioning capabilities to moderate the Burmese weather.

Mrs. Graham had gifts for all of the children of employees: brightly-colored striped t-shirts for the boys and material for a longyi for each of the girls. Each of Molly's children was pleased, but Eng Koon especially treasured that shirt! He wanted to wear it every day! Mrs. Graham had also prepared wrapped gifts for each of her employees; each woman received a light-weight sweater, and everyone was delighted.

Molly admired the beautiful, decorated evergreen Christmas tree in Mrs. Graham's home. She was embarrassed to remember the time Pastor Eastman had visited Terence, and he asked her conversationally, "Do you have a Christmas tree?"

She had responded with pride, "Oh, yes!"

When she showed him the tiny tree she had put in the window, he looked surprised, but he was too polite to comment. She had never before seen a full-sized, fully decorated Christmas tree with presents underneath it, until recently when she saw the one at the library, and now at Mrs. Graham's house. Even in this land of gold-gilded pagodas and brightly colored clothes, a tall, freshly cut Christmas tree, green boughs hung with shining lights and colorful baubles, was a delightful sight!

Chapter Twenty-One

Oasis

By April, nearly nine months into her pregnancy, Molly was quite large with the child she carried. The hot season was earning its name, and the bus ride to and from work was beyond stifling. For many weeks now, just to climb into the bus was an ordeal. With all of her strength, Molly hoisted herself up and grabbed whatever she could grab to lift herself, ungracefully, into the bus. She had trouble walking through the bus, so she always tried to get a seat near the less congested back door. But the back of the bus was especially bouncy, and she had to hold tightly to her seat so that she would not bounce out the door and into the street. She feared that the jostling on the hard bench for forty-five minutes each way might cause her to miscarry. It did not occur to her to surrender her pride and ride in Lo Yeahr's car.

A couple of the ladies that worked with Molly were pregnant at the same time, and their husbands sent them to work by car and had them picked up in the evening. Observing them, Molly found it was hard not to be envious of them or to feel sorry for herself. But she never doubted that she had done the right thing to keep her baby.

Planning for the delivery, Molly had arranged again to use the clinic of Dr. Ng and his associate. She liked the woman doctor who had delivered Lois. But, during the long rides on the bus, Molly's mind would fall to worrying about the timing of the baby's arrival and how she would get to the clinic.

She would catch herself fretting, and then she would remember to pray to the Lord for His help. "Jesus, thank-you for this child living in me!

Please help me to deliver him or her safely so he or she can grow up to honor You. I know You care about us. Help me to trust You."

Molly was later than ever coming home from work. Everything took longer: to waddle to the bus stop after work, to maneuver through a bus change mid-route, and to lumber home from the bus stop near Eight Mile. Terence was always waiting anxiously and clearly relieved to see her, but, more often than not, he questioned her about her tardiness. By now, when Terence merely mentioned that she was late, she felt his comment reflected not concern, but jealousy and distrust.

How each one needed each other! The stresses they shared weighed heavily. But instead of a united partnership against assaults from the outside, they were often divided against each other. Thus, the tenderness, affection, kindness, and encouragement so valuable in a relationship easily turned to rash judgments, resentment, self-interest, unguarded words, and hurt feelings. Molly found she could use an unkind tone of voice with Terence that she wouldn't think of using with anyone else. Sometimes after snapping at Terence, Molly was sorry, and she would make a point of sitting with him and reading encouraging verses from her Scripture book or massaging his shoulders. Other days, stretched between the demands of wife, nurse, mother, manager of the house, and library employee, she couldn't seem to find the strength and retreated, desperate to read a few Scriptures and pray alone.

Molly was relieved to find that her employer allowed a maternity leave of absence. She would be able to stay home with her baby for one month, with assurance that her job would be held for her, though the leave was without pay. Molly didn't take off any time ahead of the baby's birth, so she would have the maximum time to spend with the baby before returning to work.

Molly was feeling so big and so tired, she was more than ready to deliver the baby. This pregnancy wore her out more than the others, and she was ready to meet her little child. She wondered if her mother-in-law was right; Nye Nye was certain this baby was a boy.

"Pointed stomach, carried in the front," she said, "is a boy. Rounded, and spreading around the sides, is a girl. You will have a boy."

Whether Molly took the Prome Road bus or the Peace Pagoda bus to Eight Mile, she had to change buses at the Fraser Street stop in front of the hospital, in the market area. After work one day in late April, she got on to the first bus at Sule Pagoda, but when it was time to move to the other bus at Fraser Street, she couldn't lift herself from the bench. She couldn't expect help from any of the other passengers; being touched by a stranger would be inappropriate. Finally, with many eyes upon her and exerting great effort, she slid herself to the end of the bench and stretched overhead to barely reach the strap used by people standing on the bus. Slowly, she pulled herself up and began momentum to the steps, gravity then helping her to go down.

She wasn't sure how much longer she could do this! Somehow, she hoisted herself on to the next bus, bounced to the bus stop near Eight Mile, and struggled to get off the bus. She slowly made her way to the house, climbed the stairs with effort, and changed in to more comfortable clothing.

Suddenly, Molly's clothing below the waist was soaked. She realized that her water bag had broken, and she thought in instant panic, "Oh, my! Oh dear! The baby is coming! Lord, what to do?" She doubted that she would have time to take the bus to the clinic.

She called, "Terence, the baby is coming! What to do? What to do?"

Terence answered anxiously, "I think the chauffeur has gone. But, let me see if I can get my father's jeep."

Almost immediately Terence came back with his Number Two Sister Lily. "Oh Molly!" she said, "I wanted to visit my mother tonight, and on the way over I joked with Myo Khin, 'Oh! Maybe when we get there, we'll have to take Molly down to the clinic!' And now, here we are, ready to take you!"

"Oh, Lily, thank-you," Molly breathed with relief and prayed in gratitude to her Lord.

Myo Khin happily turned the car around and headed back in to town, as Lily chatted with Molly to ease her mind. Terence, dutiful father left to worry, would wait at home. At the clinic, a beautiful baby boy was born at eight o'clock that evening.

Molly and the nameless baby stayed at the clinic for a week. How pleasant it was to be cared for in such a hygienic place and with such expert attention! Terence came with the driver in Lo Yeahr's jeep for a visit each day. But there were no other visitors. Women were considered dirty until the menses stopped.

Once again, Terence was a proud father. Once again, when Molly went home, Nye Nye fed her very well.

A month later, Nye Nye named the baby Ohn Koon. Ohn is the main vertical supporting post in a building, and Koon, the name shared with his brother, means powerful. The meaning of the words together could be translated: "Powerful and Respected Leader."

Once again, Molly noticed, "A very big name."

The baby's head was shaved, and eggs were boiled and stained red. Nye Nye made sure the potato, yam, and ginger dish was cooked with sweet and sour sauce to dish out to relatives to announce the birth of Ohn Koon. Also she had made the special hat for him, familiarly trimming it with a patterned ribbon along the rim. With a gold pin, she attached a sprig of evergreen and a laughing Buddha image for long life.

****

Molly had been busy during her month at home, preparing to leave her newborn in the care of others. She would not be able to nurse Ah Ohn while she was away at work, so she must learn about bottle feeding. The doctor at the clinic told her how to sterilize the glass bottles, which were boat-shaped and open at each end for ease of cleaning. A sterilized rubber nipple was attached to one end, and at the other end a valve was placed to allow air to escape. Molly learned to carefully poke a small hole in each new rubber nipple, making sure the hole was small enough that the baby would not choke as he sucked, but not so small that he would be frustrated and get too little milk for his effort. She learned how to make the milk formula by boiling water in a flask, then thoroughly mixing in the milk powder to remove all lumps. The milk was poured into the prepared bottle.

Molly herself would wash and sterilize the bottles ahead of time, but Beulah, the Kayin, Christian housekeeper, would need to mix the formula. Molly taught her to carefully wash her hands when preparing the bottle and feeding Ah Ohn. She was quite strict with the maid about cleanliness. She showed Beulah how the doctor taught her to test the milk with a drop on her wrist to make sure it was not too hot. She taught her to tip the bottle in such a way as to insure a good flow of formula without introducing air pockets that might cause the baby problems with gas. After Ah Ohn drank for awhile, Beulah must lift him to her shoulder, his head resting on a clean napkin, and Beulah must pat his back gently until she heard the wind escape his mouth.

Because of the preparation involved, Beulah would have to plan ahead for Ohn's hunger. It was not considered healthy to allow a baby to cry for very long.

Too soon, Molly had to return to work. Since she had a newborn, Molly decided to work the afternoon and evening shift, though it was disheartening for her to get home late in the evening, when it was nearly time to put the older children to bed.

Terence didn't have the stamina to work long hours, and so he was home much of the time. Molly was glad he was often home. She couldn't bear to think of losing this precious baby to dysentery, so she told him, "You had better watch Beulah if you don't want your son to be sick! Make sure she washes her hands!"

At work, Molly would go to the restroom every three or four hours when she felt her swollen breasts. There she would remove her Chinese dress and painfully squeeze milk into the sink to ease the swelling and leaking, but also to insure that her breasts would continue to produce milk.

As she did this, she worried, "I know my baby is hungry now. I imagine he is getting fussy, and I hope Beulah is preparing his milk before he gets upset. I hope she remembered to wash her hands. I hope Terence is watching her." At home in the mornings, at night, and on weekends, Molly nursed her baby.

The weather had gotten quite hot, so Molly and Terence fixed a swinging cradle in the cool porch   beneath the house. Two ropes were tied to floor joists overhead, and to make a hammock, a soft cloth was tied between the hanging ropes. Molly made a small pillow for her baby, and she insisted that it be used whenever Ah Ohn was in the cradle, to support his little neck so his breathing was not restricted.

On hot afternoons, Terence stretched out in his lounge chair, a watchful eye on Beulah. Breezes swirled through the lattice openings, and the young maid pushed Ohn's cradle gently, back and forth, back and forth, until he slept soundly. Then, always a hard-worker, Beulah would scrub, or cook, or wash laundry. Sometimes, if Terence was feeling well enough, he would take a turn swinging his baby boy. And what a cheerful, contented little boy he was!

A man in a lorry truck came around to sell firewood, cut to length but not split. Calling from the street, he shouted in Burmese *"Thit thar!* Forest wood!" Terence bartered with him on the price, and when an agreement was made, the maids stacked the wood in the shelter under the house. The monsoon rains would soon begin, and the wood must be kept dry. Even in the hot season, a nice supply of wood was necessary to feed the cooking stoves.

Molly received her paycheck every other week. Always, two urgent purchases came first from the paycheck: medicine for Terence and milk powder for Ah Ohn. At Dr. Ng's suggestion, Terence had found that Digoxin, an extract taken from the foxglove plant, gave him some relief from heart palpitations. For Ohn, Molly must purchase the best powdered milk, which according to Molly's doctor at the clinic, were British brands, "Cow and Gate" or "Glaxo." The maids could do the other shopping, but Molly would purchase these things, which were only available on Cheap Row, where, unlike the name implied, beautiful homes lined the street and westerners or Anglo-Indians resided. Medications were not distributed from a pharmacy or given with a written prescription advising recommended dosages, so patients were largely on their own to determine the dose.

Each day when Molly came home from work, she first massaged her husband's neck. Then she nursed her baby. Then she directed the maids in preparing the evening meal. Then she looked at Charlene's school work.

****

One Sunday afternoon Anita came to visit Molly. Terence and Anita continued to show sibling tension, but Molly was always glad to see her sister-in-law and friend. Anita looked at the new baby with surprise.

"Oh! He is healthy!" Anita exclaimed. After staring in amazement, she added, "Molly, we were worried. We thought, 'The mother is not home. How is the baby? He must be suffering!' "

Anita admired Ah Ohn's round cheeks and said in wonder, "...but this baby is thriving! He's doing very nicely!"

Molly was pleased with Anita's response. She remembered back to the war days when Anita did not have enough milk for her baby. She told Anita, "Your husband told me about the milk formula, and the maid gives it to Ah Ohn. Also, I nurse him whenever I can. We don't have to give him goat's milk."

Anita remarked, "Yes, Sammy told me that Ah Ohn is doing very well. But I could hardly believe it. I wanted to see for myself."

She said with satisfaction, "Yes, he looks quite healthy. This is really God's blessing."

Molly knew it was true.

****

When Ah Ohn was about four months old, Terence took Molly to see a new American movie, and they took the baby along. They enjoyed the movie, "By the Light of the Silvery Moon," starring Doris Day. Ohn slept the whole time.

****

Molly was beginning to know quite well the people with whom she worked. She admired Mrs. Graham's savvy in hiring. Many of the women working in the library were wives or relatives of important members of Burmese society, and in this way Mrs. Graham gave both legitimacy and security to the library. There were the wife of a brigadier general, the wife of a lieutenant colonel, the wives of judges, the niece of the figurehead president, the wife of a professor at the university, and so on. These women of prestige usually dominated their co-workers. Generally, the tribal Burmese women did not mix socially with women of other tribes, let alone the Anglo-Indian or Chinese. Though most were cordial, they tended to keep aloof, an unsurprising result of the classist culture, and Mrs. Graham did not interfere. Molly was aware and acquiesced to her place, but she sometimes missed the friendly atmosphere of the Methodist English High School, where she recalled that races mixed as equals.

Several of the higher ranking employees had studied library science in the United States. Mrs. Graham had arranged for their training.

A few other co-workers in the library were wives of Americans or wives of locals working with Voice of America. This agency of the American government sent shortwave radio broadcasts of music and U.S. domestic programming as well as VOA news and commentary. Its first international news broadcasts had been sent to Latin America to counter Nazi propaganda. Then when the U.S. entered World War Two, broadcasts of war news were sent to Germany in the German language, countering false propaganda broadcast by Nazis. The VOA charter states that it will provide news which is accurate, objective, and comprehensive, but socialists, communists, and other critics accuse the agency of spreading propaganda.

Clara was Burmese, but not as powerful as some. She often chatted with Molly as they worked together at the circulation desk, keeping Molly informed of undercurrents at the library.

Molly's boss, Martha Khin, was an American who met her Burman husband in London where he was training with the Voice of America. When she came to Burma, Martha conformed to the Burmese culture in many ways, dressing in Burmese clothing and cooking Burmese meals for her husband. But she kept her hair short and permed, in keeping with western culture.

Martha was an efficient and considerate boss. But Molly was curious about the western woman with eastern ways. One time Clara told Molly that the sa-yar, the Burmese fortune teller, had told Martha's husband that it would be profitable for him to change his name, and so he did. Molly thought such superstition didn't fit with the western culture, so she would always wonder how Martha felt about it.

Molly liked Martha very much. She quickly saw that Martha was nice and fair to all the women in her employ. She appreciated hard work, which Molly was glad to do. Molly noted that Martha was frustrated with Doris's disappearances when the work was especially hectic. Martha would have dismissed her, Molly guessed, but Mrs. Graham soon placed Doris with a supervisor more tolerant of idleness.

Ei May Tun, the Burmese woman who was head of circulation in the children's library, did not speak or write English too well, like most of the local staff members. One of her duties was to write a monthly report to turn in to Mrs. Graham. The purpose of the report was to summarize what junior library programs had been given during the month, along with attendance and book usage figures. Recognizing Molly's proficiency in English, and preferring to consult a local co-worker than an American, Ei May Tun was quick to ask Molly for help writing the report. Before long, Ei May Tun was telling Molly just a few things, and then Molly was writing the report for Ei May Tun, who signed it and turned it in as her own. Molly enjoyed writing the reports and did not resent another taking credit for her work. The cooperation seemed to work well.

Polly, the Kayin pianist, reminded Molly that they had met in Pyapon during the war. Her father was a judge there. Polly was a Christian. When she found out Molly was a Christian and that Molly did not own a Bible, Polly gave her a small Gideon New Testament of the Bible in English. The Gideon organization, Polly said, was known for providing free Bibles around the world. Molly was immensely pleased to own a New Testament, the portion of the Bible concerning the time of Lord Jesus' life on earth, his death and resurrection, and the start of the Christian church.

Clara told Molly that the Kayin typist in the director's office had married a Chinese shoemaker. They had eloped to marry, an indication that they thought their parents would not approve the mixed marriage. After it was done, the parents conceded to the match. Clara said she saw the woman kneeling down and tracing Mrs. Graham's foot so her husband could make shoes for her. Clara commented cattily, "She knows how to lift the leg of the Americans."

Daw Ni Hta was the most powerful Burmese woman at the library, unofficially second in power after Mrs. Graham. Head of the reference library, she was one of those who had been educated in library science in the

United States. She was quite proud, very outspoken, and had a few clashes with other women who were not as subdued as Molly.

Second in power among locals, after Daw Ni Hta, was Ruth. She worked directly for Mrs. Graham. She had studied library science at Syracuse University in the United States. Daw Ni Hta was proud, but she was approachable and smiled at Molly. Ruth was snooty and curt, obviously annoyed by questions, and when she looked in Molly's direction, Molly felt unseen, as if Ruth were looking right through her. Molly didn't need to interact with her very often and gave her plenty of space.

The staff attended regular meetings, and the department managers would often give informative lessons to the rest of the workers. Mrs. Kyaw Myint, head of the cataloging department, gave instructions pertaining to her specialty, and Daw Ni Hta educated everyone about the reference library. Molly was eager to learn.

One day, Daw Ni Hta was incensed, but not at her coworkers. Mrs. Graham called a meeting of all the staff.

Daw Ni Hta commanded, "Look at these beautiful reference books... encyclopedias, technical dictionaries, almanacs...." By Daw Ni Hta's training, everyone understood the purposes of these books. She raged, "...someone has torn and removed pages! Look! Can you believe it? Someone has taken whole pages right out of the books!"

Everyone was dismayed at the irreparable damage to the lovely books. It was easy to see why someone would want to keep a page of precious information, but it was also intolerable to allow people to destroy the books, rendering them useless to others, and all of the workers felt the offense. The staff was instructed to be watchful of anyone behaving suspiciously in the reference library and to quietly watch patrons as they used the reference books. For all the differences among library employees, they were united in their desire to protect the books.

Mrs. Graham emphasized, "We don't want to make anyone uncomfortable, and we can't be watching every minute. But we want to protect these books, so that patrons can use them for many, many years. We must try to keep people from having an opportunity to damage them. We also want you who work in the Children's Library to train the children to respect the books, both the ones they use here in the library, and the ones they take home. Make sure you often remind the children never to write in books, never to fold pages or tear them out, and never to damage the books in any way. Of course, the books people take home can be inspected when they are returned, and fines will be levied if necessary. Our only recourse with the reference books is to watch them carefully."

****

Terence so enjoyed every book and magazine Molly brought home for him. One day she brought him a magazine simply called "Life." She had patiently waited her turn, since many others, library staff and patrons, had wanted to have a look at this particular issue from December of 1951. In an article called, "Decline of the Westerner," the author gave an account of his tour of free, non-communist Asia, and mentioned Burma. The news was not new to Molly and Terence, but they were anxious to read the American reporter's account of chaos and decay in Burma since her independence.

"Yes," Terence said aloud several times as he read the article. It was some measure of comfort knowing that those in far off America were aware of their hardship in Burma.

****

After work one day, Terence met Molly, as usual, as she walked from the bus stop into the yard of the old house. He did not scold her for being late, but he was frowning.

"Your son...." he began.

Noting his concern, Molly interrupted, "What son? Eng Koon? Ah Ohn? What about my son?" With two simple words and Terence's tone, Molly was frantic.

"It was so hot today, and Ah Ohn seemed very warm...."

"What happened to Ah Ohn?" Molly interrupted again.

"Beulah was swinging him in his cradle," Terence spoke quickly to allow no more interruptions. "I was in my chair watching. No one noticed the rope had frayed from rubbing against the beam with so much swinging of the cradle. Beulah pushed the cradle, the rope broke, and Ohn was thrown in to the woodpile."

"Ohn!" Molly moaned, "Where is he? Where is my baby?"

"He's okay, Molly," Terence reassured her quickly. "When he landed in the woodpile, the pillow you made for him was still underneath him. Your son just went on sleeping! Nothing happened to him! He is in the house. It is good that you made the pillow for him, because it protected him, and he is fine."

Terence added practically, "We will have to fix the cradle. We'll get stronger rope."

Then he told Molly, "Beulah is afraid you will be angry with her. But it wasn't her fault. Anyway, everything is fine."

Molly was relieved to hold her son in her arms and nurse him. She assured Beulah that she did not blame her; she knew Beulah would never intentionally let harm come to the children. Truly, Beulah, a faithful woman,

was much help to Molly. She was quite responsible with the children, and when she wasn't busy with them, she was never idle, always finding work to do. Molly was sincere in her reassurance to Beulah. But she thanked God that no harm had come to Ah Ohn.

****

Molly enjoyed her work at the library. She loved to see someone enter the library for the first time and stand just inside the door and look... and look...

and look, his face a picture of awe, as if he had just arrived in Paradise. Often people young or old would come and stay for the day, not wanting to leave the enchanting place.

Embassy photo, used by permission.

The themes presented to the children continued to circulate throughout the seasons, sometimes repeating unchanged year after year, as with Christmas, and sometimes varying. Popular subjects were the series on trains, the series on Abraham Lincoln, and the American nursery rhymes.

Mary had a little lamb. Its fleece was white as snow.
And everywhere that Mary went the lamb was sure to go.
It followed her to school one day, which was against the rule.
It made the children laugh and play to see a lamb at school!

Apparently, the appeal of a little lamb at school was universal. The local children enjoyed singing this rhyme put to music.

Something was going on all the time at the library, particularly in the children's library, and especially during the hot season break from March to May. Besides the singing and reading programs, there were all sorts of competitions. There were book-reading contests and classes and competitions involving paper-airplane folding and doll-making. Many games were taught and enjoyed, especially the quiet games popular in America, like chess, checkers and tic-tac-toe. Mrs. Graham would give prizes to winners of the contests, but she intentionally encouraged all the children.

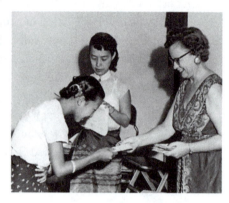

Molly helps Mrs. Graham give awards. Embassy photo, used by permission.

Molly was always learning with the children. Not only did she learn about American and other cultures, but she learned more about Burma by the way others saw the country. Rudyard Kipling, an English writer and traveler who visited Burma for a few days late in the nineteenth century said this about the Shwedagon Pagoda:

> *"Then, a golden mystery upheaved itself on the*
> *horizon, a beautiful winking wonder that*
> *blazed in the sun, of a shape that was neither Muslim*
> *dome nor Hindu temple-spire. It stood*
> *upon a green knoll, and below it were lines of*
> *warehouses, sheds, and mills. Under what new*
> *god, thought I, are we irrepressible English sitting*
> *now?"*

> *"...the golden dome said: 'This is Burma, and it will be quite unlike*
> *any land you know about."*

After working for a year at the library, Molly got her "annual leave," a one-week vacation. This was a great surprise; she did not know that she could earn pay without doing any work. She and her family did not go on a trip; very few locals traveled. But it was nice to have some extra time to spend at home with her family without missing a pay check.

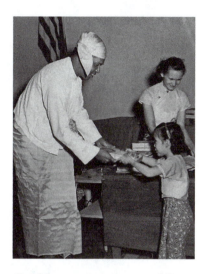

Charlene receives an award from a Burmese dignitary for her stamp collection. Martha is in the background. Embassy photo, used by permission.

Chapter Twenty-Two

A Dignitary from Afar

It was 1953, and the library was buzzing with excitement. The Vice President of the United States was coming to visit the USIS Library! No one of such rank from the United States had ever come to Burma, and besides other scheduled stops, the vice president would visit the library!

Mrs. Graham always challenged her workers to excellence, but now she was more determined than ever that everything should be perfect. Everyone caught her enthusiasm and wanted to make a good impression. Each employee labored to make the library spotless and attractive. The pages were taking special care to make sure each book was in good repair and neatly placed on polished shelves. Hazel gave particular attention to the displays and bulletin board. Papers were neatly filed or stashed from sight.

At last the day arrived. The library was closed to patrons during the momentous visit. Men entrusted with the vice president's security came in advance to make sure everything was in order. When word came that the vice president was nearing the library, Molly's heart beat rapidly in anticipation. All the employees lined up along the wall in the music hall, from which the chairs had been removed. Molly waited with the others, too thrilled to speak, terribly excited to meet this dignitary from America. She knew Terence was quite envious of her.

At last, Vice President Richard Nixon and his entourage came in to the room. Mrs. Graham, with typical aplomb, introduced her employees. "Mister Vice President, I would like you to meet my excellent staff. They are vital to the success of this library, which has become a mouthpiece of great American values to the people of Burma."

What a surprise this man was! Molly was impressed to see this smiling, friendly man shake the hand of each person. When it was Molly's turn, she felt the gentleman take her hand warmly as he spoke, "I want to personally thank-you for your fine service to the people of the United States."

Molly bowed slightly, and answered shyly, "Thank-you, Mister Vice President. I am pleased to meet you."

But she was not so quiet when she got home that evening. "Terence!" she enthused, "He took the time to shake the hand of each employee! Mister Richard Nixon! Vice President of the United States of America! He thanked me! He didn't make any speeches to us; he just thanked us! He came here to Burma! Who pays attention to Burma? If someone important comes to Burma, he doesn't bother with the library! If someone comes to the library, he does not bother with the lesser employees! Big shots will pass by us. But the Vice President of the United States took the time to shake the hand of each one! Oh, my! Terence, everyone was so flattered. You have to admire him!"

Indeed, the vice president had endeared himself to the local people. He was not pompous or unapproachable, and he did not restrict his attentions to powerful and important persons. This was a dignitary unlike any familiar to the Burmese people, whether western or Asian. Delighting the local people, Richard Nixon even rang the bell at the Shwedagon Pagoda, which, according to superstition, meant he would return to Burma one day. In fact, the people would welcome him warmly when he did return thirty-two years later as a former United States President.

Terence mentioned, "If there is one place I would like to live, it is the United States."

****

Molly couldn't afford to be sick now! She had been away from work for maternity leave, and now this! What if she lost her job?

But she knew something was wrong. She had an enduring headache, cough, and fatigue. She should be excited and energized to do wonderful work at the library and support her family, but she was dragging herself to work. At last she realized she was very ill, and she went apologetically to Mrs. Graham.

"I don't think I can come to work tomorrow," she said. She was afraid Mrs. Graham would think she was making excuses to avoid working. "I wish I could come, but I think I have some kind of illness."

Mrs. Graham was immediately concerned. "Of course, Molly! You need to stay home until you are well! You look as if you might have a fever. Go home right away, and don't come back until the fever is gone. This is important! We don't want to expose the children to whatever germs you have. Make sure you are well before you come back."

So Molly went home. The symptoms grew worse, and Terence arranged to borrow his parents' jeep to take Molly to see a doctor. The western-trained Indian doctor diagnosed her with typhoid fever. Oh! Molly remembered her hygiene classes at Methodist English High School. She recalled that typhoid is a life-threatening illness that causes high fever, often with delirium, rash, swollen and cramping abdomen, and diarrhea, sometimes leading to complications such as brain swelling and intestinal bleeding. When the illness has run its course, over four to six weeks, a patient that survives is usually emaciated and left with lingering exhaustion.

She also remembered from her hygiene classes that this was another devastating illness caused by bacteria spread through feces and passed by unwashed hands or unclean water. She would remember very little over the next few weeks, but she was determined to keep washing her hands. She couldn't bear the thought of infecting her children or her sick husband.

Bed. Bathroom. Wash hands. Bed. Bathroom. Wash hands. This was her existence.

She had a vague memory of the Indian doctor who wore Chinese clothes and drove his car to Eight Mile to see her, check her condition, and administer the antibiotic treatment. Later she would learn of his high fees for the house calls and regret the cost. But, to her credit, she kept herself clean, and no one else was infected. As soon as the fever was gone, she pushed herself back to work, and Mrs. Graham was glad to see her.

****

Charlene was excelling at school. Before the end of her first year she was advanced from lower and upper kindergartens to first grade. She would later receive another double promotion in grade school.

Mrs. Logie made personal comments on every student's report cards, and Molly would always remember one note in particular about Charlene: "She is a gem." "Gem" was an English word Molly had not encountered, so she looked it up in the dictionary.

"Oh, a precious stone," Molly read, "Or an outstanding person or thing." Molly was pleased.

Eng Koon had begun attending school with Charlene. He chose for himself an English name after reading a book from the library about an Italian boy named Anthony who liked to fly kites. Eng Koon also enjoyed flying kites with his father, so he took the name Anthony, or Tony for short.

Even from a young age Tony was very independent. Molly attended a parent-teacher meeting and met his first grade teacher, a Burmese woman with an English name, married to an Anglo-Indian, Molly guessed. The teacher enthused, "Tony is doing so well in class! Did he tell you he has come out first in the class?"

Molly was surprised, "No, he never told me."

"What? He didn't tell you?" The teacher was also surprised. "Oh, yes, he is an excellent student!" She went on, "Did he tell you his poem was chosen to be printed in the school's magazine? The first issue of 'Swaying Palm' will be printed soon, and Tony's poem will be in it."

Molly said, "I didn't know. He never mentioned anything like that."

"Oh, yes!" The woman continued. "Your boy is very intelligent, and so creative and original. You must be very proud of him."

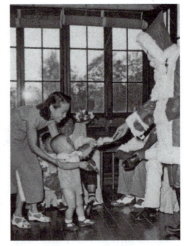

Molly returned sincerely, "Yes. I'm glad you told me. Now that you have told me, I am proud of him."

Tony was also given a double promotion.

Lois was impressed by her older siblings' school work, and she imitated them. She often pretended she was in school and would stand up straight and confidently recite things she had learned from watching Charlene and Tony. She looked forward to being old enough to join them.

Ah Ohn was a toddler now, and in December, Molly made certain that all of

Embassy photo, used by permission.

her children attended the USIS Library Christmas events. Then the children went with her to the party at Mrs. Graham's home. The Indian page was dressed as Santa again, and he was relishing the role with frequent and convincing calls, "Ho, ho, ho! Merry Christmas!" A photographer with the embassy caught the moment when shy Ohn, coaxed by his mother, received a gift from the intimidating creature.

As usual, Mrs. Graham was generous with Christmas gifts to her employees. The women all received Cover Girl compacts, with a mirror and face powder. Oh, the ladies treasured these! And the men employees were delighted with brightly colored Hawaiian shirts.

****

The glitch in Tony's educational rise happened in second grade. He suddenly stopped doing his homework.

When word of this reached Molly, she asked him, "Why aren't you doing your homework?"

Tony pouted, "I don't know.... Because you don't do it with me."

Molly realized in this excuse Tony's need for her attention, and she resisted the urge to scold him. In fact, she didn't argue with him at all. She said agreeably, "Okay, Tony. Take out your geography book. I'll go over it with you." Her tutelage was thorough. After a week or so of this special treatment, Tony decided he preferred to work on his own.

Molly's parents had moved to Tamwe, in east central Rangoon.
Terence said, "Let's borrow my father's car and go for a drive to see them." This photo was taken in Tamwe.

Molly introduced to her own children the new book that was so popular among the children at the library, Charlotte's Web. They loved to hear the imaginative tale of the heroic spider who made great sacrifices to save the life of her friend, Wilbur, the pig.

****

Keeping good maids was always a concern. A girl would make some money and then want to return to her village. When Molly was between maids, the wife of Indian Gardener was kind to help her with the care of the children. But she didn't like to help too long. One day the wife of Indian Gardener met Molly with an angry look. Tony was naughty, she said. Tony climbed the lattice to the roof, she said. She yelled and yelled, but Tony would not come down, she said. Molly asked Terence why he did not tell Tony to come down. Terence said he was asleep. Molly asked Terence if he heard the woman yelling. Well, he said, she was always yelling.

****

Tony got very sick, and his skin was a very strange yellow color. Molly took him to the hospital, and he was diagnosed with jaundice, but the cause was unknown. While he was still in the hospital for treatment, after about a week, he started feeling better, and to entertain himself he took his slate around to others in the ward to play tic tac toe. Those adult patients would later tell Molly, "Oh, your son is so bright! He beat us!"

To hear that Tony was active relieved Molly. She really felt Tony was getting well when she heard him chanting the Burmese nursery rhyme he loved:

> *Ah po JEE, oh!*
> *Car GOHN GOHN.*
> *Mer-they-bar HNIT ohn!*
> *Now HNIT kar--*
> *Der sound MOAN--*
> *Pwe GHEE bar ohn!*

This translates:

> *Oh, old man*
> *With bended back!*
> *Don't die yet!*
> *Next year--*
> *November--*
> *Come and see the concert!*

****

Like her siblings, Lois advanced through the grades with scholastic excellence and confidence. When Lois was in first grade, her teacher compared Molly's daughters. She told Molly, "I noticed that when Charlene was bullied, she would go hide in a corner and cry quietly. When Lois is bullied, she fights back. Your younger daughter is a fighter."

Molly understood the teacher meant to inform her of the girls differing personalities. But as the words settled in Molly's mind, she understood the implication that her daughters were being bullied. Molly knew Tony was bullied as well, even by some of his relatives. In fact, she had heard from her children that Lo Yeahr had started calling them "Jesus Eggs," a derogatory reference to the Christian custom of decorating Easter eggs as a symbol of new life. Being Christian had seemingly drawn a target on the backs of her children. Having a sick father had painted that target even darker, and like people everywhere, peers were quick to take advantage of any perceived weakness. Though Molly knew that teachers at the Methodist English High School did their best to train their students to respect one another, even this affirming haven was spoiled by unkind human nature. As the evening went on, Molly felt this concern effervescing uncomfortably to the top of other concerns, but she didn't know what she could do.

Another remembrance burdened her and added itself to the unhappy thoughts. She recalled coming upon a sister of Sit Hong. After they had greeted one another, the woman told Molly, "Oh Ngood! I see how your mother-in-law treats your children. Her children and other grandchildren grab things and she says nothing. Your children are polite, and they never ask for anything. Your mother-in-law spoils the others, saying 'Oh have this and take that!' while she ignores your children and gives them nothing. She should not treat them this way! This is not right!"

At least Molly was satisfied to hear that her children had heeded her firm instructions, "When you go to the house of Ah Ngen and Ah Yeahr, don't touch anything. Don't grab anything. Don't ask for anything. Don't stand around hoping for favors." But, of course, she did not like to hear that her children were treated unfairly.

That night, exhaustion of the body was no match for agitation of the mind, and the sleep urgently needed for the former was prevented by the latter. Molly realized, as the restless, tormented thoughts continued hour after hour, that she was quite powerless to protect her own children. She bullied herself with blame for what she couldn't do, until, gradually, she remembered she did have one extreme weapon against all peril threatening her children and herself: she could pray to the One Sovereign God who loved her, loved her children more than even she loved them, and who was willing and able to intervene for their welfare. So she did brandish this weapon and did pray as her family slept. Her tears dropped down her face as she prayed, and as tears and time passed together, Molly trusted Lord Jesus. As she trusted Him, He lifted from her the worry and the guilt, and He gave her peace.

Other things Molly did not know would have further upset her sleep. She knew the children played police and thief around the huge soy sauce jars. This was harmless entertainment, she thought. The leeches that found them in the tall grass did no great damage. They also climbed trees or used slingshots to bring down the mayan dee and mango fruits that grew in the compound. She often heard about these amusements. What she didn't know was that the children, Charlene, Tony, Foke San, Gabriel and others, played on the brick wall around the deep, open well, chasing and daring each other. Oh! The children could not swim, and no one would have heard the cries of a child who fell into the well! The house of Indian Gardener was nearest to the well, but even he could not have heard or been summoned in time to rescue a drowning child. When Molly found out about these escapades many decades later, she was faint at the thought. She thanked the Lord for His protection.

****

Nye Nye was very close to and admired the head nun who directed the nunnery at the Chinese temple. The woman did not dress like the other nuns; she wore ordinary Chinese clothes, particularly black silk, befitting a woman over forty. Neither did she shave her head like the other nuns. But she was very knowledgeable about Buddhist writings. In fact, she had given up material things to study the writings. Through her, Nye Nye purchased a room at the nunnery to have a place to stay in her old age in case her children, particularly her first son, did not fulfill their duties to take care of her.

****

At work, Molly heard upsetting stories about unintended consequences of the international development program called the Colombo Plan. Conceived by an Indian ambassador to China, and initiated at a conference in Colombo, Sri Lanka in 1950, the plan was to encourage economic development of South and Southeast Asian nations. People from willing nations, such as Britain, Australia, the United States, and Canada, sent capital, technological assistance, and skilled workers to train and develop inexperienced laborers in Asia as together they built airports, roads, railroads, dams, hospitals, and factories. The plan was a good one, and much was accomplished through this collaboration. However, Inya Lake was becoming infamous as the place where young girls, pregnant and abandoned by foreign exploiters pledging love, would drown themselves.

"So sad. So sad," Molly thought. She hoped Terence would not hear of this ongoing tragedy. It would only fuel his fears for Molly and solidify his stereotype that men of the west were licentious and shameless, preying on innocent Asian girls. She wondered how men coming from Christian countries could behave so horribly. She knew God forbade such behavior.

****

Clara's son was eight years old, ready for the *shinbyu* ceremony. Burmese parents are expected to honor Buddha's legacy by sending their young boys to be novice monks, even if only for a week or so. The *shinbyu* ceremony starts with a street festival, or *pwe*, with music, treats, and tea provided for the community. Guests are invited to attend a party at the home any time throughout the day, and *mohinga* was warmed for each new group of guests. Besides other guests, everyone working in the junior library was invited to Clara's house for the party in the boy's honor, and Molly attended.

According to custom, the boy wore princely, embroidered silk robes. Everyone sat on mats at a round, low table. Molly watched and did what others did. A big basin of water was brought for each one to wash hands, and then a meal was served. Molly was concerned about eating out of a single soup bowl with a common spoon. She knew germs could be spread this way, but she would not risk offending. Also, everyone ate his food with his hands.

Another table, long and rectangular, accompanied by chairs and set with forks, was set up for the western guests. Molly noted the faux pas that some of these guests did not remove their shoes when they entered the house, but the hosts were tolerant.

The boy was blessed by attending monks. In this way he was supposed to receive the blessing of Buddha himself.

After the party, the young boy was to give up his comfortable life for that of an ascetic. His head was shaved, and he traded his princely robe for the golden yellow robe of a Burmese monk. Then he left in a procession to the temple to study with the monks, taking a generous gift for the temple.

Novices like Clara's son learned Buddhist instruction from the monks and joined their daily morning trek through the streets to receive food, candles, and other charitable gifts. In fact, lines of saffron-robed monks, often with many novices, were familiar in Burma. Each monk and novice carried a lacquerware bowl for the purpose of receiving donations of rice. Molly knew her mother-in-law was a generous donor to the monks and their novices.

****

A new employee to the library was a tall, lanky, Kayin woman. Gloria was proficient at speaking and writing English, as well as at typing and filing, and so she was valued in the cataloging department headed by Mrs. Kyaw Myint. Molly marveled to watch Gloria easily type something in English, using all of her fingers, and then switch to typing Burmese on another typewriter equipped with the curvy Burmese alphabet. Polly had left the library, so Gloria also became the new piano player for junior library functions. Like many Kayin, Gloria was Christian and piano-playing, and Molly learned that she played piano for weekly services at her church.

Molly would also learn that Gloria had worked in the Secretariat, the administrative seat of British Burma, the very place where Aung San and his cabinet members were murdered in 1947, just six years earlier. Mrs. Kyaw Myint knew Gloria prior to her being hired and had asked her to apply, recognizing the urgent need for someone of her abilities at the library

Like most women in Burma, Gloria had kept her maiden name, which, Molly mused, was unheard of in Chinese culture. There were many other cultural differences between Chinese and Kayin, but Gloria and Molly found much they did have in common, and they became good and lasting friends.

One day Gloria eyed their superior co-workers, and she whispered confidentially to Molly, "We are small flies!"

She and Molly often laughed quietly together about their low status in the social order. Neither woman was offended by it and accepted it as an unalterable condition, like an immoveable wall one must acknowledge and walk around to get anywhere.

Evelyn McCabe had become Mrs. Graham's assistant in place of Miss Rosenfeld. Mrs. Graham also had a new boss, whose office was in the U.S. Embassy.

****

Always of concern to Molly was paying for the children's schooling. Several times, as funds ran short, Terence and Molly were prepared to take the children out of school. Each time, Mrs. Logie said, no, she would find scholarships for them. What a blessing to have this advocate, along with whatever generous donors helped their children receive the best education! Taking charity was not easy for them, but they were grateful.

Ah Ohn was able to start school at the Methodist English High School at age four because the school had just opened a nursery school for students so young. The school continued to produce students who achieved top scores in testing, followed by St. Paul's Boys' High School and St. John's Convent Girls' High School. Like his siblings, Ohn was eager to join this fine establishment of education.

In nursery school, Ohn learned this song with his classmates, motioning adorably to each line:

> Two little eyes to look to God,
> Two little ears to hear His words,
> Two little feet to walk in His way,
> Two little lips to sing His praise,
> Two little hands to do His will,
> And one little heart to love Him still.

Ohn's parents had no trouble choosing an English name for him when they saw Lois's upper kindergarten math text book written by L. G. Owen. The English name Owen was very similar in sound to his Chinese name, so Ohn became also Owen. Before long, he too was excelling at school and his teachers had no complaints.

A maroon school bus was now available to transport the children to and from school. Little Owen sat on the wooden bench next to his brother, and, nearly every afternoon, he fell asleep leaning against Tony. When they arrived at the Prome Road bus stop, Tony would waken Owen with a gentle nudge.

"He drooled all over me," Tony complained to his parents with mock offense. For the rest of his life Tony would fondly tease Owen of this. "You drooled all over me!"

****

Grandmother Wong was too old and unwell to travel. Several times, Molly made time to take the four children by bus to Kamayut. They left the bus at the proper stop, walked down the hill, and tramped noisily across the familiar wooden bridge over the shallow water where the water cress grew thickly. Molly waited as the children peered into the water for a bit, and then they went in to the little wooden house that was raised on stilts.

Molly was happy to see her dear grandmother and to hear her whisper, "Hello, Low-see doy." But it broke Molly's heart to see her so weak and bent over. She wished she could do more to help and comfort her.

Later Molly heard her grandmother was bedridden. Molly kept thinking she should take the children for another visit. And then Molly heard the precious woman was gone.

****

More than a million people worldwide would die from the Asian flu epidemic, which hit Burma in 1956. Everyone at the soy sauce compound was sick: Nye Nye and Lo Yeahr, all of their children, the maids, the chauffeur, Indian Gardener and his family, Terence, Charlene, Tony, Lois and Owen. Everyone was sick, that is, except Molly. Somehow she escaped the chills, high fever, sore throat, headaches, and coughing that lasted at least a week, and the muscle aches and fatigue that lingered many days more. Molly was troubled with concern for all of the ailing ones, especially for her weak husband and the young children; fevers were spiking, and the patients lay motionless, except to cough. They spoke little, except to complain of their bones hurting.

Schools and businesses were closed because of the epidemic, but Molly could not have left her family to go to work even if the library were open. Instead, she went from patient to patient, leaving the compound only to go to Cheap Row to buy antibiotics. The flu was caused by a virus, not a bacteria, but the antibiotic could prevent a secondary infection to patients with lowered resistance. Anyway, anxious to do something helpful, Molly was determined that some treatment was better than none, and her confidence was in the medicine of the west.

She also knew that fluids were important to flush toxins from the body, and with her limited kitchen skills, she boiled pork or chicken to make broth to go with vegetables for a light soup. She also made the easily digested *conjee* as the British said, or what the Chinese called joke, which was rice made with much water to soften it. She seasoned it lightly with salt fish or fermented bean curd and parsley-like *cen*, or coriander leaves, sprinkled nicely on top. Molly coaxed the patients to take these healing foods. Gradually, the family members recovered, and at Eight Mile there were no fatalities.

****

Lo Yeahr had borderline diabetes, and he developed gangrene in his foot. Ngood observed the blueness in his toes and foot, and even the blue cast creeping up his leg. He went to the hospital after pressure from his son-in-law Dr. Ng. To prevent the gangrene from spreading, the doctors at the hospital amputated the toes of his right foot. They talked of amputating his leg, but Lo Yeahr would have none of it!

"I would rather be a ghost with his legs on instead of a ghost without legs!" Lo Yeahr insisted.

A Chinese monk was in the hospital ward with Lo Yeahr, and he told him of another monk who was experienced in Chinese medicine, who might be able to help Lo Yeahr. Nye Nye sent Ah San to the monestary to look for the monk. Two or three times a week, Ah San would bring the monk to treat Lo Yeahr's wound. Within a month, the wound had hardened into a scar. Molly was surprised to see Lo Yeahr on his two feet again, tramping the ten-acre compound.

Chapter Twenty-Three

Inquisitive Lady

Molly's parents had moved to Myeinigon, on Moo Zajee Street, not too far off Prome Road but much closer to downtown Rangoon than Eight Mile. Whenever Molly went to visit her parents, she made a mental note of houses in the area with a "for rent" sign in the yard. She had started to consider that an hour-and-a-half or two hours on a bus every day, back and forth between Eight Mile and work, was quite taxing and time consuming. Moving to this neighborhood would save more than half of the time bouncing around on hard benches.

In truth, proximity to Nye Nye was wearing on the family as well. Even with her work schedule, Molly could count on seeing Nye Nye every day while they lived at Eight Mile. She could expect to feel her displeasure, to receive her withering looks, and to hear her pointed stories and scolding.

"Oh, Puck Ken's wife, she is such a good wife! She carries water; did you know that Ngood? She mops floors and cooks dinner. Such a good wife! It is hard to find one like her anymore."

And nearly daily, "Huh! You don't follow me to worship the ancestors! That is why Puck Ying is sick! Take my advice: Go make fun of Je-sus!" She spat the name with derision. "Then come with me to worship the ancestors! Do not be foolish!"

In fact, for the years they lived at Eight Mile, Molly felt trapped when at home, with nowhere to hide, at the mercy of her mother-in-law's domination. Day after day it was the same; Nye Nye could come at any time, and when she came, Molly would suffer.

Molly would remember God's promises, and she would pray daily, reminding God of these. "Please, do not fail me. Please, do not forsake me. Please give me strength and courage and patience and love...." God had not forgotten His promises, but repeating the words, she acknowledged her dependence on Him and extended her trust to Him.

Still, the circumstances were difficult to bear. In the years since they had become Christians, nothing had changed. Nye Nye had all the evidence she needed: Molly had caused Terence to become a Christian, and his rebellion had angered the gods, who were causing Terence to be sick. Nye Nye felt a cultural and moral obligation to put relentless pressure on the family of her eldest son.

Nye Nye, too, was exhausted, tired of having to tolerate, remonstrate, and support these rebellious people. She often implied the burden on her to care for Terence's family. Surely, everyone was suffering.

It was painful enough for Molly to be so near her continuous, simmering displeasure, but Nye Nye's sphere of influence spread wide. Molly didn't like having her children or Terence subjected to the indignities of ostracism and bullying.

A few times when Molly came home from work, she found that the lorry driver had dumped a load of wood at Nye Nye's house. She would hear Nye Nye encouraging Lois and Owen, "Oh! You are doing a good job! Pile them up nicely!"

Molly saw that her two youngest children each carried a single piece of wood from the pile and stacked it neatly near the house. Others of Nye Nye's young children and grandchildren were watching, too precious for menial work. Lois and Owen seemed to be enjoying the project, but Molly resented that her children were being put to work like servants. Besides the humiliation of it, Molly worried that the children might get splinters from the wood or contract a disease. And the work was not easy for them; some of the pieces of wood seemed nearly as big as Owen. He was scarcely five years old! But Molly did not dare complain.

To assuage her concerns about disease, Molly thought, "Maybe I should give them some antibiotic, just in case." She knew where to get an unlimited supply.

Most of all, Terence suffered. Unlike his wife and children, he had no escape. Some days he would complain bitterly, "Ah Ma was here five times today! Every time she fussed at me, 'Why are you being so stubborn? All you have to do is turn back from this... Je-sus!'

"She says the name of our Lord with such disgust," he said sadly. "She won't listen when I try to explain about diseases; she insists that I am sick because the gods are angry with me. Then she says, 'Follow me to honor the ancestors, and then you will be well. Stop this curse upon yourself and this shame upon your family!'

"Then she accuses you of influencing me, Molly. I argue with her! I can think for myself! You didn't make me become a Christian! God called me to be a Christian!"

Molly knew it was difficult to bear up under this harangue day after day. But sometimes when she should have offered sympathy to Terence or thanked him for standing up for her, she would scold him for arguing with his mother. The pressures on everyone were intense.

Also, because Terence was bored, he liked to sit by the Evergreen Restaurant at the Lee compound. He found some pleasure in his difficult life by watching the patrons come and go. But, the man who once took such pride in his appearance sometimes didn't have the energy even to comb his hair.

Someone complained to Molly, "People don't like to see a sick man when they come to the restaurant. Terence is hurting our business."

How unfortunate that Molly had to broach the difficult subject with her husband! She mentioned the complaint and suggested, "If you look sick, people will worry. You must try to look nice."

Terence was angry with her.

She pleaded, "At least comb your hair. Make yourself presentable. Have a pleasant face. Don't hold your chest."

The family very much depended on the elder Lees. But something needed to change.

So it was that the Myeinigon neighborhood looked so appealing. Molly didn't make much money, but she figured carefully and thought they could barely afford to rent a place to live. She had noticed a sign advertising rooms of a house just a couple of streets away from her parents.

Of course, Terence would have to make the decision, but she didn't need to convince him. Molly pointed out that she would save a little bit on bus fares and be home sooner to give him attention. Neither needed to mention more; it was understood between them the freedom they would gain.

Soon the family was moving to Boe Moe Street in Myeinigon. Molly could sense the excitement of each family member.

The owner of the long, two-story house was an old, single, Burmese woman, who lived in the upper story on the one side, and her married sister lived below her on the first floor. The Terence Lee family took the other half of the house. Downstairs was a living room, kitchen, and a shared bathroom. Terence loved to sit in the living room to read. Upstairs were two small bedrooms and a larger open area. Terence slept near the window in the bigger room upstairs; Molly slept in one bedroom and the maid in the other. The children, draped with mosquito nets, slept on mats on the floor in the living room downstairs.

The rented space was much smaller than that of the old house at the soy sauce factory, but the building was sturdily built with wood. The shared bathroom had a hole to squat over, a pull chain to flush, and a water source. What a wonderful, greatly missed convenience was running water! The family was poor by most standards, but they felt their wealth when using the water faucet and the bathroom. Some of their neighbors had to take buckets up the street to get water from a common tap. Only a block away was a squalid camp where people lived in thatched-roof houses and open sewers. So Molly and her family counted their blessings.

They all got along well with the owner, on the few occasions that they saw her. The younger sister was a frequent visitor and a nosey gossip. Terence immediately disliked her. *"Jee hlee,"* Terence called her in Cantonese. "The woman must know every matter," he said. From then on, she was privately known to the family as "Inquisitive Lady."

Even apart from the nosey neighbor, there was little privacy. Other neighbors, whether they were arguing with each other or petitioning the gods, could always be heard through open windows, and the aroma or odor of whatever was cooking could not be missed.

Gossiping was not the Inquisitive Lady's only fault. As Molly had sometimes experienced from other ethnic Burmese women, she would have to stand and endure the Inquisitive Lady's rude sizing-up for her dress, and especially, for her unimpressive jewelry. Molly didn't care that she disappointed the woman. What few pieces of expensive jewelry Molly owned, she rarely wore. Simple pearl earrings were good enough for her to wear in public. She had too little interest or means to impress people.

Molly's earnings barely paid for rent, food, and medicine, but the family also afforded the small wages of a much-needed maid. Molly could hardly go to work and leave Terence at home alone. The maid did the cooking, cleaning, and laundry, and she kept an eye on Terence.

One luxury which was purchased on the family's meager income was a radio. As before the war, these were rare in Rangoon, and the few owners of radios were thoughtful enough to turn them up loud and face them toward the street so whole neighborhoods could benefit. People would often stand in the street to listen. Long, lonely days, when his wife and children were at work or school, were difficult for Terence, and Molly felt strongly that he needed this distraction.

Molly was pleased to have relatives just two streets away, where Johnny's family lived on the first floor of a very modest home with Molly's parents, and Byu Goo, Moonlight and Dorothy lived on the second floor. A monastery and a pagoda were also nearby. Anita was just a couple of miles away in a much nicer neighborhood.

Molly could not miss the rumors that her father's wealth had been diminished by his habit of gambling. She thought it quite possible, but she never knew for sure. She did know of other families whose fortunes were lost by this addiction.

Molly was not aware that Tony had to teach young Owen to defend himself against bullies here. The older brother was an experienced and capable trainer; as a grown man, Tony confided to Molly that it was not unusual for three tormentors at a time to bully him. He would say to them, "Come along." Like his father, Tony had become a fighter. He needed to defend himself and Owen, but he had also become, perhaps, too quick to take offense. For Owen's benefit, one time when their parents were away, Tony arranged a boxing match, with gloves, between Owen and an aggressive peer. With Tony's coaching, Owen was able to inflict enough damage to be left alone after that.

Waiting at the home on Boe Moe Street, Terence continued to look for what might be in Molly's hands when she came home from work. "What have you brought me?" he would ask eagerly. Sometimes the library would discard a magazine, and then an employee or patron could keep it, so Molly was able to give such a thing to Terence to own. He loved the science and technology magazines.

Molly liked to keep the discarded Sears and J.C. Penney catalogues, from which she cut out pictures of the latest fashions for girls. She took the pictures to the daughter of the Chin's old servant and friend, Pwa Pwa. The young woman was an excellent seamstress and could look at the picture and make the stylish dresses for Charlene and Lois at an affordable price.

Even if Molly did bring home books or magazines, often Terence would first greet her with "Come! Come! Come! My neck hurts! Please rub it for me!" Molly knew just how to rub the pain and tension from him. Sometimes she fussed at him that she was tired too, but she cooperated with his requests, and she sensed in her fingers the comfort she gave him.

****

Molly often arranged for the children to take a bus to the library after school. School ended early, around 1:00 pm, so the children could spend much of the afternoon with Molly at the library. The children would finish their homework and then spent marvelous hours gorging themselves with literary pleasures carefully selected by the USIS Library staff. Molly and her children rode the public bus home together when she got off work at 5:15.

When Tony got home from the library, he always dumped down his school bags and went out to play. Molly rarely noticed him studying, and forgetting his time at the library, she was surprised that he excelled.

Sometimes the children would go home after school instead of to the library. Lois especially enjoyed walking to her grandparents' home two streets over and spending the afternoon with her Auntie Dorothy. The woman and the girl shared an interest in fashion. Even as a girl, Lois learned to perm and style her aunt's hair.

****

One day Martha Khin asked the staff, "Does anyone know someone who can teach sewing? The girls could benefit from learning this skill."

Molly replied, "My sister Dorothy is very good at sewing. She has learned from our mother; she needs only to see a dress and she can copy it. She speaks Burmese too. Only, her English is not very good."

"Oh, that's no problem, Molly." Martha replied. "In fact, knowing Burmese is excellent. And Chinese too? That is a wonderful bonus!"

"I will ask her if she will come and teach the children," Molly promised.

In this way, Dorothy worked at the library teaching sewing classes to the girls during one hot season. She asked the girls to bring their dolls, and she helped them to sew clothes for the dolls.

Lois was an eager student, and Dorothy continued to work with her after the class. Lois became a proficient seamstress.

****

There were many changes in library staff over the years. Martha Khin left suddenly and quietly. Molly assumed she was leaving work to care for her five children. Then Clara whispered something about The United States Federal Bureau of Investigation. She described it as an intimidating, secretive organization, called "The FBI" for short. She said the FBI did something called a "background check" on Martha. Someone said that Martha had joined a communist organization as a teenager!

Molly was indignant. "Is this true? But even if it is true, she was only a teenager! What a shame! Who knows what one will do as a teenager?" Poor Martha! She was an asset to the library.

Ironically, Martha was replaced by a woman of the Mon tribe, typically fair-skinned, who was an outspoken critic of the United States. She had graduated from Rangoon University and then, recruited by Mrs. Graham, she studied library science in the United States for two years. She often said with great severity, "There are ugly Americans, and there are good Americans." Molly wondered what happened to make her so dislike the people.

Except when discussing the United States, the new junior library director was a jovial person. Her husband was an Anglo-Arakan and an officer in the Burmese army, but Daw Su Su was not aloof as some of the wives of powerful men. She could be domineering, but she was much less serious and less easily offended than some of the high class tribal Burmese women.

Daw Su Su quickly took Molly into her protective care, sympathetic to Molly's difficult situation. She advised "Bow poh," a term for a friend of another race, "Don't spend your money on meat. Eat vegetables. You can buy yellow beans, dahls, lentils, and graham, like the Indians. You will save a lot of money."

Molly was skeptical. Terence was mostly vegetarian, but Molly doubted he or her children would eat the stuff Daw Su Su recommended. She doubted even that her maids would eat those unfamiliar foods.

Nevertheless, Molly appreciated the concern. Molly addressed her boss sincerely, "Oh, Daw Su Su, thank-you so much for your advice. You are very kind to think of me."

Daw Su Su found out Molly lived near her in Myeinigon. She said, "Oh, Molly. There is no need for your children to take the bus to school. You can save some money. Have your children walk to my house, and they can ride with my children to school." She had hired a private VW bus, and so Molly's children did often ride to school with Daw Su Su's two sons and contributed to the cost of that transportation.

About this time, Molly began to think her Chinese clothes were impractical for work at the library. The Chinese skirt showed too much leg for modest work attire, and it was awkward for discreetly climbing into a bus. Besides, she did not care to stand out on the bus or at work. The other women at work wore either longyis or western dress. Her sisters-in-law, Anita and Lily, had already switched to wearing longyis.

Anita observed, "The Burmese people like you better in a longyi. They treat you less like a stranger."

So Molly bought herself a longyi, the simple, versatile, colorful piece of cloth sewn into a tube, with a wide black band sewn across the top. She looked at the single, long side seam with brief dissatisfaction. She had learned, by demanding Chinese instructors, to sew a double seam, first wrong sides together and then right sides together, sealing the raw edge inside the seam. But she decided this was not the time to be fussy about the plain seam.

Clara had given Molly instructions. At home Molly stepped into the tube, positioning the seam on the left side so as to be concealed in the fold, and tucking in the band at the waist. She practiced pulling the fabric flat across her stomach and tucking in the surplus cloth tightly at her left hip.

Molly knew that wearing the tube in this style for women is more accurately called a htamin, though Burmese are lenient about the terminology, often lumping htamins and longyis together as longyis. The men positioned their knot in the front, forming a large fluff of fabric, and this style was the one technically termed longyi. Though both men and women wore brightly colored fabrics, the print of the fabric was significant, women wearing the floral patterns in horizontal drifts, and men often wearing checks. For formal occasions, men also wore a short, solid-color coat.

No matter what the clothing was called, Molly felt insecure in the skirt, worrying that the tucked fabric would loosen and fall to her feet. She walked around the room and then tried re-tucking the longyi. Again. And again. As she practiced, she was able to fasten the longyi somewhat more securely. Just in case, she decided she would always wear a slip underneath the longyi to lessen the consequences of a falling skirt. Until she was comfortable that she could gird it snugly, she also pinned it. Often she opposed tradition by tucking in the skirt on her right hip, where she seemed to be able to fasten it tighter. She wore the modest, sleeved, Burmese blouse to complete the ensemble.

The first day she wore the longyi to work, Molly approached Daw Su Su. As she spread her arms to present herself in the new attire, she asked, "See? Now am I looking like a Burmese girl?"

Daw Su Su did not hide her amusement. Bent over in laughter, she managed to speak between guffaws, "No! Oh, no, bow poh...! Ha, ha...you have a light complexion, and ... ha, ha, ha... Molly, your hair...!"

"What about my hair?" Molly asked, feigning offense, but entertained by her boss's reaction.

Still laughing, Daw Su Su said, "Now tell me which Burmese girl has short, permed hair, like you?"

Molly hadn't thought of that, but of course it was true. Burmese women wore their hair very long; it was their pride. Molly had styled her hair like the modern Chinese women she knew, and she didn't plan to change that. Of course, she couldn't change her facial features or skin tone either.

Daw Su Su pointed out Molly to the others in friendly teasing. "She thinks she looks Burmese!"

Knowing the laughter was not unkind, Molly joined it. Well, she didn't look Burmese, but she did feel less conspicuous. She determined to buy another longyi.

Daw Su Su also teased Molly about her Burmese speaking. Molly thought she spoke Burmese well, but she laughed at herself with Daw Su Su. Daw Su Su was so good-natured that Molly could not be offended, and she was eager to improve her skills.

****

Molly began hearing unpleasant rumors, which at first she dismissed as unfounded. Mrs. Graham, it was said, would be leaving to go to the United States, but this time she would not be coming back. This was inconceivable! Clara heard that Mrs. Graham's boss felt she had been in Burma too long, and she was to be reassigned. The State Department liked to keep employees moving around, she said.

Too soon the foretelling rumors became reality. Mrs. Graham clearly did not want to leave Burma. She had come with her husband before the war, and her husband's body was buried in Rangoon. She loved the native people, and they loved her. Burma was her home, and the library was her child.

But, Mrs. Graham was forced to prepare to leave. She did this as she did all things, with resolve and grace, though her misery was apparent. Library employees mourned the prospect of her leaving.

Daw Ni Hta and Ruth, who knew about these things, took up a collection from the other employees and purchased a lovely Burmese-made silver tea set. When Mrs. Graham hosted a party at her house to say farewell, the staff presented the silver tea set to Mrs. Graham.

She was so pleased. "Oh!" She said, her voice faltering with emotion, "It is so beautiful! Made in Burma! It will always remind me of my friends in Burma! I will think of you all when I am serving tea!"

She repeated, "I will think of you all," and it could be assumed she would be thinking of her friends in Burma whether or not she was serving tea. It was a sad party.

Library patrons, young and old of several races, also mourned her leaving. For many citizens of Rangoon, the library had become a second home, where days passed pleasantly as mind and body were refreshed. Doors propped open, fans stirring the air across the cool marble floor, oppressive heat rising up to the high ceiling, this was a cool, all-seasons oasis from both the stifling heat and the torrential monsoon. Many also found that stimulation from books in the library was a welcome respite from both stifled economy and stormy political conditions. Mrs. Graham was as responsible as anyone for making this place a sweet and stable refuge, and the local people sensed her parental role as fondly as Mrs. Graham felt it.

Inevitably, Mrs. Graham was gone. Mourning endured as her presence was sorely missed.

Chapter Twenty-Four

A Job Well Done

Evelyn McCabe became the new director of the library. Even though she was known to the staff before her promotion, it took time to get used to the change, and liking her seemed, at first, a betrayal to Mrs. Graham.

Molly noticed right away that Mrs. McCabe was quite different from Mrs. Graham in personality and in leadership style. She was reserved and quiet, and if she needed to talk to someone, instead of sending for her to come to the office, Mrs. McCabe would go to the person. Molly also pictured Mrs. Graham, hand on her hip, long-stemmed pipe in her mouth, admiring her domain. Mrs. McCabe was more humble. She was not the commanding presence and dynamic promoter that Mrs. Graham had been, but she ran the library with efficiency and creativity. Molly learned to love her as she loved Mrs. Graham.

Mrs. McCabe wisely resisted making disruptive changes, but maintained a comfortable flow of day to day operations with just enough variety to express her own touch. In this way, Molly felt, patrons enjoyed comforting sameness with an occasional flavorful dash of change.

About the same time, Ei May Tun, circulation director, was moving to Bangkok because her husband was transferred there. All these years, Molly had been writing the monthly reports for Ei May Tun, never mentioning to others that she was doing this function. Reflecting the pride she felt in the work of the library, Molly aptly and enthusiastically described the story hour topics, the programs, the competitions, the games, the crafts, the decorations, and the eager participation of the locals.

Molly continued to write the reports after Ei May Tun left, and she instinctively took over many of her other duties as well, recognizing what needed to be done and doing it. She started researching subjects to teach the children and enjoyed learning topics in greater depth than she had done previously.

One of the books that made a big impression on her was about the United States' President Abraham Lincoln. This President was in office when the United States was violently divided by civil war after a block of states seceded from the United States over the slavery issue. Those in the South had become dependent on forced labor and thought their economy could not be sustained without it. Those in the North felt it was wrong to enslave people, and they were trying to limit slavery. Officially, the northern states fought to keep the Union from being divided, but the underlying cause of the war was the ethics of slavery.

Molly could see the tension of slavery in America as she considered the historic Declaration of Independence, in which the colonies in America declared their Independence of Great Britain at the start of the Revolutionary War. Near the beginning of the document is the statement, "We hold these truths to be self-evident, that all men are created equal, that they are endowed by their Creator with certain unalienable Rights, that among these are Life, Liberty, and the pursuit of Happiness." This sounded good in theory, but prior to the Civil War neither the law nor the practice treated all men equally, some robbed of liberty and pursuit of happiness on the basis of race.

Molly read about the "Emancipation Proclamation," an executive order President Lincoln signed in January 1863 during the American Civil War. This order gave freedom to millions of slaves, and was followed in 1865 by the ratification of the Thirteenth Amendment to the United States' Constitution, abolishing slavery in the United States. Molly learned that President Lincoln is considered a hero by many for keeping the United States united and for ending the practice of slavery in that country.

Molly wasn't sure what effect the book had on the children, but it made her think a lot about slavery. She was aware that throughout Burma, countless Chinese, Indian, and Burmese maids, slaves or hired, were treated badly, with endless work, poor quality food, little or no pay, and frequent beatings. This poor treatment was rationalized by ideologies of karma and fate. Maids, like many animals, were beaten without remorse because it was supposed that they had done something to deserve being reincarnated to a lowly, abused position. Abusers often felt they were doing their duty, cooperating in the training of subordinates. Molly wondered if, as she taught about Abraham Lincoln, the children also sensed the injustice of people owning and mistreating other people.

On serious subjects and light-hearted, Molly threw herself into the role of teacher. She studied and taught fables written by Aesop, a Greek story-teller of the fifth century B.C. One story she liked was about a lion who threatened to eat a mouse that woke him. The mouse told the lion to let him go and he would repay the favor one day. The lion laughed, thinking it impossible that a mouse could help him, and the mouse escaped. Later, when the lion was caught in a net, the mouse chewed the cords of the net to free the lion. Molly told the children that they should learn from the story not to look down on the small size of another, for each individual has something to contribute. Molly, a small fly, was glad to contribute to the work of the library.

Another fable was about a slow tortoise who proposed a race with a bragging fast rabbit, and all the forest creatures came to watch, expecting the hare to win easily. The cocky hare ran far ahead, and, certain he had plenty of time, he stretched out to rest. He fell asleep, and the slowly plodding tortoise passed him and won the race. The moral of the story became part of the vernacular of the children, reminding them to persevere: "Slow and steady wins the race!"

Another favorite of Molly's was "The City Mouse and the Country Mouse." The city mouse visited his cousin in the country. The country mouse was a rough fellow, but he was hospitable to his cousin and shared his stores of food. The city mouse didn't care for the modest fare, and he invited the country mouse to his home in the city, expecting to impress him. They did indeed enjoy a few bites of a great feast when a ferocious dog barked at them and chased them. The country mouse left in terror. The moral was "better beans and bacon in peace than cakes and ales in fear." Molly would think of this moral when both peace and the comforts of wealth were elusive.

Also, finding much to learn in this story, Molly told the children they should not think less of someone who is different. Quietly, she thought of Byu Goo showing up in her ridiculous field worker's hat and her irrational fear of a water faucet. Her lack of sophistication had seemed so comical to a young, city girl at the time, but what a treasure Byu Goo was to the family! And, Molly thought, though she herself was Chinese, she was able to teach something of value to these children of various races.

Finally, Molly pointed out that the story shows how we become accustomed to our own surroundings and learning another way of life can be difficult. Molly had needed to adapt to her life already, but she would again find herself in changed circumstances, feeling awkward and unsophisticated, needing to adapt. Though most of her life was lived in cities, she would later think of herself as a simple, country mouse.

****

At Christmas, Mrs. McCabe kept the programs much the same; drastic changes would be foolish when expectations for the now traditional celebration were so high. But Mrs. McCabe put her own creative mark on the decor, suggesting silver bells and streamers. The children learned to sing the song "Silver Bells."

Molly knew how the Christmas programs should go. She helped organize children of employees for acting out the nativity. Charlene, very earnest and serious, was a beautiful little Mary. Lois, bright and sweet, was an adorable angel, able to recite her lines perfectly. For Tony, Molly borrowed Anita's bridal jacket and a Chinese hat to dress him as one of the kings who came to adore the newborn baby Jesus; he presented an air of royalty very well, yet also knelt humbly before the Lord Jesus. Gloria's son was cast as another of the kings from the east, wearing a traditional tribal Kayin satin gown, red with embroidery, and a golden paper crown, shining brightly. Doris's youngest son was the third king, and his costurme reflected the family's Indian heritage. A worker in the reference library found a humble robe to dress her son as a quiet, tender Joseph. The children all relished their roles and performed the magnificent event with sweet innocence. Everyone sang, "We Three Kings" as Gloria played the piano. The program was very popular, as usual, and the young actors performed many times to meet the demand of their audiences.

Molly wrote her usual glowing report, detailing the programs and how much they were enjoyed by the community. Only, this time the paper did not have Ei May Tun's signature. Several weeks later, recognizing the author, Mrs. McCabe came quietly to Molly.

"The State Department was pleased to receive your report on the Christmas programs at the library," she said.

"Wow," Molly thought. "I didn't know the report would go to the State Department."

"They sent a letter complimenting your work. They said the report was so vivid, they felt they were in the building." Mrs. McCabe smiled, "You made me look good too, Molly. Thank-you."

Molly hadn't thought about that, but she understood. Molly was only writing what she felt was true, but Mrs. McCabe was doing a good job managing the library in Mrs. Graham's absence, and Molly was glad to make that known.

****

Tony's teacher told Molly at the end of the school year, "Your son did so well in the fifth grade, he doesn't need to go to sixth grade. I have discussed this with the principal, and we're giving him a double promotion. Next year he will go straight to seventh grade."

Molly said, "Really?"

His teacher said, "Yes. Didn't Tony tell you we were considering this?"

Molly said, "No. He never told me."

****

Molly continued to enjoy doing the duties of the circulation director of the junior library. Neat and descriptive reports were filed promptly, children were enjoying the classes Molly taught, and things were running smoothly. Naturally, Mrs. McCabe allowed Molly to continue doing the duties of circulation director of the children's library. But Molly did not act in this position for very long.

Mrs. McCabe had already shown she was capable of maintaining the high standards set by Mrs. Graham, and under her leadership the library employees had continued to work in a spirit of cooperation and professionalism. Indeed, the native workers at the USIS Library were generally quite happy with their employment, as the women were paid more and given a better work environment than they could hope to find anywhere else in the country. The high-class women were pleased with and proud of their positions. But Mrs. McCabe had not considered that merely allowing Molly to act in a superior position was an intolerable breach of propriety, causing growing discord and endangering her best efforts

Soon, Molly couldn't miss the frowns of displeasure, the jealous words, and the outright anger directed at her. Mrs. McCabe also became aware of problems and asked to speak privately to Molly.

Before Mrs. McCabe could speak, Molly blurted, "You must move me!"

She explained, "I understand what has happened. The Burmese don't want an outsider taking this position. I am Sino-Burmese, Chinese by race and Burmese only by birth. You must give the position to someone else. You have no choice. I have no choice. I cannot work when everyone is my enemy. It's okay. You must find someone to replace me.

"But," Molly pleaded, "Mrs. McCabe, I do really need a job."

Realizing the work environment in the children's library would not return to normal for her, Molly suggested, "Maybe you can move me to cataloguing."

Mrs. McCabe's relief was evident, and she was clearly having the same thoughts. "Yes, I could use you in cataloguing. Thank-you for understanding, Molly."

Molly was disappointed. She loved working as circulation director of the junior library, and she felt she was good at that job. But, she understood the situation, and she did not dwell on her loss.

The women of influence insisted that Clara should have the position as head of the junior library circulation, arguing that Clara had worked at the library longer than Molly. Others would cover for Clara's shortcomings, particularly in English. Mrs. McCabe agreed.

Molly was thankful to still have a job at the library, and she was willing to learn more about cataloguing and the library of Congress designations for books, and to type the catalogue cards and book pockets. She enjoyed working for Mrs. Kyaw Myint and found the woman polite and respectful, though her husband was a general. Mrs. Myint even showed sympathy for Molly and sometimes helped her greatly by giving her a ride to work.

****

Molly was of the belief that one's words should give others a "tall hat," not with insincere flattery, but with appropriate, generous compliments. She tried to apply this policy of praise to children and to adults. Raising her own children, she tried not to scold them too much, fearing it would discourage them. For instance, if Lois brought an English paper home, Molly would find something encouraging to say, like, "You use words very well to tell an interesting story. So nice, Lois!"

Molly also made a point of saying complimentary things to her co-workers. She was very conscientious about trying to please her boss. She wouldn't think of ignoring a request, or leaving a job unfinished, or doing a job differently than instructed, or avoiding work, or any sort of insubordination.

So, she was shocked one day to hear Mrs. Kyaw Myint say, "I am disappointed in you, Molly."

Molly felt the words as a physical blow and replied urgently, "You tell me what is wrong, and I will correct it."

Mrs. Kyaw Myint said with mock offense, "I am wearing these new diamond earrings. Everyone here has commented on them, except you. I have had many admirers today, but you have said nothing."

Eager to make amends, Molly said, "Oh, let me have a look! Oh! Mrs. Kyaw Myint, your diamond earrings are so beautiful! Really. They are so big and shimmering like a pagoda! I don't know how I missed noticing them right away!"

Mrs. Kyaw Myint smiled at her, "Thank-you for the compliment, Molly."

Molly knew that Mrs. Kyaw Myint did not need her flattery. But in this gentle way she showed Molly that she should be considerate of the culture in which she lived. Burmese women took much pride in their jewelry. Molly should not forget the courtesy to take notice.

Chapter Twenty-Five

Industrious Hands

Mrs. McCabe had been working with Daw Su Su and Ruth behind the scenes. The women wrote beautiful letters to the State Department explaining how much Mrs. Graham was missed by the local people. They explained the importance of her diplomatic presence and the regard in which she was held in the community of Rangoon.

Before long, word came that Mrs. Graham was returning, and when she did, she was exuberant! She was received with a hero's welcome!

The misfortune in this happy event was that Mrs. McCabe was sent to work in Madras, India. Then again, perhaps it was not misfortune, but the providence of God.

Mrs. Graham instituted a change at the library. She felt a need for a young people's library for older children. She put Gloria in charge of this library, and Clara remained in charge of the younger children's library.

Mrs. Graham was in her mid-fifties now, but she still wore vivid clothing. This seemed odd to Molly, but nice. It was odd, because Molly knew that Chinese women over forty were expected to wear reserved clothing. But the bright clothes fit Mrs. Graham's radiance.

Mrs. Graham must have read her thoughts. She said, "Molly, some people think you should wear dark or pale colors when you get older. No, Molly! Wear brighter colors as you get older!"

Molly was approaching her forties. She would keep this in mind, but unlike Mrs. Graham she did not care to stand out.

****

Terence was not often able to work construction any more. Owen had followed him to a construction site, where he watched his father supervise concrete work, but Terence tired even after a short walk.

Though Terence often could not leave the house to work, he was not idle. Particularly in this difficult time when Molly's paycheck barely met their needs, and they were no longer receiving help from Terence's family, Terence was obsessed with doing what he could to help. Molly never knew what project he might take on next to try to help his family. While her first impulse was to worry and scold that he was taxing himself, she knew she must let him try. His body was

Molly and her children, December 1960

weak, but his mind was active. He always felt better when he was mentally engaged and productive, and he needed to contribute to the welfare of his family. Molly admired her husband's diligence and persistence.

So she tried to be supportive of Terence's projects. One of his ideas was to make sanitary napkins. From a German magazine Molly had brought from the library, Terence read about a machine that could make them efficiently. But Terence did not need the machine, because he found cheap labor in his children. Often the maid would lend a hand too, eager to make a little extra money working on the simple assembly line.

It was not unusual for Molly to come home and find everyone working around a table covered with supplies. Each one, even eight-year-old Owen, who was unaware of the product's purpose, was busily cutting cotton, or packing cotton onto a light mesh, or folding and stitching the mesh securely using a treadle Singer sewing machine. Several napkins were packed into a bright blue and yellow box and added to the satisfying towers of boxes filling the space in the room. Tony would deliver these to some of his father's friends at Indian shops in town, and the packages always sold quickly. As Terence astutely recognized, the demand was great and the supply was limited.

Molly was pleased to see Terence's quiet pleasure and pride in the activity and to see the industry of the children. The extra income was welcome, but Molly could see the benefits exceeded the monetary return.

However, as time went on, Terence found he could not keep up with the stress of the enterprise. His heart palpitations worsened with physical exertion. Even when the maid brought friends to help with the work, they could not keep up with the demand. Also, competitors were copying and underselling him. Terence thought of buying the machine from Germany to mass produce the napkins, but he never quite profited enough to come up with the payment. So Terence sold his business to his friend Rudy, who had a factory sewing clothes, especially camisoles and the latest must-have undergarment for women, brassieres. Rudy would find this new product from Terence was quite profitable as well.

Another project Terence tried was to make salted eggs. He arranged dozens and dozens of eggs on a bed of salt and set up a fan to blow air over them to dry them. He thought the preserved eggs would sell well, but they did not.

Molly did not tell Terence, but she sometimes borrowed money from her brother Johnny. Sometimes she would send Owen to this uncle to ask for money so they could buy groceries until payday. Also Molly would borrow sometimes from a cousin of Terence, a son of one of Sit Hong's sisters, who

was very kind to them. But she always repaid debts quickly.

****

The Terence Lee family continued to move methodically through time, moments packing together tightly to fill accumulating years. Each parent and child performed duties as well as he could, parents working hard to provide for their family and children diligent at their studies, all while trying to live in a way pleasing to God.

For several years, as family members focused on their own urgent circumstances, they remained somewhat insulated from the troubled march of Burmese history that accompanied each of their own steps through time. But, more and more, the events of the nation could not be ignored by the family.

Ever since the country became independent of Great Britain in 1948, U Nu had ruled as Prime Minister with a bicameral parliament and a figurehead president. During his tenure, Burma continued to be fraught with violence. Not only were different native tribes competing for power and independence from ethnic Burmese rule, but white flag communists, red flag communists, socialists, anti-fascists, federalists, separatists, Muslims, army rebels and so on, were all vying for power, and many of these were supported by interests outside of Burma.

Nationalists from China, fleeing communism, continued to spill over into northern and eastern Burma. In fact, the Nationalist Kuomintang army had taken control of many remote areas in the North.

America's continued support for Chinese Nationalist forces in Burma angered the Burmese government, which was added to ongoing ire and distrust toward Great Britain, China, Japan, and others. Consequently, all foreign interests were treated with growing suspicion, and most foreign aid was eventually rejected.

U Nu expressed his suspicion of foreign interests this way: "Take a glance at our geographical position – Thailand in the east, China in the north, India in the West and stretching southward, Malaya, Singapore, and so on. We are hemmed in like a tender gourd among the cactus."

Economically, the situation in Burma had begun to improve toward the end of the 1950's, and U Nu had some success in convincing factions to surrender their arms for democracy. But some said his preoccupation with astrology and superstition made for an ineffective government, and the country remained precariously unstable. The parliament was divided, and after a no-confidence vote nearly removed him, U Nu relinquished his position in 1956. A year later, the acting Prime Minister asked the army chief of staff General Ne Win to take over as Prime Minister to restore order. But, a landslide victory in general elections returned U Nu to power in 1960.

Though Burma had become increasingly closed and inwardly focused, the nation received a surprising international plaudit in 1961. U Thant of

Burma was elected as Secretary-General of the United Nations, a prestigious position held for the first time by a non-westerner. Incidentally, a young woman working in U Thant's administration was Aung San Suu Kyi, daughter of Aung San, the assassinated national hero who had worked for Burmese independence from Great Britain. She was a Methodist English High School and Oxford graduate.

****

Molly was anxious whenever she heard of the ongoing perils experienced by her Uncle, Old Man Thunder Voice. Chou en Lai, foreign minister to China's Chairman Mao Tse-tung, made a number of visits to Burma over the years. Each time a diplomatic visit was scheduled, Old Man Thunder Voice was arrested, without charge, and imprisoned for the duration of Chou en Lai's stay. Only because he was a known supporter of Chiang Kai-shek and the nationalists, not Mao Tse-tung and the communists who had wrested power in China, the uncle was jailed, ensuring that his thunder voice was silenced while the communist leader was in town. Molly knew that her uncle did not deserve to be treated like a criminal.

****

Molly was surprised when Mrs. Graham called her to go with her to the embassy, and they went in to a meeting room. Others from the library and the embassy were already there, including some department heads and the cultural attaché.

It was 1961, and Molly was recognized for having worked at the library for ten years. A photographer snapped a picture as the U. S. Ambassador shook Molly's hand and presented her with a ten-year pin and a certificate. He expressed appreciation for Molly's dedicated service. Others in attendance applauded. Mrs. Graham grinned with pride through her pipe.

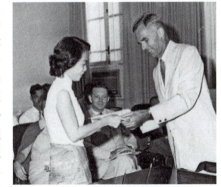

Embassy photo, used by permission.

****

Terence continued to read the science magazines and architecture books, planning for the future of his family. He loved to draw sketches and schematics of his dream house, with many variations, but always with a long veranda across the front.

In one of the science magazines Molly brought home for him, Terence read about a hospital in Vellore, India, that specialized in heart surgeries, showing success particularly on mitral valve repair. Terence was excited to read of this, certain the surgeons in Vellore could help him. But on Molly's salary, they could not afford such a trip or such an expensive surgery. He was frustrated and stewed on this for some time.

"I think I'll write to Mr. Chrisman," Terence told Molly one day. He and his American friend had been corresponding across oceans and continents for many years. "Maybe he could buy an inexpensive used car in the United States and ship it over here. I could sell the car for a big profit, maybe enough to pay for the trip to Vellore and the surgery. If there is any money left after the surgery, maybe I can pay him back."

Molly was doubtful. Would the Chrismans really do this great thing for them?

Chapter Twenty-Six

Tyranny and Despair

In the hot season, March, of 1962, the struggling country of Burma met with shocking and drastic changes. General Ne Win and his army forcibly seized power and sent Prime Minister U Nu to the infamously brutal Coco Island prison in the Indian Ocean, 200 miles from the Burma coast, in so-called "protective custody." Claiming that parliamentary democracy was unsuitable for Burma, Ne Win removed the legislature and terminated the constitution. In April, General Ne Win's Revolutionary Council devised a blueprint for governance called "The Burmese Way to Socialism."

The treatise of the usurpers began, "The Revolutionary Council of the Union of Burma does not believe that man will be set free from social evils as long as pernicious economic systems exist in which man exploits man and lives on the fat of such appropriation. The Council believes it to be possible only when exploitation of man by man is brought to an end and a socialist economy based on justice is established; only then can all people, irrespective of race or religion, be emancipated from all social evils and set free from anxieties over food, clothing and shelter, and from inability to resist evil, for an empty stomach is not conducive to wholesome morality, as the Burmese saying goes; only then can an affluent stage of social development be reached and all people be happy and healthy in mind and body."

A socialist economy, with common ownership and central planning, was said to be a fundamental concept for the "sufficiencies and contentment of all." To this end, "it is imperative that we first reorientate all erroneous views of our people." All arts and literature were to be conformed to this purpose. The armed forces would be built up to defend, or more accurately to enforce, the socialist economy. Any private enterprises which could not be confiscated would be regulated by "fair and reasonable restrictions."

By mentioning the intent to modernize agriculture and industry, those of the Revolutionary Council seemed to think it would happen in spite of destructive action. They confiscated land and businesses and put inexperienced people in charge of farm cooperatives and factories. Every aspect of society was micro-managed. It was said that health and culture would "flourish in direct proportion to the tides of socialist success like the lotus and the water's height." Faith was placed in the people, the peasants and the working classes, so said The Council. But it was the people's duty and responsibility to cooperate with progress, ergo to cooperate with those highly evolved, fittest, and powerful individuals of The Council, who defined progress and the means to it. Darwinist dogma prompted so-called superior beings to exploit the lesser, all the while claiming the best of intentions.

So began a tragic spiral of societal disintegration. Many natives initially welcomed the change, which came with myriad promises of fairness and mutual well-being. But the result was a repressed, unjust, isolated, bankrupted country whose government squandered its natural wealth and ruled its populace by fear.

In the library, little was said verbally about the upheaval. Many of the local women working at the library had husbands formerly in positions of power. Suddenly, many of these men had been stripped of power and were in danger of being exiled as political prisoners. Fear was spoken on the face of every woman, and political comments were taboo. Patrons were also cowed. But the staff tried to maintain business as usual as the situation continued to worsen over the months.

****

At Rangoon University, where students had a history of peaceful protest dating back to British colonial times, students were bristling at the Revolutionary Council's regulations leveled at them: the University Council of professors was eliminated, and all university affairs were controlled by the Revolutionary Council. Unauthorized gatherings were prohibited, dormitories were locked at 8:00 pm, and study hours were fixed. Besides these rulings, peculiarly random orders were also levied, such as the one that stated a student could not eat meatless meals for only a few days, but must eat vegetarian meals for an entire year. On Saturday, July 7, 1962, the students organized a protest. Tony, a high school student, was curious.

Molly was at home when Tony came bursting through the door. He stood immobile, just inside the doorway, staring at his parents. His face was ashen, filled with horror.

"What is it?" Molly asked.

To his hesitation, she blurted out the only explanation she could imagine, "Did you see lightning again?"

Once before Tony's face had looked pale like this. He had witnessed a man trying to find cover from monsoon rains and cowering beneath a tree. While Tony happened to be watching, the tree and the man were hit by lightning. The man was killed instantly, his body charred.

"No, Mom!" His voice was tight with fear. At first his words were unclear, and neither Terence nor Molly could make sense of them.

"Slow down, Tony! What is it?" Terence coaxed.

Tony began again. "I was at the University.... It was terrible! You won't believe it! There were many students. A big crowd. They were protesting against the military government. I was sitting on a wall. I was watching. The military came. Some of the student leaders were arrested, and other students started shouting against the military...."

Tony could hardly speak the words. He said hoarsely, "The soldiers shot the students. ...Killed them with machine guns. Many students were dying. The soldiers didn't stop. They kept shooting. Everyone was running. I ran home as fast as I could."

"Oh! Tony!" Molly cried.

Silence filled the room as the horror lingered, grotesque as Tony remembered and as his parents imagined. When Tony spoke again, he was still hoarse, but his voice was stronger with resolve.

He said emphatically, "I can't stay here. I'm going to run across the border to Thailand!" Tony's young face was tightened with determination.

His father matched his determined look, "No! Tony! It's too dangerous!"

"It's too dangerous here!" Tony answered his father.

Stunned by the prospect, at first Molly could not get past the single word, "No! No! No! No!"

Terence told Tony sternly, "You don't understand! It isn't easy to go to Thailand! There are steep mountain ranges and deep canyons and rivers to cross! The thick jungles are full of malaria!"

Molly added, "Even if you find your way and survive the jungle, who is going to take care of you in Thailand? We have no relatives there. You are not thinking ahead! You are thinking of things theoretically, but the reality is very difficult!"

Tony said, "Then get me to the United States, Mom. You have to find a way to do it! I won't stay here!"

"What?" Molly opened her empty hands helplessly to Tony and cried in despair, "How am I going to do it? I don't know how to do it!"

The next morning the student union at the university was obliterated by dynamite. Ne Win's public response was unapologetic.

"I have nothing more to say except that we will meet knife with knife and spear with spear. That is the only solution," he bellowed.

"No!" Tony told his parents. "The students had no knives and no spears. They were unarmed."

Ne Win said publicly that seventeen students were killed.

"No!" Tony argued angrily to his family. "Many more students died. At least a hundred."

Later, a shaken medical student Molly knew, who came often to the library to study, told her very quietly, "They said only a few students died. But I saw bodies stacked up in the morgue. Hundreds died."

Molly thought, "These Burmese have no respect for human life! These Buddhists won't kill bedbugs or mosquitoes, because they say they respect life! Then they do this to students!"

The University was closed. Tony was tormented.

Molly asked at the consular office and found out Tony could go to the United States to study on a student VISA. But he must have a sponsor in the United States.

"What to do, Terence?" Molly asked.

Everyone had to be careful about expressing dissatisfaction. But, Ne Win had become very unpopular, so even though it was dangerous to speak ill of him, local people occasionally took the risk in cautiously creative ways. Weeks after the massacre of students, word trickled through the city that Ne Win had traveled abroad for "a medical check-up," and with his tendency to sniff, people gossiped, "He has a bad nose!" Disguised as sympathy, "Maybe he's going to die!" was a wishful whisper Molly heard more than once.

Other whispered rumors among locals occasionally surfaced. "Ne Win never sleeps two nights in the same bed," and, "An armed guard is posted outside whenever he sleeps." The unfortunate implication was that, apart from natural causes, Ne Win would be difficult to remove from office.

Insults, *ning deh*, Burmese for "to put him low," were sometimes too satisfying to resist at first. But the cruelty, power, and reach of the government became formidable in the capital city. Soon most residents were cowed into complete silence, dissent given free voice only within carefully guarded minds.

****

In January 1963, The Burmese Socialist Programme Party published a more detailed paper describing its ideology, "The System of Correlation between Man and His Environment," which was an unprecedented, confusing treatise combining paranoid nationalism, humanism, Marxism, and Buddhism. Posing as logical and scientific and promising benevolence, it was neither on the first two counts and resulted in the opposite on the third. Darwinist snobbery had corrupted the thinking of Burman minds as it had corrupted others: The powerful few dictated, scolded, and enforced by cruel military might their own moral code, which they claimed to base on their highly evolved understanding of material, animal, and phenomenal worlds, of which man, they said, is a blended image. Weird postulations were stated as unarguable fact, such as, "In (man) combine the material body with life, mind and matter in their correlation, and the ceaseless process of mutation."

These self-appointed superior beings of the BSPP, masked in mock humility, promised to usher in a utopian world of mutual cooperation in which man would no longer exploit man as in "the slave system, the feudal system, and the capitalist system." Of course, the military government elite had only supplanted the former elite, becoming far worse exploiters and oppressors.

Widespread shortages resulted as shops across Burma were confiscated and inexperienced people were assigned by the government to run the shops. No longer did a maid enjoy shopping. Molly would send her to get a half pound of sugar, or a can of evaporated milk, or even a small piece of material for sewing. This used to be a simple process.

"Ma Ma, Big Sister," the maid would complain to Molly later. "I went, as I was told, to 'People's Shop Number Four.' I stood in a long, long line, far down the street. The people in the line are not friendly, as they used to be at the shops and markets. I waited all morning, and finally, just as I got near the front of the line, the shop manager came out and said, 'Whatever we have in the shop has all been given out. You come back tomorrow.' "

"Hmph!" Molly would say unhappily, complaining to Terence. "Tomorrow may be the same thing. Even if they give you what you want, they give you just a little bit."

Unable to solve that problem, Terence changed the subject to one that might have a solution. "I think I will write to Mr. Chrisman. Maybe he can help us get Tony to the United States."

Molly nodded. "Yes. But be careful what you say to him. I have heard that the government is reading all of the mail that goes out of the country. If they don't like something, we might go to jail."

Terence promised to be careful.

****

Tony was completing his studies at the Methodist English High school and would graduate in February of 1963. The government had allowed the Rangoon University to reopen, so Tony wanted to begin taking classes there as soon as he received his high school diploma. He was not afraid to join the students on campus, and in fact, he felt a camaraderie with them. The only problem was that because he had skipped a grade, he was too young, at age 15, to be admitted.

"Mom! You have to get me in!" Tony insisted. "You know people. You can do something. Maybe you could tell the principal I'm sixteen."

Molly was upset. "Goodness! You are telling me to make up a lie for you? You want me to lie to my high school teacher?"

"You have to!" Tony pleaded. "I have to go to college!"

Molly continued to argue with him. How could she purposely lie to anyone, especially to Mrs. Logie?

But she was weakening. She was glad that for the moment Tony wasn't talking about going to Thailand, and she was pleased that he wanted to further his education. She didn't want to disappoint him, and what was he going to do anyway, if he didn't go to college? He might get into trouble.

"Mom, you think about it. You have to figure out something." Tony was not to be dissuaded.

Several days later, Molly happened to remember an old book with crumbling binding that belonged to Terence. It contained family records, including dates of births and deaths, written in Chinese calligraphy.

She thought to herself, "Suppose I write Tony's name there as if the grandfather wrote it down. I will put his birthday one year older and see what they say." So she carefully did that, trying to match the handwriting of the characters. She was ashamed to do it, but she rationalized that she was helpless to resist Tony's determination, for he worried her day and night. Besides that, he really should go to college.

She gave the book to Tony, and he was happy. He showed it to Mrs. Logie, who asked a board member to translate the Chinese to English for her.

He read, "Lee Eng Koon, son of Lee Puck Ying, son of Lee Sit Hong, son of Lee Ah Poi was born on..." he had to consult a chart to translate the date from the Chinese calendar, "...October twenty-third, nineteen forty... six."

Tony told his mom later, "Mrs. Logie just said, okay, thank-you."

Oh my. Molly didn't feel better after getting away with the deception. She was very sorry to trick Mrs. Logie. She knew she was "bearing false witness," breaking a commandment from God, and she was ashamed. Molly confessed her sin, and God was patient with her.

Tony applied to and was accepted into Rangoon University. The Burmese government told students what course of study to take. Tony was assigned to attend military medical school.

Tony fumed to his mother, "What if I don't want to be a doctor? What if I don't want to serve the military? They say if they give me an education to be a doctor, then I owe the military ten years of service. I'm not going to do that!"

But what choice did he have? As she listened to his anger, Molly worried about what he might do.

Charlene was already in the civilian medical school at the University, and Molly worried for her as well, knowing that the Burmese government could send her anywhere after she graduated. Many new graduates were sent to the border where there was always much fighting. No one would care that she was a woman; she could be sent there anyway. The fact that she was Chinese would not endear her to Burmese officials.

Molly mentioned to her former boss and friend Daw Su Su that she wanted to buy a copy of *Grey's Anatomy* for Charlene, to assist her in her studies. Daw Su Su, ever helpful to Molly, had an acquaintance who was head of a hospital in Rangoon. From him, Daw Su Su obtained a copy of

Grey's Anatomy, and she proudly presented it to Molly without charge. Molly received it tactfully, and Charlene accepted it tactfully from her mother. But it was a very old edition, with torn and missing pages. Charlene studied with friends who owned the latest copies, and the girls helped each other to learn the material. In fact, when one of the girls in the group of friends failed a course, the rest rallied around her and tutored her so she could pass the exam the next year.

Tony's friends in college were older than he. One friend especially looked after him. He told Molly, "Tony sleeps in chemistry class. He had the same material in high school, and the class bores him, so he leans on my shoulder and falls asleep."

Molly sometimes heard stories from her children about their college classmates. Men and women attended classes together, and sometimes couples would fall in love. If their parents consented, the couple could get married. If their parents did not consent, the couple might elope to get married. Afterwards, they might hide out with friends until the angry parents calmed down. Eventually most parents would agree to the match, if the thing was already done. However, especially if the marriage was mixed race, the parents might not agree at all and shun the couple.

****

In the midst of social upheaval, Molly's papa became very sick. His face was sallow yellow, his eyes lost their brightness, and he barely had the strength to maintain ever important appearances. According to Chinese custom, he must not show his children a "bad face." Molly could see through the facade and knew he was suffering, but he did not complain and was very brave. She knew she was expected to be brave too. She conformed to expectations, but in her heart she was rebelling. It grieved her to see the magnificent tiger weakened,

Chin Hone Foo, posing with a cigar for show, though he did not smoke

but more so to see him try to remain the tiger. She wanted her father to be human, to express his suffering, to help his children prepare for his passing.

He was seen by a Chinese doctor who offered a mix of herbs. Papa did not improve.

"You live or you die," Molly forlornly told Terence, frustrated again by Chinese medicine.

A stream of relations came to visit. "Why do they come only when you are dying or after you die?" Molly sadly asked Terence. He had no answer.

When Papa was critically ill, he went to an Indian hospital in Rangoon. An Indian doctor trained in the west treated him.

"He must be desperate," Molly told Terence. She complained again, "Western medicine is sought only when it is too late."

Indeed, if the doctor could have helped him before, he surely could do nothing at this late stage. Papa, Molly's imposing Papa, died.

A western autopsy showed officially that he had liver cancer. Someone said that maybe the illness was brought on by the large doses of quinine Papa had used to protect himself against malaria. No one had told him how much to take.

The Chin dong took care of all the funeral arrangements. Papa's casket was placed in the hot street for many days as a stream of noisy mourners came by. A beautifully embroidered cloth covered the impressive coffin, and a large photo of Chin Hone Foo hung from one end. Though he was not as prestigious as his older brother, Molly's papa was still an important figure in the clan, and clan members in hoods and sackcloth made a satisfying clamor.

Molly knew her mother consulted a Chinese almanac to determine the favorable time for burial. On that day the elaborate procession to the cemetery began. The coffin-bearing truck led the family, riding in many cars, to Chinatown. The truck was highly decorated, with finely sewn tapestries draping the sides. Once in Chinatown, Chin Sen King, Chin Sen Kee, and Chin Sen Phat, wearing sackcloth, got out of the cars and walked after the coffin-bearing truck. They made a procession around the neighborhood, and many other mourners joined them or watched as they chose. Chinese musicians accompanied the mourners, playing on trumpet-like instruments and keeping rhythm with a cacophony of gongs and cymbals. Then the mourning marchers got into cars again and proceeded to the Chinese cemetery some distance away.

At the cemetery, a spread of food was produced, including many chickens, vegetables, and fruits. Molly saw her mother also setting plates of food before other grave markers in the cemetery, neighbors of her husband in this resting place. After sufficient time for the deceased to partake of the food, the feast was taken home, and the family ate what was left.

****

Mr. Chrisman actually did it! He bought Terence a car and sent it half-way around the world to him! What an amazing friend! What a sweet answer to prayer! Terence felt in his bones this was his opportunity to be well again!

He had no trouble finding a buyer among the Burmese elite in a country where the current climate made finding a car next to impossible. With funds from the sale of the car carefully hidden with their own little savings, Terence and Molly began to wheedle and persevere through the bureaucratic tangle to leave the country. At least for medical reasons the government was more lenient about travel, wanting to show it was a benevolent government, after all. So, enduring a personally challenging but administratively generous wait of just a few months, Terence received an appointment for a government-approved doctor to check him, and this expert confirmed that Terence was very ill. More paperwork inched its way through the system.

Meanwhile, Molly wrote to Mrs. McCabe in Madras, India. They had been corresponding ever since Mrs. McCabe moved there, so Molly informed her that she and Terence would be traveling to the Vellore hospital, on the outskirts of Madras. Molly hoped she could briefly see her friend while she and Terence were there.

Molly received a quick and gracious reply. Mrs. McCabe wrote, "Molly! Come and stay with us! You and your husband too! I will send a driver to pick you up at the train station in Madras!"

At last the paperwork was in order; "Slow and steady wins the race." Molly and Terence flew from Rangoon to Calcutta, where they managed to get a taxi to take them to a hotel for one night. The traveling was very taxing on Terence, and he clutched his heart nearly all the time. Even though Terence was sick, he was full of hope, and he was able to direct Molly what to do all along the trip. This was a great comfort to her.

Molly had never seen such crowds of people as she saw in the streets of Calcutta. Beggars were everywhere. Children, dirty and wearing torn clothing, would hang on to her skirt even as she passed short distances from the airport to the taxi, from the taxi to the hotel, and later from the taxi to the train station. They looked at her with imploring faces, urgently crying, begging. Terence could not resist their pitiful looks, and handed coins to a few. Oh, then they were mobbed by children! Hundreds of them came running, crying out piteously.

Molly felt both sorry for them in their obvious poverty and afraid of the mob of them. She remembered hearing about how the people in this city had suffered during the war, and she thought of Puck Hee eating grass to survive. She deeply pitied the children, but she could not give coins to all of them! How does one begin to address such need? It tore at her generous spirit to pull herself away and hurriedly pass them. But she would never shake the image of them.

The next day they took the train to Madras, and as promised, Mrs. McCabe's driver greeted them at the train station. Molly didn't know how the Indian man recognized them, but perhaps he noticed that they were the only Chinese couple wearing longyis. The man was quite friendly and chatted as he drove them to Mrs. McCabe's house.

"Please, Molly, call me Evelyn." It was not the first time Mrs. McCabe had encouraged Molly to do this, but it seemed unnatural to Molly's Asian instincts. Molly would sooner call her, fondly but respectfully, "Auntie." But Molly would try to accommodate Mrs. McCabe's-- Evelyn's -- western preference for first names.

Evelyn was warm and welcoming, showing comforting hospitality. Evelyn's mother, who insisted on being called Donna, was living with her, and Molly remembered she had been with her daughter in Burma also. Donna also was so kind to the traveling couple.

Mother and daughter shared a beautiful, big house and several servants. Oh! It was really grand! Perfect, Molly thought practically, for diplomatic entertaining and to help the local economy.

Molly felt very much in good care, but it was more than common hospitality she felt. Until now, she hadn't thought about the hardness of her life. She was just doing her best to get through. Her thoughts were preoccupied with, "I have to do this. I have to do that," not, "Poor me."

But she sensed that Evelyn and Donna felt her difficulty and sincerely longed to do what they could to ease her suffering. She thought the servants and driver were especially kind as well. Molly felt their compassion and was moved by it. She would always be touched to remember this time.

Molly wasn't sure whether the hospital would have a place for her to stay while Terence was being examined. She felt she must go with him, but she wasn't sure where she would sleep.

Evelyn removed all concerns. "While Terence is in the hospital, please stay here, Molly... among friends. Our driver can take you to the hospital whenever you want to go to be with Terence."

So Terence was admitted to the hospital, and Evelyn's driver took Molly to be with her husband for several hours every day. Otherwise, she was indeed in the care of kind friends.

The hospital staff was also compassionate. Terence became friendly with the interns, and he and Molly were photographed with them. The loving attention in Madras and in Vellore was good for both of them. All week, Terence was flying on high hopes.

At the end of the week, Terence and Molly waited to meet with the doctor. When he came in to Terence's room, Molly tried to read his expression, and she was not happy with what she saw. There is no easy way for a doctor to give, or for a patient to receive, bad news. But both doctor and patient in this case tried to ease the difficulty of the other. The doctor was kind. Terence was brave. The heart was too enlarged for the surgeon to risk operating. Terence would not likely survive a surgery, and so the doctor would not dare to do it.

After the doctor left, Terence was overwhelmed with discouragement. "All this effort and expense wasted.... I thought God would use the surgeon to heal me. I thought I would get well. "

Molly tried to comfort her husband, "At least we tried, Terence. Don't talk about the effort and expense. We had to try."

She knew he was already thinking how hard it would be to write to Mr. Chrisman with the news, "The surgeon will not operate. The heart is too enlarged."

Evelyn and Donna met Molly and Terence as the driver brought them back from the hospital. Their faces were full of hopeful anticipation.

It was hard to say out loud, "The surgeon will not operate. The heart is too enlarged." Molly said it, so Terence wouldn't have to say it. She added, "But at least we tried."

Taking her lead, Evelyn repeated, "Why yes, at least you tried."

The women continued to offer their love and comfort. After another gentle night at the McCabe home, it was time to leave.

Molly thanked them profusely. "You have helped us so much! We were strangers here, and this is a difficult time, but you have made things so easy and nice. I was hoping to get a little room near the hospital. I didn't know how I would pay for it. Instead you have made me feel welcome and at home with you. I'm sorry, I cannot even give you a gift. I can only give my thanks. When I am in trouble, God always sends someone to help me, and this time He sent you to help us. Thank-you! I will never forget your kindness."

The Indian driver clearly felt compassion for the couple, and he tried to make the trip to the train station as pleasant as possible. He took a scenic route and pointed out landmarks along the way. He photographed them at

a few places. At one place, they found someone else to take the picture, so that the kind driver could pose with them. Terence and Molly were able to wear their smiles at Marina Beach.

Once on the train, it was more difficult to be cheerful. The stop in Calcutta was harder even than before. With the forlorn children grabbing and begging, sorrow seemed to fill the world as it filled their hearts.

Terence and Molly each dreaded returning home and having to tell, over and over, "The heart is too enlarged." Molly despaired seeing her husband look so defeated. She had one solace, her Lord Jesus. She prayed to Him for comfort, for faith, for strength. Molly knew Terence was reaching for the same solace. But they were grieving.

****

Grief sat heavily on Molly. Adding to the weight of personal sorrow, distressing sounds beyond her own fog could not be ignored, sounds of the continuing political turmoil in Burma.

The government continued instituting an epidemic of edicts, and the results were expressed well in an article in the American magazine *Time*, August 30, 1963, titled "Burma: The Way to Socialism and Havoc." This article was passed around the library quietly, from one grim soul to another, as each one read what subscribers outside of Burma could glimpse of their misery, the devastating results of Ne Win's policies for Burma's citizens and the repression and hopelessness of their experience. But Burma was nearly forgotten by other nations of the world as they focused on conflict in Vietnam.

Molly never saw the government documents, "The Burmese way to Socialism," nor "The System of Correlation of Man and his Environment," but sometimes snippets reached her ears. She thought, "Nonsense sounds so good! Where is the justice? Where is the happiness? They make the words sound so good, but the result is so bad!"

The Revolutionary Council promised to be progressive, non-discriminating, and diligent in scientific research, but their methods were to steal property, coerce citizens, and jail or kill opposition. The Revolutionary Council promised to adapt the government to Burma's specific needs and to be self-policing, which means they were tyrants with no accountability. Anyone who dared to speak such things was quickly silenced.

****

The next pestilence in Rangoon was the institution of street spies. A head man was assigned to every street. Molly complained in angry whispers to Terence, "Everything you do, he will know what's happening. If you want to go somewhere, you have to tell him where you want to go. And when you come back, you have to tell him that too. If you want to go visit your mother in another part of the city, you have to go and report to the head man."

Molly imitated the conversation, her voice turning from pleading, "Oh, please, I must go away...." to demanding, "Where are you going?" to pleading, "Oh, my relative is sick...." to demanding, "Tell me, where are you going and when are you coming back?"

Molly exclaimed, "Terence! You have to give the head man the time you will come back, and when you come back you have to go and tell him, 'I have come back.' How do you like that? He is very stern with us! And he can report anything bad about you; you never know, you see?"

Of course, Terence could see perfectly well. But Molly dared not vent her anger to anyone else, and so he listened. Terence could do no more to comfort his wife.

Also, the government mandated *mark bone din*, government-issued identification cards. Everyone, even little children and old people, must have a card. Everyone must have a picture taken at his own expense, and this photo was fastened to the card with the person's name and address, signature, fingerprint, and religion. Tony didn't need a picture, as he had an extra one from his passport application, but purchasing the rest of the photographs for the ID cards was another expense Molly had not expected. This was a minor complaint. Much more gravely, it was a way for the government to control people. The cards were needed for jobs, for education, and for travel. Even to purchase anything at the shops, one must show the *mark bone din*.

Molly was hoarse with indignation as she complained to Terence. "It's very, very difficult! People are becoming very unhappy, but nobody dares to say anything. You say something, and you'll be in prison! You just have to tolerate it!

"Each day the government is making changes! The ground is shaking under us! But when the government people start to talk, you think, 'Oh! What pretty words! That sounds so nice!' You start to believe them. 'Oh, yes! Up is down, and black is white!'

"Many people are trying to leave the country, Terence. And do you know what? I am praying to my Father in Heaven! We are powerless, but He is our source of power! Everything impossible is possible for Him! I am praying to Him, 'Oh, Lord, please open up a way for us to leave this country, because it is not a good system to live here.'"

Terence nodded in agreement and repeated his dream. "If there is one place I would like to live, it is the United States of America."

Tony took the opportunity to repeat, "Mom, you have to find a way to get me out of here."

She tried to distract Tony. She found the means for him to take judo classes. She also bought him a guitar, and after a few lessons Tony was able to teach himself. But he persistently reminded his mother that he wanted out of Burma.

Chapter Twenty-Seven

Daring Letters from Burma

Tony's friend and classmate Vernon had gone to London, and Tony kept a correspondence with him that revealed much about the times. Tony wrote in October 1963 that he had seen Vernon's mother in front of the Rowe Company. Tony heard from her that Vernon was working long hours, and he advised his friend to take care of himself, to find some friends, and to enjoy some recreation, maybe at one of London's amusement parks. He described the weather and the situation in Burma as "hot." He wrote:

"I heard that you were homesick for Burma, but try to stick it out. 'Home' here isn't a very healthy place. Unrest amongst the students and monks is occurring and top politician leaders have been taken under 'protective custody.' Only God knows what kind of position our country is in now. At least in England you would be able to live in complete freedom and the word 'democracy' would mean something. I wish I had hypnotic eyes and (could) picture what this place would look like in the next five years."

Tony also wrote that he would like to be a physicist. But, he added sarcastically, in the wisdom of the Burmese government he was studying medicine.

Vernon replied quickly, fearing for Tony's safety, and he advised him to write anonymously.

Tony answered in his next letter that he wouldn't discuss "hot" topics, so it wouldn't be necessary to hide his identity. Tony mentioned that he hoped to have a big surprise to tell Vernon in a few months. He reiterated, "Stick to London! Don't think of coming back here."

In November, in a letter including talk of girls and classes, Tony complained that he disliked biology and repeated his wish to study physics. Vernon had misinterpreted the 'surprise' Tony mentioned in a previous letter. Instead, Tony hinted, the surprise was that he hoped to write soon from where their mutual friend wrote, which Vernon would know to be the United States. Everything was arranged except for Tony's "house leaving certificate (i.e. PP)," meaning passport. If he could get that "exit ticket," Tony would be able to study physics, perhaps in as early as two months.

Tony couldn't give Vernon all the details, but the dear Chrismans had agreed to sponsor Tony. He was anxious to get his passport so he could go to the United States and begin his studies at a junior college.

Tony also wrote that things were not going well in Burma. He creatively used code words to inform Vernon of risky subjects, though he was surely dangerously blunt at times:

"On Saturday night (ie 2nd) eight army officers and men in jeep and three men students in Opel car had an accident. Result: fistfight; 1000 students surrounded Kamayut police station and bombarded it with stones and bottles, army Dodge jeep passing by overturned and burned, driver and passengers nearly killed. In the old capital of Burma, Yul Brynner's followers in yellow sweaters found with Guy Fawkes ingredients. A-men entering campus do so at own risk...."

Vernon would have no trouble understanding Tony's codes. Guy Fawkes was a rebel in British history who planned to assassinate King James I using explosives. Yul Brynner was a stage and film actor, well-known for his shaved head. Those who followed Brynner's hairless style and wore yellow "sweaters" alluded to bald and saffron-robed monks of Burma, some who were found with explosives. Tony indicated that, in spite of military power, the army men were at risk on campus.

Surely tempers were flaring. In many incidents around the city, monks and students were bravely showing resistance to the oppressors and courageously representing a defenseless people. Mobs also became indiscriminately violent.

Tony asked Vernon to let him know if his letters were-- and he drew a triangle. This was the symbol, as on the back of the United States' dollar bill, of the "All seeing eye," or the "Eye of Horus," an Egyptian god said to be all seeing. In this way Tony, fearing the censors, asked if his letters were being opened before Vernon received them.

Later in the same month, Tony explained by letter that his P.P. had been denied. "New law by cabinet: no private individual except top ranked member of G. may leave our teak curtain. Our mixture of Profumo and Castro broke off negotiations ... in the dense jungles of ours."

Referring to John Profumo, a British minister of war, and Fidel Castro, a former guerilla warrior who assumed military and political power in Cuba, Tony was cryptically speaking of General Ne Win. Profumo resigned his position after revelations of a scandal involving a prostitute connected to Soviet spies, and Fidel Castro also had a reputation for being unfaithful to his wife, as did Ne Win. Tony's comparison of Ne Win to Castro was an especially apt one. Ne Win seemed to pattern Burma's government after the socialist Cuba of Castro, a cruel tyrant, who in 1960 seized all news media; arrested teachers, professors, and moderates; forced one-party rule; instituted neighborhood watches; and made labor unions illegal. As Tony indicated, the Ne Win government banned international travel from Burma, claiming the resistance of tribal groups made it necessary. Tony used the phrase "teak curtain," a comparison of Burma's invisible but dense barrier surrounding her to the "iron curtain," the political and military border between Europe and the eastern European nations of the Soviet Union, behind which barrier was no escape and no accountability.

Tony also wrote, "We are having a little 'Auschwitz' here. Occupants being mainly pressmen, leaders, educated men, etc.; large masses of people have been taken under detention." In this way, he let Vernon know that Burma's government was imprisoning and killing its citizens as the Nazi's did in Auschwitz, the infamous concentration and extermination camp in Poland from 1940 to 1945. Tony also mentioned their mutual friend and classmate, the late Mi Mi Taik, the eldest son of the first president of Independent Burma, who was killed when Ne Win's soldiers arrested his father at their home on the night of the coup.

Tony assured Vernon that he had not given up hope, though his application was rejected. "East Berliners are brave and clever aren't they? Their exit from East Berlin was done by ingenious thinking. Maybe my problem may be solved in the same way." Tony also mentioned, Queen Sirikit's kingdom, a reference to Thailand, and said he was trying to make connections. He said that Vernon should not reply until he has heard again from Tony, though it may be many months.

Molly didn't know what Tony had written to his friend until many years later, when Vernon gave her the precious letters. She was not wrong to worry that Tony would disappear one day in an attempt to cross the border to Thailand, the kingdom of Queen Sirikit. As his letter indicated, after his passport to the United States was denied, he was making plans, like a few ingenious East Berliner's escaped East Germany, to escape Burma.

****

Terence became deeply depressed after the fruitless visit to the hospital in Vellore, and Molly was very concerned for him. Often he would cry out loudly to God, "Oh Lord, why me?" Sometimes, unable to fight the nebulous enemies of illness, poverty, and loneliness, he would vent his anger on Molly.

Slowly he began to engage in life again. Eventually he was able to find his voice to praise God in the midst of his suffering. Molly was comforted when she heard him softly singing a favorite hymn:

> "Fairest Lord Jesus, Ruler of all nature, O Thou art God and man, the Son Thee will I cherish, Thee will I honor, Thou my soul's glory, joy, and crown."

****

Molly was surprised to hear that her sister Moonlight had married an older man, Mr. Wu. Then she was shocked to hear that Mr. Wu already had a wife before he married Moonlight. Molly knew her father would not have approved of this match for his daughter. Clearly it was a boon to Mr. Wu's face, acquiring a second wife from a prestigious family, but the Chin face suffered; Moonlight's position as Number Two Wife was not flattering. Besides all of that, hadn't Moonlight seen the painful consequences of multiple wives within a family?

Molly's children knew the children of the first wife. "My Auntie is now their step-mother," Charlene noted with embarrassment.

Other family members would later tell Molly that Mr. Wu was formally introduced to relatives living and dead at her father's funeral, but Molly had no memory of this. Maybe only the men were privy to this ceremony, or maybe Molly was distracted.

Moonlight's choice was awkward, but Molly couldn't tell Moonlight what to do. There was no social or socialist prohibition of such relationships in Burma, and Ah Pa was no longer present to forbid it. Likely it was Ah Pa's dying and death that made Moonlight feel the need to have a husband to provide for her. Older Chinese women did not have many options.

Moonlight lived in Mr. Wu's fifth floor apartment on Thirty-Fifth Street near the Sule Pagoda, a little more than a block away from the USIS Library. Soon, Mr. Wu rented another apartment for her, one more accessibly located on the second floor of a nearby building.

Moonlight visited Molly with a proposition, "Why don't you move to the fifth floor apartment? It would be convenient for you to go to work."

Molly was very interested. "Oh, that would be nice! I wouldn't even need to take the bus; I could walk to work. The children could walk to the library whenever they wanted."

Moonlight was embarrassed to mention, "I'm sorry, Ah Ngood. If it were up to me, I wouldn't ask for this. But, you know, my husband will expect a salami, a one-time side payment, besides the monthly rent, to sublet the apartment to you."

The request seemed reasonable. Molly said, "Of course. But, you know I don't have extra cash. I do have some jewelry. A little bit."

Moonlight answered, "Oh, I'm sure that will be fine. Just a few things that I can show my husband."

Soon the family was moving again. Terence struggled to climb the first flight of stairs. He stopped often, holding his chest and panting. It was clear that he could not climb the steps to the fifth floor, and there was no such thing as an elevator.

Charles, a friend of Charlene's, was helping the family to move their few possessions. He and Tony each grabbed his own right forearm and the other man's left forearm to form a seat for Terence, and in this way they carried him slowly up the steps. All three had to stop and rest several times before the heights were reached. After that, Terence rarely came down from the apartment. Every few months he would slowly descend from the mountain, usually to see a doctor, and then he would be carried back up by the young men.

But Terence was pleased with the apartment. He did not miss the Inquisitive Lady. He especially liked the south-facing balcony, where he could perch above the city and enjoy the fresh air when the sun was not too hot and when the rains were not too heavy. He could not see past the buildings

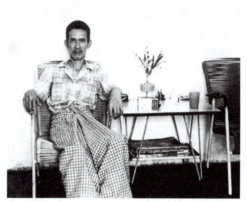

on Strand Road, where expensive hotels boasted views of the Rangoon River, but it was still a pleasant view of the city, and watching the street helped to pass the time. The embassy was just beyond Strand Road on Merchant Street, and Terence liked having Molly close while she was at work.

A co-worker was leaving the country, and she had a sale of some of her belongings. Molly found some excellent furnishings for the apartment: a set of chairs with aluminum frames and brightly-colored, plastic straps woven to form the seats and backs. Some people called these "lawn chairs," but they were ideal for the apartment: cool and comfortable for the Burma heat, inexpensive, cheery and colorful, and conveniently portable. In the set were two regular chairs, a table, and a reclining chair. Terence was happy with the purchase, and when he wanted to sit on the balcony, someone would carry out the recliner for him.

The apartment was hot, but the family was used to heat. There was only one bedroom, but the children were satisfied to sleep in the fairly large living room. Molly purchased a roll of linoleum, and when it was night, this was rolled out on to the cement floor; then the children placed their woven bamboo mats on this surface. Molly had often heard both her mother and mother-in-law insist that layers such as this were necessary to avoid getting arthritis from sleeping on a cement floor with only a mat, so she took this precaution for her children. The apartment also had modern plumbing.

Charles was an art student with a good-natured little dog. Pets were unusual in Burma. Charles's family had found a way to move to Hong Kong, and he couldn't take his dog along. He brought the dog to the apartment for Owen.

Charlene with Hercules' mother, who found another home, and Owen with Hercules

"His name is Hercules," Charles said. Owen immediately loved the little dog, and they became fast friends. He would often take his pet for a walk past the Strand Hotel.

Owen also found some other boys in the neighborhood, and they often played soccer together in their bare feet. The boys liked to fish at a Rangoon River jetty too.

Molly did not mind the short walk to work; it was so much better than riding the buses. But a few times she was accosted on the way. One time a wild man jumped in front of her and showed her a picture of something obscene. She challenged him angrily, "What?" and continued walking.

****

Tony's first letter to Vernon after moving to the Thirty-Fifth Street apartment was sent in February of 1964. He wrote about attending the latest Methodist English High School's graduation ceremonies, Vernon's high ranking in absentia, Mrs. Logie, and classmate crushes. In the only serious turn, he stated that his P.P. must be settled "by hook or by crook" by September at the latest. He did not explain, but he was counting on being in the United States to begin classes by then.

The next letter was also light-hearted, advising Vernon not to become a boozer like the comic strip character Andy Capp and asking about snow and about fish and chips. Tony also talked about girls, and about the new "shake" and "hitchhiker" dances. He said that locals were still in "Twistville," meaning that they were enjoying the popular "twist" dance. Again referencing East Germany, he closed the letter *Auf Weidersehen* and asked if Vernon remembered his Deutsche: *Vergenern Li nicht*, meaning, "Make a break." Tony was delicately telling Vernon of his planned escape.

In his April 10, 1964 letter to Vernon, Tony told of taking his college exams and of expecting poor grades, as he was indifferent about answering the questions. He continued to voice dislike of biology, quietly rebelling against the government mandate of his course of study. He said his botany practical paper did not go well. "This subject exasperates me." Officials would find they could not make him learn what he did not care to learn.

Tony talked of his summer holiday in Ngapali, reached by a Fokker F 28 airplane. His Aunt Lily and Uncle Myo Khin had felt sorry for him and took him along with their children to the Ngapali beach on the Arakan coast. Few people traveled for vacation, and this was a special treat for Tony.

He expressed hope that Vernon had enjoyed his holiday trip too. He recalled that some of the cities Vernon planned to visit were mentioned in Arthur Conan Doyle's "Hound of Baskerville," the original Sherlock Holmes mystery.

Tony closed the letter with sarcasm. "Incidentally, the educational system in our country is to be thoroughly changed for the better. Vocational Schools will be opened and the Government will do the selection of the students for these schools. Exceptionally bright students must attend the medical and engineering fields. This is done in the hope that it will fix the future of our Socialists State. Whew! The old system of freedom of choice of vocation had only bettered the capitalists and imperialists! Foreigners, especially Indians, are leaving by the thousands for their respective homelands. We sanction the spirit of nationalism and patriotism in our country. Well that's for now. I hope I shall not be forced to visit 'Auschwitz.'"

Surely Tony was assuming that censors reading his letters would have a poor command of English and little insight into world history. Nevertheless, he knew imprisonment for his incendiary meaning was a real possibility.

Members of the busy Revolutionary Council continued their progressive decrees. In March 1964, all political parties were outlawed except The Burmese Socialist Programme Party, and the other parties' assets were confiscated.

On May 15, 1964, residents of Burma faced another shocking event. The Council deemed all fifty and one hundred kyat bank notes to be worthless! For a few days, citizens could stand in long lines to declare possession of these bank notes and exchange some of them for replacements. The government claimed to be countering the rampant black market in this way.

Molly stood in line, which extended far down the street. Molly heard whispers, "Don't change all your money. The new money will be worthless." These skeptics recalled the Japanese forcing citizens to trade British bills for worthless Japanese currency. But Molly could not afford to save any money back, and one could only guess whether or not the old bills would ever be worth anything. In fact, this time the old paper money lost all value, and those who saved some, or had the bad luck of owning too many to trade in, were poorer for it.

Tony commented on this turn of events in his May letter to Vernon. He was apparently emboldened that he had not yet been arrested. He was trusting that a veil covered the eyes of censors.

He wrote, "The demonetization of one hundred kyats and fifty kyats notes took place suddenly. Momentarily there was sudden panic in the country…. The Government gave the people exactly one week to declare the amount of delegalized money they had in their possession. Heavily affected were the rich people who had not put their money in the bank but who had kept the money in their homes. Yesterday the cash were finally declared and a final counting of the declared money showed only 1/3 of the total money. This brings about a deficit about two thirds of the money unaccounted for. Compensation of two hundred kyats per head will be given to persons declaring demonetized notes."

Tony told of other difficulties. "The Indian nationals here in Burma are having a rather tough time. The Indian Embassy had declared that they would accept the valuables of the Indian nationals leaving Burma for good and keep them in custody."

Molly heard stories of Indian women trying creative means to take their jewelry with them when they left Burma. Some would hide jewels in small containers of curry. Those unfortunate women who were caught were jailed until the slowly moving Burmese government got around to deporting them. Their jewels were confiscated.

Tony added in his letter to Vernon that even as he was writing at twelve midnight, a loud speaker on a jeep could be heard blaring government propaganda. Molly had learned to tune out these annoyances. Sometimes the message was, "Rice will be available at The People's Shop Number Four tomorrow." Sometimes it was more nice sounding words and promises that continued to spin the Burmese world into chaos.

Tony mentioned to Vernon that a mutual friend was "missing." What a simple word full of frightening implication! This was to be the last of Tony's letters from Burma.

****

Tony continued to pester his mother, "Get me out of here, Mom! You have to find a way to get me out! I will not go to military medical school and serve the army for ten years! I won't do it, Mom! If I have to, I'll go across the border to Thailand!"

"No! Don't do it, Tony!" Molly tried to reason with him, hoping by repetition the arguments would have an effect on him. "It sounds easy to do, but it is not! How will you survive in the jungle and find your way to Thailand? What will you do when you get there? Don't do it!" Molly pleaded.

****

Terence had been to visit his parents, and he returned with terrible news of Lily and Myo Khin.

"Myo Khin was working as usual in his shop. Some military police came." Terence was frowning. "They told Myo Khin that the socialist system must nationalize private businesses."

"What does that mean?" Molly asked.

"The military police said, 'Your shop belongs to the People of Burma now. So you must leave,'" Terence voiced the command gruffly.

He continued, his voice sounding helpless, "Myo Khin didn't know what was happening. He just said, 'Huh?' He was shocked!"

"They just came and said they were taking his shop?" Molly sat down heavily. "What did he do?"

"What could he do? He couldn't argue with the police. No one would dare do it. By now we know there is nothing we can do, or we get arrested or shot.

"So he got up and went to his safe to get his money. They said, 'No! You cannot take anything from the shop. Everything belongs to the People of Burma. The safe also belongs to the People of Burma!' They put a seal on the safe, identifying it as government property.

"So Myo Khin went to get in his car, and the police said, 'No! That car belongs to the People of Burma!'

They told him, 'You must leave now!' Just like that, all at once, Myo Khin was bankrupted! He was dazed. He just left the shop. As he left, the military police put a seal on the door and a seal on the car. What else could he do? Myo Khin walked home with nothing but his jacket."

"Oh, Terence! That's terrible!" Molly hardly knew what else to say.

"That's not all!" Terence shook his head in disbelief even as he continued.

"Oh my! What else?"

"A few nights later, some people came to his house… people from the military government. They knocked on the door and asked for Myo Khin."

Terence was breathless, "Then they grabbed him and handcuffed him! They arrested Myo Khin! And they took him away!"

"What?" Molly cried.

Terence continued, "Lily thought, 'Huh? What happened?' No one knew why they took him. Lily didn't even know where to look for him. She had to go to all the different prisons around Rangoon to try to find him. At each jail, she was met with a frowning guard holding out his hand. She had to take presents, bribes, to the jailers just to get information. At last she found the jail where they are keeping him, and she took some food for Myo Khin because the jail food is hardly fit to eat. Then Lily had to give the jailers more "presents" so they will give the food to Myo Khin."

Molly was angered by the injustice and said, "Poor Myo Khin! Poor Lily! And no one knows why they arrested him? They can just come and drag him away like that? In the dark? Without a warrant?"

She worried, "Oh, my! What will happen to him?"

As the atrocity touched her deeply, her anger was stirred. She demanded, "Terence, how would you like it? With your sweat you build up your business. Then military police can just come and take it and take the safe with the money you have earned! And then -- you are arrested!"

Molly thought of freedoms and rights protected for citizens in the United States: freedom of religion, freedom of speech, freedom of the press, freedom of assembly, freedom of movement, freedom from unreasonable search and seizure, due process of law, the right to public trial, the right to a trial by an impartial jury, the right to be informed of accusation, the right to bear arms.... But here, freedoms and rights were summarily seized and trampled by the Ne Win government.

Counting the offenses, Molly raged to Terence, "We have no freedom of speech! If anyone is found speaking against the government-- if you are joking in the street or purposely say something against the government or anyone in the government, right then you get arrested. Right then and there! And if they don't arrest you in the street, they will come to your home at night, in the middle of the night, knock on the door, and ask for this person. If you say, 'I am that person,' straight away, they handcuff you and take you away and maybe your family will never know where you are kept!"

Molly was just getting started, and as she continued, she forgot to be quiet. "There is no due process of law or trial by jury! There is no freedom of press or assembly! And there is no freedom of movement. The grouchy head man is watching the activities of each family. This is not only annoying and inconvenient! Terence, this is frightening! They are controlling us!

"Besides taking away our rights, they have ruined the economy. If you want to buy anything, you have to go to 'People's Shop Number One or People's Shop Number Four!' Then you stand in line. And when your time comes to get the thing, the shop people say, 'Whatever we had in the shop is finished. You have to come back tomorrow.' And the next day maybe the same thing could happen to you. You have to stand in line forever. Day in and day out.

"All this government knows how to do is to squeeze your neck!"

She suddenly saw and understood the warning look from Terence. She must guard her words. She hoped she had not been heard through the walls of the apartment.

Chapter Twenty-Eight

Progressive Government

The government remained destructively busy. The "New University Education Law" was passed, suddenly making Burmese the only legal language of instruction in all the schools. Tests already taken in English had to be retaken in Burmese, so Tony had to retake exams he had passed in English. Lois and Owen, also more adept in English, were suddenly forced at the Methodist English High School to learn all courses in Burmese, textbooks replaced overnight. Uniforms were issued by the government, and the children had to recite socialist slogans in the classrooms. Because more and more things associated with the west were banned from the country, seasoned teachers were replaced by unprepared ones, and tested policy was replaced with nationalism and superstition. Educational standards fell. Students were made to stand in respect as their teachers entered a room, perhaps because less qualified teachers could not inspire respect by their abilities to teach.

The continuing upheavals in so many areas of life made for a very unstable and unpleasant existence. No one knew from one day to the next what would be the new abnormal normal, the latest foundation whisked away, the firm handhold removed, the succeeding inconvenience or trauma. The only sure thing was uncertainty.

In 1965, all mission schools and hospitals were nationalized. Most foreigners were forced to leave Burma, and the USIS Library was among the casualties; it was to be closed. Mrs. Graham told the senior staff, and the news trickled down to Molly. With this announcement, an air of quiet mourning permeated the library. Each employee, from the superiors down to the small flies, was distraught, though Mrs. Graham tried stoically to hide her misery, and the wives of former government officials, by necessity, were without opinion.

Those who had enjoyed coming to the library were also in mourning. The youngest patrons of the library were tearful, the young adults were silently angry, and the old patrons were demoralized.

Molly often heard the sad refrain, "This was so good for us. Why would the government take it away?" But it was no use challenging the inevitable. The powerful few were making the decisions, and protest was futile and foolish.

Mrs. Graham tried to find jobs for many of the library employees. The U.S. Embassy had a few openings. Gloria, a very capable woman, found a secretarial job with Voice of America at the embassy. Gloria was so proficient that Molly would tease her that she should have been a boss, not the secretary. But others were not so fortunate. Many of the Burmese women employed at the library did not speak or write English well. This, plus having a useable skill, were prerequisites for the embassy.

One by one, the women and the page boys left the library, each with solemn regrets that such a rewarding job and such a marvelous place were not to be found elsewhere in Burma. Only Molly was left with Mrs. Graham. The two women spent weeks together packing books into boxes to ship to schools and other libraries. Mrs. Graham was determined that the precious books should help someone somewhere.

Molly was grateful to still have work. But what would she do when she had finished helping Mrs. Graham? She knew of no businesses in Burma requiring the minimal, two-finger typing skills of a Chinese woman. A government office might need a secretary, she thought, but the Burmese government likely would want to hire a Burmese girl. Besides that, she was afraid to work for the government.

But she had to find work somewhere. Who would want her?

As had become her habit, Molly prayed about this concern. "Oh, Lord Jesus! How will we survive? How can I support my family? My husband cannot support us. The children are still in school. I am the only one who can work. I must support my husband and my four kids. You provided this wonderful job for me at the library, but now I am going to lose it. You have helped me many times before, Lord Jesus. Anytime I don't know what to do, You help me. Will You help me again?"

Molly was focused on her own thoughts when Mrs. Graham spoke. Molly noticed Mrs. Graham was struggling to control her emotions as she taped shut another box, "The government says we are doing spy work here, Molly! We are not doing spy work! We are a library, for goodness sake! We are showing the culture of the United States to the people of the host country. We are sharing information... important information about the whole world. It is a benefit to the local people. In closing the library, the leaders of Burma are hurting their own people." It was the only time Mrs. Graham hinted to her that she disapproved of the Burmese government.

What could Molly say? For a moment she couldn't think of anything.

But confronted by Mrs. Graham's deep sorrow, and momentarily forgetting her own, Molly found sincere words to try to comfort her. "You have helped so many people, Mrs. Graham! So many people have learned wonderful things in this library because of you! We have heard some students say they became doctors or engineers because of the library. My own children love to learn, and they are all good students because of the library.

"My goodness, Mrs. Graham!" Molly went on with great feeling, "Think of the comfort and pleasure you have given my husband, so that, even stuck in his house, he could read and see pictures and learn about wonderful things all over the world. Many people have stories like this about how the library has helped them. Your efforts have not been in vain."

Mrs. Graham gave Molly a smile and thanked her, but sadness quickly returned to her face and voice, "It looks like this time I will be leaving Burma for good. Did you know, Molly, I came here with my husband David? We came to Burma as missionaries just six years after we married. Then the terrible war came, and I became a confidential secretary to the American Military Mission, and David joined the mobile hospital unit with Dr. Seagrave. Then we had to evacuate from Burma, running just ahead of the Japanese soldiers. After our escape, David and I signed up to teach for a year at Ginling College in Chengtu, China. Then we went back to New Delhi to work with the Office of War Information. After the war, David was offered the position of Director of Evangelism at the Karen Theological Seminary. But before he could formally accept, he suddenly died of a heart attack here in Rangoon."

Mrs. Graham paused, lost in her thoughts. Then she added, "His body is buried in the cemetery here."

Molly was so sorry for Mrs. Graham's loss, which obviously left a gaping wound even after all these years. She had rarely seen this vulnerable side of Mrs. Graham. Molly was also surprised that Mrs. Graham had been a missionary. Mrs. Graham did not exhibit the humble nature of most Christian missionaries Molly had met. Perhaps her role as Director of the USIS Library forced her to become more commanding.

Mrs. Graham's strong voice was now choked with emotion. "This has been my home for nearly thirty years. We first came here in 1937, and now it is already 1965. I love this place and the people here. I have so many... attachments... to Burma."

The women were quiet for a few minutes. Molly was about to offer another sympathetic word, but Mrs. Graham changed the subject and her tone of voice.

She said, "I'm so glad the paperwork finally went through for Tony to get his passport to study in the States! Oh, Molly, what a relief! I know you were afraid he would try to run to Thailand! Did he arrive in Florida okay? Have you heard from him lately?"

Molly replied, "Yes! He is in Florida. His sponsor, Mr. Chrisman, lives there, and Tony was staying with the Chrisman family. Oh my goodness, Mrs. Graham, he worried me so! 'Mom, get me out of here!' Finally, the Burmese government allowed students to travel.

The Terence Lee family, minus Tony

"But he is not staying with the Chrismans anymore. I think Tony was too independent. Mr. Chrisman wrote us and said Tony insisted that he wanted to be on his own. Mr. Chrisman didn't think it was a good idea. He was concerned for Tony, and he said that he tried to talk him out of leaving. But Tony was determined, and Mr. Chrisman said if we agreed that Tony should go out on his own, against his advice, we should sign a letter relieving him of responsibility.

"Meanwhile, Tony was writing to me, 'Mom! I want to be out on my own... roe, roe, roe!' Terence and I talked about it, and Terence agreed, 'Oh, Tony is very independent. He likes to be on his own!'

"Terence was too sick to write the letter, so I wrote to Mr. Chrisman, saying 'Thank-you very much for having my son stay with you. You are so nice. But I know my son is very determined....' And I relieved him of responsibility. Tony knows English very well, and he is very resourceful, so I think he will be okay," Molly concluded.

"How old is he, Molly?" Mrs. Graham asked.

"He was sixteen when he left. He is seventeen now," Molly answered. She noticed Mrs. Graham's look of concern.

She said, "After I wrote to Mr. Chrisman, I wrote to Tony and said, 'You are on your own. You'd better be careful what you do. Don't do all the wrong things.' "

Mrs. Graham cloaked her countenance and spoke with assurance, "Tony is a good boy, and he is strong. I'm sure he will be fine."

"We don't hear from him too often. But he seems to be okay. Mr. Chrisman wanted him to go to a junior college while he adjusts to living in the United States. Tony is very busy with his studies," Molly said.

Day after day the women continued their labors. They were sad to be about the business, and sadder to think of finishing the job. They did not broach serious subjects too often. Instead, they focused on their work, taking satisfaction in, at least, being busy.

****

Mrs. Graham met Molly with a little more brightness one day. As they were sorting through periodicals, she said, "Molly, I want you to apply to work at the embassy. They have another opening for a secretary. I sent some of the others over there to apply, but they couldn't do the typing. The people at the embassy asked me, 'Don't you have any girls that can do the work?' I said, 'Yes, I kept one back to help me, and I am sure Molly can do the work. You will be very happy with her, but she must help me close the library first.' "

"Oh, thank-you, Mrs. Graham." Molly was nearly breathless with gratitude. She was pleased to see that God was perhaps opening a door for her.

"You know how things work here, Molly," Mrs. Graham continued apologetically. "I had to send the others first, to try for the position. I knew they would have trouble, but I had to give them a chance. I just sent another one over to try for the position, but she could not do it. At least, she doesn't seem too upset that she didn't get the job, and it is good news for you."

"Thank-you," Molly repeated. "I will do my best."

"I know you will, Molly," Mrs. Graham replied. "I am sure of it."

It is true, as Mrs. Graham said, that the library was not a front for a spy agency. But the library did put thoughts into heads about human liberty, rights, equality, and dignity. These were dangerous ideas from the view of the socialists, and it is no surprise that they wanted the wonderful library closed and the devoted Zelma Graham sent away from Burma.

****

Molly went to work as the secretary for the Budget and Fiscal Officer, Arthur Parolini, at the United States Embassy. The B & F Office was a small department which handled all the financial affairs for the embassy, including providing paychecks and setting budgets. Also, all of the American government employees came periodically to the department to exchange some of their money from American dollars to Burmese kyats, so they could do shopping in Burma.

The staff of office workers consisted of two Indian and one Anglo-Indian accountants, an Indian cashier, and Molly as secretary. Molly worked for the two American managers of the department, Mr. Parolini, who was the head of the department, and the Disbursement Officer, whose office handled all the cash. Molly also typed all of the correspondences of the Head of Accounting, an Indian man, Mr. Samson. Molly didn't handle cash, but she did all the typing of memorandums and letters for the department, as well as typing the tedious tabulations of numerical data.

Before long, Mr. Samson confided to Molly, "You are doing a great job here. The other women sent from the library to apply for the job did not do so well. That last girl was asked to do some typing. She sat at the typewriter all day, until five o'clock, and she could not type one short memo. We all felt sorry for her."

Molly reflected again about the lack of skills of some women at the library. But she also knew Mrs. Graham did not hire many of those women for their secretarial or librarian abilities, but to give the library legitimacy. In this way they surely earned their pay, besides the work they did helping the children.

She felt sorry for the poor woman who could not type the memo. With very little instruction, maybe she could have done the job.

But, unlike most of the other women at the library, who had enjoyed second incomes for their families while doing pleasant work, Molly needed a job. Desperately. She reflected on how God had provided again for her to have work, and she thanked Him every day.

Molly also felt an urgency to improve her skills. Yes, she could type, but her method was, as she said, "any old how," pecking out letters and numbers inefficiently. She saw others using all of their fingers to type very quickly. After the scare of losing her job at the library, she felt compelled to do something to improve herself, to be in a better position to provide for family. She prayed to God for guidance. Soon, she found that she could take classes locally and for a reasonable cost, so she signed up for training in typing and shorthand.

It was challenging to fit this schooling into a busy, difficult life, and it meant having to take the bus after work to attend the classes. Of course, her family still needed her at home. More fatigued than ever, she arrived to the appartment on Thirty-Fifth Street to Terence's pleas for a massage, "Come! Come! Come!"

But the sacrifices were worth the effort, for soon she was proficient at the touch typing method. Looking only at the text and not at her fingers, she could rapidly type fifty words a minute. She also learned the Pittsman shorthand method so that she could make and recognize little curves and lines representing whole words, and in this way she could write down what a person said as fast as he or she could speak, eighty words a minute. She earned her certificate from the Rangoon Shorthand and Typewriting School at the Rangoon Young Women's Christian Association, better known as the YWCA.

At work, Molly discovered that Mr. Jacobs, one of the accountants, was a deacon at the Immanuel Baptist Church. Molly hadn't known him well because she wasn't able to attend church often, even though she lived within walking distance now. But Terence couldn't make the trip down the mountain every week, and he did not like for her to leave him alone, though he must tolerate her going to work.

Molly found the work at the embassy demanding, and there was rarely a moment of rest. She was always writing something, typing something, tabulating something, or filing something. Sometimes she took dictation, but usually Mr. Parolini preferred to write out his thoughts and give these notes to Molly to type. The most tedious work was typing for the head accountant, because he required extensive, over-sized charts, with rows and columns of numbers. Molly used a very large electric typewriter for this tabulation. Every number must be typed accurately, and if she made a mistake, the error must be erased and corrected, and then the page did not look so neat. But the most important thing was to be accurate.

Molly also needed to type stencils without error to make duplications. A special typewriter made the stencils, cutting the letter shapes into card stock or plastic, so the finished surface could be inked over and over to make many copies.

Or, to make a few carbon copies of a letter, layers of typing paper were alternated with "carbon paper," which was inked on one side, and when it was struck by the raised letter on the hammer of the selected key on the keyboard, it left a duplicate residue on pages following the original. One had to press the keys quickly but firmly to give enough force to make the imprint on the last copy. Usually not more than three or four copies could be made at one time. Molly observed that the latter copies were always fainter and more blurred than the first copy, but it was not her fault, only a characteristic of the process.

As Molly fit into the routine, she found that June was always the busiest month, called the "fiscal month." There were many reports required, and Molly and Mr. Samson put in many extra hours in the evening and on Saturdays to get the work done. The benefit was overtime pay. The unfortunate consequence was being away from her family, and Terence missed her more than ever.

The man who worked for the disbursement officer was a very flashy guy. Molly noticed his big, expensive looking watch and his nice clothes. She thought he must make a very good salary. He and the disbursement officer handled all the cash.

A good, fast typist will learn to think of words, not individual letters, as she transposes handwriting. So it was not possible for Molly to miss the meaning of what she was typing. One day she was startled to read about large sums of cash being missing from the department, the responsibility of the disbursement office. The letter explained that the guy working for the disbursement officer, the flashy guy Molly had noticed, was found to be responsible for theft, and the letter went on to explaine the time and effort it had taken to prove this.

When Molly returned from her lunch break, one of the accountants was waiting to talk with her. "Molly, I want to ask a favor of you."

"What is the favor?"

"Do you know anything about this case of money being missing?"

Molly knew the issue was confidential. She knew she must keep her mouth shut, so she played dumb. "Money missing? Oh my? What happened?"

"Someone in the department is accused of embezzling money. But I know he didn't do it."

Molly wasn't so sure.

"We are local people," the man continued. "We must stick together. We must help each other."

"Oh, they wouldn't trust a local person like me to type something like that. Maybe Mr. Parolini gave the work to one of the American secretaries in administration," Molly suggested.

"Well, if you see anything about this, Molly, if Mr. Parolini asks you to type anything about this case, let me read it," the man said. Molly thought he seemed angry. He repeated, "We need to help each other."

Molly brushed him off, repeating, "I am sure Mr. Parolini will not trust me with something like that. He won't trust locals with classified information."

She deflected further questions in this way and prevented the ire of her co-workers, but she would not break the trust of her boss. Her lack of forthrightness with the man seemed a necessary deception. She didn't dare offend him by bluntly telling him she would not help him. Sometimes people in Burma, Molly knew, would retaliate against even slight offense by doing something drastic like kidnapping children and blackmailing for their return. She had heard of such things, and she would not dare risk this. Anyway, the man didn't need to know that she knew anything.

Molly was glad the typed letter was hidden safely in her desk. She was relieved to hand it over to Mr. Parolini without detection.

Mr. Jacobs had heard Molly being pressured, and he confided to Mr. Parolini, so that he would use an American secretary for confidential reports. Molly appreciated Mr. Jacobs' intervention for her.

The thief was taken to court, and the embassy was surrounded with scandal. Molly felt sorry for the disbursement officer, the thief's boss. The scandal reflected poorly on him.

Molly learned to keep confidentiality on other matters as well. When it came time for employee reviews, individuals would come to Molly and ask, "Have you typed mine yet?"

Molly was consistent in her reply, "No, no. Nothing has come yet." Again, whether reviews were good or bad, Molly did not intend to break the trust placed in her. She mused that, anyway, she did not want to be the cause of boasting or of depression by revealing the content of the review. She wanted to ask, "If you are a good worker, why do you worry?"

Then there was rivalry among the employees, particularly between Mr. Jacobs, the second accountant, and his boss, Mr. Samson. Molly had to be very diplomatic and listen to the comments of each about the other, making sure she never repeated a word of it. She remembered the Scriptures, "live peaceably with one another," and, "blessed are the peacemakers." She knew how difficult that was to do, even among Christians, and even in her own home.

Terence couldn't come down from the mountain on his own to spy on her, and Molly thought the less said the better about her male co-workers. Only a few co-workers were Americans, and they were the perceived threat. The accountants were Indians, and Indians were not known for flirting, but for being good at accounting.

Still she sometimes had to defend herself to her husband, "I'm Chinese, Terence. The American men know that Chinese girls have good reputations. We don't flirt around. We are faithful wives and devoted mothers."

In case Terence thought Molly was an exception, she emphasized, "You know I don't flirt! Men don't come around me and flirt! They know better!" she said with defiance. "They respect me. They don't come around me and do stupid things."

"You are too jealous," she told him again and again, turning from a defensive posture to a scolding one. "You don't trust your own wife! My life is hard, Terence, and you make it harder with your jealousy." Now she couldn't resist adding, "At least you can't spy on me anymore! You can't get past the armed marine that guards the embassy." That should quiet him!

Molly was ashamed whenever she argued with Terence, and it seemed they argued often. But when they read the Bible together, they did not fuss. When they read the Bible together or prayed together, they found themselves in perfect agreement. It was a good feeling.

****

Indeed, Molly was pleasant to her male co-workers, but in a strictly appropriate way. And none of the American men at the embassy were ever inappropriate to her.

Molly enjoyed a friendly exchange with one particular marine guard as she came and went every day. He was a likeable, young, dark-skinned man of African descent and of small stature. Molly doubted he was more than a teenager. He regularly greeted her by her first name, "Hi Molly."

Forgetting that she had once been terrified of marines, she explained to the young man one day, "I want you to know that, in this culture, it is considered rude to call a stranger or an acquaintance by his or her first name. This is especially true if you are addressing an older person."

"Really?" He answered with surprise. "Where I come from, it is considered friendly to use a person's first name. I'm sorry ma'am."

"It's okay. People know you don't know," Molly reassured him. "I am not offended, and you may continue to call me Molly. I only told you because I think you should know about it. You should call a woman my age Ma Ma for 'Big Sister' or Daw for 'Auntie.' "

"Yes, ma'am," he said respectfully, "I'm glad to know this. Where I'm from, people, especially women, don't want to be thought of as older. They like people to call them by their first name. It makes them feel young."

"How odd," Molly thought. "I didn't know people find me younger if they use my first name."

But she liked the young man, and they continued to exchange pleasantries. Another day, she had a special favor to ask of him.

"Leon, would you consider visiting my husband, Terence. He has never seen an American Marine in person, and he would love to meet you. He is very sick and can't come out too much, but he would like to see a real United States Marine. This would mean a lot to him."

"Of course!" Leon said sincerely. "That's easy! Where do you live?"

"Oh, it's not too far... just a couple blocks. But it isn't easy to get to our apartment." Molly was concerned that he would be dissuaded, but felt she must explain. "We live on the fifth floor. You would have to climb many stairs to get there."

"Molly, it's no trouble!" the fit guard assured her. "It will be good exercise. I'll bring my friend, and Terence can meet two American Marines."

"That will be wonderful!" Molly beamed.

They agreed on the date. As promised, Leon brought his friend, a big, muscular white man. Molly asked the maid to serve them coffee, with cream and sugar, and cake and cookies. The maid, clearly impressed, bowed deeply as she served the visitors. The marines enjoyed conversing with Terence, graciously answering his questions and satisfying his curiosity. Molly hardly heard the conversation, but she was pleased with the effect on Terence. He was enjoying his role as host to these fine Americans.

****

Molly was invited with the rest of the staff to have a meal at the home of her boss. She found the address in Washington Park, and Mrs. Parolini fixed a delicious meal for them.

Molly didn't finish her meal, and Mrs. Parolini worried, "Oh, Molly, don't you like it?"

"Of course!" Molly said, embarrassed to be singled out.

"But you didn't finish! Can I get something else for you?"

"Oh, no. I am quite full," Molly assured her. Mrs. Parolini did not seem convinced.

Later, Mr. Jacobs kindly explained to Molly that the western custom did not match the Chinese custom in this regard. He was aware that the Chinese are offended if you finish your food and don't accept more. To them, leaving something uneaten on the plate indicates you have finished. "The Americans," he generalized and overstated the case, "are offended if you don't finish the food on your plate. They think it reflects poorly on the cook."

Oh my! If Molly had known this, she would have made an effort to finish every scrap! She considered herself fairly familiar with western culture, but it seemed there was always something to learn.

****

In 1967, more frightening rumors came. As Molly heard, some Communist Chinese, called "Red Chinese," had crossed the border into northern Burma. The native tribal people said the Chinese men were mean to them. These few were so offended that they got more natives to go back and face the Chinese. They were having words, and angry speech escalated to fighting. Molly heard that more Burmese came to join the fight, and the skirmish became a violent, mob-driven battle. Soon, throughout Burma, retaliation exploded against Red Chinese and "White" Nationalist Chinese alike.

In Chinatown in Rangoon, men from the dong, trained in Kung Fu, banded together and armed themselves with spears, swords, and sticks. These men formed a human barrier around Chinatown to guard the residents. Finding the protective wall formidable, the lawless mob passed Chinatown, instead targeting isolated Chinese. Molly heard of mobs breaking into homes, throwing all furniture and possessions into the street, ripping up mattresses to look for hidden jewelry and money, stealing what was wanted, and igniting remaining possessions in a huge fire in the street. The families dared not do anything to protect their belongings; even so many were beaten. Rioters also stopped cars in the streets, looking for Chinese to brutalize.

But humane Burmese citizens in Rangoon quietly rebelled against the mob. They said, "This is too much for any race! No one should be treated this badly! We have to do something!" Citizens cordoned off streets with railings and posted guards.

The mobs came through and asked, "Are there any Chinese people living on this street?"

The civilized protectors of their neighbors would answer, "No, no Chinese. Only Burmese. We don't allow you to pass this street. We keep our street clean. No Chinese. Have peace of mind."

So, satisfied to hear that there were no Chinese on the street, the mob would go to the next street. Often they would find the Burmese of that street also assuring them that no Chinese lived there, frustrating the volatile passions of the mob.

By widespread support of kind Burmese willing to make a stand to protect their neighbors against the mobs, Molly's family members, scattered throughout Rangoon, were protected from the rioting crowd. At the Thirty-Fifth Street apartment, sympathetic Burmese neighbors protected Terence, Molly, and the children, as well as another Chinese family. But the threat was real, and Owen witnessed looting and ransacking of homes and businesses in adjacent streets. For a few weeks, Molly and her children dared not leave the apartment for work or school.

Until this frightening ordeal, Molly had hesitated leaving Burma. To go through the process of leaving with a sick husband and four children, or three since Tony left, seemed a greater burden than to stay.

But now she said to Terence, "How can we live here? Any time the mob can kill us! What if they get past our neighbors?

"The mob doesn't care if we are Red Chinese or White Chinese! Anyway, we don't have labels on our foreheads!" Molly stroked above her brow as she said, "See! There are no words, 'Chiang Kai-shek,' or 'Mao Tse-tung,' on our foreheads to tell the Burmese on which side we are! They see Chinese as Chinese! When they find Chinese, they beat them up! Any time they can walk into your house and throw out your things! They have no shame! And they rip your bed and take what they want and burn the rest!"

She continued to vent her fears, but not so loudly that the neighbors might hear, "In just a few minutes, our lives could be wrecked! And the government is not protecting the Chinese citizens! Some people say the government is behind the attacks! We are no longer safe!

"But where could we go, Terence? Maybe Taiwan?" Molly suggested, knowing other White Chinese who had emigrated there. "Or to Hong Kong like your father's sister?"

"If there is one place I would like to live, it's the United States," Terence said, as he had often said. "I would like to live in Hawaii," he added wistfully. "It is so beautiful there, Molly. Every day it rains a little bit at one o'clock in the afternoon, and by two o'clock the rain is gone, and it is sunny again. The ocean is so blue and lovely. The trees and flowers are lush."

Molly frowned, and said with irritation, "You been there, Terence? You talk as if you know the place!"

Terence returned, "I know it is beautiful, Molly. I have read about it. I have seen pictures."

Her husband was always the dreamer. She was the sensible one, considering realistic ways to protect the family and get them safely out of Burma. He was stuck in this impossible dreaming of going to the United States. Hawaii!

From working at the embassy, she knew it was not easy to get to the United States. In fact, because of her proficiency in Taishan Cantonese and Mandarin, as well as having a good understanding of the Hong Kong dialect, Molly was often called into the consular office to translate for a Chinese family wanting to immigrate to the United States. So she knew what was what. The highly educated had preference, or people with skills, and of course one always had to know someone, particularly a close relative, living in the United States already. Such advantages would put a family on a quota list to wait, and maybe someday, after many months and years, the family would get a call to go.

What skills did they have? Whom did they know? They had no reason even to be put on a list. Tony was not a citizen of the U.S. and could not help his family to get there on a permanent basis, at least not yet. Charlene was not yet a skilled doctor. So any chance of going to the United States was a long, long way off. Molly had explained all of these facts to Terence, but it didn't matter. Terence would still dream, and she would have to be the one to get serious about saving the family. But he was so weak, she would not argue with him this time.

****

Charlene was progressing well in medical school. Molly was proud of her. Some of the girls in her classes were afraid of the real skeletons they had to study and dropped out of medical school. But Charlene was not afraid. One day she brought home a real human skull and laid it on the floor of the apartment. Her family shared her fascination with the object. Molly had once aspired to be a doctor; now her thwarted ambition was being accomplished by her eldest daughter.

The family anticipated Tony's letters. He could not be open in his communications; obviously his letters from overseas were opened and scrutinized by censors. Molly and Terence must be even more discreet in their letters; the slightest suspicion could attract the military police and send them to prison. So Tony talked very casually about his classes. He mentioned that an English professor had taken a special interest in him.

When Tony graduated from the junior college, this professor sent a letter to his parents. He praised Tony's hard work and academics. He assured Terence and Molly, "He will find his way in America." Molly was proud of her son's accomplishments and was pleased by the recognition extended by this professor. Terence read the letter over and over to himself.

Each of the children, so far, had received an award of distinction when he graduated from the Methodist English High School. Charlene's distinction was in chemistry, Tony's was in physics, and now Lois had received a distinction in English and was pursuing a degree in business commerce.

Owen was also excelling in High School. Molly never had to worry about him. He told her one day that he had been baptized at the Immanuel Baptist Church. Molly didn't know of his intentions until after his baptism, but she was very pleased. Even when he was quite young and the rest of the family could not attend, Owen had taken the bus alone from Myeinigon to go to the church nearly every Sunday. He went early to attend the Sunday school classes too.

Owen was present with his uncle Wayne when his Grandfather Chin's casket was opened three years after his death, and Owen would never forget the odor or the vision. He saw black rubber shoes still on the feet of the degraded corpse. Indian men were hired at a nominal fee to clean the bones and rebury them.

Chapter Twenty-Nine

Cigarettes

The State Department continued to move people. Arthur Parolini left Burma and was replaced by Margery Palmer, Molly's new boss. Miss Palmer was a pleasant, kind woman. Also, Molly would always think of her as encircled by a persistent fog of cigarette smoke.

After the first few months of settling in to her job, Miss Palmer took a special interest in Molly. She asked many questions about Molly's family. She was curious about Tony and inquired about his progress in the U.S. She asked about Molly's work experience, and she asked to confirm how long Molly had worked for the United States.

Molly hadn't stopped to think about it. "Well, let me see. I started working for the USIS Library in 1951. I worked at the library for, hmm, fourteen years until the Socialists closed the library in 1965. Since then, I have worked for the U.S. Embassy. I've been at the embassy for over two years now, so altogether... that's more than sixteen years."

Besides her duties as secretary to Miss Palmer, to the Disbursement Officer, and to the Head of Accounting, Molly continued to be used by the consular office to interpret for Chinese families wanting to emigrate from Burma. Truly, anyone who had a way out of Burma was taking it. Especially since the riots against the Chinese, people of this race were no longer willing to wait out unhappy business conditions in the land of their birth, and they were leaving Burma in a steady stream. Molly never heard the embassy's American personnel openly criticize the Burmese government, but the staff members clearly felt sorry for local citizens of every race and tribe and tried to help as they could.

Molly continued to worry about how she could get her own family out and where to take them. She thought Hong Kong, Singapore, or Taiwan would be the most likely destinations. She knew from relatives that some were also going to Canada or Australia. Hong Kong, as a British colony, was a good first step to one of these other nations, she knew. What to do? Most people getting out had a close relative somewhere, one of millions of Chinese dispersed throughout the world, but Terence and Molly were not in good standing with the Lees and doubted they could count on help from those few overseas.

She prayed, remembering her hope and her help were in her Heavenly Father. She spoke to Him nearly constantly throughout each day, but now she lifted up this new concern, with trust and sincerity. "Lord God, You are such a great and loving God, and I am grateful that You have helped me so many times. Please help me again. Help me to find a way to leave Burma. I don't know how to do it, but I have to get my family out. This is no longer a safe place for us. Even if my children can be educated here, what kind of job can they have? This is not a good place to live. Please get us out. Please show me how."

As was her established, familiar way, she spoke all that was in her heart to her Friend. "Lord Jesus, the United States is the best place to go, for the democratic life and freedom of speech and freedom of everything, and I could see my son, Tony, again. But I don't have a close relative that is a citizen to petition for me to go there. Please open a way for us to get out of Burma somehow." Each day and night she often repeated the prayer, "Please get us out!" as Tony had once pestered her.

She explained to God that if she could get her family to Taiwan, then maybe in several years Tony would graduate, and maybe he could find a good job in the United States, and then maybe, eventually, he could get his citizenship and petition for his family to come over, and they could all be together again. Maybe this is how God would answer her prayers. But she didn't know how even to do the first step, to get out of Burma. She pleaded, "Lord God, please, open a way for us."

****

At work one ordinary day, consular officer Michael Joyce called Molly to his office. Molly was prepared, as usual, to translate for a Chinese family wanting to immigrate to the United States. But as Molly walked into the office, she sensed something unusual. She looked around the empty room, confused. Maybe a Chinese family had not yet arrived for their appointment.

"Where are the people?" She asked simply.

Mr. Joyce replied, "No, Molly, this time it is for you."

"What is for me?" she asked, perplexed.

"Sit down."

Molly sat, trying to hide her discomfort.

"How many years of service do you have, Molly?" he asked seriously.

She wondered why that was suddenly so important. Maybe she had earned another service award. She repeated, as she had told Miss Palmer recently, "I worked at the USIS Library for fourteen years, and I have worked two years now with the embassy. Sixteen years all together."

He said, smiling, "Okay. Wow! You qualify to have a special VISA to go to the United States. Do you want to go?"

Molly was incredulous. She thought, "Do I want to go? To the United States? What is he talking about?" But no words came from her mouth.

He asked again, "Would you be interested in taking your family to live in the United States?"

Now emotional words broke from the floodgate. She said emphatically, "Yes! Of course! Oh, Sir, that is exactly what I want to do! I have been praying to Lord Jesus to go there! Everybody tries to go to the United States! I too... but I didn't think there was a chance for me."

"Yes, Molly. You have a very good chance. If you want to go, you can go."

"Really?"

"Yes. You can go because you have more than fifteen years of service to the United States Government."

As Molly tried to comprehend what was being said to her, Mr. Joyce explained. "Any foreign national who works at least fifteen years for the United States government, in any branch of service, as long as it's part of the United States Government... be it air base, or navy base, or embassy, or agency, like the agency for international development, or any of the other branches... qualifies for a special immigrant VISA. So if you have fifteen years of service, you can go to the U.S., if you want to go."

"Of course I want to go! Yes! I have more than fifteen years of service! I have more than sixteen years of service," she reminded him.

"Do you have anyone in the United States? Any relative?"

Molly thought, "Oh. Now I am in trouble."

She explained, "My oldest son is studying at a university in the United States. He will graduate with a Bachelor of Science degree in Chemistry. That is what he told me. I really want to see my son. But he is not a citizen." She frowned and confessed, "And my husband is very sick...."

"It's okay, Molly. If you are interested, you and your family can go. I can help you. I must write a memorandum to the Secretary of State, Dean Russ, to ask for his approval. The reply will come in a couple of months. When the reply comes, I will call you. I don't think there will be any problem, and you won't have to be on a waiting list, like most immigrants. The problem will be with the Burmese government. That will take much longer."

Molly nodded, thinking of the bureaucracy she had encountered with the Burmese government. She thought she knew what to expect.

Mr. Joyce cautioned Molly not to tell others of her plan to leave Burma. Without another word, she understood that this was good advice. She had lived long enough under the threatening shadow of the socialist government to understand the need to keep secrets. Spies were everywhere and eager to be rewarded for digging up dirt on anyone about anything. It wasn't that she didn't trust her friends, but someone might accidentally say something that could put her joy into jeopardy. People in Burma had learned to be very cautious of every word spoken, which even if said innocently, could be used by powerful individuals to jail or abuse anyone. Already Molly felt she was suspect, being Chinese and working for the United States Embassy, so she would be very discreet, exposing her secret only to those who needed to know.

Molly left the office overwhelmed with thrill and awe. Surely her co-workers wondered what had happened to her.

She could hardly wait to tell Terence! She might get his hopes up for nothing, if the plan didn't work out. But he was so close to her, like a part of herself, she must share this news that was too good to keep from him, news which seemed to be an amazing answer to their prayers.

Oh! He was so very excited! He began making plans. After meeting up with Tony, he said, they would move to Hawaii. He thought they would build a little house there, and when he was not too tired, he worked feverishly on sketches of houses and detailed floor plans, always with his long veranda across the front of the home. With pride and anticipation, Terence would show his drawings and share his ideas with Molly.

"Maybe I can get treatment in the United States," Terence said. "The doctors there are quite advanced."

Molly was cheered to see Terence encouraged. He had gotten so thin. Terence was always a trim man, but now his skin hung loosely on his bones. He did not shave or dress neatly as in the old days. He was tired all the time, and his heart gave him trouble at the least exertion.

Every few months, his heart would race frighteningly, and he would cry out to Molly, "Take me to the hospital!" If Molly was at work, he would send someone for her and wait for her to come home. Then she would hail a three-wheel taxi and take him to the hospital. There, the London-trained, Arankanese cardiologist could stabilize his heart with a shot of digoxin. Terence would be admitted for a few days, and then, a little stronger and his heart beating at a normal rate, he would be discharged. Charlene's friends would be called upon to lock arms and carry him up the flights of stairs to his flat and to the simple pleasure of his lounge chair on the fifth floor terrace.

There, in the warm sunshine, holding his heart, his imagination carried him far from the dusty street below to a lush, tropical island. He had often imagined himself there, but now, he felt it was more than a flimsy, fanciful dream; it seemed a reality just waiting for the struggling family make their way into it.

Molly's spirit was lifted by the apparent stunning answer to her prayer. Amazing! This was better than she thought possible!

She knew God cared about her circumstances, that He loved her and was willing and able to intervene. She also knew He sometimes answered "yes" and sometimes answered "no" to her prayers. She could not explain the mind of God: Terence's life was spared, and yet he remained sick. She dared not complain, because she was glad her husband was still with her. She kept trusting that God was working for good in their lives, even when life seemed hard, because she knew that God is worthy of trust. In difficulty, she continued to exercise thanksgiving and to count her blessings.

But now, the sudden, amazing response to her prayer filled her with humble awe, gratitude, and joy.

****

The daughters of Terence Lee had many suitors. Charlene sometimes had two young men lingering in the flat at once, though she was often too busy with her studies to acknowledge them. Sometimes one suitor would not leave as long as the other was there, causing long battles of will. They watched each other with wary, sour expressions, inadvertently annoying Terence until he was so frustrated he would chase them away. Then suitors took to waiting on landings up the five flights of stairs.

Charlene said in exasperation to her mother, "I don't know what I'm going to do!"

Lois was known as the "hair band girl" for the modern hair bands she wore. She loved to sing in the choirs at school and at church, and she had an angelic voice. But she was too flirtatious for her father's liking, and many Burmese boys were chasing her. When a Burmese girl in Lois's class killed herself in her home, word circulated that she was pregnant and took her own life rather than face the shame of being pregnant without a husband. Then it was really too much for Terence to bear that his daughter seemed unaware that her flirtations could have unintended consequences.

Terence admonished Lois, "Don't pay attention to those boys. You had better study." He was so weak, and it pained Molly to see the stress this was putting on him.

To try to mollify Terence, Molly gave Lois a stern scolding in front of him. This seemed to chasten Lois and to satisfy her father's anxiety for the moment. Alone with Lois, she pleaded. "Why do you do this to your father? He is so sick! Please don't upset him!"

Terence also confided to Molly that he was afraid Lois would run off and marry a boy, forcing them to approve the marriage after the fact. He feared the boy would be Burmese.

Molly was also concerned about Lois. But she didn't understand Terence's prejudice. "Why do Chinese have to marry Chinese? Why do we come to another one's country and then look down on him?" she thought.

They could not complain about Lois's studies. She was smart and resourceful, and her grades at the Burmese business school, called B-com, were stellar. The Burmese government had assigned her this course of study based on her aptitude. Fortunately, strong-minded Lois did not rebel in this.

****

Owen's little dog Hercules became sick. The pet had painful sores, which he scratched without relief, and his fur was thinning. Veterinarians were scarce in Rangoon, but Owen heard of one about five miles away. He walked the distance to see the vet, holding Hercules to his chest.

The vet diagnosed the disease as mange and gave Owen a shampoo to treat it. But he cautioned Owen that the condition is difficult to cure.

Molly didn't know that the dog was ill or that Owen had made the ten mile round trip trek until later. With the needs of the family so great, he did not want to complain or to ask for bus fare.

Several times Molly saw Owen lying on the floor and staring at the black ants crawling around him. For long periods, he would keep very still on his stomach, chin on his hands, palms down, just studying the ants. Molly wondered if this was normal, and she worried that there might be something wrong with Owen's mind. Or, she comforted herself, maybe he would become a scientist and study insects one day.

****

Several weeks went by, and Mr. Joyce called for Molly again. It wasn't until she realized it was just the two of them in Mr. Joyce's office that she thought, "Oh! There must be news!" She waited quietly, her face flushed with anticipation.

Sure enough, Mr. Joyce was pleased to tell her, "I have good news for you! Molly, you have been approved to come to the United States...." He gave her a few moments to express her joy and gratitude, which were profuse! Molly could not maintain professional decorum, for the emotions were too much to hold back. The news was blossoming possibilities for her family!

"Mr. Joyce," she said through her tears, "this is my dream!"

She thought to herself, "Oh! Things are happening so quickly! This will be so easy!"

Mr. Joyce was smiling at her pleasure. Then, as if he had read her thoughts, Mr. Joyce cautioned, "Now for the hard part. It will be very, very difficult to get through the Burmese government. You may have to wait a long time. Go ahead and get started. When you get your Burmese passport, come and see me."

He added, "I will be sorry to let you go, Molly! Who will translate for me? But, that is my problem."

Of special concern to Molly was Charlene. Mr. Joyce warned that she may be too old to be admitted to the U.S. on Molly's VISA. Once Molly was in the U.S. she could petition for Charlene to join the family.

Well, God was working out everything else. Molly would have to trust Him to take care of Charlene too.

Molly was in an enchanted fog as she returned to her desk. It was hard to believe this was really happening. She and her family were really headed for the fabled ghem sun, the Golden Mountain.

When she told Terence that evening, he was overjoyed!

****

Tony was attending the university on the west coast, Mr. Chrisman's alma mater. Terence marked this new location on his map of the United States, as he had traced all of Tony's movements. Tony wrote that he often worked three jobs at a time to help pay for his studies. He seemed to enjoy working as a resident assistant; in this capacity he supervised and advised the other students living in the dorm. He was also an assistant to a professor, often grading papers. Sometimes he cleaned dorms, and he regularly worked as a busboy at a restaurant.

Usually, he wrote upbeat letters home, but he wrote one letter to his family that made Molly's heart ache: "It is Thanksgiving, and everyone has a home to go back to. But I am here alone, washing windows for the University."

Well, soon they would be with Tony again. Thank God! The family would be reunited in the United States. Wonderful!

****

Molly wasted no time in carefully filling out all the required forms and taking them in person to the Burmese emigration department, forced to begin revealing her secret to low level bureaucrats. She did everything she could think to do to prepare for the move to the States, so the family could leave quickly when the paperwork was finished. She knew that she would be permitted to take from Burma only fifty U.S. dollars each of their own money for herself and Terence, and twenty-five dollars for each child. Besides this, she could take only one tical of gold, so she had a jeweler make for Terence a twenty-two carat gold ring of this size, designed with the letter "L" for Lee. She bought fabric to have a couple of nice articles of clothing made for each family member to take when they left the country.

Molly also confided her good news to Miss Palmer. She suspected that Miss Palmer had initiated the invitation to immigrate to the United States.

Miss Palmer told Molly, "This is very important. If you need to communicate anything to your son, you had better give the letters to me, and I will send them through the embassy's mail service. We call it the APO, or

Army Post Office. I'm afraid if you go through the mail service of Burma, your letters might be thrown away."

In this way, plans began to take form. "I am only permitted to buy plane tickets from Burma to Hong Kong," Molly wrote to Tony. "After that we will have only one hundred fifty dollars between the four of us. Figure out what to do for us then." Tony was able to respond that he would find a way to help them once they got to Hong Kong.

Molly went to Puck Ken, or Edward, Wat Hong's son, for help in filling out some of the initial paperwork, like affidavits attesting to the family member's identities and upstanding characters. She knew to go to him because he had gotten a birth certificate for Tony when he went to the United States. Cousin Edward was not only a relative and a respected community leader, but he was also a legal clerk. On nice days, he set up an office, consisting of a stall with a desk and chair, outside the courthouse. For a small fee he explained procedures and could have his people do small jobs inside courthouse. Puck Ken was very helpful to Molly.

But months passed without a word from the Burmese government about the travel passports authorizing them to leave the country. Molly went regularly to check on the progress, but her paperwork was always sitting on the first desk. She saw no movement to the next desk. She could get no answers as to why this was the case. The officials said everything was being done that could be done, and they were so busy they couldn't say for sure what was the problem with Molly's case. So, Molly waited a few more months, and still nothing had changed.

Molly had not confided her secret to her friends at the embassy, except for Miss Palmer, nor any other friends or relatives, other than her immediate family and Edward. As much as she wanted to shout the news to everyone that she was moving to the United States, she must hold her tongue. One casual word might get the whole process stopped. It was hard to keep such a secret!

From her position at the embassy, Molly was aware that sometimes people wanting to leave Burma had started the process and given up after two or three years of frustration. She really couldn't afford to keep waiting, because Terence was in such poor health. Neither could she afford to give up; the cost of quitting was too great. Molly continued to pray about these concerns to her Heavenly Father.

One day Molly recognized a notable Chinese gentleman as he came to the consular office. She knew him to be connected to both her parents and

Terence's. She thought he was a relative of her mother-in-law, and she knew him to be a staunch White Chinese, a compatriot of her father and uncle.

After the gentleman finished his business with the consular officer, Molly risked calling him aside and confiding in him about her predicament. She concluded anxiously, "Everything is taken care of on the U.S. side, but I can't get out because of the Burma side."

He said, summing up the problem concisely, "Ngood, you are about to go to America. But the Burmese government can stop you because you are a Burmese citizen."

"Yes." Molly found assurance in his knowing tone, and she anticipated his advice.

"So you can change your citizenship. If you want to be quick, I can get you a Taiwanese passport. Or I can get a Chinese passport. I will guarantee it for you, so you are no longer considered a Burmese citizen. If you relinquish your Burmese citizenship, they cannot hold you. It will get you out of Burma, to Taiwan or China, but it may still take some time to get from there to the United States. Or you can declare that you are stateless." He explained the procedure to Molly of claiming to have no citizenship at all.

"Whatever you want to do," he assured her kindly, "I can take care of it by seeing some people outside the court. There is a table outside the court. Someone will type all these things for you. You have to pay him a certain amount. Sometimes he is Chinese. Sometimes he is Burmese. These people know all the lawyers inside. You don't have to go to the courtroom. They will have it all done for you. If you want, I can do this for you. I can bring the paperwork to you. All you have to do is sign the papers."

"Oh, yes, our cousin does some legal jobs outside the court too. But, I didn't know we could change our citizenship," Molly replied. She thanked him sincerely and said she would let him know what they wanted to do.

That evening she discussed the possibilities to Terence, and she asked him, "What must we do? Do you want to be a Chinese or Taiwanese citizen? Or should we remain Burmese? Or do you want to be stateless? Our distinguished friend says he can help us get a Taiwanese passport quickly.

"I am worried, Terence. If we are stateless, this may make the Burmese Government mad, and maybe they will kick us out before we have any place to go."

Terence suggested, "Why don't we try a Taiwanese passport?" So Molly gave some money to the gentleman to get the paperwork done for her.

Then she heard from someone else, "Don't use the Taiwanese passport! Because with the Taiwanese passport, you can only reach Taiwan. Use the stateless passport!"

Molly was frustrated and confused. She disliked disturbing the consular officer about her personal business, but with Terence's urging, she agreed that she must ask him. She arranged a meeting with him.

She asked bluntly, "Do you recognize the stateless passport?"

Concerned, Mr. Joyce answered, "Why, Molly, what happened?"

"Someone told me if I use the Burmese passport, the government can hold me back. A friend helped me get Taiwanese passports for my family, but someone said with these we can get only to Taiwan, and really we want to go to the United States. I heard that the stateless passport is okay, that the Burmese won't hold me, and that the stateless passport is recognized by the United States. Is this true?"

He looked relieved and chuckled at Molly's industry. He said, "Yes, actually, yes. Stateless passports were originally designed for refugees. The first ones were created for refugees of Russia when Lenin revoked the citizenship of hundreds of thousands of people. But yes, if you decide to use the stateless passport, I can give you a VISA on that, and you can go to the States. Then you can join your son."

That helped Terence and Molly to make up their minds. Molly did get stateless passports for herself and her family.

****

A new American employee had arrived at the embassy. When Mr. Ray Bridges came to get his paycheck, he made friendly conversation with Molly. After a few visits, he showed her a picture of himself at a Buddhist monastery in Thailand, not as a tourist, but as

Ray is the monk wearing glasses

a participant! In the picture he was dressed as a monk, and his hair was shaved, like a monk. Molly knew this meant he had spent a week or ten days at the monastery to become trained as a novice monk. This was confusing to Molly, because she thought Americans were Christians, and she could not believe Mr. Bridges was a Buddhist. Feeling the futility of Buddhism surrounding her, she could not fathom its appeal.

She learned that Mr. Bridges spoke several languages fluently, and that he had served the State Department of the United States in Laos, Vietnam, Thailand, and Cambodia before coming to Burma. He humbly explained that Lao and Thai languages were very similar, so it wasn't all that impressive that he knew both of these languages among others.

Molly liked Mr. Bridges. He was friendly, jolly, and optimistic. He seemed always to be joking. It was a pleasure to be around him.

As the weeks went by, Molly observed that Mr. Bridges was different from most Americans at the embassy. Other Americans could be friendly, polite, and even gracious. But Mr. Bridges went out of his way to immerse himself into the native culture and to befriend the local people of every race and rank. He invited to his apartment many of the local people, like chauffeurs and mail room workers. He hired a local cook to serve meals to these guests. This was so unusual, to entertain low level workers that were barely acquaintances, that Molly often heard others mention it.

Particularly the Indian men in the mail room talked of him. "Mr. Bridges is a very nice guy. He asks us over to his place after work and gives us a treat," said one.

"He invited us over for a meal at Christmas," said another. "He gave each one of us a watch!"

Another added, "It's very strange, though. He beats a big gong when we come. It's very noisy."

The secretary to the Administrative Officer was an American woman friendly to Molly. But she did not like Mr. Bridges. She lived near him in Washington Park, and she complained, "Why does he hit the gong? It is so loud!"

Molly said, "A gong? Hmm. In Chinese culture the gong is sometimes used to welcome people. Buddhists sometimes strike gongs to make announcements or to call people to meditation. But I don't know why Mr. Bridges uses a gong. He's an American."

****

One day Mr. Bridges met Molly in a hallway, and he had a request of her. "I have been to many different Buddhist temples. I've been to the

Lao temple, the Cambodian temple, the Japanese temple, and the Burmese temple..." he told her, "...but I want to see a Chinese temple. I wonder if you could show me around a Chinese temple."

"Oh, are you a Buddhist?" Molly laughed. She had decided he must be joking with her about being a monk.

"Yes," he answered seriously.

Molly saw that he was sincere. She explained to him, "Oh, I could take you there, but I could not show you how Chinese Buddhists worship. I am a Christian, so I cannot do the things one is supposed to do in the Buddhist temple. As soon as you go in, you are supposed to fold your hands together and bow to the statues, and then you are supposed to light the incense stick and burn paper money for each god and goddess. There are so many! One for the earth, one for the door, one for the kitchen, the goddess of mercy, the Jade Emperor, gods of rivers and mountains and cities and stars and such a lot of gods! But I cannot do these things in the temple, because I am a Christian."

Mr. Bridges seemed surprised, "I see. I didn't know." He thought all Chinese in Burma were Buddhists.

"Yes," Molly said, "I have not worshiped at the Chinese temple since I was a little girl and followed my mother."

Mr. Bridges showed his disappointment.

Molly thought a moment. "Maybe I could ask my sister Dorothy to go with us. Then she could do the ceremonies. There is a Chinese temple on Hume Road." Dorothy could not go alone with Mr. Bridges, so Molly would have to escort them to the temple.

"Thank-you, Molly," Mr. Bridges said, "I really appreciate it."

The next time Molly went to visit her mother, she made the request of Dorothy. Molly was surprised by her reluctance, and Molly became more insistent. She was irritated by her sister's shyness.

"He's a nice man, Dorothy. You don't need to be afraid of him. All he wants is to see the temple. You know I cannot do the ceremonial things."

Finally Dorothy relented, but she qualified her help. "Don't ask me to talk to him!" she insisted. "You know I don't know English."

It was true that Dorothy did not have the advantage to be well-educated in English. Her education in all areas had suffered because of the war.

But Molly scolded, "You know some English! Don't say you don't know!" She continued to chide her little sister, "Don't worry. Don't be self-conscious. He's a nice man. He won't criticize your English."

"Okay, okay! I said I will go."

The trip to the temple went smoothly. Dorothy demonstrated ceremonial things as Molly explained to Mr. Bridges.

Soon after, Mr. Bridges invited Molly and her family to come to his apartment for dinner. "And bring your sister too," he encouraged.

Terence was too sick to go along. He was jealous that Molly was going without him, but she convinced him it would be a good experience for the children to visit the American man and that it would be rude to refuse.

Dorothy did not want to go. "Oh, no! You do not need me! I do not have to demonstrate temple things this time! And I will not know what you all are saying."

Molly coaxed, "You should come! You know enough English to understand what we are saying. I will do all the talking. It will be a good experience for you! If I did not work at the United States Embassy, you and I would never meet an American. They are nice people, and Mr. Bridges is very nice."

At last Dorothy was coerced, but most of the time she turned her back on the others. Mr. Bridges was indeed a gentlemanly host, and Molly and the children enjoyed themselves.

Mr. Bridges loved cats, and he had a cat at his apartment. He told his guests that he had purchased canned cat food from the United States, but some of the food had not been used by the expiration date printed on the cans, so he threw them away. A few days later, his Indian cook said, "Master, why did you throw away that food? I found it and took it home, and my family enjoyed this very much!"

Mr. Bridges did not have the heart to tell the man the food had been intended for cats or that it was old. No harm had come to them, so Mr. Bridges and Molly and the children laughed at the mistake. Molly translated the story for Dorothy, but she was disinterested.

****

Terence received an unexpected and very kind letter from the United States. It was from Cousin Edward! He explained that he had established himself in San Francisco, and he offered his assistance. "If you ever come to the United States," he wrote, "Come first to San Francisco in California. I will help you."

This gracious offer from the Lee Wat Hong branch was a great encouragement to Terence and Molly. Terence wrote back to him that they would gladly accept his kind offer.

But the months continued to drag by without progress in the Burmese bureaucracy! Still the paperwork sat on the first official's desk! Still the officials were blasé about Molly's urgency!

Maybe the delay was just the usual Burmese casual work ethic, as in the expression, "If you don't finish today, you finish tomorrow." Maybe it was caused by long breaks to sip tea. Maybe it was something more.

As the months passed, Mr. Joyce was replaced by Mr. Butcher. Mr. Butcher was replaced by Mr. Bigelow. Still no word from the Burmese government about clearing Molly's now stateless passport and giving her a VISA to travel.

A Chinese family that Molly knew from translating for the consular came to see him again. They had at last obtained the necessary paperwork, allowing them to leave Burma.

After the meeting, Molly asked the woman quietly, "Did you have any trouble getting your paperwork? How did you get it done?"

The woman laughed. But it was not a joyful laugh.

"What?" Molly asked. "What is funny?"

The woman stared at Molly a moment, her sarcastic smile gone. She said quietly, "You don't know?"

Molly said, "No. What?"

"These people eat coins," she said, using the Chinese expression for those who demand bribes.

Molly was confused at first. The woman continued in low but emphatic words, frowning, "You have to give presents to the officials. Each table. Do this, and then you will see your papers move."

"Really?" Molly asked. "Money?"

"Money might be okay, but you have to be careful. If you make your intentions obvious, you can be arrested for bribery. Or you can give them something they want, but even then you must be careful."

Molly blurted, "I don't have much money, and what do I have that the Burmese officials want?"

The savvy woman thought for just a moment. "You work here at the United States Embassy, right? Why don't you get some cigarettes from the commissary? Everyone wants to get some of those American cigarettes. I am sure the officials will be excited to get something new to smoke."

Molly thanked the woman. She did not explain to her that she was not allowed to buy things at the commissary.

Molly had to ponder her predicament for a while. There was no question in her mind that she would have to cooperate with corruption to get out of Burma. But what to do? If she gave money and was caught, she might be thrown into jail! But what did she have to give that would make her papers move and get her family out of danger and reunite them with Tony? How could she hurry the officials so that Terence could get the medical treatment he needed?

She discussed this new information with Terence. He gave it serious thought, and then he said the suggestion of the cigarettes was a good one.

Molly reminded him, a bit impatiently, "I'm not allowed to go to the commissary, as I told you. And even if I could go there, I do not have any U.S. dollars. You must have U.S. dollars to buy anything at the commissary."

"Ask someone to help you," Terence suggested.

"I don't know any Americans well enough to ask this big favor," Molly insisted.

"I think you will have to ask someone for help in getting the cigarettes," Terence repeated.

Praying to God, Molly said, "Oh Lord, thank-you for opening the way for the U.S. immigrant VISA, but another obstacle has come up. How do I get the American cigarettes to please the Burmese officials, so they can move my papers and give me the passports? Show me what to do. So often, You have sent someone to help me. Will You send someone to help me now?" She repeated this prayer many times over several days.

****

Mr. Bridges approached Molly at her desk. He told her, "I'm going down to the cafeteria for a coffee break. Will you join me?"

First Molly had to ask, "What is a coffee break?" Mr. Bridges explained that the phrase meant he was taking a short break from work to relax and drink coffee. He explained there was a cafeteria in the commissary.

Molly insisted, "No! Mr. Bridges, I can't go there! The commissary is not for the locals! Only American personnel can go there! The embassy is very strict about this."

To emphasize her knowledge of the rules, she added, "We cannot go up to the second floor, because that's a classified area. And we cannot go down to the commissary; that is for Americans only!"

Mr. Bridges said with emphasis to match hers, "Molly, you can go to the commissary if you go with me!" He smiled, "If I take you, they will let you go in."

Chastened, Molly replied quietly, "Oh. I didn't know that." Curiosity aroused, Molly relented. But she cautioned Mr. Bridges, "Okay. But I cannot be away for very long. Maybe a short time."

So she did join Mr. Bridges for a coffee break in the commissary. It was a fascinating place in the basement of the building, with a little café and many, many shelves of wonderful and sensible items for sale. She recognized one of the locals working there, wiping a counter with an intriguing object. The thing seemed to be much more effective at cleaning than a rag. Molly asked the Anglo-Burmese girl about the object, and she replied kindly that it was called a "sponge."

Molly repeated, "Oh, a sponge! Very nice!"

"Oh yes! Very nice!" The girl chatted about the virtues of the sponge.

Molly did not take long to notice the cartons of cigarettes. She wondered, "Maybe I could ask Mr. Bridges to help me. Maybe this is what the Lord God is showing me." She was quiet as she sipped the coffee. She could hardly keep from eying the cigarettes as Mr. Bridges spoke, as if she had to make sure the neat stacks of cartons remained there. What if someone came and bought them all? But, she could not gather the courage to broach the subject with Mr. Bridges.

Later, when Molly discussed this with Terence, he agreed, "Yes, Molly. Why don't you ask Mr. Bridges to help you? It can't hurt to ask him."

Molly wasn't sure she knew him well enough to ask such a favor. But she was desperate. After a few days, with Terence's urging, she approached Mr. Bridges.

"Do you think you can help me buy some cartons of cigarettes from the commissary?" she blurted.

"Why, Molly, have you taken up smoking?" Mr. Bridges teased.

She hoped she could trust him with the truth and knew she must take the risk. "I have to please those guys in the Burmese Emigration Department so they will pass my papers so I can get our passports approved to go to the United States."

Before Mr. Bridges could answer, Molly added, "If you will do this for me, I can only give you Burmese money to make the purchase. I cannot give you U.S. dollars, because I don't have any. And I know the commissary sells everything in U.S. dollars."

Mr. Bridges frowned as he understood Molly's predicament. But he considered a moment and told her kindly, "That's okay, because I need some Burmese money. I like to buy things from here to send to my friends, so I can always use some Burmese money."

Noting her concern, he assured her, "Don't feel badly. You will help me. In fact, I'm looking at some carved items I want to buy to send a friend."

Greatly relieved, Molly said, "Oh, that's good! Thank-you so much for doing this great favor so my family can go to the United States! I will bring some Burmese money for you tomorrow."

Mr. Bridges bought two cartons of cigarettes for her and said, "That's enough, Molly. Just give a few packs to each one."

Molly could hardly wait to show Terence her prize. Together they admired the treasure and thanked God. As soon as she could arrange it, she went eagerly to the Burmese Department of Emigration.

But she showed no excitement when she did the errand; she was demure and careful not to make a disturbance. She didn't say, "I give you this. Now please move my papers along!" She quietly talked to one officer about her paperwork, acknowledging that he was very busy, but could he be so kind as to check on her case? And then she discretely placed the cigarettes on the corner of his desk. She went to the next official, and the next, making certain each official in the large room was happy.

Each one in turn was already watching and waiting for his present, but no one said "Thank-you," only something very formal like, "We are doing everything possible to expedite your paperwork, Mrs. Lee." But Molly noticed the difference in their attitudes. Instead of looking indifferent, everyone was smiling and pleasant.

****

Terence had a pen pal in Minnesota. They had been writing to each other for many years, ever since Molly brought home a magazine from the USIS Library with an advertisement for international pen pals. Having heard Mr. Chrisman's health was not good, and happily unaware of the magnitude of his request, Terence now asked this pen pal, Larry Teien, and his wife, Marlene, to sponsor his family to come to the United States.

Larry, a friendly man employed in public relations, casually agreed, not realizing that he would be investigated. Even his financial stability was scrutinized so that he could support the Lee family if they couldn't find work. Nevertheless, Larry did not hesitate to keep his word, and his wife was also supportive.

When Terence heard of the conditions of sponsorship, he rushed to send a letter to assure Larry that he would not need to support them. Everyone in the family intended to work.

The family had to leave the Thirty-Fifth Street apartment to return it to Moonlight. If they vacated the flat without preparing for other renters to move in immediately, then squatters, protected by the government, could move in, or the government could confiscate the flat. Usually an occupied flat was not brazenly taken. So it was better to return the flat to Moonlight when she had another family ready to move in to it right away.

Terence arranged quietly with his mother to stay at Eight Mile for a short time, a few months, before going to the United States. The old house was occupied, so the family moved in to the remodeled pawn shop with Nye Nye and Lo Yeahr.

****

Mr. Bridges had invited Dorothy and Molly and the children to his place several times. Molly's mother reciprocated on her daughters' behalf, inviting Mr. Bridges to join her family for a Chinese meal. Molly's brothers came with their families, and Molly and her family attended.

Molly was chatting when Mr. Bridges leaned over and said to her, "Everyone is talking. Who is listening?"

Molly teased, "You are." Then she added, "We are talking and listening at the same time."

Mr. Bridges laughed heartily.

Moonlight suggested, "Let's give Mr. Bridges a Chinese name." After some discussion, the women decided on, "Liung," a clan name meaning, "Gift from Heaven."

Byu Goo and Ah Ma at the Chinese temple. Photograph by Mr. Bridges.

Molly heard her mother observe to Byu Goo, speaking in very polite, gentle language, "Ah, this man has very long ear lobes like Buddha. He will have a very long life. He also has big lips, the upper lip protruding, like Bud-

dha." Byu Goo nodded approvingly. This was done without Mr. Bridges'
understanding, because he did not know the dialect.

At first, Molly was embarrassed by this personal critique of Mr.
Bridges. But later when she saw him at work, she thought he might enjoy
the observation, and so she told him, "My mother read your facial fortune,
and she approves."

When Molly explained further, Mr. Bridges laughed. Also, he was
flattered by the comparison to Buddha.

After that, Mr. Bridges planned an excursion to a different Chinese
Buddhist temple on the outskirts of town, and he invited Molly's family to
join him. At first, because of the riots against the Chinese, the women were
afraid to travel. Mr. Bridges was able to calm their fears. Even Molly's mother
went, with Byu Goo, Dorothy, Wayne's family, and a family friend. Molly
went along too, leaving the children at home with their father. Mr. Bridges
took several pictures at the temple. Molly enjoyed seeing her mother and
Byu Goo looking so cheerful.

Chapter Thirty

"I Couldn't Get Him."

During the hot season, for the first time, Terence turned pessimistic. "I'm going to die," he told his wife.

She argued with him, "No Terence. You are going to live. We are going to move to the United States. The paperwork is almost ready. We are almost there, Terence. We are going to see Tony again. We are going to find treatment for your heart."

Terence shook his head sadly, but he didn't argue any more that day. Every few days he would repeat, "I'm going to die." Molly would not hear the foreboding word.

****

Finally, things seemed to be falling in to place. It was May 1968. Before the hot season, Owen had graduated from high school. Terence wrote in his son's autograph book to remember and strive for three most important things in life: good health, good education, and good morals and ethics. Tony was graduating from the university in the United States. Charlene was graduating from medical school in Burma. Paperwork was now moving within the Burmese government. Documents, attesting to the children's school work, and certificates, verifying each family member's good standing and that no accusations were leveled against them, were all approved and ready to be translated at the embassy. Molly had given the paperwork to the secretary, Mable, a local Indian woman, in the consular office.

Terence was unable to attend his daughter's graduation ceremony. Mrs. Lee also did not attend, but afterward she put on her fancy Chinese dress, reserved for grand occasions, and insisted on posing for a picture with Charlene. She told Charlene to put on her four-cornered cap and her graduate's gown. Molly stood for the photo as well.

****

From the soy sauce factory on Prome Road, Terence wrote the following letter to Tony on June 3, 1968:

Dear Tony,

This is the first time I have written after so many months. But I am following your letters and [am] the first to read [your letter] when it arrived. We are now processing to apply for our traveling papers. It may take many weeks, according to the regulation here.

Ever since we returned here, I was not well at all, like I was in Myeinigon. Always something happened. Due to salty water in the well, I often got swollen and have to take extra diuretic to relief me of the water retained in me. This week I have stomach trouble, so always something quite bothering.

Your sis is going to sit for the ECFMG exams here in September. Her present work keeps her very busy and she has lost weight much. James still keeps her company in the work, sent her home, have dinner in the house. Charlene seems to have no quarreling problem with him unlike with Charles. Charlene has the right to choose her own man. Your ma and I only point out the pros and cons of the two. At present James wanted to go to Australia. He has also passed the ECFMG and can also go to the states. We are not encouraging him to follow us because he has not even declare his love to Charlene because he knew Charles is waiting out in [Hong Kong]. Charles is so good that he offered to buy plane tickets for us to fly out to Taipei and to be his guest in H. K. But we wish only to buy ship tickets up to H. K. from here. This we hope to save for you some dollars and your burden will be lighter. This travel problems we will choose if later depends on any conditions that may develop later. James has a large number of brothers and sisters whom he must take care, where Charles will follow us any where we go.

Lois is learning steadily and much interested in ping pong games. Owen has grown quite tall. Yesterday he went to have his first suit made. The material was bought two years ago. He still needs a pair of shoes for his new size foot.

I presume you will be working very hard for your coming exams. With your additional duties besides your class work, we hope you can go through the exams fairly well.

I wonder how long the convocation will take place after the exams. If that day should arrived, which your ma and I have hope and waited all these years, I hope you will spend some time and money to take some good beautiful photographs with cap and gown together with your friends and professors so that we can show them to grandma and pa, (to make them talk). It will be a great souvenir. Please keep well.

Dad

(Each of us plan to work there when we arrive, so you can save for your further study. Including me.)

****

A few days later, clutching his chest, Terence said very seriously, "Molly, I don't think

I will be able to go to the United States. You must go and take the kids."

This was unthinkable! Molly told him, "I cannot go and leave you here! You must go with us,

Terence."

Terence shook his head sadly.

Later in the day, Terence cried out to Molly the familiar words, "Get me to the hospital!"

It was a weekend, and Molly was glad she was home, so she could take her husband right away to the hospital. She spent most of her time with him over the weekend. When she had to return to her job the next week, she took the bus to see him after work each evening.

Terence had been in the hospital a few days already when Molly waited after work for a ride from her father-in-law. She was a little late getting to the hospital. Terence's father did not stay, because he was too superstitious to go in to the hospital to see his son, fearful of meeting a ghost that would make him sick.

When Terence saw Molly, he complained, "Why are you so late?"

She explained defensively, "Your dad! I came with your dad, and he had to stop a couple places before he dropped me here. It was nice of him to offer to come for me, Terence. He hasn't offered before. Usually I have to wait for the bus."

"Oh," Terence said quietly. "I didn't know."

Charlene was sitting on the edge of her father's bed, and Charlene's friend Phyllis sat beside her. Phyllis's mother was seated nearby, and Molly took the chair beside her and spoke to her. Many other patients lay in beds, and their visitors huddled around them, filling the large ward with people and their murmuring.

Phyllis was talking with Terence. Molly heard her ask, "Why don't I say a prayer for you?"

Instead of speaking to God in her own words, as Molly often did, Phyllis recited the prayer Lord Jesus prayed with his disciples, called "The Lord's Prayer." Molly had known this prayer since her days at the Methodist English High School. She bowed her head with the others as Phyllis spoke.

Our Father, which art in Heaven, Hallowed be Thy name.
Thy kingdom come. Thy will be done, on earth as it is in Heaven.
Give us this day our daily bread.
And forgive us our debts as we forgive our debtors.
And lead us not into temptation, but deliver us from evil.
For Thine is the kingdom, and the power, and the glory forever. Amen.

After the prayer, Molly's eyes were drawn to Terence. Phyllis's mother was still talking to her, but Molly couldn't keep her eyes off of him. His head rolled slightly to one side and the other, then he closed his eyes, and his head dropped forward. Molly felt something was different.

She said to Charlene, "Check your Dad."

Charlene looked at her father and then quickly ran to get the doctor in charge of the ward. Molly would never forget the sight of the young doctor in a longyi, jumping onto the bed and pressing repeatedly on Terence's chest. Someone quickly drew a curtain around the bed, leaving an image in Molly's mind of the frantic doctor on the still body. From the sounds, Molly knew the doctor continued the anxious effort to compress Terence's heart, trying to make it start pumping again. Charlene was also behind the curtain.

After several minutes passed, the young doctor came out and said quietly to Molly, "I'm sorry. I couldn't get him...."

"What?" She asked quietly. She heard, but did not understand.

"I couldn't get him," the doctor repeated. "I'm sorry."

Charlene said, "Go home, Mom. We will take care of things."

Molly felt the eyes of the other patients and visitors as she left the ward mechanically. She couldn't believe that Terence was really dead. All these years, she had known he might die from his weak heart. But when it happened, she couldn't have been more stunned.

It was June 21, 1968, at 5:30 pm. The "time of death" was significant to the hospital culture, and all paperwork was marked with it. Whether or not such details were significant, the death of Terence was life-changing for Molly. For so many years, her life had revolved around this man, and surely she had grown to love him and to depend on him.

She hardly knew what to think. She couldn't imagine a future without him.

As a season of numbness entered her, she did have a few lucid thoughts. She was grateful that she had gotten to the hospital in time to see her husband once more before he died. She hadn't been there even a half hour! She would have always regretted it, if she had come too late! She thanked God.

And she was grateful that Phyllis had been praying with him just before he died. It was the only time Phyllis and her mother had come to visit, and Molly thought it was good for Terence to hear the beautiful prayer as he was leaving this world. She thanked God.

She was trying to count her blessings. She really was trying. But the loss was great. It was as if a part of herself was removed, and she carried the wound.

In the immediacy of coping with Terence's death, Molly was at a loss of what to do. She could no longer ask Terence for his advice. But she remembered she could pray to God for help, so she did this, and help came.

Molly agreed with hospital staff that Terence's body could be taken to the morgue instead of being displayed in the street. The day after his death, Molly took his good clothes to the morgue, expecting to dress his body for the funeral.

Charlene met her and said, "Give them to me."

Molly asked, "Why? Who is going to dress him?"

Charlene answered, "James has offered to do it for us." James was one of Charlene's suitors, as Terence mentioned in his last letter to Tony. He had been a medical student a year ahead of Charlene and was now also a doctor. He was quite fond of Charlene.

"Oh." Molly was relieved. "I thought I would have to do it."

Mr. Jacobs, the second accountant from the embassy, who also was a deacon at the Immanuel Baptist Church, came to Molly and offered, "I will do the funeral service for you, if you want."

She was grateful.

Molly's mother-in-law summoned her. When Molly was seated across from her, Nye Nye dropped a stack of bills on the table in front of Molly and said simply, "Buy him a coffin."

Molly saw the pain on Nye Nye's face. She knew Nye Nye was blaming her for her son's ruined life and tragic death. But her help was sincerely appreciated. Molly bowed her head slightly and humbly said, "Thank-you, Nye Nye."

The family friend, Rudy, offered to drive the family to the service in his car. Molly gratefully accepted.

Charlene took care of many of the details for her mother. She put an obituary in the newspaper. "Lee Puck Ying, (Terence Lee), son of Lee Sit Hong... will be buried at the Baptist Christian Cemetery...."

Molly didn't expect to see many people at the funeral; she thought that Chinese and Burmese acquaintances would avoid a Christian ceremony, and she didn't know many western people. She knew she could not expect to see Terence's parents. They believed it was a bad omen to attend the funeral of one's own child.

But, surprisingly, hundreds of people did attend the service. Even in her numbed state, Molly was amazed that many from the Chinese community came, a moving salute of respect to Terence and his family. She noticed with appreciation that Terence's Number Five Sister Fe Yin and her husband were in attendance.

As Mr. Jacobs had promised, he took care of everything about the service. He spoke appropriate things, comforting at the time but not retained by Molly's mourning mind. Then he instructed that the coffin to be lowered into the hole in the earth. Even after seeing the finality of the coffin in the ground, Molly still couldn't comprehend that Terence was really gone.

****

The official coroner's report stated the cause of Terence's death was digoxin overdose. The very thing that had calmed his rapid heartbeat, giving him some measure of relief for so many years, was the thing that caused his death. The digoxin had been such a help to Terence, there was no point regretting its use.

As the days and weeks and months went by and the reality of Terence's death seeped into her, raw and wrenching mourning continued sporadically and unpredictably, and tears sprang often from the deep well of sorrow. Molly kept thinking of how close they were to going to the United States together. She was very sorry that he was not going to be able to live out his dream. She wondered what she could have done differently to make the paperwork move more quickly.

After a few weeks, Molly returned to work. She was glad for the busy schedule and the distraction of typing dry memorandums and rows and columns of numbers.

Miss Palmer told Molly that she was sorry for her loss. She said the service for Terence was very good.

"Oh." Molly apologized, "I'm sorry, Miss Palmer. I didn't see you there."

"No wonder, Molly. There were so many people."

"But I should have spoken to you."

"It's alright Molly," Miss Palmer said gently. "You didn't need to talk to me. You were busy grieving."

Molly was moved by her boss's compassion. "Thank-you for coming," she said sincerely.

According to Chinese custom, Molly must wear white or black mourning clothes for three months. She chose a white jacket to go with a black longyi. She wore no make-up.

Chapter Thirty-One

Flight to Freedom

It was several months before Molly could focus again on getting her children out of Burma. Leaving without Terence didn't seem right, but she remembered his words just before he went to the hospital for the last time. "You must go and take the kids." She must find a way to continue this path without him.

Molly was grateful that Nye Nye let them stay at Eight Mile. But she felt an incentive to renew her efforts to leave the country when lights started going out in the evenings while Molly's children were studying. Clearly Molly was wearing out her welcome with Nye Nye.

Molly felt a seed of anger threatening to grow in her. She thought defensively, "I make very little money, but still I give Nye Nye something for the electricity. She should not treat my children this way, turning out the lights while they study." Then, as soon as she recognized her need, she prayed that God would help her to be free of the unpleasant burdens of anger and bitterness.

Molly calmly told her children not to be angry, reminding herself in the process. " 'Do not let the sun go down on your anger,' " She quoted from the Bible. " 'Forgive seventy times seven.' "

Her children did not roll their eyes when Molly repeated these verses familiar to their ears. They listened respectfully to the words Molly had earned the right to speak, by which she had lived through many difficulties.

She expounded, "We must find a way to show grace when we are unjustly treated, as our Lord Jesus taught us by His example. Remember to be grateful that Nye Nye is letting us stay here in her house. It is kind of her. We will work around this. Let nothing bother you. You can use a candle, and you will study by candlelight like Abraham Lincoln. Anyway, we won't be here much longer."

****

Molly realized that nothing was happening with the paperwork now sitting in the consular office.   She suspected the reason for the delay.

She purchased a silk longyi and wrapped it in a bag. She took it to work with her and placed it on Mable's desk.

"Oh, Mable," she said casually. "I thought maybe you could use this."

Mable smiled pleasantly, but made no reply. Within a few days the paperwork was completed, all of the translations were done, and all of the copies were made.

Years later Molly would hear that someone complained to the consular officer that the secretary was expecting bribes. He was very concerned and asked this person to mark the bills he gave Mable for the bribe. Mable accepted the sum and put it in her desk drawer while she went to lunch. When she came back to the embassy, Molly heard, the marine guard would not let her pass, and Mable never worked at the embassy again. Molly liked that Americans did not allow these things to continue.

****

At age twenty-five, Charlene was too old to travel as a child on Molly's VISA. Once Molly was in the states, she would petition for her daughter. Still, leaving Charlene behind was one of the hardest things she would ever have to do. It was a comfort to know that Nye Nye would let her stay at Eight Mile a while longer. Nye Nye respected Doctor Charlene, and Molly thought if anyone could keep Charlene safe, it was Nye Nye.

Molly reasoned this way: "I hate to leave her. Maybe she will not be able to follow us. I have heard that in other countries, educated people, like engineers and doctors, are stopped from leaving. Luckily, Burma has not realized yet how much they need these people, so they still let them go, especially if they are not Burman. Maybe because she is Chinese, they will be glad for her to leave. I pray they will let Charlene go. We have to take this chance for our family. Freedom is most important. I would rather lose all my money or whatever I own and get our freedom. I have great faith in the United States, because I have read about the democratic life there. I love the system. It is good for Owen to start college there. It is good for Lois to finish college and find work there. It will be good for Charlene to go there in a few months, and she cannot join us if I don't go and petition for her. We must do this for our future freedom. God is making a way for us. I must trust God and follow where He leads me. I must trust Him to take care of Charlene."

Tony was barking orders from across the Pacific Ocean. Communication was facilitated by Miss Palmer, who, as promised, let Molly use the official U.S. mail system, avoiding the local censors and slow-downs.

"Fly to Hong Kong. It will be good for you to stay with Charles's family for a few days to rest for your big trip," Tony wrote. "I will send him money for plane tickets to the United States. You must buy tickets to San Francisco. I have spoken with Dad's cousin Edward. He will pick you up at the airport, and you can stay with him a few days to rest. I will also send money for you to buy coats in Hong Kong. Make sure everyone has a coat, a heavy, wool coat. It is very cold here."

Tony with the Teien family.

Tony also wrote that he had "hitchhiked" to Minnesota to meet their sponsors, Larry and Marlene. He found them to be kind and eager to sponsor the family from Burma.

Hitchhiked? Ah, Owen could explain hitchhiking to his mom: Tony had walked along the road with his thumb extended, a hand-signal indicating he wanted a ride from a passerby. The driver would pull over and explain how far along the road he expected to drive. Tony would accept a ride if the driver was headed the right direction. Grinning, Owen showed his mom the "Hitchhiker" dance that had made its way to the Burmese youth, pumping his right arm with thumb extended over his right shoulder, then repeating the motion with his left arm, then rotating his fists around each other in a winding motion, more "thumbing," and cool hops left and right. Molly enjoyed watching Owen dance. Hitch-hiking sounded to Molly like a fun way of traveling; she was mercifully unaware that some who picked up hitchhikers preyed upon them, making the practice risky.

Molly was surprised to receive a letter from Larry in the United States. He spoke highly of Tony. "I didn't know your son spoke English so well! And he is talented! He plays the guitar very well! I was so surprised. He seems to be a very nice young man. I am quite impressed by him."

****

Molly prepared the few possessions they were permitted to take from Burma. Their Burmese cash would be exchanged for one hundred U.S. dollars as they were leaving the country. They could each take a small bag of clothes. They could not take any jewelry, except the one tical gold piece, and they would not risk trying to take more. Anyway, most of Molly's jewelry had been sold to pay expenses. She would buy three plane tickets to Hong Kong; emigrants from Burma were on their own to figure out how they would travel from there to their final destinations. If Tony wasn't able to send money for plane tickets, they would be stuck in Hong Kong until they could somehow make enough money to continue to the States.

Any cash Molly had left would go to Charlene. A condition of her leaving Burma was that she would need to pay for her college education, since she was not going to pay it off working for the government.

****

Molly sadly tore up the precious letters from Tony and the kind letters Terence had received from Mr. Chrisman and Larry. She couldn't risk arousing the suspicion of Burmese officials as she was searched.

Mr. Bridges had offered kindly, "Molly, is there anything I can help you get to the United States, like maybe some pictures? It is risky, because I would have to send them with my boxes of personal items before I return to the United States. They would be stored in a warehouse for awhile. Sometimes these things get lost."

"Of course!" Molly was delighted by this offer. "Maybe my pictures will be lost, but if I leave them here, no one will want them. They are precious to me, so it will be worth trying to save them! Thank-you Mr. Bridges! You are very kind!"

She brought him the treasured little box of photographs. Most of these were ones Terence had taken: the pictures of herself frowning at him when she was a student trying to study, the photo of the apple green Morris open coupe surrounded by relatives, a couple pictures from Namhsan, many pictures from Terence's construction job in Moulmein, pictures of her with Charlene and Tony among the petrol cans at the house across from the soy sauce compound, pictures of her Chin family in Maymyo, and photos of her smiling and embracing her four children. She also had a little stack of pictures given to her by the embassy photographer, pictures of herself and co-workers at the USIS library.

Mr. Bridges asked a favor of his own. "Molly, when you get to the United States, will you stop and see my mother? I know you are arriving in San Francisco. I was wondering if you could go to Albuquerque, New Mexico for a few days on your way to Maryland. My mother will show you hospitality, and you could rest before flying east."

"Yes! Of course!" Molly eagerly accepted the invitation. Mr. Bridges seemed such a kind man, she was glad to cooperate with his request and to receive his mother's hospitality.

"Then she will know you are real people and that you don't live in trees," Mr. Bridges added.

"What?" Molly was startled by his comment and searched his face. He grinned at her.

"I want my mother to see that you are human beings," Mr. Bridges said.

"What? Of course we are human beings!" Molly was incredulous. She studied him again to try to interpret his meaning. She suspected he was joking with her.

Mr. Bridges was smiling, but he was not entirely happy. "I told my mother about you, suggesting you could stop by for a few days, and she asked me, 'do they live in a house or in a tree?' I told her, 'These people live in houses like you.' She has no awareness of people from other countries. She has seen pictures of primitive people in National Geographic, and she thinks everyone from another country is primitive. She thinks if you live in Burma, you look different, you must live in trees, and you don't speak

English. I want her to see what real Sino-Burmese people look like. She will see, too, how well you speak English."

Of course, Mr. Bridges would never mean to say primitive people were not fully human. But he was irritated that his mother was stereotyping people of foreign lands. Molly would show his mother that foreign people could be quite refined.

Molly smiled, "I will be glad to visit your mother. After we spend a few days with my husband's Cousin Edward in San Francisco, we will go to Albuquerque before continuing to Maryland."

Now that the time of their departure was near, Molly worried about whether or not she would be able to find work to support her children in the United States. She risked discussing this with a few close friends at the embassy. The answer was always the same; her typing and shorthand skills would be useful in the United States. She should be able to find work.

****

At last all was ready, every detail was in order, all the documents were procured, and the plane tickets were purchased. In the final few days, Molly gave away most of her belongings, keeping only what she could carry in her suitcase.

Molly expressed gratitude to the maid for her service and gave her most of her clothes. The young woman accepted gratefully, but she cried pitifully.

"Oh, *Ah Ma Gyi*, Big Sister!" she blurted. "You have been so good to me! What will become of me now? When I work for a Burmese family, I must sleep on the floor! If they are dissatisfied with me, they might beat me! They will give me inferior rice to eat. They will not care about me."

Molly was surprised by her fear. "You are not inferior to me!" She insisted. "What I eat, you eat! What I do, you do!" She tried to comfort her, and not knowing what else to do, she wrote for her a complimentary letter of recommendation.

Owen had his own difficult arrangements to make. He found a home for his little dog, Hercules. The pet had been a great comfort to him.

Mr. Bridges had contacted his mother, and she would be expecting them. He was still poking fun at her. "She asked me, 'Do they eat bacon? Do they eat eggs? Do they eat bread?' I told her, 'They eat everything you eat.' It's important for you to spend a few days with her," he repeated, "so she can see you are human."

****

At last, Molly had to say her "Goodbyes," realizing that she may never again see people very precious to her. She went to visit Ah Ma.

"Mama, I am going to *Me Kok!*" Ngood said.

Mama was overjoyed. She was glad her daughter would escape the terrible things happening in Burma and go to paradise on earth.

"Once I get settled there, I will try to get you over," Ngood told her. "I can petition for you to come and live with me. But it may take some time."

Ah Ma smiled and nodded. But how would her sheltered mother fare beyond her apartment, let alone beyond Burma?

Molly noticed that Ah San was missing from the Lee compound. He had recently completed his master's degree in chemical engineering at Rangoon University. Molly was surprised to find out that he left ahead of them for the United States. Though she had helped him with the application process, she didn't know that his paperwork had gone through, his secret being kept even from her.

In parting, Nye Nye was kind as she spoke words of good fortune to Ngood, "I wish you a better life, a free life, in the United States."

Number Four Sister Fe Heng startled Molly with her words, "Ah khlow, sister-in-law, when you go to America, you can find yourself a good husband."

She knew Fe Heng's comment came from the best of intentions. A Chinese widow's good fortune would be to remarry well in the land of wealth.

"Thank-you for your kind thought, but I will see to my children and make sure they get good educations," Molly replied.

The actual moment of leaving Charlene behind was painful. Molly reminded herself that Charlene was in the care of Nye Nye, and in the greater care of God. Charlene would be very busy in the meantime, working to repay the Burmese government.

Miss Palmer gave Molly an envelope and instructed her to take it with her to the United States. "It should help you to find work. It is a letter of recommendation."

Molly read the words, though her eyes were clouded with tears by the end:

"To whom it may concern:

Mrs. Molly Lee has had long service with the American Embassy in Rangoon. She began her career in May 1951 with the U.S. Information Service and worked in the library until this activity was curtailed in 1965. At that time she joined the staff of the embassy Budget and Fiscal Office where she did the secretarial work, filing, typing of reports and general office work.

I have known Mrs. Lee since December 1966 and have found her to be a conscientious employee, willing to accept new tasks and taking pride in completing her work neatly and accurately. She exercises good judgment when a decision is needed. Her quiet, pleasant personality has always been an asset to the office.

Mrs. Lee's knowledge of English is extremely good. Because of her knowledge of Chinese her services as interpreter were used by other offices in the embassy. She also is proficient in Burmese.

Mrs. Lee's presence will be greatly missed; however, I am happy that she has an opportunity to live in the United States. From my acquaintance with her children I feel sure they will enjoy their new surroundings and can look forward to successful futures. Mrs. Lee has the best wishes of all of us who worked with her for a happy and fruitful new life.

This letter is my personal recommendation of Mrs. Lee's services and cannot be considered as an endorsement by the United States Government.

Sincerely,
Margery J. Palmer
Budget and Fiscal Officer"

Oh, Miss Palmer gave her a tall hat!

****

Just before boarding the airplane, Molly, Lois, and Owen were to be searched by emigration officials. Molly dreaded having the humiliation of her body scrutinized by a stranger. But she had nothing to hide. No material thing was worth the risk of slamming shut the door to freedom.

The woman led her to a private room, signaled for Molly to sit down, and she did the same. The two women sat quietly looking at each other. Molly was confused and felt awkward, but she waited in silence. The woman continued looking without expression at Molly, not hinting at what to think or to expect. Molly averted her eyes to the floor, waiting in misery. After some minutes, the woman stirred, and as Molly looked, she caught the signal to follow. Oh dear! Molly could not guess where the woman was taking her.

She was surprised to be led back to Lois and Owen and to be dismissed. In a few quick whispers she found that her children had similar treatment.

She feared that something was dreadfully wrong; maybe a real search would come later. Maybe they were going to jail instead.

But, they were told to stand in line to board their plane. As her fears began to subside, Molly looked at the airplane. "Pan American," was written across the side of the big plane, and the name filled Molly with hope. She observed that the plane did not look like the rough, military transport she had taken to Maymyo.

Once inside the plane, Molly admired the plush seats that faced the front of the plane instead of hard benches that lined the sides. The interior seemed to her designed for royalty. A row of little windows lined each side of the airplane, flooding the compartment with cheery light. Owen took the seat next to the window, Lois was in the middle, and Molly sat on the aisle, protective of her children. A stewardess instructed passengers to fasten their seat belts. Molly tried to prepare her children for what was to come. She remembered that on the flight to Maymyo she felt as if someone were pushing her off the bench and pulling Charlene from between her legs as the plane took off, and she instinctively reached her arm over Lois and Owen to keep them from sliding.

Oh, but this was better! It still felt as if she were being pushed as they sped down the runway, but she was pushed into the comfortable seat, not off of a slippery bench. The sound was very loud and powerful, but it was more muted than she was expecting. Molly looked to see if Lois and Owen appeared fearful, but their faces showed only excitement as they peered out of the window. Molly also turned to look. The speeding ground fell below, and, so quickly, her perspective became completely new. Sides of big buildings became little rooftops, and cars and people became tiny, moving toys.

Within moments, she had left behind her home, her family, friends, all that was familiar, with hardly a chance to say "Goodbye." Molly would miss her loved ones, but she could not regret this path. This was an opportunity, a provision, which must be embraced with all eagerness and readiness. Hope replaced despair; excitement replaced lethargy; already the cautious breath of freedom replaced stifling oppression. Molly felt the metaphor of her flight up into the wide open sky like a bird set free from captivity in Burma.

Her still tender heart tugged with unavoidable sorrow that Terence was not with her for this splendid emancipation. She felt so sorry. Oh, Terence wanted so much to go to America!

Molly prayed, "Lord, I have no control over this matter. I cannot bring Terence back, and I must go on with my life without him. Please help me to do that."

Molly recalled the precious moment when Terence spoke the loving words, giving up his own dreams, letting go of his protective grasp on Molly, and blessing his family. The words moved her more now than when he first spoke them: "Molly, I don't think I will be able to go to the United States. You must go and take the kids." The memory saddened her deeply, but she felt she was right to honor his wishes.

Then she envisioned a vibrant and well Terence, and she imagined his youthful grin at her. She didn't know if Terence could see her from Heaven, but she knew that he had been restored to good health in that beautiful land of no more tears, and she was comforted.

She tried not to worry about Charlene, but the strings of her heart were tied fast to the daughter left behind, tugging painfully with each mile of separation as the airplane hurled through the sky. Molly prayed to God, nearly without ceasing, asking Him to give Charlene safety until she could make her own escape. Again, God comforted her.

The thrill on the faces of her two youngest children was contagious. Molly leaned into Lois to join their experience, drawn with fascination to the alien ground below.

Molly thought of her childhood when she climbed the roof of the four-story house and saw the sights of Chinatown from her perch. Oh, but this was different – she saw a miniaturized world in stunning panorama! Burma spread below her, with golden pagodas gleaming in the sunlight like scattered jewels. Beyond the city of Rangoon, the countryside spread in patches of green and gold and brown, and bumps of mountains sat on the horizon's edge. The great rivers, viewed one by one, appeared only as long, winding brush strokes to the Andaman Sea. The airplane had flown so high into the sky as to leave scarcely a shadow below, as if Molly was already forgotten by the land of her birth, where she had invested a lifetime of work and influence; afterall, she was approaching fifty already and would probably not live too much longer.

Oddly, having left the earth's surface, they seemed to be moving quite slowly. Then, as they went over the moutains, the airplane's shadow raced up and down the spectacular topography, a reminder of the impossible speed at which they were advancing. As they were alternately over the nearly-touched mountain peaks and the bottomless crevasses, the plane's shadow ballooned and diminished. Well, maybe Molly's own shadow would land somewhere and still have a bit of influence.

Molly viewed the rugged jungles bordering Burma and Thailand. Oh my! How could anyone escape Burma over such terrain? She thanked God that Tony did not try this. What they passed over in minutes or an hour could take a healthy man many days to traverse.

Seeing the world this way, Molly mused, "What is grand to men is small to God." Once again, she was awed by God's personal attention to her, providing this lavishly appointed ride to the Promised Land.

Molly reminded her children of their geography lessons: after Thailand, they would cross above Laos, then the troubled land of Vietnam, before reaching the waters of the South China Sea.

Molly noticed Owen, peering rapturously out the window.

She said, "Owen! Write down what you see!" Owen accepted her advice and alternately studied the window and his journal entries.

The plane had climbed to a high altitude and then leveled off. Stewardesses informed passengers that seatbelts could be removed. Soon after, an American Marine came to speak to Molly. She had noticed several American personnel on the plane that she recognized from working at the embassy, and she was acquainted with the man, but she was surprised that he came to speak to her. Until now, they had only spoken casually, "Hello," and "How are you?"

"Hello Molly," he said familiarly.

"Oh, hi," she said, trying to conceal her wonder about his attention. She asked conversationally, as if they often had these friendly chats, "Are you going back to the States?"

"Yes, I am," he replied.

"Will you be coming back to Burma?"

"No, I don't think so. I'm going back for furlough. Then I will be sent to another country."

He said, "I have to give you something."

Molly was startled, "What?"

He handed her a small, neatly wrapped package and explained, "This is from Margery Palmer."

"Oh, thank-you so much!" Molly effused. She had no idea what might be in the package, but she was grateful that her boss had thought of her, and that this agent was kind enough to deliver the gift.

"Oh sure," he replied in a friendly way. Then he confided, "Miss Palmer insisted, 'Don't give this to Molly at the airport! Don't give it to her anywhere except in the airplane when it has left Burmese air space!' "

Molly was unsure what was meant by "air space," but she thanked him again. Was it polite to open it right away or to wait?

He urged her, "Open it!"

Inside was a pretty coin purse. Molly thought it was a lovely gift, but the marine repeated, "Go ahead. Open it and look at what's inside."

"Oh, I thought the gift was the purse," Molly answered meekly. "It's very nice."

Lois and Owen were watching as Molly opened the purse. She pulled out a twenty dollar bill! Molly had rarely even seen a U.S. note, with the exception of the three bills she was permitted to carry from Burma. Molly showed the children. "This is not Burmese money! This is a real U.S. twenty dollar bill!"

The man explained, "Miss Palmer wanted you to have it, in case you need a little extra."

Molly marveled at the generous gift, and she let each of the children hold it in turn. "Oh, this will help me! Thank-you! Thank-you!"

The man, pleased to have completed his duty so successfully, returned to his seat. Molly wondered, "How will I ever thank Miss Palmer? I may never see her again."

"See how the Lord works for me?" she asked herself, determined to always remember His provision. "It is a blessing

Margery Palmer

from the Lord." Even late in life she would think of this kindness to her and feel like crying for overwhelming gratitude.

Molly meditated on the goodness of her God. As she did so, eventually, a mere whisper of a thought quieted a nagging question. Maybe it was Molly's brother-in-law, an immigration officer, who had secretly intervened for her and her children and spared them the indignity of a strip search before leaving the airport in Rangoon. Did he take such a risk for her? She would never know for sure, but no matter who was the agent, Molly saw it as more of God's grace to her.

Chapter Thirty-Two

The Golden Mountain

But the flight home to freedom would come in increments. The first measure of the trip, from Mingaladon Airport to Hong Kong International Airport, took several hours. Molly and the children would spend a few days in Hong Kong to rest and prepare for the next leg of the journey. As promised, Tony had sent money for them to buy their plane tickets to San Francisco and to buy coats. Tony knew that Hong Kong had high quality, inexpensive goods from all over the world, and this was a good place for the travelers to do necessary shopping.

Charles picked them up at the airport and took them to his home. The multistoried buildings in his neighborhood were crowded together like people on a Rangoon city bus! The towering structures appeared modern and stylish, but they were so close together that even clothes, hanging to dry on bamboo poles in the scant "air space," hung limply as if they too were confined. People poured like a flood from the apartments, so that in the streets Molly felt there was scarcely room to move!

Charles wanted them to do a little sightseeing, and on one excursion they took a ferry boat from the island of Hong Kong to a peninsula of the mainland, *Kowloon*, "Nine dragons." The area is surrounded by eight mountains, and according to legend, the emperor counting them was the ninth dragon. It is one of the most densely populated regions of the world. Molly would not remember anything about the area, but she would never forget the fear of crowding on to that boat with so many other people. She was sure the boat would sink!

But what a relief for the three refugees to be away from the stifling worries of Burma and in the warm hospitality, even pampering, they found in Hong Kong! The host family was kind and wealthy, the food was lavish, and the accommodations lacked nothing.

Molly noticed the family members entertained themselves hour after hour playing Mahjong. She had not experienced such leisurely living since her childhood, and she was surprised to find she did not aspire to it. Of course, for now she was glad for the respite, but she also had an inkling that she would very much miss having work to do.

Soon, Molly and the children were on their way to San Francisco. Molly was divided in emotions: she was thrilled to actually be going to the United States, but unable to stop mourning that Terence was gone and that Charlene was left behind, and feeling a little trepidation about the future. Was she doing the right thing? She prayed to God for peace and tried to focus on the future of her children, as Terence had instructed.

The duration of the flight was enough to eventually tire the travelers and to somewhat diminish the thrill of flying, but they continued to look with wonder at the expansive ocean waters, the coastlines, and the landmasses, and to be in awe of the immensity of the planet earth. Unlike a well-labeled map, the sights below were unknowable, and the travelers were mystified and mesmerized. Also confusing, somewhere along their journey above the earth, they crossed International Date Line, mysteriously going back to the previous calendar day, though they were not experiencing the events or the place of the day before. Hour after hour, even in fatigue, anticipation was swelling as they approached the land of their dreams.

What a thrill as the airplane began its decent! What a joy as the airplane touched down on the runway in San Francisco! After so many hours of thwarted movement in the speeding plane, the enthusiastic international visitors went bustling to the U.S. Port of Entry. Here they were inspected by customs to see if they had any illegal substances, or any goods on which they must pay a duty, but neither were found in Molly's party. Molly dutifully handed over the chest x-rays of herself and her children, proving they didn't have tuberculosis; otherwise they would have had to go to quarantine. She was relieved that officials seemed happy with all of her paperwork

They entered into the airport to face a crowd of people waiting to meet their parties. Molly, Lois, and Owen scanned the unfamiliar, unresponsive, foreign faces.

At last Molly recognized the large frame and smiling face of Terence's Cousin Edward! What a comfort to be swept along with his confident expertise and hospitality!

Edward was a jovial fellow and caring of people. He seemed especially to care for these relatives needing help. After his formal greeting, he urged them to the carousel.

"What's that?" Molly asked.

"That is where you get your luggage," Edward answered. "That is why I have come to take care of you. I know you will not understand these things. Watch. Soon you will see your luggage. Tell me when you see what belongs to you, and we will have to grab it."

Sure enough, just as Edward explained, a long, snaking curve of luggage came along on a conveyor system. People gathered around it, waiting. Sometimes, someone from the crowd would go and snatch a suitcase or two. Molly noticed some of the suitcases were not taken and continued on the conveyor until they disappeared from view. What if she missed her suitcases? Would these, containing her last few possessions on earth, also disappear?

Molly watched anxiously. Soon, she recognized her own bags, and she pointed to them and shouted with great animation. To Molly's relief, Edward skillfully removed the bags from the moving table. What a wonderful place was this United States!

Edward's wife was an excellent hostess, and she served familiar Chinese cuisine. Molly would remember especially enjoying the Chinese noodles. Ah, no wonder Nye Nye had great admiration for this woman!

After the travelers had a little rest, Edward showed them some of the Chinese restaurants, temples, and Cantonese shops of San Francisco's Chinatown, the largest Chinatown outside of Asia. They were able to walk to the vicinity from Edward's house, but Molly was amazed by the steepness of the walk. Edward said the area was called "Seven Hills" and the streets went up and down sharply. This was nothing like the flat ground of the flood plain around Rangoon.

Molly asked Edward, "How come we don't feel good?"

He said, "You must be having different hours." He explained the condition often referred to as "jet lag," when the traveler's body needs time to adjust to a drastic change in time zones.

516 | GENTLE MOON

"Your bodies are still used to Burma time," he said knowingly. "Right now it is noon in San Francisco."

"Yes." Molly could see the sun was high in the sky.

"But in Burma, the sun has not yet appeared. The sun cannot be two places at the same time. In Burma it is around one o'clock in the morning. Your body is used to that time. Your body wants to sleep now."

"But I can't sleep all day and stay up all night! I don't want to live this way in America!" Molly moaned. Thinking this was a permanent condition, she was quite concerned.

"Oh, it will not last too long," Edward consoled her. "Do not worry. Your body will adjust. You will be fine in a few days or maybe a week."

They also saw Edward's sister, the first of the family to come to America. She told Molly that many Sino-Burmese lived in the area. They would sometimes hear a Chinese person speaking Bumese as they rode a bus, and a friendly conversation would develop.

A few days later, Edward suggested they see some sights before leaving San Francisco. He took them on a taxi ride to the famous, steep, winding Lombard Street with eight hairpin turns in one block. Molly thought of the switchbacks on the dusty road near the Gokteik Viaduct when she and Terence were on the way to Namhsan. But she smiled to think how different was this compact switchback with modern apartment buildings in two straight rows down the hillside and the road zigzagging down the middle. There hadn't been a house in sight along the sweeping switchbacks near the viaduct.

Edward also took them to see the area around the San Francisco Bay. He showed them the Golden Gate Bridge, a six lane, 1.7 mile, suspension bridge. Edward explained that the bridge was completed in 1937, when Molly was fifteen, allowing travelers to drive north of the San Francisco Peninsula across the bay without the need for a ferry service. Molly could see the spectacular bridge was both beautiful and an engineering marvel, and she wished Terence could have seen it with her; so many things reminded her of Terence. Edward also pointed out Alcatraz, an island in the San Francisco Bay which was the site of a maximum security federal prison, in use from 1934 to 1963 to incarcerate some of America's most notorious criminals.

Other than these little trips, the family did not go out from the house. Edward understood the travelers most needed time for adjustment and rest.

Edward was very concerned about Molly's plans to cross America with her children. He asked about her side trip to Albuquerque and made sure the family would be in good care. He needed to be satisfied about every detail of their travel plan. "Are you sure Tony will meet you in Maryland?" he asked several times.

At last convinced, he comforted Molly, "Good. Tony knows a lot. We do not worry about him. I have full faith in him to help you become adjusted to living in America."

It was good to have this break before they continued on their journey. But after several days, the travelers were ready to continue to Albuquerque.

****

Just before the plane landed in New Mexico, Molly worried aloud, "Oh dear! How am I to know who is Mrs. Bridges? And how will she recognize us?"

Lois answered confidently, "Don't worry. I will look out for you."

Sure enough, at the airport, Molly was staring blankly into the wall of anonymous faces, when Lois said, "Look! There she is!"

Molly asked, "How do you know that is Mrs. Bridges?"

"She looks just like her son!" Lois stated matter-of-factly as Mrs. Bridges came quickly to them. After Lois mentioned it, Molly could see the resemblance.

"Oh, I'm so happy to have you visit me!" Mrs. Bridges greeted them enthusiastically.

Later, Molly was amused at herself when she realized that Mrs. Bridges would have had little trouble picking out their Asian faces and her Burmese dress from the passengers streaming into the airport gate from the flight from San Francisco. She noted that even without Lois's skill, Mrs. Bridges was easily identifiable once Molly noticed the sign she carried, which said, "Mrs. Lee and family."

Mrs. Bridges could not have been more hospitable, and the stay with her was enjoyable. "Call me Irene," she said immediately.

Irene took the family to her house and introduced them to Ray Bridges' step-father, Walter. Molly would learn later that Mr. Bridges loved this man very much.

Irene led them to bedrooms. To Molly and Lois, she said graciously, "This is your room," and to Owen, "This room is for you." Then she pointed out the bathroom, and said, "This is where you can take a shower."

She cooked a nice meal for them. Then, recognizing their fatigue, Irene asked if they'd like to have showers before going to bed. The weary travelers considered this an excellent plan, and Molly suggested the children go first.

Then Molly took her turn. She had never seen facilities like this, with a bathtub and shower combination. When she had finished the refreshing shower, she stepped out of the enclosure and was stunned to find water all over the bathroom floor!

Molly didn't know what to do! She couldn't find anything to clean up the mess, so she dressed quickly and called to Irene for help.

"Oh, I'm sorry. I should have told you to put the shower curtain inside the walls of the bathtub, or the water will run on the floor," Irene explained kindly.

Molly was mortified. "Oh, I am so sorry. I didn't know what to do."

"Never mind," Irene smiled, "I will wipe the floor." Immediately, she was on her hands and knees, mopping up the water.

"Let me do it!" Molly pleaded. But Irene kindly refused.

So Molly took the opportunity to speak in Chinese to her children. Irene did not need a translator to understand the brief exchange.

Molly scolded Lois and Owen, who seemed to have figured out the trick to showering in America. "Why didn't you tell me?"

"Mom!" Lois said, "Common sense would tell you to put the curtain inside!"

Chastened, Molly confessed, "Your mother has no common sense." She was humiliated at the time, but she told the story on herself with much laughter in later years.

Irene put Molly at ease. "Please don't worry. Everything is fine again."

Molly learned that Irene had a little café, and she took them there for a big breakfast each morning during their stay. No wonder Irene was anxious to know whether or not they liked bacon and eggs. Particularly at the café, Irene bossed her husband, "Wal--ter! Do this!" And, "Wal--ter! Do that!" Molly noticed too that the waitresses seemed afraid of Irene. But to Molly and her children, Irene could not have been more friendly or gracious.

Molly was curious to know whether Irene and Walter were Buddhists like Mr. Bridges. She didn't see any of the usual statues or an altar in the home. Finally she asked bluntly, "Are you Buddhists?"

"Oh, no!" Irene laughed. "We are nothing."

This seemed to satisfy a question in Molly's mind, because she could understand Mr. Bridges believing in Buddhism if he had started with nothing, no faith, like his parents. She felt that a Christian who had truly experienced personal intimacy with God could never turn from Him.

Molly and the children enjoyed their visit with the Bridges. She was fascinated by a few hot air balloons floating by one day; she had never seen such a thing! But, Molly was eager to be moving on to her destination, and after a few days Irene took them to the airport for the conclusion of their journey.

Chapter Thirty-Three

Adjustments in Paradise

Molly was quiet on the flight as she anticipated seeing Tony. It had been so long, nearly five years, since she had seen him. She had buried the pain of being separated from him, knowing it could not be helped, but now she felt how dearly she had missed him. So much had happened since her son left home. So much.

The airplane arrived at Baltimore-Washington Airport and the passengers disembarked. Molly searched the crowd, looking for the familiar teen-aged face. At last Molly saw someone coming toward her with recognition. Was this Tony?

Tony was not the sixteen-year-old boy that left Burma; he had both the appearance and the countenance of a man. Molly should have expected this. Instead, she felt it very strange to see Tony looking so transformed, and she would sometimes stare at him, trying to rectify her memory with the present vision.

Tony quickly took charge, and Molly was glad to let him do so. Noting the role he had taken, Molly remembered the Chinese proverb to women, "When you are young, obey your father; when you are married, obey your husband; when you are older, obey your son." She wasn't sure Tony knew the proverb, but he was surely living it out. Later, she would resent Tony's bossing, but not at this moment. She was comforted to submit to his strength.

"Come along. We'll get your luggage and then drive to the house. I've rented a house for us in Kensington," Tony told them. "It is very close to a library, just a couple of doors away, so Owen can walk there to study." Tony was clearly pleased that he was able to arrange this.

To his mother, Tony said, "I did not want Lois and Owen to grow up in Chinatown in San Francisco. They need to adapt to their new country." "Owen, I want you to repeat your senior year of high school here," Tony commanded. "And Lois, I want you to repeat your last year of college courses. It will reinforce what you have already learned, and it will give you both time to adjust to your new country and to grow up. This country is very different from Burma."

They hadn't even left the airport yet! Tony had given much thought to his family and felt an urgency to advise them.

As they were leaving the airport, Tony demanded suddenly, "Where are your coats?"

They opened up their bags and proudly showed him that they had obeyed his orders to buy coats. But he frowned.

"I told you to get heavy coats! You have no idea how cold it is here in the winter! You are not in a tropical area anymore."

Molly thought to herself, "I know about cold weather! The nights in Namhsan were sometimes very cold. But it is true that Lois and Owen have never experienced this."

"This is February!" Tony exclaimed as if they should understand February in Maryland. "Well, these coats are better than nothing. Put them on."

Wow! When they stepped out in to the air, Molly understood his concern. This was much colder even than Namhsan! She had never experienced such cold. Strange things happened to her. Her skin tingled, almost burned, painfully. Then she felt numb. After awhile, her body shook involuntarily; how strange!

"I did not do anything to make myself move! But my body is moving!" she exclaimed.

Tony explained casually that the shaking was called "shivering."

He drove them to the house on Knowles Avenue in Kensington. As they drove, they saw the wonderous thing they had seen only in pictures or, recently, on distant mountain tops: Snow! This beautiful, pure, and sparkling thing covered everything and made this new world appear like a fairyland!

When they got to the house, Tony urged them to go inside quickly. But they couldn't pass the snow; for the first time, they had entered the fairyland of the pictures, and it was delightful! Molly was as curious as the children, and they all had to touch it and taste it and pack it and throw it! But after experiencing snow for a short while without gloves, their hands were so cold the skin felt afire and bones throbbed with pain. They were ready to obey Tony's instructions to hurry into the house.

"Stand over here by the radiator until you warm up," Tony commanded.

They all complied, standing near the wall around a fascinating machine which produced heat. It was a metal thing looking like a row of long dragon teeth, standing about waist high and painted to match the wall. Molly vaguely remembered seeing something similar in Cousin Edward's house in San Francisco, but she had not been aware of its function. Studying the contraption, she could see no place to put burning coals or fire wood to account for the hot air breathing from it.

"This is the living room. Through there are two bedrooms," Tony explained, "One for Owen and me, and one for you, Mom, and Lois. We have a bathroom there too. The kitchen is that way, and the stairs to the basement are there."

No one wanted to leave the warmth of the radiator, but Molly was curious about the basement. The only basement she had seen was at the Embassy. While they were warming, Tony told them how he had gotten the money for the plane tickets, plus the deposit and furnishings for the house.

"You are lucky! I have not been working long enough to save enough money for all this," he explained. "So, I went to a bank and found someone who believed in me. The bank was willing to take a risk; usually they don't loan money to a young guy like me. With the loan, I got everything we need. But we will have to pay back the money with interest."

This too was new to Molly. What was all this talk about loans and interest? But she understood that they owed money to a bank, and while she was grateful, she was not comfortable with this debt. Even so, she saw the great benefit of the loan and did not think they were simply lucky, but blessed to be in God's care.

"Here is our telephone," Tony said as he pointed. "This is our phone number. You can give it to other people so they can call you. But we cannot often call the numbers of people who live far away. It is called, 'long distance,' and it is very expensive. To call overseas is even more expensive. We won't do it."

Molly was impressed! Only a few rich people in Burma owned private telephones. In fact, Nye Nye had gotten a telephone not long ago, but who would use it? Molly wouldn't think of asking to use her mother-in-law's telephone! Of course, Molly had seen others using a telephone at the embassy, so she had an idea of how to use it. Now there was one right here in her house! She could use it any time! Wonderful! She could hardly wait to try it, but who to call?

Among the furnishings in the home was a box on legs which had a glass screen on the front and some knobs below. Tony turned a knob and the glass screen was glowing. Molly could see images on the glass and hear voices coming from the box.

Tony said, "This is called a television. I bought it for you to enjoy." He took great pleasure observing the immediate attention his family gave the television.

Molly said, "It looks a little bit like the movie screen we saw at the Palladium in Burma. But it is much smaller. And where is the projector? Tony? We can keep this here in our own house?"

Tony nodded, and Molly marveled, "We don't have to go anywhere outside to see it! How wonderful! But we will be forever paying the bank. It must be so expensive."

"No, Mom," Tony said. "We will pay off our debt in a short time. You remember, 'Slow and steady wins the race.' We will pay off a little more every month."

She touched the glass to test the material and to see if she could feel the images. A little snap of static electricity startled her, and she pulled back quickly, but Tony promised the television was not dangerous. Each family member could hardly keep his eyes off of it.

As Molly would discover, not everything she saw on the television was wonderful. She watched what her children watched, and so they protected her from some of the explicit shows that would have shocked her modest sensibilities as America jumped into the mire of the sexual revolution, abandoning values Molly admired and lived, such as commitment, faithfulness, self-control, self-sacrifice, and devotion to family. Nevertheless, the family quickly became addicted to the gripping stories of soap operas, reminiscent of Chinese opera, though these new operas were never-ending and without music. Also they enjoyed watching detective shows. Lois especially liked Perry Mason, and began to see herself as a detective or a lawyer.

Immediately shocking to Molly's ears was widespread, public criticism about President Johnson, who had just left office. To hear openly critical words about a leader was still frightening to her, and she almost felt she should turn off the television for her own safety, lest she be arrested for listening to such things. Incidentally, the new President was Richard Nixon, and Molly thought of him as an old friend.

The stove and oven were wonderful things to Molly. But she had to stare, confounded, because here there was no evidence of charcoal at all, just buttons and knobs and a mysteriously appearing flame.

She remembered the charcoal stove they had used at the apartment on Thirty-Fifth Street. It was the best Molly could buy, with a grill onto which charcoal pieces were laid, and clay feet onto which the pot was put, but if the draft did not carry the smoke away, the fumes from the charcoal smoke were intolerable to Terence. He would cough terribly, gasping for breath. Molly was pained to remember this.

But she smelled no smoke from this stove. "How did this fire come out?" Molly wondered. "Where did it come from? Is there a fire under the house?"

With a slight turn of a knob, Tony became a magician, making the flame bigger or smaller. He enjoyed the amazement of his family.

Tony had carefully provided for the family, and Molly didn't want to complain. But she noticed there was no screened cupboard in the kitchen to hold the food. She would remind him later that they would need to get one, as well as the cups to stand the legs in water so ants couldn't get to the food.

Then Tony showed them a refrigerator, or "fridge," as he called it. What a wonderful thing! One could put things inside the fridge and make them cold. In this way, food like milk, vegetables, and meats could be kept fresh for many days, and one didn't have to buy fresh food daily! Molly didn't see a way for ants to get into the fridge, so perhaps the screened cupboard standing in cups of water would not be needed after all.

Tony explained about the freezer, a section of the refrigerator that kept foods even colder, so they actually got hard and frozen and lasted even longer. "You can put meat in here," he said. "But not the fresh fruits and vegetables. Also, you must put the ice cream in here; it will melt in the refrigerator section."

"Ice cream!" Molly exclaimed. Suddenly, she felt she was the young, privileged girl again, sitting on the steps of the four-story house, waiting and hoping for the Indian man who brought ice cream to the well-to-do neighborhood. She would hold the precious little annas to pay for the rare treat and a saucer on which to receive it. She had sometimes seen the Indian men churn the wonderful stuff. Then they would dip it into little metal, cone-shaped tins, pack the tins in a big, ice-filled bamboo basket, and carry the heavy load on their turbaned heads, calling out the Hindi words, *coo fee*, "ice cream!" When she purchased the ice cream, (she liked to get at least two servings at a time), the kind Indian man would press it out of the tin and on to her saucer. Eating ice cream didn't happen regularly, because it melted quickly, so the men must be sure of interest before starting the tedious project. But when it happened, it was pure delight!

Once again Tony had the privilege of showing his family more wonders in the new country. "Look," he said, "there are different kinds of ice cream here: Chocolate and strawberry."

Oh my! As if vanilla flavored ice cream was not treat enough, now they had choices! And all they needed to do was to open the top part of the refrigerator here in their own house, and right there was the splendid stuff!

As they saw the bedrooms, Molly reminded her son about an urgent matter. "Tony, we must get mosquito nets for the beds. You forgot to get these for us."

"No, Mom," Tony was amused. "There are no mosquitos in the winter. Besides, mosquitos aren't too bad here, even in the summer. If necessary, in the summer we can spray for them. But see, the windows all have screens, so the mosquitos can't come in. No one here uses mosquito nets."

Molly was too tired to ask what was meant by "spraying for mosqui-tos." She had not noticed that the windows were screened, and the screens gave her some comfort.

Noting the care with which Tony had chosen the neighborhood for Lois and Owen, Molly was reminded of the famous Chinese story *"Mung Ji"* about a poor mother who was very picky about choosing a neighborhood in which to raise her son and encouraging the right companions for him. In the story, the boy grew up to be a scholar. As she fell asleep that night, Molly thought Tony had chosen well. Still, she felt uncomfortable without mosquito netting draped around her.

****

Tony wasted no time taking Lois and Owen to the library. Owen would never forget the admonition Tony gave him. Pointing to the shelves of books, he said seriously, "Read all of these, and you will do well." Owen would try to do this.

Tony took them all to a grocery store. "Now, Mom, you know English. Just read the labels. Look. Here is milk. Three and a half percent, two percent, one percent, skim...."

"What is this percent?"

"It just tells you how much fat is in the milk. You are used to whole milk, see? That is three and a half percent. See?"

"See what? Why so many choices? Why is milk not milk? Why is whole milk not one hundred percent? If it is whole, it should be one hundred percent."

"No! No! Listen! The percent tells you the amount of fat. Whole milk has none of the fat removed, so it has three and a half percent of fat in the total." Seeing her resistance, he said, "Never mind arguing. The point is, in America you have many choices. You must get used to it."

"It's so confusing!" Molly complained.

"Mom, just read the labels."

He led Molly to the canned vegetables. "Look. There are many kinds of beans here. You can buy them canned, or in another section you can buy fresh, or in another section you can buy them frozen."

Molly did not see the variety of options as an advantage. She was overwhelmed.

Tony continued to guide his family, "Maids are not cheap to hire

Owen's high school photo

here, and most Americans cannot afford a maid. Anyway, I am sure we cannot afford one, so we will have to do everything ourselves. Everyone must help. Lois, you will do all the laundry. I will show you how to go to the laundromat." Lois did not look too happy. "Also, you must apply to the University of Maryland right away, so you can apply for scholarships and start taking classes. Owen, we will enroll you quickly in the local high school."

Tony kept his word, and within a few days, Owen was headed to American high school. Molly instructed Owen to wear the suit she had specially made for him before they left Burma. She wanted him to make a good impression, and indeed, he looked very distinguished. Tony tried to argue with her, but she was determined.

That evening, the usually good-natured Owen was dismal. He informed his mother that he did not intend to wear a suit to school again. All of his classmates were dressed very casually in torn blue jeans and t-shirts. As he tried to fit in to an alien world, at least he could wear similar clothing.

Tony smiled at his mom. He did not need to say, "I told you so!"

Owen recounted that he had also found himself out of place when he stood in respect as the teacher entered the classroom. Students in America apparently did not have this custom.

Still, he felt welcomed by some classmates. A tall American guy and an Asian American greeted him and asked his name. Unable to understand Owen's shy, quiet response, the former said to the latter, "Let's call him Fred." Soon, Owen was invited to join the debate team, and he accepted the challenge as a way to advance in English language skills.

Owen didn't mention to his mother a startling behavior he observed in a school hallway. A boy and girl were kissing, an exhibition which he had never seen in Rangoon.

****

One day, soon after they arrived in Maryland, Lois suddenly cried out, "Wal--ter!" It was such a perfect imitation of Irene Bridges crying out the name of her husband that Molly laughed out loud. Lois often repeated the imitation at unexpected times after that, and though Molly knew she shouldn't make fun of other people, Lois's imitation was so funny that Molly couldn't seem to resist laughing. Well, Molly could also laugh at herself, a little, when the children told Tony about Molly's mishap with the shower curtain. Tony nearly fell to the floor in laughter.

Molly admitted, "I was a country mouse!"

****

Every day brought new adventures and learning experiences. One day there was ice on the trees and the sidewalk. Oh! It was so very pretty! But, one moment she was upright, walking with ease, happily enjoying the scene around her, and the next moment, she was on the ground, sore and humbled. Ice and snow were lovely but must be respected, she concluded.

Sometimes Tony was frustrated with Molly, thinking she was too slowly adapting to change. "Mom! You don't need to boil the water here! The water is safe! You can use it right from the faucet!"

Molly didn't believe him. She had been educated about dangerous organisms that could lurk in water, and she would not take chances. However, she enjoyed watching the water fill the sink. Except at the embassy and the library in Burma, she did not have the privilege of using sinks like these in the kitchen and the bathroom. The big house at the soy sauce factory had modern sinks but no water source to fill them. Even when she had enjoyed the pleasure of an indoor water source in her own home, it was limited to a faucet and a bucket.

Now, Molly was pleased to have even a sit-down toilet in her house! She had experienced these at work and at Mrs. Graham's house, and she thought it was luxurious comfort to sit rather than to crouch. Still, she remembered the complaint of her Burmese friends at the USIS Library, "How can you make anything when you sit down?" She had to agree that squatting better produced results.

Tony was also upset that his mother saved many things. In Burma, on the rare occasion when something was purchased in a glass bottle, the bottle itself was kept. Sometimes a purchase was made especially to own the useful bottle, rather than the contents. Boxes and newspapers were saved and reused. Here in America, Molly found, many things were sold in nice bottles or boxes, and the basement made a nice area to collect such items for future use.

But Tony disagreed. "Mom! We don't save all this stuff! Throw it out!"

****

Molly quickly made arrangements to go to Baltimore to discuss Charlene with an immigration officer. She explained the situation to the man and then asked urgently, with unusual forcefulness, "Now! How is the fastest way to get her out?"

The officer explained that Charlene could come on her own with the quota system as a doctor, but that would require a wait of a year or more. Instead, he told Molly that since she held a green card, which authorizes non-citizens to live and work in the States indefinitely, she could petition for her "unmarried daughter" to join the family, and hopefully things would move fairly quickly, perhaps taking only a few months.

Molly showed him the documentation on her daughter.

"Oh, I see she is an illegitimate child," the man said.

"Illegitimate?" Molly asked, unfamiliar with the word, but not liking the sound of it.

"She was born without a father's acknowledgement of paternity. When she was born, he did not admit that she was his offspring-- maybe before you and your husband were married?" the man asked, not unkindly.

Molly was shocked and offended! Uncharacteristically, she raised her voice in anger, "No! My daughter is not illegitimate! Where I come from that is a great insult, sir! Charlene was the first child of my husband and me, and we were married before she was conceived! Why would you say this rude and untrue thing?"

Would false rumors about her chastity continue to haunt her? She and Terence were married in Namhsan before they had relations! In fact, she and Terence had made vows at two ceremonies before Charlene was born! Chastened, the man said, "Hmm. There must be some mistake, Ma'am. According to this document, Charlene was '...born out of wedlock to Terence and Molly Lee.' 'Out of wedlock' means her parents were not legally united to each other by a wedding. I mean to say, Ma'am, this means that when she was born her parents were not married."

"Yes! I mean, no!" Molly urgently explained, "Out of our wedlock– you know, from our being wed to each other – Charlene was conceived!" Molly felt her face was flushed. She added for emphasis, "Our daughter was born... after our wedding."

The man risked an apologetic smile and repeated, "Oh. Here in America we have an expression that a child 'born out of wedlock' is a child whose parents are not wed to each other. I didn't mean to offend you."

Calming somewhat, Molly explained, "That's just the Burmese English, the Burmese way of saying things in English. It's not my fault. These are the words of the Burmese lawyer that wrote this document." As she realized the reason for the confusion, her anger at the official cooled, and she did not blame him. But, Molly's sense of humor needed time to find amusement in this mistake.

The official helped Molly file the necessary paperwork. Then all she could do, the man said, was to wait.

Yet Molly knew there was something more she could do. She fervently prayed to her Lord, asking Him to help Charlene to come to the States as soon as possible.

Tony sent Charlene and her friend James applications to fill out and return, which Tony would then take to a local hospital. Upon receipt of the applications, the hospital was pleased to accept both candidates. When they arrived in the United States, they could start right away repeating internships. Miss Palmer had continued to assist with correspondences.

****

Tony returned home late in the morning one weekend to find Lois and Owen were still in bed. He was angry.

"Mom!" He scolded, "You must not let them do this! You cannot let them be so lazy! I will find jobs they can do. We can use the extra money." Soon, Lois was using her math and English skills working as a teller at a bank, and Owen was washing pots and pans in the kitchen of a hospital and making deliveries for a local drug store. Tony bought Owen a bicycle and put many reflectors on it and on his clothing, so that people driving cars at night could see him as he made the deliveries.

"Don't drive on the road if you can drive on the side!" Tony cautioned. "People in cars are supposed to share the road with people on bicycles. But don't trust them. Be very careful."

Tony also arranged for Owen to work a summer job as a busboy at a restaurant. "You can do like I did," Tony said. "You can start as a busboy, and when you are old enough you can work as a waiter."

After a couple more months, Tony said kindly, "Mom, don't you think it is time for you to look for work?"

It is true that after all the tension in Burma, the strain of months and years of secret planning and waiting to come to the U.S., the stress of moving from Burma, the challenge of adjusting to the new country, and the difficultly of life without Terence, Molly was exhausted. Other than her passion to bring Charlene to the United States, Molly had little ambition or energy to do more than the basic activities of life. Recognizing her sluggishness, she also gave herself the excuse that the children could adapt more easily to differences in America. She had come to depend on Tony's leadership, even though she often resisted it, and she was content to be in his care.

When Tony gently confronted her, Molly knew he was right about looking for work, but she hardly knew where to begin. In fact, she dreaded beginning. She had come from Burma buoyed with confidence that "The Lord will take care of us!" She had trusted that she could leave Burma with nothing and that God would help her find work to support her family in the land of opportunity. But her confidence in herself had waned.

Tony urged her to apply with the State Department, so that she could add to her years of service with the United States Government. He knew the pay and benefits she could earn would be much better than any other place. When she contacted the department, she was encouraged to apply, and soon she was offered a job with the Agency for International Development. There were only a few formalities to take care of before Molly could start working.

But Molly had been watching the television that Tony bought. From the television she had seen news footage of race riots in Washington D.C., and she was frightened. The riots stemmed from the April fourth assassination of Martin Luther King Jr., a civil rights activist famous for nonviolent demonstration for racial equality and justice. While standing on the balcony of his hotel, he was murdered by a crazed, escaped convict. This shocking crime against the man of peace ironically triggered violent riots by disenfranchised people of African decent in cities across the United States, particularly in Washington, D. C. Federal troops were called to restore order in the capital city, but before this could be achieved, in just a few days, some were killed, hundreds were injured, hundreds of buildings were burned, and damages were in the millions of dollars.

Molly had stared in horror at the brutal, unrestrained, angry crowd hurting people at random and destroying the property of innocent people. The television brought the violence in to her own home. The ordeal recalled to her the nightmare of riots against the Chinese in Burma, but she had heard of most of the atrocities from other people. Instead, Molly experienced this present terror as an eye witness!

She also began to see televised Vietnam War protests. Already she had learned to fear hippies, the long-haired, unshaven, glassy-eyed men, who appeared dirty and lazy to her when she first saw them leaning against light posts or lying on the sidewalks of San Francisco. She observed on the television that mobs of hippie protestors demanding "peace" were often violent and destructive.

"They demand peace," she observed, "but they themselves are not peaceful."

Molly thought of how the involvement of the United States had rescued the world from aggression, occupation, and oppression of the Germans, the Italians, and the Japanese. She was sorry for the oppressed South Vietnamese people and that American support for them was waning.

She also felt personally threatened by the violence. Molly had been in the United States just a few months, and sometimes, staring at the frightening images on the television screen, she wondered why she had come. She did not expect such horrors in America, and the capital, Washington D.C. seemed to be a hub of protests. In Kensington, Maryland, only ten miles from the nation's capital, she felt much too close to the violence already. She had no intention of going closer.

So, when Molly found out that to work for the State Department she would have to go by bus to Washington, D.C. and walk to work from the bus stop, she was afraid.

"No! No! No!" she said emphatically to Tony. "No way! I'm not going there to work! I have seen this place. If any car stops at a traffic light and the door is not locked, the rioters come and yank it open and force you out! They might beat you or kill you! I have seen this! They might want to kill me! Nothing can stop them! No! I won't go!"

Tony quickly understood there would be no arguing with his mother on this. He read the classified ads in the newspaper and found that General Electric in Bethesda was looking for a secretary.

He coaxed, "Look, Mom, it's not that I want to tell you what to do, but you'd better go interview at this GE. It's a good company."

Chapter Thirty-Four

Revelation

Molly sent her resume, and when the call came to make an appointment for an interview, she gathered her courage. Tony took her to the interview.

She talked to a friendly woman in the personnel office. Molly had no trouble passing a typing test, but afterwards, unfamiliar with one of the words in her test, Molly asked, "What is the meaning of this 'car-o-mel'?"

"It is a kind of candy," the woman answered. "It's an old-fashioned name for caramel."

"I have never heard of it," Molly confessed, concerned that a lack of such knowledge might hurt her chance to get the job.

The interviewer assured Molly that it would not be held against her. She smiled knowingly, "You'll learn to like caromel."

Molly then was sent to one of the managers needing a typist. She answered his questions politely.

When she returned to the personnel office, she gave an envelope to the woman she had seen before and said timidly, "Here are some letters that may be useful for you."

The woman accepted the envelope. She read the recommendations from Miss Palmer and Mr. Parolini.

"Molly! Did you show these to the manager?" the woman asked with urgency.

"No," Molly answered quietly.

"Why not?" the woman admonished gently. "These letters say wonderful things about you! The manager would want to know about this, so he will want to hire you."

"Oh, I'm sorry," Molly apologized. "In Burma, it is considered rude to brag about yourself."

"This is not bragging, Molly. This is letting people know what you can do, so they know you are a good person to hire," the woman insisted.

"Oh." Molly was meek and worried that she had already done something wrong.

"It's okay, Molly. I will see that he gets a copy of this," the woman assured her.

****

Tony was helpful in preparing Molly for her first day of work. "Mom, all the women here in America wear socks made out of sheer nylon. 'Panty hose,' they are called. You will have to go and buy some of these to wear to work."

"What? 'Panty hose?' What is this 'panty hose?' " Molly felt some irritation that Tony was bossing her. "I never had to wear socks in Burma. It was too hot. No one wore socks."

"I know, Mom, but listen. The women here wear them. You and Lois should go to the store and buy some panty hose. You must have these to wear to work with your dresses. Buy some more American dresses too; you can't wear your longyis here. You want to fit in with the rest of the women. And buy shoes, with heels."

So Molly and Lois went to the store and found packages which said clearly on the front "panty hose." They also bought the other things, as Tony instructed, and confidently carried their purchases home.

On the first day of work, Molly slid the silky things over her legs and pulled the panty top to her waist. No problem. But, throughout the day Molly was having to pull up the baggy things. Every time she walked, the socks sagged and felt as though they could slide right down to her ankles and bunch up in a heap on the floor! Molly tried to hold the waist band of the slippery things through her clothes as she walked or stood, so that the mortifying thing would not happen. Periodically she would go to the ladies room to try to hoist up the socks and smooth the wrinkles. Other women did not seem to be struggling as she was, though Molly could see that they too were wearing similar socks.

She was waiting for Tony that night. He got her in to this mess, and she was annoyed with him!

When Tony heard what had happened and saw Molly demonstrating the awkwardness with which she had to hold up the panty hose, he doubled over with laughter!

"Mom!" he squeaked between laughs. "There are different sizes! You must have gotten a size too big for you! Look at the packages! Small! Medium! Large! Extra Large! Mom! Of course, you need a small size!"

The next day, wearing the right sized panty hose, was better. Okay, maybe it was kind of funny that she had purchased the wrong size. But, Molly thought it was a shame she had not been around to see Tony doing stupid things when he first came to America. She would like to have laughed at him.

****

Molly quickly opened the letter from Moonlight. What a thrill to receive mail from Burma! Molly could hardly wait to have news of loved ones so far away! But she would have never guessed the news expressed in her sister's beautifully written characters.

"Oh! Dorothy is engaged!" Molly exclaimed with surprise and pleasure.

"So soon since I left?" She marveled. As she quickly scanned the figures, top to bottom, right to left, she puzzled, "I wonder who the groom is? Anyone I know?"

"You will never guess," Moonlight wrote, enjoying from afar her sister's curiosity, and teasing, "Someone you know."

Then Molly read, "Your friend from the embassy, Ray Bridges."

"What about Ray Bridges?" Molly thought.

Then she understood the meaning: "Dorothy is engaged to Ray Bridges!" She shouted in surprise, and her children came running to see what was wrong. On hearing the news, Lois explained to Tony about Mr. Bridges and his parents. She assured him that no one had foreseen this.

Molly remembered that Mama and Byu Goo had admired Mr. Bridges' facial fortune. She smiled and shook her head in disbelief at how that memory had advanced to the present circumstance.

She had to wonder, how did Mr. Bridges convince her? Molly thought of Dorothy as a jungle princess, independent and untamed. She had refused many suitors. How did Mr. Bridges get her to accept his proposal?

But, after the initial surprise, Molly quickly grew to like the idea. Mr. Bridges was a nice man. He would take care of Dorothy, and she would have so many enviable opportunities. In Mr. Bridges' position, he would likely continue to travel all over the world, and surely he would want to take his wife with him. Molly recalled that Mr. Bridges once told her he had been around the world many times. She thought that sounded exciting, and surely Dorothy would think so too.

Molly also thought American men were generally more appreciative than Asian men of women. An American man might help a woman put on her coat or hold a door open for her. Molly never saw such a thing in her culture! She had heard recently that some American women resented this, as if accepting help implied a weakness, but Molly liked it. And though some American men were notoriously flirtatious and sexually exploitive of women, Ray certainly did not fit this category. As she continued to approve of the match, Molly was also certain Mr. Bridges would never take a second wife.

Answering the pleas of her children, Molly read the letter to them. Only two months after Molly and the children had left Burma Dorothy became engaged to Mr. Bridges. The couple would be married later that very month, in May.

"I had no idea that Mr. Bridges wanted to marry my sister," Molly told them. "Now I see why he was glad for her to show him the Chinese temple. Maybe he was looking for a wife. Now I see why he wanted us to meet his mother." Molly laughed.

***

At last, Charlene had repaid the Burmese government for her scholarships and received approval to immigrate to the United States. Molly was amazed and grateful to God at the quickness in which the bureaucracies of the two countries moved. A thousand words could hardly describe the mother's relief, one fine day in May, to have all the children together with her again, and she thanked the Lord.

Molly was anxious to take some financial strain from Tony. She told him that she would take over repaying the bank for the loan for the plane tickets and home furnishings as well as paying for the rent.

Tony said, "No, Mom. Let Charlene do it. She will be making some money as an intern. I will ask her to take over the payments to the bank, and you will help pay our rent and buy our food."

She did not argue with Tony, and Charlene was happy to help the family in this way. Charlene did not live with the family in Kensington. She found a place to live near the hospital where she would be working.

****

Tony had to keep training his mother. When he had been checking on his car, she said to him helpfully, "Don't forget to shut the bonnet."

"It's not a bonnet, Mom," he corrected. "Americans call it the 'hood' of the car, not the 'bonnet.' 'Bonnet' is a British term. Here a bonnet is an old-fashioned hat some women wear at Easter."

"British speak English. Americans speak English. English is English," Molly replied with frustration, conveniently forgetting that Chinese is hardly Chinese, with each dialect unrecognizable from others.

Tony argued firmly, "No, Mom! You had better learn the way Americans say it. You have to use American English."

"I didn't know," Molly said, chastened.

Another day, she mentioned that she had bought a nice "toeMAHtoe" at the grocery. Again Tony corrected, "We don't say toeMAHtoe here. We say, "ToeMAYtoe."

"I didn't know," Molly said. It was hard to suddenly change her pronunciation of the vegetable. When she forgot, Tony would get frustrated with her and correct her.

But the hardest American expression for Molly to understand was the term used for the liquid that fueled cars. She told him innocently, "Maybe you should stop and get some petrol for the car."

"What?" Tony looked at her as if she was speaking a language foreign to him.

"Petrol," she repeated. "The car needs petrol."

He laughed. She thought this was not a good sign.

"Oh, Mom! They don't call it 'petrol.' Don't talk that way! No one will understand you! It's not called 'petrol' here," Tony insisted.

"What do they call it?" Molly asked.

"It's 'gas.' You put 'gas' in the car," he explained.

"Gas?"

"Gas!"

Aha! Molly was certain she knew better on this one. "What gas? Oxygen? Helium? Hydrogen? No, this is not a gas you put into the car! This is a liquid! It is petrol."

"That's the British word," Tony scolded lightly, also certain he was correct. "In Burma they say 'petrol,' short for petroleum. Americans use the word, 'gas!'"

"But it is not a gas!" Molly said impatiently.

"Okay, Mom," Tony conceded, and countered, "But, you have to learn the term here so people will know what you are talking about."

She wanted to have a good argument for him, but she couldn't think of one. Still, she couldn't remember to conform to that idiom for a long time.

When Tony took Molly to a movie theatre to see a movie, she stood, prepared to sing, "God Save the King!" She was proud of herself for thinking quickly. She would not embarrass herself, she thought, and prepared to sing instead, "God save the President!" But Tony laughed at her.

"We don't do that here, Mom," he said between guffaws.

****

After several months of sending Lois to wash clothes at a laundromat, and considering four family members were now providing pay checks, Tony said that they could afford to buy a washer and dryer. Then Molly took over the washing duties, amazed at the simplicity of dropping things into a machine with a little powdered soap, pushing a few buttons, and then moving the marvelously fresh and cleaned wet clothes into the dryer to be dried. No one thought of such a thing in Burma! Molly thought of how the maids worked so hard to scrub the clothes in a bucket and then hang them on a line to dry.

Lois did not escape doing laundry, however. When she started her classes at the university, she did laundry for students who paid for the service, and she also did cleaning at the dorm. In this way she paid for her shared dorm room.

Tony also bought a vacuum cleaner! Marvels filled this new world! The noisy machine on wheels had a hose on it that one put to the wooden floor to suck up all the dirt into a canister. Oh, my, the ways of Burma seemed so old fashioned! Molly thought of how the maids scrubbed the floor with coconut husks, or swept up dirt with, of all things, a straw broom!

Shopping was always a startling experience for Molly. Toys! She was amazed at the number of toys that were made for children! She thought to herself, "I grew up my children without any toys!"

Really, a kite, a ball, soy sauce pots, a sling shot, trees, a slate, and ants were all the toys they needed.

One time when Molly was shopping with Tony, she could not contain her excitement when she saw a sponge for sale. "Oh Tony! I saw this once when I went to the commissary at the embassy! It was just like this! The woman who worked in the commissary said it was very nice, very useful. She said it was better than a cloth to wipe up things and to soak up everything. It takes just a little squeeze, she said, to take the water out of it! She showed me this! I touched the sponge after she squeezed it, and it felt dry! No wringing and wringing like a cloth." Molly demonstrated with exaggeration the motion of wringing a cloth.

"Really, this is the best thing!" she enthused. "Very helpful! I really like it! I never knew before where to get it!"

Tony was glad to accommodate his mother. He purchased the delightful object for her.

****

Tony told Molly about his time in the United States before his family came. She did not realize that when he left the Chrismans, he slept in a park for a while. He saw a sign near a pond that read, "No fishing!" But he was so hungry, he caught a few fish anyway, and he cooked the fish over a little fire.

"What?" She said. "Why did you leave the Chrismans if you had nowhere to go?"

"Mr. and Mrs. Chrisman were very good to me," Tony assured her. "Mr. Chrisman encouraged me a lot, and Mrs. Chrisman cooked things I liked to eat. But I like to be independent. I was okay, Mom."

He continued very seriously, "But it was hard sometimes. I always remembered the Scripture in Isaiah 40, 'But they who wait for the Lord shall renew their strength, they shall mount up with wings like eagles, they shall run and not be weary, they shall walk and not faint.' You know, Mom, my Burmese name is *Min Thaing*, 'High Eagle.' God gave me this verse to encourage me to be strong in Him and to keep going."

Tony told her that when he had finished his studies at the junior college, one of his professors gave him fifty dollars. Then he hitchhiked to

Atlanta and wrote for a newspaper for a short time. He used *Min Thaing* as his pen name.

"Oh, yes," Molly remembered. "When you wrote to us from Atlanta, your father marked this on his map of the United States. He always tracked your movements."

Tony said that one time when he was riding a bus in Atlanta, a black woman accosted him. He recalled, "When she got on the bus, I stood up to give her my seat, but she started yelling at me, and I thought she was going to strike me. She said very insulting things and spat at me. I had no idea why she was mad at me. Then she called me Viet Kong and accused me of killing her son. I realized her son must have died in the Vietnam War, and she thought I was Vietnamese. I tried to argue with her, but she wouldn't listen. Other people on the bus were glaring at me too. So I said, 'Oh! I am going to make a lot of money here in this country!' "

"Tony! Why did you say that? The woman was grieving for her son!" Molly scolded.

"Well, she was angry at the wrong person," Tony defended himself.

Tony said he hitchhiked to Washington, D.C. and surprised his older cousin Gabriel Ng with a visit. On the way, Tony did not want the expense of a hotel, so one night he stayed at a place offering a couch on which to sleep. During the night another traveler, an old man, crawled over to Tony. He thought Tony was sound asleep and tried to take the Shan bag from Tony's clutch.

"Fortunately, I'm a light sleeper," Tony told his mother. "I grabbed the man's hand and said, 'What are you doing? Don't do that to me! That bag is all I have!'

"The man answered, 'Oh, please let me go! I won't do it again. I wanted to have a look and see if anything is useful to me. Please let me go, and I will leave you alone.'

"I told him, 'Okay, I'll let you go. But don't do like this to any other person!'

"He said, 'Okay,' and he left me alone after that," Tony said.

Beginning to realize the challenges he faced, Molly exclaimed, "Tony! How did you manage by yourself? You were so young!"

"Mom, I am High Eagle!" He smiled as he reminded her. Then he added seriously, "I also like the song 'Onward Christian Soldiers' that I learned at the Methodist English High School. I would sing it to myself for encouragement. I always remember I am a soldier for the Lord. I must move forward."

"Onward Christian soldiers, marching as to war
With the cross of Jesus, going on before,
Christ the royal Master leads against the foe.
Forward into battle, see His banners go."

"This song helped me to stay strong," Tony testified.

Molly understood this song was not a call to violence, but to inspire Christians to live faithfully and courageously for Christ. She remembered that Scripture speaks of defensive and offensive armor to use against forces of evil: truth, righteousness, the gospel of peace, faith, salvation, God's word, and prayer. She too had used these weapons in spiritual warfare, and she understood the powerful effect the song had on Tony.

Tony went on telling about his journey to see Gabriel. He mentioned that one gentleman who gave him a ride was a marine glad to have the company. The marine taught him to drink beer.

Tony told his mother, "Mom, a man must drink. Those who cannot drink are not men. That's what the marine told me."

"What?" Molly exclaimed.

"A lot of people here seem to think that way, Mom. I had to learn to drink to fit in with some people," Tony said. He added, "I don't drink too much. I'm a social drinker."

"Did you ever make it to see Gabriel? When he was born in Namhsan, he was red and skinny and wrinkly. I sometimes fed him his goat's milk from a bottle." Molly laughed as she added, "I called him "Little Monkey.""

Tony had heard before about his mother's affectionate name for Gabriel. He continued telling his story, "Yes, Mom. I went to the address you had given me. When I knocked on the door, Gabriel answered, but he just stared at me, frowning. 'Who are you?' he demanded."

The cousins had been close, but perhaps five years passed since they had seen each other. Gabriel did not recognize him.

Tony said, "I told him, 'I am your cousin!' But Gabriel still didn't know me. He said, 'How?' So I told him, 'Your mother, Anita, is the sister of my father, Puck Ying. Terence. I am Tony!'"

"Tony! Come in!" Gabriel welcomed him, and years of separation were quickly bridged.

544 | GENTLE MOON

Tony needed a place to stay and a way of making money. Gabriel's landlady allowed Tony to stay as Gabriel's roommate in the rooming house. A Jewish Iranian friend of Gabriel's taught Tony survival skills, and not all of the skills were kosher. He managed to age Tony a few years so Tony could work with him as a waiter serving liquor.

Gabriel was working as a taxi driver to pay for his education. He taught Tony to drive a car, a very helpful skill in the United States. After driving in the D.C. area, Gabriel had a plan to give Tony more driving experience. He and his Iranian friends got into the car with Tony and directed him to drive to New York City to see the World's Fair.

They were all excited to see the fair; it emphasized new technology and was quite impressive. But most memorable to Tony was Michelangelo's magnificent Pieta, on loan from the Vatican. The young travelers were enthralled by this stunning marble statue of Mary, the mother of Jesus, holding Jesus' lifeless body on her lap.

The adventurers then went to see Niagara Falls, knowing it was also in New York. But they underestimated the distance involved, and it was a long journey. Tony returned to Washington having had many hours of practice driving. After Tony got a license, Gabriel was able to help him find a reliable used car for less than $500.

After going to North Carolina and working there for a while, Tony made the long drive west across the country to San Francisco, where he met up with Cousin Edward and his family. Edward was glad to see his cousin's son and extended hospitality. Edward's sister also reached out to him, and she offered to let Tony spend summers with her in San Francisco as he worked to earn money for his university classes.

Tony told Molly that at the university he made good use of his judo lessons, continuing to study this discipline to earn the required physical education credits. He told of being paired to fight with a student who towered over him. The rival was big, but he was slow, and Tony easily outmaneuvered him.

He told of the challenge of working at any job he could find to afford classes while keeping up with his studies. He did not have the leisure time many of the students enjoyed. But he was proud that he himself paid for his classes and earned his degree in chemistry.

Tony did not attend his college graduation or take pictures, as his father had advised, because he could not afford appropriate clothes. He met a friend of the family in San Francisco who had been able to bring out of Burma a couple of the treasured pieces of jewelry Molly's mother had given to Molly at her wedding. Then he headed for the east coast in his Volkswagen Beetle. He stopped to eat in Boston, and, as an afterthought, he took Molly's little package of jewelry into the restaurant with him.

"Lucky I did, Mom," he said. "When I came back, someone had stolen my diploma." He had to write to the school to get a replacement, which was not as nice as the original. "At least your things were not stolen."

Molly thought of the hardships Tony experienced. She asked him, "Why, Tony? Why did you have so much trouble?"

Tony had learned from his mother to count his blessings. He said he didn't know why. But he said, "At least all of those difficult experiences taught me to be wise and street smart. It also made me care more about others."

Molly had observed in her life that God could use difficulties to teach her something good. She was glad that Tony also understood this.

Every time they would eat at a restaurant, Tony reminded Molly, "I always leave a big tip. I remember how I used to look forward to those tips."

****

Molly saw that she inconvenienced Tony by forcing him to drive her to work. He admitted that sometimes he should have stayed longer at his job, but he had to pick up Molly at GE in the evening and take her home.

So, she took on a brave task, joining Lois and Owen in taking driving lessons. Her children teased her that she would have trouble learning this new thing, a skill so different from anything in her experience. But Molly practiced parallel parking diligently, and she surprised everyone, including herself, by passing her test the first time, earning her license even before her two younger children. Poor Owen missed a stop sign and had to retake the test, and Lois had trouble with the parking test the first time she tried it.

Molly couldn't resist teasing them, "You thought your old mom would have trouble with this! But I have passed my test the first time!" She did wonder if the officer grading her driving was more patient with an older lady.

After this, she was driving with growing confidence, even in rush hour traffic, when her car suddenly quit moving forward, right there on a busy highway! So she got out of the car, leaving it with the engine running where it had stopped in the left lane. She dodged oncoming traffic, enduring the rude horns blaring, while praying a familiar prayer, "Lord Jesus, please send someone to help me!"

She was grateful to see a Japanese car dealership just beyond the next exit, and instead of following the road, she hiked cross-country, the shortest route, through a ditch. Entering the business disheveled, she breathlessly explained her predicament to the wide-eyed gentlemen working there. When she mentioned the car was still in the traffic and still running, the men were clearly concerned. One man quickly offered to go back to the car with her to try to fix it, and there they found a scowling policeman hovering over the disabled and traffic-tangling car. She was sure he would give her a ticket as he scolded her for leaving her car in the way of other vehicles. His irritation softened a bit when he realized Molly was new to driving and new to the United States. She sensed passing motorists were also initially angry until they saw her Asian face, and then, she thought, they became more amused than angry. She much preferred to be a source of comedy rather than offense. The young mechanic from the car dealership was able to get the car moving and kindly offered to drive Molly's car to the dealership for repairs. She left the policeman smiling and forgiving.

She called to him, "God bless you!" as the mechanic drove her away.

****

Miriam, the receptionist at GE, was a good friend. She often invited Molly to take a walk with her, to join her for lunch, or to shop during their lunch break.

One day Miriam commented to the manager, Mr. Santucci, "How long do you think it will take Molly to adapt?"

Mr. Santucci replied, "I think one year."

Molly didn't say anything, but she was a bit offended. She thought she was adapting well. She told Tony about it later.

"I think he is right," Tony said. "It may take a year or more."

"I'm not so stupid!" Molly told him gruffly.

"No, Mom, you are not stupid," Tony acknowledged. "But it takes time to adapt. Everything is so different here. Don't be offended. You are doing a great job."

Besides learning to adapt to a new country, Molly found things at GE were very different from work at the U.S. Embassy in Burma. She used a large keyboard to type accounting data into a computer terminal. Oh, this was so much easier to enter the information and to correct mistakes! No more having to make erasures! And no more typing stencils or using carbon paper! She could use a copy machine to make as many sharp copies of a report as she wanted, simply with the touch of a few buttons.

At first she was only typing bills and letters. But a co-worker, Carolyn, noticed her abilities and informed Mr. Santucci. Molly had noticed another lady talking on the phone much of the day, and Molly assumed this person was making business calls. Then the person was no longer seen at work, and Molly was given more duties, including responsibility for many national accounts like British Petroleum and Gulf, on which she was to code and calculate sales commissions as well as type pertinent information into charts.

She had picked up some terminology and sayings at work. One policy of which she was certain was this: "The customer is always right."

One day Molly received a phone call, and the man identified himself as Mr. Hearst. Then the man yelled at her and accused her of making mistakes that cost him a lot of money. He was very angry and rude.

Molly had never experienced such a disrespectful scolding. She had no idea who this man was or why he was angry with her. In spite of Molly's self-control and her dislike of calling attention to herself, she suddenly found herself crying uncontrollably.

Miriam, the receptionist, noticed her, and asked, "Molly, what's wrong?"

With involuntary sobs, Molly replied, "I don't know who this guy is! And he is yelling at me, bombarding me, 'you did this and you did that!' He said I made mistakes that cost him his commissions. But, I try to be very careful. I know the customer is always right, but I don't know what mistakes I made."

Miriam told their supervisor. Mr. Santucci asked Molly to explain what happened.

Then he told Molly, "Hearst is not a customer, he's a salesman for GE out of New York. And you didn't make any mistakes, you are fixing the mistakes the other girl made. She was very careless, and she sat talking on the phone instead of doing her work. That is why we fired her and gave you her work. I'm glad we did! You are very good at your work, Molly. No, Hearst is not a customer, so if he yells at you, yell back at him!"

Molly was at a loss. "How do I do that?"

Mr. Santucci said, "Never mind, Molly. I'll talk to him." So Mr. Santucci immediately called Mr. Hearst and scolded him.

Then Mr. Santucci called Molly to the phone, saying, "Mr. Hearst wants to apologize."

"No, no," she said, eyes to the ground. "I am too much afraid of him."

"Well, okay, but if you have any more trouble with him, you just tell me," Mr. Santucci said protectively.

Molly had no more trouble with Mr. Hearst. But it took months to correct all of the mistakes someone else had made.

****

Carolyn also befriended Molly. At first, Molly didn't know why she couldn't understand her. The woman seemed to speak English, but then again, the words seemed very unlike English. Molly knew that Americans spoke English with a different accent from the British English she had learned at school, but after working at the library, the embassy, and now at GE, she was able understand Americans quite well. Molly wondered if Carolyn came from another country, but when she asked Miriam about it, Miriam smiled.

"No, Molly, she was born and raised in America," she said, "but she's from the south. She has a thick southern accent."

At first it was very hard for Molly to make out what she was saying. She didn't want to keep asking Carolyn to repeat herself, but sometimes she had to do it. It seemed to her that Carolyn was putting an extra curve and an extra curl to her words. After a while, Molly got used to her.

****

Molly worked at GE for several years, but she found the environment very demanding as people found out what she could do and increased her work load. And for Molly's liking, there was too much unhealthy competition and infighting between peers wanting promotions and raises in salary.

So, when she heard about a job opening, she thought, "I wonder if I have a chance." She applied and was accepted to the GE Clearing House for Alcoholism. Her new boss, Maude, a woman from Sierra Leone, was pleased to find someone not only with secretarial skills, but with library cataloguing experience. Molly was pleased to find a more peaceful work environment.

As Molly became immersed in her job and learned about alcoholism, she recognized that the symptoms of hidden alcoholism were very familiar: drinking from early in the morning to late at night, mood swings, irritability, withdrawing from others, flushed face, loss of appetite. Molly was shocked to realize that Nye Nye fit the pattern well, and she felt compassion for her.

"We didn't know," she thought, though Molly now understood her father-in-law's insightful complaint to his wife, "You drink, and then you find fault with people."

With the realization that much of Nye Nye's crossness could be blamed on port wine and Johnnie Walker whiskey, Molly's lingering resentment toward her mother-in-law vanished. Surely Nye Nye herself did not know what was happening to her.

Molly was contrite as she realized she had not been completely forgiving of her mother-in-law. She knew God does not expect us to forgive only when we fully understand the situation. We must forgive as He has forgiven us: abundantly and absolutely.

****

When Molly saw Dorothy, expecting to see her joy, she felt instead her sister's unhappiness. Dorothy said their mother had convinced her to accept Mr. Bridges' proposal.

Dorothy quoted Mama, "Ah Haing, you are alone. I will die soon, and you will be by yourself. Mr. Bridges looks like he will have a long life, and he is kind-hearted. You should marry him. The situation in Burma is frightening. You are the only one that is not settled. He is a good man and will live a long life. You should marry him."

Ray was assigned to return to the United States soon after he married Dorothy and was forced to wait some months for his bride to receive permission to join him. He anticipated her arrival, planning to pick her up at the airport and to take a slow, romantic, scenic train ride to their home. He met Dorothy at La Guardia airport, and found that she was airsick and had a migraine headache. The train ride only added to her misery.

Many things in the new country were difficult for Dorothy. For instance, she did not like the feeling of being closed up in her house; she wanted windows open for fresh air, even in the winter months. When Ray mentioned this to Molly, she reminded him, "You married a jungle princess!" Molly realized she herself had trouble adjusting to America, and she had much more western exposure than her sister prior to coming to the States.

Dorothy also found it difficult to adjust to a life of traveling with Ray, or to his absence if he traveled without her. Ray had his own challenges with traveling. He once told Molly that prostitutes in the Philippines tried to seduce him, but he crossed himself and pretended to be a priest to divert their advances. Molly was amused that the Buddhist used a Catholic facade to free himself from unwanted attention.

But Molly enjoyed traveling with Dorothy. When the couple lived in Germany, Molly visited and took a European tour with her sister. Molly was delighted with all of it! She was fascinated by Pompeii and awed by Rome. Of things like the Sistine Chapel, the Pieta, and the Mona Lisa, she would later exclaim, "I saw the real thing!"

Ray and Dorothy remained faithful and committed to each other, and affections would grow over the years. Ray knew very little Burmese, but his code words to Dorothy when they were at functions together were *moh ywa dare, moh* for "sky" and *ywa* for "rain," plus *dare* for the end of the sentence. This was the Burmese expression for rain falling, or "it's raining," and it was his signal that he was ready to go home.

They had a Down Syndrome son together, and they were devoted to him. Molly said that seeing her sister and brother-in-law celebrate when their sweet little boy learned to tie his shoes made her realize that she had taken many things for granted with her children. She understood too that her children had been expected to do much for themselves.

****

When Molly left Burma, Byu Goo and Dorothy still lived with Molly's mother. After Dorothy married Ray and left Burma, Ah Ma went to live with Moonlight and Byu Goo went to live with her son, Ah Hop.

Almost a year had passed after Molly came to the United States when another letter came from Moonlight. Molly loved these letters from her sister, and she opened this one quickly to enjoy the latest news.

But the news was grave. Byu Goo had hit her toe on a dirty nail at the fresh market, and this had made her sick.

Molly thought of the clean stores in America as compared to Burma's muddy markets. She knew Byu Goo would have worn an open sandal. She read further.

Moonlight said a poison called tetanus had caused Byu Goo to become delirious with a very high fever and to have terrible and painful muscle spasms. Already she was very sick when they took her to the hospital, and she soon died there.

Oh! Byu Goo was gone! Oh, how terrible that she had suffered so!

Believe it or not, Moonlight remarked, just that little scratch had caused her to die. Molly had not heard of this frightful thing.

Molly mourned the loss of Byu Goo, but she was also very anxious about how her mother was coping with the death of her cherished friend. She read more of the letter. As Molly expected, Moonlight said their mother had grieved terribly over Byu Goo.

"No wonder," Molly thought. "They were like twins. Always together. They were rarely separated for very long."

Molly also recalled that Byu Goo often told Ah Ma, "I hope I live long enough to take care of you. If you are dying, I will take care of you." Now the faithful friend would not be able to care for Ah Ma.

Molly felt it was more important than ever for Dorothy to get Ah Ma to come to the United States. She knew Dorothy and Ray were working on that very thing.

But there was more to Moonlight's letter, and Molly continued to read. Slowly, Moonlight explained that Ah Ma was mourning after Byu Goo's death, and after just a few months, Ah Ma went into a deep sleep and never woke up. She died a few days later. Moonlight said that doctors told her that Ah Ma had diabetes, which caused her coma.

Reading of Byu Goo's death was shock enough. Now Molly had to comprehend the death of her mother, and as the news of double loss seeped into her, she was filled with sadness and regret. She longed to see the dear women again. She was sorry she had not been present in their time of need.

Through her tears, Molly read that Ah Ma died during the Chinese New Year celebrations. In ordinary circumstances, many people would have attended her funeral, but because of superstition surrounding the New Year, most people would not dare to attend a funeral at that time. Only a few of the closest relatives attended. This did not upset Molly. She imagined a quiet, peaceful farewell for her timid Mama, without the phony mourners.

Molly ached to lose her mother. She wished she could be with her family in this time of loss. But Molly would not consider going back to Burma. Even if it were not for the impossible expense of flying there, Molly was afraid that if she ever went back to Burma, the government would not let her leave. All she could do was to send a letter to Moonlight.

****

Mourning for her mother brought back mourning for Terence as if he had just departed this world. But God did return one special loved one to Molly. Anita had made her way to the states, and Molly was glad to see her sister-in-law and dear friend. They often visited together and loved attending church together at Forcey Bible Church.

As they talked one day, Molly confided to Anita, "I am so sorry Terence never got to come to the United States. I feel so bad! It was his dream! If he had come, I think he could have gotten medical treatment to make him well. I wish I could have brought him here before it was too late."

Anita's response surprised her. She said gently, "No, Molly. It is the Lord's will. Don't you see that it was a blessing in disguise? The Lord is kind to you. He is merciful. How could you work if Terence came to the U.S.? And if you went to work, who would take care of him? How could you afford his medical care? Anyway, Molly, it is the Lord's will. You did everything you could do for Terence. It was time for him to go be with the Lord."

Anita's words comforted Molly. She realized she was not to blame that Terence did not live out his dream. She knew he was now in Heaven, a place even better than Hawaii, in perfect health and happy to be with his loving God. She still greatly missed Terence, but she stopped feeling guilty that she had somehow failed him.

As the months passed, Anita's perspective helped Molly consider God's guiding hand in her life. "The Lord is kind to you," Anita had said. Sometimes Molly's life seemed very hard to her. But Anita had noticed that God was also paying attention to Molly and showing kindness.

Molly attended a Bible study at the church. In the study group, someone mentioned that King Hezekiah of ancient Judea once became sick and was near death. The prophet Isaiah told him he would not recover. But the king passionately petitioned to God that he might live longer, and Isaiah returned to tell him that God had answered his prayer. He would live fifteen more years.

Molly had a thought, and she excitedly did the arithmetic in her head. Terence's vision came in 1950, the year before she started to work at the library. He died in 1968. Why had she not noticed this before? Terence had lived eighteen years after he was expected to die!

She recalled the cherished memory of the night of his vision, when his life was spared. Molly reflected on the words she had passionately prayed to her Lord, "The children need their father! Please, let the children grow up first.... Perhaps when they finish school... or finish college.... Perhaps then they will be able to stand on their own feet.... Perhaps then they can get along without their father. Lord Jesus, please have mercy on us, and let Terence live!"

She recalled her husband's urgent words about that sacred night, "Don't forget! You must always remember!"

Molly now considered the work of the Lord with awe. When Terence died, Charlene had just finished medical school in Burma, and Tony was just graduating from college in the United States. Charlene was a somber and mature young woman, and Tony was strong, already living independently in the United States. Tough and savvy Lois was well on her way in college, and good-natured Owen, conceived after his father's life was extended by the Lord, had just completed high school. The children had grown up, just as Molly had pled to God that night. They had all finished high school, and two had even finished college! They were responsible and capable children. Not only had their father lived, sparing them the greater hardship and the greater shame of a dead father than a sick father, but, by living well, he had set a good example for them and shaped their characters. By God's grace, Terence showed his children courage, dignity, and faith in terribly hard circumstances.

Molly was moved with gratitude to God for His gracious attention to her prayer. Even in her loss, she praised God. Eighteen more years with her husband was a tremendous gift! Her effusive praise resembled that of Mary, the mother of Jesus, in her spontaneous hymn now called the Magnificat, beginning "My soul magnifies the Lord!"

In Molly's version, she praised:

"How marvelous! How wonderful!

You have worked in my life!

Even in Burma, that remote place, You heard my prayer!

I called upon You in faith, and You heard me!

Look! My husband was going to die!

Everyone knew it!

The folk doctors said he would die!

The doctors with western training said he would die!

His face was blue! His hands were swollen!

His whole body was bloated!

But You made him live again!

You let him live for me and for his children!

Eighteen years! Who would think?

And now his children have grown!

You paid attention to me!

You heard your little Molly in that distant place!

My God, You never fail!

Small things! Big things! It doesn't matter!

You hear the prayers of those who trust You!"

This revelation would be a memorial to Molly for the rest of her life. When the heaviness of mourning brought her low, she would grab on to these truths: God did love her. God did care for her. Almighty God had heard her and had compassionately answered her prayer. He was and would always be worthy of her trust. These remembrances would encourage Molly throughout her life, especially during other times of trouble and sorrow.

Chapter Thirty-Five

Old Friends and The Faithful One

America was not the idealized place Molly had envisioned from watching the best of 1930's and 1940's era American films in Burmese theatres. In some ways, America disappointed her. Knowing of the strong Christian roots of America, she had assumed a greater Christian influence, and she expected more kindness, more generosity, more selfless and moral living. It seemed to her that robust Christian impact on society was fading, and this concerned her.

Molly worried that the more America denied her own roots and borrowed from other religious beliefs or from socialist or humanist ideals, the less the nation would be the land of opportunity, productivity, mutual respect, and freedom. Socialism was especially frightful to her, and she felt grave concern with every step the United States took in that direction.

She observed that freedoms in America which could be used for disciplined thriving were often used for self-gratification. Precious rights were unappreciated. Children were becoming less treasured. People of minority races were not always treated with equality, and Molly felt that she was sometimes treated as inferior because of her Asian face.

It is also true that Molly did not dwell on negative things. As Daw Su Su had often said, "There are ugly Americans, and there are good Americans." Surely this could be said of any nation and race. In America, Molly found there were still many kind people who lived with the values of the idealized old films and who maintained unashamed faith in God. She found many people respected and affirmed individuals of all races. She concluded that she unquestioningly would choose the guaranteed freedoms, though often perversely used, of the United States over the repression of Burma.

****

From the time he was a child, Owen often talked of wanting to be a doctor, but Molly thought it was a passing dream. When Owen finished high school in the United States, he reasserted his intentions. "I want to be a doctor."

Molly and Tony tried to dissuade him. The course work would be too demanding in this new world, they thought.

But Owen insisted, "I watched my father die. I could not help him. I want to help people get well."

Owen had once worried his mother by concentrating on ants for long periods of time. This same ability to concentrate and notice details would help him in his medical studies and then in caring for his patients.

Owen continued to be a man of faith. About his hardships, he observed, "If I did not experience poverty and loneliness, I could not be a better physician taking care of people."

Charlene married James and they both worked as doctors. After finishing internships and residencies, they found work at hospitals in the area.

Tony went back to college intending to earn a master's degree in chemistry so he could have a career in research. But after one semester of study, he told his mother about the other students, "All those guys have long hair. I don't want to be like them." He associated these students with unkempt, undisciplined, drug-damaged hippies. Like his mother, Tony had witnessed the long-term, devastating effects of mind altering drugs. He would not be a part of that culture.

Instead, he got his master's degree in business. When he was passed over for a promotion at his job, though he felt he was the more diligent and more effective worker, he left his job to do consulting work, and then he started his own business. He fulfilled his promise to the woman on the bus in Atlanta, "I'm going to make a lot of money here in this country!"

He shared his prosperity by employing many, and he was a loved manager. One lady of African descent, for instance, habitually showed up late to work. Instead of firing her, he asked an assistant to find out why she was late. She explained that she had to see her son off to school before catching a bus to work. Tony told his assistant to buy her a car and to arrange for her to repay him slowly. Molly would hear many such stories when she attended annual business meetings with Tony.

Lois completed her double major in accounting and computer science. She moved to Texas to work and earned her master's degree there.

****

Five years after Molly and the children arrived in the United States, they could take citizenship tests to become citizens of the United States. They studied the three branches of government: executive, legislative, and judicial, and the way each is intended to protect the people from abuse of power and overreach of the other branches. They studied the U.S. Constitution, The Bill of Rights, and some U.S. history and geography. Much of this was familiar to them, because of Molly's work at the USIS Library. The Bill of Rights was especially meaningful to Molly. She was grateful for each freedom guaranteed: speech, the press, religion, and peaceable assembly. Molly knew personally the value of protected rights to bear arms, to have a trial by jury, to have legal defense if charged with a crime, and to be protected from soldiers invading a home and from police searches without a warrant. Molly was proud when she and her children became U.S. citizens, and she was eager to exercise her right to vote.

****

Most of Molly's birth family migrated to the United States after her. Of her siblings, only Moonlight and Clark stayed in Burma. Moonlight's husband died shortly after Molly came to the United States. Because of her low status as a second wife, no children, and no other means of support, Moonlight was impoverished after his death. In veiled Chinese figures, Moonlight conveyed her need to her sister in the land of the Golden Mountain, and Molly found clandestine methods to send money to her. Wayne proposed marriage between Moonlight and his barber in Virginia, amusing his sisters, but Moonlight died only a few years after Molly left Burma. Ah Hop, Byu Goo's son, remained in Burma also, and he wrote often to Molly and Dorothy.

Most of the Lee family also migrated to the States, Number Two Sister Lily being the only one to die in Burma before permission was given for her and her family to immigrate. Foke San, as sixth son, stepped up to be a great help to the Lee family, bringing most of them to the States and caring for his mother in her old age in America, generously supporting her lifestyle and hosting big dinners in her honor. He also fulfilled the duties Nye Nye expected upon her death. When the Burmese government planned to bulldoze the Chinese cemetery, Number Three Sister Fe Yone brought from Burma the ashes of Lee Sit Hong and the two children who died in infancy, and Foke San had these buried with his mother's ashes. Puck Koon went looking for Puck Hee, an old man by then, who had taken the difficult job of a travelling doctor to little villages in China. When the brother was found, Foke San was able to petition for and bring Puck Hee to the United States, and he cared for this brother, the gentle poet. Each one of Molly's family by marriage were very kind and often generous to Molly through her old age.

Anita's son Gabriel brought Terence's ashes to the U.S. for Molly, the Christian cemetery also slated for bulldozing. Gabriel had located his uncle Myo Khin in Rangoon, and, at the cemetery, he took a picture of this smiling uncle wearing the saffron robes of a Buddhist monk. Myo Khin's son tells that his father was imprisoned for two years without charge, and that his father did not recall receiving any of the food and gifts his wife brought to the jail, though she had paid the jailers the bribes they demanded to give the things to Myo Khin.

****

Many of the Lee children became Christians. Number Three Sister Fe Yone told Molly, "We tried to convince Mommy to become a Christian before she died. Fe Heng and I told her about Jesus. We even got a Chinese Bible for her to read."

Molly asked, "Did she read it?"

Fe Yone replied, "We don't know. We gave it to her, but I don't think she read it."

Fe Yone said that when her mother was on her deathbed, they coaxed her again to believe in Lord Jesus. Nye Nye answered that she was afraid to believe in Jesus; she was fearful that something bad might happen to herself or to her children or grandchildren.

Molly said sadly, "We caused that."

"I know," Fe Yone said. "Ah Ma always said, 'I don't want to be like Puck Ying.' We tried to say, 'No! Mama! His illness had nothing to do with angering gods. He got sick from germs!'"

Molly said, with emphasis, what by now Fe Yone also knew, "Terence had a rheumatic heart which was caused by rheumatic fever! I think he contracted the fever on the crowded boat ride from Pyapon to Rangoon during the war. He was never too well after that. If he had been able to take penicillin, maybe his heart would have been fine." Molly was sorry for Terence and for Nye Nye.

Molly heard from the television of western interest in Chinese medicine, and she was surprised. She realized that many of the herbal concoctions of her mother and mother-in-law, and of Chinese doctors and monks, may have had value to heal after all. Only, the potential remedies needed the thorough testing of the west to sort out anecdotal or even harmful ones from those with true medicinal worth. She wondered what valuable knowledge had been lost with the passing of people like Ah Ma and Nye Nye.

Guilty by association: brothers Chin Hone Ohn and Chin Hone Kam with Chiang Kai Shek in an earlier era.

****

Molly heard from her cousin in London about her uncle, Old Man Thunder Voice. For many years, the Burmans in power had unapologetically imprisoned him for the duration of each visit of foreign minister Chou en Lai, but they had released him each time the dignitary left Burma. After the socialists came to power, needing very little suspicion to imprison a man, they jailed him indefinitely. After many years, they arranged for him to be deported to Taiwan. He was not allowed to go home at all but was sent from the prison directly to the airport, wearing the same humiliating clothes he had worn in the prison. Some of his family, mostly the offspring of the second wife, went with him. If Old Man Thunder Voice expected a hero's welcome in Taiwan for suffering for the cause, it was not to be. He took the demanding job of going out every hour, every day and night, to ring the gong through the streets to chime the hour.

The family of the third wife stayed behind and kept the property in Burma. When the London cousin, a son of the second wife, went to Burma to visit, the third wife's family treated him with suspicion. They feared he had come back to claim property, but this man had no envy or expectations. He and his family had left Burma with no material possessions, but they went to various parts of the world where each one had opportunities to live and work and thrive in freedom.

****

When she became financially stable, Molly felt she must find a way to repay the Chrismans. She could never compensate them for all that their friendship had meant to Terence and his family, but she could attempt to pay for the car they sent to Burma and a little something for Tony's care. The Chrismans had moved, but Gabriel was able to find a current address. Molly wrote first to Mr. Chrisman to make sure the address was correct. Mr. Chrisman was thrilled to hear from her and answered quickly. Molly then sent him a check, and when Mr. Chrisman responded by telephone to thank her, he sounded very emotional. He was quite ill, he said, and Molly's gift and gratitude were an encouragement to him.

****

Molly and Mrs. Logie

It was difficult for Molly to stay in touch with people who stayed in Burma. But she corresponded with many old friends who returned to the states: Gloria, Mrs. Logie, Mrs. Brown, Mrs. Graham, Evelyn McCabe, Miss Palmer, Martha Khin, Mrs. Kyaw Myint, and others.

After Owen was elected as a Newark city councilman, he traveled to a "Newarks of the World" celebration in Newark on Trent, England. His mother went along, and they met up with Molly's dear teacher Mrs. Logie in Birmingham for a wonderful reunion. Mrs. Logie cooked mohinga for them.

Molly was also able to see Mrs. Graham a few times when Mrs. Graham traveled to Washington, D.C. In January of 1975, Mrs. Graham wrote from her home in Hawaii:

Dear Molly,

GREETINGS TO YOU AND TO ALL THE FAMILY -- even though it is too late for Christmas or New Year greetings.

Reason for no cards was that I spent most of the month of November in the hospital for an operation – serious, but not dangerously so, thank goodness. I am getting along all right now, just too slowly to suit me.

My older sister Ruth came out to be with me and will stay now through March. She likes it here, too, and says she is coming to stay permanently some day. I doubt it, though. She missed the "little ones" – the grand-nieces and nephews.

Ruth did all the Christmas shopping and mailing for the family and the children, and all the writing of cards to them and to mutual friends. I am just now able to start catching up on my own special friends with whom I do not want to lose touch.

I was so glad to have your nice long letter with all the news of the children. They are all doing so well – you must be proud of them – and you are really to be congratulated on the wonderful job you have done, Molly dear. If I and our library programs contributed a little to your lives, I am so glad. But it was you who held them together after their father's death, and your example of hard work inspired them, I am sure.

I, too, think of the happy days together in Burma and get homesick at Christmas time for Burma and those happy times. I sit out on my lanai late at night, watching the stars, and thinking of the years past.

I am planning on going home for the summer months at our cottage.... I will probably go directly to Washington for the last week in June, and then go on up to the cottage for the 4th of July and rest of the summer. So, will be looking forward to seeing you and hopefully all of the children, including your new grand-daughter. How does it feel to be a grandmother?

Zelma Graham

I would agree with the children that it is time for you to stop working and live with one of them. Maybe after your son Owen graduates, you will consider it. You have worked hard all your life – maybe it is now time to take it easy. And you know, it really isn't hard to do. I am thoroughly enjoying doing nothing!

My love and very best wishes to all of you and looking forward to seeing you in June.

Zelma

A few months later, Molly would receive a note from Mrs. Graham's sister, Ruth, and the following article from a Honolulu newspaper:

Mrs. Zelma S. Graham, retired Foreign Service Officer, died quietly in her home here on April 15 at the age of 71. She has resided in Honolulu since her retirement in 1971 and has been active in international programs, serving on the Board of the United Nations Association and acting as host "Mother" for numerous East-West Center grantees. Mrs. Graham is best known for her work in Burma where she was unique in the Foreign Service in that she served 22 years in one country.

The library system which she established in Rangoon, Mandalay, and Moulmein was regarded by Washington as its most successful cultural project abroad. In 1959, she was the only living recipient of the Distinguished Service Award, the highest honor bestowed by the United States Information Agency, for "her unusual and significant contribution to American-Burmese relations through the development of an outstanding American Cultural Center program and the achievement of mutual understanding and respect among a broad representation of Burmese leaders and people." While the libraries were so outstanding that the Burmese government used them for research, they were unique in their children's library sections where over 14,000 Burmese children held library cards. Her annual "Children's Christmas Party" was attended by over 6000 children, each of whom received a gift lovingly wrapped by Mrs. Graham and her Burmese staff, and lasted for a month with sections scheduled five times a day in the library. In1962, with the onset of the military government in Burma, Mrs. Graham had to supervise the dismantling of the libraries which she established in 1948. Her last foreign assignment was in Kuala Lumpur from 1966-1968 where she was equally beloved by Malayans. Because of her contributions to librarianship, she was regularly called in as a consultant throughout Southeast Asia.

She and her husband, David W. Graham, first went to Burma in 1937 as Baptist missionaries. During the war, they worked with Dr. Gordon Seagrave, known throughout the world as the "Burma Surgeon." After the Japanese invasion, she and her husband joined the army, and her duties included service in India, North Burma, West China, and Thailand. She acted as secretary to both General "Vinegar Joe" Stilwell and to General Frank G. Merrill during these years. Following the death of her husband in 1946, she went to Columbia University for library training and then accepted the assignment to return to Burma....

****

Evelyn McCabe wrote Molly shortly after this, and excerpts of her letter follow.

...Yes, Zelma Graham's death was heartbreaking. We had looked forward to seeing her when we visited Mike in Hawaii. Zelma was in Mike's hospital clinic a couple years ago. I was so pleased when he told me he saw her name on the operation list and went in to say hello and to tell her that he was sure there was only one Zelma Graham—the one his mother and grandmother had loved. Of course they had never met, but I had told Mike that Z.G. had retired and was living in Hawaii...."

...Yes, I'll never forget our Christmas of 1000 bells and those precious children singing 'A Partridge in a Pear Tree.' We all worked hard, but I think we all loved it—I know I did. And I remember your little ones in Gene Schaffer's 'Twas the Night Before Christmas' and Jamal's Santa Claus jumping down the chimney!"

****

Molly felt the importance of her work at the GE library to help inform people about alcoholism, and she enjoyed her job. But when Charlene became a doctor and couldn't find good care for her two daughters, Molly asked herself, "Which is more important, my granddaughters or making money?" The decision for her was an easy one, and she quit her job to take care of the girls.

Some friends from work scolded her, "Why are you giving up this good job to become a nanny?" But Molly loved the children and considered it no great sacrifice. She knew how hard it had been to leave her own young children in the care of others. She would give Charlene peace of mind that her children were in loving care.

Molly taught the girls many things, including love for their country. They held flags and marched around the house, singing, "America the Beautiful" and "God Bless America." They also spent a lot of time at the local library. And Molly taught them the hymns and words of faith.

****

Molly continued to suffer many sorrows over the years. While she was caring for her two young grandchildren, their father James was trying to move a new mattress down steps, and he fell and hit his head. Molly and the children witnessed the accident.

Molly impulsively cried out to the girls, "Daddy fell down!"

Realizing something very serious had happened, her two-year old granddaughter would repeat the words over and over again in the next weeks, "Daddy fell down!" James's colleagues at the hospital tried to save him. But he, only thirty-four years old, died a few days later. An autopsy showed a very small tumor in his brain.

Molly tried to console Charlene, but Charlene comforted her mother, saying, "It is God's will."

Charlene was remembering that God is always good and could be loved and trusted even in this tragedy. In some mysterious way which she may never comprehend, God was still working for Charlene's good even as He allowed tragedy to wound her. She would seek Him for comfort.

Charlene later remarried. Her groom was also a doctor, and he also had two children. The couple had another daughter together.

At age forty-two, Tony was diagnosed with liver cancer. A transplant extended his life, but less than a year later he was failing again, the disease destroying Molly's vibrant son as it had destroyed her father. Molly saw Owen, now a young radiologist, look at his brother's x-ray when the cancer returned. His face changed, and he ducked quickly into Tony's library. Molly followed him there and found him weeping.

"Owen?"

"Mom. There is no hope," he cried. "It has spread to the portal vein and to the pancreas. No chance...."

When Tony was dying, he wanted time alone with each loved one to exchange a few last words. When it was Molly's turn to go to Tony, she tried to speak, but her voice failed, and she began to cry. She tried again but could not control her emotions. She thought, "This is no good for Tony!"

She began to recite the Twenty-Third Psalm and found her voice was steady. She saw that Tony was listening closely.

"The Lord is my shepherd, I shall not want; He makes me lie down in green pastures.
He leads me beside still waters; He restores my soul.
He leads me in paths of righteousness for His name's sake.
Even though I walk through the valley of the shadow of death, I fear no evil; for Thou art with me;
Thy rod and Thy staff, they comfort me.

Thou preparest a table before me in the presence of my enemies;
Thou anointest my head with oil, my cup overflows.
Surely goodness and mercy shall follow me all the days of my life;
and I shall dwell in the house of the Lord for ever."

When someone else was taking a turn to speak to Tony, Molly noticed from the next room that Tony's breathing had become loud and raspy, and she asked Owen, "Why is he breathing like that?"

Owen answered softly, "Mom, his body is shutting down."

She thought to herself, "What is the meaning of 'shutting down?'" But she didn't want an answer.

Then Tony stopped breathing.

Molly's wounded heart bled in the silence. "Oh, he is gone!"

Already Molly had experienced the terrible breaking of bonds between herself and her husband as he left this world! She had lost a son-in-law, and now she had lost a son! Oh, this was so painful, so tragic! How could this be endured?

A quiet voice in her soul reminded her, "I will never fail you. I will never forsake you."

Molly mourned deeply. She did not understand why James and Tony died so young. All she could do was to submit to God and leave the understanding to Him. God was not indifferent to her suffering; He too experienced deep sorrow, and He was very near to comfort her. Only by clinging to Him could this next thing be survived.

Tony's only child, a daughter, was seven when he died. His wife would be left alone to raise his daughter and to run the company he had founded.

Lois suffered two divorces, a serious car accident, and financial loss. Molly worried and grieved for this daughter. But she knew God loved her. God did care for her. He had proved Himself many times before. He was and would always be worthy of her trust.

Of Owen's first children, twins, one had a rare disease. Molly traveled with Owen and his wife when they moved to central Ohio for Owen to begin working there. She sat in the back seat caring for the infant girl as the ailing boy was held by his mother. On the drive to the Midwest, the family had to make frequent stops at gas stations to use electricity to operate a suction machine so the child could live a little longer. Once in central Ohio, he was hospitalized, but he did not survive infancy. Now Molly had lost a grandchild! This again seemed too much for the tender heart.

Had God failed her? Had God forsaken her? No, surely not. Her prayers pleading for healing were not answered for this little baby, but she knew Lord Jesus was near. She must trust Him.

Molly had learned that the aim of Christian faith is not to find a way to get God to answer her prayers the way she wants, though He listens compassionately to every prayer, and He very often intervenes. The point of faith is to know Him, trust Him, love Him, and follow Him, and to experience His intimate love. Even in the hardest circumstance, the loss of loved ones, Molly could find "the peace that passes understanding" and a persistent, quiet solace, not in present circumstances, but in knowing the almighty and loving God.

Molly herself would have remarkably good health until she was in her nineties. Then she suffered severe sciatic pain and rarely left home because of it. She felt, then, greater compassion for her husband, understanding the difficulty of having to endure lasting pain. No wonder he cried, "Come! Come! Come!" when she came home from work, hoping to find some comfort in her touch.

How could she live faithfully when every day was filled with pain? Again, she rested in God, knowing He was reaching also to her. She knew that she did not earn her suffering from bad karma. God was not punishing her. Instead, she was living in a fallen world, full of disease and decay and evil, cursed as a result of every person's rebellion against God.

Again, Molly knew she was not left to suffer alone. She remembered that Jesus left His heavenly home to share our sorrows. She thought of the cross, which Jesus hated but willingly endured as the worthy Redeemer for the sins of all people, reconciling God's holy need for justice with His deep, perfect love for imperfect people. Jesus went to the cross for her; she should be faithful to Him.

Molly loved God, and she trusted His promise that He was working all things for her good, even when she could not see this work. As always, Scripture brought her comfort: "We do not lose heart. Though our outer nature is wasting away, our inner nature is being renewed every day. For this slight momentary affliction is preparing for us an eternal weight of glory beyond all comparison."

As Molly looked back on her life, she observed that her experiences had often seemed without purpose, troubled, and confused. But as she neared the end of her years on earth, she recognized the help and providence of God as He led her on a well-tended path through each phase of her life. Truly, God never failed her nor forsook her.

She thought, in hindsight, that when God blessed her, she could be grateful for that blessing. Oh! God had richly and graciously blessed her life! Molly was struck with how often God had sent someone to help her.

When she thought of the hard times in her life, she also found a reason to be grateful, for in these times she learned more surely that God was very near her, helping her, loving her. Molly realized that even in the hardest times, she could find blessings to count and reasons to praise a worthy God. Only in these hardest times could she prove her love for and faith in God, who is always good.

On May 28, 2016, Molly Lee was awarded a high school diploma together by the Methodist English High School, (now Basic Education High School No. 1 Dagon), in Yangon, Myanmar and Granville Christian Academy in Ohio, USA, seventy- five years after the bombing of Rangoon interrupted her studies. She is shown above with Pastor Gary Kirkpatrick as she encouraged fellow graduates not to lose faith, no matter how great are life's difficulties, because God never fails us. Photo used by permission Barrett Lawlis/ The Advocate, Newark, Ohio.

****

Molly would ask her children and grandchildren, "Was I right to come here?" Each one in turn answered her, "Of course, Ah Ma!" "Of course, Grandma!" Beginning in extreme poverty when they arrived in the United States, her children embraced opportunities and worked hard to prosper. Grandchildren also excelled.

Molly once thought her Chinese name, Ngood Yin, Gentle Moon, was a foolish name, considering that the massive satellite around the earth could hardly be gentle. Perhaps she had given away too much appreciation of the poetry of her culture for the logic of the west. But, as a friend pointed out to her, the moon gently reflects the glorious light of the sun. Molly, Gentle Moon, also gently reflects the glorious light of the Son of God, and so she is very well named.

Molly expressed one main purpose in telling her story. She said, "See how the Lord works in my life? I really want to tell people that the Lord works in my life. You believe in Him. You trust Him. You really think it is so hopeless, but He gives what you need. He turns it around for you. For me. He always sends someone to help me. I want people to know they can have hope."

Afterward

I met Molly at an evening service at our church, Spring Hills Baptist. Soon we were good friends, participating in the same home group and attending other Bible studies together. I began to hear intriguing pieces of her story. I was impressed by this vibrant eighty-something woman who was effervescent in the joy of the Lord, though she had suffered much in life.

One evening, she told our home group about the night of Terence's vision. As she spoke, we were captivated, anticipating every word. She told about how her mother-in-law had blamed her for making Terence a Christian, which, her mother-in-law said, angered the gods, who caused Terence to be sick. She told about the doctor seeing Terence and advising that he would not live through the night. She told about her mother-in-law preparing her son for death. Molly told about her own desperate prayer, pleading to God to spare her husband's life until her children could stand on their own without a father, even specifying in her prayer about their finishing school.

Molly spoke in tones of undimmed awe about her husband's vision, the compassionate Being, the stroking of his hand, and Terence's urgent insistence that Molly remember for him. She told about the chamber pot. When she finished, we were all silent.

Molly didn't realize that she had built the story to a climactic tension and failed to resolve it. We all wanted to know!

Finally someone quietly asked the question filling the room, "Did your husband live?"

"Oh, yes!" Molly answered emphatically. "Another eighteen years! Until the children were grown!"

Our cheers exploded! We were delighted to share Molly's joy in the lovingly, miraculously answered prayer!

****

As the years went by, Molly would tell me once in a while, "People tell me I should write my story, but I don't think I can do it." I thought of helping her, but my life was busy.

Then one of my dear sisters was debilitated by a brain tumor, and I dropped everything to help care for her. It was a long and painful year, and then my precious sister died. I mourned.

Months later, I decided I wasn't going to pick up where I left off, saying "Yes" to everything that I thought might be pleasing to God. I was going to try to be very conscious of what God wanted me to do. I attended a Bible Study, "Discerning the Voice of God," by Priscilla Shirer. Everyone in the group expressed a passion for wanting to follow God's leading. I had a list of several things I thought God might be leading me to do, but I wasn't sure which one or ones. Writing Molly's story was on the list.

One young woman, Pam, expressed what many of us were feeling. "I want to do what God wants me to do, but I don't know what that is. I just want a phone call, and then I'll gladly do what He says!"

As we learned in the study, God chooses the way He reveals His will.

Around that time, our home group planned to celebrate Valentine's Day by showing a memento and sharing a story about a loved one. I asked Molly to bring something to share.

"I had to leave Burma with nothing!" she exclaimed. "You remember that I told you, I had to leave everything behind! Only fifty dollars for me, twenty-five for Lois, and twenty-five for Owen."

"Then, tell a story about you and your husband," I suggested. "You did not have to leave your memories behind."

On Valentine's Day she did tell a story. She told of her engagement, arranged without her knowledge, announced suddenly by the arrival of mooncakes. She told briefly of the escape to the hill country, the hurried wedding against her wishes, and the perilous ride in the tea truck. She expressed her gratitude that God had protected her, even though she was not yet a Christian. We were all enthralled, fascinated by the life of this tiny saint.

On the way home, my mother said, "Someone needs to write Molly's story!"

I wondered if God was speaking to me through my mother. I asked God for confirmation.

A few days later, another member of the home group, Oneta, called and spoke to my husband.

"I need to talk to Deanna. I think there is something she is supposed to do," Oneta said.

My protective husband replied, "Are you sure it's not something YOU are supposed to do?"

She said, "No. I can't do it. I think God is telling me that Deanna is supposed to write Molly's story."

Neither Oneta nor my mother knew about my prayer and the list I had discussed with the other Bible study group. In fact, when I informed my mom I was thinking about doing it, her response was, "I didn't mean you!" She never thought of me taking on such a project.

I was anxious to tell my "Discerning" group to see what they thought. Pam told me, with awe, "You got the phone call!" I hadn't thought of that. We all laughed, enjoying the mystery of God's ways. They all encouraged me to write Molly's story, and I was excited to do it.

From the beginning, I was drawn to Molly's joy in the Lord, though she had experienced much hardship. As I said, I had recently lost my sister and was hurting. I wanted to learn more deeply how one experiences suffering, yet grows stronger in faith and joy.

I told Molly that I thought God wanted me to help her to write her story, and the two of us were eager to get started! That was in the spring of 2008.

Imagine my thrill when, months into the project, I discovered Molly had pictures! She had told me repeatedly that she left Burma with nothing. It didn't occur to her to mention that her future brother-in-law brought some of her photographs. I stared at the faces of the people becoming well known to me.

Over the following years, people would sometimes ask, "When do you expect to have the book done?"

I would say, "Two..." "Four..." or "Seven years ago!" I never imagined it would take me over eight years to write the story!

I was learning about Burmese culture, Chinese culture, British culture, mid-twentieth century culture, the Second World War, Buddhism, socialism, and so on. Much of it was foreign to me. Molly would mention cheroot, or tiffins, or nats, or Guan Yin, or the Burma Road and I would stare at her blankly. With Molly's explanations and the information highway, I was becoming educated.

As the years passed, memories came to Molly like lost jigsaw puzzle pieces. I never told Molly, "You've told me that story before," so that as I listened again, intriguing new details would occasionally emerge after being forgotten for many decades.

For instance, she told me many times of the "escape to the hill country," and each time I would pepper her with questions about the village of Namhsan. This observant woman could tell me very little about the village or the people, and I would think, "She must've spent at least a year or two there. Why does she remember so little?"

Of course, the decades of closeting painful memories would be explanation enough. In fact, Molly couldn't remember at first how she got to Namhsan. She thought that she must have gone there with her family, so I wrote it that way, researching what she might have seen and guessing what she might have done on the trip. I was hoping this would trigger memories, and she would say, "That's just how it was!" as she did sometimes. But no, it wasn't right. Then she thought maybe she went in the caravan of trucks with her in-laws. I wrote it that way, but that wasn't right either. Eventually she remembered that her protective fiancee would not let her out of his sight, and so she travelled to Namhsan with Terence.

After hearing the story many times of the escape to the hill country, I was stunned when Molly mentioned that when the family was in Namhsan her father commanded that she and her sisters cut their hair and wear their brothers' clothes. Until that time and subsequent mention of the Japanese soldiers actually coming to the village, I hadn't realized that she and her sisters were precarious prisoners hiding in their hill country refuge, leaving the relative safety of the house only to go to the outhouse. I mentioned to Molly that she had not told me this part of the story before. She said she had not thought of it for many years.

New details came not just from Molly's slowly unfolding layers of memory. As the years went by, I found I could learn more and more information on the internet. With the devastating cyclone Nargis of May 2008, the scarcely noticed, languishing country of Burma, also called Myanmar by correct phonetic pronunciation of the country's historic name, was suddenly in the news. After a few weeks of heightened public interest, I found that the sparse information on Google satellite maps was updated, so that I could actually see the streets of Rangoon.

I was curious to find the street of Molly's childhood home. But where was Maung Khine Street? Eventually some road names were added to the map, and I asked Molly about them, but this only confused her. It was some weeks before I found out that the government in Burma had changed the names of many roads in Burma, claiming that this action was to be further liberation from the occupation of Britain, though critics said that it was only meant to distract from the failings of Burmese officials. Some weeks later I found the comparable Rosetta Stone for identifying Rangoon roads, a list of former and corresponding current road names printed online by some precious soul. Spellings could be variable, such as Mg Khine or Maung

Khine Street, but at last I could pick out the road and even the roof of the still-standing four-story house where Molly grew up!

Even so, it took Molly a little while to embrace the discovery. When I showed Molly the map image with old road names penned in, I asked for her confirmation, "Were you this close to the water?" of the wide Rangoon River. I was surprised that she had not mentioned this.

She said strongly, "No!" And then slowly, reflectively, "Yes." We concluded that her sequestered Chinatown experience rarely induced her to venture south toward the river, and she did not realize that warehouses and docks were just beyond the next block. It was not a place for a little girl to explore, nor did it appeal to the teenager whose attentions were on the English school northeast of home. Designed for international shipping, not sightseeing or recreation, neither were the docks the place for the young man, Terence, to woo Molly.

During the years of our writing, I could find more and more historical data online. I could find U.S. military lists of sorties to confirm it was Allied planes flying over Pyapon at the time the Lees were daily hiding in the cemetery. I wondered whether a little more digging would reveal the name of the gunner who restrained from firing on the terrified man, now loved by us, while he was heroically racing away with a pony cart to deflect machine gun fire from his family. But there were other trails to follow.

After fruitless months of periodically Googling the American Baptists, I located a research arm, The American Baptist Historical Society. I was able to contract a researcher to find information for me on the pastors who served the Immanuel Baptist Church, but she also found information on the Grahams, the Chrismans, and others. This helped to fill in many of the remaining mysteries, to my benefit and yours. I incorporated much of this information into the story rather than to tack it on at the end.

I was privileged to hear from a few of Molly's relatives as well. Dr. Owen was very helpful instructing me on the likely order of events, clarifying confusion, and adding facets to his mother's story. He even contacted friends and former classmates scattered around the world, or remaining in Burma, to help me with some detail or other.

Foke San was also able to clarify and expand family history for me. For instance, Molly never knew that after Lee Ah Poi died, Wat Hong assigned Sit Hong to manage a rice mill. But when Wat Hong died suddenly, at age 34, creditors swamped Sit Hong to collect on debts, and intended to foreclose on shops, a rice mill, a lumber mill, and the soy sauce factory. "At that critical moment, my father went into severe shock, fainted, and had to be cared for many months. My mother, (who was never exposed to any business dealings), jumped into action, borrowed an unsecured loan and paid some of the creditors thus saving the main grocery shop, the soy sauce factory, and a few pawn shops." It was the husband of a friend of his mother's, San said, who loaned her the money and saved the family from ruin. This insight added to my great admiration for Mrs. Lee, the hero among women, and my compassion for Lee Sit Hong who experienced great hardships, as a child from threatened kidnapping and loss of his mother, and as an adult from sudden financial collapse at his brother's death, war, and a hostile governance. As I learned from Molly and others, each person was doing his best through difficult and harrowing circumstances.

Rumors and differing perspectives about lost wealth circulate in the branches of the families, but the Lee and Chin children who left Burma did not need to depend on the wealth of earlier generations. In countries providing education and promoting business, they would make their own prosperity. No one I spoke with wants to dwell on material losses of the past, but all of my sources agree that WWII and the socialist take-over in Burma were severe detriments to prosperity.

I came to love Molly dearly through the years of our book-writing adventure together. As she openly told me her story, I was surprised to find I also came to love many other wonderful, dynamic characters by her telling, including relatives, teachers, classmates, and saints from America who reached out to a nation broken by war to build libraries, buildings, hope, and life-long friendships.

Molly's husband is such a tragic figure, yet admirable, persevering, and of enduring faith. When I mentioned to a great-niece about Molly's arranged marriage, she asked, "Did Molly come to love him?" I knew that I had come to love him through Molly's telling, so I guessed the answer. But, recently, I asked Molly directly, and she said, "At first, I thought he was a spoiled brat, and I tried to correct him. But, yes, I learned to love him. He appreciated me. And I admired his honesty and the way he loved people. He was very generous. If someone was sick, he would buy medicine for him."

And through Molly's eyes I saw that Mrs. Lee, though harsh with Molly, must be admired for her strength of character and rising to challenging circumstances. As I have been told, and as the saying hints, Chinese culture expected mothers-in-law to be demanding of their sons' wives: "The patience of a daughter-in-law results from her desire to become a mother-in-law of the future." Mrs. Lee can also be understood for trying to reform her seemingly wayward son and daughter-in-law; it is no small thing for a parent to see the investment and effort of parenting disregarded and treasured values dismissed by his or her children, whether or not those choices are well made. The young children of Mr. and Mrs. Lee can also be understood for learning the resentment of their parents, and their great kindness to Molly in adulthood bears the sweetness of grace.

I want to mention that much of the dialog in the book is recorded just as Molly remembered it. Other conversations, I wrote, and she when she read them, she felt that they were generally accurate in message if not actual words. One conversation is different. Molly could not really remember what Pastor Eastman told her and Terence after their baptisms. She thought it concerned being faithful to God. I wrote Mr. Eastman at his last known address, which I obtained from the American Baptist Historical Society, but I received no reply. (According to their records, if living, he would now be 98 years old.) Because it was such an important time in the lives of the couple, I tried to offer a reasonable message from a Christian pastor to new believers. The subject of God's jealousy seemed to satisfy this and felt appropriate to the story. One statement that I attribute to him came from another Baptist pastor, Tom Pound, in a sermon just a couple weeks before my deadline: "The Bible contains more than wisdom; it is God's own living, transforming Word." I hope I have not misprested Mr. Eastman.

The Author

Note: All quotes from the Bible are either King James Version or Revised Standard.

Epilogue

Myanmar has been a suffering nation for so long. As I have heard from several people, there have been reforms recently which give them hope for a better future.

One heroine in the struggle for improved conditions, greatly admired by Molly, is Aung San Suu Kyi. She is the daughter of Aung San, the champion for independence from Great Britain, and she was not even two years old when her father was assassinated. When grown, she worked for three years at the United Nations in New York City, and she married and had two sons. She returned to Myanmar to care for her ailing mother in 1988, but her people impulsively rallied around her, and she became a champion for the oppressed people of her country and a leader of the pro-democracy movement. Though she sacrificed seeing her husband and children, she remained in Myanmar, fearing that if she left her native country she would not be permitted to return; she felt compelled to support her people. For much of the time after that, she was under house arrest as a political prisoner. The military junta allowed a general election in 1990, and the National League for Democracy won a majority of votes for seats in a parliament. Many thought Suu Kyi would become prime minister, but the military refused to hand over power, and she remained under house arrest. After another election supporting democracy, Su Kyi hoped to take an administrative role, but those in power arbitrarily disqualified her for having sons of mixed race.

Others have also made heroic efforts to improve conditions in Myanmar. Notably, brave students and monks have assembled for large, peaceful, protests. Many lost their lives in the process. Our prayers are with the beleaguered and exploited people of Myanmar.

The Author

Acknowledgements

Myanmar has been a suffering nation for so long. As I have heard from several people, there have been reforms recently which give them hope for a better future.

I observe that acknowledgements most often come at the beginning of a book, but I wanted you to read *Gentle Moon* first to better understand the contributions of the people named. As I reflect on the years invested in writing *Gentle Moon*, I realize that, though the task often seemed lonely, I could not have accomplished this venture alone.

I must first recognize Molly for her willingness to share her life with us, for her candor, and for her endurance, particularly as health has waned, in answering endless questions. I note that, unless one is driven to fame, baring one's life to others involves relinquishing ownership of something precious. I am grateful that Molly trusted me to convey her story, and I am greatly blessed by the friendship that has grown between us. Molly, at age 94, did the calligraphy for the book, the several Chinese characters and the Burmese characters for Myanmar. She has wanted to do this for many months, but has not felt well. She pushed herself to do it, just before our deadline.

Other characters in Molly's story have also given up, often without expressed permission, some parts of their own personal experiences. Some will likely remember things a bit differently than is expressed herein. Maybe they or their loved ones are exposed to the reading public in ways not entirely to their preference, and I regret that. Hopefully, they will find their stories have been reflected authentically and with love.

I am grateful to those who helped inform *Gentle Moon*. I must single out Dr. Owen Lee especially, and I offer my sincere thanks. Foke San, Gabriel, a son of Lily, a son of Fe Heng, and Lois offered insights and helpful advice, and Dorothy remembered a few details her sister had forgotten. Gloria also contributed, as did a son and a daughter of the Chrismans. Vernon is recognized for saving and returning to Molly the letters from Tony, for decoding them, and for sharing them.

I'm grateful that Terence took many pictures and that Ray saved them. Thanks to the U.S. Embassy in Burma, to Lifetouch, to The Newark Advocate, to Owen Lee, and to Megan Vannatta for the use of pictures.

Friends Bruce and Robin Malone have been prayerful and practical supporters of this project from the start. Thanks to Bruce for wise counsel and experienced help publishing my book and to Robin for detailed editing and helpful feedback. Thank-you to Michael Malone for drawing the map of Burma.

Many helpers I will never know personally. Who are the devoted contributors to the information highway, diligently scanning books, documents, maps, and photos; supplying data; and writing encyclopedic descriptions? Who are the dedicated informants of Wikipedia, already having posted answers to my questions before I knew to ask them? To these unknown benefactors, I express my gratitude.

Thanks are due the American Baptist Historical Society, office of Janet Winfield, and particularly to Rachel Sherron, the student worker who did research for me. Several of the heroes mentioned herein are better known because of her work.

I also acknowledge the contribution of the late Harley Swiggum for his vision of The Writing Academy, recently disbanded, which week-long seminars I attended several times when I was a young adult, and which gave me encouragement and training to write. Thanks to the many speakers and instructors at the Academy. Several school teachers, (*Mr. Richardson, Mrs. Hedges, Mr. Profit, Mr. Cellini, Mr. Heigle, and others*), challenged me to write well.

My home group also buoyed me with prayer, encouragement, and critique: John and Wilma Burton, Arnold and Pauline Kesterson, Jim and Dixie Merrill, Merry May Rogers (*my mother*), Gary and Linda Rudolph, Jim and Betty Schuler, Jim and Oneta Shaw, Mary and Ernie Shepard, Dotti Turner, and Jim Windon (*my husband*). Oneta is noted for hearing God and for making a phone call at His urging. Thanks also to the Discerning women's Bible study group.

I thank Rick Hansen for crash reading and focused error-catching in the closing days before the deadline.

I appreciate my family members for their dependable support. Thanks for last minute reading, editing, and valued comment by Patty Hussey (*niece*) and Julie Murphy (*sister*).

I can hardly express how much the love and encouragement of my parents, Otis and Merry May Rogers, have always meant to me, or how much I miss them. My dad has been gone from us for some time, but I supposed, as I began this project, that I would first read the completed *Gentle Moon* to my mom. However, "It was not God's will." For the first five years of this project, Mama was my biggest cheerleader.

Finally, I thank my husband Jim, who would much rather watch TV than read. Supporting another one's work when you can't relate to it is challenging. He couldn't imagine how I could spend so much time on a story which he could tell in a half hour. Done. He admits to being frustrated, when I finally read a late draft of the book to him and Molly together, that I described Molly's childhood home "tile by tile." Nevertheless, in some miraculous way, he has grown to share the vision of sharing Molly's story and to be supportive of his wife. Recently he has been chopping a lot of fresh salsa and salads for me, washing many dishes, and folding laundry, all of which is greatly appreciated. Lately, as I have climbed the stairs to my computer to work on the book, I would say, "I'm off to Burma!" and he would answer, "Don't forget to write!" Also, I acknowledge that he is making a substantial financial investment in a shaky business proposition with no expectation of gain. This is profoundly against his frugal bent, and I am profoundly grateful to see his bent bend.

I sincerely thank God for the honor of Molly's friendship and for privilege of this work we have shared. To Him be the glory!

Blessings to all,

Deanna Windon

The author lives in Granville, Ohio with her husband Jim. They have two grown sons. Jim's son Eric Vannatta lives with his wife Megan in Baltimore, Ohio. Matt Windon lives in Erlanger, Kentucky.

List of Characters Alphabetically

(Omitting "Ah," "Cousin," "Doctor," "Mr.," "Mrs.," etc. Note that "Ah" is often added before a Chinese name, "to make it sound nice.")

Alice,* an English girl and accomplished student of Miss Reed's dance classes

Anita,* Choon Fong, eldest child, Number One Daughter of Lee Sit Hong and Lee Chin Htwe Khim

Anna,* a Jewish classmate and friend of Molly

Arthur Parolini, budget and fiscal officer at the embassy, Molly's boss

Baht Sook, Ngood's mentor, brother of Ngood's aunt's husband

Bartel, Miss, Molly's eighth grade teacher at MEGHS, later Mrs. Logie and principal of MEHS

Beulah, maid of Molly's

Bridges, Ray,* courier for the embassy, a Buddhist American

Brown, Mr. and Mrs., pastor at Immanuel Baptist Church and his wife, helped Molly get an application for the USIS Library

Byu Goo, beloved companion of Ngood's mother

Carol,* an Anglo-Indian girl who taught new songs from "the west"

Carolyn, friend and co-worker of Molly at GE

Charlene* (*Ngwan Hing*), Molly's older daughter

Charles,* boyfriend of Charlene, his family moved to Hong Kong

Chin Hone Foo, Ngood's father, Number Two Son of Chin Mung Yee

Chin Hone Ham, Number Four Uncle, fourth son of Chin Mung Yee

Chin Hone Kam, Number Three Uncle, third son of Chin Mung Yee

Chin Hone On (*Old Man Thunder Voice*), Number One Uncle, first son of Chin Mung Yee

Chin Sen Kee (*Johnny**), "New Machinery or Intelligence," Molly's middle surviving brother, Number Four Son of Chin Hone Foo and Chin Wong Po Sun

Chin Sen King (*Clark**), "New Scenery," Molly's oldest surviving brother, Number Three Son of Chin Hone Foo and Chin Wong Po Sun

Chin Sen Phat (*Wayne**), "New Abundant Riches," Molly's youngest surviving brother, Number Five Son of Chin Hone Foo and Chin Wong Po Sun

Choon Fong* (*Anita**), "Spring Flower," Number One Sister of Terence, (*married Sammy Ng**)

Chow, Mr. and Mrs.* Yunnanese friends who asked Terence and Molly to
    manage their home

Clara,* worked at the circulation desk with Molly, invited Molly to her
son's shinbyu ceremony

Clark* (*Chin Sen King, "New Scenery"*), Molly's eldest surviving brother,
    Number Three Son of Chin Hone Foo and Chin Wong Po Sun

Daisy, maid of Molly's

Dolly,* Molly's cousin, eldest daughter of Number One wife of Number
    One Uncle, studied in Hong Kong, very modern

Donna, mother of Evelyn McCabe

Doris,* worked at the circulation desk with Molly until Martha Khin
    moved her to another area

Dorothy (*Ngood Haing*), youngest sister, Number Five Daughter of
    Chin Hone Foo and Chin Wong Po Sun

Durham, Gwendoline, Miss, teacher of 3-4th grade at MEGHS

Durham, Miss, teacher of math and geography at MEGHS,
    later Mrs. Mogran

Durwan, doorman at the four-story house

Eastman, Mr. and Mrs., pastor of Immanuel Baptist Church and his wife,
    baptized Molly and Terence

Edward * (*Puck Ken*), cousin of Terence and son of Lee Wat Hong

Ei May Tun,* head of junior library circulation, Molly assisted her with
    reports

Eng Koon (*Tony*), "Supreme Power," Molly's older son

Lois (*Ngwan Har*), "Lasting Glory", Molly's younger daughter

Evelyn McCabe, replaced Mrs. Graham as director of the library, then
    transferred to Madras

Fe Heng, "Wise Fill-in," Number Four Sister of Terence

Fe Lan (*Lily*), "Wise or Pretty Flower," Number Two Sister of Terence,
    (*married Myo Khin*)

Fe Yin, "Wise Swallow," Number Five Sister of Terence

Fe Yone, "Wise Appearance," Number Three Sister of Terence,
    (*married William**)

Foke Loke,* "Lucky Good Material Things," Number Seven Brother of
Terence

Foke San,* "Lucky Mountain," Number Six Brother of Terence

Frank,* husband of Molly's sister Ginger*

Gabriel* (*Get Lee**), first son of Anita* and Sammy*

Get Lee* (*Gabriel**), first son of Anita* and Sammy*

Ginger* (*Ngood He-ung*), "Moon Fragrant," Ngood's younger sister,
    (*married Frank**)

Gloria,* a small fly with Molly in the library, started in cataloging and
moved to head of young people's library, also worked at the embassy after
    the library closed

Gracie,* helpful Kayin classmate at MEHS, Molly and Yim Sie visited her
    farm in Insein, wanted to be a doctor

Graham, Zelma, dynamic founder and director of the USIS Library

Grandfather Chin (*Chin Mung Yee, "Great Scholar"*), migrated from China
    to Burma, father of Ngood's father, built four-story house

Grandfather Wong (*Wong Ngood Lao, "Moon Observatory"*), titled "Excellent Scholar," father of Ngood's mother

Grandmother Chin, Ngood's father's mother, never met by Ngood

Grandmother Wong, Ngood's mother's mother, called Ngood "My Little
    Mouse"

Han Yee (*Po Han*), Ngood's Aunt, her mother's youngest sister

Haung Se'ung, Foke San's nanny

Hearst, Mr.,* salesman for GE

Hem, Papa's Sino-Indian attendant

Hlai Pwa, "Lesser Grandmother," Second wife of Grandfather Chin,
    mother of Tuck Sook

Hop,* son of Byu Goo

Indian Gardener

Irene Bridges,* mother of Ray Bridges*

Jacobs, Mr.,* accountant at embassy, deacon at Immanuel Baptist Church

James,* a boyfriend of Charlene, a medical student

Jean,* Chinese classmate year ahead of Molly at MEHS, introduced Molly
    to dance class

Johnny* (*Sen Kee, "New Machinery or Intelligence,"*) Number Four Brother
    of Ngood

Joyce, Michael, consular officer at the embassy

Judy,* Japanese classmate who shared Molly's shame, daughter of Dr.
Sato*

Khin, Martha, head of the junior library, Molly's boss at the USIS library

Kyaw Myint, Mrs.,* head of cataloging at USIS Library

Larry and Marlene Teien, pen pal of Terence, sponsored family to come
      to the US

Lee Ah Poi, father of Lee Wat Hong and Lee Sit Hong, grandfather of
      Puck Ying, migrated from China to Burma

Lee Chin Htwe Khim, Puck Ying's mother, "Nye Nye" to Ngood

Lee Go Wan, Mrs., teacher of Mandarin at Chinese school

Lee Sit Hong, "Honoring the Generations," Puck Ying's father

Lee Tin Hone, Miss, teacher at Chinese school

Lee Wat Hong, older brother of Lee Sit Hong, uncle of Puck Ying

Len, Ngood's cousin, daughter of Number One Wife of Ngood's
      Number One Uncle

Leon,* young marine at the embassy

Lily (Fe Lan), Number Two Sister of Terence, married Myo Khin

Linsdale, Mrs., taught biology and botany at MEGHS

Louise,* classmate at MEHS, daughter of a Burmese judge, wanted to be a
      doctor

Lo Yeahr, "Old Dad," Ngood's father-in-law, Lee Sit Hong

Mable,* secretary in consular's office

Mar-Meng, "Horse Face," one of two beasts said to drag the dead to hell
      for judgement

Martha Khin, head of the junior library, Molly's boss at the USIS library

Mary, Molly's cousin, daughter of Number Two Wife of Ngood's
      Number One Uncle

Ma Seng, maid of Molly's

Maude, Molly's boss at GE Clearing House for Alcoholism

McCabe, Evelyn, director of USIS Library in Mrs. Graham's absence,
      transferred to Madras, India

Michael Joyce, consular officer at the embassy

Miriam, receptionist and friend of Molly at GE

Moonlight (Ngood Ming, "Moon Light"), Ngood's oldest sister

Myo Khin, married Number Two Sister of Terence, Fe Lan

Nellie, Molly's cousin, daughter of Number Two Wife of Ngood's
      Number One Uncle

Ng, Gabriel *(Get Lee*), first son of Anita* and Sammy*

Ng, Sammy* (Dr. Ng*), married Terence's sister Anita*

Ng, Stanley,* older brother of Sammy,* married Cousin Dolly*

Ngood (*Molly*), first name shared with her sisters, but Molly was called by this name

Ngood Haing, "Moon Sweet and Nice," (*Dorothy**), Ngood's youngest sister

Ngood He'ung, "Moon Fragrant," (*Ginger**), Ngood's younger sister

Ngood Ming, "Moon Light," (*Moonlight*), Ngood's oldest sister

Ngood Yin, "Moon Gentle," (*Ngood*), (*Molly*)

Ngow-How, "Cow Head," one of two beasts said to drag the dead to hell for judgement

Ngwan Har, "Lasting Glory," (*Lois*), Molly's younger daughter

Ngwan Hing, "Lasting Grace," (*Charlene**), Molly's older daughter, oldest child

Ni Hta, Daw,* head of reference, second in power at the library after Mrs. Graham

Nye Nye, "Respected Madam," Ngood's mother-in-law

Ohn Koon (*Owen*), Molly's younger son, youngest child

Owen (*Ohn Koon*), Molly's younger son, youngest child

Palmer, Miss Margery, Arthur Parolini's replacement as budget and fiscal officer at the embassy, Molly's boss

Papa, (*Ah Pa, Chin Hone Foo*), Ngood's father

Parolini, Arthur, budget and fiscal officer at the embassy, Molly's boss

Phyllis,* friend of Charlene

Po Han (*Han Yee*), Molly's Number Four Aunt, her mother's sister, a teacher

Po Har, Ngood's Number Three Aunt, lived next door to four-story house

Poi, Lee Ah, father of Lee Wat Hong and Lee Sit Hong, grandfather of Puck Ying, migrated from China to Burma

Polly,* Kayin pianist at USIS library, met Molly in Pyapon, gave her a Gideon New Testament

Po Sun (*Mama*), Ngood's mother, eldest Wong sister

Po Swe, Ngood's Number Two Aunt, lived in Moulmein

Puck Hee, "Hundred Times Great," Number Two Brother of Terence, a doctor and poet

Puck Hem, "Hundred Times Add-On," Number Five Brother of Terence, died at age five

Puck Hong, "Hundred Times Healthy," Number Three Brother of Terence, died before age one

Puck Ken (*Edward**), cousin of Terence and son of Lee Wat Hong

590 | GENTLE MOON

Puck Koon, "Hundred times a Gentleman," Number Four Brother of
    Terence
Puck Ying, "Hundred Times Heroic," Terence
Pwa, Ah, "Grandmother," name Ngood called her Grandmother Wong

Pwa Pwa, "Grandmother," name Ngood called the servant at the four-
story house
Pwe Sah, tea broker, generous Buddhist at the warehouse in Mandalay
Ray Bridges,* courier for the embassy, a Buddhist American
Reed, Mrs., dance teacher
Reid, teacher at MEGHS, tutored Molly in Burmese
Reid, (Big Reid), principal of MEGHS
Rita,* sister of Molly's brother-in-law William*
Rudy,* Chinese businessman and friend of Terence
Ruth,* powerful woman at library, assistant to Mrs. Graham
Sally,* Persian classmate at MEGHS, wanted to be a doctor
Sammy Ng,* (Dr. Ng*), married Anita*
Samson, Mr.,* head of accounting at the embassy
Santucci, Molly's boss at GE
Sato, Dr.,* Mrs. Lee's Japanese doctor and friend
Sawbwa, "Lord of the Heavens," hereditary ruler of one of the semi-
    independent Shan States
Sen Kee (Johnny*), middle surviving brother of Ngood, Number Four Son
of Chin Hone Foo and Chin Wong Po Sun
Sen King (Clark*), oldest surviving brother of Ngood, Number Three Son
of Chin Hone Foo and Chin Wong Po Sun
Sen Phat (Wayne*), youngest surviving brother of Ngood, Number Five
Son of Chin Hone Foo and Chin Wong Po Sun
Sit Hong (Lo Yeahr), father of Puck Ying
Stanley Ng,* older brother of Sammy,* married Molly's Cousin Dolly*
Su Su, Daw,* head of junior library after Martha Khin left, Molly's boss
        Tan, a Chinese classmate whose full name was difficult
        to pronounce
Teien, Larry and Marlene, pen pal of Terence, sponsored family to come
to the USTony (Eng Koon), Molly's older son
Tuck Sook, young uncle and playmate of Ngood
Vernon,* a friend of Tony's, wrote him from England
Walter Bridges,* step-father of Ray Bridges*

Wat Hong, older brother of Lee Sit Hong, uncle of Puck Ying

Wayne* *(Sen Phat, "New Abundant Riches")*, Number Four Brother of Ngood

Wells, Mrs., ninth grade teacher of Ngood at MEGHS

Westbrook, Mrs., personnel office worker in embassy

Wong, Miss, principal at Chinese school, taught old Chinese writing

Wong, Mr.,* benefactor and carnival organizer in Namhsan

Wu, Mr., married Moonlight

Yim Sie, adopted child of neighbor and classmate of Molly

Zelma Graham, dynamic founder and director of the USIS Library

List of Characters by Relationship

The Chin family:

Grandfather Chin, Molly's paternal grandfather, Chin Mung Yee, "Great
Scholar" [Two wives: Grandmother Chin and Hlai Pwa, "Lesser
Grandmother"]

Papa, Ah Pa, Molly's father, Chin Hone Foo, "Abundant Wealth"

Molly's father's brothers:

Number One Uncle, "Old Man Thunder Voice," ChinHone On, "Abundant
Peace," [Four Wives: #1 Wife (*deaf*); #2 Wife; #3 Wife (*Burmese*); #4
Wife (*sister of actress*)] |

Number Three Uncle, Chin Hone Kam, "Abundantly Gleaming"

Number Four Uncle, Chin Hone Ham, "Abundantly Admireable"

Grandfather Wong, Molly's maternal grandfather, Wong Ngood Lao,
"Pavilion to Enjoy the Moon," (*titled Excellent Scholar*)

Grandmother Wong, Ah Pwa, Molly's maternal grandmother, Chou Fone
Mau, "Pheasant Tail"

Mama, Ah Ma, Molly's mother, Wong Po Sun, "Treasure Graceful or
Precious Coral"Molly's mother's sisters: #2 Po Swe (*Moulmein*); # 3 Po
Har (*next door*); #4 Po Han (*teacher*) "Han Yee"

Molly and her siblings:

Ngood Ming, "Moonlight"

Ngood Yin, "Moon Gentle," Molly

Ngood He-ung, "Moon Fragrant," Ginger,* (*married Frank**)

Sen King, "New Scenery," Clark*

Sen Kee, "New Machinery or Intelligence," Johnny*

Sen Phat, "New Abundant Riches," Wayne*

Ngood Haing, "Moon Sweet and Nice," Dorothy*

Chin Household attendants:

Pwa Pwa, like a grandmother, an older servant of Molly's mother

Byu Goo, like an auntie, a personal attendant and friend of Molly's
mother

Ah Hop,* "Agreeable," son of Byu Goo

Ah Hem, Papa's Sino-Indian attendant

The Durwan, doorman at four-story house

Chin Family Associates:
Mr. Wong, benefactor of the Chin family during the war and carnival
organizer in Namhsan

The Lee family:
Lee Ah Poi, "Poi" means "to keep company," Terence's paternal
grandfather
Lee Wat Hong, "Wat" means "alive," "Hong" means "clan" or "family;"
could be translated, "Keep alive the Descendents," Terence's uncle
Lee Sit Hong, "Sit" means "branch, "Hong" means "clan" or "family";"
could be translated "Honor this Branch of the Generations," Lo
Yeahr, "Old Dad," Terence's father
Lee Htwe Khim, "Beautiful Green Piano," Nye Nye, Mrs. Lee, Terence's
mother
Terence and his siblings:
Choon Fong,* "Spring Flower," Anita,* Number One Sister of Terence,
(married Sammy Ng*)
Puck Ying, "Hundred Times Heroic," Terence
Puck Hee, "Hundred Times Great," Number Two Brother of Terence,
a doctor and poet
Puck Hong, "Hundred Times Healthy," Number Three Brother of Terence,
died before age one
Fe Lan, "Wise or Pretty Flower," Lily, Number Two Sister of Terence,
(married Myo Khin)
Fe Yone, "Wise Appearance," Number Three Sister of Terence, (married
William*)
Puck Koon, "Hundred times a Gentleman," Number Four Brother of
Terence
Puck Hem, "Hundred Times Add-On," Number Five Brother of Terence,
died at age five
Fe Heng, "Wise Fill-in," Number Four Sister of Terence
Fe Yin, "Wise Swallow," Number Five Sister of Terence
Foke San,* "Lucky Mountain," Number Six Brother of Terence
Foke Loke,* "Lucky Good Material Things," Number Seven Brother of
Terence
Gabriel,* Get Lee,* "Everything Fortunate," first son of Anita* and
Sammy*

Lee Household attendants:
Haung Se'ung, Foke San's* nanny
Indian Gardener
Ma Seng, maid of Molly's
Daisy, maid of Molly's
Beulah, maid of Molly's

Lee family relations, friends, and associates:
Dr. Sato,* Mrs. Lee's Japanese doctor and friend
Dr. Ng,* Sammy, married Anita*
Mr. and Mrs. Ng,* traveled with Lees to Namhsan, and later stayed with them at soy sauce factory
Stanley Ng,* older brother of Sammy, married cousin Dolly*
Sammy Ng,* Dr. Ng,* married Anita*
Cousin Edward,* Puck Ken, son of Lee Wat Hong

Molly's playmates and classmates:
Cousin Len, daughter of Number One Wife of Ngood's
  Number One Uncle
Cousin Mary, daughter of Number Two Wife of Ngood's
  Number One Uncle
Cousin Nellie, daughter of Number Two Wife of
  Ngood's Number One Uncle
Cousin Dolly,* daughter of Number One Wife of Ngood's
  Number One Uncle
Tuck Sook, young son of Grandfather Chin, Ngood's uncle and playmate
Yim Sie, adopted child of neighbor and classmate of Molly
Gracie,* Kayin classmate at MEHS, wanted to be a doctor
Sally,* Persian classmate at MEHS, wanted to be a doctor
Louise,* Burmese classmate at MEHS, wanted to be a doctor
Jean,* Chinese classmate year ahead of Molly atMEHS, introduced Molly to dance class
Anna,* Jewish classmate
Judy,* Japanese classmate who shared Molly's shame, daughter of Dr. Sato*
Alice,* English classmate and accomplished student of Miss Reed's dance classes
Tan, Chinese classmate whose full name was difficult to pronounce
Carol,* Anglo-Indian classmate who taught new songs from "the west"

Molly's teachers:
Miss Lee Ting Hone, teacher at Chinese school
Mrs. Lee Go Wan, Mandarin teacher at Chinese school
Miss Wong, principal at Chinese school, taught old Chinese writing
Ah Baht Sook, Molly's mentor, a brother of her aunt's husband
Miss Reid, teacher at MEGHS, helped Molly learn Burmese
Miss Reid, "Big Reid," principal of MEGHS
Mrs. Reed, gave dance lessons
Miss Gwendolin Durham, taught third-fourth grade at MEGHS
Miss Durham, later Mrs. Morgan, taught math and geography in high school at MEGHS
Miss Bartel, later Mrs. Logie, eighth grade teacher, later principal at MEGHS
Mrs. Linsdale, taught biology and botany at MEGHS
Mrs. Wells, ninth grade teacher at MEHS

Molly's children and their friends:
Ngwan Hing, "Lasting Grace," Charlene*
Eng Koon, "Supreme Power," Tony
Ngwan Har, "Lasting Glory," Lois
Ohn Koon, "Powerful and Respected Leader," Owen
James,* a boyfriend of Charlene, a medical student
Charles,* a boyfriend of Charlene, moved to Hong Kong
Phyllis,* a friend of Charlene who visited Terence in the hospital
Vernon,* a friend of Tony's, wrote him from England

Pastors and adult friends:
Mr. and Mrs. Chow,* Yunnanese friends who asked Terence and Molly to manage their home
Mr. and Mrs. Chrisman,* Mr. Chrisman hired Terence to help rebuild after the war and they became lasting friends
Mr. Eastman, the pastor of Immanuel Baptist Church who baptized Molly and Terence Mr. Zimmerman, the pastor who named Lois
Mr. Brown, the pastor who visited Terence and helped Molly apply to the USIS library
Rudy,* Chinese businessman and friend of Terence

Co-workers at the USIS Library:
Rita,* sister of William,* helped Molly to apply to work at the library
Mrs. Graham, dynamic founder and director of the USIS Library
Miss Westbrook, personnel office worker in embassy

Miss Rosenfeld, manager of library in Mrs. Graham's absence
Martha Khin, head of the junior library, Molly's boss at the USIS library
Mrs. Evelyn McCabe, replaced Mrs. Graham as director of the library,
    lived with her mother Donna, transferred to Madras
Ei May Tun,* head of junior library circulation, Molly assisted her with
    reports
Mrs. Kyaw Myint,* head of cataloging at USIS Library
Daw Ni Hta,* head of reference, second in power at the library after
    Mrs. Graham
Daw Su Su,* head of the junior library after Martha Khin left, Molly's
    boss
Gloria,* a small fly working with Molly in the library, started in
    cataloging and moved to head of young people's library, also
    worked at the embassy after the library closed
Ruth,* powerful woman at library, assistant to Mrs. Graham
Doris,* worked at the circulation desk with Molly until moved to
    another area
Clara,* worked at the circulation desk with Molly, invited Molly to her
    son's shinbyu ceremony
Polly,* Kayin pianist at USIS library, met Molly in Pyapon, gave her a
    Gideon New Testament

Co-workers at embassy:
Arthur Parolini, budget and fiscal officer, Molly's boss
Miss Margery Palmer, Arthur Parolini's replacement as budget and fiscal
    officer, Molly's boss
Mr. Samson,* head of accounting
Mr. Jacobs,* accountant, deacon at Immanuel Baptist Church
Leon,* young marine who guarded embassy
Michael Joyce, consular officer
Ray Bridges,* courier for embassy, a Buddhist American
Mable,* secretary in consular's office

Co-workers at GE:
Mr. Santucci, manager, Molly's boss
Miriam, friend and receptionist
Carolyn, friend and co-worker
Mr. Hearst,* salesman from New York
Maude, Molly's boss at the GE Clearing House for Alcoholism

Other friends in US:
Larry and Marlene Teien, a pen pal of Terence and later sponsors of the family to come to the US
Irene and Walter Bridges,* Ray's* parents

Those names marked with * have been changed to protect privacies. Some expressly asked us to change their names, and other names we changed as a precaution. Particularly, some with ongoing connections or remaining overseas wanted their names changed, so we often applied their preferences to others. Some names we did not change because they belong to public figures, have common names, or are deceased. Others have given direct permission to use their names. We confess it was sometimes troubling to guess or to find out how people would want to be represented. We hope we have properly respected the wishes of all the delightful people mentioned in *Gentle Moon*.